PENGUIN BOOKS

PAST CARING

Robert Goddard was born in Hampshire, England, in 1954, the son of a naval electrician. He was educated at Price's School, Fareham, and Peterhouse, Cambridge. Since 1978 he has lived and worked in Devon, most recently as an educational administrator. He married in 1984, and he and his wife now live quietly in Exeter. *Past Caring* is his first novel; a second novel, called *In Pale Battalions*, will be published later this year.

PAST CARING

ROBERT GODDARD

Penguin Books

PENGUIN BOOKS
Viking Penguin Inc., 40 West 23rd Street,
New York, New York 10010, U.S.A.
Penguin Books Ltd, 27 Wrights Lane, London W8 5TZ
(Publishing & Editorial) and Harmondsworth,
Middlesex, England (Distribution & Warehouse)
Penguin Books Australia Ltd, Ringwood,
Victoria, Australia
Penguin Books Canada Limited, 2801 John Street,
Markham, Ontario, Canada L3R 1B4
Penguin Books (N.Z.) Ltd, 182–190 Wairau Road,
Auckland 10, New Zealand

First published in Great Britain by Robert Hale Limited 1986
First published in the United States of America by St. Martin's Press 1987
Reprinted by arrangement with St. Martin's Press, Inc.
Published in Penguin Books 1988

LIBRARY OF CONGRESS CATALOGING IN PUBLICATION DATA
Goddard, Robert.
Past caring.
Reprint. Originally published: New York: St. Martin's
Press, c1986.
I. Title.
PR6057.033P3 1988 823'.914 87-7272
ISBN 0 14 01.0600 6

Printed in the United States of America by
Offset Paperback Mfrs., Inc., Dallas, Pennsylvania
Set in Times Roman

To Vaunda

PAST CARING

Prologue

"Yes, I have re-entered your olden haunts at last.
Through the years, through the dead scenes, I have tracked
you.
What have you now found to say of our past?
Scanned across the dark space wherein I have lacked you?"

The words recur to me now, for I have passed through my own wasted years and dead scenes and am left with the same, remembered longing. If you had told me, my elusive quarry, what to expect from a quest after your past, I would never have embarked upon it. Your shade, which I tracked and moved in, envelops me now in this place of your displaced being. What would you do? I know—there is no need to say. But first, there is a tale to tell.

One

The spring of 1977 found me, newly past thirty, a bad case of wasted talent in a largely waste city—an unemployed, divorced ex-schoolteacher of foundered promise and dismal prospect. London, that grey month of March, seemed to echo my self-pity.

That morning, the echo was a painful one in my head, fused with the dull ache of last night's beer and a well-worn theme being pursued by my increasingly reluctant host in the kitchen of his Greenwich house. It was Saturday, so the throb of traffic from Maze Hill was muted, the light, too, decently suffused as it struck the table where I sat, sipping strong black coffee. Jerry sat opposite me, washed and shaved, dressed and clear-headed—just four things he was and I wasn't—scanning the shares pages of *The Financial Times*.

"Millennium up again," he said.

"They would be," I replied. The last thing I needed to know was that my former employer was continuing to prosper, but it didn't surprise me. Millennium Properties had always been astute in their purchase and promotion of historic buildings, but their only concession to scholarship was to hire over-qualified menials like me to fudge together their tour booklets.

Millennium had given me the first half-decent job I'd had since leaving teaching. But, in an unguarded moment at a Christmas party, I'd confided my contempt for their historical standards—which were as transatlantic as their parent company—to completely the wrong person. After that, it had just been a question of resigning before they could sack me.

I'd been in debt even before that and the loss of a salary soon meant the flat in Richmond had to go. That's when Jerry, a friend from schooldays, had offered me his spare room in Greenwich, to help me through a bad patch. But the patch had spread to two months and Jerry's patience was beginning to wear thin.

"Did I mention that Tribune are planning to open a new regional office in Crawley?"

He had. And he'd mentioned that they'd be recruiting staff as a result and that, if I was interested, he could put in a word. I was, in fact, monumentally uninterested. Jerry was an earnest, hard-working actuary for the Tribune Life Assurance company, where he was doubtless highly thought of. But I could never thrive in his world and it wouldn't have done me—or Jerry—any good to try. Yet explaining that to him was supremely difficult. Not only would his sense of efficiency be affronted, but his over-serious, understated personality would fail to comprehend how Tribune Life—thirty-eight hours a week in modern offices with increments for the industrious and special rates for staff—could be ideal for him but anathema to me.

"Yes, you did. I'm looking out for the adverts when they start staffing it."

It was a lie, of course. I wasn't looking out for those or any other vacancies. My pretence was designed to appease Jerry and still my own secret fear that it wasn't so much insurance as any career that I couldn't face.

I seized on a distracton exercise: opening my morning mail. There were two letters, neatly propped by Jerry against the toast rack. One was a credit card statement. The other looked more promising: a Portuguese stamp and writing I recognized at once.

"This one's from Alec," I announced, hoping that his news from Madeira would take us off the questions of my unemployment and homelessness. Jerry only knew Alec Fowler through me and I only knew him because we'd shared a landing at university. He was one of those students sophisticated beyond their years who made the rest of us feel gauche and schoolboyish. But I was quick to learn and he was eager for company in his riotous life. Alec surrounded himself with those—such as me—who liked to regard themselves as free-thinking radicals. Cambridge in the late sixties was a forcing house for our self-indulgent brand of student chic which held that smoking pot and decrying established ideas was a new and important social development. With Alec's rogue intellect to guide us, it seemed credible. Ten years on, it appeared unbelievably naïve and—which we would have hated more—irrelevant. Yet it retained a freshness and an optimism that marked it out in my mind from the years of disillusionment since.

While I had filled those years by acquiring, then losing, a wife, child and teaching career, and England had stumbled through oil price rises and three-day weeks, Alec had contrived always to enjoy himself. Questioned but not charged, warned but not sent down, over the Garden House riot, he had appeared to devote all his study time to political freesheets but had still come out with a first in English and then, in his own words, drifted with purpose: Paris ("looking for the spirit of '68"), then Venice ("to see it before it sank") and Crete ("to teach English and study the Mediterranean light"). These spells away were punctuated by trips home, when he would descend on me to relive our student days in drunken weekends that were more than once the despair of my wife.

Alec's real ambition, as he often told me, was to break into journalism. This seemed always about to happen but never had yet. He was in New York at the time of Watergate but couldn't persuade anybody to print what he wrote on the subject. He was taken on by a Montreal evening paper at the time of the Olympics, but the job fell through before the Games even began. Then it was time to forget journalism for a while and repair his finances with a six-month teaching contract in Madeira.

Only he hadn't come back at Christmas as scheduled, just when his company would have been the tonic I badly needed. I'd written to him several times and this was his first reply. I read the letter aloud to Jerry, hoping it would take his mind off my job-seeking and flat-hunting efforts—or lack of them.

"Hi Martin,

How are you? Sorry all's been quiet from me lately, but I've had a lot on—more of that in a moment. Sad to hear about Millennium, but you're probably well off out of it. Congratulations to Jerry for putting up with you for so long.

The teaching stopped at Christmas and you wanted to know what I've been doing since then. Never one to let the grass grow—no pun intended—I've started, wait for it, an island newspaper. Madeira's full of the English—in retirement or on holiday. My idea was to give them a monthly magazine: a glossy English language affair full of photographs of Madeira's natural beauty (which is considerable) and current affairs (which aren't), to tell the tourists what to see and where and the ex-pats about what's going on. I had a head start because there was simply no competition. What's more, there's a friend of mine here who's as good a photographer as I am a journalist (fatal combination?) and came in with me, plus lots of shops and businesses keen to advertize to the English, who are their best customers.

There's also a South African hotelier in Funchal who put up the money to start us off. *Madeira Life* was launched last month and so far (fingers crossed) it's going well. Leo—the hotelier—arranged a cocktail do to butter up all the right people. I tell you, if this goes on there's some danger of me becoming an establishment figure. More to the point, it could pave my way into Fleet Street.

But not for a while yet. I'll have to do my apprenticeship here first. Which brings me to an idea I've had to brighten your life. Why not drop whatever you're doing—which is nothing much according to your last letter—and come out here for a holiday? The Portuguese couple I share this house with are away for the next month so I can easily put you up. Madeira's beautiful in the spring. I could show you round, you could tell me what you think of the magazine and we could talk about old times.

What do you think? Let me know soon, Cheers, Alec."

"Will you go?" said Jerry, a little too quickly for my liking.

"If I can possibly manage it, I'll be there like a shot." I was more confident than I might have sounded. I had a few hundred in a building society to cater for emergencies and this could definitely be classified as one.

"Well, why not?" said Jerry. "A holiday would do you good."

By Monday night, I was able to telephone Alec to suggest a date. After several false starts and through a forest of static, I heard his familiar voice down the cable from distant Madeira.

"Glad you can make it, Martin. It'll be great to see you."

"Hope so, but it's sooner than you might have expected. I've got an option on a spare seat aboard a charter flight on the 31st."

"Take it. That'll be a good time—I'll be between issues and able to show you the sights. And the sooner you come the better—it may be worth your while."

I dictated the flight number and time to him before we gave up the struggle with the static. Only after I'd put the phone down did I reflect on what he'd said and wonder whether he meant the trip might be worth more than just a holiday. Now the magazine was taking off, did he have something to offer to an old friend's advantage? It was no more than the glimmer of a pleasing suspicion, but it carried me happily through the week before my departure.

It was in a mood of well-being and optimism that I boarded the charter flight to Madeira. Amid the holiday-bound happy families, I felt out of place, but a few in-flight drinks passed the time well enough, until, that is, stormy weather began to jostle the aircraft.

As we buffeted down towards Madeira, I peered out of the window for a sight of it, my knuckles on the arm of the seat turning as white as the wavetops which I found myself taking all too close a look at. There was, though, a smudge of green somewhere ahead of us and soon we hit something I hoped was the runway and braked violently to a halt. I stumbled from the aircraft instantly sober, tugging on an anorak against the drenching rain and trailing behind the others into the terminal building.

There was no sign of Alec as we cleared customs and the rest of the passengers began to disperse, but just when I was beginning to fret, I saw him bounding down some steps from an upper floor of the building.

"Hi, Martin," he called, strolling towards me with a casual wave of greeting. He looked fit and well, tanned and relaxed, sandy hair turned blond by the sun, more like a lifeguard than a journalist as he clapped me on the back and smiled broadly.

"How are you, old son? You look bloody awful."

"Thanks, Alec." I grinned ruefully. "So would you if you'd been through that landing. I thought we were going to ditch in the Atlantic."

"A bit hairy, eh? It didn't look too bad from the bar."

"What does?"

"That's more like it. Actually, the runway is a bit on the short side. I didn't tell you because I thought it might put you off. This weather doesn't help. You must have brought it with you—it's the worst day of the year. Trust a pessimist like you to arrive when Madeira's looking at its worst." Alec was right: I'd always expected the worst from life and generally got it. He'd always hoped for the best and sometimes been rewarded. That's why I'd spent an idle winter in London and he'd exploited the potential of an island in the sun. He was also right that it wasn't at its best that day. The taxi driver wore sunglasses and drove as if the roads were dry, but all I saw as we sped round hairpin bends along the coast road to Funchal were dark cliffs, angry seas and louring clouds—more like Cornwall than the tropics.

"Don't worry," Alec assured me, "weather like this never lasts. Madeira's a beautiful island, believe it or not. Not that the Madeirans do much to keep it that way." He pointed through the stair-rod rain at an abandoned building site. "They've got all the Latin vices"—we lurched through a pothole and I nodded agreement, while hoping the driver didn't understand English—"and only one virtue: they're letting me get a magazine on the road. I know it's the back of beyond, but it's a start." After countless false starts, Alec's hope was intact. And so, miraculously, were we when the taxi wound down the hills and bends into Funchal: a smear of grey and brown buildings round a semi-circle of hills above a broad bay.

Alec's house was a haven—cool, dry and peaceful, three things it hadn't been outside. I slumped down in the lounge with relief, while Alec kept his scatter-gun appraisal of life on Madeira from the kitchen.

"It'll be black coffee," he shouted. "Milk's like gold dust here. But you look as if you need it straight anyway. There's a copy of the magazine on the table. Take a look."

Madeira Life, April 1977: bold lettering on a glossy cover, adorned by a smiling, dark-haired girl in a striped dress and bolero jacket, clasping bunches of mimosa, their bright yellow blooms starting from the page.

I leafed through the issue. Clever and perceptive pictures, and Alec's punchy prose, drew me on through a diary of events and a page of local news.

"What is the big story on Madeira at the moment, Alec?"

"There's never a big story, Martin. I just dress up what there is and pander to my readers' prejudices."

"And they are?"

"Predictable. The same as English exiles anywhere, I guess: Why are the locals so loud and lazy?"

"And where can you get a cheap dinner?"

"You've seen my piece on the Jardim de Sol. Actually it's a very good restaurant. I force myself to eat out every week to safeguard my readers' palates. Funchal's full of good, cheap eating places—and some bad ones. It's important to know the difference."

"I can imagine. Ah, this looks like your knowing eye."

I'd passed a centre spread on the Flower Festival and come to an array of darkly promising, thickly encrusted wine bottles: "'Old Madeira—Does Any Still Remain?'"

"You're bound to become a connoisseur of the stuff here. The trade's dominated by the English families—always has been—so it's a natural subject for them to read about."

"And for you to sample on their behalf?"

"You said it. But that piece is about 1792 vintage and whether there mightn't be a few stray bottles left. Napoleon was offered some on his way to St. Helena but wasn't fit enough to drink any."

"Sad."

"Yes—but typical. Madeira's out of the main stream of world events. Famous people only come here before—or after—their prime. As you'll see."

I thought I already had, for here were sepia prints of Churchill, his unmistakable, bulky frame perched on a stool painting a seascape and, in another shot, posing with his wife on some arabesque balcony, with palm trees in the background.

Alec came into the room then, carrying a tray, and glanced over my shoulder. "Churchill wintered here often after the war," he said. "He liked painting up the coast at Camara de Lobos." He set the tray down on the table and poured us coffee. "What do you think of it then?"

I closed the magazine and looked up. "It's good Alec," I said. "Very good. Colourful, lively, informative. I'd buy it."

"You think it's got a future?"

"It certainly deserves one. And you'll know whether there's a market for it." I sipped appreciatively at the coffee. "In your letter you mentioned a backer."

"Exactly. I ingratiated myself with the right man there. Leo Sellick's South African and therefore well in with the English. He made a packet buying and selling land when hotels were springing up all over, and still owns one at Machico, east of here, where there's the only decent beach on the island. He's obviously got an eye for investments, so it's encouraging that he's put some money into *Madeira Life*. He also knows all the right people, who would otherwise freeze me out. He bends their ears up at the Country Club and makes them think well of me."

"He sounds invaluable."

"He is. And with his help, I'm going to make a go of this."

I wished him well, genuinely but not without a tinge of resentment. Alec had fallen on his feet again, while I still hadn't found mine. His enthusiasm meant we didn't have to dwell on my own news, which was negligible anyway. But I did entertain him with an embroidered version of my departure from Millenium. In this, I'd resigned on the spot, rather than under coercion on New Year's Eve. Historian though I was, I didn't mind laundering the past when it suited my purpose.

Later, after dark, the rain stopped and Alec took me out to a restaurant he wanted to cover for the magazine. It was small, hot, crowded and cheerful, full of Latin laughter and bustling, seedy waiters. Alec ordered up two steaks of espada—a deep-sea fish—in shrimp sauce and a hearty bottle of dão to wash them down, then another when we started to relax.

"Tomorrow," he declared confidently, "I'll take you straight to the high spot of your stay."

"What's that?"

"You can meet Leo. He lives up at Camacha, in the hills north-east of here. When he heard you were visiting me, he insisted I take you up to have dinner with him. And believe me—it's not to be missed. He's a generous host and his quinta's a lovely place."

"Quinta?"

"Estate, if you like. But you'll remember quinta from port bottles at Cambridge. We got through a fair amount of Quinta do Noval together, I remember."

"Our concession to conservatism."

"And out of my price range here. So have another glass of this stuff, which isn't."

So I did, and the evening dissolved in drink and debate about British and Portuguese politics, students then and now, journalism and Madeira. Already, I was enjoying myself. An old friend and a new setting were taking effect.

Madeira was a different place when I woke next morning. There was a deep blue sky visible through the open window of my room, a chatter of birdsong from the garden, warm sweet air to fill my lungs as I rose and gazed out at sun-drenched Funchal, its rooftops already shimmering in a heat haze. Walls that had been grey when we drove in the day before were glaringly white, tiled roofs that had been brown were bright orange, the city clustering on a verdant green hillside above a broad blue ocean. My head was thick but the air was clear, the prospect bright.

Alec went out after breakfast and returned with some bread, cooked chicken and mangoes. "A picnic lunch," he announced. "We'll need it later. Are you ready to start?"

"What's the hurry? I thought we were going out to dinner?"

"We are—on foot. But it's a six hour walk to Camacha, so get your boots on."

"I didn't know we'd be doing any hiking."

"I told you—I'm a reformed character. And you look as if some exercise would do you good. Besides, it's a beautiful walk."

Alec started cutting sandwiches. "We'll take my rucksack," he said. "Pack anything you want for an overnight stay. We won't come back tonight."

Well, Alec had said Leo Sellick was a generous host. As for the beauty of the walk, I took his word for it. And at least there was dinner at the end of it.

We walked down to the harbour and boarded a battered old red and grey bus to carry us out of funchal. It lurched and juddered up steep-cobbled, high-walled roads, engine protesting as we climbed ever upwards.

"We're going up to Monte," Alec shouted into my ear above the diesel roar. "It's a route taken by lots of English settlers in the past, up into the hills where the air's cooler and supposed to have healing qualities. Monte's full of rest homes for wealthy pulmonary patients." Fumes wafted through the window as the bus strained round a hairpin bend. "Of course, they didn't travel by bus." I could understand why.

The bus wound up into the hills until the air became fresher and the streets broader. We were at Monte, cooler and more peaceful than Funchal and, yes, more English as well. We left the bus and walked down a cobbled street past steps leading up to a large, white-fronted church with two rounded belfries and a statue of the Virgin Mary prominent in a niche in the centre of the facing wall.

"Our Lady of the Mount Church," said Alec. "Emperor Charles of Austria is buried there."

"Did he come here for his health?"

"If so, it didn't do him much good. He died young."

We pressed on through Monte to the Hotel Belmont and turned along a cobbled road past banks of blue and white agapanthus into the settlement of Babosas. Here a railed lookout gave us views over the whole sweep of Funchal and the harbour, the hills above the city quilted with terraces and changing hue constantly as we looked, the shadows of clouds chasing each other across the corrugated slopes. I took pleasure just in looking, for the greens and blues were so much more vivid than they would have been in England, like acrylic paint after watercolour for one who'd just emerged from a winter in London.

We took a grassy path through a sunshot pine and mimosa forest heavy with scent and emerged into a narrow valley with crumbling, basalt cliffs either side. Climbing uphill, we reached the ramparts of a miniature canal where it emerged from the blackness of a tunnel. We headed east along a narrow walkway behind the watercourse.

"This is a levada," Alec explained. "Madeira's criss-crossed by them. They bring the rain down from the mountaintops to irrigate the land and drive power stations. And they're perfect for scenic walks." Almost immediately a sheer drop down basalt cliffs yawned to our right.

"Don't look down," said Alec. "Walk straight ahead and you'll be perfectly safe."

I followed Alec carefully along the path until it led away from the dizzy drops, to where pine groves and carpets of lilies flanked our route. Apart from diverting round the boundary walls of a private quinta, we stuck to the levada and its path of ochre-red earth for the next couple of hours until we came to a dusty main road crossing our path.

From the other side of the road, beside a pink-walled cottage—its garden awash with orange and purple lily blossoms—we looked down wooded slopes towards the sea, the coastline—and the humps of the off-shore islands, the Desertas, beyond it—misty in the heat.

"Immediately below us is Palheiro Ferreiro," Alec announced. "See the mansion down in the trees?"—I could make out its orange rooftops amid the greenery—"That's the Blandy quinta. They're about the wealthiest of the English families established on Madeira—a name to reckon with. They've dominated the wine trade for three hundred years. So you see, the English have always had a big say on the island."

"Friends of Leo Sellick?"

"Leo's a friend of everybody—especially people like the Blandys. And, of course, they don't live far apart."

"I'm glad to hear that."

"What's wrong? Feet playing up?"

"Let's just say I reckon I'll have earned dinner."

"We'll stop for lunch soon."

Lunch was, in fact, twenty minutes away and the other side of a short levada tunnel which we scrambled through, bent double, by the light of an ailing torch. Beyond, we sat down in a cool pine grove and devoured the picnic.

"We'll soon be in Camacha," said Alec. "Quinta do Porto Novo lies a couple of miles the other side of the village."

"And that's where Leo lives?"

"Yes. It's a lovely place at the head of the Porto Novo valley. The scenery round Camacha reminds me of England—all mist and mellow fruitfulness."

He was right. The levada soon entered another tunnel—this one impassable—and we diverted up a path to the scattered settlement of Ribeirinha, then on up a dusty road between banked verges overrun by blue hydrangeas towards Camacha. The landscape was indeed becoming English in character—apple orchards, with snowy drifts of blossom, stood between holts of willow. We passed gardens and patios where stacks of slender branches stood drying in the sun. "Wickerwork is the local cottage industry," Alec explained, "and the Camachans are masters of the craft."

We left the centre of the village by a cobbled path beside the walls of a private quinta and followed it up to where it crossed another, smaller, drier levada. We followed this as it snaked away from Camacha round the western slopes of the Porto Novo valley. More hydrangeas were in bloom here and the valley fell away beneath us in a tumble of greenery towards the sea. Cloud drifted and played round the hilltops, filtering the sun as the afternoon wore on. Once again, we were in paradise.

After about half an hour, the levada entered a tunnel and we took a cobbled track down to join the dusty red main road leading north from Camacha. We were at the head of the valley, where the road bridged the Porto Novo river and swung round to the eastern slope.

Ahead of us, round the curve, set in a peeling stucco wall that ran along the roadside, wrought iron gates stood open, with the name QUINTO DO PORTO NOVO inscribed on one of the flanking pillars. The estate within was terraced and wooded and a cobbled drive zig-zagged up the hillside towards the house, its orange roofs and white walls gleaming in the sunlight above the trees.

"This is it," said Alec. "Quite a hideaway."

We walked slowly up the drive as the still quiet of early evening settled on the quinta. There was a vineyard on the sunny slope curving away to our right, but we climbed through banks of apple trees, their blossom scattered in our path, to the house itself.

At the top of the drive, an archway led into a courtyard. A fountain, supported by stone cherubim, played in the centre. A half-walled and colonnaded gallery ran round three sides, with hanging baskets in the arches and plaster urns at the foot of each pillar, all overflowing with red hibiscus; their colour and scent filled the yard. Within the gallery, I could see carved and decorated doors leading into the body of the house and, in the middle of the side facing the arch we'd entered by, balustraded stone steps breaking the wall of the gallery and leading up to heavy wooden doors that stood open to the sweet evening air. All here was peace and silence, broken only—or rather perfectly complemented—by the water of the fountain, the buzz of a late bee, the scratch of an early cicada.

"It's a beautiful place, Alec," I said. "So warm and peaceful."

"Thought you'd like it," said Alec. "let's see if we can find Leo." He strolled towards the steps.

I lingered by the fountain, savouring the atmosphere. My eye was taken by the ridge tiles on the roof, which had been extended beyond the eaves and crafted in the likeness of dragons' heads. I was gazing up at them, admiring the handiwork, when a voice came from behind me.

"Tile embellishment is a Madeiran speciality."

The clipped vowels rendered an introduction superfluous. This was Leo Sellick, a short, wiry man, looking older than I'd expected, with a tanned and lined face, hair as white as his shirt, a thin grey moustache, keen blue eyes and a flashing smile that carried a glint of gold. We shook hands, Sellick with a grip that belied his years.

"There you are, Leo," said Alec from over my shoulder, retracing his steps. "This is Martin Radford."

"Of course, of course," the old man said, still shaking my hand. "You are most welcome, Mr. Radford. Alec's told me all about you and I'm delighted to make your acquaintance. I trust you like the dragons. I'm especially fond of them myself."

I assured him that I admired them and everything else I'd seen of the house and glanced quizzically at Alec, wondering what he'd found to say of me. But he was already grinning at Sellick and enquiring how the Quinta had fared in the storm, just a little too deferentially for my liking.

"Mr. Radford doesn't want to know how my vines are growing, Alec, and nor do you," Sellick said with disarming accuracy. "Come inside and let me offer you a sundowner. You look as if you need one."

We strolled up the steps and into the cool entrance hall of the house, then turned into a large, airy drawing room, opulently furnished in rich maroon leather and dark mahogany, with deep-piled rugs beneath our feet. One was a complete leopardskin, laid out on the hearth in front of a wide, brick-breasted fireplace, with logs unkindled in the grate. Likewise, the large fan in the centre of the ceiling was not in service. There were paintings and photographs all round the walls, flowers in vases and pots, several well-stacked bookcases, an air of tranquillity and repose. French windows set in the middle of the wall facing us led out onto a verandah and beyond that a garden. Sellick crossed to a cabinet and poured our drinks.

"There you are, Mr. Radford," he said, handing me a large cool gin.

"Thanks," I said. "And please, won't you call me Martin?"

"I'd be delighted to, if, that is, you will return the compliment by addressing this toothless old lion as Leo." I smiled: neither actually nor metaphorically was he toothless, but there was something vaguely leonine about this proud and courteous old man. He was shorter than me but stood more erect, with a set to his head and a look in his eye that spoke of scrutiny and command. He had all the English graces but a steely South

African edge to them that left me in no doubt who'd shot the leopard.

He suggested we take our drinks onto the verandah while the light held—Madeira's brief twilight was now setting in—and we followed him out happily, seating ourselves in low wicker chairs and looking down the length of a well-trimmed and tended garden. Winding stone steps led down from the verandah through oleander bushes in blossom to a terraced lawn where a bench stood by a sundial. Beyond that was a low fence overgrown with bougainvillea, a wicket gate and more steps leading to a lower terrace and what looked like a kitchen garden. A figure with a hoe could be seen among the distant vegetable rows. The ground fell away rapidly from that point towards the road and the valley floor. The opposite wall of the valley faced us, the yellow gorse scattered across it turning a dusty gold as evening fell. In the greater distance, a hazy line marked the horizon, where the darkening blue sky met the still darker sea.

"You have a beautiful home, Leo," I said.

"Thank you," he replied. "Madeira is justly called the floating garden of the Atlantic and amongst all the beauties of my homeland, I never found any of the serenity of this place." He smiled. "Here, one can truly forget the world and tend one's vegetables."

Alec grinned. "Leo's speaking metaphorically, Martin. He has a band of men to tend his vegetables."

"That is true, but I take an active interest in them, especially when they're on my plate, as I hope they shortly will be. If you'll excuse me, I'll go and check on that." He turned to me as he rose. "If you wish to freshen up before dinner, Martin, Alec will show you the way." He bowed slightly and walked away through the lounge.

"What do you think?" Alec asked after a pause.

"The perfect host," I said. "And probably the perfect patron."

"It's a little ironic, though, isn't it?"

"How do you mean?"

"Well, that I end up writing for English colonials and in debt to a wealthy South African—people I once wouldn't have been seen dead with." I had the impression Alec was getting his irony in first—before his friend from left-wing student days could point it out to him.

"It wouldn't worry me in your shoes, Alec. We've all changed and learned to accept life. Why not just make the most of it?" This was gin and fatigue talking—the recommendation would have been better directed at me than Alec. But at least it suppressed any hint of jealousy.

"Well, at least we can make the most of dinner," he said. "Come on, I'll show you where the bathroom is."

When I'd washed, I rejoined Alec in the drawing room, where I found him closing the french windows against the night; it was now quite dark outside. "Let's go through," he said and led me back into the hall and through a door facing us into the dining room.

A large, oval table stood laid for three. The shutters had been closed and the only illumination came from a candelabrum in the centre of the table. Its light sparkled in silver cutlery and the tracery of tall, narrow-stemmed wine glasses. Orchids stood, freshly cut, in vases at either end, their brilliant red and yellow petals highlighted by the white damask tablecloth.

"Leo's gone to a lot of trouble," said Alec. "You should feel honoured."

I did and, to give some little assistance, lit a taper and went over to three candles that stood on a cabinet by the wall facing the window. As the light splashed up from them onto the wall, it caught a faded sepia photograph, sombrely framed but prominently placed among several much larger paintings. Something struck me as familiar about it, so I took a closer look. Sure enough, it was what I thought: a conventional portrait photograph of a group of about twenty men, some seated, the others standing behind. It was familiar because I'd seen it before, reproduced in a history text book dealing with Edwardian politics. It was not a period I'd specialized in as a student, but in my history-teaching spell I'd become acquainted with it, and I easily identified this as a group study of Asquith's Cabinet, circa 1910. The Prime Minister sat in the centre of the front row, flanked by the assembled pride of the

Liberal party in its pre-war heyday. Lloyd George, projecting alertness and dynamism beside Asquith's vague avuncularity, was close enough to the centre to have been Chancellor of the Exchequer at the time. Standing a little pensively at the back was the young Churchill, with that bulldog set to his chin even then. Without a caption, I could not put names to the rest of these frock-coated grandees, but it was an historic picture that I peered at with growing curiosity. It seemed strange to see it there, of all times and places, and I said as much to Alec.

Before I could press the point, Sellick reappeared wearing a velvet smoking jacket and urged us to take our seats. An old, stooping Madeiran brought a carafe of white wine, then wheeled in a trolley bearing our first course.

Alec and I were hungry after our walk: we ate and drank with relish, while Sellick nibbled and sipped, savouring our enjoyment as much as the food itself. It was all delicious: deep-sea scabbard fish, sliced and swimming in a tantalizing cucumber sauce; skewered beef, flavoured with laurel and accompanied by the pick of those famous vegetable rows; rich, golden pudim; white, creamy goat's cheese. We progressed through a smooth, ruby red dão to coffee and a potent liqueur.

"Macia," explained Sellick, "is a Camachan speciality: fiery aguardente mellowed by honey from local hives."

"Talking of local specialities," I said, "I was looking at Alec's article on 1792 madeira. Is there really any left?"

"Who knows?" said Sellick with a smile. "It is recorded that Dr. Grabham, a local English resident, had some—and drank it—as recently as 1933. He married a member of the Blandy family, thus acquiring a dowry of the 1792 vintage. In all probability the last of it went with his passing."

"A pity," I said.

"Yet reassuring," Sellick replied, "in the sense that such issues—what became of an old cache of wine?—constitute the history of this little island. It may be frustrating for Alec in his search for articles, or disappointing for an historian such as yourself, but it is comforting for a South African to live where there is no history of violence and discord."

"I don't find the history of Madeira disappointing," I said. "It seems fascinating—full of exiles and romantics."

"Ah yes, those footnotes to history that are often as interesting as the main theme. But perhaps that's rather an old-fashioned attitude."

"Not in my view. I don't think history should be so . . . so cerebral. After all, it's only about people—greater folk and lesser folk—and what they've done. If history becomes more sophisticated than they were, it's missing the point."

"Excellent," nodded Sellick. "You're clearly a man after my own heart. I've long suspected that most scholarship is geared to the career of the scholar, not the enlightenment of his subject."

"Well, that's bound to be so," I conceded. "Only less than dedicated scholars could put it the other way round and they, like me, wouldn't have the energy or the opportunity to pursue the study."

"Not under any circumstances?"

"Probably not. There's no room left for novelty in history. It's all known and understood—or misunderstood. Historians these days don't write, they just sift the archives for refinements of existing theories." A vein of resentment at my exclusion from the hallowed ranks of professional historians had now become pronounced. I sensed I would regret such frankness but couldn't suppress it. Besides, though I was indeed to regret it, all of it, much later, that wasn't the reason. There was another sensation I chose to disregard—the feeling I was being led, slowly but firmly, where I couldn't say, but in some specific direction.

"But," said Sellick, "if there were something new or mysterious, wouldn't that overcome the objection?"

"It might provide the energy, but what about the opportunity?"

"That would surely be created if the mystery were sufficiently fascinating."

"Possibly, but the hypothesis rests on the existence of such a mystery. And I would contend that the scholars solved all the remaining mysteries a long time ago."

"Surely not. You also said that history was about people. Think of the thousands of names recorded in the history books, never mind the millions who aren't. There must be mysteries galore there."

"Yes, but those mysteries only exist because nobody's thought them worth solving."

"And what would make a mystery worth solving?"

"Well, if it concerned somebody significant, or changed the way we thought about them or their period."

"And where could there be such a mystery left?"

"Where indeed?" I intended the question to be rhetorical and the silence that followed seemed to confirm that we'd reached the end of our little flight of fancy. But as the smoke from Sellick's cigar climbed lazily towards the ceiling, it became apparent that we were to fly higher yet.

"How about here, Martin," Sellick said with a smile, "in this house, where we sit eating and drinking, in the middle of a mystery?"

What mystery was this? My mind cast about for an answer, but there was none. I was a stranger there, so everything was new to me, but scarcely mysterious. I recalled the framed photograph of Asquith's Cabinet as the oddest thing I'd so far come across and my eyes flicked up to it in its place on the wall. Sellick, sitting with his back to the picture, must have guessed what I was looking at.

"That photograph is part of our little local mystery," he said. "As an historian, Martin, do you know what it is?"

An opportunity to display my erudition drew me on. "Yes," I said. "I saw it before dinner. It's a group portrait of Asquith's Cabinet. I've seen it reproduced before but never a contemporary print."

"And do you know who they all are?"

"Not offhand. Asquith himself, Lloyd George and Churchill are easy. As for the rest, it's difficult to put names to faces."

"There's no need, it's done for us. Alec, would you mind handing it down to me?"

Alec rose and took the picture down from the wall. He handed it to Sellick, who turned it over and showed me the back by the light of the candle. In a firm, copperplate hand, there was written a date: 1st May 1908, which had been underlined. Beneath that, in two groups, there was a list of names which I recognised as members of the cabinet. From the positions of the three faces I'd so far identified, I deduced that the separate groups represented front and rear rows in the photograph. Recalling that Campbell-Bannerman, Asquith's predecessor as Prime Minister, had died sometime in 1908, I took the picture to be commemorative of the new premiership. My eyes ran along the names in the front row—the Marquess of Crewe, D. Lloyd George, the Marquess of Ripon, Lord Loreburn, H.H. Asquith, Lord Tweedmouth, Sir Edward Grey—and alighted upon an oddity. Between Grey and R.B. Haldane, no name figured, merely the one letter I or possibly the number 1. I remarked on it to Sellick. "What does it mean?" I asked.

"It's the front row of names, is it not?" he replied. I agreed. "How many are in that row?" I counted the faces on the photograph—there were nine. "And how many are listed?" I counted again—only eight.

"Of course," I said. "It's the pronoun I. Then this was written—and owned?—by a member of the Cabinet."

"Quite so."

I turned back to the photograph and focussed on the unidentified face between Grey and Haldane. A tall, broad-shouldered figure, handsome with a hint of arrogance in his features set off by a dashing moustache and a firm set to the jaw, younger than most of the others pictured but wearing the same sober morning dress, yet contriving nevertheless to project enterprise and initiative. I glanced along the row to Lloyd George—the shorter and stockier of the two—noting that both had a brightness of eye and a keenness of bearing that set them apart from most of their colleagues, crusty veterans, I guessed, of Gladstone's days. This was as much as I could make out by candlelight and sepia, but I was annoyed that I couldn't put a name to this particular face. I looked to Sellick for a clue and wasn't disappointed.

"Who is he, Martin, our mystery man? A promising Young Turk given his first taste of power?"

"I'm not sure. It's hardly my period. What was his post?"

"He was Asquith's new blood in the Home Office," replied Sellick with a twinkle in his eye. If I hadn't been so preoccupied with identification, I'd have taken more notice of Sellick's familiarity with Edwardian politics and perhaps concluded that he was either more of an historian than he'd given me to understand or less disinterested in our subject than his manner suggested. As it was, I was busy with a mental roll-call of politicians of the time.

"Surely," I ventured, "Asquith's Home Secretary was Herbert Gladstone—son of W.E.—and he was succeeded by Churchill . . . No, I'm wrong. Didn't Asquith ship Gladstone off as Governor-General somewhere when he came to office?"

"Quite right," said Sellick. "To Canada, in point of fact, thus making way for?"

I was there at last and just as well, for Sellick's smile was becoming slightly pained at the edges.

"A man by the name of Strafford. But that's literally all I know of him—a few years of office, then nothing—a little-known figure hard to recall amid so many famous names."

"Little-known indeed," said Sellick, "but in his day far from it. And not so hard to recall for those of us who live in his house."

"This is his house?"

"It was. Edwin Strafford retired here from England and died in 1951. I bought it at an auction after his death and fell in love with the place. Then I began to sift through what was left here and found many interesting curios, like this photograph. When I realized that Strafford had been a British Cabinet minister—which nobody here knew, or told me if they did—I found what I could about him in the history books. That was precious little, but what there was formed our domestic mystery."

The historian's curiosity in me had been aroused. It didn't surprise me that I should be ignorant of the life of such a man, but the opportunity to learn something about it in such unlikely surroundings was not to be missed.

"What is the mystery?" I asked. We had come to the nub.

"Put Martin out of his misery, Leo," said Alec helpfully. "You know you're dying to."

"Very well," said Sellick. "You will have to tell me, Martin, if this interests you as an historian. As a man, it interests me deeply." He paused to sip his coffee, then began.

"As I say, there is not much in the history books about Edwin Strafford. The *Dictionary of National Biography* devotes less than a column to him. He was born in 1876, the son of an officer in the Indian Army. He went to Cambridge, then

—briefly—to South Africa as a junior staff officer in the Boer War. He returned to England to fight his home constituency in Devon for the Liberals at the 1900 election and won, against the national trend. Then he climbed slowly but surely through the ranks of his party and became a junior minister when the Liberals came to power in 1905. When Asquith became Premier in 1908 he reshuffled his Cabinet and appointed Strafford Home Secretary at the age of thirty-two. It was a remarkable but short-lived rise. Two years later, Strafford resigned without explanation and disappeared virtually overnight—from the public eye at any rate. He left Parliament and became a totally private citizen—soon, a totally forgotten one also. He served throughout the First World War in the army, then took the post of British Consul here on Madeira. Later he bought this house and the quinta. He retired from the Consulate in 1946 and died five years later. End of story."

Sellick paused for effect. This was clearly not the end of the story.

"Beginning of mystery," put in Alec.

"That's right," resumed Sellick. "I found what little I could glean from the history books about Strafford not so much disappointing as wholly unsatisfactory. How could a man rise so swiftly—presumably on merit—then quite simply vanish without trace and, what's more, without apparent reason? One is familiar with scandal and failure in politics, but Strafford is tainted with neither. The passing mentions of his actions during two years in office—difficult years of suffragette and trades union unrest—are, at worst, neutral, sometimes laudatory. The only reason he is not given more extensive treatment is that he did not proceed with a political career like his contemporaries. It is as if Churchill or Lloyd George—of the same generation, both also promoted by Asquith—resigned abruptly in 1910, before either won fame as leaders of their country in war. Would that not seem surpassingly odd?"

"With hindsight, it would in their cases," I put in. "But who can say what Strafford might or might not have achieved if he hadn't resigned?"

"Precisely," said Sellick. "No-one can say. It is a mystery. And the fundamental mystery is why a talented, ambitious man in the prime of life chose to achieve nothing when he could have achieved so much."

"Perhaps he simply lost interest in politics," I proffered. "Or perhaps he found the public eye not to his taste. It's been known."

"True, very true," Sellick replied weightily. "And those were my thoughts too—an *enfant terrible* who burnt himself out for some prosaic reason. It seemed a pity."

Sellick rose from his chair and moved to replace the picture on the wall. He did so with reverential care, while I pondered the past tense in his last remark and waited for the next.

"It seemed a pity and it was not so," Sellick continued, resuming his seat. "As it turned out, I had been wasting my time burrowing in the reference books. I had ignored what that picture should have told me, that the answer—albeit an incomplete one—was here all the time.

"There's a fine old wooden desk in what was Strafford's study—I'll show it you later, preferably in daylight. When I was turning it out, I found in one of the drawers a large, handsomely bound volume, filled—but for a few pages—with writing in the same hand as that on the back of the photograph."

"What was it?"

"Strafford's memoir—compiled here in his retirement. It's a highly personal statement of how he came to be buried in the diplomatic service in such an obscure spot."

"Does it explain the mystery?"

"Far from it. It heightened the mystery, for Strafford does not—cannot—explain it. He recounts the circumstances of his exile, but they baffled him as much as they still baffle me."

"This sounds extraordinary."

"By any standards."

"May I see the Memoir?"

"Certainly. I will fetch it now. Can I suggest that we take this opportunity of retiring to the drawing room?"

There was no dissent. Sellick led us back through the hall to the drawing room, where the lamps had been lit in readiness for us. He went on through another door, asking Alec to pour me a drink while he fetched the Memoir.

Alec handed me another macia. "Interested?" he enquired.

"Very. It's not every day one gets to see a primary source like this."

"There speaks the true historian."

"Have you seen it?"

"Yes, but not read it. Leo's never been so forward with it before. Maybe he thinks he's found somebody to appreciate it."

Was Alec becoming sarcastic under the influence of several drinks? I'd no time to ponder the point, for Sellick returned almost at once, carrying a marbled, leather-bound tome. He waved us into deep armchairs facing the fireplace and stood, one foot on the fender, holding the book before him.

"It's a fair old read," he said, "a mix of diary and recollection. There's some irrelevant material, interesting in its own right but not strictly germane. Yet it confirms throughout that Strafford's exit from politics in 1910—and the events leading up to it—constituted the great disappointment of his life, in more ways than one. If you're sufficiently interested, Martin, I'd like you to read it and give me your opinion."

"I'd like to very much." My enthusiasm was genuine. As a student, I'd never excelled at wading through arid source documents, but there had never existed the motivation to do so, never the expectation of discovering something new or fascinating as a result. Sellick had promoted this document so well I could hardly have borne not to read it. There was, however, more promotion to come yet.

"This is probably no time for considered appraisal," Sellick said. "I hope Alec told you that you would be most welcome to remain here tonight. I would suggest that a reading of his could best be undertaken in the morning with a clear head. But never fear"—he had seen me framing a protest at this delay—"I will not leave you to lose sleep over the contents. I will tell you what I have already learnt from them. Then you will be able to judge for yourself whether mine seem appropriate conclusions."

Sellick sat beneath a standard lamp to the right of the fireplace and leafed through the book, cradled in his lap, as he spoke. "Strafford was the youngest of Asquith's prótegés and easily the most handsome. He was also unattached. He was, therefore, the eligible bachelor par excellence. He had the pick of a dozen well-connected young Liberal ladies. Yet his choice fell elsewhere and—for an Edwardian Home Secretary—it fell perversely. Strafford met and came to love a young Suffragette—a captivating creature, it would seem, but scarcely the ideal bride. These were sensitive times for politicians in their private lives. Lloyd George was forever courting disaster with extra-marital adventures and mere divorce had ruined more than one politician. So how could a Home Secretary whose government resisted female suffrage consider marrying a militant young proponent of that cause?"

"Difficult," I agreed.

"But not impossible, if he was prepared to pay the price. Morally, he could not be reproached. All such a marriage would do is embarrass the government. So, being an honourable man, Strafford proposed to abandon his political career for the woman he loved, who, in turn, undertook to detach herself from the Suffragette cause and become a devoted wife. But the path of honour did not bring him salvation. His plan was unimpeachable, yet its execution went awry in the most mysterious manner. Strafford submitted his resignation, intending that it should immediately be followed by an announcement of his engagement. But no such announcement could be made because, but a few hours after delivering his letter of resignation to 10 Downing Street, he was rejected in the most outright terms by his fiancée. She renounced their engagement for reasons she refused to disclose and asked that Strafford should never attempt to see her again. He was devastated."

"As well he might be," I said. "Why did she do it?"

"Strafford never knew. Shattered as he was by his rejection, all he could do at the time was attempt to re-build his way of life, which he had been so busily demolishing. The day after his resignation, he called again at number 10, intending to rescind it."

"Intending?"

"Yes, but it was not to be. The Prime Minister refused to hear of it, though not because he felt he was being trifled with, nor because he disapproved of Strafford's now aborted marriage. He cited other reasons which he declined to specify but which he felt sure Strafford could guess. Actually, he could not. This was a second inexplicable rejection from a source which had hitherto shown him only favour. Strafford was beside himself with despair. He brooded over it endlessly. It became the tragedy and the mystery of his life, and prompted him to compile this Memoir, many years later, when at last he could bear to commit it to paper."

"That could be the sort of mystery we spoke about earlier."

"I think it is, Martin—a mystery worthy of an historian such as yourself. Which is why I was delighted to hear you were to visit Alec, who spoke so highly of your abilities."

I glanced quizzically at Alec. This was the second time I'd heard of his advance publicity for me. "I know what you're thinking," he said, forestalling me. "But do you seriously suppose I would have spoken well of you if I'd thought it would get back to you? Leo's betrayed my confidence." He turned to the old man with mock outrage.

"Let us close with a smile," said Sellick. "It is late and I must take these tired old bones to bed. Here is the Memoir, Martin,"—he handed me the heavy volume—"for you to peruse at your leisure. Take my advice and leave it till morning —I'd value your opinion on it both as an historical document and as a personal testament. But then, we'd probably agree that they're the same thing anyway. The room next to the one you always have, Alec, has been prepared for Martin. I trust I can leave you to show him up when you're ready. Now I must bid you goodnight. Sleep well."

With that, Sellick left us. Alec poured himself another drink and we fell to a desultory discussion about the warmth of our reception. I detected in Alec's manner a slight sourness, though whether this arose from boredom, having heard the story before, or from some resentment that I'd monopolised Sellick's attention, I couldn't say. Alec himself denied the former and I dismissed the latter as an unworthy suspicion, but I was relieved when he did not demur at showing me up to my room.

Once there, I moved to the window and opened it. The shutters had been thrown back in readiness and I sniffed the cool night air wafting in across the garden behind the house. I'd hoped it might refresh me enough to turn to the Memoir that night, but Sellick had been right—it deserved a clear, wakeful head. So I confined myself to a glance at the title page in bed. One short paragraph served as prologue to the Memoir proper.

"In this volume I, Edwin George Strafford, propose to set forth the peculiar circumstances of my life and career. As a study in hubris, it may serve as a consolation for my soul and a concession to undeserving posterity."

There followed, in quotation marks, four lines of poetry:

Since as a child I used to lie
Upon the leaze and watch the sky,
Never, I own, expected I
That life would all be fair.

I took this to be some epigrammatic borrowing from a favourite poet of Strafford's, but he was not named. It put me vaguely in mind of A.E. Housman; certainly it had his fatalistic air. But I was tired and these thoughts were best left for morning. I laid the book aside and turned out the light.

I woke quite suddenly, stirred by some sound from the garden. I rose and stumbled to the window, squinting out at the glaring light of a perfect Madeiran day. Below, I could see at work the aged gardener who'd woken me. Checking my watch, I was dismayed to see that it was already past nine o'clock. So I bathed and dressed hurriedly and headed downstairs, taking the Memoir with me.

In the drawing room, the french windows stood open and, on the verandah, I found Sellick sitting by a breakfast table, sipping coffee, with a sheaf of papers on his lap. He smiled a greeting.

"Good morning, Martin. I trust you slept well?"

"Thank you, yes. Perhaps too well."

"Certainly not. You are, after all, on holiday. Sit down, relax. Tomás can fix you some breakfast in no time."

"Nothing for me, thanks. But some of that coffee would go down well."

Sellick poured me some from the pot. "You've missed Alec, I fear. He'll be back some time this afternoon. I felt sure that I could keep you occupied until his return—or, rather, that Mr. Strafford could." He leant forward and patted the Memoir where it lay on the table. "Have you made a start?"

"Not in earnest. I thought you were right about tackling it this morning. I've only glanced at the title page, which doesn't suggest it's a happy chronicle."

"One could not, in all honesty, call Strafford a happy man, as you will see. But I'm glad you haven't started reading the Memoir yet, Martin, because before you do—bearing in mind what I told you about it last night—I have a proposition to put which might interest you."

"You have?"

"Yes. Now, don't feel that I'm prying into your affairs, but I understand from Alec that you're not presently in any form of employment."

"That's true." Again, here was evidence of Alec making free with his knowledge of my affairs. It was a development I didn't care for.

"Taking that into consideration, along with your undoubted abilities as an historian, I may be able to offer you an engagement both financially lucrative and intellectually stimulating."

"You're offering me a job?" I was frankly incredulous.

"In short, I am. I have told you what I have learnt of the Strafford mystery, that the Memoir does nothing to dispel it, only increase it. There is no more to be discovered here. I feel the answer must lie in England. I am too old and too busy to go in search of it. Besides, I would not know where to begin what is essentially an exercise in historical research. But time and youth are on your side and I can supply the money. How would you like the task of finding out who—or what—betrayed Strafford in 1910?"

My incredulity was surpassed by my enthusiasm. A voice inside me said "Grab this offer—before it's taken back." The research task sounded interesting in its own right and the money that went with it could solve all my problems. But I didn't want to seem over-eager. Only that, not suspicion, stayed my hand.

"It sounds fascinating—and very generous."

"Not at all. I would finance you to find out what I want to know. If, coincidentally, you want to know it too, so much the better. But don't give me your answer now—take a look at the Memoir first, then see how you feel."

"Okay—you can't say fairer than that."

"Good. I'm glad you agree. And now, if you'll excuse me, I have some business to attend to. You would be most welcome to lunch with me later."

"Thanks. See you later, then."

Sellick made off with his papers, Tomás came and cleared the table and then I was left alone on the verandah with the Memoir. The sloping garden was shimmering in a heat haze as I settled back in my chair and began to read. It was time to let Strafford have his say.

Memoir

1876–1900

I was not born under a benighted star. I need protest no fault or handicap in the circumstances or the manner of my upbringing. I entered this life on 20 April 1876 at Barrowteign, my father's house in Devon. He was delighted to have a second son to brighten his old age, though I believe my mother had hoped for a daughter.

Barrowteign was a joy to be a child in—such a large, rambling house so filled with the memorabilia of my father's military career, such firm yet loving parents and necessarily indulgent servants, such extensive grounds of forest and moor for my boisterous yet protective brother Robert (six years my senior) to instruct me in, that I could not, for all the world, contrive a better place for a boy to learn his first of life.

My father was born in the same year as Queen Victoria and spent the middle third of his life defending her overseas possessions, notably India, where his conspicuous contribution to putting down the Mutiny won him his colonelcy. As a result, he was oft-times away from his beloved Barrowteign, that grand stone house that his father, old "Brewer" Strafford from Crediton, built as a monument to his own undoubted industry. It was, my father often told me, a disappointment to the founder of our family fortunes—whose start in life was, after all, hard and long work on that cloying red soil by the river Yeo—that his son should disdain the brewery office and take instead the King's Shill-

ing. But, as his son's military career prospered in foreign parts, it may have bolstered his reputation in the locality and I like to think that he basked in a certain reflected glory when my father's distinguished conduct in the Crimea and in India became known.

My grandfather died in 1867 and it was only this that prompted my father to retire from the army and return home. When he did so, he at once disposed of an active interest in the brewing business and, with hardly less speed, married the daughter of a local doctor—my mother, who was then only 23 and found herself quite bowled over by the handsome colonel of nearly fifty who, if the truth were told, was much more nervous than she about the whole affair, having imagined during his years abroad that he would remain a bachelor to the end of his days, and being more used to commanding men than courting ladies. The match, however, was a blissfully happy one.

I passed my carefree childhood at Barrowteign in perfect contentment, my father re-living the battles of his youth in play as surely only an old soldier can, my mother reminding me of the bloodshed which my father had also seen and chosen not to mention, my brother leading forays out onto the adjacent moorland, where we waged our own mock battles amongst the tors and bracken. These were confined to holidays when he went away to school—Marlborough, when he was eleven. I followed him at the same age.

Childers, that Classics master whom many Marlburians will remember with awe, selected me as a promising pupil and ensured that my promise, such as it may have been, was fulfilled. My father thought it a signal honour and my mother a just reward that I won a scholarship to Trinity College, Cambridge in 1894.

It was my active participation in the debates and functions of the Union Society that first drew me towards politics as a career. I saw the Union as a flawed but not unworthy recreation of the Greek demos and looked towards Westminster in the same way. My naïvety now astounds me, but, at the time, it ensured that my energies in that direction were undimmed by caution or reservation.

During my second summer vacation, I intimated my sense of

vocation to my family, who supported my endeavours with all the wholeheartedness I had come to expect. My brother Robert was now effectively head of the household by reason of my father's age and infirmity and was fast establishing a reputation of his own as a breeder of cattle. My father had been for some years an alderman of Okehampton and these factors facilitated my early introduction to Sir William Oliphant, the sitting Member for Mid-Devon. He had been in Parliament at this time for more than forty years and had already indicated that he did not propose to stand for re-election. It was my great good fortune that Sir William's recommendation, the standing of our family in the county and whatever fame I won as President of the Union in my last year at Cambridge, sufficed to secure my selection as prospective Liberal candidate in the constituency. With the next general election due in 1902, I felt that I had a good chance of so nurturing my prospects that I might then join the august assembly at Westminster as Mid-Devon's representative.

I came down from Cambridge in 1897 with a good degree and accompanied my mother on a six-month tour of France and the Mediterranean. It was, I think, a great joy for her to be shown the historical and artistic treasures of Italy and Greece by her favoured son. It was in Rome that we encountered a college friend of mine: Gerald Couchman, who had been rusticated during our last year for pauperizing a fellow-student in a card game. Couch (as we called him) was one of those fine, rumbustious high-livers whose morals bore no close inspection but whose spirit and company were alike irresistible. I paid no heed to his somewhat ruthless style of gambling—his own finances being precarious and his victims generally better endowed with wealth than good sense, it struck me as no great crime—but our tutor, the narrow-minded Threlfall, conceived a great personal dislike for Couch, who obliged him by sailing rather close to the wind. In the incident for which he was punished, Couch had no idea how ill could his opponent afford to lose. I believe that, when this finally became known to him, he waived the debt, too late to appease the wrath of Threlfall. So Couch's studies stood suspended for a year, during which time we met him whiling away his days in Rome, where he had secured an obscure teaching appointment and where his gambling adventures went unmonitored.

If like attracts unlike, I suppose my friendship with Couch could be said to exemplify that tendency. In indulging and secretly applauding his scapegrace ways, I perhaps compensated for that probity and respectability which, as a budding politician, I had to be seen to embrace but which occasionally sat ill with my youthful exuberance. Even my mother confessed to enjoying Couch's company in Rome and tolerated in him greater laxity than she would condone in others.

Couch went back to Cambridge and I went back to Devon, to be seen at shows and sales with my brother, meeting local residents in the company of my father (who appeared to see my election as his last great military campaign) and speaking at meetings with Sir William. The Liberal Party was then, in all conscience, at sixes and sevens, still striving to adjust to the retirement of Mr Gladstone. Indeed, in three short years we had three different leaders—Rosebery, Harcourt and Campbell-Bannerman—a helter-skelter progression which convinced Sir William that he had left his own retirement too late and which infused me with no very great confidence in the leadership of the party to which I was now committed. Not that there had ever been any question of my joining the Conservatives. On all issues of substance—free trade, Ireland, the Empire, the House of Lords—I was firmly of the Liberal mind, but such volatility at the helm was a trifle disconcerting. It was my brother, ever a good judge of land, who pointed out to me how it lay in this regard. For, as he said, a time of flux was ideal for a young hopeful to win his spurs.

In the short term, what was needed was patience. And just as, kicking my heels at Barrowteign, I began to exhaust mine, Gerald Couchman came to my rescue. In the summer of 1898, he at last graduated from Cambridge and took up residence in London as a young man about town, living with an indulgent aunt in St John's Wood. He invited me to stay with him there awhile and, since this would enable me to follow events in Parliament at first hand, I was encouraged to go. In the event, my visits became frequent and lengthy, so delightfully open-handed was Couch's aunt in the accommodation of guests. Her nephew led me into bad habits with a cheery smile, but I refrained from his worst excesses and kept my ear close to the ground at Westminster, where my time was well-spent.

But not, alas, reassuringly spent. There was perceptible during the spring and summer of 1899 a drift to war with the Boer republics of Transvaal and the Orange Free State that appeared, to me at any rate, to possess an inevitability borne of the most extreme and swaggering nationalism amongst the populace of London (and, I have little doubt, of Pretoria too). The low halls and taverns which Couch sometimes induced me to visit generally rebounded at this time with the most unreasoning war sentiment and caused me to doubt, for the first time, my faith in the demos. It became clear that the Liberal party would be divided should war come. Campbell-Bannerman and Lloyd George opposed hositilities and came to be roundly abused for their pains; Asquith and the former leader, Rosebery, supported them.

My position was equivocal, which met with Sir William's approval but which considerably put out my father, who judged that methods employed against the Sepoys in 1857 should be followed against the Boers in 1899; in vain did I seek to dissuade him. It was Couch who convinced me that one could carry reason too far, never being one to do so himself. We were seated at Lord's one day in June—watching Victor Trumper score a century for the Australians—when we fell to discussing what we should do in the event of war. Couch was all for enlisting at once and sampling the excitement of action. The subtleties of the dispute were of no interest to him where an opportunity for overseas adventure was concerned. To a great extent, he won me over. If war did come, I felt sure that an election would be delayed, not hastened, so time was likely to hang heavy if I stayed at home. There seemed, moreover, no substitute for first-hand experience upon which to base my own view of the matter. Accordingly, we pledged, as only young men can, to enlist together.

Fortuitously, my father was not unacquainted with General Buller, the Commander-in-Chief, whose career had started in India just as my father's was coming to fruition there and whose family home was near Crediton. Through his good offices, Couch and I were admitted that summer to the volunteer *reserve of the Devonshire regiment. When war did break out, in October, we were gazetted second lieutenants.*

So it was that, on October 11, we set sail from Southampton with General Buller and the rest of the regiment, bound for Capetown. Aboard, I encountered amongst our fellow-passengers that youthful veteran of Omdurman, Winston Churchill, like me set upon a political career, but (at this stage) in the Conservative interest. He was going to South Africa as a reporter for the Morning Post *and little did I think that I would one day sit in Cabinet with him.*

We reached Capetown at the end of October amidst a scene of some consternation, the Boers having by now invested Kimberley and Mafeking and, shortly thereafter, Ladysmith. Even to a novice such as I then was, there was a lack of conviction in the dispositions made by General Buller to cope with this emergency. He split his force into three and sought to raise all three sieges at once, a division of effort which proved disastrous. Couch and I accompanied Buller as junior adjutants north towards Ladysmith. I confess that I for one was so busily engaged in adapting to the military life in a strange country that I had little time to spare for assessing our strategy, but my instinct that it was miswrought proved sound. Buller convinced himself that the Boer forces around Ladysmith were too strong for him to lift the siege and he was right. But news of Gatacre's defeat at Stormberg and Methuen's at Magersfontein stung him into a frontal assault upon the Boer positions at Colenso on the Tugela river on December 15, only three days after reporting that a direct attack would prove too costly. That cost was a comprehensive defeat, a thousand men dead, his own command forfeited and the creation in the public mind at home of the doleful phenomenon of "Black Week", which stilled, for a moment, the bellicose clamour of the music halls.

Unhappily, the defeat at Colenso carried a bitter personal lesson for me. A battlefield far from home is no place to learn that one's trusted friend is a coward, but this conclusion was forced upon me by Gerald Couchman's conduct that day. In an action to save the ten guns that were ultimately lost, Buller took a personal hand and, therefore, we adjutants with him. In this action, the general was himself wounded and the only son of Lord Roberts was killed. I did what little I could with what fortitude I could muster, but Couch held back and, in an incident overlooked by all but me, quitted the scene in a craven act of self-preservation. I did not despise him for it, for any sane man would have felt fear that day, but I was chastened to learn that he could leave my side at such a crucial time. I did not reproach him afterwards, yet he knew that I had seen, and matters were never again the same between us.

When Lord Roberts was appointed as the new C-in-C, Buller despatched Couch and me to Capetown to await his arrival and perform what services we could in a staff capacity. We passed a long, silent, grudging journey back, Couch perhaps appalled by his own discovery about himself, perhaps resenting my silence as a reminder of it, I saying too little for fear of saying too much and reflecting that perchance the censorious Threlfall had been right all along. It might have cheered us to know that Colenso was the first and last action either of us was to see in South Africa. It might, but I must take leave to doubt it.

Lord Roberts reached Capetown in the middle of January, 1900, with the redoubtable Kitchener as his chief of staff. He at once overhauled the organization of the whole campaign and it was this greater attention to matters of supply, transport and communication that not only effected a transformation of the army's fortunes but also detained me in the Cape for the rest of my time in South Africa. My political reputation, such as it was, had evidently gone before me, for I was directed to devote some of my time—when it was not consumed in ordinary staff duties—to a tentative exploration of popular feeling in the Cape, most especially to a cultivation of the Dutch community, with an assurance of happy internal relations, when the war was over, the ultimate objective. I made little enough progress in this direction, but did what I could and always found contact with the citizenry of the Cape—its elected representatives, its magistrates and landowners, its journalists and businessmen—interesting and instructive. Couch was, at this time, engaged in the coordination of supplies, for which he developed a forte. I will say no more than that, where the distribution of food and equipment was concerned, he was not slow to introduce a commercial element to his own advantage. At all events, we saw little of each other at this time.

By the summer of 1900, the war seemed virtually over. Roberts having taken Johannesburg on May 31 and Pretoria five days later, there appeared to remain only the mopping-up of Boer resistance. It was this swift redemption of Buller's earlier blunderings that presumably convinced the Conservative-Unionist government at home that the time was ripe for a general election. It seemed to me, when I heard of it, a simple attempt to capitalize on the victorious mood of the people, but it is true to say that my view may have been influenced by the imminence of my candidature for Parliament, which I had thought to be two years away and for which I was consequently ill-prepared.

Lord Roberts showed great understanding of my difficulty and sanctioned my immediate return home. Here Couch, for all that I have said about his loss of nerve at Colenso, did me a not inconsiderable service. I had accepted an invitation to stay with the van der Merwes, an influential Dutch family near Durban, as part of my bridge-building exercise. Passing through Capetown in late August, I met Couch by chance and mentioned that I would have to disappoint the van der Merwes if I were to return to England in time to make any kind of fist of the election, which seemed a pity, this being the most overt hospitality I had been shown by the Dutch community. Couch, granted leave at this slack time, when everyone was merely awaiting the formal cessation of hostilities, volunteered to take my place in Durban. In a role where charm counted for much, I have little doubt that he did an excellent job.

So it was that I arrived home in England with but a week in which to conduct my election campaign. As I might have known, my parents and brother had already mounted a highly effective one in my absence and it was the considered opinion of Flowers, the taciturn agent whom I inherited from Sir William, that any attack upon my party's attitude to the war by my Conservative opponent would be more than offset by my own record of service in South Africa. In this he was correct. The general election of October 1900 has ever after been referred to as the "Khaki" election and if it was, as I firmly believe, the government's attempt to exploit their virtual vic-

tory in South Africa, I am happy to record that it went otherwise for them in Mid-Devon.

I shall ever recall the scene in the town hall at Okehampton in the early hours of October 5, when the returning officer announced my victory at the poll by a majority only a little short of that traditionally commanded by Sir William and a throng of red-faced Devonians toasted in cider their new young tribune. At the age of 24, I found myself a member of that most exalted of democratic institutions—the British Parliament—with everything to look forward to.

"Senhor Radford! Excuse the interruption: the master has asked me to tell you that luncheon is served."

It was old Tomás speaking, rousing me from the reverie that had followed my completion of the first chapter of the Memoir.

"Obrigado, Tomás," I said. Then, hesitantly, I sought to use a little more of the basic Portuguese I'd gleaned from my handbook. *"Oude fica o almoço?"*

"In the morning room, senhor," Tomá replied. "Please come with me."

Taking the Memoir with me, I followed him along the verandah.

"Have you been on the island long, senhor?"

"Only a few days."

"Then your Portuguese does you great credit."

"Thank you for saying so. But I think your English does you greater credit."

"No, no senhor. I have been here forty years and Quinta do Porto Novo has always had a master who spoke English. Therefore, it has not been difficult for me to learn your language, so excellent was my teacher."

Who'd taught him English? If Tomás had been there forty years, it seemed he must mean Strafford.

"You worked for Senhor Strafford?"

"Yes, senhor. I had that honour."

We'd passed through the drawing room into the hall. Tomás led me along the gallery to a large, airy room on the western side of the house, with picture windows overlooking the vineyard. At one end of the room was a grand piano and, above it on the wall, an oil painting of a savannah landscape. In the center of the room stood a table, laid with bowls and plates for a salad lunch. There was an air of newness here, more of Sellick and less of Strafford.

I tried to draw Tomás out before he left me. "You admired Senhor Strafford?"

"Senhor Strafford was a gentleman."

"Thank you, Tomás. That will be all." Sellick's voice came abruptly from behind us. Tomás nodded gravely and padded away. There was a hint of curtness in his dismissal, dispelled at once by Sellick's warmth and courtesy to me.

"I see you have the Memoir with you, Martin. Set it aside for a moment and help yourself to some lunch. I trust you will excuse the informality of the arrangement."

"It looks delicious. All this is really too generous of you."

"Not at all. I have put a business proposition to you. The least that I can do is offer some meagre hospitality whilst you consider it."

There was, needless to say, nothing meagre about his hospitality. I took some grilled tuna from a platter and some of the rice, potato and vegetable salads that accompanied it. Sellick poured me some vinho verde and offered me a seat by the window. This had been slid half-open to a wisp of cooling breeze in the midday heat. Below, the vines stood in silent ranks. This was the siesta hour and no sound broke the peace.

I'd set the Memoir down on a coffee table between us. "Have you made much progress?" Sellick asked. "You see that I cannot contain my curiosity."

"I've just finished the first chapter: Strafford's just been elected to Parliament. It's a fascinating read."

"I hoped that you would find it so. Has it helped you to form a view of my earlier proposition?"

"It's confirmed my first reaction—that I'd be delighted to accept. I feel sure it's an opportunity I don't deserve. But, if you're prepared to back me, I'll try to justify your confidence."

"I'm most gratified to hear you say so, Martin. Let's drink to your investigation."

As we touched glasses to toast our agreement, I thought of Helen again, for the second time that morning: Helen, my dear ex-wife. She'd always performed that ritual when wine was served with a meal. I remembered her tight frown of annoyance whenever I drank from the glass prematurely, now with none of the impatience I'd have felt at the time. It was odd to think of her with so little venom, odder still that Strafford's college friend, Gerald Couchman, should share her surname. For Couchman was not a common name.

"You look pensive, Martin."

"The Memoir's given me a lot to think about. To be honest, I can't wait to get back to it."

"I understand and will not delay you. But before you do, you might be interested in seeing Strafford's study. You'll remember I referred to it last night."

"That would be very interesting."

"Straight after lunch then."

When we'd finished our meal, Sellick led me back to the hall and up the stairs to a large room on the southern side of the house. When he opened the shutters, light flooded onto a scene that took me straight back to Strafford. Sellick explained that he never used the room himself and had left it as it was when he arrived. The view from the window was of the garden and, beyond that, the sea. Motes of dust floated in the sunlight and the tick of an old longcase clock by the door added to the impression of another time and place. In front of the window was a large mahogany leather-topped desk and, in front of that, a leather-seated, wheelback swivel chair.

This, clearly, was the desk where Sellick had originally found the Memoir. Either side of the inkstand were the framed photographs that must have drawn Strafford's eye every time he sat there. On the left was a studied portrait of a couple, the man elderly, with a walrus moustache but a ramrod back, the woman middle aged and elegant—surely Strafford's parents.

On the right was a less formal portrait of a young lady. She wore a high-necked dress, fastened with a brooch. Her dark hair was drawn up high and evenly from her face, with just a few strands hanging by her cheeks. Her eyes were large, dark and intent and her lips, slightly parted, seemed just about to smile. To me, she was a stranger—or so I thought. To Strafford, she must have meant, at some time, almost everything. That certainty charged not only her look but the very placing of her photograph. Strafford could have sat there and seen those eyes and, beyond, the ocean, both so deep and distant, every day of his life on Madeira. But only his Memoir could tell me what the frozen past of this room never would: what he felt when he looked at the confident, confiding tilt of her chin, fixed in time by the camera, or gazed out across the placid infinity of the ocean.

"It's as if Strafford had just left the room," I said at last.

"Isn't it?" said Sellick. "I feared it might seem morbid to leave it like this, but with so much space to spare, why not? It's easy to imagine him sitting at that desk."

"I just have. Presumably, one of these pictures is of his parents. What about the other one?"

"There's really only one person it can be."

"His fiancée?"

"That's right: Elizabeth Latimer. My enquiries have revealed that she is still alive in England, under her married name of Couchman . . . You look surprised, Martin."

"The name . . . Then she . . ."

"Married Gerald Couchman. That's right. But I'm sorry. I really shouldn't give so much away like this. Still, you must have wondered why Strafford made such a point of that friendship."

I had, and this explained it. But it wasn't the irony of Strafford losing his fiancée to his discredited former friend that dismayed me, though I was happy for Sellick to think that it was. It was the echo in my own past that his words caused. No longer was there just a coincidence of surnames. Seven years before, at my own wedding, I'd met the redoubtable Elizabeth Couchman, Helen's grandmother, then a hale old widow of eighty, and still, it appeared, alive and well. It was the achievement of her generation of Couchmans that made my marriage the social coup my family thought it was and which, in the end, helped to unmake it. Now, in Strafford's study on Madeira, I encountered my ex-wife's grandmother as the beautiful young Edwardian lady she once was and the woman who won—and broke—the heart of a famous man.

After dismay came caution. It was still possible—just—that this wasn't the person I thought. But if it was, how would Sellick react to my connection with a family that was to form part of my investigations? Not well, my instincts told me. And they went further: don't risk this golden opportunity, don't tell him. So I didn't.

"It makes it all the sadder," I said. "That and the atmosphere of this room."

"Yes," said Sellick. "There are so many echoes."

For a moment, I was alarmed. Had he found me out? No. How could he? There were echoes enough of Strafford's past without him needing to guess at those of mine—weren't there?

"I know what you mean." The truth was, I hoped I knew what he meant. "In fact, the Memoir seems so much more real here—more immediate—that I'd like to stay to read it, if that's all right."

"By all means, Martin. Stay as long as you like. I'll make sure you're not disturbed. I hope, though, that you'll join me for an aperitif before dinner. Alec's sure to be back by then."

"Thanks. I'd like to."

Sellick left then, closing the door behind him. I sat at the desk and looked out across the garden and the valley towards the sea, then back at the picture of that face and those eyes, imagining Strafford doing the same. I opened the Memoir and looked at his firm, assured handwriting, betraying nothing, no sign, no quaver that might tell me the message those eyes held for him. There was only one way to find out. Eagerly, I resumed my reading.

Memoir

1900–1909

Parliament was due to assemble in early December, 1900. By then, I had recovered somewhat from the euphoria of election night and had taken rooms in Pimlico, so as to be handily placed for Westminster. Sir William had kindly arranged my introduction to some of the leading figures of the party and my brother had quietly assured me of such financial support as might be necessary in the straitened circumstances of a fledgling M.P.

I had supposed that, in the Parliamentary Liberal Party, I would rejoice in the company of enlightened, like-minded men steering a straight course for the betterment of their country. I soon discovered that such a rosy view could not be sustained when I actually joined their ranks. I knew, of course, that the war had created a division of opinion. What I did not know, but sought rapidly to assimilate, was that on virtually no point was there universal agreement, that many of the disagreements had more to do with personal enmities than issues of principle and that possibly the only uniting factor was an interest by individuals in cultivating a political career. Such and swift was the disenchantment of the new M.P. for Mid-Devon.

But I must not do an injustice to the many able men whom I encountered at Westminster. Campbell-Bannerman, the leader, was a tough old Scottish Liberal who at once surprised me by his radicalism. He seemed determined to soldier on despite the mutterings of those who thought him mediocre. I was often told how we should revert to Rosebery or plump for Asquith as leader but, as a young and impressionable man imbued by my father with a respect for older generations, I unhesitatingly aligned myself behind C-B.

The only issue on which we might have differed was the war. But my experiences in South Africa had not endeared me to our cause in that conflict. My latter days there, spent as they were more amongst the local populace than the military, had filled me with great respect for their robust desire for independence and I felt sure, as did C-B, that the correct Liberal line was to deplore a piece of heavy-handed colonialism. In taking this view, I found an enthusiastic welcome in that most fiery spirit of the party—Lloyd George, whose accounts of speaking against the war in public almost persuaded me that I had had a softer time of it at Colenso.

Lloyd George was an inspiration. Not that much older than me, he embodied what seemed the youthful promise of the party. Instead of the non-committal crustiness I found in older members, Lloyd George could exuberantly and persuasively propound so many reforms that one was left only wondering in which order they should be introduced. Whilst laying great stress upon his Welshness, he did not trouble himself to disguise his own ambition, the very English one of being Prime Minister. I could see no reason why he should not be, indeed contemplated the prospect with some relish for my own position should he one day have charge of things. For I was not slow in developing my own ambitions and a desire to advance them.

It was certain, however, that neither the Liberal party nor its rising young men could hope for much whilst the war lasted and the public suspected our patriotism. And the war lasted much longer than I had supposed it would. So far from being virtually over when I left Capetown at the end of August, 1900, it had nearly two years to run. The Boers resorted to highly effective harrying tactics and Kitchener, now the C-in-C, responded with a scorched earth policy, destroying homesteads and rounding up the Boer population in camps. In my maiden speech in Parliament, in March 1901, I deplored the breakdown of negotiations between Kitchener and Botha and questioned what purpose would be served by the gradual subordination of a people to the extent that, finally, they felt only mute hostility towards the mother country. Lloyd George congratulated me afterwards and C-B winked a sagacious eye. There was even a quiet word in the lobby from Winston Churchill, now a Conservative M.P. but eager to befriend any fellow-newcomer to the House.

But the war did eventually end in May 1902. When news came that a peace treaty had at last been signed, I remember thinking of Gerald Couchman, whom I had not seen since leaving South Africa. I wondered how he had fared there in the long extension of hostilities which neither he nor I had anticipated. As it happened, I went up to Lord's one afternoon in June to catch some play in the Test Match. Seeing Fry and Ranjitsinhji, the most stylish of England's batsmen, both out for ducks, I beat a hasty retreat and, reflecting that Couch's aunt lived nearby, called round to seek news of him from my one-time hostess. Sadly, I learnt only that she had died the year before and that the house was now owned by strangers, who knew nothing of her nephew.

Peace in South Africa brought peace too in the Liberal party. Old feuds were forgotten and, now that the government could no longer rely on patriotism to bolster it up, thoughts turned to the next election and how the party might fare at it. The Prime Minister, Lord Salisbury, retired and his successor, Balfour, developed a knack helpful to we Liberals of offending members of his own party. One such was Winston Churchill, who crossed the floor of the House and became a Liberal in May 1904.

That spring had seen some family concerns draw my attention back to Devon. My brother had announced the previous autumn his engagement to Miss Florence Hardisty, the daughter of Admiral Hardisty of Dartmouth. Arrangements were going forward for an Easter wedding when my father died, quite suddenly, at Barrowteign. His last wish, expressed to my mother, was that the wedding should go ahead as planned. Some delay was inevitable, but I supported the idea that it should be as brief as possible. Accordingly, on a sunny St George's Day, I officiated as best man when the elder Strafford went down the aisle.

I confess that I found my new sister-in-law a rather dull

embodiment of provincial worthiness, a sure sign that London was turning my head, and cared not for the insipid watercolour painting that constituted her principal recreation. Through no fault of her own, Florence made Barrowteign seem less like home than once it did, but mine was a lone and perchance over-sensitive reaction. Florence prudently deferred to my mother in matters of household management and made a good, commonsense wife for Robert.

It was with some relish that I now devoted myself to events at Westminster. An early election seemed in prospect and we were all busy with an unofficial campaign. On 13 October 1905, I appeared in a supporting role with Sir Edward Grey, everybody's tip for the Foreign Office should we win, at a meeting to support Winston Churchill's candidature in northwest Manchester (his first in Liberal colours). An otherwise unremarkable occasion was rendered memorable by constant interruptions from an unlikely source: two young ladies. They stridently demanded of us a promise of votes for women, which they did not extract. I learned that one of them was Christabel Pankhurst, a name that later came to mean a lot more to me than it did at the time. There was great publicity surrounding the incident and the two were briefly imprisoned for refusing to pay a fine for disorderly conduct, arising from a commotion they caused in the street after being expelled from the meeting.

I was bemused and set thinking by this event, to the extent of canvassing the opinion of others. I could not, for my part, see how a Liberal government could oppose female suffrage, but we were not committed to it, quite the reverse. Lloyd George agreed with me on the principle of the case but pointed out that other, more important, reforms would have to come first. My mother pronounced herself a suffragist, but deplored militant tactics, whilst my sister-in-law had no opinion to express. I tended to take the Lloyd George view: first things first. Yet I can now see how a newspaper report of that disrupted meeting in Manchester would have read to a precocious sixteen-year-old girl, quite as intelligent as the average voting male, as the advent of a crusade. Little did she or one of the affronted speakers in Manchester know that they were one day to care a great deal more about each other than about the issue of female suffrage.

In December 1905, Balfour finally threw in his hand and resigned. C-B received the premiership that was a just reward for many years' toil, presiding over an exceptionally talented administration, with Asquith at the Eschequer and Lloyd George at the Board of Trade. My highest hopes were fulfilled when I was myself given a junior appointment. In eagerly accepting, I hardly paused to consider the nature of that appointment and thus found myself a junior lord of the Admiralty with a negligible knowledge of the sea.

I had, however, no time to brood on the point. C-B had no intention of seeking to govern with a minority (a rather obvious trap laid by Balfour) and called an election for January 1906. Matters were rather better prepared in my constituency this time and, done no harm by my new appointment, I was returned with an increased majority. Nationally, the party fared even better than we had hoped, securing an historic victory.

There was, however, no opportunity for me to bask in an afterglow of success. Back in London, there was work to be done. The First Lord of the Admiralty, Lord Tweedmouth, was a staunch old Scot who had served his time under C-B and now received his reward. His seat in the Lords made me answerable for naval policy in the Commons: an onerous responsibility but one which gave me an opportunity to shine. Winston Churchill benefited from a similar arrangement at the Colonial Office, where his Secretary of State was likewise a peer. We came to know each other well at this stage, both feeling that we could make our names in the service of superannuated seniors.

In February 1907, I became an uncle when Robert's son, Ambrose, was born. A happy child, his company made Barrowteign a more congenial place for me to spend the summer recess and it was clear that the birth of a son and heir meant not a little to my brother, now well set in the life of a country gentleman, who bore with good humour my chiding of him for becoming set in his ways.

Early in 1908, the Prime Minister's health began to break

down. In April, he was obliged to resign and, before the month was out, he was dead. I was sorry to lose his steady hand upon the tiller, but was not blind to the possibility for promotion opened up by the consequent rearrangements. Rather earlier than I had expected, I was summoned to see our new leader. Asquith was a man of whom I had once been suspicious, finding him, when I was new to Westminster, aloof and often absent. But now he was all beaming beneficence in offering me a post in the Cabinet. Herbert Gladstone, he said, had been induced to accept the Governor-Generalship of Canada. Asquith deemed that a younger, more vigorous approach at the Home Office was required than Gladstone had brought to bear. In consideration of my work at the Admiralty, he offered me the post. This was more than I had dared hope for. I accepted with alacrity. Asquith remarked that I was to form part of what he considered to be a brilliant team. For the moment, though, I was concerned only with the honour and achievement of becoming Home Secretary at the age of 32. There seemed no limit to my future aspirations.

It seems generally to be agreed that Asquith's 1908 Cabinet was a quite remarkable assemblage of political talent: a team for all occasions. With this I would not differ. Indeed, I was proud to join it and my arrival coincided with that of several other rising stars—Lloyd George promoted to the Exchequer, Churchill and McKenna admitted to the Cabinet for the first time.

Proud I was, but not blind to our shortcomings. Asquith had an incisive, lawyer's mind but seemed devoid of originality. The older members of the Cabinet resented us newcomers and, in the conflicts which arose from that, Asquith aligned himself behind those he thought would win the day, a tendency which positively encouraged collusion and intrigue behind the scenes. At this, Lloyd George, for all his apparent openness, excelled and found in Churchill an enthusiastic recruit to his radical cause. Sympathetic though I was to their reforming zeal, I distanced myself somewhat from them, being determined to find my feet before committing myself to any particular stance.

There was, besides, plenty of work to occupy me at the Home Office, where my predecessor had let matters slide.

The women's suffrage movement, by its implications both for the constitution and for civil order, now fell within my purview. I found myself torn between a wholehearted support for their cause in theory and a thorough disapproval of their methods in practice. When the Metropolitan Police Commissioner advised me that a mass meeting of all groups supporting female suffrage was to be held in Hyde Park on Sunday, 21 June 1908, I approved his proposals for policing the event and decided, without his knowing, to be present in person.

It was a memorable occasion. I was not sufficiently well-known to the public to be noticed, discreetly clad amongst the vast crowd that gathered, but I took good notice of what took place. There were speeches by Keir Hardie—of the new Independent Labour Party—and Emmeline Pankhurst, pleading their cause with great force and conviction. There was also a stirring contribution from Mrs Pankhurst's daughter, Christabel, whom I remembered from our encounter in Manchester in October 1905. It was a wholly peaceful gathering and I walked away amidst the departing throng wondering if something could not, after all, be done for them.

I conveyed my views to the Prime Minister, urging that the government should commit itself to female suffrage on a long-term basis, arguing that this would defuse much of the frustration clearly displayed at the meeting I had attended. I received a cursory answer to the effect that this was something against which the Cabinet had already set its face. In private, Lloyd George advanced a more cogent argument to me. What was the point of considering such a move when the House of Lords was certain to veto it anyway? I gained the impression that I was advancing a radical departure from agreed policy rather too soon after my appointment, so resolved to bide my time and say no more on the subject.

In the event, the suffragists proved quite capable of involving me in their campaign without any effort on my part. Later that summer, Emmeline and Christabel Pankhurst were arrested for inciting a mob to charge the House of Commons. Their case came up at Bow Street in late October. Much to my astonishment and that of Lloyd George, we were both subpoenaed by the defence. I myself was subject to some energetic interrogation by Christabel—a qualified barrister—but my experience in the House of Commons enabled me to refute her guileful arguments. My contention that the laudable theory of female suffrage was being done more harm than good by her antics cast me in a good light both in court and in the press, though I was wigged afterwards in a note from the Prime Minister for letting slip my private views.

Lloyd George invited me home for a drink after our court appearances and I expressed my fear to him that on female suffrage, as on some other issues, we were allowing more radical elements—such as the Labour Party—to steal our thunder. He agreed, pointing out that, whilst the House of Lords' Tory majority continued to veto Liberal legislation, it could hardly be otherwise. But he said he hoped to do something about that and, as events showed, he was as good as his word.

Lloyd George's fulfilment of his pledge was the Budget of 1909. Well I remember the many Cabinet meetings during March and April which pored over that gargantuan, revolutionary document. What he had contrived to do was to meet all the various claims upon the Exchequer—from an expansion of the navy to counter Germany, to the requirements of the new old age pension—by an extensive raid upon the resources of landed wealth, by income tax, super tax, death duties and, most dreaded of all, land value duties. And behind it all, as we argued the details back and forth, was an awareness that the Lords would never bear such a blow at their class. And since their rejection of a Budget was unprecedented, this was bound to bring to a crisis their repeated veto of other legislation. How it would be resolved nobody knew or cared to guess, certainly not the Prime Minister. Nevertheless, in the absence of any alternative and with Asquith's awe of Lloyd George ensuring that none would be found, we pressed forward. On 27 May 1909, the Finance Bill was issued in its final form and so was set in motion a trial of strength between the two Houses of Parliament.

Yet I remember that warm spring evening of May 27 for quite other reasons. I returned to my house in Mallard Street tired and thoughtful, wanting nothing so much as some peaceful solitude in which to turn over these portentous political events in my mind. I had resisted the Metropolitan Police

Commissioner's wish to place a constable at my door and so there was only Prideaux—my father's old valet who had come up to London with his wife to attend to my wants since my father's death—to greet me at home. He took himself off to the kitchen to instruct Mrs P to prepare supper for me, she being well-used to my irregular hours. I poured myself a scotch and sat down to peruse that morning's Times. *This was my first opportunity of the day for some rest and relaxation. I embarked upon it a single-minded young politician with thoughts fixed upon weighty matters of constitutional import, oblivious to the imminent explosion into my world of a personal but far more potent force.*

I set down the newspaper and crossed to the window, tiring for a moment of editorial speculation. As I toyed with my drink and gazed out onto the street, softly lit by evening sun, I observed a slim, elegant young lady dressed in grey, pass by the window and turn in at my door, then heard the sound of a letter landing on the doormat. My curiosity aroused, I hurried out into the hall and picked up the letter. It was, in fact, only a note on plain paper, folded in half. Unfolding it, I was taken aback to see that it read: "Whilst women are denied the vote, politicians shall have no peace".

At this point, there was the sound of breaking glass from the drawing room, splintering the quietude of evening. Glancing back into the room, I saw a half housebrick lying on the carpet where I had just been standing, shards of windowpane scattered around it. My elegant young caller had just hurled a brick through my window!

I flung the front door open and ran out onto the pavement. There she was, hurrying away down the road. Calculating that she had not reckoned upon immediate pursuit and enraged by this assault, I made after her. The street was empty, so she at once heard me running towards her, glanced round in alarm, then quickened her pace and turned right into a side road. I was at the corner in no time and saw she was only thirty yards or so ahead of me, dress gathered in her left hand as she now ran headlong in flight. She looked back again as she heard me drawing closer, shouting out for her to stop and, in so doing, failed to avoid the bootscraper by the door she was passing. She tripped and fell awkwardly against some railings flanking the door. The chase was over. I stooped over my fallen young assailant and turned her round by the left shoulder to face me.

"Do you realize . . . you might have killed me?" I said, breathless and angry.

"Are you Edwin Strafford?"

"I am."

"Then you've only yourself to blame. Did you read the note?"

"Yes . . ."

"Then you should see sense and meet our just demands . . . you're foolish, obdurate and wrong."

At this, the young lady sought to rise, only to slump back with a cry and clasp her right knee. Suddenly, absurdly, I was touched by her spirit and her injury. She had knocked her chin against the railings and this was reddening into a bruise. There were tears at the corners of her eyes so much had her leg pained her. She looked very young and beautiful, her mouth set in a frown of discomfort but her eyes flashing with determination. Strands of dark hair had escaped from her wide-brimmed hat and fell now across her flushed face. I forgot my outrage and felt, of all things, remorse for frightening her into a fall. That she, so young and vulnerable, should have been driven to this defiance, so ill-equipped to escape yet even now prepared to defend her cause, made me feel old and heartless.

"You've hurt yourself," I said. "Let me help you up."

Biting her lip, she was reluctantly obliged to accept my assistance. She flinched as she set her foot on the ground and I had to support her.

"I think," I said, "that, even if I am not to arrest you, I must insist that you accompany me back to my house."

She had no choice but to agree. Taking her firmly by the arm, I marched her back along the pavement as fast as her limp would permit. Indoors, I found the Prideaux in a fine state of consternation, Mrs P having convinced herself that I had been borne away by intruders. I explained what had actually happened and asked Mrs P to tend the young lady's injury. She led her charge away firmly but dutifully. Prideaux, who had cleared away the broken glass, asked if he should now call the police.

"Thank you no, Prideaux. For the present, a glazier will suffice." Prideaux took himself off, muttering some inaudible protest under his breath.

A few moments later, Mrs Prideaux returned with the young lady. "The little minx 'as taken no 'arm, sir. What shall us do with 'er?"

"Leave her to me, Mrs P," I replied. "I want to have a few words with her." She hesitated. "Don't worry. I shan't let her out of my sight." With this assurance, the good soul withdrew. I turned to my young guest.

"The question arises," I said, "of what is to be done with you."

"You may call the police and have me arrested if you wish."

"I think not. Your trial would provide just the sort of publicity you desire. And, besides, with Miss Pankhurst to defend you, I would be assured of a hot time in the witness box."

"As you were when Christabel was tried last autumn?"

"Quite so."

"I was there, Mr Strafford. You acquitted yourself well, but it was a sophist's victory."

"You think so?"

"Yes. It was an accomplished political performance, paying no heed to truth or justice."

Still this beautiful firebrand was prepared to debate with me. I was surprised at the force of her convictions and the intelligence of her arguments, above all at my willingness to overlook her throwing of the brick, my wish to sit and talk with her rather than hand her over to the police.

"Won't you sit down? Your leg must be hurting you."

"It is nothing. Your servant bandaged it." But she did sit down and was still a little flushed and breathless, though she had ordered her appearance since her fall, so that her dark eyes were dry and her hair in place.

"Since you know who I am, will you at least tell me who you are?"

"Elizabeth Latimer."

"And how old are you?"

"Twenty."

"What would your parents think if they knew what you had done here this evening?" It was a foolish question, the sort of question I knew I would resent in her shoes.

"If they were still alive, Mr Strafford, they would be as uncomprehending as you, though with the excuses of being older and less well-informed." I was suitably rebuked.

"I'm sorry, Miss Latimer. You must forgive any testiness on my part. It is a reaction to having a brick thrown through the window of my private house."

"You have been Home Secretary for a year now. What have you done in that time that would prevent an unenfranchised woman throwing a brick through your window?"

"But Miss Latimer, you have not yourself come of age."

"For shame, Mr Strafford. More sophistry."

She was right, and I was ashamed as I leant back in my chair and gazed across at her, wondering why, at the height of my powers and standing well in the counsels of the land, I could not match her for energy and commitment, why I should ever think that my mastery of debating techniques could excuse a politically expedient ambivalence. I recalled the scene in Okehampton Town Hall nine years before, when I had first been elected. My high hopes had since been fulfilled. But what of the electors' trust in me? Had that been rewarded, when Miss Latimer could so rightly rebuke me? I looked across at her, striving to conceal this sudden guilt, but she, gazing back, dispelled it in the most unexpected manner. Her mouth curled into a hesitant smile which was at once restrained, as if it had appeared in a forgetful moment. Her own mask, that of the amazon campaigner, had slipped, to show the beautiful, nervous young woman beneath.

"Mr Strafford—what do you propose to do with me?"

"Why, nothing, Miss Latimer."

"Nothing at all?"

"Nothing. You may go entirely free—on one condition."

"And that is?"

"That you meet me again soon, when you have recovered from your injury, so that we may discuss your views in calmer fashion."

"To what purpose?"

"Surely the man whose window is broken may attempt to show the breaker the error of her ways."

"Very well. You offer me an opportunity to show you the error of your ways which I can hardly refuse."

"Shall we say Hyde Park next Sunday afternoon at two o'clock—the seats by the Round Pond?"

"The venue seems an odd one."

"Miss Latimer, I cannot meet you in formal surroundings. Yet, as Home Secretary, I would earnestly like to hear more of how my government can so have failed that it drives the pride of its young womanhood to window-breaking. I would also like to bring you to understand that political realities preclude immediate concessions to what may appear to be the cause of justice and right. I should hope that such an exchange of views would prove educative to both parties. Yet it can only be of benefit if it remains, at this stage, confidential. I must therefore ask you not to report our meeting to your confederates."

"Mr Strafford, that is no hardship. They would pour scorn upon my failure." She blushed, as if regretting this frankness. "I will meet you on Sunday."

"Thank you, Miss Latimer. And by all means report your evening's work. I shall advise the newspapers of the attack upon my house. Privately, you are welcome to the credit."

"Though you and your colleagues are completely in the wrong, Mr Strafford, I must concede that you are at least a gentleman."

This seemed the most harmonious note we were likely to find on which to close. I called Prideaux and asked him to show her out. He did so with a disapproving grimace. I stood by the broken window of the drawing room and watched as Miss Latimer walked away down the street, still limping slightly. She did not look back, but I looked after her until she was out of sight, wondering if she would keep our appointment, whether, for that matter, I ought to keep it. Now that she had gone, it seemed an absurd thing to have agreed. Yet, already, I was looking forward to Sunday, determined in my heart to go, and do the worrying later.

Sunday May 30 duly came and I with it to Hyde Park in the sunshine. Parents were frolicking with their children by the

Serpentine as I made my way with as much nonchalance as I could muster towards the Round Pond. There I saw an old man selling balloons to clamouring children. As a group of them scampered away, a view opened up on the benches. Seated on one of them, dressed in cream and reading a book in the shade of a pale blue parasol, was Miss Latimer. She did not look up as I approached.

"Good afternoon, Miss Latimer," I said, doffing my hat.

"Good afternoon, Mr Strafford," she replied, looking up gravely from her book. "Won't you sit down?"

"It's a lovely day," I ventured conversationally as I sat beside her.

"It is indeed."

"May I ask what you have been reading?"

*"It's a new book of poems by Thomas Hardy—*Time's Laughingstocks.*"*

"Do you think that we are Time's laughingstocks, Miss Latimer?"

"We may be one day, Mr Strafford."

"One day, when women have the vote?"

"Touché."

"Alas, it was a sophist's thrust."

"It is good that you should recognize it as such."

"Thanks to you, Miss Latimer, I have lost faith in sophistry."

"I am glad to hear it, but doubtful. How can you so suddenly have lost faith in something which has served you so well in your career?"

"Let me try to explain."

"Please do."

And so it was that, on that bench in the warmth of a Sunday afternoon, with the sounds of ducks and children at play as accompaniment, I told Miss Latimer more of the effect of a political career on a politician than I had previously told anyone save myself. Perhaps my solitude had left me in unwitting need of such an opportunity. Certainly, Miss Latimer's sincerity had reminded me how much of that commodity I had been obliged to shed in the pursuit of public office. I told her how, in the effort to master each new brief, to establish a Parliamentary reputation, and to achieve good standing in the eyes of the Liberal leadership, I had perforce neglected those other aims which had been in my mind when first I solicited the support of the electors of Mid-Devon. I also explained that my rise to a Cabinet post and the small degree of fame that went with it gave me a measure of that independence necessary to implement some of those neglected aims. And in all this, I contended, there was a lesson for Miss Latimer and her fellow-Suffragettes: something could only be achieved after an apprenticeship of respectable endeavour, not simply by the power of argument, however forceful, in other words that they should emulate my example, serve their time and await their opportunity.

This was not best-calculated to appeal to an impetuous twenty-year-old. But Miss Latimer's counter-argument was based on other grounds, namely that the women's suffrage movement had served its time, since the last suffrage extension in 1884, that the presently growing militancy was a symptom of rightful frustration and that, if the Liberal Party did not soon take heed, they would lose ground to those—like the Labour Party—who would.

"Miss Latimer, you are more convincing than any house-brick."

"But, without the brick, would you have listened?"

"I have always listened to the suffragists, but I would not have listened to this one in particular. Therefore I give thanks for the brick."

"Mr Strafford, you flatter me. What matters is not whether I am convincing but whether you are convinced."

"I am convinced that you are a most remarkable young lady which my party is the poorer for having lost to the suffragist cause. How came it to have so ardent a campaigner?"

"In no very different way to that in which it has recruited many educated women who grew tired of waiting for politicians to see sense."

"Yet your example might be instructive."

"I doubt it. But my story is briefly told, so let us see. My family hails from the Forest of Dean. My mother died when I was born and my father when I was ten. I was an only child and therefore had to rely on the charity of distant relatives. Fortunately, an aunt took me in. I still live with her, in Putney.

My father had left sufficient for my education at a boarding school in Kent. There, one day in the library, I read of a meeting in Manchester disrupted by Christabel."

"I remember it well."

"It made me realize that there were many who shared my dissatisfaction with the sort of deferential existence we girls were being groomed for. As soon as I left school, I made contact with the Women's Social & Political Union. I was well-received and at once impressed by their energy and commitment. Christabel was the driving force and inspired us all, as she still does."

"To attack politicians?"

"Mr Strafford, you would hardly expect me to volunteer to His Majesty's Secretary of State for Home Affairs information about who planned or suggested such acts. I take sole responsibility for my action on Thursday evening."

"I am glad to hear it, Miss Latimer. I was not inviting disloyalty and, besides, your action on Thursday evening will never be a police matter. I am only trying to establish how matters have come to this pass."

"Then you already know. We women have waited too long and will wait no longer. Remember what I said in my note."

"Oh I do. Unhappily, it is not within the power of the government to meet your demands. If a bill for female suffrage passed the Commons tomorrow, it would assuredly be rejected by the Lords."

"That, Mr Strafford, is your problem."

"And it will be solved. Our differences with the Upper House are approaching a crisis, which will, I believe, be precipitated by this year's Budget. But the crisis will take time to resolve—at least a year. Until it is, what is the point in harrying us?"

"Lest you forget, when the time comes."

"I for one will not. But perhaps you could donate an occasional brick to serve as an aide memoire."

"I shall be casting no more in your direction. One is enough."

"Then we have achieved something?"

"I think so."

"Yet I may still forget. It would seem a pity to do so for want of your refreshing candour."

"Feel free to avail yourself of it at any time."

"I hope I may. I have enjoyed our talk here in the sunshine. Could I perhaps suggest a little outing into the countryside later this week for a further ministration of your antidote to a politician's self-importance?"

"In my judgment, Mr Strafford, you need the antidote less than your colleagues, but I would not wish to deny treatment to the valetudinarian."

"Who is pleased to hear it. My office permits me a few extravagances. One is the motor car I have recently purchased. An excursion in it might entertain you. Would Wednesday afternoon be convenient?"

"If you can free yourself from your duties for so long."

"Oh, I think I can. Besides, I would probably be doing the Metropolitan Police a service by occupying you for an afternoon. Could I perhaps collect you from your home at two o'clock?"

"A motor car at the door might prove too much for Aunt Mercy. Let us say Putney Bridge."

"By all means. I'll look forward to that."

So it was that I collected Miss Latimer as arranged on Wednesday afternoon. We drove out to Box Hill, a favourite picnic spot for Londoners, but pleasantly deserted that day. We strolled up onto the crest of the North Downs and took the air, full of the skylark's song and gentle summer breeze.

"Thank you for bringing me out here," said Miss Latimer. "It is wonderful on the downs."

"I wish that I came here more often," I replied.

"But you are too busy."

"And starved, until now, of an ideal companion."

She demurred, but did not deflect the compliment with some barbed bon mot, as she would have done the previous week. Later, in a tea shop in Dorking, we clashed briefly over the question of Suffragette hunger strikers. Just as I was about to point out that, with buttered scones before her, she was poorly placed to comment, she said the same herself. The absurdity of the militant campaigner taking tea with the dedicated poli-

tican whilst, elsewhere, civil servants might be ascurry at some new outrage, suddenly struck us and we dissolved into a laughter that drew disapproving glares from neighbouring tables. That day in Dorking, we did not care.

We returned to Putney in good time and I was invited in to meet Aunt Mercy. A small, spry, bright-eyed lady blissfully unaware of who I might be, met us in her conservatory and continued to tend her chrysanthemums whilst hearing of our outing. She insisted that her niece should show me the garden. There I took the opportunity of requesting Elizabeth's company for dinner on Friday. She accepted. This time there was no mention of curative treatment for my blindness to suffragism. This time, I said goodbye to Elizabeth, not Miss Latimer, and she to Edwin, not Mr Strafford. The fences were coming down.

Yet not all caution with them. I shunned my normal haunts for dinner, for fear of encountering a colleague, and took Elizabeth to an establishment favoured by my brother on his rare visits to the capital—The Baron in Piccadilly. I drove down to Putney on a fine evening to collect her. A maid admitted me and Elizabeth appeared from upstairs, wearing a dark blue velvet dress and presenting an appearance that is possibly my loveliest memory of her. She wore a pearl necklace and a brooch at her breast, but no other jewellery. Nor was any needed to enhance her beauty, the dark, lustrous hair drawn back from her face and the large, clear eyes gazing upon me. All in all, I felt, as we drove back towards Piccadilly, a very lucky man.

The Baron did me proud for dinner, the head waiter being as impressed by Elizabeth as I was. We spoke discursively and pleasurably, abandoning the rivalries of the suffrage for music, art and literature, our very different lives now converged in our strangely similar visions of the future. As we shared our thoughts, I found myself thinking of sharing our lives. Easy as that was by candlelight, I realized that realism would come with daylight: the Home Secretary and the Suffragette was not a viable partnership. Something had to give.

And we both gave, a little. Elizabeth could not abandon her cause, but, by eschewing militancy, she could avoid embarrassment to me. I could not abandon office, but, by saying nothing in public and telling the Cabinet in private that female suffrage must somehow be wrought, I could apply a little discreet pressure on her behalf. We did our best by each other. And for each other we seemed surpassingly good. We drove and dined often, Elizabeth introduced me to the opera and I her to cricket. We came to trust each other with confidences about intrigues in the Cabinet and the suffragist movement. Elizabeth seemed to make of me a better person and this newfound completeness took the raw edge off my political ambition. It had been charged with the difference Elizabeth made in me. And in her accounts of altercations with Christabel Pankhurst over campaign tactics, there appeared the hint of a difference that I had made in her.

With time, we became less cautious. I was down to speak in one of that summer's long, acrimonious Commons debates about the Budget. Only when halfway through did I realize that Elizabeth was in the public gallery, watching. I think it was her presence that made me risk a joke—well-received as it turned out—to the effect that, if the Chancellor's proposed diversion of funds to the tarmac-adamming of roads came to pass, many who had coughed on the dust thrown up by my own vehicle would be duly grateful and that they must include voters of both parties. That was, in a sense, a tribute to Elizabeth, who had told me "Never take yourself seriously—only what you believe in" and had been, as on most subjects, wise beyond her years.

I entertained her in the Members' tea room after the debate and she acknowledged the tribute, silently, over the tea cups. We were joined, unexpectedly, by Lloyd George. Perhaps he had seen Elizabeth and headed in our direction as a result, being one famed for his interest in the fair sex, especially a beautiful young representative of it. This fact made me slightly uneasy.

"Won't you introduce me to your charming companion, Edwin?"

"Certainly, L.G. Miss Elizabeth Latimer, the Chancellor of the Exchequer."

They shook hands, Lloyd George contriving to give Elizabeth the glad eye as he bowed and smiled. In any other company, I would have been amused by his incorrigibility; now I was irritated by it. Not that I needed to be, for Elizabeth treated him almost with disdain, to which he was not accustomed and which only our growing affection made it seem that he deserved. Still, it was not an uncongenial spectacle to one who had often enough seen the Prime Minister shrink beneath his Chancellor's wand.

Elizabeth betrayed a knowledge of politics over and above any confidences of mine and joked that even the tea in her company was Liberal (it was Earl Grey), which persuaded Lloyd George that she was that dangerous phenomenon, a beautiful and intelligent woman. The beauty and intelligence I could never have doubted, but of danger I saw no sign.

The summer passed in this carefree entrancement. Early in August, I was persuaded to indulge Aunt Mercy's passion for horse racing: Elizabeth and I took her down to Goodwood for the day. Aunt Mercy was the only one to win any money, but my sights were set on a higher prize. Picnicking on the grass with the slope of the South Downs behind us and Mercy lost somewhere in the press round the betting tent, I mentioned the impending Parliamentary recess, when I customarily got away to Barrowteign.

"I shall miss you while you're away," Elizabeth said.

"And I you. That is why I should be so very pleased if you would consent to accompany me."

"To Barrowteign?"

"Yes. Don't worry, you would be in excellent hands. There is my mother and my brother, his wife and their son. And I could show you the delights of Devon."

"And your ancestral home?"

"It's hardly that, but it is where my roots are. Won't you come?"

"If you think I would not be intruding."

"Certainly not."

"And if Aunt Mercy agreed."

"We'll ask her, but I'm sure she will."

"Then I'd very much like to go with you."

"You don't look quite certain."

"Oh, I'm certain. It's just that . . . oh, Edwin, sometimes I'm so nervous."

"There's no need to be. Just trust me."

And she said that she did. There was no need to say that I trusted her. Aunt Mercy, flushed with her winnings, expressed unconstrained enthusiasm for the proposal. A letter to my mother elicited equal enthusiasm and plans were swiftly made. Elizabeth reported qualms in her suffragist circle about such a long absence for undisclosed reasons, but she was not to be swayed by them. As soon as my official duties would permit, we were off.

The clock behind me struck seven and drew me forward nearly seventy years from the Sussex Downs to Madeira on an April evening. It was growing dark in Strafford's study now. If I'd not been so absorbed in his narrative, I'd have put the light on, but the gathering gloom seemed appropriate when I considered the bright promise of that distant summer and set it against an old man's desk far from home, with only photographs left of those he'd once held so dear.

Downstairs, Tomás sounded the dinner gong—I'd missed aperitifs. From Strafford's lost world, where I'd been all afternoon, it was a long way back to the present. So it came as a wrench to close the book and take it with me from the room.

In the drawing room, I met Alec coming in from the verandah, with Sellick behind him.

"We were wondering where you'd got to," Alec said.

"I'm sorry. I didn't notice the time until just now."

"Leo's been telling me about your deal. I believe congratulations are in order. Welcome back to the rat race."

"Thanks. I'm hoping it'll prove a more civilized race than the one with Millennium."

"Sure to be. You've done better out of Leo than I have. I think he's making a habit of rescuing English intellectuals down on their luck."

"How could I deny journalism Alec's wonderful turns of phrase?" said Sellick, smiling broadly.

"Nevertheless," I said, "we are both indebted to you, Leo. I hope you won't have cause to regret your generosity."

"I'm sure I shan't. And besides, am I not a hard taskmaster? It is Saturday, and I have let you go on working. But even the avid researcher must be fed. Shall we eat?"

Dinner was as excellent as the night before: succulent Porto

Santo melon followed by roasted local rabbit, washed down with more of Sellick's fine dão. He and Alec talked of the next issue of the magazine—and a few after that—but I said little. I was impatient to return to the Memoir. For the moment, Strafford's world interested me more than my own and dinner, even in civilized company, was no competition. My distracted state was not lost on Sellick. While he sipped malmsey and I picked at some cheese, he finally drew my attention to it.

"I think your thoughts are elsewhere, Martin."

"You're right and I'm sorry. The meal's superb."

"But your mind is on the Memoir."

"I'm afraid so."

"Don't apologize. As sponsor, I'm delighted to see it. How's it going?"

"Very well. Strafford is about to take Elizabeth Latimer down to Barrowteign."

"Ah yes. All is well at that stage."

"But not for much longer?"

"No, but don't let me spoil your reading."

"I don't think you will. Besides, such a work's bound to have an unsatisfactory ending."

"Why so?"

"In the sense that it's the story of Strafford's life written before his death and therefore incomplete. Tell me, is he buried near here or in Funchal?"

"Neither. He is buried in England, in the village of Dewford, near Barrowteign, with the rest of his family."

"He wasn't completely forgotten then, if they took him home to be buried?"

"He did not have to be taken. Strafford died at Barrowteign."

"Really?"

"Yes. I swiftly established that he was not buried on Madeira. The British Consul then made enquiries for me in London. It transpired that Strafford returned to England in the spring of 1951 and went to Barrowteign to stay with his nephew."

"What did he die of?"

"He was hit by a train on a level crossing where a railway

line traversed the Barrowteign estate. That's all they could tell me."

"I see."

"Though, as you'll read for yourself, that has a curious parallel with events in the Memoir. But I'd better say no more at present."

Beyond that, Sellick would not be drawn. His smile was sphinxlike in the candlelight, his sudden revelation and as sudden reticence all too convenient. I knew then that I wasn't the only one holding back information. In Sellick's case, he was letting it slip at intervals. Now, I was to understand that Strafford hadn't ended his days in exile, but back in England, by accident, in search of . . . what? The truth after forty years? A last sight of Barrowteign? Or something else Sellick wasn't telling me about yet? But no, he'd said the mystery of Strafford's fall was intact. I had to assume he didn't know either, yet I couldn't any longer be certain.

We went through to the drawing room for coffee. There, on a card table, stood a solitary, dark bottle of madeira.

"What's this?" said Alec. "Something special?"

"You might say so," replied Sellick. "I asked Tomás to put it out for us."

"But there are no glasses."

"That's because it's not for drinking . . . yet. You could call it a prize bottle. Take a look. You'll soon see what I mean."

Alec picked up the bottle and tilted its yellowed label to the light. "I don't believe it," he said. "I just don't believe it."

"What is it?" I said, walking to his side.

"See for yourself . . . Leo's been holding out on me."

It was old madeira . . . very old. In fact, a bottle of the 1792 vintage.

"I'm sorry, Alec," Sellick said with a smile. "Nothing could stop you writing the article when you did. Unfortunately, the time was not the ripe to tell you that there was indeed some left."

"But how . . ."

"A bequest from Dr Grabham to the previous owner of this property, discovered by me in the cellar."

"But last night you said . . ."

"That in all probability Grabham had left none behind. I know. Well, that still is the balance of probability. In fact, though, he left a few bottles to Strafford—naturally enough, as the most distinguished and discerning Englishman of the locality after Grabham himself—and Strafford left this one bottle for me to find. But I couldn't tell you until tonight because I hadn't persuaded Martin to research the Strafford mystery."

"I'm not sure I see the connection," I said.

"The connection," replied Sellick, "is my description of it as a prize bottle. It constitutes our prize, our reward to drink in Strafford's honour when your research is satisfactorily concluded. At that time, I propose that we three should gather here to commemorate the occasion by cracking open the last of the '92. I am sorry not to have told you before, Alec, but I hope you'll agree there was a good reason."

"I suppose I must," said Alec. "Can I at least write about it after that?"

"Of course," said Sellick. "As a good journalist, you should be grateful to me for providing you with the perfect sequel."

We laughed, and toasted in much younger malmsey Sellick's judgement in planning such a fitting tribute to Strafford. For me, it was a long way to look ahead, but at least there was the satisfaction of knowing that Sellick's whimsical editing of the facts could be applied to Alec as well as me.

"I think you owe me a game of snooker for this, Leo," Alec said. "It'll give me a chance of revenge."

"What Alec means, Martin, is the certainty of revenge. Clearly, I must submit. Will you join us in the billiards room?"

"I'd like to, but duty calls." I pointed at the Memoir where it lay on a low table by one of the fireside armchairs.

"Of course. We'll leave you to it, then."

They took their drinks and headed off. I wasn't sorry to see them go. I'd had enough of Sellick's conjuring tricks for one evening and felt on surer ground with the Memoir: the dead do not dissemble. Tomás brought me some coffee and I sat down with it in the armchair beneath a standard lamp. I opened the Memoir and rejoined Strafford in the year 1909.

Memoir

1909-1910

I remember that misty day at the end of August 1909 more clearly than I remember many of the days I pass here in my retirement. I collected Elizabeth from Putney and loaded her trunk into the car whilst Aunt Mercy pressed parting gifts and wishes upon her niece. Elizabeth wore a tweed dress, with a cape and a bonnet tied under her chin to ward off the chill of a long journey. I sounded the horn in farewell to Mercy as we drove off, alarming a passing dray but, strangely, settling Elizabeth's nerves. She confessed that she had been feeling somewhat apprehensive about meeting my family and was positively relieved that we were now on our way.

We passed down through Surrey and Hampshire and stopped at Salisbury for luncheon in a cosy tea room by the cathedral. The grey mist on the green with the great spire above minded Elizabeth of the Melchester of Hardy, whose Wessex we were about to enter. I remarked how odd it seemed to me that one so young as she should read the poems of one so old and sad.

"Mr Hardy is not such a sad man," she replied. "He is merely resigned to the poignant sense of loss with which every eager enterprise must one day be remembered by those involved."

"That's an old thought for a young head."

"Perhaps, but my awareness of it will not dim my enthusiasm—or any happiness it can bring." The set of her chin told me that she was to be believed. "Tell me in thirty years if it is

so." My hopes still to know her thirty years on took wing at that remark. It was as well for my peace of mind that I did not know how vain those hopes were or how right she was.

We travelled on until the chalk and pale green of Dorset changed to the red earth and deeper green of Devon and, when we reached Exeter in the late afternoon, we found the sun shining there as if it had done all the day.

"Now we are entering your kingdom," Elizabeth said as we drove slowly over the bridge across the Exe.

"Hardly that," I replied, "merely my constituency, too rarely visited since I became a minister, and my home, which I am always glad to return to."

"Your mother will be pleased to see you."

"And you," I reassured her, hoping that I was right.

Beyond Exeter, we went by winding lanes on which cars were a rarity. It was early evening before we passed through the village of Dewford on the banks of the Teign, turned onto the Barrowteign estate and sighted the big old house among the beech trees, as familiar to me as it was strange to Elizabeth.

My mother greeted us and at once turned her warmth and charm to ensuring that Elizabeth felt welcome. Robert we found in the drawing room, sucking on his pipe and looking more like the squire of the neighbourhood than when last I had seen him, yet with his bluff good humour unimpaired. Before there was time for any awkwardness to arise, little Ambrose tottered in with his nanny and, by the time his mother appeared, was being dandled on Elizabeth's knee to his evident delight. Florence looked askance at this and her apparent resentment of the possible admission of a female rival to a family over which she seemed rapidly to be gaining dominion was the only jarring note in an otherwise harmonious homecoming.

Of Elizabeth's political activities we naturally said nothing, beyond alluding to her suffragist sympathies to my mother, who took these to be comparable with her own and still counselled against mentioning them to Robert, who would be scandalized. I was less inclined to doubt this after a tour of the estate with him, during which he speculated on increasing the rents in such an unthinking manner that I detected a harden-

ing of his attitudes with age, or perhaps with marriage, that disturbed me. He was appalled by my hints of a coming clash with the Lords over the Budget and I subsequently said no more to him of such matters.

For all that, Robert was charmed by Elizabeth, as was my mother. I think she recognized in her such energy and intelligence as she might once have aspired to herself had she not accepted rural seclusion with my father. They made an instantly sympathetic pair, the elegant old lady and the vibrant young one; perhaps Elizabeth saw something of Hardy's poetry in my mother's soul. If so, it was a great deal more than she (or I) saw in Florence's paintings, which I found festooning the house to my considerable irritation. Elizabeth proved more adept than I in displaying some admiration for them, but even this could not endear her to my sister-in-law.

A central purpose of any sojourn at Barrowteign was to remind myself of all the doings in the constituency, to visit and advise those with a problem and to show myself in the area. In this Elizabeth proved a great aid. Her beauty dazzled many, her wit drew out others, her grace soothed the pugnacious few. At her behest, I played in Dewford's last cricket match of the season, which impressed the villagers almost as much as the rounds I stood them at the inn afterwards. At my behest, she accompanied me on a visit to the poor quarrying districts south of Barrowteign and there conceded that old age pensions and Lloyd George's national insurance schemes ought perhaps to take priority over suffrage reform. We continued, in short, to be as good for each other in Devon as we had been in London. Even Flowers, my assiduous agent, was heard to mutter that Elizabeth for a wife would enhance my standing in the constituency.

Not that it was Flowers' typically blunt calculation that set me thinking of matrimony. That was born of the affection that I felt deepening into love. September passed as an idyll of growing happiness and hope. Fine weather attended our weeks at Barrowteign and I often took Elizabeth out onto the Moor or down to the coast, indulgences in the beauty of nature which she had not known since childhood. So far from London and my career, it was easy to forget the difficulties attendant upon our association. Insofar as I bore them in mind, it was only as a minor problem easily overcome. Much more significant so far as I was then concerned was whether I could persuade Elizabeth to agree to marry me. I doubted not that, if I could, it would assure my future happiness.

Michaelmas was that year a peerless day of autumn brightness, every tree and every stone at Barrowteign picked out by sharp shadows in the clear sunlight of a cloudless sky. The house was quiet, with Robert off on his quarter-day tour of the tenant farms, Mother along with him to see for herself that all was well with those whose welfare was always close to her heart, if not always that of her son. Florence had gone to visit her family in Dartmouth for a few days, taking Ambrose with her. Elizabeth was eager to escape into the sunshine and I was free to indulge her eagerness.

I drove the car up into the foothills of Dartmoor that lie between the Teign and Bovey valleys and stopped where the lanes became too rough and steep for further progress. We continued on foot, I carrying a picnic luncheon in a haversack whilst Elizabeth set a disarming pace and navigated expertly by one of my brother's maps. So it was that she brought us to Blackingstone Rock, that great node of granite atop the hills above Moretonhampstead, and led the ascent. I was more breathless than she when we reached the flat top of the rock and sat down to take the view. Before us the Torridge plain stretched as far as the sea, which I could almost think I saw, so clear was the air. Behind us Dartmoor hummocked towards its wilder reaches. Down in the Teign valley, it was just possible to descry the distant roofs of Barrowteign. I gazed around in awe, breathing heavily.

"This will never do," said Elizabeth. "You have spent too long behind your desk in Whitehall, Edwin, I can see."

"Perhaps," I replied, "but I have carried a meal on my back and you have younger legs than I."

She threw a fern leaf in my direction and we laughed. The sun and the warmth seemed as undeserved at this season as our happiness, but both were there to be revelled in. I uncorked the flagon of cellar-cooled cider I had brought and we toasted the countryside of my birth.

"All over Devon," I said, "workers will be pausing from

the harvest at about this time for a draught of their native brew."

"Or worrying about their rent for the next quarter."

"Do not be hard on Robert," I said, detecting a shaft in his direction. "He's as good a landlord as they come. A little set in his ways, I admit, and beginning to take himself too seriously, but that's just the onset of middle age. Losing my breath on stiff climbs is probably a sign that I'm to emulate him."

"I'm sorry. I didn't mean to criticize Robert. He is a good man. He simply lacks his brother's vision and intelligence—and humour."

"Any humour is your gift, and a goodly part of the vision too. Florence would grind any man down. We cannot all be lucky enough to find someone like you."

Elizabeth looked down and blushed, in her a rare show of vulnerability. But it was not the altogether pleasing contrast with my plain and prosaic sister-in-law that had occasioned this embarrassment. It was the implication that she might one day be my wife. What had so often been in my thoughts of late emerged in speech with a subtlety that we both realized the other would appreciate. And it was a measure of my respect for her that I did not then attempt some awkward concealment.

"You have guessed my thoughts," I said. "Four months ago you threw a brick through my window. I little thought that it would find a way to my heart. But it has done, and more, for you have changed me as you have touched me, made of me a person I am happier to be."

"I will take no credit," she said softly, "unless you acknowledge the better woman you have made of me."

"Such mutual flattery!" We laughed then at ourselves and at each other.

Elizabeth gazed about for a moment at the view.

"It is lovely here," she said. "And it has been lovely at Barrowteign this past month. Thank you so much for bringing me."

"Thank you for coming," I said. "Alas, the time has sped by and soon we will have to return to London." For a moment we each thought of what that would mean, then I put it into

words. "I have grown so used to spending each day with you. It will seem strange and hard not to once again."

"It will seem hard for me too."

"There is of course an alternative." Elizabeth said nothing, nor I for a moment. Then I continued. "You could agree to marry me."

"What are you saying, Edwin?"

"What I am saying, Elizabeth, is will you marry me?"

"Oh, I would so like to say yes."

"Then will you?"

"What about your career?"

"It could only be enhanced by a wife as lovely as you. You have already seen how my constituents have taken to you."

"But in London?"

"There too. The Prime Minister is no ogre and would have, I judge, no grounds to object."

"Not even the grounds of my own politics?"

"Not even those. But I would not expect you to abandon them."

"Then what about your family?"

"Mother adores you."

"But surely Florence does not."

"A commendation in itself."

"You seem to have an answer to every objection."

"Only because there can be no objection to something so right."

"Then I will say yes, Edwin, with all my heart, and learn to obey my future husband."

We smiled, knowing that obedience would never be expected in our marriage, and I drew her close and kissed her, the breeze blowing her hair onto my face.

"I love you, Elizabeth."

"And I love you, Edwin."

There reached its zenith, on that high boulder in Devon, my hope for what life had to offer. It had offered me ministerial rank in the counsels of my land and I had taken it, though with what benefit to those I was set to serve I could no longer clearly see. Now it had offered me Elizabeth, whose happiness I saw as a sure, attainable objective amidst all the shifting compromises of politics. We sat atop Blackingstone Rock that bright September noon, smiling with a mutual nervousness at the certainty of our love, knowing that the granite beneath our feet could be no firmer than our trust in each other.

Yet even granite can be broken. And the first cracks were even then appearing. What I did not know until long after was that Florence, fearing her own eclipse in the family and, worse still, some sullying of her name by an unfortunate marriage, had taken it upon herself to consult her father's solicitor and to commission some discreet research into Elizabeth's background, her suspicion having been aroused by some reticence she detected in our accounts of it. At first, no doubt, she was concerned only to satisfy herself that Elizabeth was an appropriate bride for me in her own watercolour social terms. But I can imagine the horrified glee with which, on her latest visit to Dartmouth, she received the report that Miss Latimer, orphan of Putney, was an active member of the Women's Social & Political Union who had already come to the notice of the police and been fined for at least three breaches of the peace in the pursuit of militant suffragism.

So, when Elizabeth and I returned to Barrowteign and delighted my mother with our announcement, we were but shortly followed home by Florence, in a secret ecstasy of spite rewarded. She knew her husband as she thought she knew her prey and, in response to our tidings, brought some of her own to Robert's ears, couched, no doubt, in terms of concern for my welfare. Robert, decent pliable man that he was, realized (as his wife reminded him) that there was nothing to be gained by challenging me on the subject, so thought to have a word with that most pragmatic of counsellors, Flowers, who, alive to his responsibilities as my agent, determined that covert action was required to save a career which he had laboured long to protect. This took the form of an approach to the mandarins of the Liberal Chief Whip's Office, who thereupon began to move with all their dread inertia against two unwitting lovers.

Of all this, I was in ignorance. Likewise my mother and Elizabeth, who drew even closer after our announcement than before. And if Robert looked straight at times and Florence sour, I would have seen nothing in it. My mind was set on a spring wedding and the imminent resumption of Parliamentary business, strictly in that order.

In the middle of October, with the leaves falling at Barrowteign, we set off to London, my mother sending us on our way with entreaties to return at Christmas and to fix a date soon. To neither were we in the least averse. We motored back happily with the roof up against the autumn chill, talking of ourselves and the future—now conjoined—as the countryside slid serenely by. Mercy had been warned by letter and greeted us with fulsome approbation. High tea with her in Putney, Elizabeth on my arm making plans with her aunt which I was happy to indulge, made me feel glad to be back in London.

I still felt so next morning, when I reported to my office in positively buoyant mood. Despatch boxes had kept me in touch with events in my absence but I was looking forward to Meres' customarily thorough briefing nonetheless. Before there was a chance of that, I received a message to telephone 10 Downing Street at once. The Prime Minister's secretary told me that Mr Asquith wished to see me in his office at four o'clock that afternoon. He declined to elaborate.

There was much to busy myself with in the interim. Accordingly, I walked round to Downing Street that grey afternoon in a mood more of curiosity than foreboding. I was admitted without delay to the presence. I found Asquith slumped at his desk and knew at once from his posture that he was in a taciturn frame of mind. He asked me to sit down.

"Did you have a good break, Edwin?" he growled.

"Thank you, yes, Prime Minister."

"And you return refreshed?"

"Indeed—ready for the fray."

"I can guarantee some of that. I'm confident that the Budget will be passed by the Commons early next month."

"And so to the Lords."

"Quite. I am reliably informed that they will reject it."

"Then they will have to bear the consequences."

"As will we all. We will find ourselves on the horns of a constitutional dilemma."

"Surely that can only hurt the Lords."

"Alas no. We will almost certainly have to go to the country for a mandate to overturn the Lords' decision."

"If we must we must."

I had grown by now more than a little puzzled. This issue had been debated, our reaction to the Lords rejecting the Budget rehearsed, many times before in Cabinet. Our conversation now was adding nothing, so to what purpose had I been urgently summoned? Asquith rose and began pacing the room.

"At a time such as this, Edwin, we can ill afford public embarrassment. The people must respect us as the repositories of good sense in opposition to irresponsible aristocrats."

"Have we not established that position?"

"We had. I now find that it is imperilled by one minister's imprudence."

"What has happened?"

"What has happened is that the Chief Whip has told me that, during your recent stay in Devon, you became engaged to marry a notorious Suffragette."

I was taken aback. I had to set aside for a moment enquiry into how the Chief Whip had come by his information and face what appeared to be an unwarranted intrusion into my private life.

"Is this true, Edwin?" Asquith asked, facing me.

"Yes. I would quibble with your description of Miss Latimer as notorious, but she has certainly been active in the suffragist cause. And we are engaged to be married. But I can see no . . ."

"Who knows of this?"

"Our respective families and, it seems, the Chief Whip. But what . . ."

"Not the WSPU?"

"Certainly not. Miss Latimer and I proposed to say nothing about it for a while yet."

"That, at least, is something."

"Prime Minister, what is the problem?"

Asquith sat heavily back down in his chair, sighing as he did so.

"Edwin, you showed yourself from an early stage to be a calm, incisive thinker, neither a demagogue nor a sycophant. You were that invaluable asset to the man at the wheel—a young, energetic, impartial adviser, a good worker with a good brain. That is why I promoted you when I came to office. How can you therefore be so naïve as to ask where is the problem in your marrying a Suffragette?"

"I have thought it through and see no problem. My private life is just that: private. I have made no secret of my support for female suffrage in the long run but I accept that it must take its place in the queue. My fiancée appreciates that now too and has foresworn illegal acts. But neither of us wishes to force our convictions upon the other. I really do not see why two unattached young people should not marry if they wish."

"Because neither of you is unattached. You are a member of a government many of whose supporters deplore militant suffragism and would impute to you, for marrying a Suffragette, just that degree of irresponsibility of which we are now accusing the Lords. It would do immeasurable harm to our standing with the electorate, at a time when we must have popular support to force through those social reforms which a Cabinet of which you are a member considers so vital. Miss Latimer is, by contrast, a member of an organization which seeks to promote by violent means its own sectional interest above those with greater needs and fewer resources. Your marriage is not to be countenanced in these circumstances."

"Then I will resign." There was nothing else I could say. No amount of argument would sway Asquith in this mood and Elizabeth deserved such a sacrifice of me. Yet I knew, in the back of my mind, that resignation was the one card that might win me this hand, for the Prime Minister could ill-afford to lose me at a time when Lloyd George, with Churchill's willing assistance, was threatening to seize the initiative from him. I was one of the few able young lieutenants he could look to for aid. Sure enough, I saw his face fall at my words.

"Edwin," he said, "I trust it will not come to that. Your proposed marriage is not to be countenanced at this time and in these circumstances. That is not to say that there will not be a better time and more propitious circumstances. What I am

asking you—and Miss Latimer—to do is wait and keep silent for a while."

"How long would that be?"

"Let us suppose that matters fall out as we expect, that the Lords do reject the Budget next month. There would then have to be a general election—probably early in the New Year—to give me the right to ask the King to create sufficient new peers to swamp the Lords if they will not then concede. The matter would be resolved by the spring."

"I see."

"Is that too long to ask you to wait? Just a few months may see us establish for ever the right of a democratically elected government to legislate without hindrance from an hereditary upper house. These are grave issues indeed. Would you see our case weakened by the impatience of youth?"

There seemed, again, no choice in how to respond.

"No, Prime Minister, I would not. And if all you need are six months to finish the job, then you can rely upon my discretion—and that of Miss Latimer—in the interim. Do I take it that we could proceed after that without objection?"

"Of course. I have no wish to stand in your way. All I ask is your support in the trying months ahead."

"You have that without the need to ask."

When I left Downing Street, I felt disappointed by Asquith's excessive caution but consoled by the esteem for me evident in his reaction to the idea of my resigning. I proceeded at once to Putney and told Elizabeth what had happened.

"What the Prime Minister is saying then," she remarked with composure, "is that he has no objection in principle to our marrying but that he expects us to keep it quiet until his problem with the House of Lords is resolved next spring."

"Precisely."

"And you gave him an undertaking to that effect?"

"My dear, what else could I do? We had spoken of a spring wedding anyway. Is it such a great hardship to announce nothing until then?"

Elizabeth crossed to where I stood and took my hand. "No, it is not, Edwin. It is a small price to pay for you remaining a minister and I would not wish for all the world to damage your career, which, after all, may achieve so much good."

I was relieved. "I am glad to hear you say so. I felt presumptuous in speaking for you as well as for myself this afternoon."

"There is no need. We must both learn to speak for each other henceforth. But do not think"—her eyes flared theatrically—"that this will let you off the hook, Mr Strafford. The day after the Lords pass the Budget, I shall expect an announcement in The Times*."*

We laughed and kissed and were surprised by Mercy in search of her embroidery. I did not stay for dinner, leaving Elizabeth to impress upon her aunt the need for discretion whilst I penned a letter to my mother with the same injunction.

Next day, there was a Cabinet meeting at which Asquith informed us all of his expectations for the progress of the Budget. Lloyd George uttered threats to dismantle the Lords which confirmed my suspicion that the Prime Minister had need of me at this time. There was, naturally, no mention of our conversation the previous day.

Rather as Asquith had predicted the Budget passed the Commons on November 4 and was rejected by the Lords on November 30. The government's reaction was pre-ordained: we would go to the country in January and, upon re-election, force the Lords to pass both the Budget and a bill depriving them of the right to veto legislation by the threat of creating sufficient new peers to swamp their Tory majority. Asquith set about persuading the King that he should cooperate in this by being willing, if necessary, to create those peers and gave us in the Cabinet to understand that he was encountering no difficulty. There remained only the slight problem of winning the election.

I went down to Barrowteign for Christmas—Elizabeth (and Mercy) joining me a few days later in the name of discretion—and stayed on for the campaign in the constituency. This time, Elizabeth was not much seen in the area, again for discretion's sake. She chafed at her relative confinement, but was kept amused by Mother and Mercy. Robert and Florence had gone to Dartmouth for Christmas, which was probably as well. I made no attempt to determine the provenance of the communication to the Chief Whip, though I harboured various suspicions. Still and all, the impending election kept me occupied, knowing as I did that a great deal more hung upon it than was normally the case. One help to the government in general and its Home Secretary in particular was that the suffragist organizations called a truce for the campaign, hoping for their reward in the new parliament. So far as she had been able, Elizabeth had supported this move in her branch of the WSPU and it had been implemented despite Christabel Pankhurst's trenchant opposition.

The citizens of mid-Devon did not betray me. I was returned with another enlarged majority, taking me past the figures Sir William had been wont to attain. The election went less well for the party as a whole, however. We won rather fewer seats than in 1906, losing more than a few to Labour, who seemed to gain (as I had feared) by the frustration generally felt at our inability to bring about the reforms which we had promised. Fortunately, the Conservative vote collapsed. Nevertheless, we lost our clear majority and, though much the largest party, were dependent upon the Irish members to pass legislation.

When Elizabeth and I returned to London—again separately—in the middle of January 1910, it was in a mood of cautious optimism. Despite the less than clearcut nature of our victory at the polls, I had no doubt that we could at once set about breaking the power of the Lords forever. Once that was done, I could turn with a clear conscience to the sealing of my personal happiness by marriage to Elizabeth. Never at any point in this, our trial by tiresome parting, did I doubt the ultimate triumph of our love.

I left Strafford there and went up to bed. The silence and shadow of his own drawing room seemed no place to follow his chronicle into its darker phase, the phase I knew must follow, when all his flair and promise turned to pathos and despair. At first, I'd been fascinated by the transformation and how it had come about. Now, it was beginning to appall me.

Yet some of the grimness had gone by morning. The sounds and light of another hot Madeiran day reminded me of a there and then sufficient for my purposes. There was no sense in falling under the spell of my long-dead research subject. Apart from anything else, it wasn't professional. I went down to breakfast with a remedial jauntiness.

Alec was on the verandah, eating a grapefruit. I helped myself to some coffee, which stood ready, and sat beside him.

"Bad news, Martin," Alec said between spoonfuls. "Today we go back to Funchal."

"Well, I didn't expect to stay this long anyway, but I'm nowhere near finishing the Memoir."

"Don't worry. Leo's thought of that. He's asked me to get a photocopy done. He doesn't want to part with the original for long, so we'll take it with us, make a copy, then I'll return it to him."

"Fine. When do we go?"

"Pronto, I'm afraid. I need to be back in Funchal for this afternoon's soccer. As sports correspondent, I can't afford to miss the island's fortnightly big match. And that'll mean catching the bus. There aren't many on a Sunday. I'll ask Tomás what time the next one passes."

"It seems a pity to leave so soon."

"Needs must. Talking of which, Leo's in his study and wants you to look in on him there. I think he's planning a business chat. You know how meticulous South Africans are where money's concerned. Why don't you have a word with him while I look for Tomás?"

Sellick's study was on the eastern side of the courtyard. It was a far cry from Strafford's—small but pleasantly cool, with a window overlooking the fountain.

Sellick swung round in his chair clutching a sheet of paper as if it was a profitable bill of lading.

"Come in, Martin, come in," he said. "Please excuse the cheerless venue. You've come at just the right time. I'm writing to my banker"—he flourished the paper—"instructing him to transfer to your bank account the sum of one thousand pounds, to start your research off. Then you need only let me know when you need more. I trust that seems satisfactory."

I assured him it did and gave him the name and address of my bank.

"Thank you, Martin. That will have been arranged by the

time you return to England. Now, how goes the reading?" The change of subject was abrupt, as if the sordid question of money was to be given minimal attention.

"It's going well, though there's still a lot to read. But Alec tells me I can have a copy to refer to."

"Yes, and he wants to return to Funchal today. So I shall see no more of you until . . . well, until you've reached a conclusion. But I shall expect regular progress reports."

"You'll get them. I'm eager to start. I should be able to finish reading the Memoir before I fly home on Wednesday. Then I'll get straight down to it."

"Where will you begin?"

"Difficult to say at the moment. I'll decide after finishing the Memoir. But probably with the records of the time—before tackling survivors of the events in person."

"Well, that's for you to judge. Just do your best. If we can find out something, perhaps Strafford will rest easier."

"I hope so."

He rose and held out his hand. "Good luck in our enterprise." We shook hands. "You will carry my thoughts." He looked straight at me with his keen blue eyes, no smile lightening their intensity. Yes, it was a serious business. I'd thought of it as enjoyable, lucrative, rewarding, but never till then as the solemn undertaking Sellick clearly felt it to be.

We left a couple of hours later, in time for the bus Tomás assured us would pass the Quinta shortly before noon. Sellick saw us out into the courtyard, shading his eyes against the glaring sunlight. Alec headed down the drive, but I paused for a moment to wave farewell to Sellick as he stood, smiling, by his fountain. I remembered him as he appeared then—a small, dapper old man, my benefactor—longer than I did his clear calculating mind. I remembered above all the Quinta, its mood and magic as the place of Strafford's exile, where he could search forever in the solitude of his study for the fatal error he didn't know he made. Where Strafford ended, I was beginning.

Two days away in the cool uplands had made me forget the noise and glare of the capital. There was only time to drop the

Memoir off at Alec's house and bolt some lunch before setting off for the football stadium in the western suburbs. I wanted to stay at home and read some more, but Alec wouldn't have it.

Presumably, he didn't see why he should suffer alone. Maritimo, the island's premier football team, were at home in a Portuguese league match that *Madeira Life* couldn't afford to miss. The concrete stadium at Barreiros was ideal for basking lizards and well-oiled Madeirans who couldn't tell good football from bad, but to English eyes the players looked unfit and unimaginative.

"It's always like this," said Alec, as the ball was kicked lethargically around. "Mañana interspersed with melodrama. I'm sorry if it's a bit of a bore."

"It's not that. It's just such a contrast with the Quinta."

"Well, it's easy to bc romantic about Madeira if you live up there." A paunchy Madeiran with a beer bottle blundered into Alec while taking his seat. "This is as real—if not more so—than the Porto Novo valley. As an historian, you should know that."

"Perhaps it'll stop me getting starry-eyed about Strafford's Madeiran connection."

"No fear of that, Martin. You're more of a realist than I am."

"Realist enough, I hope, to notice the part you played in getting me this job."

"Nothing to do with me." He craned over a shoulder for a view of the match's first shot at goal. "It was all Leo's idea." To universal groans, the Maritimo forward ballooned the ball over the bar.

"Come off it, Alec. Leo hardly stopped saying what a glowing account you'd given of me. He seemed remarkably well-informed about how I'm placed at present. And didn't you say in your letter the visit might be worth my while? Was that the come-on or wasn't it?"

"Well, okay, I suppose so. I told him you were a well-qualified unemployed historian. I knew he might put two and two together and figure you were the man for the job he had in mind. And I reckoned it would appeal to you. And I did what I could to help a friend. What's wrong with that?"

"Nothing. Don't get me wrong. I'm grateful for what

you've done." I was and that was all I'd meant to say till Alec had tried to deny the part he'd obviously played. But his unease reminded me of a conflict of interest that wouldn't go away. Now that we were far away from the Quinta, I could at least see whether Alec would find it embarrassing.

"Sorry, Martin, I didn't mean to bridle. It must be the heat." It was certainly hot, and about to get hotter. A Maritimo forward fell over in a tackle and everyone in the ground except the referee awarded a penalty. Shouts, threats and fruit hailed onto the pitch. "That referee will need a police escort afterwards. A riot would really boost circulation." Alec was to be disappointed. It was too hot even for the Maritimo fans.

When the match lapsed back into torpor, I broached the burning question. "Obviously, I'm grateful for what promises to be a fascinating—and well-paid—assignment. But I can't deny there's something holding me back—something I can't afford to have Leo hear about."

"You can trust me, Martin. God knows you could tell Leo things which might spoil my image as the white knight of journalism."

"It's nothing like that. It's a delicate matter of declaring an interest. You see, I'm related to someone in the Memoir."

"How?"

"By marriage. Helen's grandparents, the Couchmans, knew Strafford. They're central figures in the story."

"Really? Well now, that is odd."

"It's more than odd—it's bloody awkward. How can I pose as the dispassionate researcher while knocking on my ex-in-laws' doors asking embarrassing questions about their past?"

"Surely it won't be quite like that?"

"Maybe not. But shouldn't I tell Leo?"

"What's stopping you?"

"The thought that, if I do, he might withdraw the offer."

"Then don't. It's your problem, not his. Besides, aren't there . . . compensations?"

"If you mean antagonizing Helen's family, I'm past that. And anyway, I'm in no position to bear grudges."

"Maybe not, but doesn't it . . . well, add to the fun?" He grinned at me and I found myself grinning back. Yes, there was something to be relished in delving into the secret past of a family which had never hidden its distaste for me. I'd disgraced them, but maybe not as much as I'd been made to feel. I hadn't sought revenge, but if it flavoured what I was about to do in the pursuit of truth, history and gainful employment, who was I to resist?

"Coincidence is a strange thing," I said at last.

"Don't fight it. After all, if I hadn't known you, Leo might be offering this job to somebody else."

"That's true. And I can't afford not to take it." With that, I disposed of the last of my doubts. What I'd wanted—and received—from Alec was confirmation. However much he might have oversold my talents, I felt I could do the job as well as anyone—maybe better. Besides, I wanted to do it for its own sake. Like Sellick, I wanted to know the truth about Edwin Strafford.

Next day, Alec took the Memoir off to photocopy it. Left with a free morning, I set off for an extensive exploration of the byways of Funchal. As I might have known, it was a tiring, unsatisfactory experience, which merely increased my impatience to return to the England of 1910.

I was pleased and relieved to find Alec waiting for me when I got back to the house.

"There you are Martin," he said, pointing to a pile of xeroxed sheets standing by the Memoir on a table.

"Great. Thanks, Alec." I leafed through the copies. It was suddenly odd to see the old marbled tome reduced by modern technology to a stack of new white paper.

"We'll parcel that up for you to take away and I'll return the original to Leo on Friday."

"Fine."

"Well, I've got to see my printer at two-thirty. If I don't keep after him, the magazine will fall behind schedule. Do you want to come with me?"

"Thanks, but no. Now the Memoir's back"—I patted its leather cover—"I think I'll catch up on my reading."

After lunch, Alec set off for his appointment and I chose the most comfortable camp chair to sit on in the garden, in the shade of a palm tree. Bees buzzed in the afternoon heat, but the high walls kept out the noise of Funchal, preserving the peace and my concentration. I returned to the Memoir.

Memoir

1910

The qualified optimism with which I returned from Barrowteign in January 1910 did not long endure. I had supposed that Elizabeth and I would not have to separate our lives for many more months, but I was sadly wrong. My error, however, did not lie in the causes for pessimism then apparent. These were the disagreement within the Cabinet about the nature of the proposed Parliamentary reform and the delicate negotiations with the Irish Nationalists necessary to secure their support for both this and the outstanding Budget, upon which we were rendered dependent by the narrowness of our majority. Both these difficulties were, as it transpired, disposed of with some ease.

The intractability of my own position did not become clear until an announcement by the Prime Minister to the Commons on February 21st, the content of which surprised many of his own party and dumbfounded one, namely his own Home Secretary. What Asquith said that famous evening was that, so far from having secured the King's agreement before the election to create sufficient peers to force the necessary legislation through the Lords, he had not even asked for it and that the King had subsequently indicated that there would have to be a second election before he felt under an obligation so to do. I must have blanched visibly in my seat alongside Asquith and my dismay might have been noticed had there not been so many backbenchers on hand to express astonishment at this revelation. They had been led to believe that suitable guaran-

tees by the King existed and now found themselves committed to another general election, a scarcely relishable prospect in view of the ambiguous outcome of the first. But whilst many condemned Asquith for improvidence, I had to hold my tongue before a far greater injustice. The figure standing beside me, orating upon the legal and procedural complexities in which the government now found itself, had deceived me. In the moment of that rounded pronouncement, I felt only the blackest outrage. Had he so soon forgotten his undertakings to me of the previous autumn? And if he had not, why had he left me so long to trust in a course and speed of events which could now no longer come to pass? It seemed to me that there could only be one answer: because it suited his purpose. The man whom I had to regard as Lloyd George's dupe had now duped me.

Try as I might, I was unable to confront Asquith that night. I returned home to think long and hard about how this left Elizabeth and me. I had no wish to tell her of the implications of the announcement: firstly that the constitutional crisis would not be resolved that spring, secondly that our marriage would not be deemed politic until well after a second general election, whenever that might be. It was unthinkable, after all our self-denial and patience, to wait again, who knew how long. I could not sleep for fury at Asquith, paced the empty streets that night and presented myself at 10 Downing Street the following morning at an early hour determined to see him.

In a typically Asquithian gesture the Prime Minister made no difficulty about seeing me. I found him alone, still at his breakfast, and he offered me tea and toast, which I abruptly declined.

"Sit down, Edwin," he said appeasingly. "I do apologise for greeting you thus, but after a late sitting I am up surprisingly early."

"It is about last night's sitting that I wish to speak."

"I thought it might be. My announcement must have discomposed you somewhat."

"Prime Minister, you understate the case greatly. I was shocked. May I remind you that . . ."

"Last autumn," he interrupted, "we discussed your marital ambitions and agreed they were better deferred until our present difficulty with the Lords is settled."

"And you promised that, if we won the election, it would be settled this spring, which it cannot now be."

"I promised nothing, Edwin. I expressed certain hopes to you in good faith. I hoped to have suitable guarantees from the king . . ."

"But you said you had not even sought them."

"That was to avoid embarrassment to the Crown, which is my duty. Of course I asked the King, in December, after dissolving Parliament. He said that he could not resort to the creation of peers unless two successive elections confirmed our mandate."

"You did not tell me that."

"How could I? Think of the damage it might have done party morale, not to mention our popular support if it had then been known that two elections would have to be endured if we were to have our way."

"I said that you did not tell me."

"I judged it inappropriate at that stage."

"After the election?"

"I hoped to sway the King to consent without a second election. Had our victory been clear, I might have succeeded."

This, I felt sure, was a lie. The King was not of a temperament to budge on such issues, as Asquith knew better than most. He had merely been trailing me on a string. What was I to do?

"I think you might have forewarned me of your announcement."

"I regret that I could not. Relations between an elected leader and his monarch are essentially delicate. They rely upon complete confidentiality."

"If you say so, Prime Minister. The point is: how does this leave me placed?"

"Not as badly as you may have feared, Edwin. Let me explain. We need to present the Lords with the Budget and a Parliament Bill to remove their veto. I think the latter will frighten them into passing the former. But they will jib at the bill and we will go to the country on it. If we win again, the King will be obliged to support us."

"When?"

"Timing is difficult. The Cabinet needs to agree the terms of a Parliament Bill; I hope you will assist me there. Then we need to secure the Irish votes to pass such a bill through the Commons, and you know how slippery they can be. Whatever the form of the legislation, I have little doubt that the Lords will reject it outright."

"And then?"

"We will dissolve Parliament, knowing this time that success is assured if we win."

"I cannot see that being resolved before the end of this year."

"Neither can I."

"Then you are extending the term of our agreement substantially. I am not sure Miss Latimer and I can wait that long."

"Say not that I am extending anything, Edwin, rather that we are all the victims of circumstance. I can only repeat what I told you last October: that I need your support, that the party and the country need it to secure historic reform. Does delaying your marriage until next year really seem an unacceptable hardship in the light of that?"

"I can only say that I will consult my fiancée and decide with her what to do."

"Then I pray you reach the right decision—for all of us."

He had me, as he knew, caught on any number of snares. If he had deceived me once, he could deceive me again. Yet what he said was superficially true. This was no time for what would seem to the ignorant a light-hearted indulgence of my whim. I cared deeply about what the government was striving to achieve, as Elizabeth cared deeply for the suffragist cause. The events then unfolding might serve both aims. Following the election, an all-party conciliation committee had set about drafting a bill for limited female enfranchisement which, along with several other just reforms, might come into being in the wake of a Parliament Act. Neither Elizabeth nor I wished to be responsible for so prejudicing the outcome of an election as to risk all that. And Asquith had laced his high-principled call for personal sacrifice with a hint of venal reward for those who stood by him. If he could not persuade me, he would seek to buy me. That, and his persistent duplicity, told against his argument. Yet what could tell against the facts of the matter, standing as they did beyond his control and mine?

I left Downing Street that morning my mind reeling at the complexity of what once, on a rock in Devon, had seemed so simple. I at once took a cab to Putney and reached Mercy's house with the frost still on the lawn. Elizabeth was in the drawing room with a friend, a suffragette of similar cast, who rapidly excused herself upon my arrival. Elizabeth beamed and kissed me, but uttered a warning word.

"Julia will have recognized you," she said. "I thought we were to be cautious."

"I'm sorry," I said, "but caution could not stand in my way this morning. Have you heard what Asquith said in the House last night?"

"No."

"He admitted that he had no guarantees from the King to create peers in the event that the Lords reject a Parliament Bill."

"But that means . . ."

"It means, my dear, that there will have to be a second election, probably this summer. We would not be able to marry with his sanction before the autumn at least."

Elizabeth sank down dejectedly in a chair.

"Oh Edwin, we have waited so long."

I went to her side. "I know, I know. That is why I have come here this morning, to decide with you whether we should wait any longer."

She turned her dark eyes upon me, mirroring in their anguish the longing I also felt. "You know what I want to do—marry you. But we cannot throw your career away for that."

"We can and we will if the two aims are incompatible."

"But they are not—yet."

"Perhaps not. But how long can we wait? Even coming here this morning, I took a risk. Must I take risks to be with you?"

"I don't want you to, but let us think for a moment. Perhaps the Lords will pass the bill."

"We can't hope for that."

"Let's at least wait to see if they do, then decide what to do."

Elizabeth was right, as I knew, and though I protested feebly a little longer, we followed her course. It was strange that she, the young lady, should commend patience to the older man, but her eye for the right action did not desert her. We resolved to wait, a little longer, agreeing however that any further delay would be intolerable. I was prepared, that day, to toss away the bauble of my career for the shimmer of a loving future with Elizabeth, but she held me back, and later I thanked her for that. Looking back now, I wish I had not been so persuaded. We could not then know that the road of reason on which we had embarked was ultimately to lead us apart.

I returned, still seething inwardly, to my office and all the appanages of ministerial rank which sat so ill with the inclination of my will. It was a difficult task to wait again upon events so much beyond my control, but I sought to do so, setting my sights on distant fulfilment. And Elizabeth and I still snatched meetings, by prearranged chance, and filled our letters to each other with private hope.

In that way the month of March elapsed and April wore on. By then, the Irish had been won over by the ultimate promise of Home Rule and the terms of the Parliament Bill agreed by the Cabinet. The original occasion of the crisis, Lloyd George's 1909 Budget, was meekly passed by the Lords on April 28th, in the knowledge that the real battle was yet to be fought.

That evening, most of we ministers gathered at 11 Downing Street for dinner with the Chancellor of the Exchequer, to celebrate the laggardly passage of his Budget. It was a cheery, even exuberant, affair and I contrived to affect the prevailing mood, without much success. Asquith was in good heart, though weary in appearance, while Lloyd George and Churchill contemplated in the euphoria of alcohol and cigars a triumphant summer election, followed by a resounding victory over the Lords. I strove to share their confidence and, in a quiet moment, Asquith said to me, "They're right, Edwin. By the autumn, we should be in the clear." I only wanted to believe him and, that night, in that able, talented company, I did so.

Even I could not blame Asquith for the next stroke of fate to tell against me. Suddenly, on May 6th, King Edward died. During the ten days of mourning that followed, we all soberly realised that his guarantee to create peers had gone with him and, I personally realised, the prospect of an autumn wedding. I did not feel able to bear any further delay, nor did I believe I could expect Elizabeth to. Yet our rightful response was as hard to devise as before.

The day after the King's funeral, a lengthy, ceremonial event in which I was obliged to play my part, I happened to arrive outside the tropical plant house at Kew Gardens at noon, just as Elizabeth did. We strolled amongst the exotic fronds in apparently idle discourse that was, in truth, an anxious appraisal of our circumstances.

"It is chastening to realise," I said, "that somebody as seemingly powerful as I should be so at the mercy of others. Now, my dear Elizabeth, we must wait upon the King."

"I would rather wait upon you, Edwin."

"And I on you. But the new King is an unknown quantity. We do not yet know his mind."

"On what subject?"

"On the creation of new peers. Should he be more amenable than his father, he may consent without another election."

"That would be marvellous."

"Indeed it would, disposing swiftly of any objectives to our marriage. The problem is that he is not bound by his father's guarantees and may take a harder line. We can only wait upon his word."

There, again, was the message of which we had both sickened, the message of waiting that had worn us down. Yet still we had the light tread of hopeful young lovers as we left the humidity of the plant house and strolled across the grass, our hands in secret clasp.

On May 27th, we risked dinner at The Baron to mark the anniversary of our first meeting. Strangely, that distant event seemed welcomely simple by comparison with the toils of po-

litical complexity in which we now found ourselves. And still we had to wait.

It was, in truth, not long before King George showed his hand. In early June, he explored with the leaders of both major parties the possibility of agreeing some compromise legislation that would avert an open clash with the Lords. Of this I knew nothing until a Cabinet meeting on June 6th. It became apparent, from the Prime Minister's peroration, that the King had indeed thrown over his father's guarantees to create peers. What he desired was resolution without conflict. To this end, he wanted the party leaders to meet and devise a decent settlement. Asquith favoured the idea as, to my surprise, did Lloyd George. Seeing an end to my personal suspense receding with an election into the distance, I protested that we should not become embroiled in interminable negotiation and looked to Churchill, hitherto a voluble exponent of dissolving and having done, for support. But he said nothing, significant though his exchange of glances with Lloyd George seemed. The others paraded behind Asquith's assertion of loyalty to the Crown and mine was a lone voice.

Nevertheless, I was asked by Asquith to stay behind after the meeting, along with Lloyd George and the Marquess of Crewe (Leader of the House of Lords). I was thus obliged to simmer beneath the Prime Minister's blandishments as to my and their suitability to constitute the four Liberal representatives to the Constitutional Conference. There were to be four Conservative representatives and one each of the Labour and Irish Nationalist parties.

The first meeting took place at 10 Downing Street on June 16th, a scene-setting event at which Asquith and Balfour exchanged high-sounding nothings, the Conservative peers uttered dire threats and the Labour and Irish delegates made their shrill presence felt. At a prearranged meeting in Hyde Park the following Sunday, I was unable to express more optimism to Elizabeth than that I would resist a little longer before we took matters into our own hands.

The Conference re-convened on June 20th. There was a lengthy discussion of the merits and demerits of joint sittings, quinquennial parliaments and exemptions from veto of special categories of legislation, but with no signs of movement from either side on any issue. Ten grave figures sat round a table expending more air than effort and I grew more depressed and silent with each well-trod avenue that we fruitlessly explored. A pyrotechnical attack on the Conservative peers by the Irish representative served to terminate proceedings in the late afternoon.

As if taking pity on my woebegone expression as I left, Lloyd George caught my eye and invited me into number 11 for a private discussion. At tea time, he served whisky, of which I felt in need and we both expressed exasperation with the Conference.

"You may be sure," he said, "that this will go on for months."

"I'm not sure I'll be able to stick that." He was not to know that my intolerance was rather more than the impatience of youth.

"You should do, Edwin. There might be something in it for you."

"For all of us, I hope."

"Naturally, but I meant that we, you and I, stand to profit personally from the proceedings." My ears pricked up—what Celtic ploy was this?

"I don't see how."

"Then consider, Edwin, what is the implication behind the King's action in setting up this conference?"

"That he wishes to avoid open conflict between the two Houses of Parliament."

"But in what way?"

"By bringing all sides together to reach an agreement."

"Exactly. All sides together spell coalition."

"There's been no mention of that."

"No, but there will be, mark my words. It's the only way. How, otherwise, can the Tories consent to Liberal legislation? A share in the government would have to be their reward." There was something in what he said and it explained his sudden conversion to negotiation.

"Is that why you supported this Conference?"

He wavered for a moment. "It was certainly in my mind."

"But where is the profit for you and me?" Now I was playing him at his own game.

"Isn't that obvious? A coalition could not function under the existing premiership. The Tories would never wear it. No, it would be an opportunity for bright young men of all parties, free of party dogma, to come together for the good of the country."

"And the good of themselves?"

"Why not? Who are we to refuse a golden opportunity if history offers us one? I've already sounded out Balfour."

"You've done what?"

"I've had an informal word with Balfour and he liked the idea. We would drop some reforms for the sake of others that would not be the victims of party conflict."

"Such as?"

"Such as votes for women—some women at any rate—which we've discussed before. Such as a federal solution to the Irish problem. Great gains which might be feathers in our caps."

A vision came unbidden to my mind, as mayhap it had to Lloyd George's. It was of that magical Welsh orator at the head (or near it) of a ministry of all the talents, Asquith's rein on his ambitions at last shrugged off, turning millstones to milestones at his gifted touch, hailed as a hero by Suffragettes, Irish Nationalists and any number of other discontented groups, able to persuade skilled, clear-thinking colleagues of the justice of whatever cause he might advance. Here was not merely an aspirant to political primacy seeking my support but a man hungry for power who saw in me a potential co-conspirator.

"It won't wash, L.G. Votes for a few propertied women would be worse than votes for none. As for a federal Ireland you might convince Balfour of that, but he could never carry his party with him. And if you did oust Asquith, you would break our own party in the process."

He leant forward, eyes twinkling beneath hooded brows. "Would that matter?"

The engaging iconoclast had at last gone too far. "I happen to think so," I said. "I care about the Liberal party and have no wish to see it founder on the rocks of a pointless coalition."

"Not so pointless, Edwin."

"The only point, so far as I can see, is to further your career."

"And yours."

"Perhaps. But neither is worth so much double-dealing."

Lloyd George snorted with derision and strode to the window. "You'll achieve nothing without getting your hands dirty."

"Then nothing may be preferable."

He turned. "You disappoint me, you really do."

I rose from my seat. There was only one thing to say.

"As a matter of fact, L.G., so do you." Whether or not I disappointed him, he had certainly misjudged me, and his annoyance was as much with giving himself away to somebody who might now oppose him as with the failure of his argument.

I made to leave but Lloyd George intercepted me at the door. "Stay a moment, Edwin," he said with a silken smile. "We should not fall out over a little idle theorizing."

"Not so idle, if I'm any judge."

His tone changed to one of menace. "If you are not with us, you are against us."

"All you have to do is not to involve me."

With that, I left. But Lloyd George's use of the collective pronoun had not been lost on me and we both knew that he had already involved me more than was wise. I walked away along Downing Street sadder than I was angry that we responsible men of government were now falling to exploit for our own profit that crisis of the constitution about which we claimed to feel so deeply. There was, for all that, a personal strand to my sadness—the realization that, in seeking to behave in a way that would enable me to continue with my career, I had put at risk that which I cherished above everything: my love for Elizabeth. It was time, I felt, to accord that the priority it deserved.

What would, what did, my darling Elizabeth have to say on the matter? I drove openly to Putney the following afternoon and found her and Mercy taking tea in the garden. Mercy soon found some roses to prune and left us to talk. I shall ever recall Elizabeth's serene and loving company that sultry afternoon on the Longest Day of 1910. She reclined in her chair beneath a parasol, a golden gaze above a cream dress, and sought to lead me to the right answer. She had a gift of calmness before adversity that was part of her beauty.

"I am poorly placed to advise you, Edwin," she said. "But is it not your duty to inform Mr. Asquith of his Chancellor's intentions?"

"So I think, my dear. But I have no wish to sow discord. Besides, there was something to commend what Lloyd George said."

"For him only. I feel sure you are right there."

"Others may benefit. Perhaps even your very own WSPU."

"Not by this latest private members' bill. There's nothing democratic about enfranchising a few middle-aged, property-owning women who vote Conservative."

"With the possible exception of Aunt Mercy?"

Elizabeth smiled. "Granted."

"You are right, though. It's what I said to L.G. But for him it's become a bargaining counter in his deal with Balfour. That's what appals me—that none of these issues seems to matter to him except as a means to an end, that end being Lloyd George for Prime Minister."

"Edwin, I rejoice that it appals you. I fear, however, that others may not see things the same way—others in the WSPU, for instance."

"Really?"

"Oh yes. Remember Julia Lambourne? You met her here once."

"I think I do."

"Well, she told me recently that Christabel Pankhurst secretly supports this bill—that's why the truce she called for the election's been extended. I put more faith now in what Sylvia Pankhurst thinks, but Christabel still determines policy. And what you've now said fits what I've recently heard."

"Which is?"

"According to Julia, Christabel has received intimations from an unnamed minister that, if we accept this bill as a stopgap measure and cause no further trouble, we will receive all we ask at some suitable future date. What if . . ."

"That minister were Lloyd George?"

"I think it must be."

"But L.G. can't make promises like that."

"He can if he doesn't mean them to be kept. From what you say, he's quite capable of deceiving Christabel in order to appear as the pacifier of the Suffragettes."

"That's true. Elizabeth, I've decided what to do. I shall see the Prime Minister and tell him what's happening to his precious conference. In return for my honesty, let him honour his promise to sanction our marriage."

"I pray you succeed."

"If not, we will marry anyway and damn the consequences—if you will still have me."

Elizabeth rose lightly from her chair and moved across to kiss me. "Of course I will still have you, Edwin. And you me, I hope."

"Oh yes, my darling, you may be sure of that."

Suddenly, her expression became grave as she knelt beside me. "There may be one other thing to worry about."

"What might that be?"

"I fear that, for all our discretion, some people in the movement know about us, or think they know—perhaps even Christabel herself."

"What makes you think so?"

"Well, Julia is a darling, but she talks too freely. I'm sure she must have let slip seeing you here, because I've been asked lots of awkward questions recently."

"Fear not. One way or the other, we will soon have nothing to hide." And certain it seemed that it would be so, as Elizabeth knelt before me on the lawn beneath the cherry blossoms and lent me her strength and love. But little I knew that the worst we feared was better than what was, in truth, to come.

The following morning, I telephoned Asquith's secretary from my office and arranged to see the Prime Minister in his room at the House of Commons, at five o'clock that afternoon. I was there in time to sit in on a low-key debate in the Chamber before walking smartly up to Asquith's room even as Big Ben began to strike the hour.

The Prime Minister looked up wearily from his desk as I entered, his blank expression unmoving. "What can I do for you, Edwin?" His tone would have seemed tart had it not been so tired.

"It concerns the Conference, Prime Minister."

"Please sit down." I did so. "I daresay it is not going as well—or as quickly—as you had hoped. Alas, it cannot be helped."

"You will know from what I said in Cabinet that I have no faith in the Conference as a solution to our problems."

"I also know why it is a blow to your particular ambitions, Edwin. But they can form no part of what the government judges to be best."

"I accept that, of course, though you have more than once implied the reverse." I had not intended to sound a carping note and instantly regretted it, but Asquith scarcely seemed to notice, his eyes fixed on some indeterminate point in the middle distance.

"If that is why you have come," he said at last amid his languor, "there is nothing that I can offer you."

"It is not why I have come, so let us say no more of it. What has brought me here this afternoon is the state of the Conference about which I had such doubts but which I am doing my best to make a go of."

"As are we all."

"I think not. I have recently become aware that a member of our own delegation may be pursuing schismatic objectives under the cover of negotiations with the Conservatives."

Again, there was no visible reaction from Asquith. "Be so good as to explain."

"Secret negotiations have commenced geared towards replacing this government with a coalition in which those party to the negotiations would have their reward and from which others—including yourself—would be excluded."

"And you accuse one of our delegation of this clandestine negotiation?"

"I do."

"And who might that be?"

"The Chancellor of the Exchequer."

"I see." There followed only silence.

"After Monday's session, L.G. asked me if I would be interested in such a proposal, if I would cooperate with him in agreeing terms with Balfour and support them against you when the time came."

"And how did you reply?"

"I refused. That is why I am telling you now, as I felt to be my duty."

"Then I'm obliged to you."

"I thought you might wish to . . ."

"Please don't trouble yourself to continue. I think you have said enough."

"But what will you do?"

"Nothing." His inertness of pose confirmed his reply.

"Prime Minister, I don't think I understand."

"Very well, I will specify that which I had hoped to spare you." There was a visible summoning of effort. "What you say may or may not be true. I find it entirely credible that Lloyd George should engage in such activities—I have long known him to be utterly unscrupulous. But I must weigh against that possibility the known fact that you oppose the Conference. I included you in our delegation against my better judgement, because I thought that, as Home Secretary, you had a right to take part in discussions concerning parliamentary reform. Yet I know that, for personal reasons, you feel frustrated by this method of proceedings and might therefore have an interest in undermining my faith in the Conference and panicking me into an election to forestall the backstairs intriguing of which you now carry tales. No doubt you suppose that, following an election, you could marry in the knowledge that any scandal associated with it would have dissipated by the time you had to face your constituents again."

My avuncular premier had gone too far. "You may think what you like, Prime Minister. As I see it, there is no scandal associated with my proposed marriage to Miss Latimer. You originally cited your own embarrassment as the objection. It is true that I consider the Conference to be a waste of time, but it is now acquiring sinister connotations and, if you wish to ignore the threat it may pose to your own position, that is your privilege. I would advise you to take it more seriously. As for myself, you are mistaken if you impute dishonourable motives to me. I have always sought to deal properly in this matter, whilst others have delayed and dissembled. You confess to doubts about the probity of some of your colleagues. I believe those doubts are now handicapping the execution of the government's duties. I will therefore have to review my part in the government."

I rose to leave, but Asquith held up his hand in a gesture that was more conciliatory than his words had so far been. "Stay a moment, Edwin. I may have spoken hastily and have no wish to impugn your honour. I confess that there has been so much duplicitous dealing since the election that I sometimes distrust even the trustworthy. I hope you will see why I cannot afford to act on what you have said. As for your own position, I urge you to remain. Your talents are much needed, your candour hardly less so. There is, I fear, no inducement that I can or will offer in the present circumstances. Stay if you will, go if you must. But do not set terms for staying which I cannot meet."

"Thank you for saying that." I rose a second time. "Let us say no more for the present. I will consider what to do for the best."

Asquith also rose. "Consider well, Edwin. But remember—we have need of such as you."

"I will."

Spontaneously, I shook his hand, then left quickly. He had, I noted, wrenched some decent sentiments from his soul, but this seemed to require more effort than had once been the case. By his lights a good man, he appeared to me to have withered beneath his load of responsibility, a worthy advocate worn down by advancing too many dubious arguments in the service of causes he only half-believed in. He had never lied to me, only misrepresented; never promised, only hoped; never acted, only reacted.

I made my way to the Embankment and walked west beside mother Thames, in need of its breezes to clear my thoughts. I felt not outraged by Asquith's indecision but saddened that he should have so little grasp on events. Anger was reserved for myself, for having allowed him to deceive me with his pious hopes, for having thought there would be some end to his procrastination. Now I knew there never would be and that Elizabeth and I were waiting upon his instinct for infinite delay. He might have believed my report of Lloyd George, but I knew now that he would do nothing about it, as he had himself admitted. Rather he would ignore it—and any other problem—until the moment when a crisis was forced by hands other than his. Elizabeth and I were in no position to impose a crisis, which left us only one recourse.

At Battersea Bridge, I turned inland from the river and made my way home, where I knew that solitude awaited me in which to decide what to do next. The Prideaux had gone down to Devon for their annual fortnight with their daughter's family in Bideford. So there had been nobody to admit the figure I saw standing by my door as I came along the street. Drawing closer, my heart leapt at the realization that it was my beloved Elizabeth. She was clad soberly in grey, as when once she had come there with a housebrick concealed in her reticule, gazing about her now quite as anxiously as she had that day. But, at my approach, she smiled and waved a gloved hand. I joined her at the door and snatched a kiss.

"This is very forward of you, Mr Strafford," she said with a laugh. "To kiss me in the street."

"May I not so greet my fiancée?"

"Of course. It was only that . . ."

"We have endeavoured to be cautious in our displays of affection. But I hope such circumspection can now end, Elizabeth. Come inside and I will explain."

I showed her into the drawing room and took her cape, explaining the Prideaux' absence as I went to hang it up. She in turn explained her presence on my doorstep, although I had sought no reason for such a happy manifestation.

"I walked up from Putney this afternoon half-hoping to find you in. I wondered whether I had given you sound advice yesterday."

"Don't doubt it," I said, returning to the room. "We have discharged our obligations in exemplary fashion. Would that others had."

"Such as the Prime Minister?"

"Such as he indeed." I sat her down on the sofa next to me. "I have just returned from seeing him."

"What happened?"

"I told him of Lloyd George's proposition and how I thought the Conference would be undermined by his activities."

"What did he say?"

"He said that he could not act upon such information, even if he believed it, which he was inclined not to do because he thought that I had a vested interest in wrecking the Conference. When I challenged him on the point, he backed down, but not with sufficient conviction to warrant my reconsidering my next move."

"Which is?"

"To resign . . . and marry you as soon as possible."

Elizabeth's mouth broadened into a smile, then she as suddenly looked down. "Oh Edwin, I don't know whether to laugh or cry. To marry you is all I want to do, but not at the expense of your career."

I took her by the hand. "Elizabeth, my career is not worth that much, especially not in this tainted administration. We have waited too long as it is and should wait no longer."

"But . . ."

"No buts, please, my darling. We took oaths of love last Michaelmas which should now be honoured. I should never have asked you to indulge in the charade of recent months. And be assured: it was a charade. The day Asquith has long spoken of, when he is prepared to tolerate the embarrassment of our union, will never come. He will always advance a plausible reason for its delay. Now I will save him the trouble. Let him cope with Lloyd George unaided. Let Lloyd George forward his own grubby schemes without my assistance or opposition. I will leave them all to it and devote myself to making you happy."

"Are you sure?"

"As sure as my love for you." I drew her to me and kissed her. "Marry me, Elizabeth."

"I will, Edwin, I will."

"The sooner the better now. I will resign tomorrow and apply for a special licence."

"If you are to sacrifice high office, I will relinquish what paltry political career of my own I have. I will resign from the WSPU and sunder all links with the suffragist movement."

"I do not require that of you."

"Just as I do not require anything of you, Edwin, except your love and your hand. But permit me a small sacrifice to stand beside your far greater one."

"Very well."

"What will you do without politics?"

"I will remain an M.P. for a little longer yet and consider my options. Business, journalism—who knows? Let it all be a grand adventure, starting with our wedding."

I poured two glasses of sherry, the best libation I could muster, and we toasted our mutually assured happiness, infecting each other with a sudden release of nervous gaiety. To know that all the waiting was at an end was to know that a better, brighter day would dawn now for both of us. We stood by the window, arm in arm, looking out at the few passers-by, all of them unaware of our joy, then turned away to look at each other.

"Nobody out there will be able to say that our action is unsuitable for people in our positions because we will have abandoned those positions to take up far happier ones."

"Like any good politician, Edwin, you convince me."

"But unlike many politicians, Elizabeth, you can believe this one."

"I will always trust in you."

We touched glasses and drank again in the summer sun shafting through the new glass of the window, then kissed and returned to the sofa.

"A glass of sherry in a house shorn of servants is no way to celebrate our decision," I said. "Might you be free for dinner, Miss Latimer?"

"With my future husband, always, though I am hardly dressed for the occasion."

"If I can abandon a conference, cannot you abandon convention for an evening?"

And, of course, she did. We summoned a cab and proceeded at once to The Baron for dinner at what had by now become our usual table. If less gorgeously dressed than usual for such an occasion, Elizabeth was certainly more radiant than normal, her eyes forever on mine as we drank and ate and talked, with a kind of feverish relief, of the rest of our lives together. For once, and, as it seemed, forever, we forgot the Liberal party and the suffragist movement and thought only of ourselves. The months of anxiety and suspense were at an end and, in their wake, came all the pleasure in each other which we had so long suppressed. The beautiful young woman who was soon to become my wife shared my delight with all the wholeheartedness I could have hoped for.

Around ten o'clock, we left The Baron and I summoned a cab to take Elizabeth home to Putney.

"It seems a pity," I said as the cab drew up, "that our homes lie apart."

"I no longer feel that they do," said Elizabeth.

"Nor I. On such a balmy night, would you like to walk with me back to what will soon be your home as well as mine? I could drive you out to Putney in my car." At this stage, I was merely reluctant for us to part so soon and so early, as was, I think, Elizabeth. So we walked slowly and happily, arm in arm, through quiet residential roads back to Mallard Street. As a chill crept into the night, I put my arm round Elizabeth's shoulder, reflecting with slight but pleasurable dismay that we had hitherto punctiliously avoided such intimate proximity. My beautiful bride-to-be yielded to my caress as we went and, by the time we arrived at my door, it seemed not so much intolerable as wonderfully unnecessary for us to part for the night.

We went into the drawing room and I poured a nightcap.

"Thank you for the happiest evening of my life," Elizabeth said.

"And thank you for mine," I replied. "Just think: it is the first of many more. There is a sense in which our marriage begins tonight."

"I feel that too, Edwin." I was uncertain how far I had been speaking metaphorically and Elizabeth's response did not suggest she was any clearer on the point. I walked over to hand her a glass, but instead set it down on a table and took her in my arms.

"Stay with me, Elizabeth."

"Forever, Edwin."

"And tonight?"

She paused for a moment to look at me, then spoke. "I am yours."

I cradled her in my arms and carried her upstairs to the bedroom, in a progression that seemed the most natural thing in all the world. There we celebrated in the flesh our marriage of the mind. For the first time, we were each other's in the fullest sense, unaware of our ecstasy that this was not the glorious beginning of our life together but its poignant end.

So it was that, when the rays of morning crept across the room, I awoke with Elizabeth asleep against me, seeing only bright promise in the day ahead. I slipped out of bed and made some tea. When I returned, Elizabeth had donned a dressing gown of mine and was sitting up in bed, bashful and discomposed, but not unhappy. I sat down beside her with the tray.

"Without the Prideaux, we must shift for ourselves," I said. "Would you care to risk some tea brewed by me?"

"It is as well the Prideaux are not here, Edwin. They would be scandalized."

"No doubt, but there is no scandal, my love. All such thoughts are behind us. By the time the Prideaux get back, we will have fixed a date for you to become Mrs Strafford. In all but the formal sense, you already are."

Elizabeth took my arm. "Let it be soon."

"It will be, never fear."

I now prevailed upon Elizabeth to try some of my tea, but, before she had finished the cup, she began to fret about Mercy, who was bound to be concerned about her whereabouts. The least censorious of ladies, Mercy would nevertheless be worried, so then we hurried, which helped besides to cover some of our embarrassment. I left Elizabeth to dress and busied myself downstairs.

Soon it was time to go, only Elizabeth's expressive look conveying that this was a different young girl in grey to the one who had come to my door the day before.

"I'll call a cab to take you to Putney," I said. "I'll walk to the Home Office and . . ."

"When will I see you again?"

"Before the day is out. There is a Cabinet meeting at eleven, where I'll hand my letter of resignation to Asquith. Afterwards, I'll come straight to Putney and take you to the Court of Faculties, so that we can apply for a special licence."

"Come as soon as you can. It will seem an age however soon it is."

"Are you worried about Mercy?"

"Only because she will be worried. My return will put her mind at rest."

"Then we had better arrange it in short order."

We went outside and I hailed a cab. Elizabeth lingered by my front door as the cab drew up.

"Are you not anxious to return to Putney?"

"Of course, but, somehow, this parting now seems wrong."

"A brief but necessary one, I promise, whilst I perform the obsequies in Downing Street and you settle your aunt's nerves. It will only be a few hours before we are re-united."

"Yes. I'm sorry to be so silly."

"Never silly, Elizabeth, only lovely. Go now and remember, I will love you forever."

We kissed as lingeringly as we could with a cabbie on hand, then Elizabeth climbed aboard and they clopped off along Mallard Street, I waving after her. "Look out for me this afternoon," I cried.

"I will," I heard her faintly call, words I thought soon to hear her use in more ceremonial setting—but never did.

I returned to the house to pack what official papers I had into a valise, then set off for the Home Office. There, Meres was his usual efficient self, unaware that my only task that morning was to write one letter. It was swiftly done—an unadorned one-sentence notification of my immediate departure from office. I sealed the envelope and, with it, my fate and walked smartly round to Downing Street to join my fellow-ministers at number 10.

The Cabinet meeting was unremarkable. I said nothing, not even when the matter arose of the bill to enfranchise female occupiers. It came as no surprise to me that Lloyd George spoke in favour of giving it a second reading, nor that Asquith quietly acquiesced in this. I cast a last ritual vote against, but finished in the minority.

As the meeting was breaking up, I drew Asquith aside and handed him my letter.

"I'd be obliged if you found an early opportunity to read this, Prime Minister," I said.

"Of course, Edwin, of course," Asquith muttered, but his attention was on a conversation with the Foreign Secretary. I slipped quietly away, content to go without further ado.

I lunched at the House of Commons, then strolled down to the Embankment and, so fine was the afternoon, decided to walk all the way upriver to Putney.

I arrived at about four o'clock in the orderly precincts of Mercy's house and knocked at the door, expecting it to be opened either by Elizabeth or their maid. Instead, a stranger appeared before me—a stockily built young man with a querulous set to his expression.

"Can I help you?" he said, with no hint that he meant to.

"I don't believe I know you sire, but my name is Strafford and I have called to see the young lady of the house."

"Miss Latimer is not at home."

"Really? Then the elder Miss Latimer?"

"Is in, but has asked not to be disturbed."

"And who precisely are you?"

"A friend of the family."

"A new one, it would seem, for I've never met you. Kindly stand aside."

He had nettled me by his tone, but it was the unexpected coolness of my reception at this customarily welcoming door that was trying my patience. The man did not clear my path and I might have had to force an entrance, but Mercy appeared then in the hall, clearly upset, and asked him to admit me.

"What's going on, M?"

Mercy's usual smile had vanished. She spoke in a manner she had never used before. "How dare you come here? Haven't you done enough?"

"What are you talking about?"

"You know full well, young man. If my brother were still alive, he would know how to deal with one such as you. As it is, all I can say is that the hospitality of this house, which you have so vilely abused, is forever denied you."

This was surely not dear old Aunt M speaking; I had called at the wrong door, stepped over a threshold into a nightmare in which I did not belong. There was only one way back.

"Where is Elizabeth?"

"She is upstairs with Julia, distraught, as you must have known she would be when you were shown in your true colours."

"What colours? What does this mean?"

"It means that a man I respected and my niece loved has been exposed for what he is: a fraud and a villain."

The man at the door had come up behind me. "Shall I make him leave, Miss Latimer?"

"I think that would be best . . . unless he will go of his own accord."

"M, this is madness. I'm not leaving until I see Elizabeth. Has she told you of our intentions?"

"Her intentions—her hopes—are shattered. Yours do not bear description. Cannot you be content with that?"

The young man laid a hand on my shoulder. I made a last appeal to reason, as much my own as that of those around me.

"Call this young lout off before I hurt him. I demand to see my fiancée."

The man seized my collar. This was too much. I shook him off, spun round and lashed out in all my baffled fury. My fist caught him square on the chin and sent him reeling back into a mirror that hung on the hall wall. He and it crashed to the floor. Mercy screamed. My own violence had only made the nightmare worse.

"Stop this!"

The voice was Elizabeth's. She was speaking from the top of the stairs. I looked up to her there, expecting to see my dearest love in all her radiant calmness, hoping even now that she could turn my world back upright again. She was still in her grey dress, but all else had changed. Her face was a mask, tracked and puffed by tears. She was trembling and sobbing even as she spoke.

"Edwin, you have ruined me—you have ruined us. Why come here to twist the knife in my wound?"

I ran to the foot of the stairs and looked up at her imploringly "What wound, Elizabeth? For God's sake, tell me my offence."

She grasped the banisters for support. "It is too much to ask me to put into words the depth of your deceit. You compound it now by feigning ignorance."

A young lady appeared at her elbow whom I recognized from a previous encounter as Julia Lambourne. At sight of the figure sprawled on the floor behind me, nursing a split lip, she cried out and rushed down past me to attend him. I remained staring up at Elizabeth, searching in her eyes for the trust I had somehow forfeited.

"Elizabeth, I will say it once more. Remember all that we have meant to each other and believe me: I do not know of what I stand accused. I have stood by you and my word in all our dealings. This very day I have resigned office for your sake. What has happened?"

"I remember what you meant to me, what I thought I meant to you. But it was a lie, a mockery. You cannot escape the truth, Edwin. It has found you out, but not soon enough to save me. If my pleas can in any way touch you, grant this one: leave now and never attempt to see me again. One day, I may be able to forget, even forgive, but only so long as I never have to hear your voice or see your face—that were once so dear to me—ever again."

"Elizabeth, this morning you agreed to marry me."

Elizabeth cried out, put her hand to her face and ran back from the head of the stairs, out of my sight.

"Mr Strafford, please leave." Mercy had spoken unevenly from behind me.

I turned to confront them, Julia now supporting the man as he stood glaring at me, Mercy trembling visibly beside them. Julia spoke.

"Mr Strafford, you have assaulted my brother and piled further distress upon that which you have already caused Elizabeth. We would all be glad if you now left."

I stood in the hall, poised between that tableau of accusing faces and the hurt and wrong I felt from the words flung down at me by Elizabeth. I was dumbstruck, adrift in a nightmare, the real, sure world of the night before, the year before, receding from my faltering grasp. With every denial I was held to further my guilt, with every wild flailing I descended further into the morass. A silence hung over the motionless group until I felt I would cry aloud at all its mute injustice. Instead, I walked quietly to the door, Julia and her brother parting to let me go, opened it and strode from the house.

Before I had gone a hundred yards, a sense of hopelessness and loss overwhelmed me. A short distance ahead was the church where I had thought to marry Elizabeth one day soon.

I could not bear to enter a building with such associations, but sat on a bench amongst the gravestones and wept. After a little while, a lady passed by, bearing flowers to a grave. At this, I composed myself somewhat and left, wandering east by streets I knew not in no particular direction; motion was all I sought, as if by pounding a pavement through throngs of strangers I could beat out the shock of my rejection.

In Wandsworth, a tavern was opening its doors for evening trade as I passed. So I abandoned my grim patrol and entered, hoping to drink myself into a merciful oblivion. The publican was clearly curious that such a well dressed and spoken customer should cross the threshold of his large, sawdusted alehouse, but my money satisfied him. Hunched in a corner as the inn filled slowly through the evening, I drank cheap beer until all my senses, even of loss and sorrow, were blunted. Then I could bear to be alone, so left and took to the streets again.

Some hours later, I found myself on Westminster Bridge, the familiar bulk of Parliament before me. Now I no longer felt part of its hectic life, dislocated in a self-imposed exile from love and politics—from all that I had thus far lived for. I stared down into the murky, turbid waters of the Thames, tempted to think; for a moment, that there, if anywhere, my hurt could be healed.

"Don't I know you sir?"

A voice had spoken from behind me. I turned from the parapet to face a policeman.

"Yes, surely it's Mr Strafford."

"No longer your master, constable." I must have reeked of alcohol.

"Don't you think you should be going home, sir?"

"But where is home?"

"Where the heart is, according to the poet, sir."

"Then that's why I'm on this bridge, constable. My heart is with the river, flowing out to sea."

"I'll call a cab to take you home, sir."

He walked me to the Embankment and put me aboard a hansom. But I discharged the fare some way short of Mallard Street and wandered again wherever my steps took me.

At last, with dawn breaking, I did return home, for want of anywhere else to go. A milkman was on his rounds, whistling as he went. He passed a word with a postman, who had just stepped back from my door. All was unforced jollity in Mallard Street, until my bleak homecoming.

I opened my front door and, in so doing, stirred a letter on the mat. Recognizing the hand as Elizabeth's, I seized it and wrenched it open, desperately scanning the contents for some sign that all might yet be saved.

6 Sutler Terrace
Putney.
23rd June 1910

Dear Mr Strafford,

I write following your visit here this afternoon, since there seems some possibility that you will seek to brazen out your deceit of me. Be clear, then, that I wish never to see you or hear from you again. I am only prevented from invoking some greater sanction against you than this by the knowledge that incidents such as this afternoon's will only heighten my distress and that of my dear aunt. Do me one small service after all your dissembling: leave me alone.

Yours truly,
Elizabeth Latimer

It was appalling. It could not be true, yet it undoubtedly was. Elizabeth had rejected me, in the coldest and most outright terms, apparently believing me to be guilty of some vile outrage. I staggered into the study, seized some notepaper and wrote a reply.

Elizabeth
Wherein have I offended?

Edwin

I sealed the letter and went to post it, already fearing that it would never be opened. I returned to the house, a cold dread upon me. There I brewed and drank strong coffee in a bid to confront the unthinkable in a sober state, gazed blankly out at the slowly stirring street, numbed now by it all, uncomprehending but no longer disbelieving. What was to be done? I could not go back to Putney, but elsewhere life held nothing for me. I had but lately abandoned a career, which might have been an anchor of a kind.

This last, I resolved, was one area in which I could act, and action alone assuaged my anguish. I washed and shaved, striving to keep a grasp on what had, until today, been a life of order and progress. I donned clean clothes and set off for Downing Street, arriving shortly after nine o'clock. Asquith's secretary received me and presented some objections to my seeing the Prime Minister, but I was not in the mood to be trifled with and he seemed to recognize this.

Asquith was in his study, reading The Times. *He glanced up quizzically at my entrance.*

"To say that I'm surprised to see you, Strafford, would be to put it mildly."

"No doubt, Prime Minister. May I come straight to the point?"

"By all means."

"I wish to withdraw my resignation."

"If this is a joke, it's in damned poor taste."

"Levity could hardly be further from my thoughts."

"Good. This newspaper"—he flourished The Times—*"will tomorrow report your going as a private decision occasioning dismay and regret to the government. You and I both know that, so far from that, it is the only honourable course open to you. So what do you mean by coming here today speaking of withdrawal?"*

"Prime Minister, I don't know what you're talking about. Two days ago, you pleaded with me to stay."

"Now, I have been given certain information which suggests you are unfit to be a minister of the Crown, for that matter a Member of Parliament."

"What information?"

"It concerns your proposed marriage to Miss Elizabeth Latimer, for which you have so often proclaimed your eagerness in past months. How you could deceive the young lady as you have, I do not know."

"In what way deceived?"

"Let that remain a matter between you and Miss Latimer. For her sake, I shall not speak of it. But it will do no good to try to outface the situation."

Had everyone conspired against me? Was I alone not to know the act for which I was to be punished?

"Prime Minister, as God is my witness . . ."

"Don't say any more, Strafford. Just get out."

"But . . ."

"Go."

There seemed no point in persisting. I turned to the door.

"One thing, Strafford." I paused, but did not look back. "Any application from you for the wardenship of the Chiltern Hundreds will be sympathetically entertained."

I left then, the final insult inflicted upon me. I wandered west through St. James's Park, bearing with me misery and despair enough for a dozen men.

So that was it. Strafford had been cast adrift. It came as some kind of consolation to a man who'd also endured a bitter transformation in life, the staples of marriage, parenthood and career swept suddenly from my grasp, that the wealthy and powerful were not immune to such impenetrable workings of fate.

Judging by my own example, I could hardly believe that Strafford was as innocent as he appeared. Conspiracy or blind nemesis were attractive alternatives to the greater likelihood of some culpability Strafford couldn't admit, even to himself. Yet, as an historian enticed by mystery, I yearned for something more sinister and as a man who'd inflicted many misfortunes on himself, I was eager to demonstrate that it was possible to attract them undeserved.

Alec returned around dusk and insisted I drag myself away from the Memoir and join him on a visit to some English friends—the Thorpes—who lived in a small quinta of their own on the hilly fringes of Funchal. Reluctantly, I went, but didn't regret going. Mrs Thorpe cooked a fine meal and her husband seemed to know everybody who was somebody on the island. I mentioned Sellick and Thorpe described him as "a good man to have on your side". There was an implication he was a worse man to oppose. As a businessman of some repute, it seemed Thorpe ought to know.

On our way home that night, I asked Alec if Thorpe, being a moneyed Englishman, might have been interested in financing the magazine.

"He was a natural candidate, but didn't fancy the economics of the operation. I tried several like him and it was the same story. Only Leo was prepared to put up the cash."

"Fairy godfather to both of us, then?"

"You said it, Martin."

The next morning, my last, the Manager of Maritimo was giving a press conference and Alec had to be there. I took myself into the garden, where it was warm and quiet and shady under the palm tree. There, in a final session before my flight home, I resumed Strafford's story.

Memoir

1910–1950

I can give no clear account of myself in the days following my rejection by Elizabeth and Asquith's refusal to let me withdraw my resignation. I went home, knowing that I could be alone there, and drank steadily until I was no longer conscious of what had befallen me. Oblivion was surely the best state for me at that time.

My family read in the newspapers that I had resigned, then found they could not contact me. Concern became alarm and, midway through the following week, Robert came up to London with the Prideaux to root me out. He later told me of the scene they found at Mallard Street and had cause to thank his instinct in not allowing my mother to accompany them. I was, by then, a drunken and dishevelled wreck of the man they thought they knew.

A doctor was called and I was put to bed, fed by Mrs Prideaux, denied alcohol and restored to some degree of normality. When I was able and when I could bear to, I told Robert what had happened. He expressed astonishment that his talented young brother should have been brought so low. It was nothing to my own shock at the speed with which my world had disintegrated. Wisely, Robert did not indulge my morbidity. As soon as I was up and about, he took me back to Barrowteign.

There, he and my mother sought to raise my spirits by arranging all manner of diversions during the summer. Even

Florence tried to jolly me along, though to the opposite effect. But I had no wish to forget Elizabeth or the tragedy of our parting. The pain was all I was left with to remember our love by. Even when I summoned up some good cheer for my mother's sake, it was a feeble and ephemeral affair. Although I no longer looked to liquor for consolation, I remained entrenched in my misery, pacing the Moor through the long days of summer, finding in that harsh landscape a determined bleakness to match my own. I wrote several letters to Elizabeth, hoping against hope for a reply. None came, then the letters began to be returned unopened. At that, I gave up.

One evening in early September, over dinner, my family's impatience with my melancholia could be contained no longer.

"The Haddows have invited us to dine with them next Saturday," my mother announced. "They're having quite a party down for the weekend. I said that we'd all go."

"You'll have to count me out, Mother," I said.

"Do you have a prior commitment, dear?"

"No. I'd just rather not go."

"Haddow keeps a fine table," said Robert.

"I'm hardly in need of food."

"It would do you good," said Florence.

"Your concern is touching, Florence, but I'm sure I'll survive without a visit to the Haddows'."

Robert decided to play the elder brother. "You've seen noone outside the household since coming down here, Edwin. Couldn't you make the effort?"

"I think not."

"Isn't that what it comes down to, though?"

"What do you mean?"

"That you're simply not prepared to make the effort to recover from what's happened. We've all tried to help you, but sometimes you don't seem to want to be helped."

Mother was alarmed by this sudden note of fraternal friction. "That's going too far, Robert."

"No, no, Mother," I said. "If that's what Robert feels, he should say so. Maybe he's right. But I'm not able to consign a marriage and a career to the past without a few regretful backward glances."

Robert snorted. "You're still an M.P., remember."

"For how much longer? I'm clearly a marked man as far as the leadership is concerned."

"But why?"

"Robert, I wish I knew."

"You were marked the day you decided to marry that woman," Florence put in.

"In what way, Florence?" I struggled to remain calm.

Florence warmed to her theme. "I simply do not understand how a man in your position can have thought to marry a shameless Suffragette."

There was a shocked pause, during which we all took in the significance of what she had said. Then I spoke as levelly as I could. "Perhaps you will tell me, Florence, how you came to think of Elizabeth as a Suffragette."

"Do you deny that she is?"

"Not at all. The point is that I have never told you that she is."

"It was obvious that there was something amiss with her. I made certain enquiries that . . ."

"Florence! Be silent!" Robert had spoken with uncharacteristic force and his wife was cowed by it.

"Would you care to explain for her, Robert?"

"Very well. Florence was naturally concerned to put at rest her doubts about Miss Latimer and sought to do so, but, in the process, discovered that they were all too well-founded. She advised me of her findings at once."

"You never said anything to me about it."

"Nor me," said Mother.

"I did not wish to worry you, Mother, and I judged that Edwin would misconstrue my interest, which was throughout in his welfare. I did, however, consult Mr Flowers on the implications of Florence's intelligence and he undertook to safeguard Edwin's position as best he could."

I rose solemnly from the table. "Whatever interests you were serving, Robert, you were actually only satisfying Florence's spite. Whatever your excuses, it was dishonourable to go behind my back to Flowers, who was without doubt the Chief Whip's informant. Had you behaved properly, I might today be a happily married man, not the miserable fool you *and others have made of me. It seems that every man's hand is against me, even my brother's. I will leave now rather than say any more."*

I had reached the door when my mother called me back. I turned to look at her. "Naturally, I exonerate you, Mother. But I cannot stay with others who have deceived me. I shall return to London in the morning."

And so I went, without a word, before breakfast, driving up the old coach road to London in reckless fury. Nowhere could I be happy. At least in London I could be alone in my misery and nearer to Elizabeth.

Not that that did me much good. I went down to Putney on several occasions in search of her, not to speak to her, but merely in the hope of a fleeting glimpse. I gained not a one and the house appeared to be shut up. Eventually, I nerved myself to enquire of a neighbour, who told me that the Latimers had gone abroad for several months in the interests of Mercy's health. She did not know where.

There was no more to be done on that front and I could raise no interest on others. I put in a few token appearances at the Commons, but now found proceedings there tiresome. I was constantly berated by the Whips for my erratic attendance and, in mid-October, my constituency party chairman wrote to me enquiring as to my intentions. I replied in short order saying that I would not seek re-election and that, unless an election was called soon, I would take steps to vacate my seat. There was no reply, which seemed to write finis to my political career.

Towards the end of October, my mother came to stay with me and we were swiftly reconciled. She reported that Robert had been so upset by the circumstances of my departure from Barrowteign that his relations with Florence had deteriorated markedly. I was prevailed upon to return at Christmas and seek to heal the breach, but I agreed only for my mother's sake.

Before then, there were other developments. On November 10, the Constitutional Conference broke down without agreement, though not without rumours reaching even my remote position in the party that there had been mooted, in its latter stages, some form of coalition. This came as no surprise to me in view of what I knew of Lloyd George's manoeuvrings, frustrated at the last, it seemed, by feeling within the Conservative rank and file. That had been the weakness in his scheme all along and maybe Asquith had been shrewd enough to know that.

At all events, this made an election inevitable to meet the King's pre-condition for the creation of peers. It was called for early December and, forewarned by my letter in October, the constituency party had a respectable candidate to succeed me in a Londoner who had lost his seat the previous January. In a sense, this came as a merciful release, since it neatly avoided having to give Asquith the satisfaction of my applying for the Chiltern Hundreds. In another sense, it left me farther adrift than ever, for I was no nearer recovering myself than I had been in the summer. The government was returned to office and my part in public life was ended.

I went down to Barrowteign at Christmas and tried to put a brave face on the festivities, but my truce with Robert was an uneasy one and Florence I blatantly avoided. Little Ambrose seemed to enjoy himself and my mother took some comfort from the apparent unity of her family, but it was not for me a season of hope.

The early days of January, 1911, were marked by heavy snow and high winds in Devon. Nevertheless, Twelfth Night celebrations went ahead in Dewford on the evening of January 5 and Robert and Florence attended to represent the family. Not wishing to walk in such weather, Robert drove down to the village. We expected them back by midnight. As it turned out, they never returned. They came back as far as the level crossing where the Teign Valley railway line crossed the estate, but were destined to progress no further.

So as far as anybody could ever after establish, their car became stuck by one wheel in a snow-filled pothole between the lines at a time when the blizzard made visibility extremely poor. The crossingkeeper was out rescuing some sheep that were also his responsibility and so there was no-one to assist Robert in freeing the wheel. He would not have been alarmed by this, since he would have known that there were no trains due at such a time. Unhappily, stormy seas had flooded the main line at Dawlish and a much-delayed express train to

Plymouth was accordingly re-routed via the Teign Valley. Proceeding faster than may have been prudent in an attempt to make up lost time, the engine driver stood no chance of seeing Robert's car as he rounded the bend just north of the crossing, braked far too late and carried the car away. Florence, who was still aboard, went with it, whilst Robert, who was presumably working on the wheel at the time, was thrown to one side.

I was called from the house, where I had been sitting gloomily by the fire, and hurried down to the crossing. There was a scene of utter confusion in the darkness and swirling snow, with the driver and crew of the train gathered by the mangled wreck of the car, carried half a mile down the track after the impact. For Florence there was no hope, but Robert we found horribly injured, lying some yards from the crossing, yet still alive. It was obvious, however, that he was not long for this world. He seemed to recognize me, clutched my hand, muttered the name of his son, then died in my arms.

A bitter night it was, with the bitterest moment—that of telling my mother, who had been asleep in bed—still to come. With one son a shadow of his former self, she had now to face the loss of another outright. There seemed no easy way to tell her after we had carried Robert's body up to the house, leaving others for the moment to extricate Florence from the wreckage. I simply blurted it out and she broke down. The doctor was called to attend to her, whilst I returned to the scene of the accident to assuage with labour my regret for harsh words exchanged which could never now be withdrawn.

A week after the event, we assembled at Dewford Church on a bright day, with the snow melting, to bury Robert and Florence side by side. If my mother was still numb with the shock of the tragedy, I was bemused that another blow should have come from an unexpected quarter to add to those I had already borne.

Yet life had to go on. In particular, Ambrose had to be cared for and this concern was a great aid to my mother's recovery. As her surviving son, I rallied round as best I could. I had always liked little Ambrose and he me, so I shared with my mother responsibility for him, assisted as we both were by his nanny, who proved to be a tower of strength. Other than with this, I was entirely occupied in management of the estate now that Robert was no longer there to handle such matters. I sold my house in London and settled permanently at Barrowteign, the running of the place keeping me busy and leaving me little time to brood. For all that the house was sadder without its master, I was at least usefully engaged in maintaining it.

Society and politics I continued to shun, falling out of touch with national affairs. When the Parliament Act was finally passed in August 1911, ending two years of struggle between the Commons and the Lords, I paid it no heed. I could never be a country gentleman in my brother's mould, but I could absorb myself in life and work at Barrowteign to some effect. It was as good a therapy as any for one in my condition. As the years slipped by, I did not learn to forget Elizabeth, but at length I adjusted to being without her. I did not succeed in becoming a happy man, but at least I ceased to be an entirely hapless one.

A man forms habits to cope with reality. Deprived of political life, I could at least read about it in the newspapers and did so assiduously. Wryly, over breakfast at Barrowteign, I read how my successor at the Home Office, Churchill, turned the siege of Sidney Street into an exhibition of his own flare for theatricality. Ruefully, I followed his successor in turn, McKenna, in his ever more desperate dealings with the Suffragettes.

As for Elizabeth, I could glean nothing of her, though I scanned the personal and social columns for anything that might tell me how she fared. I was determined to make no more active enquiries and stuck to that, for life at Barrowteign had become sufficient for me. Nevertheless, I was momentarily shaken when I read that a Suffragette had died after throwing herself under the King's horse at the 1913 Derby, but, as soon as I had established her identity, my mind was at rest again.

The following summer, that rest was lost to me. By a cruel coincidence, it was on the morning of 22 June 1914—four years to the day after Elizabeth and I celebrated so tenderly our impending wedding—that I read the following announcement in The Times:

The marriage took place at St. Peter's, Putney, on Saturday, June 20th, between Miss Elizabeth Latimer of Sutler Terrace, Putney and Major Gerald Couchman of Garrard Court, South Kensington, formerly of the Devonshire regiment.

I read the announcement again—then again. What could I do? What was I to say? The words would not rearrange themselves before my eye. They continued, however hard I looked, to shout at me in silent mockery. Elizabeth married was one thing, which appalled but did not surprise me. Elizabeth married to Gerald Couchman was quite another. Two figures from my past had only one connection and that was me. What could this mean?

"What is it, Edwin?" My mother had noticed my dismay from across the breakfast table.

"Nothing."

She picked up the paper from where I had let it fall and scanned the page. "Oh Edwin," she said at length. "I see here what it is. It is not nothing and I know how you must feel. But surely you must have expected it sooner or later."

"Not to that man."

"I paid his name no attention. Do you know him?"

"As you do. Look again."

She did so. "Good heavens. Gerald Couchman . . . surely you . . . surely we . . ."

"Yes, Mother. That is my friend Couch, however clearly our hearts say that it cannot be so."

"But I never knew they were even acquainted."

"Nor I. Nor were they, I swear, until . . . until when? That is the question."

"What do you mean?"

"I mean that it is a mystery that they should know each other, since I am their only apparent connection. And where there is one mystery may lie the answer to another. I must go to London at once."

I strode for the door and paused only at my mother's word. "What will you do in London? What is the point in going there after all this time?"

"To find out what I can."

Mother could see that it was useless to attempt to stop me.

Within the hour, I was ready to go. After a word with our bailiff on what to do in my absence, I was off. After 3½ years of avoiding even a short visit to London because of the indulgence of my emotional and political nostalgia that such a trip would represent, now I was speeding in that direction with no clear plan of action, just a new-found conviction that stoicism was no longer enough, that the sense of injustice that had all along burned within me might not merely be self-perceived.

London was subdued by midsummer heat when I reached it in the late afternoon. I sped past the carts and cabs of sprawling suburbia, leaving dust and shouts in my wake, heading straight for Putney. There, by the church where once I had wept openly for my lost love and where, but two days since, she had married, I halted. I walked slowly down the road to Sutler Terrace and viewed the house. Everything was as I remembered it: the well-tended lawns, the wistaria arch leading to the garden behind, the polished brass knocker on the dark green front door, closed to me forever four years before. I pushed open the gate and walked up the path.

Strangely, I stopped short of the door, pausing for the first time in that day's headlong rush after truth, unable to think of what I would say if that door were at last opened to me. And whilst I stood there, poised in indecision, a voice addressed me from behind.

"Are you looking for someone?"

It was dear old Mercy speaking and I could tell from her tone that she had not recognized me from the rear. When I turned, a smile dropped from her face.

"I had hoped you would stay away for ever," she said gravely.

"I would have done M, but for this morning's announcement in The Times.*"*

"Why should it have surprised you?"

"Because I did not expect to know the groom as well as the bride."

"Does that give you a right to try to spoil their happiness?"

"It may do. Where are they now?"

"On their honeymoon. They've gone abroad for a month. Don't ask me where, for I shan't tell you."

"I don't want to know."

"Then why are you here?"

"To find out how—and why—they met."

"Edwin"—it was a triumph of a kind that she should use my Christian name—"it's nothing to do with you. They met shortly after you . . . after your wedding was cancelled. Gerald was acquainted with the Lambournes, who introduced him to Elizabeth. He made her happy again. Knowing you was just a remarkable coincidence."

"Did he mention our time in South Africa together?"

Mercy said nothing, but glared and walked straight past me to the door. I looked after her.

"Well, did he?"

"He said as little of you as he could. To have known you was no recommendation. But we did not hold it against him."

She opened the door and went to enter. A crazy thought came to my mind with which to stop her on the threshold.

"Did he tell you about his actions at Colenso?"

Mercy looked back once, coldly, then closed the door behind her. There was nothing left to do or say. I walked away down the path. It was foolish, I reflected, to cast aspersions on Couch's war record when what I really wanted to cry out against was that he should have benefited from my rejection. It was incomprehensible, yet incontrovertible.

I drove slowly over Putney Bridge into Fulham, then traced my way to Garrard Court, South Kensington, a large apartment block near Sloane Square. The lift attendant gave me Couch's number, but warned me that Couch was away "consequent upon his nuptials". He was right. There was no answer.

So I booked into a nearby hotel and glumly surveyed my plight during a solitary evening in the bar. My impetuous descent upon the capital had achieved nothing. Without confronting Elizabeth—which I could not bear—or Couch, I had no hope of finding out what had drawn them together or whether it was connected with my unexplained disgrace. In the absence of any way forward, I knew that I should abandon the enterprise. But I had only to think of Elizabeth to know that I could never do that.

So, the following morning, I went to Rotherhithe and the insalubrious premises of Mr Palfrey, private enquiries agent, whose services had been called upon by the Metropolitan Police from time to time during my years at the Home Office. I had never seen Palfrey or his place of work before and neither encouraged me to linger longer than was necessary to commission some discreet observation of the Couchmans when they returned to London. Odious and, for that matter, odorous as he undoubtedly was, Palfrey nevertheless had a record that inspired confidence and I left the matter in his clammily capable hands.

I felt vaguely unclean at having to resort to such measures, but anything was preferable to nothing. It was with distaste tingeing my dismay that I drove out of London that morning and headed in the only direction I could go—back to Barrowteign. My mother was relieved to see me again so soon. I told her that I had seen Mercy, learned nothing and proposed to leave it at that. I made no mention of Palfrey.

Knowing that Elizabeth and Couch were not due home until late July, I did not expect to hear from Palfrey until some time during August. As it turned out, I had by then other matters of moment to concern me, as had we all. Five days after my return from London, an Austrian archduke was assassinated in the distant Balkan city of Sarajevo and, during July, a crescendo of ultimata exchanged between the great European powers led us inexorably from that obscure act to the outbreak of a world war.

My involvement in this was accelerated by the fact that I had, ever since leaving South Africa, remained an officer in the regimental reserve. At first, this had been invaluable to a young M.P., for in those days we were unpaid, but I had never seen any reason to sever the link after becoming a salaried minister.

So it was that, on the morning of August 4, when I read in the newspaper that we would be at war with Germany before the day was out unless they undertook not to violate Belgian neutrality in their moves against France, I also received notification from the War Office that the reserve was to mobilize and that I was to report to my regimental barracks in Exeter by noon the following day.

As one who had read the runes during previous weeks, this caused me much less surprise than my mother. But for all her consternation, I knew that, in her hands, Barrowteign and little Ambrose would be safe. By the following morning, when war had been formally declared and I was ready to set off, Mother had found consolation in the prevailing notion that hostilities would be over by Christmas. My own expectations, which I kept to myself, were far less sanguine but even they went nowhere near the ghastly reality of the next four years that drove even Elizabeth far from my thoughts.

For all my political awareness, I was as ignorant as the rawest volunteer of what lay in wait for those of us who blithely set off for France in that summer of 1914. The regiment was in good heart, convinced that our cause was just and that our abilities, honed so relatively recently in South Africa, were more than a match for the Germans. The sense of unity and purpose was infectious, though I remained cynically immune. Nevertheless, I believed what the strategists told us—that we had the beating of the enemy in short order—because I supposed that they knew their business. Had not Sir Edward Grey, my esteemed former colleague, said in Parliament that the consequences of war were scarcely worse than the consequences of peace?

The truth did not take long to confront me. The Battle of Mons in late August—into which the regiment flung itself with conviction and enthusiasm—was the beginning and end of the war we all expected. Casualties were heavy, but they could have been borne had there been some profit in the engagement. In truth, it merely marked the grinding to a halt of the German advance on Paris and the firm entrenchment of both sides along a line through north-eastern France, which was also a demarcation of the war we were due to wage.

Once trench warfare had begun, our cavalry expertise gleaned from South Africa became redundant and our generals' strategic thinking was bankrupted. I had been attached to the staff of Sir John French—Commander-in-Chief—during the Mons engagement, but thereafter found myself given a captaincy and a platoon to command at the front. From such a vantage point, I could examine at first hand French's methods of overcoming heavily defended trenches. These amounted to throwing infantry against wire and artillery in the hope of breaking through to an extent that might be exploited by the cavalry. Occasionally, this happened and a salient was created in the German trench line. Yet a salient, being exposed on three sides, was impossible to defend and, however far-advanced, was always bound to be constricted and ultimately strangled.

The persistence in such a strategy—in the absence of any other—was worse than futile, it was criminal. The pride of the regular army was sacrificed in one bid after another to make the breakthrough that would count and which never came. French made way for Haig, who was no better, indeed somewhat worse. For whereas French had fatuously hoped to convert trench warfare into the type of war he could win, Haig saw the trenches as means of wearing down the Germans by attritional methods until they no longer had the manpower to fight.

The reality this represented for the fighting man was almost certain death for the sake of a distant, weary victory. Yet most of them did not realize this. By the close of 1914, most of my regiment had been killed or invalided and replaced by eager young recruits who found themselves marching to a muddy grave for no clear reason.

I led, myself, a seemingly charmed existence. I rapidly sickened of leading suicidal advances over the top, but continued to do so because refusal required a moral courage I did not possess. I would have been accused of cowardice—and probably been shot for it—and would have felt guilty of treachery towards my fellow suffering men at arms. So I persisted in an intensifying mood of indifference to my own fate. Perhaps that was my salvation, for that indifference saved me from either impetuosity or panic, both fatal conditions. I won no medals but a reputation for leading survivors, who thanked me with their loyalty for still being alive each roll call. We fought for each other, not for the generals—whom we rightly distrusted for plotting our every gadarene rush upon the guns whilst sipping claret in safely distant châteaux—or for the public at home, who knew and understood nothing. I, especially, did not fight for the politicians, who were quite capable of fighting amongst themselves. As I later learned, the making and breaking of wartime coalitions at Westminister became merely an extension of the struggle for power between Asquith and Lloyd George, with Lloyd George the ultimate victor. More than with any of these, we hapless soldiers felt fellowship with our opponents. The sanest thing we did was lay down our guns and celebrate Christmas with the Germans between the lines at the end of that first year of war, only for that to be taken from us. Strict orders were issued warning that men would be shot for any form of fraternization. It was deemed to be bad for morale, as if killing and being killed for no purpose was not. Amidst all the madness and mutilation, I learned a lesson I never had as a politician: that we cannot properly lead those with whom we have not shared suffering.

The year 1915 came and went and, with it, a second Christmas by which the war was still not over. We who were not dead were deadened by the horror of it all. We no longer expected it ever to end. For me, an end of a kind came with that crowning insanity: the Battle of the Somme, which stretched from July to November, 1916. I picked up several bad doses of mustard gas and then, one pointless day in early September, took a shrapnel hit in the leg and my Somme at least was over. I spent the autumn laid up in a convalescent home near Brighton, my mother a constant visitor.

Just before Christmas, a relative stranger came to see me: Winston Churchill, whom I had encountered earlier in the year whilst passing through Armentières. He had then been serving as a colonel in the Royal Scots Fusiliers, having come out to France in disgrace following the failure of his brainchild: the Dardanelles expedition. Now he was home again, trying to recover his political reputation, but, whether in the trenches or in Cabinet, he was always possessed of a cherubic irresponsibility. We had first met on the boat to South Africa sixteen years before and, since he was the only one of my former Cabinet colleagues likely to seek me out, I was pleased to see him. He sat by my bed, beaming and ruminating upon the ways of the world—and of war.

"After we met in France, I wondered what had become of you," he said. "Then I heard you were laid up here, so thought I'd look in."

"It's kind of you to have called, Winston. The leg's not too

bad. They tell me I should be up and about in the New Year with just a limp to show for it. What are you up to now?"

He leant forward confidentially. "I'm back at Westminster. The winds seem to be blowing my way again now that L.G.'s at number 10."

"I read about that: Asquith out at last."

"Yes—and good riddance. He never had the heart for a war—and that's a sure way to lose one. L.G. won't let anything stand in his path. I have high hopes."

"Of him—or for a post?"

He grinned. "Both, actually."

I wished him well, without hypocrisy. A man who could sustain such zest for life deserved well of it. The war had blown away my bitterness, though not my sadness. And it was that last commodity that prompted me to beg a favour of him before he went. Favours were his stock in trade, so I had no compunction.

"Is there anything I can do for you, Edwin?"

"Perhaps there is. Just before the war broke out, I commissioned some work of which I've subsequently heard nothing. You might be able to find out how matters now stand."

"What sort of work?"

"Some minor confidential enquiries. I used Palfrey—you'll remember him. He never reported back, which was unlike him. I wrote to him last month but have had no reply—he may have changed his address. I wondered if you could ask around to see what's become of him."

"I'll do what I can, Edwin—have a word with people I still know at the Home Office. I'll let you know if Palfrey's still around."

"I'd be much obliged."

And I was obliged to Churchill, though not for news of Palfrey, for he never gave me any. I went back to France in March 1917, forgot my passing recollection of that unfinished business and found myself promoted to the rank of major but consigned because of suspect leg and lungs to tedious administrative duties at regimental field headquarters. Then, in May, I heard that Churchill had received the reward he had looked for from Lloyd George: the post of Minister of Muni-

tions. Within a few weeks, I was reassigned to oversee, with the rank of colonel, armaments distribution in our sector of the front. Churchill sent me a congratulatory note leaving me in no doubt that my appointment had been at his behest. Strangely, he made no mention of Palfrey. He may well have had more important things to think about. Certainly, I was kept busy at his bidding, taking some grim satisfaction from endeavouring to ensure that, if men had to continue fighting, they could at least do so adequately armed.

In that way I passed the remaining eighteen months of the Great War. In November 1918, it finally ground to an armistice: a mutual acknowledgement of the absolute futility of further slaughter. We who had been lucky enough to survive felt no exhilaration at victory, only relief. What we celebrated was a resumption of life. In most cases this meant the secure normalities of home and family. What I had forgotten in my own case, but remembered as soon as I was demobilized, was how little there was for me to return to.

They tried, I cannot say otherwise. Barrowteign in the late autumn of 1918 welcomed home its flawed if favoured son. My mother was overjoyed that I had survived and content with that. And so, for a while, was I. Sitting in my home, walking in the village of my birth, escorting my mother to church—these quiet domestic pleasures were balm to my shaken spirit. So long as I was engaged upon a process of recuperation, they sufficed.

Poor little Ambrose had contracted the virulent strain of influenza that carried off so many war-weakened souls that winter. I sought to hasten his recovery and occupy my mind and hands by constructing for him an elaborate model castle for Christmas. It was an intricate task in which I could lose myself and gain a degree of tranquillity. And I was gratified to see how happy it made Ambrose when presented to him under the Christmas tree. Having spent many hours in designing and building it, I was obliged to spend many more instructing him in its ways—how to operate the drawbridge, where the secret doors were, how a toy soldier might enter the keep. All this spared me the necessity of indulging his interest in my war-time adventures, which I wished only to forget.

That Christmas, playing with Ambrose, Mother beaming at us from the hearth, I was a man restored, but restored to what? I picked up some of the pieces of my life, but knew the others had all along been missing. I began to think again—though less intensely—of Elizabeth and recalled to mind the unfinished business of Palfrey's enquiries on my behalf. I might have decided that they should be left undisturbed, but, in truth, I had little to distract me from morbid reflection and that was translated into something more active by the New Year's honours list of 1919. I scanned The Times *resumé for names I knew and there one sentence struck home with a force undimmed by the passage of time: "Among industrialists honoured, Gerald Couchman, the munitions manufacturer, receives a knighthood in recognition of the outstanding production record of his company over the past four years and its contribution to the war effort during that time."*

So Gerald Couchman, coward of Colenso, had spent four lucrative years manufacturing the weapons of destruction, married to the woman I still loved, whilst I had gritted my way through four years of sustained misery in the Flanders trenches, serving a cause in which I had no faith and gaining no reward beyond an accidental exemption from death. This was too much to bear.

I said nothing to my mother, gave her no hint of what I felt, merely announced calmly that I would, the following day, be going to London for a few days to attend to some matters of business. She had not noticed the news of Couch's knighthood by the time I left.

On the first morning of 1919, I stood in my greatcoat on a chill, deserted Dewford railway station—my runabout motor having been ransomed to the post-war fuel shortage—waiting for the train that would connect at Exeter with the London express, questioning in my mind the wisdom of another stirring of my past, knowing in my heart that too much of my loss was unexplained for me to leave unasked the questions that still gnawed at me: Why did you reject me, Elizabeth? Why did you marry Gerald Couchman? Wherein did I offend?

The train carried me away from Dewford, over the very crossing where my brother had perished eight years before. At least, I reflected, his death had been an accident. My disgrace seemed a more malevolent working of fate which did not even deign to show its motive. In London, I hoped to smoke it out.

Upon arrival, I made my way to Palfrey's office in Rotherhithe, dingily unchanged in its housing beneath an arch of a railway viaduct on the fringes of dockland. There was nobody in, so I waited, as the trains rattled overhead and the sleet fell about me. It was a grey, dank place, cold as death that New Year's afternoon. But it was, for good or ill, where the trail lay. And, sure enough, Palfrey eventually returned to his haunt. I laid an arm on his shoulder as he turned a key in the door.

"Mr. Palfrey, do you remember me?"

"I don't rightly think so."

He admitted me to his office, one place made more tolerable by the chill. Perhaps he would not have done so had he recognised me at first, for he turned a paler shade of grey when I identified myself and mentioned our unfinished business.

"Lord sir, that was before the war."

"What of it?"

"I never thought to see you again, sir. So much 'as changed since then."

"Not my interest in Sir Gerald and Lady Couchman."

"Sir Gerald?"

"Didn't you know of his knighthood?"

"No sir, but it don't surprise me."

"Why not?"

"He's a well-connected gentleman—like yourself."

"My connections are sundered. What about yours? Does the Home Office still look after you?"

"We do business when there's need—as in your day, sir."

"Then what of our business, Mr. Palfrey? I paid you to obtain information, no matter that it was four and a half years ago."

"I've nothing to report, sir. Naturally, you can 'ave your advance back."

"Why nothing to report?"

"My enquiries was not fruitful."

"Why not?"

"Sir, it was business, as you say. So I'll repay the mon-

ey"—he pawed at a cashbox—"and that'll conclude our business."

"Before it's even begun?"

"As you say, sir"—and here he risked a meaningful look—"before it's even begun."

He had thrust some grubby notes in my hand. They were clammy with his sweat, for all that it was bitterly cold. Palfrey was a frightened man. Nothing could be more graphic than his return of money on a lapsed debt. I despaired of extracting anything from him and turned to go.

"One thing, Mr. Palfrey," I said as an afterthought. "You must know Mr. Churchill, one of my successors."

"Yes sir."

"Did he—or anyone else—approach you about your enquiries on my behalf?"

"No sir."

"This would have been about two years ago."

"Not then—not ever, sir."

He was lying—I felt certain of it. But there was nothing to be gained by pressing him further. I let the money fall from my hand and left him to stoop after it. As I walked away from his office, the conviction grew on me that his enquiries had not stopped but been stopped. Strangely, I exulted at this conviction, for it proved for the first time that there was something behind my disgrace beyond a whim of fate: some human, calculating force working against me. To a soldier, it was some kind of consolation—especially after the war I had just fought—to know that the enemy existed.

I booked into a hotel near Leicester Square for the night to plan my strategy. The loss of Palfrey's reconnaissance struck me as no great problem. The telephone directory yielded the information I most needed: the address of the Couchman works in Woolwich, the home address of G.V. Couchman in Hampstead. But I did not propose to beard Couch in either lair without first exploring the strange question of the silencing of Palfrey. My recollection of Winston Churchill's solicitious call upon me during my wartime convalescence was newly suspicious in this light. I had asked him to chivvy Palfrey on my behalf but all I had received was an arduous new posting at his instigation.

Accordingly, the following morning, I telephoned Churchill's new ministry—the War Office—and, after repeating my name several times, was put through to him. Parliament being in recess and his duties at a low ebb, he was delighted at the prospect of meeting me for luncheon. As a matter of fact, I had never known him refuse an invitation to luncheon however busy he was at the time. His appetite and ambition alike knew no bounds. To be fair, nor did his humanity and it was on this last quality that I was banking.

Gaspard's Restaurant in the Strand was better suited to the gourmand than the gourmet and I was neither. But Churchill set to with a will, leaving me to insinuate leading questions between courses.

"We're both lucky, Winston, to have survived that summer of 1916."

"That's true, Edwin. But I'm especially glad to see you again. You had to go through another two years of the beastly business."

"It was nearer eighteen months actually and they were spent in an interesting post that was safer than most. I thought you might have had something to do with that."

"Perhaps, dear boy, perhaps." He grinned as he spoke, then grew serious. "But don't misunderstand. Munitions movements were vital at that stage of the war. We needed calm, reliable people—such as yourself."

"It's kind of you to say so."

"Not at all—it's accurate. The public are quick to forget that my ministry and the people who helped it shortened the war."

"They've been reminded, Winston. I saw in the paper only a few days ago that one of your suppliers had been knighted."

"Well deserved, I'm sure."

"I'm glad you're sure, because I'm not."

"What do you mean?"

"I knew Gerald Couchman when we were in South Africa together. You might have met him there yourself."

"I don't think so. But what of it?"

"My difficulty is that the idea of Gerald Couchman becoming a knight of the realm makes my flesh creep."

Churchill's fork froze halfway between the plate and his

mouth. "Couchman's a good man. It's unlike you to play the traducer, Edwin."

"Perhaps I'm growing bitter in my old age."

"You're younger than I am."

Which was true. And he was running to fat, whereas the war had kept me in shape if nothing else. Nevertheless, I felt older than he looked. I tried again. "Couch's record in the Boer War was not that of a white knight and I daresay his commercial career bears no closer inspection."

"This is shameful stuff, Edwin. Couchman was my best supplier. He's done enough to put behind him any supposed shortcomings in the past. Some are better forgotten, you know."

"I thought you deplored the public's short memory."

"I was talking about the war we've just won. Good service in that deserves its reward. The women who worked in the factories made us forget those who had thrown bricks and bombs, so now we've given them the vote. Couchman's own wife . . ."

"Yes?"

My interruption made Churchill cautious. He continued more slowly. "She worked as a voluntary nursing sister quite tirelessly, I'm told. She deserves the award as much as her husband. That's all."

This mention of Elizabeth set me back somewhat. But I was determined to press on. "I stand corrected. But on the question of memory, do you remember the request I made of you when you visited me in the convalescent home?"

"I don't believe I do."

"Let me remind you. You agreed to contact one of the detectives the Home Office uses—Palfrey—and ask him the state of some enquiries he was conducting for me."

"I'm sorry, Edwin. I don't remember that. But I may well have forgotten—it was a hectic time."

"So you didn't contact Palfrey?"

"No. That's something I wouldn't forget. The party and the country were in turmoil then, so I'm very much afraid it must have slipped my mind."

"Would you be surprised to learn that it slipped Palfrey's mind as well?"

"Not entirely. I daresay the war must have affected even Mr. Palfrey."

"It surprised me, Palfrey being an assiduous man of business."

"It's true that these men normally look after their interests with great diligence."

"Quite so."

A silence fell between us and I announced that I would shortly have to leave. I settled the bill and rose to go. Churchill lingered with his coffee and cigars, wearing a hurt and puzzled expression. He bade me adieu without rising.

"Farewell, Winston," I replied, drawing on my overcoat. "I hope I've not spoiled your luncheon. Your comments about good service compensating for past transgressions—if any, were interesting."

"I'm glad to hear it."

"They leave me wondering when such a rule might be applied in my case."

I left before he had a chance to respond. What he had said had told me less than what he had not said. For such a garrulous man, this was unusual, but his culpable forgetfulness where Palfrey was concerned, taken together with Palfrey's own renunciation of duties which he had normally pursued so doggedly, betokened some form of conspiracy. Had I known that much before the war, I would have raged at their throats. Now, I was the subtle scout, in truth unable to descry the route that I must thread through the shell holes of my past. Only the reaction of others told me that there was one to follow.

It led, the following morning, to Woolwich and the Couchman armament works: a vast, whale-backed brick building behind high walls, overshadowing the smaller office building to which my attention was directed. I had arrived early, in steely rain, and mingled with the workers plodding in at dawn to the summoning wail of a siren. I had left them at the gates, reconnoitred the premises, which backed onto railway sidings, then returned to patrol the frontage and await the managing director.

He arrived at ten o'clock, by which time the rain had stopped in his honour and the factory was humming with activity. He swept in at the wheel of a sleek blue Bentley, heed-

less of an overcoated figure by the gates. But I took careful stock of Couch as he stepped from his car with a jaunty spring, immaculately dressed, hair smoothed down, cigarette in a holder, white scarf and gloves, a hint of a swagger as he strode up the steps towards his office. It was odd to see him again after so many years, still essentially the same but altered forever in my eyes, by his trespass upon what was mine. The devil-may-care hedonist had transformed himself into a man of wealth and substance. I hated him in that moment for his success in all the fields where I had failed. Honour, not disgrace, had rewarded his endeavours. The war had made, not broken him; Elizabeth, not lonely introspection, had become his wife.

We were the same age, yet Couch bounded up the steps like a younger, more confident man. It was not just a game leg that sapped my energy but I was not, for all that, a spent force. I called him back as he reached the doors.

"Couch!"

He stopped dead, then turned slowly. There was no recognition in his gaze down at me, but puzzlement.

"I haven't been called that in years," he said. "Do I know you?"

I walked to the foot of the steps. "I think so." I removed my hat: a functional act to aid his memory, neither friendly nor deferential. I looked up at him without smiling and some of the assurance drained from his features. He knew me.

I joined him at the top of the steps. "I'd appreciate a few words with you, Couch."

"All right. Let's go into my office." Even as he spoke he recovered himself somewhat. He led the way into the building. The foyer was dark, but richly decorated, with a leather settee, chairs and potted plants at the foot of a broad staircase. To the right, behind a counter, an earnest young lady in spectacles was perched by a telephone switchboard. The hall beyond ended in double doors, one of which stood open to a large room full of clerks and stenographers.

"Good Morning, Mr . . . Sir Gerald," said the bespectacled young lady. Couch did not respond, but led me up the stairs. Out of the corner of my eye, I saw the young lady pout with annoyance. At the top, we went straight into a secretary's

office. "No interruptions, Dorothy," was all Couch said to the lady behind the desk—who looked startled by his curtness—before carrying on into his office and closing the door behind us.

It was a large, airy room, thickly carpeted and hung with oil paintings of whiskery old men. There were several framed certificates of technical excellence and a world map covering one wall. Behind Couch's desk, windows overlooked the rear of the factory: the loading bay and railway sidings. Beyond them loomed the crane and gantries of Thameside wharves.

"Sit down, Edwin," said Couch. "You look as if you need to."

I sat in a leather armchair in front of his desk. "My leg tends to stiffen up if I stand on it too long," I explained.

Couch sat behind his desk facing me. "A war wound?"

"Yes. The Somme."

"Sorry to hear it . . . you were standing a long time waiting for me?"

"Some hours."

"You must have something important to say, then."

I had been simmering as we minced through these false salutations and this last remark took me over the top. "Of course I've something important to say, Couch. You've helped to ruin my life. Isn't that important?"

"Need we be melodramatic, old man?"

There was one advantage a lame war veteran had over a contemporary softened by success: a sinewy strength heightened now by anger. I rose, reached across the desk and pulled him out of his chair by the collar of his pinstriped jacket.

"We certainly can be melodramatic . . . old man, if you require it." With that, I let him fall back into his chair. He looked unnerved by this sudden show of force.

"All right," he said breathlessly. "Cards on the table. What do you want of me?"

"An explanation."

"What's there to explain? I've prospered, you haven't. It's the luck of the draw."

"Just tell me about Elizabeth."

"It was all over between you and Elizabeth before I ever met her."

"How did you meet?"

"Through some mutual friends—the Lambournes. I courted Elizabeth because I realized how good she would be for me. Eventually, I was lucky enough to persuade her to marry me."

"When did all this take place?"

"We first met, let me see, late in 1910 or early in 1911. I forget precisely when."

"Strange you should be so vague."

"I was never too hot on dates." He smiled weakly, then caught himself and stopped.

"You were married on 20th June 1914. I'll be precise if you can't."

"That's one date I remember."

"Good. What about all this?" I gestured expansively at the office and the works beyond.

"Another spot of luck." His words were invested with less relish than would normally have been the case, but he knew no other form for them. "My father died the year before we married. I hadn't seen the old man for ages, but he left me quite a nest egg. Elizabeth had taught me not to squander my advantages, so I invested some of it in this place. Bought out a small-timer named Pound, who made fireworks would you believe. Ploughed a lot into the plant—new machinery for shell casings and the like. Turned out to be just the right time."

"The war was quite a windfall for you, then." He detected my sarcasm.

"As it happened. But somebody had to make the bloody stuff and we did it well. I bid for all the contracts, got a lot of business once Lloyd George had gingered up supply, expanded no end. We met the deadlines and produced reliable munitions. The military thanked me for our contribution to the war effort."

"Don't expect me to add my thanks."

"I shan't. But don't expect me to apologize for doing well. I know it must have been hell for you in France, but I worked too hard here for what I've got. I've known bad times too. Remember when you swanned off home from South Africa to fight an election, leaving me stuck in a war that dragged on for two years?"

"Be thankful that you know why times have changed for

you, Couch. My transformation is a mystery to me. So tell me what happened to you in South Africa."

"It wasn't anything like Colenso, if that's what you think. Kitchener shut up the entire population in camps and we had to patrol them while snipers took pot shots at us. When that was over, I was posted to India, where I drank, gambled and played polo. Then I got sick of the whole business, resigned my commission and came home."

"And then?"

"Then I met Elizabeth. She's the best thing that ever happened to me."

I gripped the arms of my chair to remain calm. "She was the best thing that ever happened to me, too."

"Then you shouldn't have let her go."

"I didn't, as you must know."

"On the contrary. Elizabeth's never told me why you broke up and I haven't pressed her on the point. It's something she doesn't want to discuss. It's obviously a painful memory, best left alone to heal."

Suddenly, I found myself questioning my anger. That I resented Couch's material success was undeniable. That he had won what I had lost, the love of Elizabeth, was a thorn in my flesh. That Couch's past did not suggest an honourable or courageous man was not necessarily to the point. After all, Elizabeth was a fine enough person to have improved if not reformed him. Perhaps in me there had been, after all, not too little change.

But what was I thinking? There remained a mystery which could not be dismissed, which insisted on driving me on. What was there left for me but to seek the reason why I had been brought so low? Perhaps Couch knew nothing. Perhaps he was just the lucky beneficiary of my rift with Elizabeth: he had always been lucky at other people's expense. Yet somebody knew, for somebody had called off Palfrey from the scent, somebody not a thousand miles from the Cabinet which I had left as precipitately and inexplicably as I had lost Elizabeth. Who and why? Somebody knew but nobody was telling.

Certainly not Sir Gerald Couchman, who sat opposite me in his plushly appointed office, cowed a little but still, I could have sworn, laughing silently at me.

"Why not give it up, Edwin?" he suggested. "Why not just get on with your life and leave us to ours?"

I did not answer. There was no need. I had no life with which to proceed. There was only one other person I could look to now for the truth and it was the one person I could not bear to confront. Yet there were one or two shots left in the locker for Couch first.

"I can't help noticing," I said, "how well you've served and been served by former colleagues of mine—Lloyd George, Churchill . . ."

"Both Ministers of Munitions, Edwin. Obviously I've had dealings."

"Lloyd George is now Prime Minister. And they say he can be persuaded to name a price for any honour. What is it for a knighthood?"

Couch turned grim. "That's enough. You've no right to insult me."

"Haven't I? Wouldn't a lot of people be surprised at how a knight of the realm conducted himself at Colenso?"

"Save your breath, Edwin. Nobody would believe your malicious lies."

"They wouldn't be lies."

Couch rose and walked to the window. He gazed out at the activity in the yard beneath him. Then he turned and spoke. "We are what we are, Edwin. But strangely enough, I'm a better man than I was. I employ hundreds of people and make a good deal of money. Yet that's not what I mean by better. What I mean is that I have a loving wife and a young son . . ."

"A son?"

"Yes—born last summer. He and Elizabeth have given me a home and commitments. I'm not the young wastrel I once was, nor the coward you think me. I'm not sorry I succeeded where you failed—with Elizabeth—but I am sorry for you because of it. A lot of people have come home from the war with not much to return to. If there's something material I can do to help you, I'd be pleased to . . ."

I rose from my chair and looked levelly at him across the desk. "The last thing I need from you is charity. I'll tell you what I think and you can make what you will of it. I don't know why Elizabeth rejected me and maybe I never will. But if

I ever find that you had some part in it, I'll kill you: you have my word as a gentleman on that."

Did I really mean it? I cannot tell. In the heat of that moment, with Couch's offer of knightly largesse ringing contemptuously—and contemptibly—in my ears, I suppose I did. At all events, Couch's blanched countenance told me that he believed I meant it. He made no attempt to interrupt me.

"Just after your marriage, I hired a private detective to investigate you, but his enquiries were stopped—by somebody in a powerful position. Since I only told one person what I had done, I suspect he may be that somebody. It so happens that he was one of those Ministers of Munitions you served so faithfully during the war. I have no precise allegations to make, only this feeling that such coincidences add up to something suspicious. Maybe you are innocent—but it would be unlike you."

"I told you I'd changed."

"Not that much."

I walked to the door, but he called after me. "Edwin, think about what I said when you've calmed down." I paused and he walked to my elbow, becoming almost confidential in his manner. "You should exploit whatever advantages are available—or are offered. After all, I know you have in the past."

"What does that mean?"

"Well, let's face it, old man, I didn't marry a virgin."

That is when I struck him, before the curl of his mouth could broaden into an insufferable smile. The blow took him on the chin and sent him sprawling onto his dense Turkish carpet.

"You're wrong," I said. "You're no better than you ever were—and that's worse than I once thought."

I turned on my heel and walked out. I slammed the door behind me, exchanged a swift glance with the secretary in the outer office, then hastened from the building.

The Couchman residence in Hampstead was a large, gabled house set well back from the road in wooded grounds. Had it not been winter, I could not have seen beyond the wrought iron gates and sweeping drive. Yet the view through the bare trees afforded me no intelligence when I first made my way there on the afternoon following my visit to Couch at his works. I lingered on the sloping edge of the heath than ran along the roadside opposite the house, hoping for some glimpse or glimmer that would tell me how best I might approach Elizabeth. I had not the nerve to walk straight in, so awaited some other opportunity, which did not come my way that afternoon. A tramp eyed me balefully while he shuffled around the bench on which I sat and the light slowly failed and nothing else happened until Couch's Bentley sped up the drive and I knew that it was time to retreat.

Saturday was more promising: a bright, sharp day, with the frost still on the Heath when I reached Hampstead in mid-morning and strolled and assumed nonchalance where I could keep watch on the house. The war had taught me patience and perseverance in the long intervals between acts of conflict—had made me, in fact, savour the lull—so I was content to await my chance. The war had also given me the sapping cough which the chill air aggravated that morning and which made me more conspicuous than I had hoped. Still, I sustained my patrol well into the afternoon.

By then, the sun was stronger and, well-muffled on a bench, I could almost imagine that it was warm. Certainly I had fallen into a reverie, if not a doze, when I caught myself up at the sight of a figure pushing a perambulator down the drive. As it reached the gates, I realized that it was not—as I had feared—a nanny, but Elizabeth herself. I might have known that she would take her son out herself on an afternoon stroll and the characteristic act suited my purpose.

I had not seen Elizabeth since that terrible day of my rejection by her in June 1910. I saw, as she crossed the road, that the years had not changed her. She was still the same elegant figure, clad now in a black, fur-trimmed coat and hood, a proud young woman showing her son a small part of the world. They took a curving path that ran away from where I was seated and then circled round above me. They did not glance at an obscure figure on a bench. Why should they?

When they had reached the curve of the path remotest from me, I left the bench and hurried up the sloping ground behind it to a line of trees flanking the route that Elizabeth was bound to take. There I waited, leaning against one of the trees. I lit a cigarette to sooth my serves, realizing that my heart was not pounding merely because men with suspect legs and lungs should not run up slopes in winter.

Elizabeth's fingers were playing some game with the occupant of the perambulator as she came towards me. Then she looked up at me and I at her, at an unchangingly beautiful face so often in my mind during 8½ years apart. For all that I was a greyer, grimmer man than when last we had met, she knew me at once and did not put her recognition into words. The shocked silence was stiller than the air between us.

"You never used to smoke," she said at last, in a voice as pale as her face.

"Many things have changed," I replied, walking across to the perambulator and glancing in. A wide-eyed baby stared unblinkingly up at me. I was mesmerized for the moment by his innocent gaze, knowing that, in different circumstances, he—or someone very like him—could have been my own. Then I noticed Elizabeth's grip tighten on the handle.

"What's his name?"

"Harry."

I felt oddly cheated by the calmness of our exchanges, as if raging recrimination would have been preferable to icy indifference. I was ill-prepared to find that we were neither friends nor foes but strangers. I sought to repel the notion. "You don't seem surprised to see me."

"Gerald told me what happened yesterday. I feared you would not be content until you had seen me, though I can't think what you hope to gain by it."

"The truth."

"You already know it—that you cruelly deceived me and went some way towards ruining my life."

"I did no such thing."

"In time, I recovered from the blow—with Gerald's help—and made a new life as his wife and Harry's mother. I wish you no ill, but I ask you, as I asked you once before, to leave me—to leave us—alone. Is it too much to ask?"

"Until you tell me the truth, yes."

"I can't tell you anything you don't already know."

"You can. All you have to do is tell me how I deceived you."

Elizabeth's face reddened and she made to move off, but I placed a restraining hand on the hood of the perambulator. I tried a plea. "Elizabeth, please—in God's name."

She looked at me then with loathing in her eyes. Anger or distress I had expected, but not this clear message that I was held beneath contempt. It disarmed me, made we want to walk away and not prolong the agony. But I knew the agony could not truly be ended until we had the matter out.

"Will you listen to me?"

"Say what you have to say and have done."

"I love you, Elizabeth. I have done since we first met—you know that. I risked everything for you—I never expected to lose it as well as you. I have never deceived you in any way. I came to Putney the day I resigned from the Home Office without the slightest suspicion that anything was wrong. I was greeted like . . . like a criminal—a criminal who was not to be told his crime. That's how I still feel. It's too much to bear. Will you please just tell me what my offense was?"

"Have you finished?"

"Not quite. Have you any idea how it felt to read in the newspaper that you had married Gerald Couchman? Why him—of all people?"

"Don't try to belittle Gerald in my eyes. You won't succeed and it only increases my disgust at the way you've behaved."

"Elizabeth, I've lost you and I've lost my career because of some ghastly misunderstanding which I've never been given the opportunity to put right."

"There's no misunderstanding."

"I beseech you. Think it possible you may be mistaken."

It was odd that, at that moment, I should choose Cromwell's words to frame my last appeal. Yet it was a desperate bid and I sensed that it was the last gasp. The words came to my lips as the one possible way of planting a seed of doubt in the set, opposed mind that now confronted mine. And, for an instant, there was a flicker of her eyes, a cast to her face that spoke of some cloud across her stern resolve. Then I tried to capitalize on whatever slight inroad I had made in a manner I should have known was ill-conceived.

"Has Gerald told you about his conduct at the Battle of Colenso?"

Elizabeth looked at me then almost with pity. "Do you think that can compare?" she said softly. "Gerald may not be a perfect man, but he is a good and honest one. Colenso was one of the first things he told me about. It doesn't matter now—how could you think it would? There's trust between us—not deceit. Now let me go."

My grasp dropped from the perambulator and Elizabeth set off past me down the path. I stood at a loss, appalled by the futility of our exchange. Her words echoed in my mind—"Do you think that can compare?"—and stung me to cry after her. "Can't compare with what?"

She looked back at me. "Leave us alone, Edwin. I've nothing more to say to you. I can forgive you, if that's what you want, but never forget. Go in peace and leave us in peace."

She turned then and walked on and I did not follow. I sensed the finality of her words, that I would never see her again, would never know and therefore never have the peace she wished me. The elegant figure in black receding down the path merged with others on the Heath that day, left forever my shrinking world without a backward glance. And I stood helpless, watching her go, drained of purpose, bereft of hope. Remember this, I thought: fix in your mind this day in January when you looked your last upon your love, merging now in the distance with the gathering dusk that rose with swift and clammy stealth from the city below.

I remained in my hotel room on Sunday, deciding that other guests should be spared my company when in such a black mood. I paced the floor, stared out of the window, smoked more than was good for me and exchanged a couple of words with the maid who brought meals to my door.

The solitary confinement was an attempt to sweat out my feverish obsession with Elizabeth. To that extent, it succeeded. Our encounter on Hampstead Heath had told me that I could never hope to win her back. After that, my desire to know the reason was in danger of becoming morbid. Therefore, by Monday, I had resolved to make a clean break. It was Twelfth Night, the eighth anniversary of my brother's death, and hence no time to leave my mother to gloomy nostalgia at

Barrowteign. I decided to return to Devon straightaway to be with her.

And so I would have done, but for a message awaiting me in the hotel lobby. It was a sealed envelope delivered by courier. I tore it open in a hurry, wishing to be off as soon as possible. I was astonished to discover that it was a personal note from the Prime Minister asking me to call on him that day. What could Lloyd George want? Even my new resolve to leave well alone could not resist such a lure.

I was at Downing Street within the hour, finding it odd to enter number 10 under new tenancy. And new it undoubtedly was. Gone was the calm of Asquith's day. Instead, clerks and secretaries hurried hither and thither along passages stacked with files and packing cases. My escort, Miss Stevenson, explained that most of the staff were off to Paris within the week to attend upon Lloyd George during the Peace Conference. I expressed surprise that, in that case, he had time to see me.

"He was anxious to fit you in before going," she said brightly.

"I'm flattered," I replied drily.

"There should always be time for old colleagues, shouldn't there?"

I agreed, keeping to myself my thought that though there should be, Lloyd George was not the man to find it without good reason.

He received me in his study, a secretary bustling out as I went in. Miss Stevenson introduced me, then also left. Alone, Lloyd George eyed me a little warily and I him. Time and success had changed him, no question—the mane of hair now grey, the face more lined—but he doubtless observed that time and failure had done me few favours either. He rose from his chair to shake my hand.

"Sit down, Edwin, sit down," he said, drawing up a chair for me. "It's been a long time."

"Many years."

"And many things have changed in those years. You probably know about most of my changes but what have you been up to?"

"The war occupied most of my time."

"It would, it would. What sort of a war did you have?"

"Better than most—I'm still alive."

"I'm glad of that. Too many aren't, God knows. If only . . . well, it's over now. We have to look to the future, don't we?"

"Easier said than done."

"Not if you've a purpose. We're off to Paris at the end of the week—lock, stock and barrel—and I mean to see that this peace ensures nobody has to go through another war like the one we've just fought."

"Fine sentiments. I wish you luck."

Lloyd George's look shifted to the blotter in front of him; his tone altered. "Winston told me about your meeting last Thursday. He told me you didn't seem happy."

"An understatement."

"Or healthy."

"An exaggeration. I'm better placed than a lot of ex-soldiers who don't have my means. I've a limp and a dicey lung, but I'll survive."

"English winters and London fogs won't help your lung."

"Probably not, but I don't intend to visit London often."

"Perhaps a warmer climate would help."

"Perhaps."

"If so, I've an offer that might interest you. Our consulate on Madeira is vacant at present. I have you in mind for the post."

"I don't think . . ."

He held up his hand in smiling protest. "Don't be so quick to say no. It's a lovely island, I'm told, famed for its beneficial effects in pulmonary cases. And it's not a complete sinecure. The situation in Portugal is chaotic and could spread to its overseas territories at any time. There's a substantial British community in Madeira and we obviously want to look after them. Able, reliable men are hard to come by for assignments like this one. If it aids your health and gives you somewhere to exercise your talents, so much the better."

I hesitated to respond. I took his word for the state of Portuguese politics and the Madeiran climate, being ignorant of both. The oddity was that he was not. Since I did not for one moment suppose that the British population of a remote Atlantic island were as close to his heart as he claimed, I could only conclude that this post was tailored to fit me. Lloyd George, in other words, wanted me to go. Whether this was simply because Churchill had painted a pathetic picture of me and Lloyd George was eager to help an old friend I doubted. The alternative, that my enquiries were an embarrassment to both of them and that they therefore wanted rid of me, fitted everything I had so far learned—or rather, had failed to learn. But what was I to do about such suspicions? The only object of pursuing them was to reclaim Elizabeth and that I now knew to be beyond me. As for politics, I was beyond recall. Men do not come back from the obscurity into which I had plunged.

So, whatever the reasons, Lloyd George had offered me a comfortable niche to rest and recuperate in, forget my past and indulge myself in colonial comforts. Two days before, I would have flung the offer back in his face, voiced my suspicion that his motives were the worst, demanded an explanation. And the offer would have been withdrawn, my suspicion rejected, explanation denied me. I could no longer afford such a gesture. I felt old and tired, in need of a rest yet wanting a change. Madeira seemed to provide both. So I was tempted to accept. My head told me that it was the only thing to do now my heart was no longer in the struggle.

Yet it was a big step, as much metaphorically as actually, and my political instincts told me not to commit myself at once. Besides, though I had no wish to antagonize Lloyd George, I had no wish to flatter him with some fawning acceptance. So I prevaricated.

"It's a big step—yet I can see its attractions. I'd need to think about it."

"There's really not very much time, Edwin. I have to know before we leave for Paris."

"That's only reasonable. I could let you know by the end of the week."

"Very well. I'll hold it open until then."

"It's kind of you to have thought of me."

"With all the work I have to do here, you're lucky I didn't take the job myself."

I laughed, though he had not amused me. I knew, and he knew I knew, that the Premiership was what he had always wanted. Paris was to be his bow on the international stage. Asquith was not jettisoned to win the war but to win Downing Street for Lloyd George. From a man reputed to sell honours to the highest bidder, unconditional offers of congenial employment were inherently suspect.

Miss Stevenson came in then to remind Lloyd George that he had an appointment with the Chancellor of the Exchequer at eleven o'clock. I took the opportunity to withdraw, leaving them stooped together over their papers. I walked out of 10 Downing Street for the last time, passing at the door Bonar Law, the Chancellor, coming in—a stern, predatory figure, whose haste alone could not explain the cold lack of recognition that greeted my smile. I who once had sat in conference with him stood now excluded from his vision.

This thought dogged me as I made my way to Paddington and caught the train to Exeter. I sat alone in a compartment, watching the wintry landscape pass, seeking to come to terms with my own insignificance. I was no longer a minister, no longer an M.P., no longer a soldier. There seemed nothing left but a decent repose in sub-tropical obscurity.

My mind was more or less made up before I reached Barrowteign, though I did not tell my mother so. She was delighted to see me back, especially to brighten such a sombre anniversary, so I delayed telling her about Madeira until the following day. Even then, the medical argument won her over, for she was likely to miss me less than she would worry about me if I remained, coughing my days away, at home.

And so it was agreed. On Wednesday morning, I telephoned Downing Street to accept. The same day that the Prime Minister and his entourage set off for Paris, I received a formal offer from the Foreign Office and accepted by return. My mother reconciled herself to my departure by looking forward to holidays on Madeira with her son the Consul, whilst Ambrose occupied his days before the start of term at Marlborough in poring over atlases and encyclopaedias, rendering himself better informed about Madeira than its Consul Designate.

At the end of January, my mother accompanied me to Southhampton to see me off on the ship to Lisbon. I was sorry to leave her but glad, in another way, to be going. This was the clean break I had promised myself. As the ship slipped out of the grey Solent that cold afternoon, I bade farewell to my past as well as my home. Elizabeth had been right: to leave well alone and seek a peaceful future was all that remained to me.

It was, of course, exactly what Lloyd George had said it was not: a sinecure. Aside from dealing with some slight unpleasantness when a group of dissidents exiled from the mainland seized control (or thought they had) in 1931, His Majesty's Consul on Madeira had few duties and those he did have were far from taxing.

Madeira, I soon discovered, was a Portuguese possession in formal respects but a British colony in many others. There was a governor and a garrison in Funchal, the capital, with whom I had to ensure good relations and a substantial Portuguese population about whom I could be largely indifferent. More significant from my point of view was the sizeable British presence on the island. Some had come for the climate (as, in a sense, had I), others had come with the oceanic cable-laying companies and never left. One family—the Blandys—dominated the production of Madeira's eponymous liquor. Others were either in the staple crops of the island—bananas, sugar cane and, of course, grapes—or simply in retirement. They lived in varying degrees of luxury in sun-blessed quintas scattered along the balmy south-eastern coast of the island and passed their days drinking tea at Reid's Hotel or imbibing gin at the Country Club in Funchal—both virtually British institutions—while discoursing upon the ills of Madeira and the greater ills of the old country.

As Consul, all I had to do was look after their few administrative requirements—which was easy—and tolerate their assorted prejudices at a range of social functions—which was not. The compensations for this were several—an airy, agreeable official residence set in the hills overlooking Funchal and the harbour, an efficient secretary to discharge most of my duties at the Consulate for me and time aplenty on an island in the sun to rest and relax. I made friends among the enlightened element of the expatriate community, a few more—after I had mastered the language—among the Portuguese popula-

tion and grew to know the island well by my extensive forays on foot into the hinterland: a lush, luxuriant plot, sewn by nature, reaped by man. As one of its beneficiaries, I grew to love it.

Which is not to say that I became happy. Time to wander the Paúl da Serra—the plateau in the centre of the island that reminded me of Dartmoor—was also time for reflection. My bafflement and sadness were submerged by life on Madeira, but not drowned. Whenever I touched bottom, they were waiting for me.

Each summer, Mother brought Ambrose out to visit me and we passed a few happy weeks together. Every year, Mother was a little frailer and Ambrose a little more of a man. Eventually, Mother was not equal to the journey and, in 1930, I went home—my only return visit—for her funeral. Ambrose has been out a couple of times since then; otherwise I am quite forgotten in my homeland, which is as I should want it. For the part I played as mediator in the quelling of the uprising on Madeira in the spring of 1931 I was thanked in a speech in Parliament by the Foreign Secretary. I wonder how many M.P.'s listening that day realized that the Consul referred to was formerly one of their number.

One British resident on the island of whom I grew especially fond was that relishable eccentric, Dr Michael C. Grabham. I became a regular visitor to him and his wife, Mary, at their home near Camacha, the village north-east of Funchal which constituted the centre of the wicker industry. Grabham, who served as doctor for the area, had had the good sense to marry a member of the Blandy family and the charming lack of it to collect clocks on an island where time meant very little. He had erected a clock tower in the village and hung it with a bell from his native parish in Lancashire, which the villagers could happily ignore, and had laid a cricket pitch on the village green, which they were happy to play on in festival matches against a British exiles' XI, for whom I played and later umpired: a far cry from Fenner's.

When old Grabham died in 1935, he left me a longcase clock which I had often admired and which now adorns my study. He also left me with an abiding fondness for Camacha and the valley in which it is set, full of apple blossom and willow trees, a veritable Little England free of the associations that the genuine article has for me. Accordingly, I used a bequest from my mother to purchase Quinta do Porto Novo, a delightful residence which came into the market in that area. This sealed my resolve never to return to England and I have not once regretted the decision.

My retirement fell due in 1941 but, by then, the Second World War was in progress. Portugal remained neutral, but diplomatic resources were stretched thin. The ambassador in Lisbon asked me if I would stay on for the duration of hostilities and I felt it was the least that I could do. Generally, the war passed me by, save for letters from Ambrose telling me of his life in uniform. When it was all over, in the summer of 1945, he came out to stay with me and we compared our experiences of two very different wars. He also told me at that time of Barrowteign's virtual bankruptcy and of his intention to cede it to the National Trust. Even had I been able to bale him out—which I was not—I think I would still have seen the proposal as a fitting one.

My successor as Consul did not arrive until March 1946, one month short of my seventieth birthday. After 27 years, I was happy to relinquish the post and retire to Quinta do Porto Novo. Since first espying the place on visits to the Grabhams, I had seen it as an ideal venue for my declining years, to be spent overseeing nothing more arduous than the wine cellar, the kitchen garden and a small apple orchard to remind me of England.

Negligible as my Consular duties were, they gave me the habit of attending a desk, which I could not wholly abandon. Accordingly, I conceived the idea of compiling this chronicle of a life unfulfilled to occupy the days when rain fell on the fertile Porto Novo valley. Strangely, however, when it came to the point, I was reluctant to set it down on paper, feeling that nothing would be served by such an exercise, certainly not my own peace of mind. So the idea lay fallow, though only, as it turned out, awaiting its moment.

His Majesty's Leader of the Opposition, Mr Winston Churchill, chose to mark New Year 1950—the start of this brave new decade—by holidaying on Madeira. I was not among the eager throng at the harbour the morning his ship docked, though I had been offered a place in the official reception party. Instead, I kept myself to myself in Camacha. I received an invitation to take tea with him at Reid's Hotel, where he was staying, and deemed it churlish to refuse.

I found Churchill on the balcony at Reid's, enjoying the shade from the afternoon sun. He was gazing out across the harbour, with palm trees waving sleepily in the hotel garden beneath, a panama hat and some papers on the table before him and a large cigar clamped in his mouth. The scene was a soporific one, but when Churchill turned his eye upon me, I knew that he was still the same sharp-brained Winston that I had always known. He had plumbed the depths since last we had met—dismissed between the wars as a Germanophobe—and climbed the heights—Prime Minister and saviour of his country during the war—but looked that day at Reid's a happy, contented old man, smiling at some secret joke.

"Edwin, sit down," he said. "I can't tell you how pleased I am to see you. It's been so long . . ."

"More than thirty years," I said, seating myself opposite him and wondering if he recalled the exact circumstances of our last meeting. Waiters bustled round to serve tea now that I had arrived.

"Clemmie's exploring the town, which will spare her our chin-wag about old times. You're looking well, I must say—Madeira's been good for you."

"Madeira's good for everyone, especially an underworked, overpaid British Consul. You're looking pretty fit yourself—how's leadership?"

"Between you and me, pretty deadly in opposition. I'm longing for an election so I can get back to Downing Street."

"It's where you belong. We had our differences at times, Winston, but let me say this as somebody who stayed in his quiet burrow during the war—you did a damn good job. The country owes you Downing Street."

"Thank you, Edwin, it's kind of you to say so."

"But I must confess to one reservation."

"I know it—the fact that they've made an old Tory of me!"

"Well, it takes a bit of swallowing. I remember when you stopped being a young Tory."

"Time rings in its changes, you know. I hadn't reckoned on

one irony right here, though. They've put us in the suite L.G. once used."

"Yes, they would. He came with his wife in . . . oh, it must be 1925."

"You heard he married Miss Stevenson eventually—when he was eighty?"

The comment struck a chord in my mind. Lloyd George, the old charlatan, had truly had his cake and eaten it too—Prime Minister and belted earl before his death, he had survived countless divorce scandals and lived to marry the secretary with whom he had betrayed his wife. I, who had wished nothing more than to marry the lady of my choice, both of us being free to do so, was allowed neither political career nor wedded bliss. Such was my punishment for wanting success and happiness. When Lloyd George, Churchill and I sat together in Asquith's Cabinet forty years ago, who could have guessed that they were marked out for fame and honour whilst I was destined for the most resounding failure.

It was too late to begrudge Churchill any of his achievement or my lack of it. He might have detected by a flicker of my eye that his mention of Lloyd George and Frances Stevenson was indelicate in view of my own circumstances, but he could be forgiven, for having forgotten them. There was plenty of harmless talk for us to indulge in: his anecdotes of the mighty at war in the world, mine of the petty at peace on Madeira, our shared rememberance of the lost Edwardian age. He told me of his plans to go painting down the coast at Camara de Lobos. I invited him and Clementine to dine with me at Quinta do Porto Novo before they left and he accepted.

In fact, the dinner engagement was never kept. News came from England that Attlee had dissolved Parliament. The election for which Churchill had thirsted was nigh. He sped home by flying boat as soon as the weather would permit.

It was this brief interruption to my obscurity that prompted me to re-open these pages. We had not mentioned the name Couchman. We had not spoken of the past that really mattered to me or Churchill's part in it, whatever that may have been. We had not even touched on his reasons for wanting me to come to Madeira, assuming he had any or that it was not all Lloyd George's idea. We might conceivably have done so after several glasses of malmsey at Quinta do Porto Novo—I shall never know. And that is why I felt slightly cheated by his precipitate departure and why the idea recurred to me of setting down on paper the perverse course of my life. I harboured the notion that, in the process, I might divine the flaw in my character rendering all that seemed so incomprehensible a just fate for one such as I.

It is the autumn of the year now, and of my days, with winter in the wings. And I was wrong, as so often before. There is no lesson in any of it, unless it be that life can never be truly explicable. Injustice remains as mute as ever.

Where are you now, Elizabeth? Do you still, sometimes, think of me? If so, what is it that you think? What did it really mean, I wonder? For I shall ever seek the truth that you denied me. My tragedy is that I shall surely never find it.

E.G. Strafford

Quinta do Porto Novo,
Camacha,
Madeira,
October 1950.

Two

The skies over Gatwick were an insipid grey. The platform where I waited for the London train smelt of railways and—distantly—of asphalt. Madeira was suddenly all of its two thousand miles away and England, on an April afternoon, was, for better or worse, home. With a job to go to now, I could confront its realities with some sort of equanimity.

I was back at the house in Greenwich, with dinner on the go, before Jerry returned from the office. I entertained him with anecdotes of Madeira in general and Alec in particular, but he was unable to disguise his relief when he heard about the job.

"It sounds just the thing for you, Martin."

"I think it is, Jerry—an historian's dream. But it means I'll be dodging round the country exploring lines of research for—well, for as long as it takes. Which means you won't see much of me here."

"Do you want to use this as a base?" It was the question I was hoping for.

"If that's all right by you. It'd be useful to keep my stuff here."

"Certainly." Jerry had drunk more than his usual from the bottle of Madeira I'd opened—my request was well-timed. "You don't want to carry everything around with you." Then, as if to reassure himself: "Where will you make a start?"

"I just need to make some notes on the Memoir. Then I'll be off to see people mentioned in it who are still alive. And I'll certainly go up to Cambridge to use the libraries and pick some brains."

It was exciting, even as I spoke of it, to think that the quest for Strafford's secret was about to begin. The first step was never in doubt, it was straight back into my own past, to test at first hand the link which bound me to the Couchmans and the Couchmans to Elizabeth.

It was late, too late really, when, after a stiff drink I faced up to telephoning my ex-wife.

"Shaftesbury 4757."

"Hello Helen, it's me."

"Martin: how are you?" Her voice was flat and apprehensive.

"Fine. How's Laura?"

"Nervous. Have you forgotten she starts school next week?"

"No, of course not." Naturally I had, though her fifth birthday, in February, should have reminded me. Still, it was an opening. "That's why I've called. Would it be okay for me to come down and see her before then?"

"When were you thinking of?" The apprehension had frozen into a certainty: the one blot on her civilized social landscape—her ex-husband—was about to reappear.

"How about tomorrow?" I was eager to begin my investigation and this visit was a pretext to do just that.

After a lengthy pause and the rustling of what could have been a calendar: "All right. We're not doing anything in the afternoon. You could look in about two."

"Right. I'll see you then."

"Fine. I must dash now, Martin. See you tomorrow. 'Bye."

The phone went down. I hadn't expected the conversation to be as short as that, but it didn't surprise me. Helen had never believed in making life easy for me, before or after our separation. Little did she know that I'd just come across a way of making her own life unexpectedly difficult. How difficult even I had no idea.

I got to Shaftesbury two hours early, two trains and a bus having taken less time than I'd allowed. I'd only ever been there to visit my daughter, on sufferance, and the whole town seemed always to grudge my coming. For me, it didn't sit mellowly on its hill above Cranborne Cross. It was always sunless and suspicious, Gold Hill and the green horizon conspiring behind a grim, grey mist.

That day, it was the same. With time to kill, I made for The Ship Inn in Bleke Street. Usually I'd called there after visits to Archdene, not before. Today, it didn't seem to matter if Helen guessed I'd been drinking. And The Ship was a warm and welcoming place, so I sat by the bar and drank pint for pint with a talkative tractor salesman from Yeovil.

Elizabeth, I remembered somewhere around the third pint, had read a lot of Hardy's poetry and, here I was, paying him the unintended compliment of opening my investigations in his very own Shaston. Not that I'd read any of his poems, only a couple of the novels, but the lines Strafford had quoted from one keep coming back to me. "Yes, I have re-entered your olden haunts at last." I hadn't yet, but, already, it felt as if I had.

Haunts no, the trail yes. It led out of The Ship at two o'clock and down Tout Hill. Archdene was the smartest and last of four thatched cob cottages backing onto the hill Shaftesbury stood on—something of a well-kept antique, in fact, which was appropriate, considering that Helen's new husband, Ralph Corbett, prowled the market towns of Wessex dealing in well-kept antiques. Even I had to admit that he had good taste and Archdene reflected it—an old cottage, yes, but expensively restored with a big garage dug out of view into the side of the hill so as not to spoil the olde worlde impression. It could have graced the cover of the county magazine and probably had. No father could object to his daughter being brought up in such surroundings, especially one with no alternatives to offer. But I did, of course.

There was no answer to the doorbell. I looked round the side and noted, with relief, that Ralph's Range Rover wasn't in the garage. Then I saw Helen, near the top of the sloping garden, stooping over a vegetable row. Her hair was tied back rather severely and she was wearing jumper, jeans and gumboots—very much the country lady. I didn't call out—wouldn't have known what to call—but walked up the path towards her. Crocuses and daffodils were in bloom on the rockeries around the lush; terraced lawn and the vegetable garden above looked well-turned and neatly plotted. All this was Ralph's influence. Helen was no gardener—hadn't been anyway. But she'd always been pliable and had slipped well into her new role.

She heard me coming and looked up with her tight little frown. She wasn't surprised to see me but there wasn't the hint of a smile.

"Hello," I said, panting from the short climb.

"Hello Martin. Laura's not here I'm afraid"—pre-empting any question from me. "When we agreed two o'clock yesterday, I'd forgotten that she'd be at playschool till three. They have a little group to prepare them for the real thing."

"That's all right. I'm late as it is."

"How was the pub?" This was her way of telegraphing that it was obvious I'd been drinking.

"Fine—Shaftesbury's well off in that line."

"So I believe. But we hardly visit one."

"Not much time, I suppose, with all this garden to keep up."

"It's certainly a busy time of the year. Come into the house and have some coffee," she said after a pause. But there was no crack about sobering up, which was a minor victory for me.

We walked down to the back of the house, through the extension Ralph had built and into the kitchen—flagged floors and stripped pine furniture with an old-fashioned but brand new range in the wide chimney breast, Saabatier knives and Le Creuset saucepans hung up like objets d'art, filtered coffee served in a Dunoon mug.

"I'll have to go and collect Laura in half an hour," Helen said. "Do you want to come with me or wait here?"

"Is it far?"

"No. Just round the corner."

"Let's walk then."

"I'm sorry she wasn't here to meet you." What she really meant was she was sorry to have been alone when I arrived. Actually, it suited my purpose.

"Never mind. It gives us a chance to talk. How's your family?"

"You mean Mummy and Daddy?"

"Yes."

"They're fine. What makes you ask?"

"Just curiosity. I never wished them any harm."

"They'd be pleased to know that."

I ignored the edge to her remark and got in before she could sharpen it. "What about your grandmother?"

"Thriving."

"Good. I liked the old girl."

"You only met her once." Another edge to blunt.

"That's true." I dodged the issue of where. This wasn't the time to remind Helen of our wedding. "But she was very . . . impressive."

"Still is."

"How old is she now?"

"87, 88. Something like that."

"And still keeping well?"

"Very, when I last saw her."

"Where does she live now?"

"Still at the house in Miston. Why do you ask?"

"Where exactly is that?"

"West Sussex. But why do you want to know?"

"Just curiosity."

"Come on. When have you ever been curious about my family? Hostile, indifferent, yes. But curious?"

"Historians are always curious about the past." This impersonal half-truth was my way round the acerbity that was creeping in. Whatever else, I didn't want a slanging match.

Helen put down her coffee with a crash. "You're getting a bit pompous, aren't you, Martin?" Then she noticed she'd spilt some of the coffee on the table, swore demurely and fetched a cloth. "You're practising history now, are you?"

"Sort of." It was true, in a sense. But Helen wouldn't understand what sense. She'd talked about history as if it was a profession like medicine or the law, but sarcastically, knowing it wasn't. "I'm researching the history of the Suffragette movement." I grabbed at a convenient lie to explain my interest without it seeming sinister. "Your grandmother is the only person I know who was around at the time, who could give a first-hand opinion."

"You don't know my grandmother." She wanted to deny me that. "And I can't believe you're researching anything."

"Why? It's an interesting subject."

"Maybe. But when I say I can't believe you're researching it, what I mean is that I think you're lying."

"Why should I be?"

"I don't know. But I don't trust you." I couldn't blame her for that—she had a good reason not to. "And I don't want you bothering Nan."

"I'll try not to do that." I wasn't going to try very hard.

The polished brass antique clock on the wall chimed the quarter. "It's time to collect Laura." She began piling the cups in the sink, making enough noise for me to tell she was angry, a reaction I'd hoped to avoid.

She put on an anorak and made for the door, so I followed. We walked quickly and silently along the lane, following the curve of the hill round to where a small Victorian school stood in a playground behind mesh fencing. In an annexe of the building, we found Laura in a babbling little group of children waiting to be collected.

Laura looked surprised and greeted me with childishly deliberate formality, deterring me from kissing or embracing her. I was reduced to a meek hello. To be honest, I'd never been at ease with her or she with me. Our exchanges were always stilted. They made me feel like a least favourite uncle. So we walked mournfully back to Archdene, talking about play-school (which she liked) and "proper" school (which she thought she was looking forward to), while Helen walked sightly ahead, chatting to a neighbour and her red-headed son and avoiding any explanation of who I was. They stood at the gate for a few minutes, finishing their conversation, while Laura and I went in. Laura sat on a stool in the hall and began unbuckling her sandals. My eye was caught by the large index book standing next to the telephone. It was a record I could rely on Helen to keep accurately, so I riffled through it and, sure enough, came to N for Nan: Quarterleigh, Miston, West Sussex. Telephone; Midhurst 5376. I made a note of it.

Only then did I notice that Laura's saucer eyes had followed every move, so much more interesting than some stiff new sandal buckles. "What are you writing down, Martin?" she asked. (Helen had weaned her off "Daddy" years before and I couldn't complain.)

"Just an address."

"Whose address?"

"Your great-grandmother's." She wrinkled her nose. "Nanny Couchman."

"I like Nanny Couchman," she said, smiling at the thought. It was the first time she'd smiled since we'd collected her. That, and the buttercups on her dress, suddenly moved me. Why was my own daughter a stranger to me? I knew the reason and it didn't help.

"I like her too. I thought I might visit her."

Helen came in then. "You should have had those sandals off by now," she said, still annoyed, but with me not Laura.

Laura made another prod at the buckle, but her mind wasn't on the job. "Martin's going to see Nanny Couchman."

Helen shot a glare at me, but kept talking to Laura. "Never mind about that now. Let's see to those sandals." She stooped and undid them for her. "Now, into the kitchen and I'll make you some tea." Laura scampered off down the hall. Helen was left with an opportunity for inquisition. "Is this true?" It was more an accusation than a question.

"I'm considering it. I told you so."

"To ask about the Suffragettes?"

"That sort of thing."

"I don't believe you. There's something else."

"Why should there be?"

"I don't know. But there must be."

"If you say so." I was tired of being conciliatory, but I shouldn't have been—it was my best line.

"I don't want you bothering my grandmother."

"It'd be no bother."

"I'll be the judge of that. I don't want you bothering any of my family. We agreed you wouldn't. Remember?"

I remembered. But it was an agreement I couldn't afford to honour. "What we agreed was that I could see Laura whenever I wanted. I haven't abused that, have I?"

"No, but only because you don't care about her."

"How would you know?"

"Because I know you." This was getting messy—and out of hand. "Now listen"—and I did, because she could still command me, which was one of the things I hated her for—"Leave Nan alone and the rest of my family, or I can make it impossible for you to see Laura. Do you want that?"

"Of course not." But how could I avoid it? "This is getting us nowhere, Helen, and I must go." It seemed the best thing to do. "I'll say goodbye to Laura and go now—if that's all right." I didn't wait for her agreement.

It was, in all conscience, a hasty exit. Laura was as surprised to see me go as she had been to see me arrive. Helen had been painfully near the truth when she'd said I didn't care. I did, of course, but not enough. I knew that I'd really only come to glean what I could of Lady Couchman. The rest was a pretence I couldn't persist in. So I left, so abruptly that it can have left Helen in little doubt that she'd been right to suspect me.

A steely, filamentary rain was falling now. I followed the lanes in a broad curve round the foot of Castle Hill and climbed back into the town up cobbled Gold Hill, with its famous view of Cranborne Chase shrouded in cloud. I was eager to be away, but there was a long wait in the High Street for a bus to Gillingham station. A boy and a girl in school uniform stood at the stop, kissing and giggling. They both looked too young for it, but it was, for me, that afternoon, a chilling portent. I couldn't turn away and I certainly couldn't disapprove. The boy went off into a nearby shop at one point and I looked at the girl, leaning against the stop, russet hair tumbling over her raincoat collar, a haughty hint of beauty in her face, but chewing gum energetically and eagerly accepting the cigarettes the boy brought back. I was relieved when the bus came. They clattered to the rear while I sat at the front with my holdall full of secrets.

On the train to London, I considered my next move. Strafford's Elizabeth was alive and well and I now had her address in Sussex. That was the obvious place to go. But something made me hesitate. I didn't feel quite ready. When the train stopped at Salisbury, I got out, on a whim, and walked down to the cathedral. The rain had stopped and a watery sun was shining now on the old mellow building. There was only one tea shop with a good view of the Green, an old-fashioned little place full of high-backed settles and dimpsy alcoves, knots of garrulous county town ladies tangled at small wooden tables overloaded with teapots, cakestands and white lace doilies. I was only just in time to be served and sat alone, sipping coffee by the window, the sun-splashed lines of the cathedral curved by the bullseye panes.

This had to be where Strafford and Elizabeth had stopped on their way down to Barrowteign all those years ago, when everything was going well, when they could debate Hardy's poetry and smile at each other over the teacups. It was eerie to sit there nearly seventy years later, with so little changed—apparently. But we'd changed—they and I—and not for the better. When I left the shop, I went and sat on a bench at the edge of the Green and watched the light fade on the noble cathedral. Then I walked slowly back to the station—but never got there. I wasn't in the mood for a dark, solitary train ride. Sellick was paying well and I passed a pub just short of the station where the noise from the bar was cheery and welcoming. So I booked a room there for the night and spent the rest of the evening sampling the local beer. I drank too much of it—of course—but it didn't prevent me from waking with a bright idea, and I was at the reference library as soon as it opened its doors to a warm, hazy day.

It took no particular skill to plump for the *Dictionary of National Biography.* Sure enough, in the Supplement covering deaths between 1951 and 1960, I found him. Sellick had told me of finding the entry himself and that it had said little. He was right. It seemed to me that a former Home Secretary might have warranted something fuller. But no, the measured biographese was aimed at the surface and found its mark.

"STRAFFORD, EDWIN (1876-1951), politician, was born at Barrowteign in Devon 20 April 1876, the second son of George Strafford, colonel in the Indian Army. He was educated at Marlborough and Trinity College, Cambridge . . ."

It went on in the same vein. After Strafford's own chronicle of his life, it was dull and skeletal.

"When Asquith became Prime Minister in 1908, he persuaded Herbert Gladstone to retire from the Home Office and appointed Strafford in his stead, swift recognition indeed for the promising young M.P." We know, we know. "Whether the speed of his rise went to his head or his onerous responsibilities proved too much for him must be a matter of conjecture"—conjecture I didn't much like and which wouldn't have pleased Strafford—"since he remained but two years in the post before resigning shortly after the commencement of the Constitutional Conference of 1910, called in an attempt to resolve . . ." Yes, but what about that resignation? "No sure reason for Strafford's departure was given at the time and none has emerged since. The commonest theory held is that he lost patience with the Conference as a means of settling the dispute between Lords and Commons and sought to panic Asquith into more desperate remedies. If he thought other ministers would follow his example, he was sadly wrong and if, as may be guessed, he made that familiar mistake of the overweening young, to suppose himself irreplaceable, he was promptly disabused of the notion. One so swiftly raised was as swiftly brought low. His fate resembled that of Lord Randolph Churchill in resigning the Exchequer in 1887. Both gestures were simply ignored and only the makers of them suffered as a result. Like Churchill, Strafford drifted into a twilight world and became the despair of his friends and colleagues." Where was the evidence for this? The writer disliked Strafford—that much was clear. "He left Parliament at the general election of December 1910 and lived thereafter mostly in Devon until the outbreak of the First World War, when he joined his regiment in France. His war career was without distinction." A damning little sentence that struck in my throat. "At its end, he was appointed H.M. Counsul to Madeira, a post which he held from 1919 until his retirement in 1946. He coped well when rebels exiled from mainland Portugal tried to seize the island in 1931, and earned thereby the thanks of MacDonald's government. Otherwise, the obscurity and remoteness of his posting were such as to render him entirely forgotten in the public mind at home." The writer seemed to take pleasure in emphasizing the point. "Strafford remained in Madeira after his retirement, although it was on a visit to his nephew at Barrowteign that he met his death, struck by a train on a level crossing in the early hours of 5 July 1951. He was buried in the churchyard of the nearby village of Dewford." Nothing was made of the irony that Strafford's brother had died in similar circumstances forty years before. It annoyed me. While I was struggling to solve the Strafford mystery, some hack had penned this dismissive obituary without knowing there was even a mystery. I braced myself for the summing-up.

"It was perhaps inevitable that some—or at any rate one—of the young men promoted by Asquith should turn out not to have the capacity for high office. That was Strafford's deficiency and it was unfortunate for him that there were so many other able contemporaries—notably Lloyd George and Winston Churchill—with whom his rapid decline stood in such stark contrast." The bibliography was virtually non-existent: *The Times* 6 June 1951, private information, personal knowledge. For that read ignorance and aspersion. Who'd written this? Three initials—M.E.B.—protected the guilty party. I thumbed through the list of contributors to identify him.

M.E.B.: Marcus Everard Baxter. Double-take: I knew him. Marcus Baxter was my Director of Studies at Cambridge, a drunk and a bore but also, in his day, a gifted historian, an acknowledged expert on twentieth century British politics. His judgement mattered—more than mine would to anyone else. Marcus Baxter cutting his historical teeth on a character assassination for the D.N.B. I could have done without. But, if the old soak was going to set himself up as judge and jury on a wronged man, I'd lead for the defence. At least it was someone to bounce ideas off in Cambridge and, if I could discredit his treatment of Strafford, so much the better.

Baxter's lofty pronouncement gave me the fire—dampened in Shaftesbury—that I needed to find Elizabeth, the one surviving person who might know everything. After one night in London, I set off for Miston.

I liked what little I saw of Chichester, that demure little cathedral city that preens itself on the warm coastal plain of Sussex, but I could spare it no time now. Buses north from there across the South Downs were rare, so I took a taxi. A jowly, garrulous cabbie drove me up past Goodwood Racecourse, telling me—which I could have guessed—that most of his fares stopped there.

"I suppose so," I said, vaguely, my mind flitting to the Goodwood of long ago, with an invitation being issued and accepted to spend a few weeks in Devon. I wondered if the old lady in Miston ever thought now of the young girl at Goodwood.

"Not a gambling man yourself, sir?"

"Not on horses, no." But on other things maybe. Perhaps my journey was a gamble in itself.

"Which village did you say it was?"

"Miston. Do you know it?"

"I know where it is, right enough. Quiet little place just over the Downs. What's the address?"

"Just drop me in the centre. I'll find my way from there." I didn't want this man spraying gravel round a quiet Sussex driveway. I wanted to arrive silently and in my own good time.

We topped the Downs in sunshine. They looked clean and green and peaceful, sheep with their lambs dotting the slopes. Below us, a small wooden-spired church stood in a cluster of thatched roofs. As we came down the hillside, I spotted the sign: MISTON—PLEASE DRIVE CAREFULLY. We didn't, of course, lurching to a halt by the war memorial in the centre of the village.

I paid the driver off and looked around me. The little post office-store on the other side of the road was closed for lunch. Further along, there was a gentle hum from the pub—a solid, welcoming, four-square English pub, the sort I liked, full of simple rural pleasures, though not simple rural customers to judge by the pair in pin-stripe suits who emerged as I watched and loaded themselves into a company car. Like most other English villages, Miston wasn't self-sufficient anymore. It had been once, I thought, turning to look at the memorial behind me: a rough-hewn Celtic cross above a cairn-shaped stone bearing the names of the village's young men who'd "laid down their lives in war that others might live in peace". I wondered what they'd make of expense account businessmen at the bar of their Royal Oak, then forgot them. After all, a pub was a good place to seek directions.

They told me how to find Quarterleigh and, after a couple of pints, I made my way there down a narrow, musty lane past a terrace of timbered and tile-hung almshouses, with an arched and pillared gallery running the length of them in which hung heavy-scented flower baskets. Beyond the almshouses, the lane broadened in front of the church, an unpretentious flint structure behind yew hedges on the lower slope of the Downs. Doves were cooing in the rafters of the wooden spire and rabbits scattered from the tumbledown graveyard at the sound of my lifting the latch on the gate. It seemed a pity to disturb their peace, but the barmaid had been specific—"Quickest way is through the churchyard into Croxon's Lane. Quarterleigh is the house beyond the Rectory."

One path led to the door of the church. Another led across the graveyard to a kissing-gate in the hedge. I headed towards it, my eye wandering over the gravestones, some overgrown or askew, others newer and well-tended. It felt strange, but seemed right, to be approaching Elizabeth by this old, silent path. Then I stopped dead. Hard by the track there was a clean, white, marble tombstone. The inscription on the stone was clear and stark: "Gerald Victor Couchman, Knight Bachelor, Colonel (Devonshire Regiment), died 26th September 1954, aged 78 years. Rest in Peace." So, here was one of my quarry, at rest in a Sussex churchyard. But at peace? Not, perhaps, if he knew what I was stirring up in search of his past. There was space on the stone for another name, that of his widow, but it was blank. I pressed on through the gate.

The lane beyond traced a contour along the foot of the Downs. On the other side of it, the ground sloped gently towards the brook that ran through Miston. I walked by the entrance to the Rectory and on to the next drive: gravel—newly chipped—with white, wooden double gates standing open between flanking forsythia bushes, vivid yellow in the afternoon sunshine. The boundary was marked by a waist-high flint wall but, beyond that, a banked rockery of aubretia and rose bushes topped with miniature firs, blocked any view of the house.

I hesitated at the gate. I'd never been there before, met Elizabeth only once—fleetingly—at my wedding. Then, and until now, she'd been just one of those hostile, disapproving

Couchmans, not Strafford's lost love, the enigmatic temptress of his tragic past. Once a symbol, now a shadow, what of the lady herself? I set off cautiously down the drive. It curved past a broad lawn to the front of the house. Quarterleigh was a half-timbered, thatched house in immaculate repair, the cob lightly washed in pink, the windows leaded and flowerboxed, smoke curling gently from the chimney, honeysuckle trained in an arch round the door. What could be more peaceful, more serene, less suspicious? Nothing, I surmised. But then, why should it be? Why should an old lady expect nemesis to call in the middle of a soft spring afternoon?

It was not Elizabeth who answered the door. It was opened too quickly—almost flung open. I was surprised, but not for long. The reason was standing before me. Henry Couchman, my celebrated ex-father-in-law, had lost none of his bloodshot pugnacity since the last time I'd seen him, eyeing me distastefully in the divorce court three years before, a proprietorial arm round his daughter then, a silent warning-off in his glare. The glare and the meaning hadn't changed. He was the man in possession, a man of means and solid virtues confronting the disgraced intruder.

Henry did not speak. It was one of his justly famed qualities. As a largely silent Member of Parliament, he'd risen like damp in the Conservative party, been a junior minister under Heath, commanded still an impressive majority in his constituency, did not welcome scapegrace sons-in-law. When they'd been excised from his family, he didn't expect them to show their face again.

I broke the silence. "I didn't expect to see you here."

"I'll bet you didn't, my lad." Henry's patronizing tone was unaltered. But whereas once he could use it to make me squirm, now I had a secret advantage. An overbearing father-in-law came down a peg or two when he was also a baby who'd stared up at Strafford from his pram with blank incomprehension.

"Is she at home?"

"Not to you." He almost smiled then in his superiority. Strafford was wrong, I thought. You could never have been his son.

"Does that mean she's here?"

"No. She's gone away for a few days."

"Where would that be?"

"Why do you want to know?"

"I wanted to speak to her, that's all."

"Now listen, Martin." Henry puffed himself up with that familiar prelude to an overbearing lecture. "My mother doesn't know you and doesn't want to know you. Those of us who do know you wish we didn't, and I certainly don't propose to allow you to bother an elderly lady. When I heard you'd be coming here . . ."

"I suppose Helen told you."

"Naturally." I might have known she would. Even now I could hear her daughterly tones down the telephone to Henry, concern for her grandmother camouflaging her hatred of me. If only I'd been more subtle, or sober, in Shaftesbury. But that would have been beyond me and now the damage was done. Elizabeth had been spirited away, leaving Henry to stand guard. But why? "God knows why Helen puts up with your visits. If I were Ralph . . ."

"But you're not." Actually I'd never seen that much difference between them. It was just that Henry was a man of more substance, so he felt he had more weight to throw about.

"By God, Martin, if I were, I'd have seen you off years ago for the bloody nuisance you are. Maybe access to my granddaughter isn't my affair, but my mother's peace of mind certainly is. The last thing she needs is you sniffing around."

"After what?"

The question knocked him off balance. He began to bluster in his party political manner. "What . . . How can I say?" He seemed to recover himself. "We don't know what you're up to, Martin, and we don't want to know."

I saw a slight advantage and tried to exploit it. "I was hoping to speak to your mother about the past—the Suffragette era. It interests me as an historian." Henry snorted derisively. "It might interest her too. What I don't know is why it should worry you."

There was a flicker of uncertainty in Henry's steely glare. "You don't worry me, my lad." Strangely, that was the first moment when I felt I did.

"Something does, Henry, sufficiently for you to whisk your

mother away at a moment's notice and lie in wait for me here."

"Lie in wait be damned." His colour, which was always red, was getting redder still. "I came down here to catch up with some paperwork in peace and quiet." Now he was making excuses. "I have better things to do than . . ."

"You've got a funny way of showing it."

"Listen to me, my lad." He advanced menacingly.

"No, listen to me. What do you know about Edwin Strafford?"

He stopped in his tracks. "Who?" It didn't seem too much to imagine that he had no need to ask.

"Edwin Strafford. A friend of your father—and your mother—at different times."

"Never heard of him."

"Really? A Cabinet minister under Asquith—surely you should have done?"

"Why?"

"That's what I'd like to know."

"There's nothing to know. You're talking in riddles, man."

"I admit that. But it's a riddle I'm trying to solve. Edwin Strafford was once engaged to your mother."

"What of it?"

"You do know of him then?"

"I didn't say that. I daresay my mother had many admirers when she was young."

"This one also fought with your father in South Africa and was later thrown over for him by your mother."

Henry drew closer, so close I could smell the whisky on his breath. "I don't know what bloody fool game you're playing, but I advise you to stop it for your own sake."

I knew Henry's moods well enough to know that it would soon be time to stop. But I decided to try one other line, on a hunch. "It's just innocent research, Henry. Nothing for anyone to feel guilty about. Edwin Strafford's been dead for 26 years. But you did meet him once."

Henry wouldn't remember the meeting I was referring to. But he reacted as if he did—that or some other meeting. "Guilty? What the hell are you implying? I've never met the man."

"I rather think you have."

"I've nothing to say to you, Radford. Get yourself off my property."

"All right. I'll go quietly—for the moment." I turned and walked as casually as I could away up the drive. It was no time to point out that Henry wasn't on his property, but his mother's. Or perhaps he'd meant a different kind of property—the past, a family secret, a meeting I didn't know about. I heard him close the door firmly behind me. But I wasn't finished with him yet.

I walked back through the churchyard, past Couchman's grave. He'd outlived Strafford by three years, still been on the scene when his old friend came home to England in 1951, to meet his accidental death. Had they met then? I'd touched a nerve by referring to Henry meeting Strafford. If he really had, when else could it have been?

Back in the village, I followed a footpath that led down beside some cottages along the banks of the brook that ran through Miston. Soon, I was in a field carpeted in buttercups and daisies, with the church opposite me over the stream. I crossed a stile into a wood that grew down to the banks of the stream and followed the path through bracken and bluebells to a point exactly opposite the rear of Quarterleigh. Shaded in the dappled light of the wood, I had a clear, secure view of it. The back garden of the house ran down to the opposite bank. A conservatory was built onto the back of the house, with a paved area in front of it. To one side was the garage, with the bonnet of Henry's Jaguar extending beyond the open doors, to the other a large greenhouse and a terraced kitchen garden. The rest of the garden, lushly grassed and flower-bedded, sloped down between rhododendron hedges to the river, where the yellow heads of daffodils merged with the waving reeds at the bank.

I stayed where I was for a quarter of an hour or so, till I started to get cold and bored, concluded that Henry wasn't coming out, and gave up the vigil. As I climbed over the stile out of the wood and emerged into the open, my eye was caught by a flash of light from an upper window of the house. Looking back up at it, I thought I saw a figure draw back from view and didn't find it hard to imagine Henry peering out through binoculars that had caught the sun. If so, he'd spotted me and knew I'd been watching. But I knew something too: the Henry who'd blustered me off the premises and who might have caught me spying was a frightened man. The question was: why?

I went back to The Royal Oak and booked a room for the night. That evening, I sat in the bar, drank beer and played darts with the locals. I dropped the name Couchman a couple of times but learnt nothing. They knew a rich old widow lived at Quarterleigh but that was all. She was neither an eccentric recluse nor a local celebrity. The landlord remembered Sir Gerald, when I mentioned seeing his grave, as a well-spoken, free-spending whisky drinker who called regularly in the lounge bar and gave good racing tips.

I slept soundly and woke with a clear plan. Elizabeth was out of my reach, for the moment. The only clue to follow was Henry's denial of meeting Strafford. If they'd ever met as adults, it could only have been when Strafford came home in the spring of 1951. He'd gone then to Devon to visit his nephew—and died there. So that was where I would go, to try for weakness another part of the wall.

During a blank weekend in London, I wrote my first report for Sellick, which wasn't as easy as it should have been. In telling him how my search for the truth was going, I had to gloss over some of the truth that I already knew: that to the Couchman clan I was a pariah, that Henry Couchman would have resented me even if he hadn't resented my questions. But I left Sellick in no doubt that Henry knew something and held out the hope that in Devon I might find out what.

I wonder now, looking back, that I could have had so few misgivings about editing the truth to suit my purpose. It never once occurred to me that I was doing what I was trying to prove others had done.

Three

I didn't set off for Exeter until Monday afternoon. I'd arranged to stay with friends, so there was no need to hurry. Somewhere after Taunton, the train began to wind through the deep green fields and brick red earth that spoke of Strafford's homeland. I'd never been there with those associations in my mind before, never heard a station announcer pronounce Crediton in a Devon accent and thought that that was where old Brewer Strafford had come from. It gave the city echoes. It wasn't any longer just the place where I spent an odd weekend with my friends the Bennetts, wasn't just a genteel cathedral city astride the river Exe. It had acquired a past and a share of the mystery.

From St David's station, I walked down beside the river to the Exe Bridge—now a multi-lane roundabout, not the simple stone structure that Strafford's car had once rumbled over on its way to Barrowteign. There I caught a bus up into the modern housing estate on the high ground west of the river, where the Bennetts lived in their proud little detached property, complete with patio doors, open plan front garden and integrated garage—a happy, suburban couple with no qualms about leading a settled, ordered existence. They never minded my gentle chiding of their domestic routines because they kept alive that played-out English virtue: tolerance. Nick and Hester had met me—as well as each other—during teacher training. I'd been Nick's best man and he'd been mine, Alec being—as usual—out of the country at the time. But that wasn't the sentiment that kept us friends. It was simply that Nick and Hester had stood by me during my exit from the teaching profession, had been fully aware of the circumstances but never once reproached me. When others had turned their backs, they'd invited me to stay with them for a few weeks and ride out the bleakest period. It was a kindness I'd never forgotten.

As I came up the road, I spotted Hester kneeling on the lawn, gouging at some impertinent weed with a trowel. She was wearing dungarees that, with the long flaxen hair flowing down her back, made her look too young and delicate for the task.

"It's only trying to remember when it was a meadow," I said, coming up behind her.

Hester jumped like a startled hare—she had a gift for not hearing people coming. "What?" she cried, swinging round to look at me with her large, intent eyes—eyes that always made me think I should have married her rather than Helen—or at least tried to. "Oh, it's you!" she said, smiling with recognition. And that earnest, trusting smile always made me think again: Hester deserved someone better than me—and she'd got him.

She bounced up from her kneeler and delivered me a smacking kiss. "Come inside," she said with bubbly enthusiasm. "Drag Nick away from marking for a moment."

Indoors, we found Nick sighing over a stack of exercise books. He looked up with a careworn, crumpled grin. "4B are bad enough without you turning up" he said. "But at least it's an excuse to stop. How's tricks?"

And I told him—as best I could—while Hester started dinner and Nick treated himself—and me—to some relaxing gin and tonic and assured me how lucky I was to be out of teaching.

"Especially," he enthused, "when you land a cushy research number. What I wouldn't give to be writing my biography of John Clare"—the pet project he'd never had time to start—"rather than ploughing through that . . ." He gestured despairingly at the pile of ink-stained books and gulped some more gin rather than select a suitable epithet. "But what brings you down here?"

"Strafford's family lived at Barrowteign—a National Trust property in the Teign valley."

"What are you looking for there?"

"Anything I can find."

So he wished me luck, as did Hester, over the excellent dinner that followed. As Hester pointed out, I was looking well and sounding happy, so temporary or not, the assignment couldn't be bad. She was right. And so far the job had done more for me than I'd done for it. The next day gave me a chance to put that right.

Nick gave me a lift to the bus station on his way into school next morning.

"Have a good time," he shouted as I got out. "Think of me while you're swanning around Barrowteign this afternoon." Then he disappeared in a cloud of exhaust fumes.

The bus that struggled up the hills west of Exeter dropped me at Farrants Cross on the Moretonhampstead road. It diverted to Dewford only on Thursdays—and this was Tuesday. But a fine spring Tuesday, so I didn't mind wandering down the empty lane into the Teign valley, the only sound birdsong and the trickle of water seeping from the fields. To my left was a high, overgrown embankment. Nick's map showed it as a disused railway line: the old Teign valley route that in sixty-odd years of uneconomic working had seen three accidental deaths in one local family. Who'd have thought it, to see it now brambled and benign beneath a blue sky?

Further south, the valley opened out a little. The disused railway became just a scar across the fields beside the river that I could make out from the higher vantage of the road. Then I saw what I was looking for: a bunching of trees in parkland and, nestled in amongst them, tall slate roofs and red sandstone walls: Barrowteign, waiting unchanged to receive me.

The road descended into a slight hollow and I lost sight of the house. Further on was a crossroad. The signpost indicated Dewford to the right, various hamlets to the left. But a separate National Trust board—BARROWTEIGN: HOUSE AND GROUNDS, OPEN APRIL 1 TO OCTOBER 31—pointed also to the left. So I followed that, dipping down slightly between fields to an old stone bridge across the river. Just the other side, the road forked. Another National Trust board directed me to the left and there, ahead, were tall stone pillars flanking a gateway. The road led through them past a newly painted sign: BARROWTEIGN. There was no high wall, no lodge, just fir trees shading a mossy bank with new fencing along its top. I stopped between the pillars, savouring the place and the moment. Statues in the likeness of barn owls had been carved at the top of each pillar. They gazed down stonily at visitors and held a small shield between their claws. Time and weather had erased any device the shields might once have borne.

The drive turned abruptly away from a direct route to the house, although a gated road, marked PRIVATE, continued that way through an avenue of lime trees, their leaves bright green and inviting in the sunshine. It looked to me as if that could once have been the main drive, because there were no trees shading the tarmacced route that I followed away from and then back towards the house. And if I hadn't been on foot and looking out for it, I'd certainly have missed the shallow trench—like an empty moat—that the road crossed a little further on: the railway line, bisecting the park once but now, with its fences and rails gone, its ballast all but grassed over, just a minor undulation beneath a motor coach's wheels. I was puzzled: there was no sign at all of a level crossing or its keeper's cottage.

The road topped the bank on which the house stood, ran past a stable yard now serving as a car park and broadened into a gravelled square at the foot of wide stone steps. These led up to a paved area running along the foot of the house behind a low-clipped yew hedge. I paused at the foot of the steps and looked up at the building: a grand but unpretentious frontage, red sandstone with some lighter stone facing round the windows: wooden doors beneath a rose-windowed arch, the familiar stone owl now placed as if holding the lantern above the doors, tall tracery windows on the ground floor, fewer, though in the same style, on the floor above, oriel windows above that beneath the steep slate roof. Either end of the frontage stood gabled cross-wings bellied out by bay windows.

The porch led straight into a hall, dark despite the high

windows, panelled and roofed in wood, with a huge granite fireplace and, at the far end of the hall, broad, shallow stairs that led up to a half-landing, then divided either side and went on up to balconies that ran round three sides of the hall.

An old lady perched sparrow-like at a desk by the fireplace sold me a ticket and a guidebook and said her piece. "The Hall is a Victorian imitation of medieval tradition: a place for the feudal lord to entertain his vassals. In this case the first Mr. Strafford sometimes held parties for his brewery workers here. But the tradition soon died out. The staircase is solid teak, and leads to the bedrooms. You'll find a guide in each room."

I thanked her and went on. On the other side of the fireplace, well-lit by the windows facing it, was a full-length portrait. There he was, founder of the family, looking just as I'd expected from his grandson's description: a proud, stout, red-faced man, dressed in a rather faded Georgian style, posing in his own hall and grasping the lapels of his tail-coat with self-satisfied firmness. The small plate read: THOMAS STRAFFORD (1789-1867), but the picture said far more.

In a dark lobby behind the hall I found another family portrait: an alert, dignified figure in military uniform—Colonel George Strafford, M.C. (1819-1904), who "extended the estate and refurbished the house on the death of his father. Colonel Strafford was a Victorian country gentleman, a local alderman and charitable benefactor, but no businessman. The family's brewing interests were sold off during his time."

Into the dining room: a long rectangular table laid for dinner, a canopied fireplace, a smaller breakfast table in a bay window looking out into the garden. Another portrait, this time of Robert Strafford, tweed-suited in waders and casting a fly in the tumbling waters of the Teign. "Mr Robert Strafford (1870-1911) took especial pleasure in country pursuits—hunting, fishing (his efforts greatly enhanced the reputation of the Teign in angling circles) and cattle-breeding (a Royal Agricultural Society gold medallist, 1906-1907-1909), his prize-winning breeds are still to be seen in the park."

Then into the library, lined with shelves full of leatherbound Victorian books, a globe, chairs and one long table in the centre: more of a working library than most such places. Yet I was disappointed: what I'd looked for, some sign of my Strafford, had eluded me. I could imagine him being there. But why no formal portrait? Why no "Mr Edwin's study"?

On his own in the library the guide was looking bored and listless in his chair in the window, so I decided to tap his local knowledge. He was an amiable looking old fellow in blazer and regimental tie, with a clipped moustache and a knowing eye.

"Excuse me," I said.

"Can I help, sir?"

"I hope so. I've enjoyed the tour of the house but it's left me wondering about the family."

"Oh yes, sir?"

"Yes. I'm an amateur historian and I remember there was a politician named Strafford at the turn of the century. Any connexions?"

"My word, yes. A younger son of the Colonel, if my memory scrves. But something of a black sheep, if you know what I mean." He winked. "Some sort of scandal. He had to go abroad. Left his mother in the lurch, his brother having died by then."

"I don't recall any scandal."

"No sir, well that sort of thing was kept quiet then, wasn't it?" I decided not to correct him. "Anyway, that was the beginning of the end for the family. By the time Mr Ambrose—young Mr Strafford—came of age, the estate was in bad shape. After the war, he passed it over to the Trust."

"And what became of young Mr Strafford?"

"Oh, he still lives here. Well, not in the house, but on the estate. Not so young anymore, of course. We see him about quite a lot. Lodge Cottage is just down the drive."

"I didn't see it."

"No sir, you wouldn't. The road up only follows the old drive halfway. Lodge Cottage is on the private half."

"Would there be any objections to my calling on Mr Strafford?"

"Shouldn't think so, sir. But you'll not find him in at this time of the day."

"No?"

"Not as a rule. The Greengage in Dewford is your best bet.

And that's where he's most . . . sociable, if you know what I mean."

"I see. Thanks. I may look in there."

Out in the garden again I had no difficulty in finding the turn in the drive where the gate marked PRIVATE led up to Lodge Cottage, but decided not to venture further. The guide knew what he was talking about and I needed a drink. So I headed back to the bridge over the Teign, up to the main road, then took the lane into Dewford: a scattered village strung across the valley side—all ups and downs, narrow bends and muddy gateways. Dewford had none of Miston's olde world charm. It was a working Devon village almost visibly in hock to the tourist trap across the valley. As for the Greengage, it was no place for expense account lunches: a low dark bar full of farm workers eating pasties and drinking lager. Just to be different, I ordered traditional local cider and shouted to the landlord above the clatter of a fruit machine about whether Ambrose Strafford was in. But no. "He allus' goes into Newton Tuesdays. You'd best try this evenin'." I swallowed my cider and left.

It was a nuisance, but it gave me time to explore Dewford. Further up the hillside was the church, its stone tower looming over yew trees. I entered the little graveyard through a dark lych gate and didn't take long to find what I was looking for: the Strafford family plot. Three generations were there, from Thomas Strafford's plain if oversized tomb to the weeping angels that flanked "Robert Strafford of Barrowteign in this parish, also Florence Strafford, his dear wife, formerly Florence Hardistry of Dartmouth, taken together by tragic accident, 5th January 1911; united in death as in life." Dwarfed beside this magniloquent memorial, one small stone bore the briefest of inscriptions: "E.G.S. 1876-1951; R.I.P." That was it. Nothing more. But there were fresh daffodils in the vase formed by the stone. And it was a green, peaceful spot, quite a sun trap in the afternoon in fact, not such a bad place. Suddenly, I wished I'd brought flowers. My only tribute was the Memoir in the napsack over my shoulder and what I proposed to do with it.

I spent a quiet hour wandering round the church, then

walked back to Barrowteign to have a leisurely tea in the refreshment room housed in the old servants' wing. When the house closed at six o'clock, I made my way out down the old drive from its higher end, also marked PRIVATE, and soon came to Lodge Cottage in its grove of lime trees by the disused railway line. The cottage was a modest, whitewashed little property fenced in with its own well-kept garden. The railway was just an uneven grass track with nothing left of the crossing except a cream-painted, five-bar gate now part of the boundary of the cottage garden. An old lineside shack a little distance upon the track looked to have been converted into a garage. There was still a cattle grid on my side of the crossing, but the gate had been replaced by a fence. There was no sign of life in the cottage, but I went in through the low wicket gate and tried the knocker: wrought iron in the likeness of an owl. There was no answer.

Back to The Greengage. It was quiet now, and emptier, in early evening. The fruit machine was silent, blinking mournfully in a corner. Two men played darts with hardly a word. A wisp of smoke curled from a small log in the grate. A grey-muzzled sheepdog lay on the hearth, cocking an ear and opening one eye as I came in. The landlord stood polishing glasses with practised deliberation. Seeing me enter, he leant across the bar and whispered something to his only other customer, a gray-haired old man in a voluminous sheepskin coat, who nodded and sent up a plume of smoke from his pipe.

I ordered a pint of beer and savoured the first gulp. My companion at the bar, perched on a stool with his back against a pillar, sent up more smoke and turned to look at me. His grey hair extended in a white mutton-chop whiskers to meet his moustache, yellowed by pipe-smoking. He had the red nose and cheeks of a drinking man, but the rheumy eyes and laugh lines of a man happy in his drink, not inflamed by it. A pewter tankard stood on the bar in front of him. My eye shot to the device inscribed on the side of it—the Strafford owl. I no longer had any doubt who my companion was.

"Good evening," I said hopefully.

"Evening," he replied, then puffed out some smoke. I had to restrain a cough. "Ted here tells me that some anxious young bugger's been looking for me today. Would that be you?"

"I was certainly hoping to speak to Mr Ambrose Strafford."

"That's me."

"I thought it might be. My name's Martin Rasford. Pleased to meet you." I put out my hand. He looked at it quizzically, then smiled and shook it. "Can I buy you a drink?"

He drained the tankard. "Wouldn't say no." The landlord refilled it from a cask of cider that stood on the bar.

"I went round Barrowteign this morning. It was a fascinating tour."

"Glad you liked it." He didn't look it.

"It made me curious about the history of the family."

"It's all in the guidebook."

"There wasn't much about Edwin Strafford."

"Why should there be?" His eyes narrowed.

"They oughter've printed your story 'bout your uncle, Ambrose," the landlord put in. "That'd sell a few copies."

"Looks like Ted here's aching to tell you all about it," snapped Ambrose.

"No, no," Ted grinned. "You tell it better, Ambrose."

"What is the story?" I asked.

"Go on," Ted said to Ambrose. "Why not tell him? I've heard it 'nough times—bain't no secret what you think."

Ambrose ground his pipe stem between his teeth and looked stubborn. The door clinked open behind me and two men came in. Ambrose winked at me with the eye Ted couldn't see from his side of the bar. "Don't let us keep you from your customers," he said. Ted huffed off towards them. "Ted's a bloody windbag," Ambrose resumed. "He'd probably say the same of me. I don't mind people knowing what I think—when I know what they think."

A show of frankness was called for. "I'm a student of history, Mr Strafford. Your uncle was a famous politician in his day. I thought there'd be more about him at his family home. It struck me as odd there wasn't. In the churchyard his gravestone merely states that he died in 1951."

"What more do you want?"

"I don't know. I was hoping you might tell me."

"All right, Mr Radford. You want the gospel according to Ambrose Strafford? Then come sit at the prophet's feet. It's warmer by the fire." He picked up his tankard and moved over to where the sheepdog lay asleep on the hearth. The one log on the fire was burning low. Ambrose bent gingerly, took another from the fender and propped it against the flame. The bark began to burn with a slight sizzle. He eased one foot against the dog's rump. "Move yourself, Jess," he said. The dog did so without complaint. Ambrose lowered himself into a rocking chair while I sat on a hard chair opposite him. "Ted'll complain about wasting fuel, but these spring evenings still have a nip in 'em. Smell that wood?"—the new log was giving off a sweet scent—"Apple: a lovely burner. We used to have lots of apple to burn at Barrowteign."

"But not anymore?"

"Oh, they still give me some for my little cottage. But it makes me feel like a bloody servant." He gazed into the back of the fire, then smiled. "I can't complain. They've been generous in their way. When I came home after the war, Barrowteign was in a bloody awful state: they'd billeted some Yanks there and buggered some of the best pasture with tank practice. The Trust rescued me from queer street."

"Was your uncle no help?" I was still playing the innocent.

"He was abroad—in the diplomatic service. Didn't know much about it. Besides, he wasn't rolling in money himself."

"A former Cabinet minister?" I tried to sound incredulous.

"You didn't make a fortune in politics in those days, Mr Radford—any rate, not if you had my uncle's scruples. Besides, it was a hell of a time ago. I can't remember him as an M.P."

"Why did he leave Parliament?"

"Don't the historians know?" He grinned gently.

"They know he resigned from the Cabinet and later gave up his seat—but not why."

"All he ever told me was that his fiancée broke off their engagement and he was so knocked up by it that he couldn't carry on his duties."

"Wasn't that rather drastic?"

"It might seem so to you, but my uncle was a man of feeling and integrity—not like these bloody carpetbaggers we elect nowadays. And there was more to it. I know that he tried to withdraw his resignation, but they wouldn't let him. Don't ask me why. I don't think he knew himself. It was as if somebody had it in for him—somebody powerful, somebody nameless."

I didn't take him up on this but suggested another drink and waited at the bar while Ted poured them. I looked back at Ambrose, wreathed in pipesmoke in his rocking chair, an old, eccentric figure in tweed and sheepskin. I knew from the Memoir that he was seventy and the cider alone made him look it, but his eyes were like beacons in a sometimes foggy head and he had the storyteller's art of conviction combined with entrancement. He was, and looked, a ragbag of many things—gentleman drunk, crude countryman, aging redneck. I couldn't trust him but I couldn't resist him either. I knew he was drawing me on to some favoured, festering revelation and I half-knew what it must be. But I wanted to hear him say it. Maybe I already knew I would trade for that his dead uncle's words that he'd never heard before.

"There's a disused railway line across the Barrowteign estate," he began again, after a quaff of cider.

"I know," I said. "I saw the track bed where it crosses the drive."

"You've sharper eyes than I thought then." He looked impressed. "It's been blotted out quite a lot of the way. Never made any money, you see. It was opened in 1903, not long before I was born, and closed in 1958—just 55 years' existence: hell of a waste of all those bricks and tons of earth the navvies sweated blood to shift. The Great Western had their reasons though. They needed a fall-back for when the coastal route was flooded. In those days they didn't just cancel trains because of high seas, like these bloody jokers British Rail. They gouged a line through whatever was in their way as an alternative. I expect you think I'm rambling: bloody old fool, you're saying to yourself."

"Nothing of the kind." Which was true, because I knew the point he was leading up to.

"Well, in those 55 wasteful years, that pipsqueak of a railway line—that over-engineered wet weather alternative—claimed three members of my family. They called 'em accidents. Death pacts, I'd say—and worse. However much the GWR paid my grandfather to cross his land, it wasn't enough. Barrowteign's the only flat land in this part of the valley, so they had to go through it. You put a crack express on the route in an emergency and it's the only bit of it where he can work up any speed. And that's how the Teign Valley railway line claimed my parents."

His eyes widened and his thin voice strained oratorically: he was enjoying himself. Of course, I'd heard it all before—and read about it in the Memoir—but Ambrose made it sound different. That diverted express on the evening of 5 January 1911 bearing down on Robert's car ceased to be a ghastly accident and became an avenging fury scenting as victim the Strafford blood line. It left Ambrose orphaned and the family maimed. Edwin became a crippled regent, the Straffords' Fisher King, unable to lift the curse that laid them waste. "By 1951 the National Trust had taken over Barrowteign and settled me—of all the bloody ironies—in the crossingkeeper's cottage on the railway line where my parents had been killed.

"My uncle arrived one wet evening in the middle of May—without warning. I'd thought he was in Madeira. Then, out of the blue, there he was on the bloody doorstep, just as I was lighting a pipe and thinking of stepping down here for a jar. Old Jess—this one's mother—didn't bark, which was unusual, so I might've guessed it was him—hair more white than grey, stooped but still square-shouldered. He was in his greatcoat, carrying a battered old leather suitcase. I'd not seen him for six years but somehow didn't feel surprised that he was there. He wouldn't say what he'd been up to, only that he'd been in London and would I mind putting him up for a while? 'Course, I didn't mind. But he wasn't the uncle I remembered from my visits to Madeira. All he wanted was pen, paper and silence. He had a whacking great book in his case and spent hours at a time scribbling in it. God knows what it was about. When I asked, he turned . . . well, furtive: that's the only bloody word for it. And that was something he'd never been before. It rattled me, I can tell you."

My ears had pricked up. Strafford, writing in his great book. What could that be? His Memoir had finished the year before. What, then, was this?

"He hardly went out during the day. The odd stroll after dark. One trip into Exeter. He wouldn't come into the village with me. I couldn't work it out. It just wasn't like him. But in another way it was. The sad reflection there'd always been in his eyes was in his mind and voice too. That was the only difference. It was as if he was hiding from something, but didn't much mind if it found him anyway. 'Course I badgered him, but he wouldn't tell me a bloody thing. 'It's just a flying visit,' he said. 'Treat it as an old man's farewell.' What the hell did that mean?"

"Quite a lot, judging by what happened."

"Too bloody true. About a week after he arrived, he had a visitor. I came back from here one afternoon and they were in my little bit of garden. My uncle and this other chap. About the same age—but frailer, well-dressed in a cashmere overcoat, for all that it was bloody May. They were arguing. No, that's the wrong word. There was just this cold fury between them which made me think of winter. Old men don't argue—'cept when they're drunk, like I do. They haven't the energy for it—take my word on that. But these two were at odds: no question. The stranger was bald and red in the face. I remember he looked strung between pleading and bluster. As for my uncle, he was calm and grave—like a carved image.

"Soon as I showed up, the stranger left. He shot me a glare and made off to his car—a bloody great Bentley with a chauffeur in it—tucked away up the drive. He didn't speak—I remember that. But it was like he was biting back some oath. As for my uncle, he wouldn't discuss it. 'Just a passer-by seeking directions,' he said. Beyond that, he clammed up.

"That night though, we talked about the family and Barrowteign, about my parents—'cos he remembered 'em and I hardly did. He told me how he'd often thought it should've been him killed on the level crossing, not my father, him, with nothing to live for, not my father with a wife, a young son and a future. What little he had, he said, he'd leave me to remember him by. That amounted to a house in Madeira—I sold it. But it didn't seem like the remembrance he had in mind that night.

"After that, he took to mooning round the crossing quite a lot. I'd see him there as I came up the lane—like a bloody stormcrow in his flapping coat, almost like he was standing guard over something. It made me restless. And Old Jess. She'd wake in the middle of the night, barking at nothing. But was it nothing? Sometimes I'd think there were footprints in the garden where I'd not stepped, sometimes things moved, paint chipped round windows when it shouldn't. But with a railway on your doorstep, who the hell could be sure of anything?

"The night before my uncle died though, there was something to be sure of. To settle my nerves, I'd been in the juice till late and slept like one of these logs. If Old Jess barked, I didn't hear her. But there was some bloody commotion— a glass breaking somewhere—so I turned out. I found 'em in the parlour. My uncle fully dressed and alert—as if he hadn't been asleep—holding this young feller in an arm lock. Bulky character with an ugly, pampered face—'bout your age—lots of huff but no bloody puff to judge by the way my old uncle had wrong-footed him. He was snarling something when I came in, but I can't remember what—I was still full of sleep. I was all for having the blighter banged up for the night as the police house. But my uncle wouldn't hear of it. He just bundled him out with a kind of dismissive contempt. Called him a 'worthless felon' and this chap took off without another word. Only he was no felon. No felon I ever met dressed as well as him or got the worst of run-ins with 75-year-old men. Besides, break-ins are rare enough round here now. Then they were bloody unheard-of. We both knew there was more to it. But my uncle still said nothing.

"That's why it's one hell of a coincidence to swallow that his death the following night, when the train hit him on the level crossing, was an accident. Like everything else about that man, there was more to it."

"But what?"

"Murder, young man. Murder premeditated and concealed. But murder it was—plain as the nose on your face."

"What did the Coroner think?"

"Nothing. The man was bloody incapable of thought. All he could talk about was safety standards on unmanned level-crossings. Strangers after dark—intimations of violence—

were an unknown world to him. Anything I said was just the bloody cider talking."

"Was there no evidence?"

"I'm not talking about evidence. I'm talking about feelings, suspicions, certainties." He prodded his finger at me with each noun, then suddenly relaxed with a kind of deflation. "If I had some evidence, somebody might've listened to me."

"It's never too late."

"After 26 years, young man, it's just an old bore's fireside story. Something to entertain strangers." He looked wistful at the thought. I couldn't not tell him the one thing that might alter everything.

"It's a fascinating story. I believe every word of it."

"Good of you to say so."

"No, really. I believe it because it fits so well with some information I have. Something you won't know about. Something that could be said to constitute evidence."

His brow furrowed. He peered at me with his hooded eyes. "What information?"

"All in good time." I leant forward. "Why don't we take a look at the crossing? You could tell me exactly how the so-called accident happened and I could see for myself. Then I could tell you what I know."

"This is a bloody fine turn-up for the books. I'm supposed to be the storyteller, not you." He smiled at the thought. We'd been in the pub some time—it was filling up now—and I was anxious to continue our conversation in private. The element of the unknown I'd introduced looked to have persuaded Ambrose to do the same. "Okay. Let's go. I could do with a walk. There's nothing to see but I'll show you anyway. Then you can contribute your twopenn'orth."

He hauled himself out of the rocker, stirred Jess gently with his boot, seized his stick from beside the fire and led me out, greeting a dozen red-faced drinkers as he went who all seemed surprised—if not sorry—to see him leaving early.

It had grown dark outside and, though the last tinge of blue hadn't yet left the sky, the stars were out—so much brighter than in the city where I usually saw them that I stared up at them in surprise.

"It was like this that night," Ambrose said, so close to my ear that I started. "Still and moonlit. But it was a full moon, so there was a chalky light making everything plain as day—no weather for accidents."

We set off back the way I'd come in daylight, down the lane out of Dewford to the main road, then over the ancient stone bridge across the river. Ambrose said nothing, as if, like me, in awe of the night. His boots grated on the tarmac, his dog pattered beside him and, somewhere, a fox barked. Otherwise, the stillness and silence were uncanny. It might have been a night in 1951, not 1977, for all the difference it made in the darkness of the Devon countryside.

It made, of course, one big difference. There was, as we left the main drive up to Barrowteign and followed the lane to Lodge Cottage, no railway line across our path, only one of the crossing gates, serving now a different role.

Ambrose kicked up some gravel with his boot. "That's some of the bloody hardcore," he said. "I kept it as a drive to my garage. I built a cucumber frame out of sleepers and trained clematis round a warning sign. There's not much else left—the gate, some fencing, the cattle grid. It doesn't tell you a hell of a lot, does it?"

"I suppose not." And it didn't. To the south, the line petered out unevenly on flat ground beside the lime trees. To the north, beyond the black outline of the garage, was the blacker shape of a shallow cutting. Leaving me standing on the line, Ambrose went into the garden and unlocked his door. Stepping inside, he turned on a lamp above it which lit up the scene a little more. "What exactly happened, then?"

Ambrose walked across to the fence and leant on it as he spoke to me.

"Trains from Exeter used to come out of the cutting on a slight curve and accelerate over the crossing. They always whistled and, anyway, you got to know their times. There wasn't really any danger. My father was unlucky. He got his car stuck on the crossing in snow and a diverted express ploughed straight into them. Just one of those bloody things, I suppose."

"But not in your uncle's case?"

"No. Some days the visibility's poorer here than it was that night. And there wasn't a breath of wind. So if he was standing here having a quiet smoke—which he did most nights—he'd have heard the train miles off and, if not, still seen it in bags of time."

"But he didn't?"

"You tell me. The driver saw nothing wrong till the last moment—a figure crouched low on the track. Hit him at full speed. Death would have been instant. At least it was a painless way to go." He puffed at his pipe and the smoke made me think of the train that night, bearing down on the crossing, Strafford helpless in its path.

"Perhaps he just didn't hear. Old men's faculties do fail."

"Not my uncle's. It's my belief he couldn't move. At the inquest, the driver talked about seeing somebody else near the crossing—moving quickly. Not much more than a shadow. The Coroner disregarded it."

"Where were you at the time?"

He snorted. "I was at The Greengage. The landlord then—Ted's father—kept pretty relaxed hours. And events had unsettled me, so I wasn't averse to staying after time—more's the bloody pity. While I was up there, somebody—the shadow the driver thought he saw—disabled my uncle and dumped him in the path of the train. That's how I see it."

"But you've no proof?"

"Not a bean. Unless you can put some where your mouth is." He laughed, more, I think, because he felt sure I'd been joking than because he didn't want to sound harsh.

"I think I can. You could call it your uncle's side of the story."

"Then come inside, young man. I've waited a long time to hear that."

I shuddered slightly in the warm night air. I'd gone all the way now and committed myself to showing him the Memoir. It wasn't at all what I'd intended in my guarded approach to him at the pub, but, somehow, the place and the person had seduced me. Strafford had once told his nephew he could have what little there was to remember him by, so who was I to hold it back?

We went into the cottage, the entrance hall low and a little musty. Jess, who'd been waiting for us on the mat, jumped up and led the way into a small front room. There was a faint glow from the fireplace and the curtains were open on a bay window overlooking the moonlit garden and what was once the railway line. Ambrose turned on a standard lamp and began gouging at the ashes of the fire with a poker while I looked around.

The room was crowded and dusty, more like an attic than a lounge. The wallpaper, whatever its original colour, had turned the shade of Ambrose's tobacco. Bookshelves, fitted in each alcove, climbed to the ceiling. These, various chairs and several tea chests wedged behind the chairs overflowed not just with books large and small, but folders, sheets of card and paper, empty picture frames, newspapers, albums and portfolios. In amongst all this, room had been found for a couple of wingback easy chairs either side of the fire. There was a bureau by the wall with so many pulled-out drawers, used envelopes, scraps of paper, stubs of pencil, empty cheque books and stray pipe cleaners in it that the flap couldn't have been closed in months. Amid the debris stood a glass tumbler with a shallow pool of cider in it. On a folding table behind the door stood a large, old-fashioned valve radio and a scatter of plastic pieces from an airfix kit. Finished articles—a Spitfire, a bi-plane and what looked like H.M.S. *Hood*—were arranged on top of a tallboy in one of the corners. There were several Indian artefacts—a carved ivory elephant, a brass casting of Kali, various trinkets and bric-à-brac—jockeying for space with some seedy-looking cacti in pots. Under the window was a round wicker basket with a blanket in it. Jess climbed in and looked quizzically at us, as if wondering why we were so active at such an hour.

Ambrose had added some smaller twigs and a log to the fire and coaxed it into some sort of life. "That'll burn nicely now," he announced, stooping behind one of the armchairs and raising an earthenware flagon. He pulled out the cork stopper. "D'you want a drink?" I'd had enough already but I agreed. "Sit down. Make yourself at home." I cleared a newspaper and one of his pipes out of a chair—the upholstery pockmarked with burns and nicotine stains—and sat down. Ambrose fetched some tumblers and poured us generous measures.

"Cosy little place you've got here," I said.

"Don't soft soap me, boy. It's a bloody tip and you know it. But Jess and I have come to like it." He chuckled. "Besides, I keep a warmer bar than Ted." It was true—the logs were burning nicely. "Now tell me about what you said outside."

"It's here." I patted the napsack that I'd looped over the arm of the chair.

"What the hell is it?"

I didn't keep him in suspense. This time, I told him the truth—about the new occupant of Quinta do Porto Nova hiring me, about Strafford's Memoir, about what it contained and what it didn't contain. Ambrose listened quietly, puffing at his pipe and staring into the fire. Without waiting for him to ask, I took the Memoir out of the bag and handed it to him—with a kind of reverence in the gesture. He looked at it with bemusement.

"Is this all there is to it, then?" he asked. "You walk in—the man from bloody nowhere—and hand me my uncle's last testament on a plate?"

"Not exactly. My arrival is, as you say . . . fortuitous. But you could've seen it a long time ago. It was at the Quinta waiting for you."

"Irony, thy name is Strafford. Maybe that's what he meant about an inheritance. I thought it was just that rambling old adobe in Madeira. I sold it without even going over to take a look—bloody shortsighted of me." He peered at the cover of the Memoir, cradled in his lap. "One thing. This looks pretty much like the book he was writing in when he was here. Did he send it back to Madeira before he died?"

"Maybe. But there's a discrepancy. That Memoir finishes in October 1950."

"Hmm." He leafed through the pages. "The old bugger's hand—no mistake. But not the same book you say? I never found the one he wrote in while he was here. I scoured through his effects—which God knows were few enough—and couldn't have missed it. But it wasn't there."

"Then what happened to it?"

"You tell me. Maybe he lost interest and destroyed it. Maybe he sent it back to Madeira and it's been lost. Maybe it was this one and he was just amending or updating it."

"That could be." Actually, I didn't see how it could. Ambrose rummaged between the cushion and the arm of his chair, fished out a battered pair of half-moon spectacles, perched them on his nose and began to read. I refilled my glass—there was a standing invitation—and thought, suddenly, of Nick and Hester. Shouldn't I tell them I wouldn't be back that night? "Do you have a telephone?" I asked. No answer—eyes glued to the Memoir. "Ambrose! Do you have a phone?"

He looked up sharply. "Course not—tomfool gadgets. There's a box in the village."

"That's a long way."

"Then don't go. Shut up and leave me to read. Have another drink."

"I just have."

"Typical of the ingrate young. Well, read something yourself. God knows, there's enough here."

My mind was on a different tack. "Those effects of your uncle you mentioned . . ."

"Two birds with one stone. There wasn't much—clothes I burned—a few bits and pieces. One book. Have a look at it. Maybe it'll shut you up." He hauled himself out of the chair, navigated unerringly to one of the shelves and shuffled through a stack of books, clicking his tongue. "Here"—he plucked one out—"a collection of poems. That was all. We Straffords are a mawkish lot given half a chance."

He tossed it down to me, then settled back in the opposite chair with the Memoir. I looked at the book he'd fetched—a slim, battered, well-thumbed volume: *Satires of Circumstance* by Thomas Hardy—first edition, 1914. I might have known Strafford would have chosen Hardy for his travelling companion. The titles of the poems were redolent of the mood of the Memoir: 'The Going', 'Your Last Drive', 'Rain on a Grave', 'Lament', 'The Hunter', and so on. One, 'After a Journey', had had its page marked and its title ringed in red. I read it through—wistful, allusive, elegiac like the others, but I saw no more than that in it. Which was just one of my mistakes.

It was morning. Grey light was shafting through the grimy bay window. White ash lay in the grate. I was still in the armchair, neck wricked like it was broken, my back aching only slightly less than my head, my throat protesting at the merest swallow. So this, I thought, is a cider hangover. I kicked a half-glass of the stuff as I struggled up, spilling it on the threadbare hearth rug, cursed and hoisted the remainder up for safekeeping on the mantelpiece. There, I was reassured to see, I'd put *Satires of Circumstance* some time during the night, probably for the same reason. The Memoir was there too.

I rubbed my eyes and coughed speculatively. My senses were beginning to work again. There was a smell of bacon frying somewhere, and Ambrose whistling tunelessly. I followed the signs out of the room, down the short passage and into the kitchen—small, low-ceilinged, flagged floor. Opposite me, the top half of a stable door stood open onto the garden. To the right, on a rickety table beneath a window, there was a large teapot, with some cups and plates—decent but old and chipped—a bottle with some milk in the bottom, a marmalade jar with a knife standing up in it like a tin soldier, a much-gouged pat of butter and half a loaf of bread surrounded by crumbs. Jess was eating from a bowl by the door, but stopped to look at me. There was a big old range in the chimneybreast to my left. Ambrose stood by it, resplendent in a spotted and stained butcher's apron, prodding bacon, eggs and tomatoes round a vast, black, encrusted frying pan. He cocked one eye at me and stopped whistling.

"You look bloody awful," he said. "Want some breakfast?"

"No thanks. Tea, if you have any."

"Loads in the pot. Help yourself." I slumped down at the table and poured some into a willow-pattern breakfast cup. Ambrose decanted his meal onto a plate and sat down with it opposite me. "Cider disagree with you?"

"Lack of practice"—between sips—"I suppose."—"You seem fine."

"Ah, but it was an abstemious evening for me. I had all that reading to do."

"Did you finish?"

"'Course I bloody finished." He gave me an egg-smeared glare. "And had a couple of hours for a stroll at dawn while you were sleeping off the cider."

"What do you make of it, then?"

He poured tea from a great height into his cup. "First, Martin, I feed the inner man. Then I think." So I had to wait till he'd soaked up the last of the fat from his plate with the bread, tossed an end of rasher to Jess, drained the pot and lit his pipe, before he resumed. "It took me back," he puffed, "in both senses. I'd thought about him, remembered him of course, but it's not the same thing. He was a remote, reticent man to me—absent in mind if not in body. Now—long after—he becomes different. A whole man with a story to tell—a tragedy, I should say."

"It does seem to bring him alive."

"But what about his death, eh lad? Doesn't it just raise as many questions as it answers? The dark forces moving against him—who the hell were they? Lloyd George? Churchill? This man Couchman?"

"I don't know."

"And why did Elizabeth ditch him?"

"That's the central question. I'm sure the rest turns on that. But just asking her won't help—as your uncle found."

"Then what?"

"It seems logical to suppose that, in some way, he was discredited in her eyes. There were several people who stood to gain from that."

"Who?"

"A list of suspects isn't difficult. He knew Gerald Couchman to be a cheat and a coward—enemy number one. He defied Lloyd George over his plans to oust Asquith—enemy number two. He was the reason Elizabeth Latimer withdrew from Suffragette circles—they were therefore enemy number three. Your own mother disliked him enough to snoop into his fiancée's background—enemy number four."

"Poor old Mother," he mused. "I couldn't bear to have any of her pictures down here, you know. Left 'em all up at the house. Can't see her blackening her brother-in-law's name, though."

"She wanted to split them up."

"Granted, but by blackening Elizabeth, not my uncle. No, that's too devious. Besides, she's dead and gone."

"So?"

"So what about his death? Strangers sniffing round, breaking in, rowing with him. Then an accident that stinks of murder. What the hell's that got to do with my poor old mother?"

"Nothing, I suppose." I hadn't believed it myself. "But nothing with Lloyd George either—he died in 1945—or the Suffragettes."

"Then this blighter Couchman?"

"Again, unlikely. I was stretching a point to say he might have had it in for your uncle. He wasn't in touch at all at the time of the engagement—not even in the country." We'd talked in a circle and got nowhere.

And that's how we went on. Ambrose was subdued and soulful away from the cider, puffing at his pipe with the look of a bemused, slightly pained, old man. I was holding out on him, not telling him about my connexion with the Couchmans or my encounter with Henry. I was afraid he might insist on seeing Henry and blow any chances I hadn't already blown myself. I was happy to pump good old Ambrose for all he was worth, but keeping him in the dark suited my purpose. I saw a link between Henry's panicky denials of knowing Strafford and heavy-footed intruders at Lodge Cottage in 1951. But I wanted more to go on before trying to prove it. Historical instinct—plus the fact that Henry was himself a politician—prompted me to suspect a political conspiracy against Strafford, but I wanted to test that idea in scholastic circles in Cambridge before going any further. Ambrose had told me all I expected to get out of him. So I began to regret even showing him the Memoir and decided to tell him no more. It was another mistake, of course—more culpable than any before. I should have trusted Ambrose—as he trusted me. But I was incapable of that.

After breakfast, we took Jess out for a stroll round the grounds. Barrowteign was just opening for business, the first visitors trickling in. But it was still quiet and peaceful as we ambled among the horse chestnuts and looked up the sloping ground to the broad frontage of the house. There was still dew on the grass and mist lifting only slowly from the trees. Ambrose stirred last year's conker cases with his stick and contemplated what had once been his home.

"I never go up there now," he said. "Too many bloody memories, I suppose."

"Did your uncle, when he stayed with you?"

"Not that I can recall." He sucked his pipe. "'Course, there were workmen swarming all over it that year—restoration they called it. Tarting up I'd say, from what I've seen." He shook his head dolefully. "He asked me a lot about what they'd done, though, where they'd put all the stuff they moved."

"And what had they done?"

"Chucked a lot. Stowed the rest in the attics. A lot of stuff I've forgotten is probably still up there under the dustsheets." He sighed. "Best place for it, I suppose."

We turned away from Barrowteign, left the grounds by a stile Ambrose knew and walked down across the river. It was getting warmer all the time and we seemed to be making for The Greengage.

"Hair of the dog, Martin," Ambrose said. "That's what you need. I just need a bloody drink. My uncle came here with me at midday after that break-in, the day before he died. It was a scorcher—early June—and we sat outside and drank beer to calm our nerves. Mine needed it after that, God knows, and though my uncle didn't show it, I reckon his did too." We turned in at the door of the pub and he looked across to the small garden behind it, with chairs stacked on tables and an early season look about it. "The drink must have made him sentimental. I remember him talking about that toy castle he made for me when he came home from the Great War. What had I done with it?" Then, almost as an afterthought: "It was a bloody good castle, though."

We were Ted's only customers at that hour. He stood polishing glasses and holding them up to the light, while I winced through my first drink and Ambrose made smoke. His eyes sparkled through the haze and altogether he looked remarkably unlike a man who'd just had a sleepless night. He was busy recollecting the mysterious past, to him more refreshing than any rest.

But not to Ted. "You still blatherin' on 'bout that, Ambrose?"

"I'm not complaining," I put in.

"Maybe you would if you'd 'eard it many times as I 'as."

"Facts are facts," Ambrose snapped. "I didn't imagine that housebreaker. Have you forgotten that?"

"I remember right 'nough. I remember Constable Sprague comin' in and askin' my old dad and me if any strangers 'ad been askin' after your uncle 'afore that blessed break-in. 'Course they 'adn't—not 'afore like."

"Wait for it, Martin," Ambrose said with a grimace. "Ted will now torment me with what he failed to tell the Coroner." In a tone of mock enthusiasm: "Well, Ted, did anyone ask about my uncle *after* the break-in?"

"Somebody did."

"But you didn't think to mention it to Sprague?"

"Well, it weren't 'afore the break-in were it, like 'e asked. It were after."

"But it was before he died, wasn't it? The afternoon before, to be bloody precise."

Ted nodded slowly. "Might've been."

"It was when you first told me, Ted, far too late for the inquest of course."

"Dain't prove nothin', do it?"

"No," Ambrose said with a sigh.

And nor did it. What did we have? Strafford lying low in Devon while a person or persons unknown tried to find him. Why? Strafford dead in a bizarre accident. Just that or something more sinister? A cidery old nephew cultivating conspiracies at the fag end of his family fortunes. Or was he really onto something? I had to believe the latter if only out of respect for Strafford. But I badly needed substance rather than suspicion and that's what Ambrose couldn't give me.

I phoned Hester from The Greengage, assured her I was all right and said I'd be back with them by evening. Ambrose volunteered—which was good of him—to drive me to Exeter, so we walked back to the cottage, collected the Memoir and climbed into his ancient, rusting Morris Minor. Jess hopped into the back and we took off up through the valley at a mad speed. Ambrose talked as he drove, and smoked, and kept turning to me to emphasize points, none of which made for a restful journey. He had no difficulty extracting from me a promise to send him a copy of the Memoir or keep him posted on my research, but I was, at the time, more concerned about the horse-box we were overtaking.

As we approached Exeter, he quizzed me about Sellick and I found myself being evasive. "It's just that he has the money to indulge his interest in an historical mystery." Ambrose signalled his doubts about that but I didn't share them. He didn't know Sellick and I was in no mood to indulge him.

"What's next on your bloody agenda then?" Ambrose asked as we pulled up in the Bennetts' cul-de-sac, the prim little properties looking a thousand miles from Barrowteign.

"Cambridge: to find out what the historians make of it all."

"Just go on digging, lad. Believe me, there's something buried."

"That's what I think, too." I picked up my bag. "Well, thanks for all your help."

"Don't mention it." He smiled and shook my hand firmly. Then he gave me one of his endearing winks. "I'll go on digging too, remember that. Together, I reckon we could come up with something—one hell of a something."

"I'll keep in touch."

Hester and Nick were good enough not to be annoyed by my failure to turn up the night before and I entertained them with an account of my lost 24 hours with Ambrose. I spent the next day in the City Library looking up old local papers for mentions of the fatal accident.

There was a brief paragraph in an issue of 5 June 1951, a fuller report of the inquest two weeks later. As Ambrose had said, there was much talk of the safety record of the Barrowteign crossing, none of the death being anything other than accidental. As for the driver's recollection of a figure running away from the scene at the time, the Coroner asked the jury to bear in mind how upset the driver had been by the collision. This was tantamount to inviting them to ignore that piece of evidence, which they duly did. The Coroner conjectured that an elderly man alarmed on the crossing by the approach of a train might easily have stumbled or trapped his foot between the rails in trying to hurry away. The jury went along with that and brought in a verdict of accidental death. One short sentence describing Ambrose's evidence showed how little attention he'd been given. And it had rankled ever since. On Friday, I returned to London for a weekend in limbo. I was keen to go up to Cambridge straight away, but the college couldn't offer me a guest room till Monday. I knuckled down to writing another report for Sellick, making as much as I dared of Ambrose's allegations of foul play. As far as it went, it was accurate and honest. I felt more confident now, more in control. Little did I know that my peace of mind was merely self-delusion.

Four

I peered through the grime on the window of a grubby, jolting old Eastern Region train at that sprawl of derelict sidings you pass through just outside Liverpool Street station. Sunlight on that sea of rust only added to its bleakness. Yet it was familiar as well as bleak: a starting point on my once regular journeys to Cambridge. I remembered—as I always remembered—shivering at the first sight of those hostile stretches of Essex on my first journey twelve years before. At first intimidated, later seduced and lastly appalled by the alien pleasures of that city in the Fens, I was nevertheless still drawn to it and secretly welcomed the opportunity Sellick had given me to go back again. After all, despite my carpings, for all my reservations, Cambridge had given me three years a good deal nearer the top than the seven years since. Pampered, narcissistic, overweening—all of those things it was, and more. But was that so much worse than what I'd become?

Princes' Hall, the grey eminence sandwiched between Corpus Christi and Pembroke Colleges, had always been a world unto itself. It was no different that cool evening, with a sheet of mottled cloud slung across the sun, as I paid off the taxi and eyed the place, through the black and gold arrow-topped railings on its front wall, with the same suspicion it had always seemed to reserve for me: a grass and cobble court, Tudor cloisters down one side, a Victorian hall on the other, a Gothic chapel at the far end. "Good for history," those who'd advised me to apply to it had said, and they'd been right—for a certain kind of history: long on knowledge and memory, short on imagination and humanity.

Next morning, I went early to the University Library, that towering structure on the left bank of the Cam with a spire to rival Salisbury, but dedicated to a different kind of god: learning of the dessicated, bibliomanic variety. The writings of all the leading politicians of Strafford's day were there. I waited for them to be fetched from the archives in the huge reading room—silently aswarm with students cramming for finals—and felt a secret pride at my more subtle errand. In fact, this part of it told me next to nothing. Virtually every Cabinet colleague of Strafford's had left some testament to posterity—memoirs, letters, diaries, autobiography—but after a day sifting through them I'd gleaned nothing, except added respect for Strafford as a writer and a man.

The scantiness of the references was, like the dog that didn't bark, suspicious in itself. And nowhere was there any substantiation of Baxter's surmise that Strafford had resigned in order to panic Asquith into an early election. That, I consoled myself over a currant bun in the Library tea room, was the weak point where I could open my attack on the well-armoured historical hide of Marcus Baxter.

I chose the hour before dinner to call on his room—a spacious, three-windowed apartment over an arch to the left of the chapel—and was in luck. When I knocked, his hoarse, bellowed "Come" was at once familiar.

It was always said of Baxter that he didn't so much enter a room as invade it. When it was his own, he didn't inhabit it so much as infest it. There was about him a strange combination of the seedy and the glamorous, the louche and the honourable. An aroma distinctive of his proud perversity—or was it an odour?—hung around the room and transported me instantly back to my many previous visits, all of them more deferential than this one. There was still a mix of old books, fine whisky, stale onions and cheap cigarettes in the air, still the look of an old bull remembering spring about Baxter as he glared up at his visitor. He was seated on a utility chair, rasping into a pocket dictating machine, while the velvet-upholstered *chaise-lounge* by the window, where he could have had a good view of the court, was piled instead with books and papers, and the wooden swivel chair behind the crowded desk stood empty. The room was given over completely to books and papers, the only decoration being a small bust of Cromwell on a pedestal in one corner and a drinks cabinet entirely stocked with malt whiskey in another. Unless, that is, you counted Baxter himself—a short, stocky, weatherbeaten figure with the look of a prizefighter about him, blue towelling bathrobe wrapped over his day clothes, high tar cigarette in the corner of his mouth, grey and balding but still with that widow's peak that lent a devilish air to the crumpled face.

"Who's that?" he barked, peering through the fug of his own creation.

"Martin Radford—remember?"

Baxter may have meant to smile, but the effort of keeping his cigarette where it was converted the expression into a crooked leer. "Naturally, my boy. Class of '67." His memory was intact, as I might have known. "What stone have you crawled out from under?"

"Teaching, you might say."

"Best thing—for you and it. Have a drink." As ever, he made no move to fetch one for me, so I poured some myself. "What's your excuse for creeping back here? You know I don't encourage it."

"Why is that?" I asked, topping up his own drink and trying not to be nettled.

"Because, my boy, the ones who come back to tell me how successful they've been tend to be those I thought the least of." He consented to remove the cigarette from his mouth, but only to swallow some whisky.

"That's all right then." I cleared a space on the *chaise lounge* and settled in it. "I've no successes to tell you about."

"Then I'll agree not to say what I thought of you."

"What about you? How are the books going?"

"I've got a biography of Bonar Law coming along."

Time for a dig of my own. "Wasn't he rather a dull dog?"

"That's the whole point. I don't want gossip column stuff getting in the way of politics. Did he drink? Did he go with women—or young boys? Who cares? Did he create an Irish problem to dish the Liberals?—that's more like it."

"I'm doing a little bit of historical research myself at the moment."

He snorted into his whisky. "Better late than never."

"That's why I dropped by. Noticed from the records that you'd been there before me."

"Where?" Baxter made it sound as if I was insulting him.

"Edwin Strafford. Home Secretary under Asquith. You wrote his D.N.B. entry."

Baxter grinned. "Radford, this must be the first time you've read anything I've written. I trust you were impressed."

I ignored the sarcasm and threw in some of my own. "I found the length manageable but the conclusions questionable." It could've been him commenting on an essay of mine.

"Ho, ho. Strong words indeed. As always, Radford, I must ask you: where's your evidence?"

"It's more a question of where's yours? Do you remember how you explained Strafford's sudden resignation from the Home Office in 1910?"

Baxter flapped his hand at an imaginary fly. "Of course I do. Strafford was just a busted flush. Wanted to be a politician with clean hands. When he found he couldn't be, he tried to pressurize Asquith into calling an election and scrapping the Constitutional Conference. I think he regarded compromise as sordid. Too much of a gentleman to be involved in that. Too big a fool to see that his resignation was pointless. No power base, you see—no political nous."

"But how do you know that's why he resigned?"

"Why else? It fits the picture: an empty gesture by an irrelevant dilettante."

"It sounds like pure prejudice to me."

"Then what do you think?"

"I've got hard evidence that he resigned in order to marry a Suffragette."

Baxter threw up his hands and guffawed. "And Bonar Law was Jack the Ripper. Thank God you quit teaching, Radford."

I tried to stay cool. "I think you'll find my evidence a good deal more convincing than yours."

"I doubt it. What've you got?"

"A memoir left by Strafford—newly discovered among his papers in Madeira."

A primary historical source was pure gold to Baxter, so, for all his sneering, a prospector's glint came into his eye. "Could be interesting. But don't make the old mistake of believing what a politician says about himself."

"In this case I do. It shows that Strafford tried to withdraw his resignation immediately after submitting it but wasn't allowed to—something conveniently overlooked in your DNB piece."

"I'd heard that, but it only confirms what I think of him. Lost his nerve as soon as he realized how weak his position was. Asquith would hardly have wanted him back after that. If your Suffragette nonsense was correct, why did his ardour cool so quickly?"

"It didn't: he was thrown over."

"Then why didn't Asquith take him back?"

"Exactly what I'm trying to find out. I believe one or more of his Cabinet colleagues conspired to ruin his reputation."

"Who—and why?"

"Lloyd George seems favourite. He tried to entice Strafford into secret negotiations with Balfour to form a coalition and oust Asquith."

"When?"

"June 1910—immediately before his resignation."

"Then your chronology's out. Lloyd George *did* discuss the possibility of a coalition with Balfour—but not until the autumn of that year."

"Then either Lloyd George was lying when he told Strafford about it or we simply don't realize how early he started exploring the idea."

"Or Strafford's led you up the garden path."

"I don't think so."

"Well, since you're here at this time, do you want to be led into Hall? I'm going across." He rose, flung his bathrobe over the back of the door and struggled into it. I agreed readily enough and followed him out onto the court, where evening sun was shining on the cobbles—wet from an afternoon shower—and gowned figures were beginning to trickle in to the summoning dinner bell.

Then came the first sign that Baxter was thinking about what I'd said to him. "Why should Lloyd George need to ruin Strafford," he pondered, almost to himself, "just because he refused to participate in negotiations with Balfour?"

"Because Strafford then knew enough to discredit Lloyd George in the party's eyes and scupper the negotiations before they'd even started. It's my belief Lloyd George feared Strafford's youth and ability enough to need either his complicity—or his head."

Baxter stopped in his tracks and pursed his lips against his finger. "Your version has all the appeal of a skimpy garment on a beautiful woman, Radford—eye-catching, but not much use in bad weather. First, verify your source—let the U.L. take a look at it. Second, spend a few months with all the other contemporary material. Third, assemble your case. Then come back."

"I don't have time for all that."

"Then you don't have time for history."

I bit my lip and we went on into dinner. Baxter was greeted jocularly at high table; he introduced me cursorily and inaudibly. In the seat opposite us, an etiolated figure wrapped in the folds of an oversized gown measured his porcelain profile against the candlelight and raised one hand feyly in welcome. "Marcus," he said, in a whine forgivable only for its vintage, "that you are come once more amongst us is unexpected justification for my risking again the perils of the chef's rabbit pie."

"Do cut the crap, Stephen," Baxter retorted. "Radford, meet Stephen Lamzed, our foremost art historian. Not here in your day. We poached him from King's."

"Pleased to meet you." I tried to sound non-committal.

"Enchanted." Somehow, Lamzed contrived to look it. His face, framed by long silver hair, was a mosaic of wrinkles, but I could have taken them for the cracked oil of an Old Master till the moment he wet his lips with the long, thin tongue of a lizard catching insects in the desert. "If you will permit me to say so, Marcus, it is too long since you last brought glad company to our table. To what do we owe the pleasure?"

Baxter smiled slyly. "Radford's investigating a Suffragette romance."

Lamzed winced. "What say you, young Radford?"

"You could put it that way. I'm researching an episode of Edwardian history that touches on the Suffragettes."

Lamzed began checking the cleanliness of his cutlery. "I confess that the study of women being forcibly fed and—which is worse—shouting at men holds no attractions for me, but it is much a vogue of late. Is not the history faculty a hotbed of feminist causes, Marcus?"

Baxter raised his eyebrows above nearly closed eyelids. "Hardly that."

"But I am not daily regaled with tales of the dark lady of Darwin? Is not the siren of the Sidgwick site the talk of every common room in Cambridge? And is she not a proponent of just such study?"

"Who do you mean?" I asked.

Baxter wrenched a bread roll in half. "He means there's a few lectures easier on the eye than me and one in particular who gets a good audience simply by being female and under fifty."

Lamzed's wrinkles organized themselves into a grin. "Marcus, you underestimate yourself. But it is certainly the case that Miss Randall enjoys a following which, even if less academically pure than your own, is nonetheless a shade larger and conspicuously more enthusiastic." Baxter returned the grin through clenched teeth and swayed out of the way of a bowl of soup. I waited for my own to arrive before pressing for details.

"Miss Eve Randall," Baxter explained, siphoning soup noisily from his spoon between phrases, "is a research fellow at Darwin. She gave a course of lectures last Michaelmas term on Edwardian protest movements. Well-received, I'm told."

"You didn't hear any?"

"They clashed with some of my own on imperialism. Stephen could no doubt give you the respective audience ratings." Lamzed bowed in acknowledgement. "Anyway, she's giving six more this term."

"Weight of popular demand," Lamzed breathed over the table.

"Edited highlights," Baxter continued, "for the benefit of those too starstruck to concentrate last time."

"Would it be worth my going along to one?"

Baxter let his spoon fall with a clatter into the now empty bowl and began to pick his teeth. "Why not? If you really want to work up a Suffragette angle to Strafford, you could bounce the idea of Miss Randall. I don't think she'll thank you for some hearts and flowers theory, though. She sees the Suffragettes as sexless Amazons."

Lamzed peered suspiciously at a solitary asparagus tip that he'd fished from his soup. "Wednesdays at ten," he intoned. "Queue early to avoid disappointment." I decided to do just that. Which was, though even I could be forgiven for not realizing it, another mistake. While Lamzed simpered on about the declining art of male lecturing—and Baxter cracked his teeth on rabbit boones—I quickened my pace down the steepening slope.

The Sidgwick site at ten the following morning—a cool, nondescript sort of day, with a scattering of distracted students around the stark, grey blockhouses of the arts faculty. It had been a new development when I'd first been a student there—a triumph of soulless 'sixties architecture—but was now looking older than its years: concrete stained, façades peeling, extractor fans straining. I sat outside the coffee bar watching the changeover between nine o'clock and ten o'clock lectures, then filed in at the back of a crocodile of students for the one we'd all been waiting for.

I sat at the back of the room and looked around, first self-consciously, then curiously, at the students, all busy comparing their reactions to last week's lecture and snapping open files with excessive enthusiasm. They looked younger and more serious than I'd expected: so many pimply youths and blue stockings. But perhaps that was just incipient middle age.

Still, there was no doubting the respectful nature of the hush that fell on the room a few moments later. A tall, elegant figure entered by a side door and walked briskly, but without hurrying, to the lectern: Eve Randall, a cool, grave beauty in a lemon dress beneath an academic gown, standing serene yet unsmiling at the head of the room. Her entrance was like a window opening in a stuffy room, but there was a keen edge to the breeze it let in. Her features had a fine distinction that made you catch your breath and the dark, lustrous hair curled on her shoulders with an alluring bounce, but the flashing eyes and slightly raised jaw told you the cat had claws. Not that there was any need for her to show them—the audience was in her power.

She spoke for forty-five minutes, fluently, without notes, calmly ordering and disclosing arguments in a beguiling sequence that made you want to agree with her, made you want her to be right. Her voice and her lecturing style were like a chilled apertif: enticing you to the main course. But the appetizer was all we got. Soon, the lecture was over and we were left with scraps of memory. For my part, the content of the talk had been inconsequential. She'd placed Suffragettes in the van of pressure politics, pioneering a way of reacting to unacceptable circumstances in a democracy. The fact that I didn't agree with that didn't really matter. The point was that I and everyone else there went along with Eve Randall because of her haughty, mysterious beauty—her style, her flair, her magnetism—not the logic of her thesis. "The extreme lengths of personal denial and humiliation to which these young women were driven illustrate the increasing failure of the Edwardian political machine to solve its problems. More lastingly, they removed British women forever from a Victorian walled garden and confronted them with the challenging but not always pleasing truth that they could only achieve change in society by sustained and united effort." So she ended, until the following week, though I don't suppose I was alone in regretting that she didn't continue.

A number of students—mostly girls—clustered round their idol afterwards, asking questions. I left them to it—I wanted to tackle her alone. I sat outside on a bench while the next bustle between lectures subsided. About five minutes later, the figure I'd been waiting for emerged from a side door of the hall. She walked well—I'd noticed that when she'd arrived for the lecture—and moved now gracefully but purposefully across the paved arena to the History Library—that ugly prow of brick and glass that was the site's crowning folly of modernist architecture. I'd been there often enough in the past to guess that Eve Randall would have been allocated one of the hutch-like offices in the upper reaches of the building and, while she went up in the lift, I checked a nameboard, traced her and made my way there by the stairs.

The door was open. A gown was draped over a chair behind the wood and tubular steel desk. The occupant of the room stood by the metal-framed window, gazing out at the red brick turrets of Selwyn College, while an electric kettle came to the boil in a corner. I tapped on the door and she turned to look at me.

A black lambswool cardigan had been put on over her dress. It softened the donnishness but not the conviction. I put her age at about my own, but without my grey hairs or ragged edges. She looked like a woman in perfect balance: between youth and maturity, character and beauty, womanhood and professionalism. This harmony expressed itself in an easy perfection that I'd viewed from afar in the lecture theatre and admired now at closer quarters. She'd dressed demurely for the occasion, but there were voluptuous hints to the fit of her clothes that I wasn't slow to take and her hair swayed with an almost calculated freedom as she turned her head. There was still no smile, as if the solemn scrutiny of her eyes must come before any courtesy.

"Miss Randall?"

"Yes." That was all—no reciprocal question as to who I was.

Steam gouted from the kettle to my left. "Shall I switch that off?" I asked.

"Please."

I did so. "I was at your lecture and came to tell you how much I enjoyed it."

"Thank you for saying so. It's good to hear."

"I'm sure you must have been told the same before. I believe the course has been very popular."

"You've not been before then. I don't think I recognize you."

"You wouldn't. This was my first time."

"Are you an undergraduate?" She looked doubtful.

"No. I'm not at the university at all." Then she looked suspicious. "I graduated some years ago from Princes'." I hoped that might sound better. "My name's Martin Radford."

She stood quite still for a moment. Her eyes, which had all along been intent, now stared at me. For a moment, I had the impression she was about to ask me to leave, as somebody with no business being on the premises. Instead, she slowly smiled, disconcertingly, with an air of relish. Then it broadened into something altogether friendlier and I felt at ease.

"I was just making some coffee. Would you like some?" I agreed and turned the kettle back on. She walked across and prepared two cups. "Won't you sit down?"

"Thanks." She went back and sat behind the desk. I took the only other chair available. It left me squinting slightly into the sun, with Eve silhouetted against the light. She'd arranged the furniture, I suspected, so as always to be at this advantage over visitors.

"Do you have a particular interest in the Suffragette period, Mr Radford?"

"More a specific one. I'm carrying out some research that has a bearing on the Suffragette cause."

"Really? We're in the same business then."

"Not exactly. I believe you're preparing a book on the subject."

"That's correct."

"Well, I'm not doing anything like that." I sipped some coffee. Eve remained quite motionless. "The Suffragettes are just one aspect of my assignment. But, as an expert on the subject, you might be interested in that aspect."

"You flatter me, Mr Radford. I've amassed a good deal of information on the Suffragettes. I'm not sure I'd call it expertise."

"I think most people would. What do you know of Edwin Strafford?"

"Home Secretary from 1908 to 1910. A moderate. Had he not resigned, McKenna might never have been there to introduce the Cat & Mouse legislation. The government might have coped with the situation better."

Now for a hunch—how much did she really know about the Suffragettes? "Or Elizabeth Latimer?"

She repeated the name and thought for a moment. "One of

the Putney set. She, Miriam Fane, Julia Lambourne and the Simey twins were followers of Christabel Pankhurst. From about 1906 to 1908 they were known as the Five Furies in Suffragette circles because of their daring stunts. They fell away after that and by 1911—when Christabel resumed her militant tactics after a truce—Lambourne and Latimer had certainly moved into the gradualist camp and soon out of the picture altogether."

I was taken aback. I'd got used to Strafford cropping up in books and records but it was new to hear Elizabeth spoken of in the same way—Strafford's Elizabeth, the Elizabeth I'd looked for in Sussex. "I didn't realize she was so well known."

"She wasn't. But I've gone so deeply into this that there aren't many active Suffragettes who I haven't heard of."

"What about a link between Strafford and Elizabeth Latimer?"

She sipped her coffee for the first time. "That's new to me. What sort of link?"

Then I told her about the Memoir and the broken engagement, the mystery and the broken man. Baxter had predicted hostility to this hint of feminine vulnerability in Suffragette ranks but none came. When I'd finished, Eve said nothing. Instead, a timer went off on a shelf behind me and made me jump, so long had the silence been.

"I'm sorry," she said, without stirring. "That tells me I'm late for a seminar. I must go. But the Strafford memoir interests me greatly. Can I see it?"

"I was hoping you'd agree to look at it."

"I'd love to. Could you bring it to my rooms in Darwin tomorrow afternoon? We could have a longer talk about it then."

She told me her room number and we agreed two o'clock. It had gone better than I'd hoped. Eve Randall was hooked and so, in a different way, was I. Still, I knew better than to spoil a good impression by hanging around. I rose to go.

"Tell me," she said, "are you a teacher?"

The question surprised me. "No. I used to be. Why do you ask?"

"What else do you do with history? I've often wondered."

"Not much . . . until a job like this comes up."

"A stroke of luck for you then?"

"Very much so." Just like, I said to myself, meeting you. I thought about our fortuitous encounter all the way back to Princes'. And the more I thought about it, the more I relished the prospect of our appointment the next day.

Darwin College is a small, discreet, graduates-only institution tucked away on an eddy of the Granta just below the Mill Pool and shielded from Silver Street by high walls. It doesn't encourage visitors. As an undergraduate, I'd always thought of it as having the withdrawn smugness of unexplained wealth. In fact, this was the first time I'd crossed its threshold, found its miniature, punt-laden backs sheltered from prying eyes behind a wooden eyot, trod its immaculate lawns beneath the sycamores and weeping willows, entered its private world.

Eve Randall's room was on the first floor of the older red brick section of the college. I climbed the stairs with the copied Memoir in a fat ring binder, feeling, absurdly, the nerves of reporting ill-prepared for a supervision with a stranger. Only I wasn't ill-prepared, so I dismissed the sensation as mere weakness and put my best foot forward.

Eve received me in a high-ceilinged lounge with tall windows looking out across the garden to the river. Pastel shades suffused the room. Even the daffodils in a vase on the bookcase seemed to have been chosen for their pale petals. The curtains were floor-length, the carpet thickly-piled, the wallpaper a restrained matt. A large print of Suerat's *Bathers at Asnières* dominated one wall. At the far end of the room, one curtain had been drawn to shade a pinewood harpsichord. Patterns—any signs of fussy femininity—were notable by their absence. Overall, the atmosphere was cool, but with a promise of softness; a sort of dignified caress.

Unlike the day before, Eve wore perfume—faint and barely distinguishable from the flowers in the room, but heightening the sense, as she stood near me, of privilege at being admitted to this place. Nor was she concerned now to appear, as she had, formal, almost regal, in her dress. That afternoon, she could have been one of her own students in her open-toed sandals, tight, dazzling white jeans and pale blue, collarless

French-style blouse, belted at the waist. Could have been, but for the sheer quality of her looks. She wore neither make-up nor jewellery, her hair fell unbraided to her shoulders, but there was a penetration to her gaze, a hint of nascent smile on her lips, that deprived her beauty of simplicity and added a layer of the beckoning unknown.

She asked me to sit down on the wide, pale green couch, using my first name in a way which suggested I was being admitted to something more than just her presence, then served lemon tea in shallow Chinese cups.

"So Martin, tell me more about the Strafford Memoir."

As I did so, Eve sipped her tea and listened with an intent delicacy. Was it the Memoir or me that was being examined? At the very least, it felt like both, so that I was speaking not merely for Strafford, because he couldn't speak for himself, but also for Martin Radford, because he'd been so seldom heard.

"What Strafford never knew," I said, "and what I'm trying to find out, was why he was rejected. So far, all I've got to go on is suspicion. Maybe you can give me some evidence."

"Evidence of what?"

"Of conspiracy. I suggest that to split Strafford and Elizabeth Latimer and discredit Strafford in the process was a desire common to some members of the Cabinet and some leaders of the Suffragettes. That shared motive suggests to me the possibility of a conspiracy."

"To what end?"

"To remove Strafford as an obstacle to Lloyd George's ambition. To prevent Strafford depriving Christabel Pankhurst of an able lieutenant and so ridiculing the movement. To foster an alliance whose objectives were political power for Lloyd George and votes for women as a reward for their assistance."

A butterfly passed by the open window and a punt cast off from the Darwin moorings below. Inside the room, Eve indulged her gift for silence and immobility, while I waited for her response. I'd never stated my claim so explicitly before and had partly shaped it for her benefit. To my own ears, it didn't sound quite good enough.

"None of this fits with my perception of the personalities and motivations involved in the suffragist movement." She paused, as if weighing the words, which hung heavily in the air. "That doesn't mean it's inconceivable. As one attempting to compile a definitive account of the Suffragettes' struggle, I'd be foolish to close my mind to possibilities which are at odds with my preliminary conclusions." Gloom had been followed by reprieve. "I'd like to read the memoir, then tell you what I think."

I handed the Memoir across to her and thought, in that instant, of Ambrose, whom I'd regretted even showing the document. Yet now I was happy to entrust it to a virtual stranger not because—whatever I might pretend—she was likely to put it to better use than Ambrose, but because it was the one sure way I had of impressing her. The Memoir was my passport to more of her company.

"I'll return it within 24 hours," she said.

"Keep it longer if you need to."

"No. That will be sufficient." The professional had spoken.

"Perhaps we could meet for lunch tomorrow to discuss it."

Another pregnant pause, part of Eve's mental and physical poise, which conveyed significance in the most trivial thought or act. "I'd like that . . . Do you have a car?"

"Not in Cambridge." (Or anywhere else.)

"Then I'll drive you. Suppose I were to collect you from Princes' at noon?" She'd taken the initiative and I was happy to surrender it. I agreed and made to go.

"You have lovely rooms here," I said, pausing by the door of the lounge.

"They've adapted very well."

"So light and airy. And you admire the pointillistes?" I gestured at the Seurat.

"I admire their pleasure. Art is an antidote to history."

"In what way?"

At that, she nearly smiled—for the first time. "Historians need to be reminded occasionally how much pleasure the past contains. To hear the music of Handel played on a harpsichord or see those bathers at Asnières as Seurat saw them is to realize how much of life history misses."

"You may find the Memoir restores some of that life to history."

"We shall see."

Yes, I thought, we shall. I caught myself smiling for no reason as I walked along Silver Street back to College that afternoon. I say no reason, though it was in fact that I felt my luck to be changing at last. As indeed it was.

I positioned myself early outside Princes' next day, leaning against the railings with as much nonchalance as I could summon. A silver MG eased throatily to a halt ten minutes later and Eve invited me to hop in. The roof was down in the bright and breezy weather and her hair and the white scarf round her neck had been ruffled by the wind. She wore dark glasses, a navy blue guernsey and white slacks, as if for yachting. At once, a third side of her was shown to me. I'd seen the cool professional and the temptress in repose. Now here was the young woman of action and means.

We drove, very fast but with studied expertise, out to a village south of Cambridge. During the journey, I tried to draw Eve out about the Memoir, but she kept distracting me with questions about Princes'. So it was not until we were seated in a sunny corner of a pub garden, with a flat village green, some elm trees and a Norman church in front of us, sharing a platter of fine beef sandwiches, that I got anywhere on that score.

"What do you think then?" I asked, sipping at my beer.

"I think it's a lovely day."

"I meant the Memoir."

"I know." She smiled. "I'm sorry." She needn't have been —her smile was worth any tease. "The Memoir is a fascinating document. Particularly for me. I've tended to concentrate on female writers of the period. The book I'm writing is very much the Suffragette viewpoint. To that extent, Strafford is tangential to my theme. But the novelty and vitality of his chronicle make it a tangent worth following."

"And what about my theory?"

"It's certainly a possibility." At last, I thought: an open mind, willing to be convinced. Neither of us, of course, was ingenuous in our readiness to entertain the theory. I hoped Eve saw in it promising material for her book, for all that it clashed with her theme. For myself, the more such study was likely to throw us together, the better it suited me.

"Only a possibility?"

"At this stage, yes. But let's put it to the test."

"How?"

"What we need is corroboration. I've had access to a vast quantity of documentation on the period. We need to cull through it again, looking specificially for anything which might tell us how or why Strafford was disgraced. If we can establish a connexion with existing evidence, then there might really be something to build on."

"You really think it's worth a try?"

"I do."

"Well, I'll drink to that." I chinked my glass against hers and thought at once, as I had before with Sellick, of Helen and our marriage. Sitting there with Eve on a spring afternoon, it seemed to me that, at long last, I was wholly glad to be rid of that part of my past, unreserved in my conviction that I was now doing something infinitely more worthwhile.

I'd never been meticulous enough to make a good researcher, but Eve soon showed she didn't suffer from the same deficiency. She produced—already typed—a list of autobiographies, diaries, memoirs, old magazines and newspapers, which were to form the basis of our enquiries. It meant me sifting through them all in the U.L. and other libraries on the look-out for any link—however slender—with Strafford and my theory. These were sources Eve had already examined but, clearly, our only hope of substantiation was to go through them again. So it was a task I was happy to undertake.

"I'll look through all the material I have," Eve said as we sped back towards Cambridge, "but pressure of work obliges me to leave most of it to you."

"That's as it should be."

"Not really. I'm not completely disinterested, you know."

"You mean your book?"

"I'm committed to finishing it by Christmas. If your theory stands up, it could become something of a scoop . . . I'd have to talk to my publisher about a co-author."

"An acknowledgment would do." We laughed. "Or perhaps you could make an advance."

"What sort of advance?" Her tone of voice played with the idea that my pun had been intended—as it had.

"How about your company for a little trip down the river on Sunday? That's one occasion when I can't visit libraries and it's May Day. I could celebrate by trying to remember how to punt." I felt undermined by the pause which followed. "Of course, I realize you're probably pretty busy at the weekends."

We drew to a halt at the first set of lights into Cambridge. "Leave me to worry about how busy I am, Martin. I'd enjoy a day on the river. Cambridge is a close little community, as you must know, never short of rumour. It's refreshing to meet somebody who isn't—any longer anyway—associated with it."

I went back to my room at Princes' with the Memoir and the reading list, feeling, it struck me, rather as Strafford must have felt about a Sunday appointment 68 years before, with Elizabeth in Hyde Park: a tremulous relish of playing with fire.

May 1st was a day of fragile spring brilliance, better than I could have hoped. I walked round to Darwin while the city was still cool and quiet, pausing by the Mill Pool to look upstream. The river was calm, empty and perfect for punting, a quaint activity with just the right romantic edge for my purposes that day.

Eve was dressed all in white—calf-length pleated skirt, a high-necked blouse with fluted sleeves. She donned dark glasses and a wide-brimmed straw hat and we walked round to Scudamore's Yard, where I hired a punt for the day.

We set off slowly up the Granta, with Coe Fen on our left. I concentrated on giving a competent display of punting technique, while Eve reclined on a cushion and asked how my first day in the Library had gone.

"Fruitlessly."

"Give it time. Research isn't a quick business."

"That's what Baxter said."

"Is that Marcus Baxter?"

"Yes." A pause while I hauled the pole out of a muddy reach. "Used to be my Director of Studies."

"A respected figure in the Faculty."

"He spoke highly of you too."

"Flattery indeed."

"Baxter's no flatterer." I grinned ruefully. "Praise from him has to be earned. You're a rising star, Eve. Beautiful, female history fellows are a rare commodity here. How did you manage it?"

She laughed. "Beauty I deny. Sex was an accident of birth. As for my career, being a woman is a handicap, undeniably. The fact that it shouldn't be only drives me on."

"So writing about the Suffragettes is a labour of love?"

"In a sense. More, perhaps, the paying of a debt of those who had more to struggle against than I. But an historian can't afford to be starry-eyed. They had their faults and made mistakes."

"Such as?"

"They too often failed to exploit their natural advantages."

I ducked as we passed under Crusoe Bridge and pondered the point. "Does that mean you think they should have fluttered more eyelids than banners?"

Eve extended a finger at a passing mallard. "Well, we know one, don't we, who swayed a minister of the Crown?"

"Can we believe it was for some sinister purpose?"

"Nothing is ever quite what it seems, Martin, as Strafford discovered. We all have ulterior motives, don't we?"

"Do we?" I didn't quite know what she meant.

"Well, I'm not only interested in how Strafford was brought down. I'm also concerned to make my name as a writer. And what about your mysterious sponsor?"

"No mystery. Leo Sellick's just a wealthy man indulging a whim. Who are we to complain? Still, I'm prepared to volunteer my ulterior motive."

"Which is?"

"To lure you out for trips like this."

Eve smiled seraphically, settled back on her cushion and pulled the hat down over her eyes. "Wake me in Grantchester. Punting that far should make you question your motives. And mind the decoys."

I laughed, but Eve was right. My punting days were too far behind me for us to reach Byron's Pool, which had been my objective. I tied up at an old landing stage on the banks of a field, with the church tower at Grantchester showing beyond some not too distant trees and persuaded Eve to walk through the lengthening grass to a gate which gave onto a track into the village. We reached The Red Lion shortly after noon and took lunch at a metal trellis table in the garden.

"How's the intrepid punter?" Eve asked with a smile as I gulped my beer.

"Temporarily demotivated. It's seven years since I last did that sort of thing."

"Was that when you graduated?"

"Yes. I remember coming down here the morning after a May Ball. Mid-June it was: very hot."

"And who was your companion on that occasion?"

"A leading question."

"Forgive the historienne her curiosity."

"That's all right. My companion later became my wife, later still my ex-wife."

"I'm sorry."

"Don't be. I'm not." And I wasn't. But that was about the last wholly accurate remark I made as we drifted on to a discussion of Eve's university teaching career and my school-teaching experience. It was an inevitable but uncomfortable subject for me, even more so than my marriage, but it was easy—all too easy—to present my withdrawal from both as a reasoned reaction against boredom and indifference, almost, indeed, as a bold assertion of individual integrity. It was, in many respects, a prepared speech: camouflage I'd long prepared for a truth which could only do me harm in other's eyes, not to mention my own.

"So you see," I said, "there's not much to show for those seven years since I was last here."

"There's more than you might think. I'm impressed by anyone abandoning a career—for the right reasons."

"I only had to do that because I'd entered it for the wrong ones. I'm sure that doesn't apply in your case."

"No. I don't think it does." She was firm on the point. "It might have done at one stage. When I graduated from Durham, I walked straight into a bursary to study for a doctorate at Berkeley in California. I never finished it, till now. The book is its final form. But I wasn't ready for it then. A publisher in San Francisco persuaded me to become his personal assistant. When it became clear that he wanted something more personal than I was prepared to provide, I came home. Only later did I do an M.A. at Manchester, then persuade Darwin that I was the woman they wanted. Now they've given me some lecturing, things are going really well."

I felt the same—things were going well. After lunch, we ambled back across the field towards the punt, lazily anticipating the more leisurely journey back. I pushed off from the bank and poled back towards Cambridge. The going was indeed easier downstream, but that wasn't the reason life seemed sweet. The broad skylines of the Fens symbolized the fresh air that had blown into my life. More specifically, Eve Randall, her figure rousing in repose, drew me on with the languid promise of her gaze as it flicked up from the rippling water to meet my own.

We didn't see each other after that until Wednesday afternoon, when I called at Darwin on my way back from the University Library to bring Eve up to date on my research. A bearded, sweatshirted student was leaving as I went in and I found Eve dressed soberly for the supervision that had just taken place: mauve angora jumper over a heavy purple skirt, hair gathered in a bun—schoolma'amish, with a suppressed sensuality that made me want to unfasten her bun and kiss the pout off her lips as she said, in mock censure, "Deserting the Library before closing time, Mr Radford?"

I contented myself with a smirk. "Seeing double from too much small print. The newspapers seventy years ago used microscopic type, you know."

"I do know, Martin," she said with a smile. "I think they had more to say than the tabloids of today."

"Not about Edwin Strafford."

"Another blank?"

"I'm afraid so."

She made tea while I sat on the couch and gazed out through the window at the river, remembering with relish our outing three days before and wondering how I could arrange another.

Eve came back with the tea. "I'm glad you called," she

said, setting down the tray. "I'd have contacted you today, anyway."

"Oh yes? Thanks." I took the cup from her hand.

"I'm going to London tomorrow. Coming back on Friday. I've got to see my publisher and I thought I'd take the opportunity to have another look through the Kendrick Archive."

"The what?"

"Julia Lambourne—who crops up in the Memoir and was one of the Five Furies—died three years ago. Her married name was Kendrick. She bequeathed a large quantity of correspondence and miscellaneous documentation pertaining to the suffragist movement to Birbeck College. It's not yet been properly evaluated, though I had a look through it last year in connexion with my book. Now, I'd like to take a second look."

I sat up abruptly, spilling some tea into my saucer. "Eve, you should have mentioned this before. Julia Lambourne was close to Elizabeth Latimer. Her brother tried to warn Strafford off when he visited the house in Putney at the time of the rift. Surely this could be just what we're looking for?"

Eve sipped her tea calmly. "Don't get too excited, Martin. I remember nothing that's likely to help us. But, obviously, it's worth checking."

"Any chance I could come too?"

A pause of deliberation. "I think you'd do better to carry on here. Duplication of effort would be wasteful." I'd seen other advantages to a joint visit to London, but Eve's quiet tone brooked no argument. "Besides, Professor Davis at Birbeck is very protective about the Archive. He knows me, so there won't be any problem, but . . ."

"Point taken, I'll soldier on here."

"You won't have to wait long to hear if I find anything. I'll be back Friday evening."

I seized an opportunity. "How about dinner then? I could take you out and you could tell me what—if anything—the late Mrs Kendrick has for us."

Eve set down her cup and smiled. "That would be lovely, Martin. I'll look forward to it after the noise and grime of the city."

After tea, she walked down with me to the garden and along the gravel path towards the gate into Silver Street.

"I haven't thanked you properly for taking me out on Sunday," she said. "I enjoyed it very much."

"I'm glad. So did I. While you're in London, I'll have to get used to doing this job on my own again." Reaching the gate, we stopped.

"Not for long." So saying, she leant forward and kissed me, lightly but for long enough to plant a suggestion of more to come in my receptive mind. "Take care while I'm away. See you on Friday."

"I'll call about seven." She raised one hand in acknowledgement before disappearing round an ivy-clad buttress. That was Eve's way—to go quickly and leave me thinking. As I think I did, more about her and less about the Kendrick Archive than I should have.

Thursday, with Eve in London, seemed duller in prospect than it proved in reality. I posted another report to Sellick—which said nothing because there was nothing to say—then made my way to the University Library for another dutiful day with the reading list. I stationed myself at a small table in the cavernous reading room with *The Women's Victory & After* by Dame Millicent Fawcett and tried to concentrate.

About an hour later, as I was debating with myself whether to break for coffee, the muted, bookdusty atmosphere around me was rent by a stifled curse to my left of "Oh shit" as half a dozen books crashed to the floor. I jerked round, as did several others with pained expressions, to see Marcus Baxter stooped purple-faced over the fallen pile, muttering to himself as he scrabbled to retrieve it. Breaking off, he dumped his briefcase—with enough force to suggest that he blamed it for the incident—on a chair and, glaring up, caught my eye.

"Radford," he rasped. "Don't just sit there gawping. Give me a hand." I did of course, while retaining a supercilious expression calculated to annoy. We stacked the books on the table. "Why are you hanging around here?" Baxter went on, eyeing me biliously.

"Following your advice: spending time with sources on Strafford."

"Found anything?"

"Not yet."

He grinned crookedly. "Then you've been looking in the wrong place—as usual. I noticed something only the other day that'd repay your careful study, if you know what I mean by that." I had the impression he'd have spared me the last shot if I hadn't just witnessed his embarrassment.

"What was it?"

He fastened his briefcase. "I'm going for a smoke. Come along and I'll fill you in."

We descended to the tea room, where coffee and cigarettes improved Baxter's mood—a little. I pressed him for details of his find.

"Have you been through Hobhouse?" he barked. I took it that he meant Charles Hobhouse, Financial Secretary to the Treasury and later Chancellor of the Duchy of Lancaster under Asquith.

"I've read *Inside Asquith's Cabinet,* if that's what you mean."

"It isn't. That's just extracts from his dairies. I mean the unedited version."

"Then no."

"Typical." He stubbed out a cigarette in his saucer. "Well, if you had, my boy, you might have seen this." He rummaged in his bulging case. "Following your conversation last week, I thought I'd check the chronology of references to Lloyd George's secret talks with Balfour in 1910. I remembered that Hobhouse mentioned them in his diaries."

"Over and above what he says in *Inside Asquith's Cabinet?*"

"I've told you before Radford, you can't get away with skimping. Ah!" He pulled out the piece of paper he was looking for and flicked it across the table at me. It was a photocopied page of manuscript, covering three dates in October.

"What does this tell us?"

"It's Hobhouse's diary for October 1910. Look at the entry for Monday the seventeenth."

I read it aloud. "Disturbing conversation with Birrell this afternoon. He told me that Lloyd George and Balfour had for some time been meeting at secret venues over and above the

Constitutional Conference. It was the first I had heard of such a thing and Birrell implied that their objective was to form a coalition to carry through agreed—though diluted—reforms. Lloyd George had evidently declared to Birrell quite openly that he aspired to the premiership of such a coalition. The price for this would be paid by others. Asquith would have to be 'put out to grass' and Churchill passed over because the Tories 'would not stick him at any price.' As for opposition from within the party, Lloyd George had pooh-poohed it. 'Anyone who wants to,' he had said, 'can go the way of Strafford.' What did that mean? Birrell—who replaced Strafford in June as a delegate to the Conference—did not know and nor do I, unless it is that there was more to Strafford's resignation at that time than met the eye."

"'More to his resignation than met the eye,'" echoed Baxter. "Isn't that what you're looking for?"

"It's exactly what I'm looking for. This is marvellous."

"Don't get carried away. It's only hearsay—contemporary, recorded hearsay, but hearsay nonetheless. It's not much to go on."

"Yes it is. It's somebody other than Strafford quoting Lloyd George to the effect that Strafford was deliberately removed from the office."

"Not quite. It's somebody quoting somebody else quoting Lloyd George . . . tenuous, I'm afraid."

"But . . ."

"And Lloyd George could've been flying a kite. He 'aspired to the premiership'. When the coalition was actually floated, Balfour was to be Prime Minister—in name anyway. Asquith was to be 'put out to grass" with a peerage presumably. It never happened. The party—people like Hobhouse—wouldn't have worn it. Maybe the idea that Strafford was deliberately jettisoned was wishful thinking, designed to impress: as it did."

"But taken together with Strafford's own account . . ."

"It begins to take shape—as an attractive possibility. Work at it, Radford, and you might have something." The past taskmaster had spoken.

"I will. Can I keep this?" I held up the copy.

"Certainly, my boy. Treat it as a memento of my scholastic integrity." He smiled and, for once, I had to smile with him.

I decided to leave the Library early that afternoon. After Baxter's revelation, there didn't seem much point in lingering. I'd discarded Fawcett straightaway and gone for the full version of Hobhouse's diaries, but they contained nothing else on Strafford to compare with what Baxter had given me. It rankled slightly that I'd had to rely on him to point me in the right direction, but it pleased me even more that he'd seen fit to toss me a crumb.

What I most wanted to do was carry my discovery to Eve in triumph, show her that there was substance in my theory and, for that matter, in me. Because she was in my mind and I was in the Library, it was no more than idle curiosity that made me look her up in the University Calendar. But there was a shock waiting for me in her listing under Darwin College: "Miss E. Randall, M.A. (Couchman Fellow)." Couchman Fellow? What could it mean? I turned feverishly to the section on endowments and found it there.

"COUCHMAN RESEARCH FELLOWSHIP: The Fellowship was instituted in 1955, under the Will of the late Sir Gerald Couchman, to facilitate research and teaching in the Humanities at one of the postgraduate colleges of the University by a suitably qualified woman. The Trustees (the Vice-Chancellor, the late Sir Gerald's executor and the Master of the College at which the incumbent is to be resident) appoint the fellow annually and have discretion to re-appoint in appropriate cases." There followed a list of the Fellows since 1955, with, at the bottom, "Miss E. Randall, M.A.—1976".

Why hadn't she told me? The question rang like an alarm bell in my head.

There could be no misunderstanding. Eve's fellowship was in the gift of the Couchmans. The more I thought about it, the more I dimly recollected being told sometime that the family had exercised its generosity in this way—another piece of conspicuous superiority that grated on my marriage to Helen. That was all it had been: a minor, forgotten irritant. Now it was a torment, not by its existence, not even by Eve's occupation of it, but by the fact that she hadn't told me. In all fairness—all logic—she should have done.

I went down to the river and walked up the Backs, trying to make sense of it. After all, I told myself, Eve wasn't to know of my connexion with the Couchmans any more than I was to know of hers. I was afraid anybody who knew of mine would refuse to accept me as an objective researcher. Did Eve fear I would think the same of her? If so, we were in an absurd stand-off.

I turned in at the back gate of King's College and walked over the bridge towards the Chapel, too lost in thought to have any taste for the architecture. At first shocked, then dismayed, I now felt only a pervasive uncertainty, the ebbing of a shallow confidence. What was I to do? Trust Eve's integrity or mine? If she had as little of it as me, I was lost. Yet everything told against that. She had too much grace and beauty for me to judge her by my own standards. I was wrong, I told myself, as I tramped past the Old Schools and turned up Senate House Passage, wrong to feel slighted over this. Why should Eve tell me something which—strictly speaking—wasn't any of my concern? Surely I could rely on her to resolve any conflict of interest in her own way. Above all, what right did I have to question her impartiality while at the same time suppressing evidence that I was even less impartial? She'd said none of us was disinterested and she'd been right. Had that been a signal, a warning not to expect too much of her? If so, I decided, it was time to heed it—expectation wasn't my prerogative. But hope remained.

I drank a lot that night: my normal refuge at times of stress. The stress was wanting Eve back in Cambridge but not knowing whether to say anything to her about the Couchmans when she was back. The stress was being nearer the truth but farther than ever from peace of mind.

After a wretched night I spent the morning patrolling Great Court at Trinity—Strafford's old college—lost in thought, a few more drinks at lunchtime, then a walk through the Botanical Gardens to clear my head—which it didn't—and on to the railway station. I spotted Eve's MG in the car park and lay in wait on the platform, knowing that, some time that afternoon, she must step off the London train.

Several trains came and went, each washing a wave of dead faces past me, while I sat on a bench, watched movements in the goods yards and wondered what I'd say when the waiting was over.

Somehow, I knew the train Eve was on when I saw it nosing up the long straight line towards the station, knew which first-class compartment she would elegantly descend from and knew then, if I'd ever doubted it, that I could say nothing to her about the Couchman Fellowship. For what did I think when I saw her through the crowd, in dark glasses and cream three-piece trouser suit, looking askance and apart on the suddenly busy station?—a superior, supremely desirable being singled out for me from the ruck around us. What did I think? I thought I would follow her to the ocean's edge.

"Martin," she said with a flashing smile, "this is an unexpected pleasure." The greeting kiss was brief but far from casual. "It's great to be back—and to see you here."

I took her bag and smiled too. "It's great to have you back." All my doubts dissolved as we walked towards the ticket barrier. "I couldn't wait to see you—I've got some news." But not, of course, the news she didn't want to hear.

"Same here. We can swap over dinner."

"It's a deal."

She said she was tired after the journey and would I drive her back to Darwin? I surprised myself by how well I piloted the MG through the city streets. I wondered if any of the passing students who saw the stranger in the sports car recognized their dream lecturer by his side and found myself hoping they did. I'd booked a table at Shades' in King's Parade because it was small, quiet and generally empty even on a Friday night. We walked up to it through the still of early evening. Eve dressed in a black suit over a flounced, white silk blouse, fastened at the neck with a silver brooch, elegant perfection walking with her arm in mine, talking of the contrast between Cambridge and London, flirting on the fringes of our respective revelations.

That game continued through the apertifs and whitebait till the wine flowed with my steak and her veal and we came to the crunch over dishes of tender meat.

"As soon as I saw you at the station," she said, as the candlelight twinkled at her brooch, "I knew you were dying to tell me something."

"But you said you'd not returned empty-handed either."

"That's true."

"Then ladies first."

"Isn't it the woman's right to choose? I choose to hear your news first."

"All right." I conceded with a smile. "But it's not really my news. Baxter pointed me in the right direction."

"Really?" She raised her eyebrows.

"Yes. The diaries of Charles Hobhouse. A *bon mot* from Lloyd George about Strafford's resignation, with lots of implications." I removed the sheet of paper from my pocket and passed it across the table. "Look at the entry for 17th October 1910."

Eve pursed her lips and read through it, then sipped some wine. "What did Baxter make of it?" She was less obviously impressed than I'd hoped.

I sat back in my chair. "You know Baxter. He requires signed affidavits for any conclusions—except his own. Said it was still flimsy. But, taken in conjunction with the memoir—which he hasn't seen—doesn't it reinforce the idea that Lloyd George was out to get Strafford?"

"No link with the Suffragettes, I see."

"Not yet. But isn't it a start?"

"Oh yes." She shot me a reassuring smile. "You've done splendidly, Martin. We could look on it as a breakthrough, except . . ."

"Except what?"

"Except for what I found at Birbeck—in the Kendrick Archive. So many papers, documents, notes, letters—not properly catalogued yet. And there, amongst them, the answer. So simple, really—it shouldn't be any surprise."

Is this it? I thought. Do I get truth served, sweet and simple, as an extra course: bathos in the evening? Does the high priestess just roll me a secret, like a cigarette she doesn't smoke? Can she pass me Strafford on a serviette? If she can work the oracle, what's to be my votive offering?

All those thoughts, in the second between sentences. But all I said was "What is it?"

"Elizabeth Latimer couldn't marry Strafford because he was already married."

"He was what?" I felt as if the restaurant chair was about to flip me, Sweeney Todd-like, into the world of turned tables and discarded masks.

"Married. Amongst the Kendrick papers, I found a marriage certificate: Strafford's, dating from his years in South Africa. He married—and evidently deserted—a Dutch girl there."

"Are you certain?"

"Only that the certificate is there—or rather, here." She reached into her bag and brought out a buff envelope, which she placed on the table between us. I fumbled at the flap, pulled out the folded, yellowed, crinkled sheet within and held it to read in the candlelight.

No mistake. The name was there, recorded for posterity in some rough Boer registrar's jagged hand. Edwin George Strafford, aged 24, and Caroline Amelia van der Merwe, aged 21, joined in matrimony at Port Edward, Natal, on 8th September 1900.

"I don't know what to say."

"Do you believe it?"

"Do you?"

"It looks genuine, Martin. It feels genuine. It seems awfully like the truth. I feel sorry that my suspicions have been confirmed."

"You suspected this?"

"Not exactly. Something like it. Something disappointingly conclusive. I'm afraid it was always on the cards that Strafford would turn out to have discredited himself."

"But Eve, the Memoir. This goes against everything he wrote in that."

"True. But I fear it's not unprecedented for people—especially famous people—to present their past as they would wish it to have been. There's no reason to doubt the veracity of the Memoir—as far as it goes. It's simply that Strafford edited out the one ugly truth he couldn't face."

"But how could he? How could it remain hidden in the circumstances?"

"I was thinking about that on the train. This document was in Julia Lambourne's possession. It was she and her brother who were on the scene in Putney to protect Elizabeth at the time of the split, right? Therefore it's fair to conclude that Julia uncovered this information and showed it to Elizabeth to save her from a bigamous marriage. She'd presumably decided to check Strafford's credentials when she first realized how close he was to her friend. The enormity of her discovery may have made her hesitate to reveal it, but, when she learned of Elizabeth's seduction, she could no longer hold it back. As for not making it public, how could they, when to disgrace Strafford was also to ruin Elizabeth? Shc would have had to admit to adultery, then a considerable social stigma. And what good would it have done the Suffragettes for the public to know that one of their brave, responsible young ladies claiming the right to vote was happy to take a roll in the hay with a Cabinet minister? No, everyone was better off burying the truth—including Strafford."

The waiter came to remove our plates. I had no stomach for dessert. We ordered coffee. "It still doesn't make sense. Why did Strafford pour out his soul in that memoir if it was built on a lie?"

"It wasn't. An impetuous, regrettable marriage doesn't make Strafford a bad man. It doesn't mean he didn't love Elizabeth, or mourn their separation as much as he claimed. It doesn't even mean that your own theory is invalid. If Lloyd George really did want to get rid of him and somehow found out why Elizabeth had broken off their engagement, then the information might certainly have persuaded Asquith that Strafford should be decently ostracized."

"But Hobhouse's quote makes it sound as if Strafford's removal was so much more contrived."

"Useful, perhaps, as a threat to other potential opponents of Lloyd George. To anyone who didn't know better, Strafford's fall was exemplary—*pour encourager les autres*."

"I don't know, Eve. I thought I knew Strafford, thought I knew his mind. Now, it seems, I must think again."

Eve reached across the table and touched my hand. "Then take time to think again." I opened my hand and grasped hers. "Then we'll decide what to do—for the best." When we left the restaurant, we walked down through King's College, past the dark, looming outline of the Chapel, to the river, and talked of Strafford again.

"I have an idea what we should do about this discovery, Martin," Eve said, "but it's important you should decide. Do you want to drop it—or carry on?"

"How can we carry on?"

"That's up to you."

"And you."

"Let's say both of us."

"All right. Let's say that."

"Last Sunday was good."

"Yes, it was."

"Then let's do something similar this Sunday. I'll drive you somewhere—we could picnic if the weather's fine."

"I'd like that."

"Well, regard that as your deadline. Tell me then what you feel we ought to do. Reveal the truth about Strafford after seventy years—or leave it buried?"

We walked across the bridge towards Queens' Road, our hands joined now, saying nothing but pledging silently to give Strafford what he'd asked for: justice, suddenly a less pretty thing than I'd once thought.

Eve had given me, had given Strafford, a day's grace. It was a dull, wet day in Cambridge: slate grey clouds scudded across the flat landscape. There was only one thing I could do to help me make up my mind, so I did it: immured in that cheerless guest room of Princes' Hall, I read the Memoir through again, from start to finish, only this time acutely, unsympathetically, like an interrogator looking for inconsistencies, inaccuracies, giveaways.

You couldn't really say I found any. Eve had been quite right. As far as it went, the memoir left no room for doubt. But the certificate, flourished without warning from the past of a distant country, focused my attention on its fateful date: September 1900.

"Passing through Capetown in early September, I met Couch . . . and mentioned I would have to disappoint the van der Merwes . . . Couch volunteered to take my place in Durban . . . So it was that I arrived home in England with but a week in which to conduct my election campaign."

The election that year had been held on October 4. That would place Strafford's return to England "but a week" before around September 27. A sea voyage from South Africa? Say two weeks. So he'd have left Capetown around September 13. Damn: there was time enough for him to have married Miss van der Merwe in Port Edward on September 8.

"Couch volunteered to take my place in Durban." Not Port Edward. Did he really? Presumably not. Then why say it? Unless Strafford was laying an alibi, reassuring himself that, no, he didn't really commit the van der Merwe madness, that foolish fling in South Africa never happened at all, couldn't for that reason touch him so long after, so far away. Yet it did happen. I'd seen his upright, fluent, English signature on the certificate and there it was again, at the end of the Memoir, little changed by the intervening fifty years.

I paced the tiny room, glowered at the rain-lashed wall of Pembroke College across the alley from my window, and wondered: who was she, Strafford? Just some poor, pretty maid you wanted to forget? Is that what you thought? That Elizabeth shouldn't be denied you just because of a senseless soldier's lapse? "That was in another country, and besides the wench is dead"? Only she wasn't, was she?

Later, I began to feel anger rising against Strafford. I felt cheated, deceived by him, a little as Elizabeth must have felt. In that mood, I went out to drink away the evening, roamed the bars and pubs whetting my resentment with alcohol. The Couchmans' concern to keep me away from Elizabeth in her dotage, to dissuade me from reopening an old wound, suddenly made sense. More than that, it seemed a decent thing for them to do.

That, in itself, gave me pause for thought. I didn't know Elizabeth, but I knew her son and her granddaughter—all too well. Decency was a quality they identified with what was neat and seemly. And, when drunk, I naturally thought of Ambrose, and the mysterious, threatening visitors to Lodge Cottage the spring of Strafford's last journey home. Who would fear an old, disgraced man? Nobody. That answer wouldn't go away and nor would the growing conviction that there was something wrong with the story—or this version of it, presented to me by somebody whose objectivity I knew to be as questionable as my own. What about that, after all? The one revelation that hadn't been made the night before.

I raced back to Princes' and read the South African sequence in the Memoir over again. "Couch volunteered to take my place in Durban." Couch the coward, cheat and . . . what else? Did Couch go to Durban after all? Perhaps they both went to Port Edward. Who were the witnesses to the wedding? I'd forgotten to look, would have to check. But, if Couchman knew of it, perhaps even connived at it, was it he who betrayed Strafford, alerted Julia Lambourne, maybe Lloyd George as well, then casually helped himself to a distraught Elizabeth? That would explain his fear of Strafford, why he tried to buy him off, why, perhaps, he finally had him killed off. And Henry? Could I detect his podgy hand in a nasty little murder of a helpless old man?

I'd arranged to meet Eve on the Fen Causeway at noon. Neutral ground was fitting, I suppose, for an occasion that might well decide whether we joined forces or went our separate ways. I made my way to the rendezvous across Coe Fen, breathing deeply and trying to blow away a thick head. Certainly, Saturday's rain had left Cambridge clean and fresh. The only haze left was in my mind, surrounding Eve. I couldn't forget my dream of her—the perfect, nubile temptress. Yet, in the waking world, she was sharp-brained, giving just enough to make me want more but without dispelling one atom of her mystery.

There was another rub: the Couchman connexion. A marriage certificate, conjured like a rabbit from a hat: so convenient, so unanswerable. Alone and clear-headed in a rational moment, I questioned that. If Eve was simply doing the

Couchmans' bidding, what better than to produce a piece of paper, like a black cheque, to buy my silence?

If that was so, I realized, Eve would lead me to a policy of inaction. Let the dead bury the dead, let Strafford and his friend or foe Couchman, with all their secrets and deceits, rest in peace. It wasn't the historian's line though, certainly not that of the thrusting young academic out to make a name for herself. So which line would she choose and which would I follow?

As soon as I saw the low, sleek shape of the silver MG heading my way along the Fen Causeway, I knew it didn't really matter which line she chose. Whichever it was, I was bound, in all my knowing weakness, to follow.

We drove out along the Colchester road to the Gog Magog Hills and walked around the wooded slopes of the Wandlebury earthworks until we found a sunny grass slope to spread the car blanket against the damp of Saturday's rain.

Eve had brought cold chicken, crisp salad and chilled white wine to lull me into well being. If that wasn't enough, there was the distant view of a village cricket match and, of course, Eve by my side. She was dressed in the white jeans and blue peasant-style blouse she'd worn the first time I'd visited her at Darwin, ten days before. Was it really only ten days? It seemed longer to me, as we sat together on the hillside, as if she'd been around me—or in my head—for as long as I could or cared to remember.

"Have you come to any conclusions, Martin?" she said.

"Let's look at it this way." I was thinking aloud now, tailoring my conclusions to fit Eve's expectations. The full range of my reactions weren't for her consumption. "I could tell Sellick that Strafford compromised himself by pretending never to have been married and that that alone explains his fall from high office. But I'm far from sure it would satisfy him."

"Why shouldn't it?"

I couldn't give Eve the true answer to her question, couldn't tell her about Ambrose's not so fantastic claims, because to do so would point the finger at her sponsors, the Couchmans. And to do that would open a door of doubt in our relationship which I wanted to keep firmly closed. So what did I actually say? "Because, I suppose, he's paid a high price for what would be a disappointing conclusion."

"Surely that's the risk he took when he commissioned this research."

"True, but you implied we didn't have to give up here. We could go on digging for more."

"That's not quite what I had in mind."

"It isn't? Then what?"

"What I meant was: you could use the certificate to write an abrupt but fitting finis to your work for Sellick—or we could put the certificate to work for us." The last phrase had silent reverberations.

I looked at Eve in puzzlement. "How?"

"I said I wasn't disinterested, Martin. I made sure you knew that. You also know I'm writing a book about the Suffragettes as pioneer feminists. I don't want it to be an abstruse, inaccessible work. Genuine human interest would give it depth."

"What sort of human interest?" I was beginning to catch her drift.

"A young, idealistic girl fights for what she knows to be right. She is seduced by a politician of charm and intelligence and he seems to be persuaded by her of the rightness of the suffragist cause. But he takes no practical steps to put that persuasion into effect and has all along betrayed the girl by not revealing the truth about himself. In effect, a microcosm of the problems afflicting the Suffragettes. Told to leave politics to the wiser, better sex, they find that sex incapable of organizing its own affairs, let alone the country's. With that theme, we'd be on to something of a coup."

"We?"

"Naturally, Martin, what I'm proposing is a partnership."

A partnership in crime, I thought, with Strafford as its victim. But any kind of partnership with Eve was too attractive for me to reject, so all I could do was stall. "How would Strafford come out of this?"

"Badly, I'm afraid." She leant closer to me across the blanket. "How could it be any other way, Martin? We have clear evidence of his deceit of Elizabeth. As historians, how can we close our eyes to that?"

"I suppose we can't." Strafford, I thought, why aren't you here to stop me condemning you? I can't remember you or your Memoir when Eve lies so close to me.

"Then surely the logical extension of that is to mine Strafford and his questionable Memoir for our book." *Our* book—not that.

"But what do we tell Sellick?"

"Nothing for the moment. He won't expect to hear anything definite yet. Until he does, he doesn't need to know that we're moving in a different direction, does he?"

So, softly in the spring sunshine, with the taste of her wine in my mouth and the touch of her flesh in my mind, Eve led me in the direction she wanted. Who was I betraying? Sellick, Strafford or myself? All of us, really, but Sellick was far away, Strafford was dead and I, well, I was prepared to trade whatever was necessary for whatever kind of partnership Eve was prepared to offer. I leant forward and kissed her in an act of willing abandonment.

Eve pulled away with mock sharpness. "Are there any Strafford-style secrets in your past you should tell me about, Martin?"

"None, except a poor marriage and a better divorce."

"In that case, you've nothing to worry about."

After the picnic, we strolled around the earthworked slope, hand in hand. Eve pointed out unusual specimens of orchids and I listened, not to learn more of the exotic blooms, but simply to hear more of her voice.

Whether through her concentration on the flowers or mine on her, we were surprised by stormclouds billowing in from the west and caught in a downpour on the uncovered hillside. Through vertical, drenching rain, we ran to the car and mopped ourselves down. We were soaked through, Eve's jeans and blouse clinging to her. There was nothing for it but to drive straight back to Cambridge.

Eve dropped me at Princes' Hall, where I changed hurriedly. Then I walked to Darwin, the sun now perversely shining. I followed the gravel path round from the Silver Street gate, past the rain-beaded lawn, and looked up at Eve's room, where, at that moment, a curtain twitched back to reveal her, standing solemnly, wrapped in a yellow bath towel, with wet hair tumbling onto her shoulders in pleasing disarray. She caught my eye, but didn't pull the curtain back, instead smiled and waved her hand gently in greeting.

When I reached the room, she was wearing a kimono and welcomed me with a formal, dampish kiss. She smelt of bath oil and spring sunshine, looked, if anything, even more ravishing rumpled and unready than in any finery.

"I made a pot of coffee," she said. "Have some while I get dressed."

I walked over to a small table by the window, where she'd stood the coffee, poured some and sat drinking it in an armchair splashed in aqueous sunlight.

On the table, next to the coffee, stood a file and some papers, including the envelope that had contained the marriage certificate and, underneath it, several photocopies of the certificate. I picked one up and looked at it with more concentration and less shock than when Eve had first unveiled it. Strafford—his name and signature—was still obstinately there, along with Caroline van der Merwe, joined by a minister of the Dutch Reformed Church at the Veltenschrude Chapel, Port Edward, Natal, in the presence of . . . blast, nobody I knew, no familiar ghost like Couchman, just two names which meant nothing, but, then again, no van der Merwes either, which was odd. Why was no member of the family on hand for the biggest occasion in a young girl's life? I looked at the addresses. Strafford's was shown as Culemborg Barracks, Capetown and Miss van der Merwe's as Ocean Prospect, Berea Drive, Durban. I seized an atlas from Eve's bookcase. Port Edward was a dot on the map of South Africa, about a hundred miles south of Durban—a long way to go for a wedding. With no relatives witnessing the event, it smacked of an elopement—even, perhaps, an abduction.

Eve returned to the room, wearing jeans and a sweater.

"Any clues there?" she asked, seeing me with the atlas. I told her of my tentative conclusions. She stooped by the table and poured coffee. "You could be right, Martin," she said. "But does it really matter?" I was shocked and obviously looked it. "Let me explain." She sat down on the couch near me. "For our purposes, it's surely the effect, not the circumstances, of Strafford's South African marriage that counts.

The Memoir gives us his side of things, distorted to suit. What about other people's?"

"Such as?"

"Such as Julia Lambourne. The personal papers in her archive may tell us how and why she came by this evidence." She sipped her coffee. "And then there's Elizabeth. I expect you realize she's still alive."

"Oh yes." It sounded simple to say, though it wasn't. This was the first time we'd spoken of the present-day Couchmans and I dallied with the idea that Eve would now volunteer her connexion with them. But she didn't. "So what's the next step?"

"Glean what more we can from the Kendrick Archive before tackling Lady Couchman." I had a mental picture then of Elizabeth, the Elizabeth I knew from the Memoir, grown old gracefully, serving tea and angel cake in the drawing room at Quarterleigh even as we sat debating her past in Cambridge, unaware, in her antimacassared world, of the old grievances conspiring to catch up with her. "I'll go down to Birbeck tomorrow and make a start."

"What would you like me to do?"

"Keep on with the reading, Martin. I want us to be equally knowledgeable about the Suffragettes before we announce ourselves. I won't be gone long—I'll certainly be back for my lecture on Wednesday."

"Fine. I'll be there." It wasn't fine, of course. I was already deciding to spend the time trying to verify the certificate, however immaterial Eve thought its details to be, and I should certainly have asked myself: if you're prepared to let Eve trust you to carry on reading at her direction while actually following an independent line, how can you be so sure she's really only going to London to look at the Kendrick Archive? But her persuasive talk of "announcing ourselves"—the seductive promise of a literary partnership delivering me material and emotional success on a plate—made me forget all such doubts.

Next morning, I saw Eve off at the railway station and walked slowly back to Princes' Hall, wondering quite how I could find out more about the van der Merwes of Boer War Durban.

What was waiting for me at the college, however, drove such thoughts from my head. As I strolled through the gate into First Court, one of the porters dashed out of the lodge.

"Mr Radford," he said, "I've got a message for you here. I was just going to deliver it to your room."

"Thanks." I raised my eyebrows in mild surprise. I hadn't expected any mail to reach me there. In fact, it wasn't mail, but a telephone message taken by the porter. I started to read it as I walked across the court, then stopped dead as it sank in.

"Mr Radford: please ring Alec Fowler urgently on 01-836-2387."

A London number. What was Alec doing in the country? It suddenly seemed an age since I'd seen him in Madeira. He'd given me no clue then that he might soon follow me home. And what was so urgent? Alec had often in the past popped up from nowhere, on the end of a telephone, suggesting we drink away old times, so I shouldn't have been surprised, but the message, reaching me on a dull morning in the grey precincts of Princes' Hall, held a tinge of foreboding for me. I couldn't say why, unless it was that, so soon after I'd agreed with Eve to play Sellick along while we went our own way, Alec's appearance on the scene seemed a sinister coincidence.

I dialled the number from a payphone on one of the student staircases. It was a hotel in Drury Lane. They put me through to Alec's room and he answered straightaway.

"Martin. Great to hear you. Thanks for ringing." He sounded a touch more businesslike than usual. "How's it going?"

"Slowly but surely. But, more to the point, what are you doing in London? You never told me you were coming."

"Bit of business came up unexpectedly. Contact of Leo's in the holiday trade—you know, some bucketshop billionaire. Possibility of a link with the magazine—for which read money. I'm over to butter him up, persuade him to sign a few cheques, so that Leo doesn't have to stand all the losses. Thought I'd look you up while I was here. It wasn't easy. Jerry was even less helpful than usual, but I tracked you down in the end."

"How long are you here?"

"Rest of the week. But I'm working to a tight schedule. Could you come down to London for a jar?"

"All right, Alec. How about later today?" It struck me that meeting Alec while Eve was away would be the best thing all round. I didn't want him blurting out something about my marriage to a Couchman and, come to that, I wanted to keep Eve to myself.

We agreed on a pub halfway between Liverpool Street and Drury Lane—one Alec knew from friends at the City University, a large, dark alehouse in Clerkenwell, full of frosted glass partitions and smoky alcoves. I was there by one o'clock on a drizzly London afternoon, to find Alec consuming British beer and a Fleet Street daily with the enthusiasm of a man breaking a fast. He was perched on a bar stool and shot me a flashing grin through his Madeiran tan and the fuggy interior of the pub as I walked in. We greeted each other and retreated to a table.

"Cheers," I said, gulping the first of my beer. "How do you like it back in England?"

"Beer great, weather lousy. 'Twas ever thus. Now tell me how the research is going."

"Like I said over the phone: slowly but surely."

"You've been at it a month now."

"That's right. Leo should have had three reports from me."

"He has. The last one arrived just before I left. Gather you've stirred it up with the Couchmans but dug up nothing in the archives."

"That's about it."

"No breakthroughs then?"

"'Fraid not. But don't look so disappointed—it's a slow kind of job."

"What's come out of your Cook's Tour of the Couchmans' unwanted past so far then?"

"I've managed to rub Helen and her father up the wrong way. Of course, I'm a past master at that."

"But what about this nephew of Strafford's you dug up in Devon?"

"Ambrose? A real gem—of the rough-cut variety. He's convinced his uncle was murdered."

"Oh yes? Who by?"

"That's the $64,000 question, Alec—or however much Leo's prepared to pay." We exchanged a smile at that. "Thrown under a train in 1951 by . . . well, take your pick: Gerald Couchman, his son, MI5, Winston Churchill."

"The KGB?"

"You've got the picture. But seriously, the accident stinks. I reckon Ambrose's right."

"And it was murder most foul?"

"Could be. I'll have a clearer idea when we've spoken to Lady Couchman—her testimony's crucial, if we can get one out of her."

"We?"

I'd been caught out, but it didn't seem to matter. "Ah, well, while I've been in Cambridge, I've interested an expert on the Suffragettes in a bit of co-research."

"Anyone I know?"

"Shouldn't think so—Eve Randall, a fellow at Darwin."

"Age? Vital statistics? Marital status?—in that order please."

"Satisfactory on all counts, Alec—if you must know."

"So your co-research could extend beyond Strafford's Memoir?"

I played coy. "She's an acknowledged authority in her field."

"But no help—on the business in hand?"

"I wouldn't say that. She's found . . ."

"What?"

"Just some evidence that needs checking—but it might be exactly what we're looking for."

"You said earlier you'd not had any breaks."

"We don't want to build up false hopes."

"Don't worry about me, Martin. I've no axe to grind. But there's a lot of 'we' in this. Just how closely are you working with this dish?"

"Eve's got a book coming out next winter about the Suffragettes. It seemed sensible for us to join forces."

"I'll bet it did. This couldn't be the reason you feel so happy about working for Leo, could it?"

"Why should it be?"

"Because Leo's given you the opportunity to cultivate a

beautiful young academic—while all I get in Madeira is flowergirls and fishwives."

"Maybe." I smiled sheepishly. "But Leo can't complain, if it helps him as well as me."

"How does it help him?"

"I told you. Eve's turned up something."

"Which is?"

Suddenly, after all my earlier reticence, I was about to spill the beans. Tongue loosened by drink? No doubt. Eager to prove that I could exploit the chance Sellick had given me? Certainly. Goaded into demonstrating that I hadn't been wasting everybody's time? Probably. "The likelihood is that Leo's grand mystery is just a domestic tragedy. Strafford's engagement was broken off because he was already married."

"You have proof?"

"Eve found the certificate. Now we're trying to back it up."

Alec whistled softly. "I don't think that's the sort of discovery Leo's hoping for."

"Neither do I. That's why I'm saying nothing till the picture's complete. I'd appreciate your keeping quiet about it when you get back."

"Scout's honour."

I should have stopped there, with Alec's quip on honour. But I felt a need to expand and justify, so ploughed on. "It's an instructive little tale really." I sketched in Eve's idea of how the Strafford theme might fit into her book. I didn't attribute it to her, but Alec guessed anyway.

"So that's it." He chuckled. "Leo pays well but Eve's a better looker.

"Let's have another drink and toast whatever kind of partnership you think you'd like best."

I was happy to do that. We drank on until the pub closed at three o'clock, then made our way to Liverpool Street for my train back to Cambridge. We waited in the buffet, drinking treacly coffee served by a rotund West Indian lady. I felt a secret triumph at my position relative to Alec's. For once, I seemed set fair to outstrip him. There was no sign of the *Madeira magazine* opening doors in Fleet Street for him, whereas the Strafford Memoir had led me to Eve and all her promise. I think Alec sensed that contrast, baulked at it as much as I rejoiced. Of course, he didn't say anything of the kind.

"How long will you keep Leo guessing?" he asked, stirring his coffee distractedly.

"No longer than I need to. Once we've assembled the evidence and heard Lady Couchman's side of the story, we'll be ready."

"And what about Ambrose Strafford?"

"We may have to leave the verdict on his story open. But I hope not. For his sake, I'd like to know what really happened the night his uncle died. Again, a lot will depend on what the old lady says."

There was a crackly announcement of the train for Bishop's Stortford, Cambridge, Ely and King's Lynn. We drained our coffees and joined the file to the barrier, shouting the rest of our conversation above the hollow tannoy and the clattering and whistling of the station concourse.

"Best of luck then, Martin," Alec said, clapping me on the shoulder.

"Thanks—and you with the tourism tycoon."

"I'll need it—so will you. Be in touch."

He waved me onto the train, then I saw him stroll away through the crowd with his familiar, casual, slightly loping gait. An old friend, a good companion—and something else neither of us deserved, or, if we did, not in the way it happened.

When I telephoned South Africa House the following day, they could tell me nothing about the van der Merwes, instead referred me to the Registrar-General in Pretoria, which was no help at all.

I had better luck at the University Library, where they turned up some old street directories of Durban, dating from when Natal was a British colony. In an 1897 copy, I found what I was looking for: the household of Ocean Prospect, Berea Drive recorded and listed. Just bald names and initials, though I knew who one of them was: van der Merwe, J.G., Mrs. O.C., J.I., P.J., Miss C.A. The next copy dated from eight years later and no van der Merwes appeared at Ocean Prospect, instead a Mr and Mrs Franklin. The lapse was tantalizing. Where did they go? What became of them? Above all, what happened to Miss C.A. van der Merwe, later Mrs Strafford? The dusty old directory held no answers.

Eve returned on Wednesday. She left a message for me at the college asking me to dinner at Darwin to "hear the latest". Not that that was really the greatest attraction of the invitation. I went eagerly.

The dining hall at Darwin was small, intimate and modern. With no undergraduates at the college, there was a restrained and cultured air. Eve, wearing her gown over a pink dress, added a stunning beauty. The staff served her with a deference and attentiveness denied others, while the fellows at our table savoured her words as they would a fine wine. There were quizzical glances at me—a stranger in their midst, a mysterious escort for their enigmatic colleague. I enjoyed their envy, although, if they'd only known, my understanding was, if anything, less than theirs.

Eve and I restricted ourselves to small talk over dinner. We adjourned to her rooms for more serious discussion. It was a warm, humid night. We opened the windows for air and sat by them, sipping calvados with our coffee.

"I went through the whole Archive in minute detail," Eve said, sighing a little from memory of the effort.

"And?"

"And I needed to, to find what little I did."

"Which was?"

"The slender file on the bureau." She looked towards it across the room. "It contains copies of the only two documents—other than the certificate—which are likely to help us. Take a look."

I fetched the file and looked through it. Photocopies of two letters, both handwritten and evidently to Julia Lambourne. The first bore no address, but was dated 21 June 1910.

Julia,
Much relieved to hear that you feel able to act for us in this matter. We must not flinch from unpleasant duties when the good of the cause dictates. Annie will deliver the document to you tomorrow. It would be best not to allow Elizabeth to take

possession of it. Keep it safe and secret, since we may yet have further need of it.

C.H.P.

I looked up at Eve. "The initials are of those of Christabel Pankhurst," she said. "Annie is almost certainly Anne Kenney, her trusted lieutenant. As for the document, what can it be but the certificate?"

"I suppose it must be. The timing's certainly right. But this suggests Julia played no part in finding the evidence of Strafford's marriage."

"Perhaps she asked others to check for her. But have a look at the second letter."

Hotel des Sommets,
St. Moritz,
Switzerland.
18 September 1910.

My dear Julia,

I have felt so guilty about not writing to you. Please forgive me. At all events, here are the latest tidings, written on the hotel terrace, within sight of the snow-covered mountaintops. The air here is quite different to London, as you might imagine. I find it positively enervating, such that all I can manage some days is to sit in the sun, listen to the cowbells and read. Zola is my favourite at present. He has a keen eye for so much that is wrong with society.

By contrast, Aunt Mercy has been invigorated by the atmosphere. She tramps the Alpine meadows quite tirelessly, and has developed an enthusiasm for natural history, so much more exotic here than in Putney! I have latterly found pretexts upon which to avoid participation in her excursions. Rest assured, however, I never allow her to go without a guide.

Fatigue is not the only reason, though, for my not accompanying Aunt. Passing through Zurich at the end of August, whom should we meet at our hotel but Gerald Couchman?—that very nice man to whom you introduced me during the summer, at a time when I was scarcely fit to meet anybody socially. He promised that our paths would cross here and so it has proved. He has been at this hotel for a week now and has provided me with charming, considerate and amusing company, being sufficiently aware of my recent distress deftly to avoid preying upon the subject without, at the same time, seeming to underestimate its significance for me. Last night, over dinner, he asked if we could tolerate his company when we move on to Venice at the end of the month. Although I may have appeared less delighted at the prospect than Aunt, it was, *entre nous,* entirely the other way about.

Gerald has a happy knack of enabling me almost entirely—at least for several hours at a time—to forget my past troubles and for more than that I cannot presently ask. Be sure to pass on to Miriam, the Twins and your brother my heartfelt thanks for their support and assistance when it was most needed. To you and the sisterhood in general, I extend my best wishes and encouragement. It seems to me, as I assess matters in repose, that insofar as my experience holds any lesson for the movement, it is that we should look for victory to our own resources and nowhere else. Christabel may, as you say, have arrived at a crucial understanding with those most likely to effect the necessary legislation, but it is the kind of intrigue in which, I am sorry to say, I can place no faith.

Not that any of this, dear Julia, need blight our friendship. I am already feeling much better than I did before we left England and, when we do return, I hope you will find me very much like my old self, never to be, I suspect, wholly restored, but certainly up to—indeed, already looking forward to—a good gossip with an old friend.

With much love from
Elizabeth

Odd, and unsettling, to step outside Strafford's vision and version of events to see them from Elizabeth's oblique, understated angle. My mind played with the meanings that lay between the lines. The proof of Strafford's unworthiness handed to Elizabeth's friend by Christabel Pankhurst, who also has a "crucial understanding" with . . . Lloyd George? Was Strafford's removal one side of a bargain and, if so, did Elizabeth realize the full depths of the intrigues which she "had no faith in"?

A further thought: Elizabeth referred to being introduced to

Couchman "during the summer". I recalled, from the Memoir, Couchman assuring Strafford that he'd not met Elizabeth until after she'd broken her engagement. Though strictly consistent with her letter to Julia, the proximity of the events now seemed suspicious.

"Well," said Eve, slicing gently through my thoughts, "what do you make of them?"

"They support both our theories. The note from Christabel hints at a deal with Lloyd George. The letter from Elizabeth points the moral: that the Suffragettes would have been wise to fight for their rights without trying to persuade politicians to make concessions to them." In fact, my second remark was my concession to Eve.

"Aren't the theories basically one and the same?"

"Are they? Surely Elizabeth was expressing disapproval of any deals or compromises. And remember, she was proved right."

"In what way?"

"Well, if Christabel really did strike a bargain with Lloyd George and deliver Strafford's disgrace as her side of it, then she was taken for a ride, because Lloyd George never repaid her with votes for women."

"We don't know any such bargain was struck. We can *assume* Julia alerted Christabel to Strafford's involvement with Elizabeth and that Christabel in turn alerted Julia to Strafford's deception of Elizabeth. We can even assume Strafford's removal from office suited Lloyd George, but we can't assume there was any formal bargain."

"Surely Elizabeth, in her letter, refers . . ."

"To an understanding, nothing more. Christabel may well have negotiated with Lloyd George. After all, it was he who eventually conceded the issue."

"Not until 1918."

"True, but political favours have to be earned. That's not an operation for the gullible. Remember I criticized the Suffragettes for not exploiting their advantages?"

"I do."

"Well, maybe Christabel should be exempted from that criticism. She would never, you see, have trusted a politician. To do so was Elizabeth's mistake."

"Even so . . ."

"I think," said Eve, standing up with a silencing air of decision and walking to the window, where she stood with her back to me, "I think we would do well to concentrate on the aspect of the affair." It was a calm and modulated statement, but, unmistakably, an instruction. Her very pose, feet apart on the carpet, one hand on her hip, a lithe figure outlined against the night, seemed to place the matter beyond debate. "If, that is," she continued, "a combined approach is to prove successful." Beyond debate, then, if I wanted to remain close to her, in the working sense, or any other sense I cared or could be led to imagine. When she turned to look at me again, my own reaction reminded me that such closeness was now my prime objective. "It would seem such a pity to spoil that."

"I agree." My consent was much more than colloquial.

"Good," said Eve with a smile I'd earned like a political favour. "Then you'll be pleased to know I've made an appointment for us to see my publisher on Friday and put him in the picture as to the revised format of my book . . . and put you, as it were, on the strength. Then we'll be in a position to tackle Elizabeth."

So that was it. The deed was done, the bargain struck, unstated, implied, like any deal that was made between Lloyd George and Christabel Pankhurst. The commodity was different—a hint that my desire for Eve could be fulfilled—but the price was the same: Strafford's name and neck, on a plate, in a Memoir. "Let me have my way with him," Eve was saying, "and maybe you can have yours with me." Our eyes and words danced and dodged around the reality of the choice, but it remained there for me to see, as palpable as the night.

When I left, Eve came down with me to the garden. She'd been cooler, steelier than for some time before and I was, though still snared by my own hopes of her, unnerved by it. We strolled to the bank of the river and looked out across the mirror-like surface. The night was still and sublimely silent. Eve touched my arm and led me down onto a landing stage beneath the weeping willows, where we could sit and listen to the water dappling against the stanchions. The empty yet illuminated Graduate Centre hummed to itself across the river while a sleepless duck quacked plaintively further along the bank.

"After we've been to London on Friday, Martin," said Eve, "I think we deserve a little relaxation."

"I'm all for that."

"A friend of mine at Girton owns a cottage on the Norfolk Broads. I have a standing offer of the use of it, since she never goes there in term-time. This might be a good weekend to take her up on it. We could go up Friday night and stay till Monday, take stock of the project, mess about in her boat and generally enjoy ourselves."

"Sounds delightful."

"It's a charming place—wood and thatch, a lawn running down to the river, private moorings and a little dinghy."

"It's all right." I smiled. I didn't need much convincing. "I'm sure it would be wonderful. I can't wait."

"Business before pleasure, Martin. First we must go to London."

"Till Friday then." I leant forward and kissed her.

She kept her face close to mine. "As you say, until Friday." We rose then and walked across the lawn towards the gate. "I'll pick you up from Princes' at nine o'clock."

"Okay. I'll be waiting."

We kissed again at the gate, then I walked away down Silver Street while the night and Darwin College swallowed Eve, but left her, whole and bewitching, in my mind. She had, with the last proposal, softened the blow, made the bruise to my researcher's ego easily bearable for the sake of a weekend with her, alone but together.

Thursday, May 12th was just another day, 24 hours between me and a delicious prospect. It was cool, I recall, and wet—an interval, an interlude, a waiting time when profundity was unthinkable. But perhaps revelation often comes when you're not looking for it, resolution when you don't realize you need it. That's how it was for me.

Confined to my room by nagging rain and incipient boredom—although Eve believed me to be dutifully reading in the U.L.—I fell to playing a fatal game of what if? Strafford's

Memoir stared at me across the room, mute but accusing, so it was probably inevitable that I should think about it. I already knew I had a choice. Either the marriage certificate was a forgery—elaborate, convincing and not very likely—or the Memoir was a calculated lie—also elaborate, also convincing and, if anything, even less likely. But what if, I fell to thinking, what if both were genuine? They couldn't be, of course, but, if they were, then, strangely, everything made a weird kind of sense. If every word of the Memoir was true as far as Strafford knew, then no wonder he was shocked and baffled by his sudden fall from grace. If the certificate was genuine, no wonder Elizabeth wanted nothing more to do with him. I'd been looking to disprove one by reference to the other. What if, instead, I tried to use them to confirm each other? I didn't know how to go about that, but I knew it didn't involve seeking Elizabeth's co-operation in a piece of Suffragette hagiography that went in for cheap psychology on the side at Strafford's expense. And that, I knew, was what Eve had in mind: an academic treatise translated into a bestseller by a travesty of the Memoir. I was offered a share of the success strictly on Eve's terms, and it was only my obsession with her which made me entertain those terms. We were to see her publisher the next day, no doubt to consign to him the right to use the Memoir. In return, I was offered a weekend in Norfolk. It was appalling to realize that I thought it a worthwhile trade.

Away from Eve, when I looked out the window at the rain washing the flagstones of Princes' Hall, against a dripping percussion of water flooding from the gargoyled spouts of ancient guttering, away from the toss of her hair, the timbre of her voice, I could see her idea for what it was and reject it. But where would I get the courage to tell her so next day? Nothing I knew about myself suggested I would find it.

Eve had said she would collect me at nine o'clock, so I made sure I was at Darwin by 8.30. The bedmakers were still on the staircases, but Eve's floor was quiet and, when I knocked the door, I heard her "Come in", soft but distinct, from an inner room.

She was at the far end of the lounge, seated at the harpsichord but turned to face the door, as if she'd just been playing, though I'd not heard her doing so on my way in. She was dressed somberly, in a plain black skirt and matching lightweight jumper, hair tied back in a bun, her appearance severe against the pale wood of the harpsichord. She didn't smile and she didn't move, just regarded me with the commanding scrutiny which seemed always at her disposal and which now prevented me walking further than the doorway.

"Martin," she said. "What brings you here?" The question sounded like a dare, had that cool edge she usually blunted with warmth for my benefit. But not this time. It fractured the shafted morning air in the room, crystallized it as in the frozen moment of the pointilliste picture on the wall.

"I had to come," I replied, feeling the sentence flounder. "I've decided . . . our approach, it won't work." Eve said nothing, left me time and space to blunder into. "I still think Strafford was a wronged man . . . it seems only just to continue investigating the possibility."

"What exactly do you mean?" The second word was stressed with an impatience bordering on something worse.

I walked to the window for air, feeling surprised at my own confusion, foolish in my supposed resolve. "I mean . . . I'm not prepared to give up the Memoir to your approach." I looked at Eve across a haze of sunlight angling through the window between us. She raised one eyebrow, as if to ask me and herself how to interpret the word 'Approach' and I hurried to scotch the ambiguity. "I'm saying that . . . before committing ourselves to a particular line . . . before seeing your publisher . . . we give ourselves more time to make up our minds."

"I've already made up my mind."

A sickening preception that Eve had made up her mind, not about Strafford or her book, but about the other thing between us, the shy shadow debate in all our discussions, the delicate entertainment of an offer of love, and made it up, moreover, in a way I dreaded, made me step forward to see her clearly, drove me into some dilution of my decision.

"All I'm saying, Eye, is let's give Strafford the benefit of the doubt . . . let's keep an open mind . . . together we can . . ."

I reached forward to take her hand, a hopeful clutch at reassurance. But Eve jumped up and stepped away, letting the lid fall across the keyboard of the harpsichord with a crash like a gunshot. She glared at me, breathing heavily. "Don't touch me."

I froze, appalled and horrified, not so much by the harsh words as the simmering revulsion in her look. What did she mean? My mind raced to answer but couldn't. While I flailed inwardly, like a climber seeking holds on a smooth, sheer slope, she spoke again, with a voice from the clouds.

"I'll give Strafford the benefit of the doubt, Martin. At least he has the decency to be dead. But there's no doubt in your case, is there?"

What doubt? What case? An awful answer was laughing at me across an impossible chasm. I felt as if I was falling and remembered an old dream. Running, fast as the wind, to dislodge a cackling, misshapen dwarf from my back, hearing the thud and feeling the lightness after, pausing, free at last, to gulp some air, and then, there was the dig of his claw-like hands in my shoulders, the foul stench of his breath as he whispered in my ear, "Did you think you'd lost me, Martin? Run as far or as fast as you like . . . you never will."

I must have closed my eyes for an instant, as if to still the sensation of plummeting. There was a rustle of paper and when I looked again, Eve had thrown some old newspapers onto the seat of her harpsichord stool.

"Never mind about Strafford's past," she said. "There's yours—for all to see. Now would you like to tell me again why you left teaching, why your marriage ended? Or can't the humble seeker after truth face it about himself?"

I crouched by the stool and picked up the paper on top of the pile. I recognized it at once: *The Kentish Courier,* 6 June 1973, front page, centre right, a three-column article under the headline TAUGHT MORE THAN HISTORY: SEX SCANDAL AT AXBOROUGH GRAMMAR SCHOOL and, under that, DAUGHTER'S CAREER WRECKED BY LECHEROUS TEACHER, CLAIMS OUTRAGED PARENT. "Tom Campion, widely respected Round Table charity campaigner and Managing Director of Hammer Haulage, Co. Ltd., Axborough, spoke yesterday of his anger and outrage at the lenient treatment of Mr Martin Radford, currently suspended from his history-teaching post at Axborough Grammar School following revelations that he had used extra pre-A level tuition as cover for a sexual relationship with his seventeen-year-old pupil, Jane Campion, now undergoing psychiatric treatment and said by her father to be 'too broken up' to sit her examinations next week. Mr Radford, 26, a married man and father of a daughter himself, was yesterday unavailable for comment at his home, 15 Gales Crescent, Axborough, but Mr Campion, 44, protested that 'Radford shouldn't be allowed to sit at home on full salary when he's answerable for the corruption of my daughter. He should be brought to justice.' A police spokesman said yesterday, 'Mr Campion has spoken to us, but his daughter is seventeen and therefore over the legal age of consent. This is a matter between Mr Radford and his employers.' The Headmaster of Axborough Grammer School, Mr Hugh Wilmott, would only say yesterday that Mr Radford's conduct had been referred to the Director of Education and that he had been suspended until a decision could be made. He hoped that Jane would still . . ."

I didn't want to read anymore, knew it by heart anyway. Next in the pile was the Sunday paper that had persuaded "broken up" Miss Campion to sell her lurid story for readers to salivate over with their bacon and eggs. What had been a private, irresistible obsession became a piece of public pornography. Jane, with her demure, distraught look for the cameras, honed her image as the violated victim, while Radford, the unheard actor in every tabloid sentence, couldn't tell anyone that suspension was worse than hanging, couldn't stop the moral orgy of retribution. Somewhere here, I knew, we'd find SUSPENDED TEACHER'S WIFE WALKS OUT, with Helen quoted in all her prurient glory: "I cannot remain—or allow my daughter to remain—with a man who has behaved as my husband has." Whether the minor paragraph would be here, recording my eventual dismissal after the long, coiling agony of a committee enquiry, seemed more doubtful.

I dropped the paper and looked up at Eve. "It was a long time ago," I said lamely. "These papers make it sound . . . worse than it was."

"How would you make it sound better?"

"I don't know," I stood up and wiped my hands nervously on the sides of my trousers. "That's why I couldn't . . . tell you."

"That's why you lied."

"If you like."

"Well I don't like. I'm not some adolescent for you to dazzle and bed and throw away."

"I never . . . thought you were."

"You thought you could deceive me and seduce me with a lie as big as Strafford's. If we'd gone to Norfolk this weekend, maybe you'd have succeeded. But not now. Because I don't need you or Strafford."

"Maybe I need you."

The revulsion in Eve's eyes turned to contempt. There was no hint of mercy. "Bad luck, Martin. I'm not interested in an unemployed sex offender. Take your pathetic fantasies . . . and get out."

There was nothing else to do. I moved to the door. But there was more to say. I turned on the threshold. "I lied, Eve, because I was afraid this was how you would react to my . . . lapse."

"Is that what you call it?"

"I'm not denying anything. But can't I ever be allowed to forget it?"

"Can Jane Campion?"

"I expect she's all right."

"But you don't know?"

"No."

Eve walked round and behind the harpsichord, so that the stool, with its incriminating load of newsprint, stood between us. "Exactly. You don't want to know. You don't want to live with the consequences of your actions. You want to smash a life, grab your pleasure and go free."

"It wasn't like that."

"It may have been—for all you know or care. No wonder you defend Strafford. He did much the same thing. Well I want none of it."

I stood my ground and played the only trump I held. "I'm not alone in suppressing the truth. You never told me you were working for the Couchmans."

Eve's contempt was verging now on boredom. "This isn't a game, Martin. Just try to understand that what I've learned about you makes it impossible—intolerable—for me to associate with you. Please leave now—and don't come back."

"One question. How did you find out?"

"A well-wisher told me your seamy little secret, and I'm grateful to them." She walked slowly over to the telephone on the bookcase. "If you don't go now, I'll have you removed."

I stared at her incredulously. I realized that the shock to her of the truth about me must be great. I'd learned to live with it because I'd had to—why should she? I'd lied, yes, and worse, but did I really deserve this clinical dismissal? Every gesture of Eve's, every look, suggested that she believed I did, that, if I remained, she might actually enjoy my being turned out by porters, because degraded men don't deserve dignity.

If I'd been Strafford, I remember thinking, I might have stayed, argued and fought it out. But he'd had the strength of not knowing his crime, whereas I was in no doubt. From the truth, as much as Eve's coolly threatening tone, I retreated headlong down the stairs.

Where do you go in flight from yourself? I'd asked that before, several times since 1973, perhaps, subconsciously, even before. In the wake of exposure, publicity and disgrace, I'd even contemplated suicide. But if I'd had enough strength for that, I'd never have been weak enough to fall for Jane in the first place.

Black Friday in Cambridge. I wandered along Silver Street in a daze, not knowing what to do or where to go. I turned off and headed south across Sheep's Green, alongside the Granta, where, thirteen days before, I'd punted with Eve, where we'd smiled and flirted on the edges of intimacy, lied and lazed our way towards today's bitter parting.

Five

I sat up all that night staring out the window at the tangible nothing of night, neither wanting nor daring—from a fear of dreaming—to sleep. There was something else, I knew, offering none of the ecstasy I'd hoped for with Eve, none of the respectability I'd long ago forfeited, but at least a purpose, a cause, a scrap of honour. It was Strafford. His mystery had fallen to me, and if there was anything left of Martin Radford worth calling a man, this at least I could try to measure up to. What I'd been incapable of doing, Eve had done for me: she'd chosen what I should do.

Next morning, on the London train, I started thinking about something more prosaic but nonetheless irksome. Who'd told Eve about my past? Who'd been the "well wisher" she was grateful to? And why tell her? Who stood to gain by it?

A jealous lover I ruled out. There'd been a sign of one and, even if there had been, what would he know about me? Few people remembered a nine days' wonder four years later.

No, the answer was clear. It had to be the one person I'd told directly about my plans for and with Eve: Alec, my loyal trusted friend. He'd materialized without warning, questioned me, could have guessed what little I didn't tell him and he alone knew all about Axborough in 1973 because I told him at the time and again since, in drunken confessionals when I'd needed to explain to somebody, as well as myself, what it had all meant. Who else would have known where to lay hands on the chapter and verse of my disgrace as well as where to find the one person who would, four years on, be as shocked by it as if it had happened yesterday?

But why? It was the only answer which made sense and yet it made no sense. I felt entitled to know Alec and I felt sure I did. It wasn't his style, this mean, covert betrayal. And he'd so recently shown me his customary generosity by fixing the job with Sellick.

The train stopped at Bishop's Stortford, but my mind accelerated through another layer of deception: the job with Sellick. My talk with Alec in the pub in Clerkenwell had threatened the basis of that job quite specifically. It had implied I was about to ditch Sellick and use the Memoir for my own purposes, notably to get closer to Eve. Never mind that I'd had second thoughts later. That had been the intention Alec had wheedled out of me. I remembered our drink-loosened chat:

"I don't think that's the sort of discovery Leo's hoping for."

"Neither do I . . . I'd appreciate your keeping quiet about it."

And Alec had said he would, as, earlier, he'd spoken of his dissatisfaction with being Sellick's errand boy and later had said:

"Don't worry about me, Martin. I've no axe to grind."

But what if he had? What if all that chafing at well-paid servitude to Sellick had just been to lull me into frank disclosure? What if he'd even then been running an errand for Sellick, to check on my progress, and had known his paymaster wouldn't like what he'd heard? What if he'd reported back and been told that my dalliance with Eve must be stopped, that I must be put back on the straight and narrow? If so, Alec had had the means to do it, painfully but effectively.

As soon as we reached London, I dashed to a phone and rang Alec's hotel.

"Mr Fowler booked out yesterday morning, sir . . . No, no forwarding address . . . I believe he said he was leaving the country."

Yes, he would have done. Scuttled back to Madeira now he'd done his job. God, Alec, I thought, if you've really done this to me . . . then you're no better than I am. What was the reason? What was the bribe? What price did you hold out for?

It was a long time coming. I hadn't felt it when they'd denounced me in Axborough, hadn't been able to feel it on behalf of Strafford. But I felt it now, stirring and seething within me: anger—a rising fury at the Couchmans and all they'd done and all they represented: a falsified morality that said the likes of Strafford and me weren't permitted to succeed, weren't allowed to be happy. Well, Strafford and I could prove them wrong. It was time to put the record straight. I had to see Elizabeth, the unheard witness, before Eve could get to her or Henry pack her off again. She'd lived too long to avoid a last encounter with her past.

It was a relief to find that Jerry had gone away for the weekend and that I could be alone in the house. I felt bone weary and decided to stay overnight, even thought—and smiled at the thought—of writing another report for Sellick. But there'd be no report. I wasn't doing this for Sellick any more.

It was odd to think that I was, already, retracing my steps, yet in another way only just beginning, as if all before had been a dry run and this time the guns were loaded. Victoria, Chichester and a taxi rider to Miston by night. A room at The Royal Oak to lay up in, feeling furtive and resenting having to, feeling nervous about the morrow and knowing why. I'd waited a long time—Strafford far longer—for a word with this stubbornly living lady, the only one left with a foot in both camps, an existence shared between the real, spare presence of a room at a village inn—where the floorboards rumbled with the laughter of locals drinking after time—and the leatherbound, scarcely credible reality of a remote, remembered world. Another vigil, another dawn—a deed I couldn't dodge.

I exerted myself to wait until a reasonable hour. Even then, it was before nine o'clock when I left The Royal Oak on a ludicrously sweet, bird-chirruping, bright-as-paint spring morning. A GPO van was parked by the post office down the road and, on the other side, a butcher in a striped apron was arranging chops in his window. Old ladies were pottering through the village dressed for winter, carrying wicker shopping baskets and trailing scottie dogs on leads.

The flowers in the garden were a little more luxuriant, otherwise Quarterleigh was as it had been a month before: the white gates, the forsythia, the gravel drive and the pink-washed house, recumbent in its fold of the Sussex Downs, with honeysuckle round its door.

It was not Elizabeth who answered the door. But it wasn't Henry either. Instead, a cheery, red-cheeked dumpling of a woman in a flowered housecoat, smiling out of habit even though it was suspiciously early and she didn't know me.

"Is Lady Couchman at home?"

"Ar, she is, but she's 'avin' breakfast. It's a mite early to be callin' on folks."

"You're right. I'm sorry. But, if she could spare me a moment, I'd be most grateful."

"I'll go an' ask." She lumbered off down the hall, then stopped and turned round. "What shall I say y'name is?"

"Martin Radford. She may remember me." I hoped not, but pretence was pointless.

The housecoated lady returned a moment later. "Mrs Couchman"—there was no ladyship here, it seemed—"says you can come in, if you're 'appy to take us as you find us."

"Of course." I followed her along the low-ceilinged passage, then turned behind her into a room with two windows looking out onto the garden, so that the occupant could have seen me coming.

In a chair on the far side of a dark gate-leg table was Elizabeth. I knew her at once, not so much from our one brief meeting at my wedding seven years before—though she'd changed little since—as from all the other, better, vicarious ways I'd made her acquaintance.

She was eighty-eight years old, but looked no more than seventy of them in her starched blouse and powdered dignity. The hair was shorter, of course, snowy white and simply cut, the face lined with a filigree of faded beauty turned to fragile charm, the mouth had lost its assertiveness and gained a winning humility. But the way she held her head as I walked in, the flash of her dark, glinting, unchanged eyes, were still as they were, for all the years, in that photograph on Madeira. If I'd been Strafford, walking in from a banished past, I'd still have loved her—for her poised serenity, her look of reconciled enfeeblement, her embodiment of so many memories.

"Martin," she said. "How very nice to see you again."

I was taken aback by this kindly, regal greeting. "Lady Couchman . . . I'm surprised you remember me."

"Of course I do, my dear. We old ladies have little to do but remember. Would you care for some tea—or toast? Have you come far?" This can't be, I thought. You can't just welcome me like a favourite nephew. But she could and did. "Dora, could you possibly bring some hot water for the tea?" Dora waddled out. A black and white cat glared at me and made way reluctantly for me to sit down.

"No toast for me," I said. "I've just had breakfast at The Royal Oak."

"Really? It's comfortable there, I believe. What brings you to these remote parts, my dear?"

"You do."

"I'm flattered that a young man should want to look out this old stick."

"I came to see you a month ago, but you were away. Your son was here."

"Strange. He's never mentioned it."

"He wouldn't. We've not been on good terms since Helen and I parted."

"I'm sorry to hear that."

"In fact, I didn't think I was on good terms with any of your family."

"Well, that just shows you how wrong you can be, young man." Dora rattled in with the hot water and poured some into the pot, then pottered out humming to herself. "Dora is such a dear. I don't know what I'd do without her."

"Does she live here?"

"Oh no. She comes in mornings and afternoons for a couple of hours to attend to those things I'm getting too old for."

"You don't look too old for much."

She smiled. "Martin, if I were fifty years younger, I'd think you were trying to turn my head."

"I am, in a way. Or rather, turn your mind, back a little more than fifty years."

"Goodness—so far?"

"I'm afraid so."

"You needn't be. Reminiscence is one of the few things left to me."

"The past isn't always pleasant to recall. Look at my own."

"My dear, I may be old, but I'm not taken in by everything people tell me. You had your problems, I believe, as did Helen, and naturally I'm sorry for her, because she's my granddaughter. But you mustn't judge me by my son's attitude. Like his father, Henry is good-hearted, but inclined to be hasty. I try to judge people only by what I personally know of them."

Sensing that, if I waited much longer, I wouldn't be able to say anything to this dear old lady, I blurted it out. "Is that how you judged Edwin Strafford?"

She looked at mc as if she'd seen a ghost. Maybe she had. "Edwin? What do you know of Edwin?"

"More than you, I think. I know why you broke your engagement with him, which he never did. I know how he frittered away his life after you rejected him. I think I know what you meant to him, and what losing you meant to him."

She sat back in her chair. "Martin, you alarm me. I'm not used to shocks like this."

"I know. I'm sorry." I rose and went to her side. "Are you all right?"

"Yes, yes. I think so. But please, what do you mean?"

"Would you like to sit in an armchair?"

"I think perhaps I should." I helped her up. "It's all right. I can manage." A touch of vexation. She sank into a chair by the fireplace, recovered herself a little. "I'm forgetting myself. Do help yourself to some tea."

"Not just at the moment."

"Then please continue. I don't understand what you're telling me."

I sat down opposite her, on the edge of my chair. "Elizabeth"—the use of her name seemed to come naturally—"I have in my possession a copy of a memoir written by Edwin Strafford in his retirement on Madeira. It relates his life in full, especially the period of his engagement to you. It professes a lifelong bafflement as to why you ended that engagement. I know that you discovered he was already married. But the Memoir contains no mention of such a thing, as if Strafford never knew he was married. I have this Memoir with me today, here in this room." I pointed to the bag I'd dropped by the side of her chair.

"There must be some mistake." It was a hope more than an assertion.

"There must indeed be—somewhere. That's what I'm trying to find out. Would you like to look at the Memoir?" Without waiting for an answer, I fetched it from the bag and handed it to her. It seemed more fitting for her to receive it than anyone. It was, after all, written for her. Elizabeth held it as she might an original painting by a famous artist, not previously known to exist: cautiously, with nervous apprehension.

"Martin, my dear, you must understand how . . . unexpected this is."

"I do understand that. It was uncovered by the present owner of Strafford's property on Madeira. He's hired me to research its background."

"Which has turned out to be close to home?"

"Too close for comfort, to judge by your son's reaction to my visit."

Elizabeth smiled wanly. "Dear Henry would only have been trying to protect me. My engagement to Edwin is a painful memory. But not so painful now as it once was. If my dear husband were alive, he would probably throw this onto the fire. But I, alas, was always too curious for my own good."

"Your late husband features in the document."

"I see." She nodded her head slowly. "It is then, as you say, thorough."

"Yes."

"Having read it, how much do you know?"

"As much as Strafford ever knew. But why not read it yourself?"

"Yes"—a firm set of her jaw—"I think that would be best." She opened it carefully. "I see that it may take some time. Can you leave it here?"

"I don't think you'll want to put it down once you've started."

"Don't worry, Martin." She smiled, with a defiant hint of mischief. "It'll be quite safe with me. I am not my late husband—or my son." I believed her. "But old ladies lack stamina. Suppose you were to return later. We could discuss it then."

I had no choice. "Okay. About seven o'clock, perhaps?"

"That would seem admirable."

"I'll leave you then." I rose to go.

"Would you mind showing yourself out, my dear? Dora becomes tetchy if called upon to often." I assured her I didn't and made for the door. "Oh Martin," she called from her chair, "thank you for bringing this to me." Elizabeth was the first to have thanked me for delivering the Memoir. I was flattered by her courtesy. "And, could you fetch my reading glasses from the table before you go?" As I did so, the cat glanced up at me superciliously from the seat it had reclaimed. "It is unquestionably Edwin's hand," proclaimed Elizabeth, once she'd propped the tiny gold-rimmed spectacles on her nose. "So strange to see it again after all these years."

I wondered if she'd kept any of Strafford's letters but didn't ask. "I'll leave you to it."

"Thank you, my dear."

As I walked away up the drive, I felt vaguely cheated. Elizabeth was old, charming and accessible. Her house was no fortress. There was in her no hint of bitterness at Strafford for hurting her or at me for reminding her of it. It had all been absurdly easy. I'd come and gone like a tradesman from the village making a delivery. Only this was one debt she couldn't settle monthly by cheque. I'd be back later for payment.

An empty day, waiting on the reading speed and dozing habits of an elderly lady, gave me time to fret. I followed a chalk track up onto the Downs and back again in time for lunch at The Royal Oak. Afterwards, nervously, guiltily, I stole down the footpath by the brook to the wood where I'd spied on Henry. Quarterleigh, with Dora gone home, had a look of dormant normality. I'd half expected to see Henry's car in the garage, but there was no sign of it. I'd known there wouldn't be, had only gone there to quell an irrational fear.

That done, there was nothing to do but lie on the bed in my room at the inn and wait for evening.

A dove from the churchyard was cooing somewhere in the garden of Quarterleigh. Dora was back for another round of duty, depositing empty milk bottles on the doorstep as I walked down the drive.

"Missus said I were to expect you," she said neutrally. "You'll find 'er in the conservatory."

She showed me through. The conservatory was at the back of the house, looking down the sloping lawn to the brook, where small clouds of midges floated among the reeds. The room preserved an afternoon warmth, with rugs spread on a stone floor and potted plants exuding a musty aroma. Elizabeth was seated on cushions in a wicker reclining chair, with the cat on her lap and the Memoir, in its file, on a footstool by her side.

"Good evening, Martin," she said.

"Good evening." I looked out of the window. "Your daffodils are going over."

"All things do, my dear. Please sit down."

I moved a copy of *Sussex Life* from a canvas-backed chair and sat next to her, our seats arranged so that we saw more of the garden than each other.

"You have a lovely home," I remarked.

"I feel at peace here, which is all I now seek. Alas, it is clear that Edwin never found that precious commodity."

"You finished the Memoir then?"

"Yes, indeed. I'm seeing double and feeling heavy in the head, but I've read what Edwin had to say and I'm glad to have done so."

"And what do you make of it?"

"Ah, that's more difficult than reading. It is—what else could it be?—disturbing. Edwin's Memoir reads in every sentence like God's own truth. Only, I know it can't be. It's rather shocking to have it all told, so detailed, so personal, to have it read by a young man like you, to know that you know how I felt to love a man and be betrayed by him."

"I do see that."

"I wonder if you do. You said earlier that you know why I broke my engagement with Edwin. How did you find out?"

"A . . . colleague . . . found Strafford's marriage certificate in the memorabilia Julia Lambourne—Mrs Kendrick—bequeathed to Birkbeck College, London."

"Ah, so that's where it went. I've sometimes wondered."

"Could you tell me more about it?"

"I don't really think I could. You see, Martin, I need a little time to adjust to this."

"I understand. It's just that . . ."

"You're eager for answers. I understand too. Do you have the certificate?"

"Not here. But I've seen it. It's quite conclusive. Strafford married a Miss van der Merwe in South Africa in 1900."

Elizabeth frowned slightly. "Quite so. But you wouldn't think it, would you, to read this?" She inclined her head at the Memoir.

"No. That's just the point."

"Martin, my dear, I have a suggestion. Would you care to stay here for a few days? I'm sure it's very pleasant at The Royal Oak, but here you could be certain the Memoir was safe"—she smiled—"and I could try to answer some of your questions, in an old lady's good time."

"That's kind of you. I'd be delighted to." I was impatient to hear what she thought, but didn't want to jeopardize anything by pressurizing her.

"I'll ask Dora to make up a bed in the guest room while you collect your luggage."

"I'd better go straightaway."

"Before you do, I have a question. Who is the man who has hired you? What is his interest?"

"Leo Sellick? He's a hotelier on Madeira who brought Strafford's house when it came onto the market. When he found the Memoir, it fascinated him and he's employed me to satisfy his curiosity. I haven't told him about Strafford's secret marriage yet."

"I see. So many people curious about my past."

"It's inevitable."

"Not but for this." She was right, but the Memoir couldn't be disregarded, any more than Strafford's marriage could be, except by him. Not that I had the impression Elizabeth wanted to disregard it. I think I'd brought it to her at the right stage of her life, when there was nothing left to lose—for her, anyway.

When I got back from The Royal Oaks, Elizabeth had already gone to bed. Dora showed me to my room, then left. I settled in, feeling strangely at ease. There was a vast, feather-mattressed double bed, a broad, solid wardrobe, an empty wash-handstand behind the door, a sash window at floor level looking down into the garden.

As Elizabeth had said she did, I felt a peace in Quarterleigh. It was that sort of place, cosy, rural, womb-like. Even the creaks were comforting. I slept better than I had for days.

"Good morning, Martin." Elizabeth greeted me with her button-bright smile over the breakfast table. "It's a lovely day." Undeniably: the sun was already warm through the last of the moisture on the window. "Can you drive?"

"Well . . . yes."

"My doctor—a dear, but a terrible fusspot—has instructed me not to. So my car has few outings. I wondered if you would care to take us up on to the Downs."

"Ah . . . yes. Certainly."

"Splendid. I feel in need of fresh air. We can talk up there to our hearts' content."

Dora seemed amazed to learn that we were going for a drive. The set of her jaw suggested she didn't like some of the changes to routine stemming from my arrival.

Elizabeth appeared in a dark blue dress under a white raincoat, carrying a walking stick and sniffing the sweet air from beneath the brim of a pale straw hat. For all her frailty, she looked like a lady with a mission.

At Elizabeth's instruction, I drove north-west to Harting Hill, one of the more precipitous parts of the South Downs escarpment. We parked at the top and walked slowly east along the spiral track linking the tops of the downs. It was a fine, breezy morning, with the sheep-cropped turf firm beneath our feet, skylarks' song and the bleat of lambs blown to us on the wind. Yew-clumped slopes fell away below to the flat plain of the Rother valley. We had the chalky path to ourselves, to walk and talk.

"When Julia first told me Edwin was married," said Elizabeth slowly, treading steadily in time to her breath, "I refused to believe her. She was waiting for me in Putney with my aunt when I returned from Edwin's house, having . . . been there since the previous day."

"This would have been 23rd June 1910?"

"Is the date so important?"

"It may be."

"Well, the Memoir would confirm it. At all events, it did not take them long to guess where I had been and, though I had naturally expected them to be shocked, I had not foreseen the horror and outrage with which they reacted. Julia, you see, was something of a free-thinker and my aunt the most indulgent of guardians.

"I sought to set their minds at rest by announcing that Edwin and I were to be married at once. This, however, only increased their consternation. Julia had, you see, already told my aunt what she knew. As I say, I refused to believe it when Julia told me. It went against everything I knew and understood about Edwin. It was simply incredible."

"What changed your mind?"

"The documentary proof. Julia had not wished to produce it, but felt obliged to do when she saw that I could not otherwise be convinced. And then it all seemed to make an unpalatable kind of sense."

"In what way?"

"For nine months, Edwin had found good political reasons why we could not marry. There had been one delay after another, none of his making. Or so it had seemed. But it suddenly occurred to me that it could all have been an elaborate fraud, leading me on with a promise he could not keep until . . . until he had achieved his objective."

"Was there any other proof?"

"Why yes. Julia's brother Archie had met an officer from Edwin's regiment who recalled that he had married in South Africa. Archie confirmed that to me."

"Who was this officer?"

"Can't you guess?"

"Gerald Couchman."

"That's right, Martin. I wasn't introduced to Gerald until later. At first, I thought little of him, but . . ."

"He proved to have winning ways on holiday in Switzerland and Italy."

Elizabeth stopped in her tracks. "How did you know that?"

"Along with the certificate, the Kendrick Archive also contains a letter from you to Julia reporting Gerald's arrival in St Moritz."

"I see." She smiled. "It's disconcerting to have you know so much about me."

"Did your husband say much about Strafford?"

"Not really. He knew it was a subject best left alone."

"Do you think he supplied the certificate?"

"No. I assume Julia obtained it on her own initiative."

"Would it surprise you to learn that Christabel Pankhurst supplied it to Julia?"

"Not greatly. Christabel would not have approved of Edwin and me. She would have seen it as a form of treachery."

I told her about the evidence of a plot between Christabel and Lloyd George. I stopped myself suggesting that Couchman might have been involved.

"What you say is quite possible, Martin. Unfortunately, all it proves is that certain people wanted something to use against Edwin and he, in his weakness, gave it to them."

"Has the Memoir told you much that you didn't already know?"

"Not a great deal."

"About your husband, for instance?"

We stopped on arriving at a fingerpost in the vale below Beacon Hill. Elizabeth looked at me frankly. "Gerald never made any secret of his failings—at Cambridge, Colenso or elsewhere. It was his honesty that first drew me to him. We had a long courtship and a long happy marriage."

"I'm glad to hear it." We turned and began to retrace our steps.

"It has to be said, my dear, that there was the great difference between Gerald and Edwin. In a sense, a hasty marriage in South Africa was no worse than a loss of nerve in battle. But Edwin tried to conceal his lapse, whereas Gerald did not. They were rewarded accordingly. Gerald was a dear, good, flawed, loving man: a man I'm proud to have been married to."

"Do you think the Memoir is one last concealment by Strafford?"

"I must presume so. And yet . . . and yet, it won't quite do, will it? If Edwin was ever to have given a full account of himself, the Memoir would have been it. So how can we just write it off?"

"We can't. That's why I'm here."

We drove down to The Maple Inn in Buriton and sat in the garden under a sunshade. I drank beer while Elizabeth sipped a sherry. It all seemed innocent and rather quaint, like taking a maiden aunt out for a treat. Only our talk was of darker stuff.

"There's a question I must ask you."

"Go ahead, my dear."

"Strafford tormented himself over what he saw as an inexplicable rejection. We think he could have explained it himself but couldn't bear to. Why didn't you remove all doubts by simply confronting him with the evidence of his marriage?"

"Ah, remember that I didn't know Edwin was in any doubt —why should he have been? I presumed he never intended to go through with our wedding, since that would have been criminal rather than merely deceitful. By continuing to insist he wanted to marry me, he seemed only to be tormenting me. And the last thing I wanted was argument or denial from him. I felt distressed and betrayed, in no condition to discuss anything. I wanted Edwin just to leave me alone."

"Even so . . ."

"There was another reason. Julia told me the information in strictest confidence. I was to say as little as possible about it, which wasn't difficult, since I wanted to say nothing."

Tea back at Quarterleigh. We sat in garden chairs by the edge of the brook.

"Do you remember Strafford's nephew, Ambrose?" I asked.

"Why yes." Elizabeth smiled. "A charming boy. His parents weren't sure about me when I visited Barrowteign with Edwin in the summer of 1909. I see from the Memoir that Florence Strafford was even more suspicious of me than I'd supposed. But Ambrose—well, he had a child's trust and welcomed me to that house as one innocent receiving another."

"You never considered going back to Barrowteign?"

"Hardly."

"If you did, you'd find Ambrose still there—well, close at hand anyway. I looked him up last month: the last of his line. An old man now, of course, too fond of his cider and dwelling a bit in the past. But a generous host."

Elizabeth shook her head. "Good Lord. Dear little Ambrose—become an old man? It hardly seems possible. How is he?"

"As well as his drinking and age will allow. But . . . troubled."

"By what?"

"Doubt, suspicion, unanswered questions."

"Like his uncle?"

"No, about his uncle. What do you know about Strafford's death?"

"It was in the paper—a railway accident near Barrowteign. Gerald pointed it out to me. I think he was secretly rather relieved. For myself, I was sad but not unduly surprised. I was glad they said it was an accident but had my own opinion."

"Suicide?"

"Call it that if you like. I think Edwin just walked away from life."

"That's not what Ambrose thinks."

"I suppose he wouldn't."

"He doesn't think it was an accident either."

"Then what?"

"Murder." The setting—trickling water, a green lawn and soft sunshine—disinfected the world. I was glad of it. I didn't want to haunt this old lady with Websterian visions, just bring something into the open, into unambiguous daylight.

Elizabeth sipped tea, as if to steady her nerves. "Extraordinary. Tell me more." She said it without seeming to want more, rather with an air of duty.

So I told her more: of Strafford materializing at Barrowteign in the spring of 1951, of his strange behaviour there, and his unidentified visitors, of the night of his death, of Ambrose's lurid version of events.

"Who does Ambrose think these . . . intruders . . . were?"

"He doesn't have a clue."

"Do you?"

"A clue? Yes. The Memoir is the only clue Strafford left us. Who would have wanted—or needed—to threaten an old man returning from exile?" Elizabeth said nothing. "You said your husband was relieved to hear of Strafford's death."

"Yes, I did." A long, thoughtful pause. "Tell me, Martin, why do you think Edwin returned from Madeira?"

"I don't know. He finished the Memoir seven months before. There's no sign in it that he intended such a visit."

"Quite the reverse, to my mind. Did something happen—something change—that drove him to come?"

"How can we tell?"

"I suppose we can't. Not now."

Elizabeth remained the most gracious and considerate of hostesses, asking over dinner how much I saw of Laura these days and never referring once to my disgrace in the eyes of her family. But she also seemed more anxious than before, as if preparing—reluctantly and apprehensively—for something more significant than anything we'd so far said.

Later, as we sat in armchairs round the large fireplace in the drawing room, she insisted I have a glass of port, though she drank nothing stronger than coffee. Only then could she come to the point, and even then obliquely, with an apparently unnecessary question.

"When did I last meet Edwin, Martin?"

"Surely you don't need to ask me that?"

"I'd like you to tell me."

"Okay. It's described in the Memoir. Hampstead Heath, January 1919."

"Not so, I fear. I should have told you before, but it didn't seem relevant. Now, in view of what Ambrose thinks, it has to be said. I last saw Edwin a month before he died—in early May, 1951."

So. The tables were turned. I'd surprised Elizabeth, but now she'd surprised me. Layer by layer, we were slowly approaching the truth. But what it was neither of us who sat swapping revelations in a cottage drawing room that evening had, even then, any idea.

"Tell me more." I deliberately borrowed Elizabeth's own phrase.

"There is a poem," she said, in a cobwebbed voice, "by Thomas Hardy, which begins this story. Whenever I read it, I think of Edwin that day, though I've never spoken of it till now. You'll find a collection of Hardy's poems in the bookcase behind your chair. Could you get it out and read one to me? You'll find it in the section 'Poems of 1912–13'." I turned to it. "After a Journey." I found the page and began to read.

"'Hereto I come to view a voiceless ghost . . .'"

"No," she said gently. "Next verse."

"'Yes: I have re-entered your olden haunts at last:
'Through the years, through the dead scenes I have tracked you;
'What have you now found to say of our past—
'Scanned across the dark space wherein I have lacked you?'"

"Enough." The command struck a plangent note. "Those four lines, so evocative, so appropriate, so very much Edwin. We both loved Hardy and Edwin knew I would recognise that verse, which he used to re-introduce himself when he came back. It announced his coming."

"How?"

"Well, Gerald retired from active business in 1945 and we handed the house in Hampstead over to Henry. He'd just married and it seemed right that he should raise a family there as we had. That's when we bought this cottage. But Gerald kept an interest in the firm to the very end and would stay with Henry whenever he went up there. As it happened, what I'm about to describe took place during one of those trips, so that I was alone here apart from Rose, the housekeeper we had before Dora.

"I couldn't tell you the exact date, but it was a weekday early in May 1951. Rose came in to say that, as she'd been returning from some shopping in the village, a man had stopped her at the gate and asked her to deliver a note to me. He'd been emphatic that it was for my eyes only and had gone on to say that, if I wished to speak to him about the contents, he would be in the churchyard until six o'clock.

"The note was that verse of Hardy's you've just read to me. It wasn't signed, but I knew the hand, and, when I pressed Rose for a description of the man, it sounded like Edwin grown old. He'd come a long way and time had healed my hurts. So there was no question of my refusing the invitation, though I made myself wait until past five o'clock before going over to the churchyard.

"There was a thin drizzle falling and I could see somebody sheltering from it in the lychgate. I knew immediately that it was Edwin, still a commanding figure though a little stooped with age, his shoulders rather hunched, hands buried in his greatcoat pockets. He had his back to me as I came along the path and didn't turn round until I called his name.

"'So you came,' he said. I just nodded. 'Thank you.' I told him there was no need to thank me and asked how he was. 'Well,' he said, but, though he looked fit enough, he seemed and sounded weary—more so than even his age justified. He apologized for luring me from the house, spoke courteously but distantly, as if unable quite to believe that we were once again talking to each other. Then I put the only question I could put.

"'Why have you come, Edwin?'

"'Just to see you, one more time.'

"'But why now?'

"He didn't answer that, just asked how life was treating me. I said I was happy and content, which was true. I couldn't draw him on his own life. He said there was nothing to say about it. Instead, he wanted to know about mine—my family affairs, all that I'd done since marrying Gerald. He didn't sneer or protest, as he once would have done, just listened, rather pensively, nodded occasionally, asked more, gently inquisitive, questions. I didn't mind telling him. I could bear all the old heartache and speak to him dispassionately. It all felt curiously like an interview, as if Edwin were weighing my achievements in life. It didn't even seem particularly strange that he should be doing so."

"But why would he have been?"

"I don't know. He'd never been, except in desperate moments, an outspoken man, but that day he was more reticent than ever, like a concerned, self-effacing godparent. I thought it might be contrition as much as anything, so let him be as silent as he wanted to be.

"We went for a stroll round the village. Edwin asked about its history and character, why we'd chosen it, what I planned to do there. As I say, it was all deceptively anodyne."

"What do you mean: deceptively?"

"I mean that Edwin was probing for something, subtly and patiently, and I was letting him. I didn't object because there was nothing to object to. He didn't raise the great issue that lay between us and, out of a kind of relief that he wasn't still harbouring some resentment, I was happy to talk about almost anything else. Yet there was some purpose in our pleasantries, something I couldn't discern behind his gentlemanly interrogation. Then he said a strange thing: 'I've met Henry, your son.'

"'Of course,' I replied. 'The last time we met.' I was hoping that this didn't presage a reopening of old wounds. But it didn't.

"'Do you think he takes after his father?' he asked. I said I thought he did and that it had always pleased me to note the resemblance. He made no more of that.

"I asked how he had travelled to the village and he said that he had walked from the railway station. The nearest one then was Singleton, but that was five miles, a fair step for an old man, so I offered to drive him back.

"On our way, Edwin seemed to bring himself to say a little of what he had come to say. He left it until we were driving through Singleton—almost the latest he could, which suggested to me that he had had to screw up his nerves for it. 'The reason I came,' he said, almost in an undertone, 'was to see if I still love you.' Then, without waiting for me to speak: 'And the curse of it is that I do.'

"I pulled to a halt at the railway station. It was quiet there that evening and we were quite alone. I felt unnerved by his sudden declaration, worried that we wouldn't, after all, part amicably.

"In fact, he at once reassured me. 'Don't worry,' he said. 'I'll go quietly.'

"'Edwin,' I said, 'I'm sorry.'

"'There's no need,' he replied. 'It wasn't your fault.' His admission implied an acceptançe of guilt.

"'That's all I can find,' I continued, 'to say of our past.'

"'Then let that be all.'

"So saying, he stepped from the car and walked quickly into the booking office. He paused at the door, turned, doffed his hat to me and then was gone."

"What did you do?"

"I drove away. He didn't seem to want me to wait until his train came and it seemed fitting not to do so. The leavetaking he had chosen had a quality of . . . reconciliation. I had once offered him forgiveness. Now, at last, he had accepted it. But forty years seemed a long time to have to wait. So I was pleased to make my peace with Edwin that day, pleased that we had met just once more.

"I told Gerald about Edwin's visit when he returned from London. I didn't want to keep it from him and, if I had tried to, I daresay Rose might have let it slip. Gerald was angry at Edwin for having come, though I told him there was no need to be. Still, he remained unhappy about him being back in England and that's why he seemed relieved when, about a month later, we heard of his death.

"That's when I first felt that I really knew Edwin's purpose in visiting me. It was simply to put his mind and my mind at rest before what I am sure was his calculated and dignified exit from life. Though I had never—except for a very short time—lost all of my affection for him—because some affection must always remain where love has been felt—it was only then, after forty years, that I recovered my respect for him."

It was an attractive theory. It fitted the nature of the encounter Elizabeth had just described and, as the only witness to Strafford's state of mind at the time, she had to be heeded. What it clashed with, of course, was Ambrose's conspiracy theory. Only Elizabeth's description of her husband's "anger" and subsequent "relief" supported Ambrose, but they were points worth pursuing.

"Between Strafford's visit to you and his death," I said, "did your husband take any more business trips?"

"He may have done, my dear. I really can't remember. Why do you ask?"

"I wondered if, in view of how angry you said he was that Strafford had shown up, he might have tried to confront him."

"I think it highly unlikely."

"But not inconceivable?"

"Not quite that—what is? But I do not believe he would have done so without telling me. Gerald and I had an unspoken pact of honesty. Just as I did not hesitate to tell him of Edwin's visit, he would not, on his part, have practised any secrecy. Besides, I am sure Gerald would have gone a long way to avoid such an encounter."

I left it there. I didn't want to accuse Gerald or Henry Couchman of threatening Strafford when, to their wife and mother, such things were clearly incredible. She was prejudiced in their favour but had a right to be—a right borne of knowing them a great deal longer and better than Ambrose or I had. Between us all, prejudice wasn't hard to come by. Evidence was. I lay in bed that night thinking about what Elizabeth had said and all the questions it left me with. What happened between October 1950 and May 1951 that drove Strafford back to England? Did he visit anyone else apart from Elizabeth and Ambrose? If so, who—and why? Was his death an accident, suicide or murder? Only Strafford could tell me for certain.

Next morning, over breakfast, I broached another question to Elizabeth that I'd been wanting to ask.

"I notice your husband endowed a fellowship at Cambridge."

Elizabeth smiled and began buttering some toast. "Don't you approve? I think it was one of the best ideas Gerald ever had. He was keen to make some gift to his old university. An endowed fellowship seemed to go to the heart of the place better than a contribution to his college's maintenance fund. I though it would be splendid to provide some support for female academics and Gerald was happy to fall in with the idea, bless him. I remember him joking about it: 'Once a Suffragette, always a Suffragette.' He was right, I suppose, but when I think of the succession of Couchman Fellows that

Gerald's bequest made possible—some of them eminent in their fields now—I feel prouder of him than all the incumbents put together. It's a very happy way to preserve his memory."

"I'm sure."

"What brought it to your attention?"

"Since the present fellow is working specifically on Edwardian history, I made contact while in Cambridge to see what she thought about Strafford."

Elizabeth's eyes sparkled. "Ah, so you've met Miss Randall."

"Yes." I was surprised by the energy of her response.

"Tell me more. Henry handles all the administration of the endowment, but I was delighted when he told me the latest fellow was researching a period of history so close to my heart."

I had a sinking feeling. Elizabeth could have no idea how close to her heart Eve had thought of going. "It was Miss Randall who discovered the marriage certificate in the Kendrick Archive."

"Really—most enterprising of her." There was no trace of sarcasm in the remark.

"She's certainly that. I believe she'd thought of speaking to you about your own experiences as a Suffragette." Not to mention as Strafford's dupe and a symbol of exploited Edwardian womanhood.

"I hope she does. It's strange—and rather cheering in a way—to live long enough to see one's youth become history." She thought for a moment. "Tell me, Martin, have you ever thought of marrying again?"

"Who would have me?"

"My dear, you underestimate yourself."

"I don't think so. You see, sooner or later, they'd be bound to find out about . . . my past. And that would be that." I didn't mind referring to the skeleton in my cupboard. Elizabeth knew about it, after all, and one show of frankness deserved another.

"The past can become a burden if you let it, Martin. I believe Edwin may have found that."

"But how do you stop it?"

"We must each find our own way. We live with the past because we have to, but we don't have to live in it."

"It's difficult, when you're still called to account for it."

"Then somehow, you must clear the account."

Elizabeth was right. But how? In my case, it was surely irredeemable. In Strafford's, perhaps less so. I consoled myself with the thought that I might yet ease his burden. Inevitably I thought of my burden: Jane Campion—and what she'd lured me into. I thought of what it had cost me: Helen and Laura, a home and a career, now Eve. Then I thought, for the first time, of Jane herself. I'd assured Eve that Jane was bound to be all right. In reality, I had no idea what had become of her since 1973. She'd floated away to London that summer and out of my life. Perhaps, I thought, after the Strafford business is settled, I'll find out what she's done with herself, perhaps have that dispassionate talk with her I once promised myself, seek—like Strafford—some kind of expiation.

What was I thinking? "After the Strafford business is settled." I'd not yet looked as far as that, because it didn't seem possible to do so. It was so complex, so vast, so much a lifetime, that completion didn't seem conceivable—or even desirable. Two months before, I'd never even heard of Edwin Strafford. But what now would I do without him?

Elizabeth gave me a few days' grace—time to recover from the blow Eve had delivered, time to take stock of my suspicions. Restful and restorative as they seemed, they were also, in a sense, profligate. While I dawdled and talked gently through the enigma of Strafford's life with Elizabeth, at a pace set by the lazy buzz of bees in her garden, the equipoised movement of her grandmother clock, something more awful than awesome was gaining momentum, accelerating slowly towards the speed of inevitability which would make it an event.

There was no thunder to warn us, no humid prescience in the air, just village life in Sussex, teeming with normality. On Thursday evening, Elizabeth went out for her weekly rubber of bridge at the Sayers' house and, once Dora had gone home,

I was left alone to ponder my next move. Even the cat, who clearly saw me as an interloper, contrived to vanish.

I decided, after all, to report to Sellick again. Instinct told me that, if he really had sent Alec to check on me and alienate Eve from me, it would be foolish to let him deduce I knew that or could be rattled by it. So I set out the evidence Eve had supplied without mentioning her and summarized Elizabeth's recollections with all the blandness at my disposal, ending prosaically with a request for more money. Staying at Quarterleigh had restored my sense of proportion: if Sellick thought he had a right to interfere in my life, he'd have to pay for the privilege.

I'd just finished the report, and was wondering what time Elizabeth would return, when the telephone rang. Without thinking, I answered it, then instantly regretted doing so. Henry was on the other end.

"Martin—what the hell are you doing there?"

"I came down to see your mother."

"I told you not to bother her when you showed up last month. What d'you mean by coming back?"

"She hasn't objected."

"Let me speak to her—at once."

"I can't. She's out playing bridge."

There was a silence at the other end, then: "Listen to me, Martin. I'm telling you to get out of that house right now. Otherwise, I'll come and throw you out."

I felt confident enough to goad Henry. "You didn't tell your mother I'd tried to see her—why was that?"

"You bloody little upstart—leave my mother alone, or you'll regret it."

I put the phone down. There seemed no point in trading insults with Henry. We'd done it too often in the past. The question in my mind was: why was he so worried? All right, he had good reason to dislike me, even loathe me. But why be so defensive about Elizabeth when she clearly didn't need or want him to be? Henry as the devoted son didn't really convince. As a politician and a person, he'd always had an ugly streak. I felt sure that was what we were seeing now. I waited until breakfast next morning before telling Elizabeth about Henry's call. She didn't, at first, see its significance.

"I am sorry to have missed speaking to him. Surely he knows I play bridge on Thursdays."

"I don't think you'll have to wait long to see him."

"Oh, is the dear boy planning a visit?"

"Elizabeth, your son hates me . . ."

"Surely not."

"It's true—and understandable. The point is that he warned me not to come back when I met him here last month. He was furious to find I was here last night. I'm sure he'll arrive soon to throw me out."

"There will be no throwing out, Martin, when you are my guest. But I'm sure you're mistaken."

"We'll see."

We soon did. After breakfast, I walked into the village to post my report to Sellick. When I came back, Henry's Jaguar was in the drive. He must have made an early start from London. It smacked of panic.

I found them in the drawing room. Elizabeth had forced breakfast on Henry, who didn't seem to want it and was loudly telling her she should be more selective about who she entertained, when I walked in. Henry leaped from his chair. I could tell at once that his mother's presence was restraining him, but that only made the difference between unpleasantness and raging invective. The effort at self-control deepened his colour menacingly.

"I'm told you've been here several days, my boy."

"That's right."

"Well, it's several days too long."

Elizabeth interrupted. "Henry, Martin has stayed here at my invitation. I presume I may have what guests I choose?"

"Yes, Mother, but this guest is the man who dishonoured my daughter—your granddaughter. Our family owes him nothing but contempt."

"I appreciate your feelings on behalf of Helen, Henry, but I cannot believe she would be offended by my showing Martin a certain amount of hospitality."

"Well I'm offended—doesn't that count for something?"

"Of course. But please, let us conduct ourselves in a civilized fashion."

"It's just because he"—stabbing a forefinger in my direction—"couldn't conduct himself in a civilized fashion that I object to him sponging off you."

"Henry, please . . ."

"Hold on," I broke in. "I don't want to cause any trouble. I'll leave. After all," adding a rider for Henry's benefit, "we've discussed everything I was hoping to. I'm very grateful for all you've told me."

Henry's face was a study in baffled outrage. He turned on Elizabeth. "Mother, what have been telling him?"

"Martin is conducting some historical research into an Edwardian politician named Edwin Strafford—a friend of your father's. I've simply been helping him with my own recollections."

"Bloody hell, Mother. How can you be so stupid? Don't you see . . ."

Elizabeth rose from her chair and silenced him with a glare. "Don't swear in this house, Henry—and don't talk to me in that fashion." She walked slowly past him. "If you wish to speak reasonably, you will find me in the garden. Excuse me, Martin." She left.

Henry recovered from his brief humiliation. He turned towards me, preparing to launch a broadside. I decided to get one in first. "Where were you on the night of 4th June 1951, Henry? Or, come to that, the night before?"

"What are you talking about?"

"You said you'd never met Edwin Strafford. It isn't possible, is it, that you did meet him after all—on the dates I've just mentioned, in Devon?"

He closed on me, stared and set his jaw. "I don't know what you've wheedled out of my mother, Radford . . ."

"Only what you hoped I wouldn't."

"You're pushing your luck, my lad."

"Aren't you pushing yours?"

"I advise you to put up—or shut up." The practised politician still had an instinct for bluff.

"All right. The reason for your hostility and your mother's

lack of it is that you have something to hide and she hasn't. What she's told me helps fit together a few more pieces of the jigsaw. The picture I'm getting implicates you in a plot that ended with Edwin Strafford's death in what was supposed to be an accident." I reckoned I could out-bluff him if I had to.

"I'm warning you . . ."

"Strafford was staying with his nephew in Devon in June 1951. I've spoken to the nephew. He recalls break-ins and threats from strangers. His evidence explodes the idea that Strafford's death was accidental . . ."

Moving faster than I'd expected, Henry grabbed at my throat. I jerked back against the door frame and he ended up grasping the knot of my tie. It was a tight grip and I could feel his arm shaking. "Listen," he said between clenched teeth, "do you really think rubbish like you can threaten somebody in my position? If you want to get funny, it won't just be a question of stopping access to Laura. The police could keep a much closer eye on your nasty little life if the right person asked them to. There are all kinds of ways I could have you leant on—till you snapped. Do you understand that?"

"I understand that what's threatening you isn't me, but a fear of the truth." I was getting back at him for all the abuse he'd inflicted on me over the years, but I was also telling myself to go steady, because I'd never seen him angry to the point of violence before. I guessed that, in a similar mood, he could have killed Strafford. All I doubted was his courage, so I nerved myself to test it.

"You must be mad."

"Who's behaving madly—you or me?" There was turmoil in his face. He relaxed his grip, then let go altogether, though his hand stayed in the shape of the hold, as if reluctant to give it up. We were both bluffing, of course, both guessing what the other was trying to guess, both revealing too little—or too much—for either to be certain what the other really knew.

"I know what you think you've got over me, Radford. Vindictive scribblings left behind by that philandering bastard, Strafford." He was letting slip a hint that, yes, perhaps he had known Strafford, for the sake of telling me that he knew all about the Memoir. It was a blow, because it left me in no doubt that Eve had informed her sponsors of their connexion with the document. But it would have seemed worse if it had happened sooner. In a sense, I was relieved she'd betrayed me. It made my own disgrace in her eyes more bearable. The question was: did she alert Henry before or after she found out about my past? It made a difference, but not to Henry.

"That was only the start. I've found out a lot more since then. You're in it up to your neck."

"I'm in nothing, my lad. I'm a Member of Parliament. I'm respected—and influential. Who's going to take you and your pathetic accusations seriously when they find out what you really are? A schoolteacher who couldn't keep his hands off the girls in his class, working out a grudge against my family with the flimsy half-truths of some questionable memoir."

"You are, Henry. You're going to take them seriously, because they'll be true. You didn't mind telling everyone that I wasn't worthy of Helen and I won't mind telling your constituents why you're not fit to represent them in Parliament."

"Get out of this house, Radford. You'll be sorry for what you've said, sorrier still if you go on with this charade."

"Okay. I'll go. But it's no charade. You wouldn't be so scared if it was. And another thing—do your really think you can rely on Eve Randall to keep quiet about the Memoir?"

Henry looked puzzled, as if I'd caught him off balance. "What do you mean?"

"Just that. Can you rely on her? The fellowship's one thing, but the Memoir could make her name, used in the right way.'"

Henry's expression suggested he hadn't thought of this. But he wasn't going to let it deflect him. "I want you out of this house, Radford, out of my life and out of my family."

"You get your wish—for the moment."

I went upstairs and packed hurriedly. I could hear Henry talking loudly to Dora in the kitchen, but, through the window, I could see Elizabeth calmly pruning a rose bush in the garden, determined, it seemed, to be undisturbed by her son's boorish display. I went down with my bag and walked out through the conservatory to join her.

"I'm going now," I said. "It'll only cause unnecessary trouble if I stay any longer."

Elizabeth put down her secateurs. "If you say so, my dear. But you're welcome to remain."

"I really don't think I can."

"Well, come again any time. I've enjoyed your visit." She leant forward and kissed me on the cheek. "My best wishes—for everything—go with you."

Elizabeth's serenity had endured. Strafford had spoken of her "gift of calmness before adversity that was part of her beauty", and there it was, intact, sixty-seven years later, a long cream dress with petticoats and parasol swapped for a gardening coat over a plaid skirt, but the spirit unchanged, the beauty still evident to the discerning. Amidst all the imponderables, I knew that her wishes for me and everyone else would always be the best.

I went back to London—for want of anywhere better to go. I couldn't decide what I should do next. Henry was worried—no question about it. But I couldn't prove anything and he knew I couldn't. I'd seen all the witnesses, scoured all the records, followed all the leads. And at the end of them—nothing but suspicion, nothing you could call a case against anyone.

I closed the front door behind me, dumped my bag on the hall floor and felt the familiar, vaguely reproachful atmosphere of the house envelop me: back with nothing to show for my absence.

Then came word from another planet. On the kitchen table Jerry had left a scrawled note saying he was away, and a few letters—the usual circularized dross. But one looked different: a large envelope, addressed by hand in black ink, the writing rough and ready, postmarked Newton Abbot, May 16th—the previous Monday. I tore it open. It was from Ambrose.

Martin,

An old fellow like me shouldn't have to go to such bother to trace a young whippersnapper like you. Your friends in Exeter didn't know where you'd gone, but they gave me this address, so I hope you get this soon.

What's the flap? Well, hold onto your hat. That book my uncle wrote in when he stayed with me in 1951—we thought it was lost or sent back to Madeira—never left here. After you cleared off, I found it: a complete account of what he did when he came back here that spring and why he did it. It doesn't tell us how he died, but, hell, it tells us every other bloody thing we wanted to know—and then some. There are people around who'd be scared rigid if they knew what was in it.

No names, no packdrill—yet. Come and read it yourself first. Then tell me there's nothing in my suspicions about his death. I'm certain now that he was murdered—and so will you be when you see what I've got.

Yours aye,
Ambrose Strafford.

P.S. The old bugger chose a cunning hiding place and it's only thanks to you I looked there, so you deserve a share of the booty. And what booty! Martin, I've been waiting 26 years to strike this seam and believe me, the Couchmans have got it coming. Get in touch as soon as you can—we'll hold a council of war.

A.S.

I walked slowly into the lounge with the letter, sat down and read it again. It didn't alter. For once, Ambrose's extravagant prose didn't exaggerate the significance of his discovery. "The book Strafford wrote in." We'd pondered it, but never really thought it could be a full-blown Postscript to the Memoir. Yet now, out of the blue, here was Ambrose saying it was. He'd found it, read it and been vindicated by it. How he didn't say, beyond a dagger thrust at the Couchmans. Ambrose was old and cautious and not about to entrust his new secret to the mail. Yet he was prepared to share it with me, though how I'd given him the clue to its whereabouts I couldn't guess.

I wanted at once to read the Postscript, possess it and devour it until Strafford had told us everything. I felt like setting off straightaway for Dewford. Maybe I could get there in time to catch Ambrose at The Greengage, whisk him off back to Lodge Cottage and sit in his lumber room of a lounge, drinking cider and congratulating each other on our achievement. The marriage of Memoir and Postscript—Henry's bluff called and Strafford's secret told at last—was an exciting prospect.

It was a curse not even being able to phone Ambrose because of the old man's distrust of such implements. I settled on a telegram—the best I could do in the circumstances: GOT YOUR LETTER STOP MARVELLOUS NEWS STOP BE WITH YOU TOMORROW STOP HOLD TILL THEN STOP. The delay was irritating but no worse than that. Why should it have been? In a way, it just gave me an opportunity to savour the prospect. As it turned out, even one day was more than I could afford.

Returning from a brief shopping foray for essentials on which Jerry had as usual run dry, I didn't think anything of the red Porsche in front of the house until the driver stepped out.

It was Timothy Couchman, Helen's elder brother, immaculately dressed in black blazer and cream slacks, shirt casually open at the neck. He tossed back a lock of hair and blew smoke lazily into the air. "Hello Martin," he said with silken mockery, moving towards me with a smooth, composite sound of expensive clothes, gold cuff-links and leather-heeled shoes.

Of all the Couchmans, Timothy was the one I instinctively loathed, now more than ever. Once he'd had spare, high-boned good looks to go with natural charm. Even then I'd disliked his habit of command, his panache bordering on one-upmanship, his quality of upper-class spivvery. He'd been a third generation parasite who thought himself a predator. Well, maybe he'd grown into that. There was less refinement, more dissipation, about him now, the clear skin turned sallow, the hollow cheeks puffy. God knows what other dubious enterprises had followed those I knew about, but evidently enough to keep him in his accustomed style. His flashing smile, once supposed to be engaging, was now sabre-toothed.

"What do you want?" I was past being even initially polite, I felt sure his appearance was connected with my stay in Miston. I had him marked as his father's errand boy.

"Martin, it's good to see you after all this time." Timothy was never one to be taken aback by mere unpleasantness.

"Well, it isn't good to see you. What do you want?"

"Could we perhaps step inside to discuss it, old man?"

"Why?"

"I have a proposition for you. I believe it merits your consideration."

Maybe, I thought for a moment, Henry had sent his son to propose some compromise he couldn't stomach offering me himself. If so, I ought to hear it. "It had better not take long. I'm in a hurry."

"Aren't we all, old man?" For all his affected weariness, I could believe he was. He followed me to the door. I opened it and showed him into the lounge. He cast a superior eye over the room, then sat down without being asked. "Pleasant place —for the suburbs. I didn't know you ran to this."

"I don't." I let him make what he liked of that. He flicked ash into the grate of the converted electric fire. I fetched an ashtray from a cabinet and placed it ostentatiously by his chair, then sat opposite him.

"How about coming to the point? There's no welcome here for you to outstay."

"No call for that sort of talk, Martin." He drew lengthily on his cigarette. "Gather you've been upsetting my grandmother."

"Far from it. I get on with her better than with the rest of your family. Your father was the one who seemed upset."

He slowly ground his cigarette into the ashtray I'd provided. "Papa is certainly concerned about your . . . activities. I expect you know that"—he was suddenly serious—"if you continue to pry where you're not wanted, the whole question of contact with your daughter will have to be . . . reviewed."

"I know that your father tried to threaten me with denial of access to Laura."

"Hardly a threat. How can we reasonably allow you to continue seeing her when your conduct is becoming so . . . unstable?"

"You can try anything, via Helen's solicitor. But it won't work. How much do you know about this business?"

"All there is to know, old man. No secrets in my family." He smiled, with just a hint of irony, and lit another cigarette.

"In that case, what are you worried about?"

"Nothing."

"Then why are you here?"

He spread his hands. "Cards on the table, Martin. We're worried that your irrational inquisitiveness may arise from personal problems. Papa thought I might have a word with you—as members of the same generation—and offer what help I can."

"I don't need it."

"Don't be hasty. The help I had in mind was financial."

So that was it: a bribe. I wondered what price the Couchmans put on my silence. "Do go on."

"My thoughts are pretty vague at present, but if we could help to establish you in some more . . . satisfactory . . . occupation, there'd be no need for you to make yourself look ridiculous with this charade of historical research."

"Are you talking about putting up capital?"

"Something like that." He nodded meaningfully.

"How much?" It was time to draw him out.

"How much would you need?"

"The man I'm working for is paying me £10,000."

"I see." Another cigarette was stubbed out. "Well, naturally, we'd have to ensure initially that you weren't . . . out of pocket."

"Naturally." I got up and walked to the window. It was dark outside now. "Henry's a bigger fool than I thought to send you here with a crude bribe. I'm not interested."

Timothy turned to look at me. "Not interested, old man? It's unlike you to strike a high moral tone—and so unconvincing."

"I realize it's difficult for you to understand anybody not being for sale."

"Only when they're so obviously . . . shop-soiled. I gather you weren't so . . . pernickety . . . where Miss Randall's offer was concerned."

I made the mistake of getting angry. "What do you mean?"

"I mean that, with our interests at heart, Miss Randall could have bought your tatty little memoir for a knockdown price."

"Then why didn't she?" My mind flicked to a scene in that Memoir, when Strafford visited Couchman at his factory, was also offered a bribe, was also goaded over a woman.

"Because, I presume, she judged any price too high to pay where you were concerned. Besides, who could know then that you would make such a nuisance of yourself?"

"Are you sure Miss Randall wasn't as interested as I am in learning the truth?"

"Quite sure. Eve knows her interests are better served by tenure of the Couchman Fellowship than a hare-brained literary partnership with you." He was letting me know he was on first name terms with Eve, letting me know she'd told him all our plans. The telephone forestalled my reply.

I hurried into the hall and answered it. Nick Bennett was on the other end.

"Martin! Thank God! I've been trying to get hold of you all day."

"What's the trouble?"

"It's that weird old friend of yours—Ambrose Strafford."

"Yes?"

"He visited us a week ago, anxious to contact you. We gave him your address."

"I know. I got a letter from him."

"Well, he was here again today, much more wound up than before. He said he was desperate to speak to you."

"Why?"

"He didn't exactly say. He'd been drinking, if you ask me, rambling about threats, strangers, dark forces—whatever they might be. He claimed he was in danger and had to see you: a matter of life and death."

This sounded like Ambrose—but why so alarmed? "Was he specific?"

"No. He didn't seem to want to say much to me. And Hester found him a bit disturbing, so I didn't encourage him."

"Do you know if he'd had my telegram?"

"Yes. He had it screwed up in his pocket. He pulled it out and said that, if I spoke to you before he did, I was to tell you he would 'try to hold on', but that 'it won't be easy'. I tried phoning you while he was here, but you weren't in. He said he had to 'keep watch at Barrowteign'. Then he left."

"Did he say anything else?"

"One thing, as he was getting in his car: a message for you.

'Tell Martin to remember,' he said, 'that we Straffords have lofty memories.' What does that mean?"

What indeed? "I don't know, Nick. I don't know what any of it means. But I'm worried. Ambrose is a bit of an oddball, but he's not soft in the head. If he feels in danger, it's because he is. I should have reacted more urgently to his letter." Or not lingered in Miston, I thought.

"What will you do?"

"Get down there double quick."

"Do you want to come to us tonight?"

"I'll never get a train this late. I'll travel on the first service tomorrow morning and go straight to Dewford. Could I come and see you after that?"

"Of course."

"Then I'll phone from Dewford. Speak to you tomorrow. Oh—thanks for letting me know, Nick. It may turn out to be just what Ambrose said: a matter of life and death." Strafford's life and death were what I meant, but the phrase was to echo beyond anything I or Ambrose could have intended.

After such news, all I wanted Timothy to do was get out. I found him leaning against the mantelpiece, with his feet on the fender, blowing cigarette smoke towards the ceiling, looking so casual I felt certain he'd been eavesdropping.

"Some trouble, old man?" he said.

"My only trouble is getting rid of you."

"Easily done." He elbowed himself away from the mantelpiece and walked past me to the door. "If you see sense, Martin, just get in touch. If not, don't say you weren't warned."

"You won't hear from me."

"A pity. If you *should* change your mind, just call me. I've left my card."

A last gesture typical of the smooth-talking salesman. Timothy made his way out and I slammed the front door behind him. I walked back into the lounge and found his card propped against the clock on the mantelpiece: Timothy H. Couchman, Mercantile Consultant, 4 Padua Court, Berkeley Street, London W1. As I heard his Porsche throb into life and accelerate away, I tore the card into four and dropped the pieces into the wastepaper basket.

Then my eye trailed along the mantelpiece to where I'd tucked Ambrose's letter under a Toby jug. I pulled it out and read it through again—the abrasive, confident tones, the hints of long-awaited vengeance for his uncle's death, the eager anticipation of disgrace for the Couchmans. But nothing firm or definite on paper, all in his head, everything on a promise. I had to get to him quickly, had to find out what he meant. He'd told Nick of threats and strangers. Did he mean the old ones which had assailed Strafford, or something new? I had to know.

Six

I didn't sleep at all that night, which was probably just as well. At dawn, I went up to Paddington and caught the first train to Exeter. I arrived just after nine o'clock and took a taxi out to Dewford.

The Teign valley road was empty so early on a cool, damp morning and the taxi made good time. I looked out at the fields I'd passed on foot a month before, followed with my eye the scar of the old railway line across the water meadows. At the crossroads, I told the driver to turn left and we bowled down over the old stone bridge across the river. Along the right-hand rampart, there was a strip of fluorescent red tape from one end of the bridge to the other and, on the far side, a dark van drawn up. I could see more red tape, strung between stakes, along the bank of the river and a stocky figure in gumboots and a white coat walking away from the waterside, up through the saplings which grew down to the river. I wondered, idly, if there'd been a road accident, but the bridge seemed undamaged, with nothing out of place.

I paid off the taxi at the entrance to Barrowteign, walked past the familiar, owl-topped pillars and followed the track through the gate and under the lime trees to Lodge Cottage. It was a reassuringly ordinary, placid morning in the country-side. Already, I could imagine Ambrose sniffing the air through his kitchen door, lighting his pipe and cracking some eggs into the frying pan, whistling tunelessly at Jess and wondering when the hell that young bugger Radford was going to show up. Well, here he was.

The first thing I noticed, as I approached the old crossing, was a police car drawn up by the garage. I thought Ambrose might be entertaining the local constable to breakfast, but no windows in the cottage were open and there was no whiff of bacon in the air. I eased open the garden gate, expecting to hear Jess bark, but she didn't. The front door stood open, so I stepped inside.

"Hello! Ambrose?" I shouted.

There was a sound from the front room, some heavy footsteps and then a burly, uniformed policeman stood in the doorway. He had a rumpled, rural look but a broad, implacable bearing. "Who might you be?" he said, with guarded civility.

I was taken aback, literally. This man's large frame seemed to fill the house, never mind the hall. "I'm a friend of Ambrose Strafford. Is he here?"

"No sir."

"Can I ask . . . why you're here?"

"When did you last see Mr Strafford?"

"About a month ago."

"I see . . . you don't come from these parts, I'm thinking."

"No."

"When did you arrive?"

"Just this minute."

"I didn't 'ear a car."

"No. I came by taxi. It dropped me off at the gates. Now . . ."

"Seems a funny time to come visitin'."

"I was anxious to see Ambrose."

"Why might that be?"

Surprise was turning to impatience. "Don't you think that's my business, officer?"

The constable nodded. "Ordinarily, it would be, sir. But . . ."

"But what?"

"I'm investigating an unexplained death, so . . ."

Panic flared in me. "Whose death?"

"Ambrose Strafford's."

"How?"

"'E drowned in the river last night. Seems to 'ave toppled over the bridge on 'is way back from The Greengage. Drunk, we think."

For a moment, I couldn't think or speak. Ambrose drowned? It was impossible, inconceivable. Yet stolid policemen don't lie. "Last night?"

"Seems so, sir. Estate worker goin' into Barrowteign found 'im first light this mornin'. 'Eard his dog 'owlin' and found old Ambrose among some tree roots in the shallows by the bank, near the bridge."

I was too late—only, it seemed, a matter of hours too late. Ambrose, alive, hearty, drinking his fill at The Greengage, then—drowned, a shape in the water, by the dawn shore drifting. It was awful—but an accident? After all his portents, all his warnings? That was too much. "How do you know what happened?"

"We don't, sir. Leastways, not till we get the results of the post mortem. But it seems obvious. Ambrose liked his cider, drank a lot last night and fetched up in the river. It's pretty shallow under the bridge, so 'e must 'ave been far gone when 'e fell in. 'Cept . . ."

"Except what?"

"'Cept 'e's been rabbitin' on 'bout strangers threatenin' 'im recently."

All my hopes forbade me to believe I or Ambrose could be denied by some grotesque accident. So Ambrose drank. Well, he drank every night of his life and never had any trouble negotiating the bridge before. I felt the same way he felt about his uncle's death. Whole families can't be accident-prone. But strangers can bundle old men off bridges or onto railway lines. A thrill of horror lanced through my shock. If I'd not been blind or stupid or both, I could have foreseen this, foretold it for certain by the graven shape of the Straffords' tragedy. Suddenly, Ambrose's death was fitting—and that only made it worse. When I spoke—shouted almost—at the constable, I was voicing my despair. "Perhaps you should have listened to him. Don't you see this was no accident?"

The constable remained calm. "No sir, I don't. But that

ain't my job. What is, is to question strangers who turn up at the deceased's 'ouse at crack of dawn without explanation."

"You can question me—by all means. But I'm not a stranger—wasn't a stranger—to Ambrose."

"You're a stranger to me, sir—to the village."

"My name's Martin Radford. I came here just after Easter to research the history of the family who owned Barrowteign. I met Ambrose and he told me all he could. I came back at his invitation."

"What for?"

I decided to keep that to myself. "I'll never know now."

"If you say so, sir. I think I'll 'ave to take a statement."

I didn't object—why should I? We went through into the kitchen and sat either side of the table I'd once shared with Ambrose. There were still knives and plates on it, with breadcrumbs and flakes of tobacco scattered around and a tea towel slung over one corner. The old, encrusted frying pan stood on the range, with a lining of set fat, and there was washing-up in the sink. It seemed incredible that Ambrose's cosy shambles of a world—proud and prickly fastness of the last of the Straffords—had lost its master.

The constable pulled out a notebook and laboriously pencilled in my account of meeting Ambrose. I told him of the mystery of Strafford's death in 1951—that Ambrose and I both believed it wasn't an accident. I said I thought both deaths had the same explanation, but I went no further. Even in my shock at this loss, I didn't utter wild accusations, didn't venture what I couldn't prove. I said nothing about the Couchmans, the Memoir or the Postscript. It was my duty to record that Ambrose wasn't just a foolish old drunkard who got himself drowned, but I never really expected the police to believe anything else.

"And you say the landlord of The Greengage can corroborate this?"

"Yes—in part."

"Well, I'll check with 'im. Then I'll get your statement typed up and see if my inspector wants to 'ave a chat with you. Where will you be over the next few days?" I gave him the Bennetts' address in Exeter. "All right, sir, I'll be in touch."

"Is that it?"

"What else would you expect?"

"Ambrose spoke of threats. Then he dies mysteriously. Shouldn't . . ."

The constable rose massively from his chair. "It's not so much of a mystery, sir. You go talkin' that way and people'll think you're as nutty as old Ambrose."

I got up too. "Okay. I get the message. I must be on my way." I moved towards the hall. "Found anything here?"

"Nothing that need concern you, sir."

"I see." Only I didn't, and nor did he. Where was the Post-script? I couldn't ask this man and he wouldn't have told me if I had. He wouldn't have understood what I was driving at, couldn't have comprehended the stark disappointment of an empty, grieving cottage after the lure of a letter sparkling with life. I walked out into the morning air, changed by the knowledge of Ambrose's death, telling myself that old men who knock back the cider do tend to be a danger to themselves but hearing, all the time, another voice, in aged, grating tones, which said insistently, and all too credibly, "Don't let 'em fool you. Do you really think it could happen again?" There, in the garden, as I looked at the old track bed and remembered the prelude to another accident, I realized that, no, I didn't believe in lightning striking twice, and I wasn't going to let Ambrose die for nothing. I returned to the main drive and hurried to the bridge.

I leant heavily on the wall, feeling a strange mixture of sickness and elation, sick with shock and sadness that Ambrose was dead, elated—in a way which appalled me but couldn't be denied—by the rush of knowledge that something had at last happened. My investigations had begun to bear their bitter fruit. But how? Why? With Ambrose gone, I was further than ever from the answers.

I walked disconsolately up to the crossroads, then on into the village. The place was quiet, still gathering itself together for the business of the day. Despite the hour, I made for The Greengage, reckoning Ted, the landlord, could give me as good an impression as anybody of what had happened.

There was no sign of life at the front, but I could hear movement in the yard behind the pub, so walked round and found Ted stacking crates, with the cellar door open. He looked up and nodded recognition.

"I've heard about Ambrose," I said.

"Bad business," Ted grunted. "I told the police 'bout you."

"Why?"

"'Cos old Ambrose, 'e was bothered 'bout strangers—always 'ad been, you knows that. So I told 'em 'bout you,'cos you are one." He slammed an empty crate on top of the rest and leant on the pile. "Seemed the least I could do."

I knew what he meant. In his clumsy way, Ted had done his best by Ambrose and didn't mind letting me know he'd named me as a suspicious stranger. So I was, for all he knew. "Ambrose wasn't afraid of me."

"Reckon not."

"But somebody else?"

"Maybe."

"Could we go inside and talk about it?"

"Okay." He led me through the back door of the pub into the bar, dark and not yet ready for trade, with chairs upside down on tables. He pulled two down for us, then, without a word, drew two pints of cider from the barrel Ambrose must have supped from the night before and set them between us. "'Ere's to the ol' bugger," he said and quaffed some.

I drank some of mine. "I came down to see him."

"I know. 'E said you would. 'E were impatient to see you."

"Pity I didn't get here sooner."

"Maybe so."

"What happened?"

"We don't know. 'E were in 'ere as usual last night. Next I knew were when George Ash—our local bobby—woke me up a few hours ago. They'd found Ambrose in the river and George wanted to check if 'e'd been in 'ere aforehand. 'E 'ad Jess with 'im—we've taken the animal in for the time being."

"I met Constable Ash at the cottage. He reckoned Ambrose fell in, drunk, and drowned."

Ted grunted. "I'd 'ave said that myself, but Ambrose were a fly bugger—nobody's fool—and 'e dain't spend a lifetime suppin' cider without bein' able to walk 'ome blindfold. 'E 'ad no more 'an 'is usual last night, an' besides . . ."

"Yes?"

"You know all that guff 'e used to talk about 'is uncle—strangers, 'avin' 'ad a 'and in 'is death?"

"I do."

"Well, it were strange, but last night 'e seemed sort of... anxious. 'E asked if I remembered some bloke who came in at lunchtime and sat alone in a corner. Did I recognize 'im? 'Course I dain't. People just drop in if they're passin', specially at weekends. I told Ambrose as much, but 'e insisted this bloke 'ad been watchin' 'im, though 'e'd said nothin' about it at the time. Said 'e'd seen 'im hangin' round Lodge Cottage durin' the day and thought 'e knew 'im from somewhere, though 'e couldn't be certain."

"Did this character show up last night?"

"Not as I knows."

Who was it, Ambrose? I thought. Did you recognize one of the shadowy faces at last? I wanted badly to know, but Ambrose was dead and Ted, if he'd ever known, couldn't remember.

"Tell me," I said, swallowing some of the cider, "did Ambrose mention finding something recently?"

"No—only as 'e was keen to see you again."

"He didn't say why?"

"No. Don't you know?"

"Not exactly. I think he'd found something out—but I don't know what."

Ted drained his glass. "Reckon you never will now—supposin' there was somethin', that is."

I finished my cider too and got up to go. "What do you think? Was it all talk? A pure accident? Or something more sinister?"

Ted took our glasses to the bar. "I ain't a fanciful man," he said. "You knows that from the cold water I poured on Ambrose's stories 'bout 'is uncle." He walked back and unbolted the front door to let me out. "But both 'is father an' 'is uncle—then 'im too—in queer accidents?" He stroked his chin. "That's a bit much. That's a bit too much."

He opened the door. "That's what I think too," I said, stepping out into the road. "Thanks for the chat—and the cider."

"The cider was for Ambrose: I owed 'im a round. Chats are

free—call anytime. Things'll be quieter 'ere without that gabby ol' bugger to chivvy me up."

I reached the Bennetts' house around lunchtime, sooner than I was expected. Hester was surprised to see me and even more surprised to hear why I was early. She sat me down in her kitchen—a far, efficient cry from Ambrose's grimy palace of hob and range—made me coffee and listened to the story of my catastrophic morning.

"It's hard to believe," she said when I'd finished. "He seemed so . . . vital . . . when he was here."

"Nick said you weren't too keen on having him in."

Hester smiled in embarrassment. "I wasn't. He was terribly sloshed. I took him for a tramp."

"Not quite that."

"No." She gulped some coffee. "It must have come as a terrible shock. What will you do now?"

"I don't know. I just don't know."

I was none the wiser three hours later, when Nick came home from school. I recounted to him what had happened and we talked it over during dinner. He and Hester became the audience for my internal dialogue. Did he fall or was he pushed? The same as for his uncle. Were the conspiracies against them merely figments of their imagination or did Ambrose's "dark forces" really exist? He'd claimed in his letter to have something against the Couchmans, so wasn't it one hell of a coincidence that he should fall off a bridge just before he could deliver the goods?

Suddenly, I remembered that I'd left Timothy alone in the lounge during Nick's phone call to me. He could easily have read Ambrose's letter if he'd noticed it. I couldn't imagine propriety stopping him. And he'd left his card on the mantelpiece, where I'd put the letter, so it was surely odds on that he had. Did that really make it likely that he'd sped down to Devon in his Porsche the same night and done away with Ambrose? Hardly. Such an act was altogether too direct for his devious mind and, besides, why should he have done?

My last thought before going to bed with a good slug of Nick's whisky inside me was a depressing one. The likeliest contingency was that, intoxicated as much by visions of vengeance as The Greengage's cider, Ambrose had simply tumbled off the bridge, as P.C. Ash had surmised, knocked himself out in the fall and drowned. If so, his hopes and mine were already in the tidal reaches of the Teign—literally so if he'd been carrying his discovery with him. So near, we fondly thought, but now as far as ever.

Next morning found me on an early bus back to Dewford. There were no other passengers, so, as we jolted along the road, I was free to mine my thoughts. I judged most of the dust would by now have settled on the drama of Ambrose's death, written off as the watery end of an old boozer: the loss of a local character, but what else could you expect of him? I felt certain that P.C. Ash would have abandoned his patrol at Lodge Cottage and returned to cases of sheep-worrying. The coast was therefore clear for me to see if I could find whatever there was to find.

I was right. When I walked down over the bridge, the tape had been removed. The Teign flowed on, the bridge stood, the body gone, the evidence gathered, the book closed. Or about to open, if I could only find it.

I walked through the gate and tried the cottage door. It was locked—Ash had done his duty. As I made my way to the back of the house, I nearly fell over an old wheelbarrow, with a pannier basket inside, containing a bundle of dead flowers. A recent picking by Ambrose—or something long forgotten? It was hard to say. I came to the kitchen door: firmly bolted from the inside. I was feeling increasingly furtive, especially since circumstances were pushing me towards forcing an entry.

But there was no need. As I rounded the corner on the other side of the house, I saw that one of the kitchen windows was open—wide open, with the stay hanging loose and, yes, when I looked, gougings in the wooden frame as if somebody had jemmied it open.

I peered inside, expecting the same scene as the day before. But the kitchen was no longer merely disorderly—it was chaotic. Cupboard doors and drawers had been pulled open, the contents removed and piled anyhow on the floor. There was nothing destructive about it, but somebody had been through the place. It couldn't have been the police—they'd have had the decency to put everything back. Then who?

I dragged over an old, upturned bucket and used it as a platform to scramble in through the window. It was a squeeze, but I hauled myself over the draining board next to the sink and dropped down into the room. The injured pride of the cottage clamped itself around me in the musty, watchful silence. This was already an empty house, smelling of the neglect which intrusion only accentuated. And silent too, silent in the still, echoless manner of a tomb.

I steeled myself and walked through into the front room. The curtains were drawn shut and the gloom was forbidding; I hurried across to part them. Muted shadow had already hinted at what intruding daylight made graphic: more of the same treatment meted out to the kitchen, only worse, because there was more to this room, more accreted, personal associations with Ambrose. The furniture had been cleared of its load of books, papers, packets, models, pipes and portfolios: the whole gallimaufry of one old man's home heaped on the floor, sifted crudely for no clear purpose. Worse, beneath the table, felled but apparently unnoticed, one of the old fellow's model aircraft: a First World War bi-plane, lovingly constructed, now crushed on the floor, one wing smashed as easily and irretrievably as a moth's. I looked across to the window, where the curtains were snagged on an upturned cactus pot, its soil scattered across the carpet; I could have wept.

But I didn't. In a way, I was as much an intruder as whoever had done this. And they, like me, had been intruders with a purpose, for all the signs of vandalism and malice in their search. I turned, as they must have turned, to the old bureau by the wall. It was empty now, not the crammed glory-hole Ambrose had made of it. One of the wingback easy chairs had been pulled round to face it and used as a repository for its contents. I imagined somebody standing by the bureau, checking through its hoard and tossing each discarded item onto the seat of the chair as they went.

I'd hoped my search could be discreet and respectful. There was no chance of that in view of the mayhem I'd found. It was demeaning, but there was nothing for it but to scrabble through the heap, hoping to chance on the prize. Yet, even as I began doing so, I knew I'd find nothing. If it had been there —which I doubted, in view of Ambrose's secrecy—it wouldn't be there any longer. There was no doubt in my mind that somebody had already looked for it.

The gruesome task took all morning. I worked my way through all the rooms—and all to no avail. I had a mental picture of the Postscript as a fat, leatherbound tome rather like the original Memoir. It was therefore going to be hard to miss if I looked in the right place, but it would've been equally easy to hide somewhere—under the floorboards, behind a cupboard—which I would overlook. Lodge Cottage was small, but full of nooks and crannies and Ambrose's ingenuity could have found many obscure hidey-holes. It was, in short, a hopeless task, but one I had to attempt. My only consolation was that whoever had already been there had obviously been in a hurry and had probably therefore done a less efficient job than I could.

I gave up at lunchtime, tired and dispirited by the fruitless effort, feeling vaguely defiled by the necessity of rooting through Ambrose's possessions. I took only one thing away—Strafford's first edition of Hardy's poet (*Satires of Circumstances*), which I found spread open in the front room, with some of its pages bent back as if it had been tossed down—dismissed as being of no account. I was one up on somebody there. It meant a great deal to Strafford and to me, even more now I'd talked to Elizabeth about her last meeting with Edwin and his use of those lines from 'After a Journey'. Ambrose wouldn't have minded me taking it as a memento. Nor, I hoped, would his uncle. It was good to rescue it from the chaos and take it away for safekeeping. Yet it wasn't the Postscript and that was all I really wanted.

I asked directions to the police house and found Ash's cottage —whitewash and slate with a green-fingered garden, ivy growing over the blue DEVON & CORNWALL CONSTABULARY sign, a tiny office—of kinds—housed in a modern brick extension to one side. I peered in through the wired-glass door. It was bare and empty—a table, three chairs and a WATCH OUT THERE'S A THIEF ABOUT poster. I rang the bell—several times. It was, in fact, the cottage door which creaked open in answer. Ash emerged, breathing heavily, with an aroma of suet and gravy behind him, dabbing some of his dinner off his uniform tie.

"Mr Radford, ain't it?"

"Yes. Can we talk?"

"Best come in the office."

He opened the door, led me in and plonked himself on one of the chairs, overlapping it uncomfortably.

"I went up to Lodge Cottage this morning—just to take a look. It's been broken into."

"Broken into?" Ash's brown furrowed.

"Yes. A kitchen window forced. As far as I could see, everything turned over."

Ash got up and strode to the window. "I left it secure. Vandals, I bet."

"Out here?"

"There's a load of tearaways round 'ere whose dads work in the quarries down at Trusham. They'm as bad as any townies, believe you me."

"It didn't look like vandalism."

"Then what?" Ash shot a glare at me.

"A break-in, I'd say—a break-in with a purpose."

He looked at me with his slow, countryman's irritation. I knew what he was thinking. This man's another fantasist like Ambrose. Why can't he leave me to knock a few heads together in the quarrying community and bury these other, alien notions with the old man who dreamt them up in the first place? "I'll take a look, Mr Radford, an' notify the Trust to shut it up proper. I'll add your . . . opinion . . . to my report to the inspector. 'E might want to 'ave a word with you 'imself. That's all I can do."

"I see. Well, thanks for that. I'll be going."

He followed me to the door. "Reckon that'd be for the best, sir . . . in the long run. Why not stay in Exeter and leave this to us locals?"

"Maybe I will." I had no such intentions. "Tell me, is there to be an inquest?"

"Got to be, sir. Openin' on Thursday. But they'll adjourn till after the funeral."

"When's that?"

"Monday."

"Will I be required—for the inquest?"

"That's up to the Coroner, sir. But I doubt it." So did I. This case had accidental death written all over it and my inconvenient suggestions of something less straightforward were best ignored. "But don't worry. Somebody from the Exeter station'll call round for a fair copy of your statement for you to sign—just to put the Coroner in the picture." He smiled. It was supposed to be reassuring.

I got to The Greengage in time for last orders and told Ted all about it. But his reaction was disappointing. He agreed with Ash that it could well have been the work of Trusham rowdies. And the passage of one day had dented his conviction that something was wrong. Ash had been to see him, asked him all about Ambrose—and me—and implied it was an open and shut case. By the time the inquest came round, I doubted if Ted would see it any other way himself. What, after all, was the point? He said as much as I was leaving, long after the other customers.

"Trouble is, who's goin' to believe me if I stands up in court and talks about strangers followin' Ambrose an' all that guff? They'll just think I'm a crank like 'im—an' there's my trade to think of."

Of course. Ted's trade. Ash's reputation for running a quiet patch. Ambrose's image as a cidery old menace to himself. And me? A cocky young outsider researching the history of the Straffords and looking for mystery where there was none.

I went back to Exeter angry with all of them, including myself. What was to be done? Nothing, except inflict my mood on the Bennetts and await developments.

They came in trickles. On Wednesday, a constable from the Exeter force called with Ash's version of my statement—brief, factual and accurate as far as it went. I signed it, reckoning I'd better bide my time before making any outlandish claims.

That afternoon, after school, I persuaded Nick to drive me out to Dewford for a look at the cottage. Some National Trust workmen were boarding up the windows. The foreman told me it was a temporary measure. As far as he knew, the contents—along with the cottage—would revert to the Trust. Already, there was talk of opening it next season as an authentically restored crossingkeeper's cottage. Maybe they'd even lay a strip of track and put up new gates. From function to dereliction to tourist curio—why not? It was a twentieth century sequence which had enveloped the Straffords.

I didn't want to go to The Greengage again, so I let Nick drive me to a pub he knew—The Nobody Inn at Doddiscombsleigh, up in the Haldon Hills east of Barrowteign. It was a warm evening, so we sat in the garden—steadily filling with the jean and cheesecloth intelligentsia of Exeter whom Ted would've have no time for—and I had less and less.

"What can I do, Nick? That book was somewhere in Ambrose's keeping. How do I get it now?"

"I don't see how you can. You searched the cottage thoroughly?"

"All morning. It wasn't there."

"Already stolen?"

"I doubt it. I bet Ambrose took good care to hide it. But where?"

"Under the floorboards? In the garden?"

"Maybe—but I can't excavate the place, can I?"

"No. Not now. You'll just have to wait and see what the inquest turns up."

"I think I already know."

"Will the Coroner call you—or me?"

"I haven't mentioned Ambrose visiting you—and I won't. All round, I see nothing to be gained from blurting out allegations I can't back up."

It was the truest thing I'd said. The lull since Ambrose's death and the ransacking of his cottage threatened to unnerve me, but I sensed that, if I just waited, something would happen. It was certainly far likelier to happen if I said as little in public as possible. Only by stealth could I smoke out whatever was hidden—wherever it was hidden.

That didn't stop me attending the opening of the inquest in Exeter the following morning. I sat conspicuously alone in the public gallery while Ash briefly stated the circumstances. The Coroner issued a disposal certificate to permit the funeral to go ahead and then adjourned the proceedings for a week.

Nick and Hester went away for the weekend, ostensibly to visit Hester's parents in Tewkesbury. I wouldn't have blamed them for just wanting a rest from me. I drank at the local pub, paced around the house and wrote a further report to Sellick—telling him about Ambrose's mysterious death but saying nothing, at that stage, about the Postscript. Why build up false hopes? I thought. Besides, since Alec's visit, I proposed to tell Sellick only what I had to. He would learn of the Postscript if and when I was ready.

Monday was the day of the funeral. I travelled out early on the bus and waited at the church for the party to arrive. A pallid morning, with thin, grey drifts of cloud across a washed-out blue sky, an edge to the breeze, an ill-prepared quality to the day and the place.

The party, if you could call it that, arrived in drabs. A dapper, military-looking man in a tweed suit, who introduced himself as "Knox of the National Trust, i.c. admin up at Barrowteign, you know: showing the flag, what?" I could have done without his good cheer. Then Ted from The Greengage, trying to look solemn but appearing merely puzzled, fidgeting at an unfamiliarly stiff collar. Finally, the Vicar: doughy face, disapproving air, hurrying unnecessarily. That was all—no retinue of retainers, no host of grieving friends and relatives. We were the ill-matched mourning party and only two of us were there from choice.

The hearse arrived promptly at eleven. Knox insisted on telling me the Trust had footed the bill. The service was brief, even, at times, garbled. Then we filed out into the churchyard behind the coffin. A grave had been dug near Robert and Florence Strafford's monument of weeping angels. Some of the earth from the pile had tumbled against the small stone marked E.G.S. but nobody seemed to have noticed. With awful swiftness in the fitful sun, the deed was done. We'd thrown our handfuls of Devon soil after Ambrose into the grave, been thanked perfunctorily by the Vicar and made our way out through the lych gate.

Ted looked quite affected, said he'd have to get back for the lunchtime rush and hurried away. Knox, eager for an audience, offered me a lift wherever I was going and I accepted one to Farrants Cross. As we drove out of the village, he began to talk in the stream which the occasion at the church had reduced to a trickle.

"Know old Ambrose long?" he asked.

"Not long. But I liked him."

"Bit of a character and no mistake. Touchy, you'll allow."

"I suppose so."

"Take the last time I saw him."

"When was that?"

"Must have been the day he . . . fell off the bridge. A week ago yesterday."

"What happened?" I tried to sound casual.

"Well, it was a Sunday—always our busiest day at the house. I was putting in a weekend to help with the rush. Dashed bad time for the old fellow to choose."

"To choose for what?"

"Showed up in my office in the middle of the afternoon—just when there was a flap on."

"And?"

"Demanded some blessed key. Wanted to visit part of the house not open to the public. Demanded, mark you, not requested."

"I suppose he felt he shouldn't have to ask."

Knox looked straight at that. "Probably so. Typical of the man, though—blustering in without consideration. But, when I handed it over, as good as gold. Profuse thanks, that sort of thing. Even tried to tip me, like some blasted servant." He bridled at the memory, then smiled. "I suggested he donate it to Trust funds."

"And did he?"

"I should say not. Between you and me, I think he was too fond of the Trust. But we were fond of him: a celebrated eccentric."

The car pulled up. We were at Farrants Cross. Knox's last memory of Barrowteign's resident eccentric was as a Sunday afternoon irritant. "Thanks for the lift," I said, climbing out.

"By the way, what was the key he wanted? What part of the house did he want to visit? I thought he didn't like going to the place."
"That's true." He pondered the point for a moment. "The key? Oh, it was to the attics. There's a lot of storage space there. The old chap probably wanted to root around for something." I reeled inwardly. "Jolly nice to have met you. Cheerio."
"Goodbye." I waved after Knox's car as it pulled away. But I wasn't thinking about his courtesy. Something else was chiming in my mind. At last. I knew why Ambrose would have wanted to climb to the attics of his ancestral home that Sunday afternoon. Not to look for something, but to hide it. The Postscript, lying unsuspected at Barrowteign—waiting for me.
It was as much as I could do not to run after Knox's car and shout for him to stop and take me at once to the house. But I couldn't. Stealth, I reminded myself, was the only course.

Though I left it as late as I could bear, my arrival at Barrowteign the following morning was still earlier than most visitors'. The drive was empty as I made my way up it, past the gate which led through the lime trees to Lodge Cottage, over the trench marking the line of the old railway and onto the bank beneath Barrowteign's broad stone frontage.
The guide in the entrance hall was, I felt sure, the same lady as I'd encountered there before. I claimed to have an appointment with Mr Knox. "Major Knox," she corrected me. I was directed up the back stairs to the second floor, which housed the administrative offices. The ceilings were lower than below, the corridors narrower, the wallpaper plainer. I walked confidently past a secretary's office where a typewriter was clacking to a door marked MAJOR L.W. KNOX—ADMINISTRATOR, knocked and went in.
Whatever he'd been doing, Knox didn't seem to mind the interruption. He wheeled round from the window, which commanded a fine view of the garden, and smiled. "'Pon my soul—an unexpected pleasure." He walked across and shook my hand vigorously. "Mr Radford, isn't it?"
"That's right. We met yesterday."
"Do sit down, old fellow. What can I do for you?"

I sat in a studded leather chair and looked across the fine old desk at Knox. He'd furnished his office pleasingly from sundry contents of the house—a bracket clock on top of a bookcase, a couple of gilt-framed oil paintings of the Flemish school on the wall, an ornate inkstand between us on the desk. Barrowteign was a comfortable billet for Major Knox.

"Having never seen the house," I lied, "I thought I ought to while I was down here."

"Fine idea. Let me show you round. Pretty quiet at the moment." Not like when Ambrose came calling, I thought.

"That's very kind. There's no need. I just thought I'd look in on you."

But Knox was already on his feet. "No, no. Least I can do. Happier circumstances than yesterday, what? Come along." He made for the door. As I followed, I noticed, to the left of the frame, a wooden panel set in the wall carrying a score or so of hooks and, on them, an assortment of keys—some old and little used, others bright with the newness of security consciousness and one of them, I knew, the key I was looking for.

Knox led me out into the corridor, leaving his office open and unattended with a carelessness I found encouraging. He took me back down the stairs to the hall and commenced his own, superior version of the house tour. I didn't mind the repetition, in fact played up my role as the impressed novice of history, smiling at his every laboured witticism and trying to look in awe of his erudition.

The tour over, I insisted on buying him a drink in the restaurant housed in the old servants' wing. We had some lunch, I stood the wine and several brandies afterwards. Knox was enjoying himself. I began to lead the conversation where I wanted it to go.

"It's a fascinating house," I said.

"One of our more varied properties and no mistake."

"It's strange, but I've always found with these old houses that it's not really the grand showpiece rooms which attract me."

"No?"

"More the, sort of, curious corners tucked away."

"How d'you mean?"

"Well, the servants' quarters here—very nicely adapted as a

restaurant—the bathrooms with their great, solid tubs you could bath an elephant in. The kitchens with their copper pans and vast, scrubbed tables."

"Ah, know what you mean—eye-openers, what?"

"It's a pity you can't open more of the house to show that sort of thing."

"We're thinking of doing something with the stable block next year."

"Really?"

"Apart from that, I don't think there's anything we've overlooked."

"How about the upper floors?"

"Got to be somewhere for admin, you know." He smiled.

"Of course. What about further up?"

"That is the top. Only the attics above us."

"Nothing of interest there?"

"Hardly think so. Full of junk from family days. Incredible hoard of old rubbish. Don't think we've ever been through it properly, but everything worthwhile is on display. Between you and me, now old Ambrose's gone, we can probably ditch the lot and use the space more effectively."

"Sounds a fascinating place."

Knox chuckled. "Wouldn't have said so. Inches thick in dust, you know."

"Still, as I said, it's these curious corners that appeal to me."

"Nobody ever goes up there." I didn't remind him that Ambrose had, only recently.

"That seems a shame."

"If you really want to take a look, there's no problem. I could take you up—but you'll regret it."

"Then I won't say I wasn't warned." I touched his glass. "Have another before we go?"

"Won't say no." And, in this pliant mood, he didn't say no to returning to his office for the attic key. A large, old, brass affair, number twelve on the board, a fact I mentally noted.

At the far end of the corridor housing his office, Knox unlocked a solid, panelled door and flicked a switch illuminating narrow spiral stairs. He led the way up, stumbling at one point, to another door, opening onto darkness. He groped around somewhere to his left and found another switch which lit up the interior.

Bare, dusty boards and the sound of a water tank dripping somewhere. Planks of wood piled against one wall, an old map chest, with several drawers broken, against the other. For the rest, tea chests, orange boxes and buckets, dust and cobwebs everywhere.

There was a path between the debris to another door at the end of the chamber. Through this was the attic proper, thinly lit by daylight from widely spaced windows. It stretched as far as I could see, the length of the house, with thin panel divisions along the way but open doorways in each so that I could see beyond. It was obvious why, to Knox, the contents were just "old rubbish." They were piled in disorderly heaps, sometimes reaching to the sloping roof, sometimes blocking the path between them. Chairs standing on tables, old chests and cabinets, picture frames, boxes, bathtubs, barrels and bottles. Then more, and more, of the same: broken-backed books in tumbled piles, a huge freestanding gilt mirror, smashed in one corner, a bundle of old umbrellas and walking sticks, an ancient wind-up gramophone, an upset pot of paint with its contents set years ago in a patch on the floorboards.

I wandered through the detritus of a family home, feeling as much despair as hope. It was an ideal hiding place for anything, and that was the problem. How could I look for something specific in this vast muddle? It was the difficulty in Ambrose's cottage magnified ten times.

Ambrose! How he'd have laughed to see me trailing Knox through a chaos his administrative mind detested: a chaos of Ambrose's making—among others. What had he said to Nick? "Tell Martin to remember that we Straffords have lofty memories." Not, as I'd thought, a reference to the family's faded glory, but an old eccentric's last joke, which I'd failed to see. Now, here I was, at his bidding. But what could I see? Everything and nothing. I laughed at the answer.

"Bit desperate, what?" said Knox, thinking he'd caught my drift.

"Yes." He couldn't have known how right he was.

We passed through one panel doorway into the next part of the attic. As before, an excess of riches. Under every dust-sheet, behind every box, could have been the answer. But where to begin? A battered and strapped old cricket bat was propped against a hamper in one corner. Had Strafford once hit the village bowling for six with it? No. It was a boy's bat. Perhaps he'd instructed Ambrose in its use, on his return from the Great War.

On top of the hamper was a rusty metal wastepaper bin. Inside, a spindly lampstand minus shade and bulb and an old bottle once used as a candle holder, the neck encrusted with wax. The crooked, yellowed label read STRAFFORD'S IMPERIAL PALE ALE—BEST IN THE WEST. It must have been more than a hundred years old, the contents brewed in Crediton—before the Straffords dissociated themselves from such humble trade—and drunk long ago.

My eye moved beyond the hamper. There, in the angle of a joist, stood something else I recognized: a toy castle, about four feet square, a castellated turret at each corner, a keep in the middle, arrow-slits, tiny doors and arched windows, a drawbridge, the wood of the doors painted green, the walls carefully covered with stone-patterned paper, the battlements sawn all round to an exact pattern. It was a craftsman's joy—and that of a young boy I'd known as an old man.

A broken cobweb hung vertically from the joist. The dust around the castle had been disturbed and, yes, I could see fingermarks on the coated surface of the drawbridge. A tiny turret door sagged open on its leather hinge. The interior was dark but certainly large enough for the purpose I suspected. The drawbridge reached the height of the castle—about two feet. I judged a standard size book could have been thrust inside and longed to test my judgment. Where, after all, could have been more fitting? Ambrose's Christmas gift from 1918—lovingly carved by his uncle in a task to take his mind off the carnage of war.

My confidence grew with the memory of Ambrose's letter to me. "The old bugger chose a cunning hiding place and it's only thanks to you I looked there." Why me? Of course. My visit had prompted him, while we took our hair of the dog in The Greengage, to recall his uncle's mention of the castle on their own last drink there in 1951. What Strafford had remembered, Ambrose also remembered and, eventually, I did too. The perfect, hinted-at hiding place was before me, with Ambrose's fingermarks in the dust as confirmation.

Only one thing held me back—Knox's bemused company. "Spotted something?" he asked, noticing my rapt attention on what was, to him, just another section of the shambles.

"No, no." My denial was instinctive. I couldn't let him think there was anything of value to be found. He'd have laid claim to it with curatorial zeal. Once again, stealth was my only recourse. Stumbling on my prize, I had to walk calmly away from it—and return later, alone. "As you warned me: just dusty old junk."

"Seen enough?"

"I think so." I had. Enough to know I was on the right track. "Shall we go down?"

Knox was happy to go. To him, the attic was a door to be locked, a key on a varnished board. He insisted I have tea back in his office and sank gratefully into the chair behind his desk, like a man returning to his element.

I sustained the small talk over tea, Knox recounting how he'd stiffened the administration of the property while I eyed a certain brass key across the room and regretted not having plied him with enough brandy to make him forget to lock the attic door.

I left with a reluctance Knox mistook for pleasure in his company. "Jolly nice to have met you again, old fellow."

"You too, Major Knox. Thanks for the tour."

"Think nothing of it. Call again any time you're passing."

"Thanks. I will."

"Next time, we'll miss out those blasted attics, what?"

"Good idea." Little did he know.

I went down the back stairs to the hall. The old lady was still at her desk, handing booklets to visitors as they entered.

"I trust you enjoyed the house," she said brightly.

"Very much. Your Major Knox is a most hospitable fellow."

"A charming man—such a gentleman."

"I said I might call on him again." I tried to sound off-hand. "Do you know what the best time would be?"

"Any weekend I think, during opening hours. Major Knox

is a most punctual man . . . except Wednesday afternoons, that is. He always has Wednesday afternoons off—for his golf, you know."

"Thanks. I'll remember that." There was no danger I wouldn't. It was Tuesday afternoon. I had only to wait 24 hours and Knox would be absent from his post. The key and the attic would be at my disposal.

Lunchtime the following day: ideal, I judged, to find the administrative quarters of Barrowteign at their quietest. I followed the tour route as far as the backstairs, then headed up instead of down. The corridor on the second floor was silent, with no clack of typewriter or jangle of telephone. Knox's secretary had evidently gone to lunch and Knox himself I knew to be out for the rest of the day.

I walked slowly to his office, trying not to creak too many floorboards. Sunlight was streaming through the window behind his desk. A snatch of childish laughter came from the garden below. There, on the board by the door, was key number twelve.

It was simple to reach out and remove it and I knew I was safe from detection if I returned it before the end of the day. Hadn't Knox said nobody ever went up to the attics? Yet my heart pounded as I walked along the corridor towards the door leading to them. Strangely, it wasn't the fear of the daylight robber which had gripped me, but fear of what I was now so close to discovering. The Postscript: I'd dreamed about it, debated it, run over in my mind only that morning on the bus all the permutations of what it might contain. The prospect of certainty was suddenly intimidating.

I closed the attic door carefully behind me, locked it and climbed the stairs to the windowless ante-chamber. Then into the attic proper. Sunlight split the gloom in dust-hung wedges. I threaded my way anxiously through the hoard of rubbish. There, safe in its niche by the angle of a joist, was the toy castle.

I crouched in front of it, as Ambrose must have done, and prized gingerly at the drawbridge. It stuck fast—I hesitated to wrench at it. Then, the answer: a rusty spindle imbedded in the wall of the castle porch. It turned, squeakily but effectively—the drawbridge jerked down on a string cable.

Inside, a matchwood grille representing a portcullis. And, in the other wall of the porch, another, smaller spindle. But no, this one was broken. It hung slackly, the string perished years before—or severed in Ambrose's haste days before.

With the string gone, I could raise the portcullis by one finger lodged in the grille. I was on my knees now, peering in through the narrow gateway. Sure enough, by the dim light I could see, as I held up the portcullis, an object—a package of some kind—stowed inside. I reached in with my other hand. It felt solid and book-shaped, the wrapper vaguely waxy, tied with rough string. I eased it out from its resting place. There was a struggle to get it past the spikes of the portcullis. Then it was free—and in my hands.

It was a waxed canvas package, securely wrapped and tied. I cursed myself for not bringing a penknife, told myself to be patient as I coaxed the knot loose. At last, the string fell away. I folded back the canvas, then an inner layer of crinkled brown paper—and there it was.

It could have been the Memoir looking back at me: the same style of book—a leatherbound, foolscap, maroon-covered tome with marbled pages, standard issue, perhaps, in the Consular Service. Unlike the Memoir, most of its pages were blank, but the first quarter or so was filled with that distinctive, copperplate handwriting in diplomatic black ink that left no doubt in my mind: Strafford had left his mark. Just when I'd begun to fear never hearing his voice again, there he was, speaking to me as only he could.

There was a sound somewhere in the attic. With a start, I snapped the book shut, sending up a cloud of dust. I coughed and cursed my nerves. It was just a mouse, scurrying among the packing cases. The door, after all, was locked behind me. Nevertheless, I felt vulnerable in that labyrinth of dusty rafters. I needed air, light and time to study my discovery. I couldn't wait till I'd taken it back to Exeter, yet I couldn't stay where I was.

I left the wrapping paper and string by the castle and walked over to one of the windows: a grimy fanlight admitting a sepia beam to the attic. Outside, there was a lead fully forming a gutter, a brick parapet beyond it and blue sky. The gully was broad and dry, the brightness inviting. The fanlight opened in the centre. I wrenched down the retaining bolts and pushed the two halves apart. They stuck for a moment, then swung free.

A rush of sunlight and birdsong pierced the attic. I put my head out and looked along the gully in either direction. It was quite a heat trap behind its parapet and just the airy hideaway I was looking for. I dragged over an old ottoman and, using it as a platform, climbed out through the window.

From the parapet, I had an imposing view of the garden. A few tiny figures were moving amid the fountains and clipped hedges. Beyond them, the foothills of the Haldon range climbed eastwards. The scene shimmered in a modest heat haze. It could have been painted or embroidered—a pattern of English country house life laid out like a rug. A scene four generations of Straffords could have looked at smugly: the greenery refulgent with their ownership. But not any more. The Straffords were dead, strangers were loose in their garden—one on the very roof of their house.

Not quite a stranger, Strafford—I hope I can say that. You could have done worse than have me open your book. Whoever ransacked Ambrose's cottage, for instance. Instead, it was me, feet against the brick parapet behind the stone-faced wall of your house, back to the sun-warmed slate roof some architect designed for your grandfather 150 years ago, just so, at a lounging angle dictated by the reclining rainfall of Devon winters. It was me, with a good three hours at my disposal before I needed to worry about leaving, a vital three hours to give to you and your last, late thoughts. Perched on the apex of your ancestors, crouched at the nadir of your family fortunes, I opened your book—and a door with it, in a past still able to confound the present.

Postscript

I had not thought we would speak again so soon, fate and I. I had supposed the conclusion of my Memoir to be just that: a conclusion, permitting of no sequel, deserving of no encore. It needs not saying that I should have known better.

How came then the interruption to my unremarked and unremarkable exile on Madeira? It came explosively, like thunder on a humid afternoon. And humid it was that day, the Porto Novo valley steaming in mist which refused to disperse before the heat of the sun. It was the day before my seventy-fifth birthday, and I, having lived to an age when nothing might be thought still to be capable of surprising me, was about to discover that life had left its greatest shock for me till last.

I was on the verandah after luncheon. Tomás had removed the coffee tray and study of the previous Saturday's Times *had not prevented me falling asleep in my chair. Once I would have brooded over the leader page or gone for a walk round the quinta to forget the nonsense I had read in the parliamentary report. Nowadays I just slept—and forgot the more easily.*

I recall that, for an instant, I believed myself to be dreaming—as, mayhap, I had been—of my time in South Africa. Certainly that would account for the accent of the voice seeming somehow fitting. But then, it was not the accent which served to shock. It was what the voice said.

"Wake up—old man!" The words were brutal and barked, like an instruction, many years after I had last been instructed to do anything.

I opened my eyes and stiffened in the chair. Leaning on the other side of the verandah rails was a man I did not recognize—unusual, in itself, in the Porto Novo valley. He was a short, lean man of middle age, grey-haired but muscular, bronzed by the sun but not, I judged, the Madeiran variety. His clothes were expensive, but there was about him the look of a desperado, a gleam in his piercing blue eyes of something akin to mania. Or perhaps I would not have jumped to these conclusions had he not held in his right hand, trained across the verandah rails at me, a revolver.

"Are you Edwin Strafford?" he demanded.

"Yes." I tried to remain calm. "And who are you?"

"They call me Leo Sellick." The answer seemed oddly framed.

"I don't think I know you, Mr Sellick."

"You wouldn't."

"Then . . . what can I do for you?"

"To begin with, you can tell me if you recognize this gun."

"Why should I?"

"Because it's yours."

"I don't own a gun."

"You did once."

"I think not . . . except in the army."

"Exactly . . . in the army."

"Mr Sellick, I left the army more than thirty years ago."

"And you lost this gun more than fifty years ago."

"I think you're mistaken."

"No. There's no mistake. You are Edwin Strafford."

"I am."

"And I, God help me, am your son."

At that moment, I had no doubt that the man was mad. An armed intruder claiming to be the son I did not have could hardly be sane. Yet the fact that he was armed dictated that he be, at least, humoured. Besides, I felt an unaccountable curiosity to hear more. Perhaps it was that an old man in uneventful retirement welcomes any intrusion, however abrupt. "I have no son," I said, with an effort of sweet reason.

"Then meet the man who thought he had no father . . . until now."

"Mr Sellick, sooner or later, my servants will chance upon

us here and be alarmed if they see that you are armed. Why not sit down and put that gun away? I'd rather there were no accidents."

"There'll be no accidents, Strafford. If I decide to kill you, it'll be for the best of reasons."

He walked slowly up the verandah steps and sat in the upright chair opposite me, where he evidently felt in a dominant position. He held a panama hat in his left hand and rested it over the revolver in his other hand. I struggled, meanwhile, to take stock of him. He looked and moved like many a rancher I had encountered in South Africa: lean, tough and terse, with eyes that reached as far as the Veldt. In the context of the Boer War, such men had to be watched; they might shoot a man as easily and automatically as they would a hyena. Yet Sellick was far from home and his brow was knotted with thought.

"What brought you here, Mr Sellick?"

"A piece of paper, you could say. Take a look." He released the hat, reached into his jacket pocket, took out a folded paper and tossed it onto my lap.

It was a birth certificate and I guessed that it was his. But I had no grounds to be sure. The entry was, for all its apparent authenticity, preposterous: a fusion of names and identities which were wholly alien to each other. A stern-faced South African had burst into my life and flapped beneath my nose a document purporting to disprove all that I knew about myself. I sat for a moment dumbstruck by the outrageous evidence placed before me.

The entry read as follows. When and where born: 21st June 1901—Geldoorp Hospital, Pietermaritzburg, Natal. Name: Leo. Name and surname of father: Edwin George Strafford. Name and maiden surname of mother: Caroline Amelia van der Merwe. Rank or profession of father: Army officer. Signature, description and residence of informant: F.H. Sellick, doctor attending birth, Geldoorp Hospital, Pietermaritzburg. When registered: 24th June 1901.

It was, I assumed, an uncanny coincidence. There had been another British officer in South Africa bearing my name. He had fathered a child there. Sellick was labouring under some kind of misapprehension. Yet what kind was not clear. Was he, after all, the Leo named on the certificate? What did he want of me?"

"Is this," I said at last, "a record of your birth?"

"It is."

"Yet your name is Sellick—that of the doctor who attended the birth."

"Correct."

"Then please—explain."

"It is you who should explain. But I'll tell you a story. The part of it you don't know.

"That is my birth certificate. But it only came into my hands this year. I was raised in the Cape Province of South Africa by a rancher named Daniel Sellick. He had a fine spread on the Great Karroo. As a boy, I took him and his wife for my parents. On my twenty-first birthday, they told me the truth, or part of it, at any rate.

"My real mother, they said, had died giving birth to me. The doctor in attendance was my uncle, Frank Sellick, who, knowing his brother's wife couldn't have children of her own, and distressed at being unable to save the mother, persuaded them to adopt me as their own.

"My uncle was dead by the time they told me—the flu bug of 1918 got him, doctor or not—so I only had his story at second-hand. He'd told them that my mother, Caroline van der Merwe, was a Durban girl who'd married a British officer in the autumn of 1900. He'd almost immediately deserted her, only for her to discover that she was pregnant. It was a bad time to be carrying a British officer's child in Natal. When Botha's patriots invaded the province in February 1901, a raiding party butchered the van der Merwe household: they'd have regarded them as collaborators."

"No doubt. They were hard times."

Sellick glared at me. "You sit there so smug and fine, the English gentleman in retirement—with no conception of the suffering you caused."

"I caused none, Mr Sellick. The people and the events you speak of are unknown to me."

"Spare me your denials. Listen a little longer."

"My mother, being pregnant, was spared in the massacre —a superstition among fighting men, as you would know, but

an ironical one in this case, since it was her pregnancy by a British officer which marked out the family. Witnessing the slaughter of her parents and brothers drove her mad—God knows she'd suffered enough. She was placed in the asylum at Pietermaritzburg and, so far as I know, died in childbirth in June of that year.

"The tragedy was remote from me and I forgot it easily, as young men do. The land was good to us on the Karroo and we were happy. My father—my adoptive father—died in 1938 and I inherited the place. It prospered and I'm in semi-retirement now, with a manager to run it for me. I didn't expect many more surprises from life.

"Then, three months ago, I received a letter from my uncle's solicitor in Pietermaritzburg. My uncle had placed the full facts in his hands but didn't want them disclosed until my mother died."

"But you just said she died when you were born."

"Not so, Strafford. She wasn't so soon off your conscience. After my birth, she remained in the asylum in Pietermaritzburg: a hopeless lunatic, mindless and forgotten. She died last December. Amongst her few possessions was that birth certificate—and, in an old tin trunk, this revolver, with its holster and belt, clearly stamped as British Army issue. It's an officer's weapon—your weapon."

"No, Mr Sellick. Not mine. I'm not your father. I served in South Africa, it's true, but I never met a Miss . . . van der Merwe of . . . Durban." I had hesitated because, as I said it, the name was familiar, though not as somebody I had ever met. But Sellick misinterpreted my hesitation.

"Your very voice betrays you, Strafford. God knows why or how, but, in your haste to desert my mother, you left this gun behind, and she preserved it as the only reminder she had of her husband—other than a cheap wedding ring. But don't worry. I had the revolver looked over by the finest gunsmith in Capetown. It's in fully working order now."

"I'm sure."

"Let me tell you a little more. Let me tell you how it felt to hear that my mother had died in a lunatic asylum without ever knowing her son. Maybe my uncle would have told me of her whereabouts had he lived. But my ignorance of her wasn't

really his fault, nor her madness, nor her tragedy. No, that was the work of the dashing young British officer who married her and then abandoned her to the mercy of a Boer raiding party."

"Quite possibly. But I am not that man."

"I've spent long enough tracking you down to be certain of my facts, Strafford. My birth certificate wasn't much to go on, of course, but my uncle had said the van der Merwes were a Durban family and so I went there. No sign in the Registrar's records of a marriage in that name in the autumn of 1900."

"I wasn't even in South Africa in the autumn of 1900."

"Then when did you leave?"

"Ah . . . the middle of September, I think."

"At last, the truth. I congratulate you. My solicitor hunted the length and breadth of Natal looking for a record of the marriage. Eventually, he found it. It seems you eloped with my mother and got married in Port Edward, down in the south of Natal—obscurity suited your purpose, no doubt."

"Mr Sellick, it is your purpose which is obscure to me."

"I obtained a copy of the marriage entry from the Registrar in Port Edward. I have it here." He threw another piece of paper at me, which I inspected. Like the first, it was alien to me, for all that my name and, so it seemed, my signature, appeared on it. I stared at it in disbelief.

"When married: 8th September 1900. Name and surname: Edwin George Strafford. Age: 24 years. Condition: Bachelor. Rank or profession: Second Lieutenant, British Army. Residence: Culemborg Barracks, Capetown." The signature was uncannily like mine. I could see why, to others, it would seem the genuine article. But it was not. Even at a space of fifty years, I could tell it for the forgery it was. As I peered at the document, recollections and associations raced through my mind, amounting to far more than Sellick's threats. I could understand his anger at his father, but I was not the man he sought. And already, I was guessing who might be, and trembling with excitement at the clue now, at long last, given me, the hope it held of unravelling the besetting mystery of my life. None of this, however, was about to detain Leo Sellick.

"Well might you shiver, Strafford. Perhaps somebody's walked over your grave." I could not hope to make him com-

prehend the deeper perfidy he had unwittingly uncovered. As soon as I saw the address recorded for Caroline van der Merwe—Ocean Prospect, Berea Drive, Durban—it struck a chord. That was the address I had been bound for, as part of my diplomatic work in the Dutch community, during the autumn of 1900, when news came of a general election at home, necessitating my precipitate departure for England. Who had taken my place in Durban? Who had successfully mimicked his friend's handwriting at Cambridge? Who had the nerve to marry under an assumed name but not the nerve to charge in battle? The answer to all three questions was my old friend, Gerald Couchman.

Sellick was still talking to me. "I soon discovered which regiment had occupied Culemborg Barracks in September 1900: the Devonshires. The Regimental Archivist in Exeter supplied me with what information he had on you—your political and military career, your present address." What better than proof that I was already married to destroy Elizabeth's faith in me and make her think me no better than a scoundrel, a worthless seducer? Who gained more from our engagement being broken than the man who eventually married her? Who could be better placed than he to produce the bogus evidence of my infamy?

"I prepared myself for this encounter by a close study of your life, Strafford. You seem to have specialized in loss of nerve—running out on your wife, then politics, then your family in Devon. Now you've buried yourself here, what do you feel when you look back on it all—satisfaction? Or the disgust it causes me?"

"Neither, Mr Sellick." How could I explain that we had both been deceived—both betrayed—by the same man? I hardly noticed Sellick's expression as he eyed me across the verandah. In my mind, I saw only Sir Gerald Couchman, arms dealer, happily married man, proud father, gambler, coward, mountebank and bigamist, who had ruined me—and the woman I loved. "What I feel is . . . vindication."

Sellick glared at me. "Vindication? Haven't you been listening? You can't outface me, Strafford. I hold the proof of your ruination of a good woman, your culpable neglect of your responsibilities, your casual disposal of any moral . . ."

I rose quickly from my chair. It seemed to take him aback. "Save your breath, Mr Sellick. You have my sympathy—but you have the wrong man."

Sellick jumped up also and pointed the gun at me. "I ought to kill you now, Strafford. Haven't you even the decency to be sorry?"

I sat down again. I saw that Sellick was a real problem. I could hardly hope to convince him of the truth—it was, even to me, incredible—yet how could I satisfy him? I owed him nothing, but his father—whoever he was—did and, for that reason, I should perhaps have been more open with him. But I was an old man, suddenly in a hurry, anxious to have done with a tiresome interview and call a guilty man to book. Therefore, I had no choice but to dissemble. "Mr Sellick. Conceive it possible"—the phrase itself caused more echoes in my head—"that you may be mistaken."

He shook his head. "Not possible. You are the man. Hand me back the certificates."

"Very well." I did so. "What do you want of me?"

He smiled. It was a cruel, slavering smile, a smile suggestive of his lineage. "What I require of you, Strafford, is a public admission of your guilt, a full statement of your miserable conduct in respect of my mother." Clearly, this was a more pleasing prospect to him than any mere execution.

"Do you think anybody will be interested?"

"Oh, I think so. A candid memoir to appear in a Fleet Street newspaper. A graphic portrayal of how a former Cabinet minister conducted himself in wartime. An exposure of the truth about their Consul's past likely to interest the British community here on Madeira."

"Assuredly. And I have no choice but to comply?"

"None. I will do it without you if necessary."

"I see. Then how do you wish to proceed?"

"I have an appointment with a journalist in my hotel at seven o'clock this evening. Be there—ready to volunteer a confession—or I'll ruin you slowly, first with your family, then your regiment, then . . ."

I held up a hand. "Pray do not continue. I will cooperate."

"I thought you would. I reckoned you wouldn't have the

courage not to—and I was right. Hunting you down has been disappointing in a way. You're not worthy of the kill."

I shrugged my shoulders, endeavouring to look crestfallen for his benefit. I was busily thinking of ways to keep this aggressive South African quiet for a while—but I wanted him to think, for the moment, that he had me where he wanted me: at his mercy.

Sellick slipped the revolver into his jacket pocket. He looked at me as if I were a cornered, frightened animal. "I'll leave you to compose your thoughts then . . . Father. I'm staying in Reid's Hotel. I'll expect you there, promptly at seven."

"I'll be there."

"Be sure you are." He walked smartly down the verandah steps and away round the side of the house.

After a few minutes, I walked after him. From the side of the house, I could see down the length of the drive to the gates. Sellick had just reached them and was climbing into a waiting car. The door slammed and it sped away, back up the valley road towards Funchal, raising dust behind it as it went.

Back on the verandah, Tomás was awaiting me anxiously. "Senhor Strafford," he said. "I was concerned about your . . . visitor. He did not announce himself at the door . . . and left like he was not happy."

"We can't be happy all the time, Tomás, even in the Porto Nova valley. Will you get the car out for me, please? I have urgent business in Funchal."

I regretted the necessity for the action I next took, yet I did not hesitate for a moment. Whatever awaited me in England—where now I knew I must return—was, in a sense, pre-ordained, determined and decided the moment Couch—for I did not doubt that it was he—put my name to that marriage certificate in South Africa fifty years before. I was not about to seek out the myriad of whys and wherefores in a spirit of vengeance. Too many years had passed for that. It was, rather, with a sense of detached curiosity that I embarked upon the crowning act of my life, to test how much I still cared, to determine if it were still possible to identify an unal-

loyed truth about what had happened to me, to confront that truth and see it for what it was.

The task of neutralizing Sellick was, in all this, no more than a preliminary trifle. Yet its accomplishment was distasteful, obliging me as it did to seek favours from old friends, to wield influence where, properly, I should have had none.

I drove straight to police headquarters in Funchal and was warmly received by the Chief of Police, Carlos Garrido. We had been firm friends since the 1931 Revolution, when I had been able to prevent the authorities in Lisbon making of him a scapegoat. Garrido was not a man to forget a kindness, which was as well, since I now had one to ask of him.

"Carlos, I'll come straight to the point. I want you to arrest a man."

"Edouin, when you were Consul, all you asked me was not to arrest people. Now . . . so, who is the man?"

"Leo Sellick, a South African staying at Reid's."

"What has Senhor Sellick done?"

"Threatened me—with a gun."

"I do not allow people to threaten my friends, Edouin. Senhor Sellick will be seeing me."

"Wait. It's not as simple as that. It's true he threatened me and that he has a gun. But it's only an antique. And I won't testify against him. I just want him held for a while."

"How long?"

"A few weeks. I have to go to England and I don't want Sellick to follow me."

"It can be done—passport irregularities, threatening behaviour—detained in custody. I give you"—he paused—"one month. More I would give no man. Then: we let him go—unless you give evidence."

"I won't. We British handle South Africa's consular business—I'll arrange for my successor to drag his feet if Sellick complains. To you, old friend, I'm grateful. I wish I hadn't had to ask you such a thing."

"Then do not ask again, Edouin. This one—it is for the old times."

"One other point. The gun is the property of a . . . friend of mine . . . in England. I'd like to return it."

Garrido spread his arms theatrically. "Ah, removing the

evidence also—why not? Come here tomorrow and I will see what I can do for you."

I thanked him again and left. My next call was on Brown, the British Consul, at his official residence—once mine—on the hillside above Funchal. Brown was an amenable fellow and agreed to play his part. Between them, he and Garrido could be relied upon to hold Sellick for the duration of that month's grace which they had given me. I returned to Quinta do Porto Nova well satisfied—in the strictly personal sense—with my afternoon's work but impatient to progress to what really occupied my thoughts.

My suspicions had not stopped at Couch and any hand he had had in my estrangement from Elizabeth. For I knew that there were other, even more sinister, connotations. I passed the night rehearsing in my mind the events of 1909 and 1910, considering who had stood to gain by my removal from the political arena: Lloyd George for one, the Suffragettes for others. The evidence of my apparent deceit of Elizabeth could have been used to condemn me in Asquith's eyes as a dangerous and despicable philanderer of whom he was well rid. Could the opportunistic Couch have sold for a goodly price that means to cast me as a villain? For did I not know too much of Lloyd George's real intentions for his peace of mind?

Still and all, Lloyd George was six years dead and beyond my reach. The man at the centre of all my suspicions—Gerald Couchman—lived still, married to Elizabeth, a knight of the realm. He was the man who deserved my immediate attention.

I had forgotten one of the penalties of old age: lack of stamina. The following day, the sun shone. It was April 20th, my seventy-fifth birthday. The Porto Novo valley was a pluperfect copy of England in spring, the apple blossom in the quinta seducing me to stay with its powdery promise. Tomás served breakfast on the verandah and brought my birthday cards on a silver tray, adding felicitations of his own. Who but a madman would have wanted to uproot himself from such serenity?

I suppose it was madness of a kind: an inchoate strand in an old life which commanded me to follow, an Anglo-Saxon restlessness which refuted the Latin langour. And, overriding all else, there was the pathetic eagerness with which I checked through the cards, as I had every birthday and Christmas for thirty years, half-hoping, against all reason, that one card, one day, would be from Elizabeth. Yet it never was.

So I returned to Funchal and Garrido's office, determined to follow the strand to its source.

"We have Senhor Sellick in custody," Garrido announced. "He was with a . . . newspaperman . . . when we arrested him. Now . . . he complains loudly. Maybe the newspaperman will also. You have given me a problem, Edouin."

"I know. I'm sorry—and grateful."

"De nada. *When I say do not mention it, I mean it. Here is what else you asked."*

He pulled open a drawer and took out the revolver in its holster, attached to a waist belt and shoulder strap. Their fraying leather still had a whiff of Aldershot stores about them. They could easily have been mine.

"Thanks, Carlos. I won't forget this."

"Nor will Senhor Sellick. Do you wish to see him? He has spoken of you—not kindly."

"No. Just hold him as long as you can."

"I told you Edouin—one month. You have until May 20th."

"Then I must make haste."

"Before you do, there is something else I think you should have. It was found in Senhor Sellick's room . . . among his possessions." He drew from his pocket a paper and I guessed at once what it was. "It seems to me that this belongs to you. It is a record of your marriage." I took it from him. "I did not know you were married."

"A long time ago, Carlos." I smiled. "I was a different man then." I thanked him again for his efforts, slipped the revolver and harness into a bag and made to leave. He stopped me at the door.

"Edouin . . . I know you well. This must be something . . . very special."

"It is. You could say it's . . . everything."

"I thought it was so. For that reason, I do it for you. Good luck, my friend . . . with everything."

"Adeus, Carlos."

I arranged my departure as swiftly as I could, but it was the following Monday before I boarded the flying boat for England. It was St. George's Day, a fitting date for my first return home since the death of my mother 21 years before. Yet this visit was unheralded and—strictly speaking—unnecessary. I had given Ambrose no warning of it and, much as I was inclined to go at once to Barrowteign to see him, I knew I must first go to London and learn what I could there.

The delay before leaving Madeira had given me time to lay my plans. My principal difficulty was that so many who might have told me so much were dead. I had observed from afar the demise of my former political colleagues, as recorded in The Times *obituary columns. Before leaving the quinta, I had surveyed an old photograph I had of Asquith's Cabinet, as it had been upon formation in 1908. Of the twenty men pictured, only two still lived. I was one. Winston Churchill was the other.*

To many, it might have seemed that only one remained. For Churchill was now Leader of the Opposition with every hope of becoming Prime Minister again at the next election, whereas I had lapsed into an obscurity from which there was no returning: not, at least, until now. For the part he might have played in silencing Palfrey, the private detective, I held Churchill still suspect. We had exchanged pleasantries and anecdotes during his visit to Madeira in 1950, but that was before Sellick opened my eyes to part of the truth. Now, others too would be made to look.

The flying boat reached Southampton in cold, wet weather: colder and wetter than I remembered. Madeira had spoiled me in my dotage, prepared me not at all for the chill, grey curtness with which England seemed to receive me.

I took a train to London, booked a room in a hotel I knew near Leicester Square (or thought I knew—it had, in fact, been rebuilt since the Blitz) and took stock of England, 1951. I read the newspapers voraciously and sat in on a debate in Parliament, stifling a tiring cough which made me feel as dull and grey as the weather. The government was Labour but the debate was about an arcane dispute with Persia which would have done justice to Palmerston. Plus ça change. *Churchill was not in the chamber.*

He was my only lead. So I wrote him a letter asking if we could meet. His reply came at the end of the week, inviting me to visit him at Chartwell, his country house in Kent, on Sunday. The pallid English version of sunshine appeared, my cough abated and I recovered my momentum.

A car was waiting for me at Westerham railway station and Churchill received me alone, in his library.

He held out his hand. "Edwin, I know I broke a dinner engagement with you when I left Madeira last year, but I didn't think you'd follow me all the way here."

"Neither did I, Winston. How are you?"

"Looking forward to victory. This government is finished. Disraeli would have called them exhausted volcanoes. Now that Bevan's resigned . . ."

"Please, Winston. I'd love to sit here and gossip with you, but my business is pressing. I've lost too much time already."

He waved me into a leather armchair, beneath loaded bookshelves that reached to the ceiling. "What's this, Edwin? You've out of it now. What can be so pressing? I thought we'd chat here for a while, then join Clemmie for tea. And you've never been in Chartwell before, have you? I could show you round. I bought it with my advance for The World Crisis, *you know. The pen is mightier than the sword."*

"Very true." I thought of the stroke of a pen on a South African marriage certificate. "You could say that penmanship has brought me here."

He lit a cigar and I declined the offer of one. "You'd better explain."

"Do you realize we're the only original members of Asquith's first Cabinet left alive?"

"I suppose we must be. Lots to say then . . ."

"Yes, Winston, lots. But it won't necessarily be agreeable."

"Why not?"

"Because I don't quite know what part you played in it all. I mean my resignation."

"Edwin, that was forty years ago. Harsh things were said. What can possibly be the point . . ."

"The point is, I know now. I know what did for me. I never did before, you see. My incredulity was not for effect. It was genuine. But now I know why Asquith refused to have me in his Cabinet."

"It's more than I do."

"Then I'll tell you. I think it was represented to him that I was about to commit bigamy with a prominent Suffragette."

"Edwin, this is extraordinary. But what can I say? I simply did not—and do not—know the circumstances of your resignation."

"Perhaps not, but Lloyd George did, and you were his staunchest ally in Cabinet at that time."

His Majesty's Leader of the Opposition did not care to be reminded of redundant allegiances. "Edwin, this is becoming tiresome."

"Bear with me, Winston. Remember how you forgot to contact a private detective called Palfrey for me during the Great War?"

"Frankly, no."

"You don't remember a note of acrimony creeping into a lunch we had at Gaspard's Restaurant in January 1919?"

"No Edwin, I don't."

"Or why Lloyd George offered me the consulate in Madeira so soon afterwards?"

"Generosity, I presume."

"Or bribery?"

"I hardly think so."

"Did you perhaps tell him what I'd said about Sir Gerald Couchman? Might that have led him to want me out of the country?"

"I might have mentioned your . . . predicament. Isn't that what friends are for?"

"You tell me what friends are for, Winston. For hatching conspiracies? Cast your bread upon the waters and it will return to you after many days. I think I have the means to prove Sir Gerald Couchman, good friend to the party, to be a liar, a fraud and—a criminal. I suspect he gave Lloyd George

the means to remove me from the government, which he needed to do because I had learned of his plot to form a coalition with Balfour behind Asquith's back. I do not accuse you of complicity in my removal . . ."

"That would be as well."

"But I do suggest you kept Lloyd George informed as to my state of mind and suggested I be offered congenial employment far from home rather than be allowed to harass Couchman into any form of confession."

"I think you've said enough."

"You're probably right. But bear this in mind. If I do expose Couchman for what he is, the full story will do nothing for your reputation. With an election in the wind, it would prove acutely embarrassing."

That last was a stupid thing to have said. It was a poor imitation of Sellick and just as contemptible. But I had grown angry and spoken out of frustration at myriad injustices. Churchill looked hurt and angry. There was nothing for it but to leave at once.

But, as I jumped up from my chair, my right leg gave way —since the Somme it had never been able to bear sudden strain—and I stumbled to the floor.

The next moment, Churchill was panting from the effort of assisting me back into the chair and we were both laughing at our frailties.

"For goodness' sake, Edwin, calm down."

"I'm sorry, Winston. I didn't want to offend you—or muff my exit."

"Then recover yourself and have some tea."

"I don't think I can stay."

"As you wish. But it was you who said that we were the last ones left of Asquith's Cabinet. We shouldn't fall out."

"I suppose not. I was really only taking out on you what I can't say to—or of—the dead."

"Well, no matter. I have a broad back. Since we've both reached an age when nothing matters as much as it once did, I'll tell you something. I recall that my impression at the time you resigned was that L.G. had dished you good and proper. But I never knew how.

"It may be that Couchman placed the means in his hands.

Perhaps you know more about that than I do. It's true that L.G. showered Couchman with munitions contracts, not to mention his knighthood. You remember L.G.'s attitude to service and reward. It had a certain Welsh simplicity.

"As for Palfrey, I may have overlooked your request. I forget now if I forgot or not." He winked. "Age does that, as you should know. They were hectic times and I was seeking to re-establish myself after the Dardanelles episode. I dare say I would have known better than to pursue it. I might even have let Palfrey know that we didn't want him to do business with you. If so, I'm sorry."

"Don't worry about it." I had once, myself, worried a great deal. But Churchill was right. With hindsight, these were trifles, the necessary compromises of a political career.

"I told L.G. about our little lunch time disagreement at Gaspard's—the essentials, anyway. I'm sure that's why he offered you Madeira. But it surprised me, I remember. He dropped everything to arrange it. It was a touch panicky—unlike him. To be honest, I thought it was the best thing for you."

"I think you were right."

"Then why come back?"

"Because I'm drawn back. Once I would have demanded the truth. Now, the truth seems to demand me. And then, there's a matter of the heart."

"Then follow the heart, Edwin, not the head. Old men are free to do that."

So we went and had our tea and strolled round the garden as evening drew in. He told me how he had paced those lawns during the 1930's brooding on the Nazi menace and I told him about Madeira's little local difficulty in 1931. I stayed for dinner and then for the night. When I returned to London the following morning, Churchill and I had made our peace—a separate peace in my war with history.

But now the time had come which I had foreseen the moment Sellick had appeared at the quinta, brandishing his proofs of marriage and paternity, the time to confront him with whom a truce was inconceivable.

Who's Who *gave two addresses for Sir Gerald Couchman:*

one in Sussex, the other the house in Hampstead where I had last seen Elizabeth. I started with neither. Instead, I went to the armament works in Woolwich, or, rather, the site of the armament works. It had been removed—bombed or demolished, who knew?—and in its place houses were being erected. A board proclaimed: "Homes for Londoners by Couchman Estates." As befits an opportunist, Sir Gerald had diversified.

Churchill had told me over dinner the night before that Couch's son, Henry, was a prominent Conservative and the party's prospective candidate for a suburban constituency. There was every likelihood of his being elected. So there could be no doubt that Couch had founded a prosperous dynasty to whom my reminder of less glorious passages was unlikely to be welcome.

The headquarters of the Couchman business empire was now a modern office in Finsbury Square. In response to my enquiry, the receptionist told me that both "Sir Gerald" and "Mr Henry" were engaged at a board meeting. So I left quietly.

But I did not stray far. I stationed myself on a bench, shabbily dressed and inconspicuous, and waited. Shortly after four o'clock, a knot of well-dressed and opulent figures emerged. At a distance of twenty yards, I could distinguish Couch from the rest. He had grown fat and rather puffy round the face. He wore a mohair overcoat against the cool afternoon, smoked a cigar with the flourish of affluence, but seemed withal frail and unsteady. He was helped into a waiting car by a man whose looks betrayed him as Henry—young and thick-set with a malevolent cast to his features. I heard him say "Hampstead" to the chauffeur. As the car drew away past me, I could see Henry leaning forward intently in the back seat, energetically making a point. Couch was gazing out of the window, straight past me with an unfocussed, dissipated blankness.

I hastened to Hampstead by taxi. Yet once there, once standing in front of the gates of the Couchman residence—the house screened from the road by undergrowth—I hesitated. The sun had come out and The Bishop's Drive on a spring evening seemed altogether too sedate and tranquil to permit any outrage.

Now it had come to the point, I was nervous and uncertain.

A housekeeper answered my knock, which was more tentative than I had meant.

"Is Sir Gerald Couchman in?"

"Yes, but . . ."

"I must see him . . . at once."

"He's only just finished dinner. This is hardly. ..."

"I must see him. I think he'll agree if you give him my card." I had written on a blank postcard: "Couch: remember September 1900? Edwin Strafford." She took it away, then, a few minutes later, returned and showed me into a back room. There were french windows giving onto the darkened garden—the curtains had not yet been drawn. The room was surprisingly untidy; in other circumstances it would have been charmingly so. There was an open music box, some knitting behind a cushion on the settee, a child's playing brick on the carpet. I felt like an intruder in a family home—as I was.

The door opened and Sir Gerald Couchman stood before me. He was an ashen-faced septuagenarian in carpet slippers and a patched cardigan, trembling slightly as he looked at me.

"What do you want?" he said in a thick voice.

Of a sudden, I did not know what I wanted. Did I really want to ruin an old man if I could? Did I really think I could win back Elizabeth? I felt a sense of futility sap my spirits. In the end, all I did was hand him the certificate.

He stared at it for some moments. "What do you want?" he repeated.

"I want an explanation." He handed it back without a word. "Do you recognize this certificate?"

"No."

"I believe you do."

"No."

"It's dated 8th September 1900. The names on it are Strafford and van der Merwe. In September 1900, I was due to visit the van der Merwe family in Durban, but never did. You went in my place. That's what I want you to explain."

"It was a long time ago."

"Is that your explanation? Did you or did you not go to Durban in September 1900?"

"No. I don't know the name van der Merwe. I never agreed to take your place on any mission to Durban."

In so saying, he erred tactically. For to lie at that stage revived my dormant anger. I stepped towards him and he, in retreating, half-fell, half-slumped into an armchair. I looked at him in surprise. He was physically frightened of me. In his eyes there was a look of helplessness, a helplessness that had driven him to a pointless lie.

"Sir Gerald, I can prove I wasn't in Port Edward on the date quoted on this certificate. Can you?"

"No. But it was fifty years ago. Who can prove anything?"

"Is that what you're relying on? You must know what this means. It means I've found out. I've found out how Elizabeth was turned against me. This is how, isn't it? Not content with amusing yourself with some absurd marriage in South Africa, using my name, you then employed the evidence of it to steal Elizabeth from me."

"No."

"Sir Gerald, it's my belief that, if I took this to Elizabeth, she'd recognize it and admit it was how she was persuaded that I'd deceived her. If I then proved to her that I couldn't have married Caroline van der Merwe in Port Edward on 8th September 1900 because I wasn't there, how do you think she would feel about the man who was?"

He said nothing, so I continued.

"It's not my signature, Sir Gerald. I think that can be proven. Even if it can't, I can prove I was on the boat to England on that date." This was a lie: I could prove no such thing. I could not recollect the date of sailing, but I suspected that it was after the 8th. "And if all that only convinces her that you are the innocent beneficiary of my impersonation, I can, if necessary, arrange for your real wife to identify you as the Lieutenant Strafford she married."

He covered his face with his hand and pronounced one word: "Caroline."

I was angry then, not for myself, but for Elizabeth. I took the gun and harness from my bag and dropped it onto the cushion next to him. "On her behalf, I'm returning some lost property."

He parted his fingers and stared at it. He lifted it with one hand and flexed the leather. Then he looked at me solemnly.

"What took you so long, Edwin? Since Colenso—perhaps even since Cambridge—I've sensed you would do for me in the end. I backed a winning streak so long I thought it would carry me through. God damn you for leaving it so late."

I sat down opposite him. "Tell me about your winning streak."

"First, tell me about Caroline."

"She's dead. Died last year in a lunatic asylum." Further pretence on that score seemed pointless.

"But you said . . ."

"That was to draw you out."

"You bastard. Without her, what can you prove against me?"

"I don't need to prove anything. I can make Elizabeth doubt you enough to believe you married her bigamously, I can . . ."

"After forty years? You wouldn't do that to a woman you once loved."

"Maybe I wouldn't—if you told me the whole truth, here and now."

"Here and now. Do you know what that means? This is my son's house. He lives here with his wife and two children. Some old man from nowhere can't just walk up the path one evening and demolish all that. Henry's likely to be elected to Parliament . . ."

"The truth is all I want. About that gun, this certificate, about Elizabeth and me."

"All right. But I can't tell you here. It makes me feel . . . unclean. We'll drive somewhere in my car. Then I'll tell you."

"Anywhere you like."

"Wait here." He left the room and I heard muttering elsewhere in the house. A few minutes later, he returned, dressed to go out. "Come on." He led the way by a communicating door to the garage and his Bentley. "Usually, my chauffeur drives me," he murmured. "But not tonight."

We set off in silence, by some route he knew that took us to

Parliament Hill. He pulled up at the side of the road and wound his window down. The lights of London sparkled below us in the night. He lit a cigarette and smoked it through, then took a nip from a hip flask and began to tell me. Once he had commenced, he required no prompting. There was a quality almost of relief in his confession.

"You wouldn't understand, Edwin. The irony is that I have the title, but you're the *parfit gentle* knight, too pure for your own good—and everyone else's. It's hard to believe you still exist—here, now, in 1951. Take my word for it: it would have been better if you'd gone over the top one day in France and not come back.

"Because that's what happened in 1914—a world ended. You're out of place, out of step, out of time. The days of liberal, amateur politics—liberal, amateur anything—are long gone. Remember your touching faith in the demos? Your belief in the sweet triumph of intellectual debate? It was a sham even then. Now it's an anachronism.

"None of us is free anymore. We lost that, somewhere along the way to what they laughably call a welfare state. I'm not complaining. I turned a profit every step of the way. If they wanted to kill each other, I sold them the means. If they wanted to house or entertain each other, I sold them the homes and the cinemas. You see, I rumbled it all a long time ago. Profit is pleasure. And pleasure is life. I believe in hedonism as an honourable calling. I'll sell you a silk tie to wear with your hair shirt.

"But freedom? That was the baby that went with the bathwater. We couldn't have sat at Lord's in 1939 debating whether to enlist or not, as we did forty years before. We'd have been told. The British have become hostages to history, triumphant in a war but still queuing for meat rations while every black face round the world condemns us as imperialist ogres.

"I have to kow-tow to a load of cloth-capped union leaders who call themselves a government and they have to kow-tow to the Yanks. I suppose we ought to laugh really. It's all a bit of a bloody joke.

"Hostages to history? Yes, all of us. Even me—especially

me. Because you're my history. You're my conscience, the albatross I've looked out for all these years. I've always had a simple approach to problems: change them. You don't like the past? Then fiddle the books. Rewrite your image until it fits the bill. You'd be surprised how easy it is, as long as it's just paper and fallible memory. Not so easy when it's a real, live human being like you. Why didn't you die on the Somme, Edwin? You'd have done us all a favour, including yourself.

"The trouble with altering the facts to fit the picture is that it's a cumulative exercise. It starts as a game—a bit of a lark really. Then it gets serious, then complicated, then . . . then pleasure becomes pain because you find yourself and everyone else believing the charade—living the lie as if it were the truth.

"When did it begin? At Cambridge, I think. I was surrounded by handsome, athletic young men—the cream of England's youth. And first at cards—and later at almost everything—I found I could dupe them, gull them utterly at the drop of a hat.

"So it amused me to lure them into debts, take them for all they were worth, see how far I could lead them with lies. I almost miscalculated by getting myself rusticated, but even that didn't turn out badly.

"Then South Africa. I saw it all as a golden opportunity for pleasure and profit. And I was right. The army gave me plenty of both, most of it unofficial. But it was something else as well: plain dangerous. Colenso was a revelation to me. I mean, why did we risk our necks at the say-so of that lunatic Buller? You know what happened—I cut and run. I wouldn't call it cowardice so much as common sense.

"It was a difference of perspective. My father kept me on a short rein at Cambridge—financially. That's what separated me from all you clear-eyed young gentlemen. I knew the value of money—and of life. You took it all deadly seriously, but were prepared to stop a Boer bullet just like that. And for what? So that a few Uitlanders could get their hands on the Transvaal gold mines.

"And you? Well, Edwin, I'll tell you now what always niggled me about you. You had all the gentlemanly virtues like the rest of them. But I couldn't dupe you. You were armoured

against me with an incorruptible hide of liberal enlightenment. What was worse, after Colenso, you'd marked my card. You'd rumbled me.

"But then you still trusted me, because that was the decent thing to do. When I volunteered to take your place in Durban, you just said 'Thanks very much' and pushed off home. My nose told me this was an opportunity for pleasure and profit not to be passed up. And so it proved.

"When I got there, I pretended to be you just for the sake of it, just to see if I could get away with it. The van der Merwes were unsuspecting sobersides—the old man a magistrate and Lutheran lay preacher. They were all so impressed by me it wasn't true. They had a gruelling week of dinners and meetings arranged for me to butter up the Dutch community. I dodged most of them.

"But as soon as I met the daughter of the house, it was a different story. Rembrandt would have died for her. Whether because I was in a foreign country or because she was far from ancestral Holland I don't know, but she had a mystical lightness to her beauty, a cool, liquid apartness. You could say it was merely lust and I couldn't deny it. She was twenty, always severely dressed in drab colours at her father's insistence, but that only made it worse. Remember, I was no gentleman. But, in Durban, I enjoyed your gentleman's licence.

"Caroline fell for me readily enough but could not be seduced. She would marry me—elope to escape her father's disapproval—but otherwise she would neither give herself nor could she be taken. So, quite consciously, quite deliberately, I decided: why not? Why not push my luck? I was, in a way, getting back at you, abusing their hospitality and your identity, sullying your spotless reputation which had so shown up mine at Colenso. The beauty of it was its outrageous plausibility. Who would ever check up on a tumble in the Veldt? Who would ever know?

"So I eloped with Caroline van der Merwe. We stole out of the house and rode through the night to an obscure railway station. The next day, we reached Port Edward—as far as we could from Durban without straying into Cape Colony. I'd wired ahead to make the necessary arrangements and the cer-

emony was over in a trice. If I say so myself, it really did look like your signature on the certificate.

"Three days later, I deserted Caroline, left her asleep at our hotel in Port Edward. I thought the van der Merwes would find us soon and, besides, I'd got what I wanted. She wasn't too bright, actually, inside that trusting, princess's body. I just took my kit bag and walked away in the middle of the night, cool and calculating as you like. Stupidly, I'd left my revolver and harness in Durban. Well, who elopes carrying a gun? I had to do a lot of explaining about that. It's strange it should turn up again, after all this time.

"Back in Capetown, I read about your election to Parliament and enjoyed the joke. Then the joke turned sour on me. So far from being over, the war dragged on for eighteen miserable months. You politicians had a lot to answer for. Still, when it was over, I was posted to India and enjoyed it. An officer's life was good there, before they started agitating for independence.

"I had eight good years in India. Then I ran into a spot of bother. Caught out using mess funds to settle a gambling debt after a run of bad luck. To save the regiment's honour, I was allowed to resign my commission. Best I could have hoped for, really, but it left me down on my hunkers when I stepped off the boat from Bombay. It was the spring of 1910.

"Lo and behold, what should I find but that you were now Home Secretary? There I was, after ten years' serving King and country, penniless and unwanted in my homeland, reading in the newspaper about what an able and accomplished minister you made. It stuck in my throat, I can tell you.

"I thought I'd soon put my finances back on an even keel by gambling. The cards had always been my friends. But not any more. A question of insufficient capital, I suppose. At all events, it went from bad to worse and soon, so far from being penniless, I was up to my neck in debts I couldn't hope to pay. My luck, you could say, had run out good and proper.

"I thought you'd like to know it was desperation that made me turn to the certificate. I still had my copy, tucked away. It suddenly occurred to me that evidence of the Home Secretary's secret marriage must be worth something. But how?

You were still single, so blackmail was out of the question. Besides, I reckoned you'd break my neck if you ever detected my hand in anything like that.

"So I had to be devious. And luck smiled on me again. A fellow I knew from India—before the upset over mess funds—popped up in a gambling den I used: Archie Lambourne. I cultivated him—at first for the loans he was worth. He mentioned in passing that his sister was an active Suffragette and, in a drunken moment one night, he let slip what his sister had obviously told him, that you—the Home Secretary—were sweet on a Suffragette.

"Now that set me thinking. I took more of an interest in the Suffragette movement then, read up about their antics and leaders. Since they were at loggerheads with the government, since the suffrage was fairly and squarely Home Office business and since I knew you were secretly consorting with one of their number, it seemed to me that there was money to be made from that certificate. Pleasure and profit, you see. One breeds the other.

"I persuaded Lambourne to introduce me to his sister. And I gave her a message to take to Christabel Pankhurst: that I had damning evidence against you in which I felt sure she would be interested.

"She was. Julia Lambourne arranged an audience. I put it to Miss Pankhurst that I had heard of your involvement with a Suffragette. She'd already heard the same thing, apparently. I put it to her that, having served with you in South Africa, I was in a position to know that you were a married man. I said that I had proof and could supply it—for a fee. I cited £1000. I said that the only condition was that you should never know the source or nature of the information, on the grounds that you would undoubtedly seek to avenge yourself on me. Miss Pankhurst was very cool and said that she would think it over.

"It was a week before I heard from her again—this time via Anne Kenney, not Julia Lambourne. We were, to put it crudely, in business. Miss Kenney told me that evidence of the kind I claimed to have interested not only the Suffragettes—out of sympathy for their deceived sister—but a colleague or colleagues of yours outraged by your double-dealing.

"It was an unexpected twist. I'd expected a quick trade with the Suffragettes, not some complex political deal. But I couldn't afford to quibble. Another meeting was arranged. This time I was to come up with the goods.

"It wasn't the kind of meeting I'd anticipated. Miss Kenney insisted on blindfolding me in the cab. It was a shabby hotel somewhere—some sweltering quadrant of the East Side. And Miss Pankhurst wasn't alone. Of all people, Lloyd George was with her.

"Bit of a shaker, really. I thought at first he was going to put the lid on it. But not at all. He and Miss Pankhurst were in league. Just goes to show that the public doesn't know the half of it. Anyway, they wanted to do business. The money for the proof. Simple as that. I was to say nothing about it, dismiss it from my mind. That was no problem.

"Mmm? The date? It was the longest day—June 21st, if it matters. There was quite an interrogation, but I was an old hand at brazening it out. Besides, my impression wasn't that they doubted the authenticity of the document. I don't think they really cared one way or the other. It was a question of how it could be used.

"Secrecy seemed to suit everyone. They wanted to discredit you without you knowing. I assumed that was because they couldn't be seen to have intrigued together and it was a condition of mine from the first. We tacitly agreed that secrecy was necessary to ensure to safety. And Miss Pankhurst said that the deceived Suffragette should not be exposed to public ridicule. By that I took it she meant the movement.

"Later, of course, Elizabeth told me that Miss Pankhurst had agreed a truce with Lloyd George until the Constitutional crisis was over, that there had been talk of a coalition led by Lloyd George in which the vote might be given to women. Not that it ever happened. Lloyd George must have been flying a kite, trying to get the credit for the Suffragettes calling off their campaign.

"My luck turned that summer. The £1000 revived my fortunes. I prospered at the card table and the race track and . . . something else. I fell in love.

"I first met Elizabeth at a party Julia Lambourne arranged

—largely for Elizabeth's benefit, I suspect, to draw her back into society. It was late July, I think, held at her father's house by the Thames out at Marlow.

"Elizabeth moved through the evening like a ghost, pale, distracted and grave. Julia introduced us, but Elizabeth hardly seemed to see me. That evening, for the hand I'd had in breaking her youthful spirit, I felt regret. That night I began to care.

"Later that summer, she went abroad with her aunt. I followed and staged a chance meeting in Switzerland. We went on together to Italy. When we returned to England, I was set upon marrying her—honourably, permanently, respectably. It took a long time, not just to persuade her, but to salvage her from the shadows of depression. We'd hurt her deeply, you, I and the rest, and it took a long time to heal. And I had to change my way of life. Gambling was foresworn. I had to become a man of business.

"Fortuitously, my father—whom I hadn't seen in years—died in 1913 and left me the money with which to start up the armament works. Even if nobody else did, I smelt war in the wind and weapons I judged to be a sound investment. How right I was. Elizabeth and I were married six weeks before war broke out.

"The arms business renewed my connections with Lloyd George, who was, by then, Minister of Munitions. We had an unspoken understanding based on our previous dealings. It acknowledged the value of money. Need I say more?

"Wealth begets wealth. I found making money became second nature. And social position? Well, for a suitably generous contribution to party funds, Lloyd George provided that for me with a knighthood. Quite a joke, eh? Sir Gerald Couchman. I suppose I knew enough to make it seem wise to him to keep me sweet. And when I told him that you were back in England after the war, looking for trouble, he dipped into his pocket and catered for you too.

"I made Elizabeth happy again and she made me happy. I'm not saying I was better for her than you. But she possesses a gift for improving a man that probably had more to work on in me. It's just another irony. We have a son and grandchil-

dren by him. We have a home in the country. We're old and harmless. We're not really much of a target anymore.

"So I'm not going to beg for mercy. You have the means to destroy me and I probably deserve it. But let's not pretend you're doing this to save the regiment's honour or Caroline van der Merwe's soul. Let's not make the mistake of thinking that anybody's life is a clean sheet. If you do this, then you'll prove my point. You'll be no better than me."

I seemed still to hear Couch's voice around us in the night after he had ceased to speak, a whispered echo rustling back to me from the soft, sighing darkness. Its murmur was of mockery, of scornful, grinning, flaunted imperfection. He had been honest. He had volunteered the devious twists and turns of his fraudulent life. Perhaps for the very first time, he had told the truth. But the truth, as he would have been quick to point out, was outrageously unlikely compared with the credible charade of a life which he had painstakingly constructed. The truth, he had implied, was for our ears only. We were old enough to bear it.

Age did not prevent me feeling surprised, surprised not at the multi-layered depth of his deception but at the apparent calmness of my response to it. Where once I would have shaken him by the throat and demanded restitution, now I merely accepted his offer of a drink from the hip flask and shivered a little at a cold draught from the window.

"Can you find nothing to say, Edwin?"

"What would you have me say?"

"You could voice the disgust you must feel, or say you still don't believe me."

"Oh, but I do believe you. Not even you could manufacture such an account. It's the only version that really does fit the events, so much so that I could believe I knew it all along. Every fact—every feature—confirms it."

"Is that why you asked the date of my meeting with Lloyd George and Christabel Pankhurst?"

"In a sense. That was largely to check my own memory. The day before you met them, Lloyd George had tried to enlist me in his coalition conspiracy, but I had refused, so making me

dangerous to him as an openly declared opponent who knew of the plot. It may be that Miss Pankhurst had already approached him about your claims and that he wished to discover whether he should use those claims to remove me from his path or to bind me to him. Once I had shown my colours, he did not hesitate to choose the former course. They must have planned the sequence of events carefully, waiting until the moment I resigned before confronting Elizabeth with your evidence and simultaneously condemning me to Asquith."

"You're taking this very calmly."

"Not calmly—slowly. Let's take stock. You warned me not to cite false motives, so I shan't. Honour and truth are, in your contention, relative terms, though I can't think of anything less honourable and truthful than what you've now admitted. But let's leave aside—for the moment—the forgery of my signature, your impersonation of me, the desertion of your wife. Let's even forget the casual sabotage of my political career. Let's talk instead about the overriding issue between us: Elizabeth. What do you expect me to do about your theft of her from me?"

"Remember, Edwin, I hadn't met Elizabeth when I sold the certificate. I wasn't selling it to win her. She came later. A happy accident, you could say. Of course, I knew what you would make of it, but that at least I didn't plan."

"Yet you planned to marry her—bigamously. Do you realize what that makes you—and her—and your son?"

"Technically, it makes me a criminal, Elizabeth my mistress and Henry . . . a bastard. But it's not going to come to that, is it?"

"Why shouldn't it?"

"Because of Elizabeth. If you still love her—as I do—you couldn't do such a thing to her. And if you don't, what would be the point?"

"Revenge?"

"It rings hollow at our time of life, Edwin. As would money, if I thought I could buy your silence. No, let's not dress it up. If you did it, revenge wouldn't be the word. It's too old a crime for that. Call it by its real name: malice, pure and simple—hardly a gentlemanly virtue."

He had won, for the moment. The gambler had played his

trump. He had summoned together his failing reserves of daring for one last vital bluff. If I loved Elizabeth, I would leave old scores unsettled for her sake. If I did not, what grievance had I that could justify the destruction of his family? For who would suffer most? Not Couch. No, not he, but the innocent accessories to his crime. Mockery still hung in the night, staring at me intently from the dark void between the glow-worm trails of the city's lights. It defied me, after all the years, to sully my unjust fate with an unworthy vengeance.

"I'll think about what you've said," I announced at last. "Then I'll decide what to do."

Couch looked anxious. "Think about it? What's there to think about? If you're going to come back to punish me, you might at least get it over with." It seemed that he, like me, lacked stamina.

"No. I owe you nothing. You left me to ponder the tragedy of my life for forty years. I'm not letting you off the hook now. I'll think—and you can wonder."

"How long?"

"I don't know. As long as I need."

"And then?"

"Then I might let Elizabeth and your family know the truth—or I might not." I was making him suffer for the cunning of his bluff. I already knew whether I could confront Elizabeth with the truth about her supposed husband, but I had no intention of letting him know. So I turned his uncertainty against him and, by climbing from the car, served notice that he could look for no swift or easy absolution from his sins. For sins they were, too many and too manifest for me to appraise there and then. He might have guessed, on the strength of his own assessment of me, what my decision would be. But I saw no reason to spare his nerves the doubt.

"Can I drive you somewhere?" he said through the window.

"No. I'll walk. I need some fresh air." We stared pointedly at each other, then he closed the window and drove off quickly, the Bentley purring away into the night.

I walked slowly along the road, away from the direction Couch had taken, down towards the heart of the city, my mind full of distant memories, struggling to sharpen and sift them into clear and ordered shape. I had so long and so often rehearsed them that my inadequacy at such a moment seemed pitiful.

Not that I had long in which to mourn the pity of it. A car approached slowly from behind until its headlamps threw a stretched shadow of me across the trees flanking the road, then slowed still further to keep pace with me. It was not the Bentley, to judge by the note of the engine, but, when I turned to identify it, I was only dazzled by the lamps. I went on again and it followed as before.

After another thirty yards, I stopped again, as did the car. I turned and, this time, shouted above the noise of the engine: "Who's there?"

Suddenly, the engine died, followed by the lights. In the moments that it took my eyes to adjust to the darkness, a figure climbed from the driving seat of the car and walked round to the front of the bonnet, where I stood. He was a burly man in an overcoat, with a whiff of cigar smoke about him, and he soon confirmed what I had already guessed.

"I'm Henry Couchman." His voice was low and not without menace. "Who the hell are you?"

"What business is it of yours?"

"It's my business when a stranger bursts into my house at night and upsets my father."

"I did not burst. Your father invited me in. We're old friends. And I repeat: what business is it of yours what passed between us?"

"And I repeat: who the hell are you?"

"Edwin Strafford. Does the name mean anything to you?"

"No more than any vagrant's. Why should it?"

I was beginning to bridle at his tone. "Because I believe, Mr Couchman, that you have political ambitions."

I could almost see him puff out his chest. "I'm likely to be elected to Parliament before long. But . . ."

"Then you should study a little political history. I once sat in Cabinet with your party leader."

Now it was he who bridled. "Listen to me, Strafford. You forced my father to give you some kind of interview tonight. First at my house, then up here—in secret. He was obviously distressed by your visit and, since he's not a young man, I was concerned enough to follow you. Now suppose you tell me what you compelled him to discuss for the past hour."

I had taken my measure of Henry earlier in the day. Though I had no complaint against him, I instinctively liked him less than his father. "It was a private matter."

"You said you were an old friend of my father—yet I've never seen you before."

"Your father has."

"My father, Mr Strafford, has many callers upon his time and his wealth. It is my duty, as his son, to sift out the undeserving and the mischievous. You, I suspect are one of them. So what I'm telling you is: leave him alone."

At this, I lost patience with him. "Let me tell you something, Mr Couchman. Knowing your father as I do and, having met you, I think I know the nature of your concern. I'm sure you've often had occasion to cover his tracks."

"What do you mean by that?"

"What I mean is that your father's morals could dirty your whiter-than-white image if you weren't careful. What you really want to know is whether my business with your father has any embarrassing implications for your political aspirations. The answer is yes."

He shot out an arm and grasped my collar. He had the build and demeanour of a bully, a fleshy arrogance that bespoke an over-indulged acquisitiveness. "You're just a nothing, Strafford. If you're thinking of trying to blackmail my father—or me—then you've got another think coming. I could . . ."

What he could not do was accost me with impunity. I wrenched his arm down from my collar and stepped back a pace. "Mr Couchman, this nothing may come to loom large in your thoughts. If I have threatened your father, it's not with blackmail, but with the truth. The truth about his conduct in South Africa, the truth about the way he brought to an end my engagement of your mother."

"What . . . what are you talking about?"

"I suggest you ask your father." Fearing that I might already have said too much, I turned on my heel and walked smartly away down the road. But he was not to be disposed of so quickly.

"Strafford," he shouted after me. "Who are you? Where do you come from?"

I looked back at him. "I was your father's friend, Mr Couchman. I was your mother's fiancé. I'm from a past many people want to forget. Tell your father this: that your conduct has made his position much less secure. Tell him that you inspire in me thoughts of malice."

Leaving Couchman for the moment speechless, I strode away. A few minutes later, I heard his car turning round and roaring off in the direction his father had taken. I did not look back.

I passed the following day in solitude at my hotel. Whether pacing my room or sitting alone in the hushed lounge, contemplating racing prints on the wall, what I actually saw, what filled my mind with wistful thoughts, was the past: Elizabeth and I when we were happy together, when we were engaged to be married, before Couch walked off the boat from Bombay and back, without my knowledge, into my life.

Yet, smart as I might at the workings of Couch's devilish ingenuity—exploiting a youthful madness to gain not just money but the woman I had thought to marry—there was no denying the force of his argument that it was too late now to seek anything as crude as vengeance.

Such would have remained my view had it not been for Henry's intervention. If Couch's son was as contemptible as Couch himself—if not more so—then my conscience was easier. Or so it would have been, but for Elizabeth. It was of her that I largely thought during my lonely watch. Dared I risk seeing her, being tempted to open her eyes to what her husband had done, knowing what the truth might do to her?

I never, of my own accord, found the answer, perhaps because I did not need to. It found me, after a visit I received on Wednesday morning.

I rose at dawn and gazed out of the hotel window at the early morning business of London: street cleaners, delivery vans, a horse and cart drawing milk, a few prompt men of the City making their way. It was a scene I would not have recognized fifty years before, except, that is, for the faces. Hansom cabs had been swapped for taxis, morning suits and top hats for pinstripes and bowlers, but the people remained the same. War and rations, time and fashion could not wipe away the rogues' gallery of humanity. The faces were blank or lively, set or furtive, those of vain heroes or honest knaves.

And out of them, exploding through the flexing, yawning throng, came Henry Couchman. I could tell him by the cut of his overcoat, the set of his jaw, the young man's impulsiveness seething within the old man's complacency. He glared up at the sign over the hotel doors, then bound up the steps. I had a caller.

Within the time it took him to travel up in the lift, there was a hammering at the door. It was not yet breakfast time and, already, I felt weary.

He did not wait to be asked in. He burst past me and stood in the centre of the room, glowering as if in expectation that I would acknowledge some form of ownership.

"Mr Couchman. What can I do for you?"

"You can leave my father alone. You can leave my family alone. You can go back where you belong."

"And where's that?"

"Madeira. Anywhere provided it's far from here. You were bought off a long time ago. If what you're after is a supplement, that can be arranged. But don't be greedy. Go quietly."

"You seem to be better informed than when last we spoke."

"My father's told me everything about you, Strafford. One thing he didn't mention is what's obvious to me. You're a loser. There's nothing for you here."

"You think not?"

"I know it. You can't prove any of your allegations. But . . . I'm prepared to pay your nuisance value and have done with you. So what's your price?"

I crossed to the window and looked back at him. "Did your father suggest I might be susceptible to bribery?"

"I'm here on my own account. And I'm not offering a bribe, just a consideration to stop you harassing my father." He took a step towards me. "And to make it quite clear to you that, if you refuse to go quietly, I shall be forced to make you go."

"And how will you do that?"

"I am a man of considerable influence, Strafford. For the good of my family, my business and my party, that influence could be brought to bear on you—painfully."

"I think you've said enough, Mr Couchman. Intimidation and inducement may well be your stock in trade—like father, like son, after all—but they cannot touch me. I suggest you leave, before I say something you might not want to hear."

I opened the door but he made no move. "Listen, Strafford. If you're not on your way back to Madeira by next Monday, the consequences could be serious." He walked slowly to the door and faced me. "Old men often have accidents—if you take my meaning."

"Your meaning is clear—and contemptible. You're rapidly proving to me, Mr Couchman, that your ways are in need of correction. And that I can arrange. Now get out."

He stepped into the hall. "If you're not gone by Monday, Strafford, you'll be hearing from me." His growl had turned to a snarl. It had the note of a frightened but dangerous animal.

"On the contrary. You'll be hearing from me." I slammed the door in his face. A few moments later, I watched from the window as he emerged onto the pavement below and strode away towards Piccadilly Circus, colliding with a passer-by as he went and appearing, from his demeanour, to blame the other for his own clumsiness. I found myself wondering what Elizabeth thought of her son. Even I could not deny Couch his engaging charm, but Henry had his father's presumption and arrogance admixed with neither discretion nor sensitivity. If I had looked upon his power-stained face as a parent, it would have shamed me. I had to know Elizabeth's mind.

For she was, after all, the crux of the matter, as much a victim as I was and therefore deserving of consideration even if I did not still love her, which I sensed I did. But the suspicion had grown in my mind that what I really loved was the memory of Elizabeth as she had been forty years before, not the present, remote actuality. There was only one way to put it to the test.

From my luggage, I picked out the book of Hardy's verse that I had brought with me from Madeira; Satires of Circumstance (an apt title indeed). Elizabeth it was who had intro-

duced me to Hardy the poet, who had been reading another of his collections— Time's Laughingstocks *(apter still)—when we met in tantalizing secrecy, in Hyde Park all of a lost long ago. Perhaps for that reason, I cleaved to Hardy's work as a talisman, an antidote—for all its melancholy—to the bitterness of old age.*

Yet Hardy, in his endearing frailty, had not always been proof against despair himself. I perused his Poems of 1912–13 *and found amongst them one which seemed to capture my feelings at that moment. 'After a Journey' spoke of Hardy's return to a landscape haunted by the ghost of his dead wife and coloured by his regret for things done and undone. I too had returned to a haunted land, but, in my case, I seemed to be the ghost, to whom Elizabeth promised a form of exorcism.*

Elizabeth had not been at the house in Hampstead. If I were to find her, Couch's Sussex address (Quarterleigh, Miston) seemed likelier. Guessing that Couch might still be staying with Henry, perhaps debating how much more of the truth to tell him, I could afford to waste no time. Within an hour of Henry's ireful exit, I was at Victoria boarding a train for Chichester.

In Chichester, I bought a map and took a local train to Singleton, a village on the South Downs. From there, it was but a five mile walk through the lanes to Miston. Yet, when I came to step it out, the miles dragged at my feet. The nearer my destination I drew, the less I wanted to arrive.

I came as a stranger down a rough lane from the west into the village, its walls and gateways announcing themselves unremarkably through the misty rain as just another Sussex settlement, yet seeming, as they closed about me with all the indifference reserved for an unknown wayfarer, something more: a place of reckoning, a trysting ground whither I had come too late.

I sought directions at the post office and followed them to a lane behind the church. Quarterleigh was a thatched house set in its own grounds, an attractive blend of cosy cottage and country seat: a placid, pleasing abode, serene in its setting beneath the slope of the Downs. It could hardly have been less forbidding. Yet a 75-year-old man stood at its low white gates and hesitated to pay a call on the 62-year-old woman of the house. I retreated to the wall on the opposite side of the road, dismayed to find myself wet-palmed and trembling with nervousness. This was no way to present myself to Elizabeth. How, I wondered, would I react if she walked down the drive and saw me at that moment?

Fortunately, she did not. Instead, coming from the direction of the village along the lane, there appeared a rotund countrywoman with a laden basket under her arm and a bustling gait. She had the look of a housekeeper about her. When she turned in at the entrance to Quarterleigh, it seemed too good an opportunity to miss. I called out to her and hurried across the lane.

She consented, not without a suspicious sidelong glance, to my unusual request. Yes, she did keep house at Quarterleigh and, yes, she would take a note to her mistress, Lady Couchman, whom she believed to be at home. It was, I emphasized, for Elizabeth's eyes only and, if she wished to discuss its contents with me, she could find me in the churchyard. If she had not arrived by six o'clock—just over an hour away—I would leave. The note, which I had written on the train, was anonymous, but I had little doubt that she would guess its author. I had copied a verse from Hardy's 'After a Journey' to announce my coming and to leave open the question of whether she would grant me an audience. The choice of Hardy would, I knew, redound to the full the echo of the verse. Elizabeth, of all people, would be able to read my questing mind between the lines.

"Yes: I have re-entered your olden haunts at last;"
(Is it really a surprise to hear me again?)
"Through the years, through the dead scenes I have tracked you;"
(Why should it be, when I have never forgotten you?)
"What have you now found to say of our past—"
(Will you not grant me one boon—to speak of that which divided us?)
"Scanned across the dark space wherein I have lacked you?"
(For it is true—I have never recovered from the loss of you.)

Would she come? Did I want her to come? I could not decide.

And then she came.

"Edwin." It was her voice, as I would have imagined it, the insouciant lilt of youth become a mature assurance.

I turned and looked at her for the first time in 32 years. If she had become old, then old age was beauteous. Of course her hair was grey, her carriage deliberate, her bearing stately, but that was not what I saw. Her eyes fixed mine with a look that was there the day I forced an audience with a brick-throwing Suffragette. Her lips, had they not been set grimly for this meeting, could still, I knew, have mocked and delighted me with her smile. "So you came," I said. She nodded gravely. "Thank you."

"There's no need to thank me. How are you?"

"Well, I'm sorry to have lured you out here. It must seem unnecessarily melodramatic."

"Why have you come, Edwin?"

"Just to see you, one more time."

"But why now?"

I knew then that I could not tell her, not in cold blood. It would have been too hurtful, too callous. The time to be either, if it had ever existed, was long past. So, to substantiate my reticence, I continued to question, not denounce or proclaim. Elizabeth said she was happy and content—I could tell as much from her face. I deflected her from any discussion of what I had done with my middle age and drew her out on the subject of her family. We stood in the churchyard, at a respectful distance, conversing politely like two long-time acquaintances who had never even approached intimacy. It was, I suppose, the only way to bear all the strains of recollection. But, beyond the civilities, I was searching and scouring her life, above all her family, for some hint, some pointer to what the truth would do to her.

It was with slight shock that I came to realize from her answers that she had retained her faith in life intact. She was, as she had a right to be, a contented lady. She was careful to avoid any direct mention of the Suffragette movement or our engagement, indeed anything of life before she had married, but her passing references to the place of women in society, the experience of raising a family and the pleasing quandary of being the wife of a successful man, suggested that the attainment of wealth and comfort had not blunted her perception.

We walked round the village, then, at my request, back to Quarterleigh. Elizabeth's ready agreement confirmed that she was alone there. As she escorted me round the house and garden—all tastefully faithful to the home I would have expected her to have chosen—I could not rid myself of the nagging thought: is this where we would have lived, you and I, had matters fallen out otherwise? Is this how it would have been for us, had we grown old together? It was impossible to say.

Among the objets d'art, *there was a cabinet bearing gilt-framed photographs. There was one of a toddler and a baby, playing together, whom I took for Elizabeth's grandchildren, one also of her and Couch with Henry standing between them, wearing academic dress and looking a good deal younger than the man I had met. Elizabeth noticed me looking at it.*

"That was taken at my son's graduation—1939," she said.

"I've met Henry." It was out of my mouth before I could stop myself. I had not intended to speak of it as I felt certain that Henry would not.

"Of course. That last time we met." I was saved. She thought I was referring to seeing Henry as a baby on Hampstead Heath in 1919. The misunderstanding was a kindness.

"Do you think that he takes after his father?" It was the nearest that I had come to a direct reference to Couch and, even then, camouflaged another question which could not be put: do you realize that theirs is the shabby strain onto which your nobility has been grafted?

"I think so. The resemblance has always pleased me." There could no longer be any doubt. Elizabeth's faith was not merely intact, it was great enough to obscure the failings of her husband and son. Perhaps, having been—as she saw it—betrayed by me, she could not bear to think another man could so deceive her. In that case, my revelation would have the force of a cataclysm and the only service I could pay her

was to stave off that cataclysm, at least whilst it was still possible to do so. Couch had been right, damn his soul. How could I break the heart of the woman I loved, simply to save my name?

"Tell me," she continued, "how did you travel to Miston?" We both seemed pleased to revert to more prosaic stuff.

"I walked from the railway station at Singleton."

"That's a long way, Edwin. Surely you'll allow me to drive you back?"

"That would be very kind." She had served notice that my visit should end before it pained her. She could not have known how right she was. So I left Quarterleigh, without a backward glance, almost, indeed, with relief.

The journey to Singleton gave me insufficient time to collect my thoughts, to search for a fitting way to part, this time for good. Though I had resolved to hold my tongue as to the truth, I wanted her to know just a little of why I had come.

"The reason I came," I said as we drove through Singleton, "was to see if I still loved you." Then, before she could forestall me: "And the cursed of it is that I do." My curse, though she could not know it, was her salvation. Only my love for her saved her from the truth. My sacrifice for her sake was to let her believe the worst of me. However corrupt I knew Henry and his father to be, their disgrace was not worth Elizabeth's desolation.

We halted at the railway station, but Elizabeth remained silent, as if unnerved by my declaration. I sought to reassure her. "Don't worry," I said. "I'll go quietly."

"Edwin, I'm sorry." Her hint of forgiveness hurt me more than ever now that I knew there was nothing to forgive.

"There's no need. It wasn't your fault." It was the briefest, truest statement I could make.

"That's all I can find to say of our past." In her oblique, knowing reference to Hardy's poem, she echoed, acutely and unknowingly, all the anguish of my forbearance.

"Then let that be all." I could not stay longer without saying more. So I stepped from the car and walked over to the booking office. On the threshold, I turned to doff my hat before going in through the door and losing sight of her.

I lingered in my hotel whilst the days ticked away towards May 7th—by when Henry had warned me to be on my way—and, beyond that, May 20th: the expiry of Sellick's detention. One thing was certain: I could not go back to Madeira. If I remained in England, I could avoid Sellick and, if I left London, Henry to boot. Barrowteign drew me, as if it was, after all, time to go home, time for an old man to come to his close. If I stayed there and said nothing, who would find me or want to find me? Mine was, as experience revealed, a pious hope.

On May 7th, I took the train to Exeter and lodged for a few nights at The Royal Clarence, hard by the cathedral, fearing to complete the last leg of the journey until I had put my affairs in order. To this end, I visited the family solicitor, old Petherton—who still handled my business—and drafted a new will, as I had long intended, settling the whole of my estate upon Ambrose. Petherton, good fellow that he was, told me of the circumstances obtaining at Barrowteign following the National Trust takeover and implied that Ambrose might well have need of a bequest.

A week after my arrival in Exeter—a week of solitary tramps down the Exe estuary, soulful walks round the precincts of the cathedral, and many an hour of solitary concentration as I commenced this addition to my memoir—Petherton sent a message to me at The Clarence. His office had, it seemed, received a telephone call from somebody describing himself as "Mr Henry Couchman's private secretary", enquiring as to my whereabouts. He had been deflected by Petherton's legendary discretion, but the significance for me was that Couchman was on my trail.

Accordingly, that afternoon, I booked out of the hotel and caught a train to Dewford. Even though I had been close at hand for a week, I had not alerted Ambrose to my presence, so, when I glimpsed Lodge Cottage from the train as we rattled over the crossing, I could only imagine what a surprise it would be for him.

My impression, when I presented myself at the door of his cottage that damp evening, was that Ambrose was mightily pleased to see me, which made, for me, a happy break with the pattern of my return to England. We had not seen each other since 1945—when he had stayed with me in Madeira after being demobilized—and there was plenty for him to tell me of the years between: years of the National Trust takeover of Barrowteign and of his growing disenchantment with England.

Even Ambrose, it transpired, had grown old, and a touch curmudgeonly, in his cottaged seclusion. Once used to the ministrations of servants and batmen, he had allowed his domestic arrangements to slide into shoddiness, whilst perversely keeping an immaculate garden. He openly confessed to spending a large proportion of his time at The Greengage in the village and was bemused by my reluctance to accompany him there. I could not help that, deeming it unduly risky to show myself freely about the place.

I told Ambrose nothing of my recent activities. I claimed that I had come straight from London and he said that I was welcome to remain indefinitely. He meant it, for, ironically, Lodge Cottage was all that remained of the Straffords' ancestral home. Ambrose railed at the "wreckers" now installed at Barrowteign and, certainly, the house was in some chaos, but I had no doubt that it was purely temporary and found the changes more tolerable than he did. To me, in my present mind, a termination of Barrowteign's use as a family home seemed all too appropriate.

Over the days that followed, between his infusions at The Greengage and his energetic gardening, Ambrose sought to draw me into an explanation of my departure from Madeira, but I could not afford to indulge his curiosity. Instead, I kept myself to myself, wrote up this account, took a few strolls after dark and endeavoured to keep Ambrose from becoming bored with my company whilst not telling him too much. He agreed to say nothing in the village of my presence and I had to rely upon him not forgetting himself in his cups.

Self-imposed confinement in Lodge Cottage cast shadows of gloom across an already cheerless outlook. The work in progress at Barrowteign was one such shadow, though it afflicted Ambrose more than me. Our location, hard by the railway crossing where his parents had been killed, was another. I wondered, of an evening, when Ambrose had departed to The

Greengage, whether that very proximity drove him to drink, drove him just as it drew me with its recollections and associations, its fusion of memory and place. When, on moonlit nights, I looked at the outlined bulk of Barrowteign above us, solidly unaltered but yet so changed within, when I heard the owls hoot in the chestnut trees and let my mind play with the inky blackness that lay between the milky splashes of lunar light down the lane, then I fell prey to thoughts of natural terms and fitting ends. At times such as those, I heard a singing in the rails on the crossing just before the last down train rounded the curve from Exeter and I reflected, as I had often done, how much happier might everyone have been had it been I, not my brother, killed on that crossing forty years before. Ambrose would have had a father and Barrowteign a master, Sellick would have had no clue to follow and Henry Couchman nothing to fear.

Ten days elapsed. Then my delusion of secrecy and security at Lodge Cottage was exposed for what it was. During one of Ambrose's lunchtime absences, I had a caller. I might have lain low had he not caught my eye, watching as I was from the kitchen window as he made his way over the crossing. It was Sir Gerald Couchman, an incongruous figure in his city clothes, on foot and far from home. I went outside to meet him, feeling oddly reluctant to have him indoors. He stood on the path through the garden, a man in conflict, his breath shortened by the walk from the car, poised uncertainly between ways of approaching me.

"What do you want?" I said.

"A word . . . to the wise," he panted. "Can I come in?"

"I'd rather stay in the open. How did you find me?"

"Where else would you be? Whatever Henry thought, I didn't believe you'd scuttle back to Madeira, not after your visit to Elizabeth."

"She told you then?"

"Of course. There are . . ." He broke off with a smile. "Do you know, I was about to say there are no secrets between us."

"But that wouldn't be true."

"No. Still, Elizabeth's not to know. If you were going to tell her, you'd have done so by now. I realize that."

"Then why are you here now?"

"Because my son doesn't. He sees you as a very real threat. Frightening him, as you did, was a mistake."

"How much did you tell him?"

"Everything. He wouldn't have been content with less. Besides, between you and me, it was amusing to shatter his complacency, his assumption of respectability. I've done a lot for my son and got precious little in return."

"I'd have said you had the son you deserved."

"Maybe so. I'll allow you that one. Still, his prying into our discussions on Parliament Hill that night—following us, interrogating me afterwards—irked me into telling the young upstart just what he wanted to know. Bit of a facer for him really."

"He came to see me afterwards."

"I know. And you alarmed him. It's my own fault, you'd say, and you'd be right. I taught him the value of money too well. He believes every man has his price, so he concluded that, because you wouldn't take his bribe and go quietly, you must be raising the stakes rather than throwing in your hand."

"And who says I'm not?"

"Have it your own way, Edwin. The point is that Henry won't rest until this is settled, one way or the other. I believe he may have taken soundings within the party leadership."

"About what?"

"About whether allegations linking the present Tory leader with some form of conspiracy against you in his younger days poses a threat to their election prospects."

"What nonsense! I've nothing against Churchill. The only election prospects Henry needs to worry about are his own."

"Maybe so, but Henry and I both have influential friends, Edwin. A threat to one is a threat to all. Lloyd George may be dead but his son is a shadow minister and his government could fall at any time. Do you seriously suppose that the sort of problem you pose—the possibility of public disgrace for prominent people in the party—can be tolerated indefinitely?"

"I think it may have to be."

"Then you're making, I have to tell you, a big mistake. I say that—if you can believe it—as a friend."

I was in no mood to receive an olive branch from such a source. A claim to friendship was the one way he could still anger me. "Go to hell, Sir Gerald. And tell your influential friends to do the same. As for the egregious Henry, uncertainty will do him good, if I'm any judge. You should have manufactured some adversity for him long before now."

He coloured. "There's no point reacting like this, Edwin. What I'm saying makes sense for everyone—including you. Hand over the certificate—and go back to Madeira."

I was tempted, in that moment, to tell him why it could never be as simple as that, to tell him about Sellick and his demand for satisfaction. But I had resolved that inaction was the only honourable course left open to me, so I said nothing of the kind. "It won't wash, Sir Gerald. What I have I hold. And where I go is my own affair. If Henry tries to put pressure on me, he will make up my mind what to do, and he will make it up in just the way that he does not want."

"You're being a fool."

"From a liar, a coward and a bigamist, that could almost be praise."

I could see him wrestling inwardly to control himself. "Very well. Don't say you weren't warned." He turned and hurried out through the gate, meeting Ambrose on his return from The Greengage, as they both traversed the crossing. They passed without speaking, though Ambrose looked quizzical and, when the sound of a car drawing away from down the drive came to our ears, he asked who my visitor had been. I claimed that he was a stranger seeking directions, but I do not think that Ambrose believed me.

Nothing followed immediately from Couch's visit, yet I could not dismiss his warning from my mind, nor see what I could do about it. I could not accede to Henry's demands—which I resented anyway—without placing myself in Sellick's power. Therefore, what was there to be done but nothing? Since then, it has not needed me to indicate to Ambrose that something is amiss. Signs there have been aplenty apart from my behaviour. Jess, his dog, has been restless, as if there were strangers on her territory. Ambrose himself has claimed evidence of "snoopers" in his garden. I have slept mostly during the day and kept watch—unbeknown to him—by night. I have not detected enough for certainty, yet there has not been so little that I could say my fears—or Couch's warning—were groundless.

Last night, that which I had awaited came to pass. I had not expected anything quite so clumsy, but that was, perhaps, in character. Ambrose had turned in after a late night at The Greengage and all was quiet in the house, till Jess stirred in her basket at some movement outside. I quietened her, then heard myself the sound of the kitchen door—left unlocked, as was Ambrose's wont—being eased open.

Unlike the intruder, I knew the cottage well enough to reach the kitchen in silence. From the hall, I could hear the door being inched shut again. That was the moment I chose to burst in and catch the culprit with his back turned. Throwing caution to the winds, I seized him in an arm lock. He blundered against the table, sending a glass smashing to the floor, and I held him doubled over the back of a chair.

In the moonlight flooding through the window, he was instantly recognizable: Henry, in all his twisted fury, pinioned but protesting.

"Couchman," I breathed in his ear, "what's your game?"

"I'll have that certificate, Strafford, or I'll have you. Which is it to be?"

I tightened my hold. "You're in no position to dictate terms. Be thankful I don't turn you over to the police. Instead, I'll just throw you out, like the common thief you are."

"You won't get away with this, Strafford. I have friends who . . ."

"Be silent. If you had the means to back up your boasts, you wouldn't have crept in here yourself. You have your father's style, but none of his substance. Now, be on your way."

I was manhandling him to the door—amid many an oath—when somebody lit the gas lamp and I was dazzled by the light. Ambrose was in the room, demanding to know what the devil was going on. I told him that I was ejecting an intruder and, still half-asleep, he helped me bundle Henry to the door.

Then, gathering his wits, Ambrose asked why we should not carry him off to Constable Sprague in the village—an English landowner is wrathful when roused.

"Not worth it," I said. "He's just a worthless felon. I'd rather have done with him here and now."

So saying, I released him and Henry, for once happy to go, fled into the night. Yet I knew, even as I pronounced the words, that I could not have done with him even if I wanted to, that, though he might be gone, it was not for good.

The minute Ambrose closed the door and belatedly locked it, a weariness afflicted me and I slumped down on a chair. It may have been the exertion of overpowering Henry or the despair I felt at this ticking, timed, expiring fate whose lapping waters were enveloping me, but, suddenly, I felt older even than my years, fatigued by pointless effort. Nor was there much conviction in my claims to Ambrose that I did not know the intruder or why he should have broken in. Only the experience of recent weeks can have persuaded him that I would tell him nothing. He looked hurt by my refusal to confide in him and, indeed, as we sat silently together in the kitchen, drinking tea and feeling dawn creep across the fields towards us, I too regretted it. But, in truth, he was better off not knowing. My burden was not for sharing.

This morning, I agreed to accompany Ambrose to The Greengage. I fancy both our nerves were in need of repair. Somehow, the fact that such a perfect day—the warmest and sunniest, the most like Madeira, since my arrival in April—should follow so disturbed and disturbing a night only made matters worse. Perhaps that was why Ambrose consented to remove himself to the inn garden from his normal haunt by the bar. I preferred, at any rate, to remain in the open. Confined spaces were beginning to prey upon my mind.

Another concern was occupying my thoughts. Since Henry's blundersome advent last night, it has become clear to me that I cannot risk the discovery—in the event of my no longer being on the scene—of the evidence that this account represents. A meet hiding place for it occurred to me this morning: a gift I had once prepared for Ambrose, a place where he could find it if he ever had the dire need that might drive him to deduce its whereabouts.

So, both to learn if it was still in being, and to leave a clue no larger than a dusty corner of the mind, I asked Ambrose what had become of the model castle I had constructed for his Christmas present in 1918. He told me that it, along with much other family lumber of no great value, had been removed to the attic of the house when the National Trust took possession.

I made my excuses at one o'clock and left Ambrose to join his normal compatriots at the bar. This was a mission which I could no longer postpone. I returned to Lodge Cottage, slid the certificate between two leaves of this journal, collected some string and wrapping material, and bore the whole bundle off to Barrowteign.

The hour between one and two has been quiet, the workmen relaxing in the grounds during their lunchtime break. I, who know the house so well, had no difficulty in ascending unnoticed to these dust-laden chambers, full of the family memorabilia for which the National Trust had no use and Ambrose no room.

I have written the last few pages here, seated by a window through which sunlight has flooded onto the hoarded irrelevance of redundant possessions. Of course, I have recognized and remembered much: cracked mirrors that once reflected prouder scenes than this, chipped vases that once held scented flowers, old sea chests that my father once used on his travels. A kindly soul has deposited here a number of vapid watercolours, mates to the aqueous study of Barrowteign that I took with me to Madeira to remind me of Florence. It is not too fanciful to see all this as symbolic of my family's decline, to believe that the dust on these boards and boxes has been formed by the crumbling of a dynasty.

Once this chronicle is concluded, I shall parcel it up and lodge it within the castle I made for Ambrose. I suspect that I need not worry about whether it is ever found, or by whom. By that time, my curious legacy will be somebody else's problem. To whichever unfortunate soul, if any there be, who turns these pages after me, only this would I say. Feel for me no pity. If you wish to do me any service, render to Elizabeth whatever assistance she may need. If the facts that I have here recounted should ever become known beyond these covers, then she will have sore need of that assistance.

It is time to take my leave of this narrative, this house and, mayhap, this life. For, when I shut these covers, I will close a circle. Its perimeter was already being traced when I descried the roofs of Barrowteign, under which I now sit, from Blackingstone Rock, where Elizabeth agreed to marry me on a Michaelmas afternoon more than forty years ago. Beyond the circle, lies the shadow into which I will shortly go, unarmed but unafraid. It is now for others to decide what to say of our past.

E.G. Strafford
Barrowteign,
Devon,
4th June 1951.

Seven

So this, after all, was the truth. Or part of it, Strafford's part, his mystery untangled with a riddle. The door I'd opened led only to a labyrinth. Sellick hadn't sent me as the emissary of his dispassionate curiosity, but for some darker reason of his own, little knowing that I would discover his hand—his brutal, younger, unmasked self—in Strafford's undoing.

I couldn't grasp it all at first. The question had changed. I knew now all the secrets behind Strafford's resignation—or thought I did. That wasn't the issue anymore. The issue was what those who'd tried to stop me must, all along, have known it would become. Who or what killed Strafford? I counted off the conjectures like vegetable rows in the kitchen garden below.

An accident—not just a few hours after finishing the Postscript. That wouldn't wash anymore.

Suicide—possible, given his state of mind. Was that his "fitting end"?

Murder—it had to be. Else why would people have tried to stop my enquiries? Specifically, why should Henry have been so hostile if he hadn't been implicated? Whether he'd mobilized the forces of official displeasure or done the deed himself, it was rank with his involvement.

What of Sellick? He'd deceived me utterly, but why? To make amends for falsely accusing Strafford? Was he only seeking the truth by a roundabout route?

If Strafford's death was suspicious, so was Ambrose's. Only Timothy Couchman had known of his message to me about the Postscript. Another pointer to Henry. But there was the rub. Strafford's last plea had been to protect Elizabeth. How would accusing her son of murder, both then and now, do that?

A thought struck me. I leafed through the blank pages of the Postscript, then again more carefully. The certificate wasn't there. Perhaps Ambrose had taken it. Perhaps Henry had taken it from Ambrose, stolen it in 1977 after failing to in 1951.

Strafford's plea for Elizabeth had been before Ambrose paid with his life for trying to vindicate his uncle. That overrode considerations of sparing an old lady some heartache. She had to know.

I trembled. The afternoon was beginning to cloud over, but I wasn't cold, rather afraid. I'd convinced myself that Edwin and Ambrose Strafford had been murdered. If that was so, then I was in danger. My new-found knowledge imperilled me just as surely as Henry and whoever was hiding behind him. If Henry wasn't capable of murder, more powerful forces were, and that was worse still. Only self-doubt saved me from panic. I couldn't believe all the implications of what I was thinking, couldn't decide what to do. But I had to go on. The Couchmans, who'd despised and rejected me, had inspired a worm to turn. That old, far-sighted villain, Couch, would have realized I wasn't doing this just for Strafford, but to redeem all the other failures of nerve and character which had dogged me down the years. A flawed crusade then, a tilt at the sanctity of history with a smattering of revenge, a defiance of those who put no limit on my weakness, a clutching at straws, a last throw to be attempted only by those with nothing to lose. That's how it was for me. Not decent, simple, honest or truthful, because purity was beyond me. Just the best thing I'd ever done, because there was honour in it, however compromised.

I'd become too engrossed to notice, but it was nearly six o'clock and I was still on the premises. I climbed hurriedly back into the attic and re-parcelled the Postscript. Then, still trembling at the thought, not of what I was doing, but of what it represented, I hastened out and down the stairs. The corridor beyond the door from the attic was empty. Turning the key in the lock behind me, I made my way gingerly to Knox's office: empty. The key looped back onto its peg as if it had never left it.

Knox's secretary had evidently gone home. There was nobody to see me leave by the back stairs. The guide in the hall was preparing to close. "Didn't know there were any visitors still here, dear," she remarked, showing me out. She didn't even glance at the canvas package under my arm, though it felt to me as if it was crying theft every step of the way.

I walked into the village and phoned for a taxi. Somehow, I couldn't face a ride on a public bus. It was too exposed, too insecure. I could have had a drink with Ted at The Greengage and discussed what evidence he would give at the inquest, but I preferred to get back to Exeter and sit alone in a pub where I wasn't known, until it was late enough to go back to the Bennetts' without having to answer many questions. As it turned out, I got away with a smiling but preoccupied greeting and went straight to bed. I left the house in good time in the morning and walked into Exeter.

The magistrates' court was echoingly empty: a clerk, a yawning newspaperman, two policemen (one of them Ash), a grey-faced man who sat and looked apart, Ted Groves who nodded to me and kept clearing his throat, and a fly whose angular flight near the ceiling I watched while we waited. The Postscript was in a bag by my side—there if I wanted it, which I sensed I wouldn't, there where it seemed safest.

An official led in eight jurors, who shuffled and shifted into position in their box. Then the Coroner entered by another door, Ash's colleague called us to our feet and the business of the day commenced.

The Coroner was calm, almost casual, in his directions to the jury. He looked and sounded like a competent man, dutiful but not zealous. For this case, he hardly needed to be anything else. Ash was called and said his piece: the clear picture of an old drunk found drowned emerged from his "night of the 22nd" commentary. Then Ted, shifting his weight and overly deferential to the Coroner, an unnerved countryman not about to challenge conventional wisdom. Yes, Ambrose drank. Yes, on May 22nd as usual—but not more than usual. He held to that line as if it redeemed his reticence on other, murkier matters. The Coroner pressed him. He wanted it said that Ambrose was a helpless, drunken old fool—or so it seemed. But Ted was stubborn, and keen on his reputation as a responsible landlord. He wouldn't be shifted.

That's when I was tempted to intervene, to shout to the Coroner and high heaven that this was a farce, that he didn't know the half of it, that a supposedly simple drowning couldn't wash away the stain of a dead but restless crime. I wanted to wave the Postscript in my hand and declare: "Here's the truth, here are the names of the guilty."

And that's when a draught behind me, a stirring of stale air, told me that somebody had entered the court, somebody who moved silently and took their place in the public seating beside me. When I looked, I saw—as I'd guessed, a second before—that it was Eve.

She didn't smile and she didn't frown. Her look was frank and direct, appraising yet not despising.

"Hello Martin." She whispered the words, hardly breathed them in the courtroom hush. To me, it seemed absurd for the proceedings to continue when Eve was among us, poised in balance to a weight and occasion we couldn't comprehend, elegantly disdainful of the place and circumstance of our meeting, fixing me with a cool gaze which challenged me to pretend she was a stranger.

"Why are you here?" It was all I could say, stumbling towards some form of submissiveness.

"To see you." Was that a smile which almost came?

"But . . ."

She raised a hand in tune to the orchestration of the inquest. "Afterwards." It could have been admonition or flirtation, I couldn't tell. It was as if I'd never known her, never stopped knowing her in the way that I had. She dared me to wait in a manner which left me no choice.

I passed the rest of the inquest in a trance. After Ted, the grey-faced pathologist gave his clinical resumé of how a man had died: high blood-alcohol level, bruises and contusions consistent with a fall, death by drowning, probably while unconscious. He came and went with a rustle of the white coat he wasn't wearing.

Then the Coroner summed up. A history of drink. A dark night. A simple accident. Open and shut, like a book. The jury didn't even retire. They muttered respectfully, then obliged with their verdict. Accidental death. A brief homily from the Coroner on old men too fond of the bottle, a jab at Ted for not conceding the point, then a gathering of papers, a conclusion of disagreeable business. The policeman intoned some Plantagenet obsequy he'd said a dozen times before that ended: "Now go forth and take your ease."

It was over. Not yet eleven and we'd concluded—as we were meant to conclude—that there was nothing to say, no doubt to quell, about the death of Ambrose Strafford. I felt sick with the knowledge of my acquiescence, sick with the elation of Eve's presence, appalled by the link—the imperceptible, undeniable connexion—between the two.

We filed out of the courtroom, into the accusatory sunlight, where ease was a sham and uncertainty a practised art.

"I'm sorry about Ambrose," Eve said.

I looked at her in bafflement. "Why did you come?"

"I told you. We must talk . . . if you will." She knew I would, but goaded me by implying she could doubt it. "There's a lot to say."

"I thought you had nothing to say to me."

"That's because you forgot what I told you: nothing is ever quite what it seems." A lorry roared by in the road and the draught blew Eve's hair across her face.

"I'll happily remember."

"I can't stop now, Martin. I'll explain later. Can we meet this evening?" The exquisite torture of another postponement. Surely this was planned, this delay contrived to stretch my nerves. I scanned her face for confirmation, but only saw the ceramic perfection that hid its craft.

"Where?"

"The wine bar in Gandy Street, at eight o'clock."

"I'll be there."

"Until then, Martin. I'm sorry—I really must go." And she did go, with unhurried swiftness, taking her telling, timeless beauty with her, to her car, driving away without another word. It would have seemed curt if it hadn't been so tame compared with our last parting, would have sounded distant if it hadn't been nearer than the contempt I'd expected.

Eve arrived late. I'd just begun to wonder whether she would turn up at all when she appeared, as if from nowhere, at my table, emerging from the press of bodies as if they weren't there, simply dressed in black jeans and a plain blouse, quieter in every respect than the smoking, over-scented young beauties around us but somehow, with her assured stillness, commanding attention.

She sat down and I poured her a drink. "I'm sorry about the crush," she said, sipping her wine.

"It's hardly your fault."

"I chose the venue. Unfortunately, my knowledge of Exeter is limited."

"I didn't realize you knew it at all."

"An exchange opportunity came up at short notice. A member of the history department at the University here had gone up to Cambridge as external examiner for my papers and I've come down here to cover her lectures and seminars. With tripos in full swing, it was a good time to get away."

"Odd we should both turn up in Exeter."

She half-smiled, for the first time since we'd met again. "It was no coincidence. I leapt at the chance. Your flatmate in London thought you were down here, so I hoped to find you when I arrived. Then I read about Ambrose . . ."

"You spoke to Jerry?"

"Yes. You see, I was trying to trace you."

"But why? When we . . . last met, it seemed the last thing you'd want to do."

"I'm sure you understand regret, Martin."

"I tried to tell you about it myself."

"I know, and I wouldn't listen. Since then, I've come to see things . . . in perspective."

I was torn between protesting at the way she'd treated me and grasping at the straw she held out to me, the colour of the wine, clear and distinct in her inflexion, for all the noise and smoke. "What is the perspective?"

"The perspective is that I was guilty of . . . arrogance. I

thought that, because we'd come to . . . care for each other, I was entitled to expect your past to be unblemished."

"I never said it was that, but I did lie about my marriage and why it ended. I'm sorry for that. I'm sorry for all of it. But I can't change the past—it happened."

"I know. As an historian, I shouldn't have let myself be taken by newspaper morality. I should have let you explain, I should have helped, not joined the condemnation."

"I don't blame you. It was bound to be a shock."

"Like finding out about the Couchman Fellowship?"

"Hardly comparable. But you should've told me you couldn't be impartial."

"Oh, but I was. I kept it from you because I was afraid of what you would think, but it didn't stand in my way. I didn't tell the Couchmans what we were on to."

"Really?" I couldn't help sounding doubtful after all that Henry had implied to me.

"Really." Her expression willed me to believe her. "I don't know how they found out, but, as soon as they did, they made sure I knew your secret."

"You mean . . ."

"Didn't you realize who'd told me?"

"I thought . . ."

"It was your former brother-in-law, Timothy Couchman."

Not Alec? Just as before, when she told me of the marriage certificate, when she materialized at the inquest, whenever, in fact, she chose to, Eve had confounded me. I'd thought it out carefully, reasoned my way to Alec's guilt. But that was before I'd learned of Sellick's secret part in Strafford's past, before Eve had returned to me and suggested we could, after all, turn back the clock. "He wouldn't want our findings to implicate his grandfather."

"Naturally. And Timothy was subtle enough to know that threatening me with removal from the Couchman Fellowship would only have encouraged me to continue our research. I suppose he thought it cleverer to set me against you."

Timothy, like his father, had laid claim to Eve's complicity. It would have been in character for him to have done so just to cover up his seamy act of discrediting me. "Cleverer . . . and more effective?"

"So it must have seemed."

"Then why didn't it work?" We'd come to the crunch.

"Because I missed you." As simple, as prosaic, as touching as that. "Cambridge was a lonely place without you. What it offered me was no longer . . . sufficient. At first, I couldn't identify my sense of loss. Then I realized that you'd got under my skin. You were my loss, a loss, if you like, of humanity. Your successes and failures, your Strafford's mystery, even your scandal, are so much more real—so much more human—than the finely chiselled artificiality of Cambridge. I'd hoped you might feel flattered, Martin, that I had to follow you here."

Flattered wasn't the word. What I felt, when Eve's lips played with the candlelight and shadow as if about to smile, when she gazed at me with a sparkle of promise and a depth of mystery, was irresistible fascination bordering on hopeless infatuation. What I felt was that I was in her power and didn't mind. "What are we to do, Eve? I wish it was as simple as our feelings for each other. I wish you could just forgive my past and we could forget Strafford and the Couchmans. But we can't . . ."

"Because it's part of the bond between us?"

"And because Ambrose is dead. What was just a cerebral game has begun to hurt people. What was just speculation has become hard fact."

"In what way? All I heard at the inquest indicated that Ambrose had drowned accidentally."

"But not before finding out the truth about his uncle."

Eve raised her eyebrows. It gave me a kick to be able to surprise this serenely imperturbable woman. "And what is the truth?"

"Not what you or I thought. Stranger—subtler—than we could have envisaged. Devastating, I'm afraid, for your study of the Suffragettes."

She refilled our glasses with wine: an odd, distractive gesture. "No matter, Martin. In the context of Cambridge, your disregard for conventional interpretation is as refreshing as your personality. Hang the Couchman Fellowship, hang the book. I can find another job, re-write the book. One of the reasons I followed you was because you'd inspired me with this strange concept of truth in history. It might be uncomfortable to apply it—in your own case, for instance—but let's not funk the issue. Unless . . ."

"Unless what?"

"Unless it drowned with Ambrose. Is that what you're saying?"

I paused and gulped some wine, trying to test her with her own practice of meaningful delay. It was a poor effort. She sipped and waited for me, demonstrating with her ease that her patience could outlast mine. "No, Eve. It didn't drown with Ambrose. He discovered a further statement by his uncle, shedding new light on his resignation."

"What light?"

I tested her again with postponement. "It's a long story. This doesn't seem the time or place for it."

"Perhaps not. Perhaps it is . . . premature. After all, there's a lot for us to talk about before we turn to questions of history." Again the poise, the elegant deflection, the turning of my remark to anticipation of something I hadn't meant, but wanted nonetheless. "Let's not be in too much of a hurry, Martin. We owe each other some time."

"You must know I'd give you all the time in the world." The world's time was history, our mutual profession. The debt I'd commuted to a gift was another deflected, unintended meaning, the history I'd found myself offering her was another person's past.

"Let's start with one whole day. I have tomorrow free. We could go somewhere . . . and talk."

I agreed, naturally, enthusiastically. I didn't want to question too hard her change of heart. That she was prepared to see me again was enough. A day together, an empty space she offered to fill, a doubt she promised to still. All that I'd discovered, all the mad tumble of begged questions and suspicions spattering the years between Strafford and me, all the bleak lessons of my four-year voyage from one temptation to another, I forgot in a moment, discarded without a second thought, for the sake of 24 hours held out to me, a day that could become a stage for every variant on the theme of her beauty.

I dodged explanations where the Bennetts were concerned and planned to slip out early the following morning. I'd refastened the Postscript in its wrapping and put it away where I didn't have to see it. For the moment, I didn't want to know too much about Strafford.

But I already knew too much to forget and the Postscript, whether open or closed, confronted me with the fact. It had become a portentous, uncomfortable document, filling me with uncertainty. It was also, as I'd already concluded, dangerous to many who didn't know what it contained and some who did. Acting as its custodian was a disturbing experience.

Accordingly, I took it with me that warm, clear Friday morning, the air still fresh but the sun warm with a promise of heat later. I walked with unnecessary stealth down through the domesticated hush of the housing estate and across the river to St. David's station. There, a left luggage locker gave me just the repository I was looking for. With the Postscript under my arm, I felt insecure and vulnerable. With a key to its obscurely ordinary hiding place, I felt powerful in my knowledge of its whereabouts.

She came as I might have imagined, speeding with precision down the road from the University in her silver MG. It could have been Cambridge the first time she collected me from Princes'. She wore dark glasses, a silken scarf, a pale blue blouse over white jeans. She smiled with a restraint which might have been either distance or intimacy, daring me to express the doubts we had about each other, while hinting we could pretend instead that they didn't exist.

"I thought we'd go to Braunton Burrows," she said matter-of-factly.

"Wherever you say."

"A botanist at Darwin recommended the orchids there when she heard I was coming down here. And living in Cambridge makes you yearn for the sea."

As we passed through the pine forests of the Taw valley, Eve broke the silence which had fallen tensely between us.

"Where did you go from Cambridge, Martin?"

"London—to think. Then Miston—to work off my sadness. Lady Couchman is an antidote to any self-pity."

"So you've met her?"

I remembered my relief at the time that Eve hadn't. "Yes. She confirmed what we'd suspected about Strafford."

"Did that disappoint you?"

"Not really. She held no bitterness towards him. In fact, she suspects Strafford could have killed himself—out of a kind of remorse."

"But you don't?"

"Not now. Not in the light of the evidence Ambrose discovered."

"And you're keeping me in suspense about that?"

"For a little longer."

We stopped for a drink at a pub the other side of Barnstaple. The garden overlooked the Taw estuary, reaching in idle sweeps towards the Atlantic ocean. The air, as we sat with our chilled drinks, was charged with something other than heat.

"When we parted in Cambridge, Martin, I denied you the opportunity to . . . explain. That was wrong of me."

"Do you want me to explain now?"

"Only if you want to."

I tried. I told Eve then more of the truth about Jane and me than I'd ever told anyone. Still it wasn't the whole truth. Jane could never have been as calculating as I depicted her. But how else could I explain my squandering of what passed for respectability? I couldn't let her know how irresolute I really was.

"It's not," I concluded, "a glorious account. I don't pretend it is. But it's far from being as bad as . . . newspapers . . . make it sound."

"I realize that now, Martin. I think it may even have made you . . . a better person."

"Perhaps."

"Do you know what happened to the girl?"

"Not a clue. Enquiries from me would hardly have been welcome. Besides . . ."

"Yes?"

"Adolescents are hardier than adults tend to think. I imagine she's forgotten all about it. Married with two kids by now.

Everyone would have wanted her to forget. Nobody would let me."

"I see." She looked into the estuarine distance. "I think, perhaps, it's time we forgot the past."

"And the present?"

"You'll want to know about me and the Fellowship." She smiled slowly. "As I said, Timothy Couchman found out about our research. I've no idea how. But walls have ears in Cambridge. After we'd parted, I made no secret to him of what we'd discovered and planned. By then, it didn't seem to matter. The cat was out of the bag and there was no longer any prospect of integrating Strafford's story in my book."

"He came to see me and claimed that you'd kept him informed all along."

"A lie. Timothy's a natural liar. I should never have fallen for his line about you, but it was such a shock that I never had a chance to take stock of it. Not till after you'd gone, anyway. Not till the immaculacy of Cambridge had begun to pall. Not till I'd realized that, without flaws, people aren't real."

"If it's flaws you're after, I'm your man." We laughed at that—spontaneously and mutually, at ease with each other for a renewed moment.

After lunch, we carried on through Braunton to the coastal plain beyond: a strange, unexpected landscape after the switchback interior of field and hedgerow. There, red earth gave way to white sand and the Burrows came into view: an undulating expanse of grass-topped dunes rolling towards a distant, unseen ocean. The warmth of the sand had a steely edge, its very stillness held an awareness of instability.

Where we parked, at the edge of the dunes, there was no other car, no animal life, no sound to break the mood of heat-struck crisis. The burrows were a sparse, shifting, alien place, without association, without location. We could have been anywhere—at any time.

The atmosphere should have worried me, but it didn't. Eve had consented to take me there and that was enough. She smiled and gloried in the sun and led the way, as if she knew it, through the dunes. In the airless slacks between them, she pointed to the colourful carpets of flowers, identified varieties of orchid, bent to explain their differences of form and colour. She was almost skittish, as if taking a girlish delight at returning to her element. Her sudden lightness of spirit dazzled me more than the sun.

Beyond one orchid-rich slack, we descended a sheer slope of sand, with no marram grass to cling to. We slithered down, knee-deep in the heat-dried grains, falling together at the bottom, arm in arm.

Eve laughed and brushed herself down. "I'm glad to be back, Martin," she said.

"But we've never been here before." It was an assertion I was no longer sure of.

"Back with you, I mean." She kissed me lightly, then pulled me up and walked on, her hand in mine.

When we reached the sea, over the last grass-fringed ridge, it was a limitless mirror, laid beyond a lapped rim of flat sand. The beach stretched into haze either side of us and the sea reached as far and as wide as the sky. It was a beach you dream of, at a time you dream of: empty, as if reserved for us, perfect for whatever purpose we cared to imagine.

We sat for a while, at the foot of the ridge backing the beach, absorbing the warmth of the sun, scanning the horizon—broken only by one yacht and the distant hump of Lundy Island—and talked of Cambridge, childhood, orchids and each other: an overture of trivia with Strafford and all—or both—his works for once forgotten.

Eve lay back and closed her eyes, not to sleep but to bask in the heat. I kissed her eyelids and she smiled faintly, patient and assured in what seemed, more than ever, her particular realm.

"Now you're back," I said, "I'm free to say what I was going to say that morning at Darwin: that you make questions of history seem . . . unimportant."

"So they are, Martin."

"And you an historian?"

"But also a woman."

"I wasn't about to forget that." I kissed her again.

She opened her eyes as I drew away. "I think I was away too long."

"I thought that after one day."

"See if you still do, after this day." She smiled and scanned my face with her eyes, as if searching for something in my expression—and finding it. Then she closed her eyes again and stretched back with leisured, feline abandonment. I watched the hem of her blouse ride up over a narrow strip of flesh above the waistband of her jeans and the buttons of the blouse strain between her breasts as she arched her back. I longed in that moment, as her body slowly relaxed onto the sand beside me, to tear the clothes from her, to enter her violently where she lay, to burst the smouldering promise of her words and looks. But her studied languor forbade me, her quiet command held me back, as if saying that she would choose the moment and I would await her choice.

So I did wait, though with none of Eve's self-possession. I stood up and walked out across the sand towards the rippling edge of the sea, leaving her lying beneath the dunes. It was the hottest time of the day, the deserted stretch of beach shimmering away towards a distant headland in one direction and an ultramarine horizon in the other. I'd taken my shoes off and the heat of the sand stung my feet, so I walked out to the cooler, firmer foreshore, corrugated by the retreating tide.

I looked back and saw that Eve had stood up and was gazing towards me. But, when I waved, she didn't respond. It was as if she was gazing beyond me, into the blueness of nothing. Turning back to the sea, my eye was caught by a flash of white on the beach. I stooped to inspect it. No, not paper, but a bleached cuttle bone. I tossed it aside and stood up again.

It could only have been a few minutes since I'd looked back. Certainly, I didn't hear her approach. She walked past me silently, without speaking or glancing, strode on towards the sea. She was naked. She was Eve as I'd dreamed and dreaded she would be: finely poised between an elevated perfection of beauty and a mature peak of sexuality.

She must have known—must have planned—how it would look. Her bare feet stretching slightly with each unhurried step. The muscles of her calves and thighs working with easy elegance as she moved. The pale, curved flesh of her buttocks quivering with the rock of her hips. The line of her back reaching to where her dark hair tumbled onto bare shoulders. She must have known I couldn't withstand her.

She walked—without change of pace—into the sea, wading out until it reached her waist. Then she plunged down into it, swam out a few yards, turned, shook the spray from her hair and stood up, the water coursing down over her shoulders and breasts.

"Aren't you going to join me, Martin?" she said with a smile. Gripped by my desire for her, my dream of what she meant, my knowledge of all that went with the act about to follow, I stood for a moment immobile. Then I abandoned all the lost causes for which I might have resisted her and began to pull off my clothes.

She could have seen how ready I was for her as I ran into the sea. Half in play, half to test me one more time, she swam away down the line of the shore and I followed. At first, she outdistanced me, then slowed, as if permitting me to overhaul her, laughing breathlessly as she moved into the shallows, where I caught and embraced her, stopped her panting with kisses and ran my hands over her wet body. I felt her nipples stiffen against my chest, felt her hand move down to cradle my testicles, then one finger trace the jutting line of my penis to where the head butted against her stomach.

She gently bit the lobe of my ear. "The water wasn't too cold for you then, Martin?"

"God, you're beautiful. How was I so lucky to meet you?"

"Perhaps you deserved it."

We splashed out of the water, stumbled up the beach a few yards to where the dry sand began and fell to our knees. The force of my desire and the urgency of the moment meant we couldn't go any further. Eve began to slide her fingers up and down my penis, while I kissed her face and neck, bit softly at her nipples, ran my hand down her back and reached between her crouching buttocks for the place where I wanted to be.

She rose onto her knees as I pushed my finger into her, tensed as I felt for—and found—her clitoris with my thumb. She arched her neck back and rubbed her large, firm breasts across my face. "Oh God," she breathed.

"Is it good, Eve?"

"Oh yes, it's good . . . You must know that."

Her fingers were still working on me and I felt I would come in her hand if she didn't stop soon. I reached behind her back and lowered her gently onto the sand, parted her legs and eased her hand away. I felt unbearably eager but disablingly nervous, aware—which she couldn't have been—that this was, for me, the first time since I'd broken the bounds with Jane Campion four years before.

I lowered myself onto her. "We must stop," I said anxiously. "We can't do this, not here on the beach—not in the open."

She looked up at me and smiled. "We can't not do it, Martin. What does it matter where we are?" She touched my penis with her finger and it jerked upwards. "I can feel you can't stop now."

"I don't want to." She was right. We couldn't stop. The act was as knowing as its prologue.

"Then come into me."

I thrust into her with the dry sand patching our wet, flexing limbs. It transcended the forbidden pleasure of Jane. Eve was everything in a woman I thought had been denied me. Yet there she was, returning my frantic kisses, joining her arms round my neck and her legs behind my back, slewing with me on the sand as we moaned and moved in time to the driving rhythm of our lovemaking. Eve, who'd shown favours and withdrawn them, who'd played a subtle hand of feminine vulnerability and intellectual remoteness, who'd turned heads and conquered minds in Cambridge, was mine in the simplest, most exclusive manner.

I tried to hold myself back, but couldn't. Eve's words whispered in my ear, her firm yet yielding body beneath me, our exposed location on the beach, sped me towards a climax.

"Come on, Martin. Come for me. I want you to fill me up."

"I will, Eve, I will. I can't stop. You're so beautiful. To be inside you is . . . too much."

"Then give it all to me."

And I did. We reached a crazy, intertwined crescendo, my hands clasped beneath her parted buttocks where they scraped a hollow in the sand with their rocking motion. I felt my spine and legs stiffen and my penis sink to the root inside her, braced myself for the climax, but, somehow, remained poised on the brink, in agonized ecstasy.

That was when Eve looked up into my eyes and smiled with a timeless satisfaction divorced from the moment. She ran her tongue along the edge of her teeth in a gesture at once familiar and forgotten, tightened the grip of her legs behind my back and, with one barely audible word—"Now"—spurred me over the top.

I burst and pumped inside her with all the helpless momentum inspired by her teasing, tasted perfection. It went on dangerously long, passing a point where I thought—for one mad, fearful moment—that I could spurt into her forever and still not wipe the trace of mocking superiority from her smile. But it did end, of course, subsiding through ever gentler throbs to a twitching quiescence. Our sweat-soaked limbs, plastered with sand, stopped writhing, but remained locked together, fused in awe of our own, frightening passion. My mind, after all the doubt and evasion, struggled to comprehend the surging force of what we'd done. Eve had devoured me.

Somehow, exhausted and satiated though we were, we got back across the beach to the shelter of the dunes and fell together into a hollow of sand. We were drained by the violence of our mating, confused by the potency of the act. As the dried heat of the afternoon moved towards an over-ripe evening, Eve fell asleep on my shoulder, one arm draped across my chest and one of her legs across mine, my ribs cushioned by the softness of her breasts. I could feel her breathing against me, could feel her limbs wrapped around mine, and the feeling was a glory in her closeness, a triumph in possessing her.

With my free hand, I began to brush the dried sand from her hip and thigh where they were propped across me. My gaze moved out across the beach to the lazy, lapping ocean, to where my clothes lay in a bundle thirty yards away. I thought I should go and collect them—but not for a while. I too fell asleep.

We returned to the world by way of a country pub halfway between Barnstaple and Exeter. The locals eyed us as if they knew how we'd spent the day. Eve nonchalantly disregarded them, let them notice us kissing, smiled disarmingly at their glares.

"What now?" I said, at a genuine loss. No conversation or social occasion seemed to measure up to the enormity of what had already taken place. Eve, smiling at me over her drink, still slightly flushed from the beach, was my dazzling goddess in a monochrome world.

"The day's not over yet, Martin—and we promised ourselves the whole of it."

"It's a day I'll never forget. But does it have to be just one?"

"That's up to you." Her smile hinted at an offer of something more permanent, although, even then, I didn't think it was really up to me at all. Eve's prerogative encompassed my future.

"If I had my way, today would last forever."

"Perhaps that can be arranged." I almost believed it could be, in the way that beauty verges on sorcery, in the way that love—or the hope of it—transforms life. Most of all, I nearly believed it in the way that a man cannot help staunching a fear of the worst with a naive faith in the best.

We drove through Exeter to Topsham, a picturesque, genteelly decayed outport of the city on the eastern side of the Exe estuary. There, Eve explained, she'd been given use of the house owned by the historian who'd taken her place in Cambridge. We parked in a small courtyard behind a pottery shop and made our way out onto a narrow street lined with elegant Georgian residences, punctuated unexpectedly by openings and alleyways leading to tiny, tucked away dwellings and unsuspected gardens. It was the sort of area, once the preserve of retired naval officers, where enthusiasts for whole food and cottage craft industries had moved in with a vengeance. Cats on widows' doorsteps blinked across at feminist posters in mullioned windows.

Which category Dr Petra Sutcliffe of Exeter University fitted into was hard to say. Book End was a slender, end-of-terrace address in the Georgian sector of the street, with a rather too grandly pillared and fanlit doorway. The interior was fussily and exclusively feminine, dominated by flower-patterned upholstery on antique furniture, the works of Jane Austen, George Eliot and assorted female academics arrayed in glazed and polished bookcases.

Other influences stood in contrast to Dr Sutcliffe's self-containment. The winding staircase and porthole windows commanding views of the estuary had a tang of whichever veteran of Trafalgar had first settled there. The scent of coffee in the kitchen, the choice of perfume in the bathroom, the open files in the lounge: they, on the other hand, were Eve's, displayed carelessly but gracefully, with all her characteristic confidence.

"Petra's choice of décor is beginning to depress me," said Eve as she poured me a gin.

"How much longer do you have to put up with it?"

"Just another week. But it should be quite bearable, so long as . . ."

"So long as what?"

"So long as I have . . . uplifting company." She handed me the glass and left her hand on mine.

"Can I volunteer?"

"I was hoping you would. The best of it is"—she smiled wickedly—"that Petra would so disapprove." We laughed and toasted each other in gin. The chink of glasses, my ex-wife's foible, in the sort of home she'd have made for herself if she hadn't invested in children and county society, mocked with benign precision by one who'd perfected a combination of success and womanhood, one who understood us all better than we did ourselves.

Later we dined at a quiet restaurant in Topsham's High Street. Dark wood and candlelight suited our mood: more subtle, less frenetic than earlier in the day, yet wine and seafood sustaining the intoxicating, maritime flavour—deep beyond plumbing, heart at odds with the surface, warmly flowing around us with a cold, ebbing undertow. The subjects we moved towards were as dangerous in their way as any carnal act. Natural, innocuous and inevitable as their discussion seemed, it constituted, in face, a more complete surrender than any other that day.

"After what's happened," I said, "I don't want to keep anything from you. Now that things have . . . changed . . . between us, you should know everything I know about Strafford."

"Go ahead," she said. As simple as that, so simple I could have believed she was giving me permission rather than direction.

So I went ahead—and told her everything. Looking back, I remember how unmoved—how transfixed but undismayed—Eve was by what I'd found a shattering revelation. Strafford innocent. Couchman a bigamist. Sellick implicated. Christabel Pankhurst a traitor to her cause. Eve preserved her serenity in the face of every detail.

"Your sponsor not the disinterested hotelier you thought?" she said when I'd finished.

"Hardly."

"Mine not the injured parties they'd claim?"

"I'm afraid not."

"And Christabel Pankhurst one of the schemers?"

"It looks like it."

She smiled. "Quite a bombshell—for everyone."

"You don't look as if it is."

"Oh Martin, you mean my book? That hardly matters. Let's forget feminist first principles and go for the truth. I can be flexible. Historians ought to be, don't you think?"

"I suppose so."

"Well, you'll hardly feel any obligations to Sellick after this. How about forming a partnership with me instead?"

"A literary partnership?"

"Not just literary. Not now. But, if you like, we'll get at the truth—as historians—along the way."

"I like very much."

"Good. I hoped you would. After all, you were right about Strafford and I was wrong. Where is his Postscript now?"

"Safe."

"With these people—the Bennetts?"

"No. But secure. Don't worry. We can collect it tomorrow."

"Fine." She paused. "So—what do you think happened to Strafford and his nephew?"

"To Strafford, I don't know. But if it wasn't murder, why are the Couchmans so upset about my investigations? As for Ambrose, it's too big a coincidence to believe he drowned accidentally just after sending me that letter. Timothy knew about it, remember."

"True. But do you see Timothy being able to kill a man?"

"Frankly, no. Nor his father. But there's some connexion, I'm sure of it."

"So what do we do about it?"

"Decide when you're satisfied the Postscript's authentic. Substantiate what we can, then publish—and be damned."

Did I believe that hopeful itinerary as I sketched it over the dinner table? Did I believe that Eve believed it? There wasn't really any need to do either. For the moment, she'd stopped me caring about the end of the road. For the moment, being with her was all that mattered. The Strafford mystery was as good as any pretext—so long as we needed one.

What happened when we returned to Book End that night blended a clutch of private pleasures. The ice-maidenly historienne gave herself again to the down-at-heel outsider. A queen rewarded her subject for his tribute of the truth. An absentee hospitality was deliciously abused. A sexual act became a metaphor for a dozen other urgings and desires. I knew them all, but they made no difference. Though you know the sea is deep, the white horses still call.

And even the metaphors omitted one, crucial meaning. We sustained a continuum of which Couchman's conduct in Durban and mine in Axborough were both part. Somehow, in our different ways, we were all accessories to a betrayal of trust. But whose betrayal? Whose trust?

We enacted a different dream, in the borrowed bedroom above Topsham's period streets, from the one on the beach. Different—but the same, in a way. Less impulsive, more portentous. When we made love that night, a deed was done more shocking than any daring sexual refinement—though Eve's daring did shock me, several times, before the night was out.

I knew, of course, that I was compromising Strafford as much as myself, but I didn't know—couldn't have guessed—what that really meant. Not that it would have stopped me. Eve, in giving herself to me, prevailed over all other considerations. My only thought to the future was to ask myself whether it would always be as it was then. Even that, as it turned out, was the wrong question. Substitute ever for always. Then I'd have been nearer the mark.

Dawn. I propped open the bedroom window and watched the estuary slither into day. A mackerel sky and the grey Exe widening towards sea. A few lights on the western shore. Gulls wheeling and screeching over the mud-steeped pontoons of the riverside. An insipid summer morning in an obscure locale. Topsham and Port Edward seemed, in that moment, the same: refuges from reality, bolt holes in some wrinkle of a coastline, hidden settings for acts which would stay with the perpetrators longer than they could ever imagine.

Behind me, elegant even in sleep, one arm over the coverlet, hair fanned across the pillow in the way—yes, damn it, in just the way—I'd dreamed, Eve held the wonder of a day I hadn't thought to see. Well-used to disappointment, resigned to failure, I was already accustoming myself to unexpected triumph. The draw had been her far-away beauty shaped by her far-seeing mind. The prize was the mystery of her pliant flesh become familiar, that morning and every morning, become mine beyond hope.

Eve stirred and stretched and smiled—and proved she was really there.

"What are you thinking?" she said with a decorous yawn.

"Just that I never dared to hope it would come to this."

"And now that it has?"

"Now that it has, I'm in some danger of becoming a happy man."

Eve stepped from the bed and wrapped herself in the same dragon-patterned kimono I'd seen her in once at Cambridge—a light year's worth of weeks before. She walked across to where I was standing by the window, put her arm round my waist and followed my gaze out over the dew-sheened roofs of the town.

"To tell you a secret," she said, "I expected us to wake up together in Norfolk, not Devon."

"So did I, at one point." I smiled ruefully. She smiled consolingly. "It's strange how things turn out."

"Stranger than you'd think." With that enigmatic echo, she went to make some coffee.

For breakfast, Eve cooked ham and eggs the way she'd learned in California. We ate them in Dr Sutcliffe's intricately automated kitchen and laid plans for the day.

"The Postscript has me on tenterhooks," Eve said, sipping her coffee while I cleared my plate.

"Easily solved. I'll collect it this morning."

"You could fetch your stuff from the Bennetts while you're about it—if you want to stay."

I smiled. "You know the answer to that." She smiled back. "Okay. It's a good idea. I'll go straightaway."

"There's no hurry. But it would be convenient if you were out this morning."

"Two-timing me already?" I joked.

"Professor Pollard arranged to call at eleven to discuss how I'm finding things at Exeter. I made the appointment before I knew what I'd be doing today."

"Lucky Professor Pollard."

"Don't worry. It won't take long. And the Professor must be sixty if he's a day. But I don't want him to jump to any conclusions on Petra's behalf—especially the right ones. Why not take my car? You could be back by lunchtime."

I readily agreed. A quick whirl round St David's station and the Bennett household suited my purpose. By 10.30, I was on my way.

I collected the Postscript from the station without difficulty, relieved to find it in place in its locker. Then I drove straight to the Bennetts', intending to collect my luggage, make a few lame excuses and return to Topsham with my booty. But it wasn't to be as simple as that.

Nick opened the door and I could see from his expression that he was angry. In so calm a man, it was worrying.

"Martin—where the hell have you been?"

"Sorry I didn't phone, Nick. You know how it is." It was clear he didn't.

"I'll tell you how it's been here. We've been bloody burgled!"

That feeling: I'd had it before. Nausea. A whirling sense of accelerating motion. Of ground slipping from under my feet. It began with Nick's remark, splitting the euphoria of a self-satisfied morning.

We went inside. Hester was cleaning and dusting, re-arranging with excessive energy. She didn't look happy. Their usually carefree household had an edgy, shaken atmosphere. Something had been violated and I could believe from their expressions that it was our friendship.

"What happened?" I asked.

"When Hester came home yesterday afternoon," Nick said grimly, "she found the house had been ransacked. Drawers opened, contents all over the floor, cupboards and wardrobes emptied. It was a God-awful mess. She's been working like a demon since then to clean it up." He put his arm round her and she stopped what she was doing, looked for a moment pained by the memory of the experience.

"It was terrible, Martin," she said. "Really. Not so much the mess as the knowledge that somebody had been through everything—handling my clothes, touching all our most private possessions. It makes them seem—soiled." She shuddered.

"Was much taken?" I asked.

"Not a thing," said Nick. He looked at me darkly. "That was the strangest part of it. Camera, stereo, jewellery—all the stuff you'd expect a burglar to take. Even some cash in the kitchen. All still here. Not just left, but untouched. As if that wasn't what they were looking for."

"Then what?"

Nick sat down. "Well, I don't know. Do you?"

"Of course not."

"We expected you back last night," Hester put in.

"I'm sorry. There wasn't an opportunity to ring. Circumstances were . . . fraught."

"They were bloody fraught here too," said Nick. "To tell you the truth, Martin, I don't think we were burgled so much as searched. After all, as I told the police, everything we can account for is still here. There's only your belongings that anything could be missing from." His emphasis spoke volumes.

"I've nothing of the slightest value here." A defensive, factual remark. My only valuable possession was outside in Eve's car, safe—for the moment. But Nick was right. Their intruder had been looking for something of mine: the Postscript. It had to be. The Bennetts' home, like Ambrose's before them, ransacked, sullied in a frantic search for something that wasn't there. Relief at my foresight in using the left luggage locker was overtaken by a sickening fear of the implications. I'd only told one person that I even had the Postscript. None of which was any consolation to Nick.

"We're not fools," he said. "We're supposed to be your friends. Since the inquest, you've hardly said a word to us. Then, last night, you go missing immediately after the house is broken into. What would you make of it?"

"I'm sorry about the break-in. Maybe it is my fault. I seem to attract this sort of thing. But I can't explain anything, because I don't understand it myself." I paused. "Look, I must go up to my room."

"Go right ahead." Nick's sarcasm echoed after me. He and Hester hadn't deserved any of this. They had a right to expect the truth from me. But I wasn't ready to tell it to them. I was only just daring to face it myself.

I raced upstairs. Hester appeared to have put my room in order. My clothes were folded in neat piles on the bed. I pulled my bag out and found the Memoir where I'd left it. So there could be no question. Someone knew enough to distinguish that from the Postscript. Someone who'd also searched Lodge Cottage, who could have bundled Ambrose into the Teign, who knew what I'd only told to . . . Eve.

Ah, Eve. The hint of mockery in her smile. A deception more naked even than her body on the beach. I cast desperately for a way to discount the suspicion which had begun to grow in my mind. So beautiful. So mysterious. So it couldn't be, could it? Coincidence. Confusion. Anything would do rather than what was already looming over me with all the implacability of an unpalatable truth.

I raced from the house, leaving Nick and Hester to despair of the friend they thought they knew. I drove like a madman through the city and south to Topsham. I wanted nothing so much as to see Eve and hear her say that my fears were groundless. All she needed to do was say so and I'd believe, I knew, whatever I had to believe to explain it away.

But, as I accelerated past the Topsham town sign, I felt my headlong anxiety ebb slightly. It wasn't enough just to see Eve and hear her voice. I had to think first, prepare my case so that it wouldn't sound like the accusation it really was.

I pulled off the High Street in Topsham and parked in a narrow lane leading down towards the river. Then I set off on foot by a circuitous route towards Book End, allowing myself time to breathe and think on the way, to gulp in the breeze from the Exe and scour my mind for alternatives. If there'd been any, I'd have found them.

Ahead of me, on the left, The Passage House Inn was filling rapidly as lunchtime drew on. Laughing groups had occupied the tables in front of it, their chinking glasses out of tune with my mood. All I wanted to do was get by them quietly.

But, as I approached, two people stepped from the doorway of the pub and I stopped dead in my tracks. Eve, smiling, relaxed, in control—as always, at ease—as ever. And, at her side, not white-haired Professor Pollard, but Timothy Couchman, slickly dressed, sleekly groomed, donning dark glasses against the sun and pausing to stub out a cigarette with an expensive grate of leather on slate.

A little way down the road was parked the red Porsche. The two walked slowly away from me towards it, talking and laughing about something as they went. Timothy slipped his arm round Eve's waist. She was dressed in a simple yellow blouse and the white jeans she'd worn the day before: somehow that made it worse. As I watched, Timothy slid his hand down her hip, ran it round the swell of her bottom and patted her lightly—a casual, proprietorial signal to stay on her side of the car while he got in and unlocked the door for her. Typical of him, in a way, to get in first. Awful for me, in every way, to see how easily Eve accepted his clammy attentions.

As he rounded the bonnet of the Porsche and went to open the driver's door, he saw me. His jaw dropped, his eyes narrowed and then he smiled—with hideous condescension. Eve looked towards me as well. Our eyes met, but there was nothing there. Her face was a mask, her expression mannered to the exclusion of meaning. I could have looked forever into her beautiful eyes and seen only my own reflection, lost, distorted and alone.

"Martin, old man," said Timothy with extravagant hypocrisy, "it's great to see you." Eve spoke to him under her breath and his expression hardened.

From the night I'd given Timothy the chance to see Ambrose's letter we'd been heading, I now knew, for this moment. Timothy in search of the Postscript which incriminated his father. Ambrose drowned, his house searched. But still no Postscript. Inconveniently, I laid my hands on it. So, get me out of the way and search another house. Failing that, bribe me—if not with money then with something my past suggested I would find irresistible.

I had to get away, had to flee the scene of our meeting—a meeting of lies, a glimpsing of minds. I turned to run, to run as far and as fast as I could from what my new awareness told me about the mendacity of others and the ruin of myself. Even as I turned, I heard Timothy shout after me: "Radford—stop!" but I didn't look back. He'd have realized, as I had, that their plans had foundered at the last gasp on an unscheduled encounter, that however satisfying my discomfort, it was premature, because I still had the Postscript and couldn't now be persuaded—only forced—to give it up.

I heard his feet ringing on the tarmac as he pursued me. He wasn't far behind. But as we ran past the pub, a group of people came through the door and spilled out into the road. I threaded through them, but heard a collision in my wake. Glancing round, I saw Timothy, cream trousers darkly stained with beer, cursing a bemused, bearded young man in tee shirt and jeans. Beyond the gesticulating group, Eve stood silently by the car, her eyes looking past them straight at me—solemn, unabashed, candidly gazing. I paused and struggled for an instant with the message of her look—distant, discerning and perversely disappointed. Then I ran on.

I got back to the car—Eve's car, aware of the irony but taking from it some grim comfort. It was a petty revenge, but it was all I was capable of. I jumped in and drove fast in the direction of Exeter. The speed was a relief. It outdistanced my senses.

I went back to the Bennetts' house—a flying visit but an essential one. My mood had changed since our edgy encounter earlier and they seemed to notice. They were having lunch in the kitchen when I arrived.

"Nick . . . Hester, I can't stop to explain anything. It's all gone wrong, but I've still a chance to put it right. It's true about the break-in. It was on my account. But don't worry. It won't happen again, because I'm leaving straightaway. I really am sorry I let you in for all this, believe me."

"We only want to help you, Martin," said Hester.

"But first," put in Nick, "you owe us an explanation."

I couldn't argue with that, but I couldn't comply either. "We'll have to hold it over. There just isn't time." I ran upstairs before Nick could protest and bundled together my possessions. Into one bag with the Postscript went Strafford's copy of *Satires of Circumstance*, and, of course, the Memoir: not just an assemblage of evidence but now my loyal talismans.

Downstairs, Nick had noticed the car. "Whose is the MG?" he asked when I reappeared, ready to go.

"A friend's."

"But surely you're still suspended?"

I was past him to the door. "I said I couldn't explain now. I promise I will, when I can. But not now. There's just too much to be done."

"Martin . . ."

I didn't, couldn't, stop to listen. I ran up the short path to the pavement, flung my bags into the car and went round the other side to get in.

"Hold on, Martin," Nick shouted from the path, "you can surely . . ."

I climbed in, slammed the door and started up. Nick was walking towards me, bafflement changing to anger in his face, when I accelerated away, promising silently to return soon and make amends, unaware then of what would intervene to prevent me. The last I saw of Nick was in the rear view mirror, hands on hips, staring after me.

There was only one direction to go: east, to Miston. It had been inevitable from the moment I left Topsham, from the moment I realized how I'd been taken in just as much as Strafford. He'd looked to Elizabeth for guidance—so would I.

Unlike Strafford, of course, I had no intention of sparing her the truth. That was no longer realistic. Too many people —including me—had suffered in the cause of concealment.

The afternoon was fading imperceptibly into evening as I propelled the MG up Harting Hill and across the dip slope of the Downs towards Miston. There was an air of homecoming in the very landscape, a sensation of overdue return, an awareness of nemesis tracking me down the lanes from the west towards our resting place. Whatever lay ahead, there was now no turning back.

Eight

No turning back. That was right. After I'd driven into the drive at Quarterleigh and stopped the car, I listened to the subsiding tick of the engine cooling, while the blandishments of a soft summer evening closed around me. I hesitated, stayed where I was, struggled to adjust to my own sudden transition, wrestled with ways of taking the next, irretrievable step.

In the end, it was just as well that my mind was made up for me. The door of the house opened and Dora, plumply wrapped in a flour-smeared apron, came to investigate the noise of the car, her quizzical expression framed by the honeysuckle arch. Seeing who it was, she marched out.

"Come to disturb us again, 'ave you?" she said, with a fonder edge than I'd normally had from her.

"'Fraid so, Dora."

"Then you'd best come in. The mistress is 'ome, but Mr Henry ain't, if you takes my meaning."

"You realize I'm not approved of, then?"

"Course I do, boy. But you can't be all bad if he disapproves of you, so I'd best not turn you away. The mistress'd never let me 'ear the last of it."

Doubting if any of us would ever hear the last of it either way, I followed her into the house and through into the conservatory. Elizabeth was asleep there, in her reclining chair, some embroidery on her lap and a book lying on a stool beside her, with a marker about two thirds the way through. Dora touched her elbow and she opened her eyes at once, without starting, as if she'd not really been asleep at all.

"Why Martin," she said, "what a pleasant surprise. Just when I was beginning to think you'd forgotten all about me. Sit down and tell me what you've been doing—I'm dying to hear all about it."

"It won't make pleasant listening," I began. "Are you sure you shouldn't follow your son's advice about me?"

She smiled indulgently. "I'm too old to learn new ways, Martin. I've always believed in trusting my own judgement, not that of others. But why so solemn? Don't forget you promised to tell me whatever you found out."

"Yes, I did. But I didn't know then what it was that I'd find."

"And what was it?"

I leant forward and she looked at me intently and attentively. "There's no easy way to say it. Strafford left a further written statement: a postscript to his memoir, stating the full facts of his case. Those facts are not what you or I thought You'll find them deeply disturbing. They don't reflect well . . . on your family."

"Nevertheless, I'd like to know what they are." She didn't flinch.

"You ought to know that, if it had been up to Strafford, you'd never have seen it. It contains all that he decided not to tell you when he visited you just before his death."

"I see." She remained unshakeable.

"And his decision may well have been the best one. We could still honour it." Her very calm had shamed me into hesitation. "We could leave it in its parcel, unopened, or burn it, unread. That must be up to you."

"My dear, I don't think either of us could do that now, could we?"

"I suppose not, but it might be for the best. This discovery has brought nothing but unhappiness so far."

"Who made the discovery—you?"

"No. Strafford's nephew—the one I told you about. But he drowned shortly afterwards."

Elizabeth put her hand to her mouth. "Dear, dear. I am sorry to hear that. How did it happen?"

"An accident—according to the inquest."

"You sound sceptical."

"I am. I suppose that's why I'm here really." A lie, but I couldn't face telling her the truth, that spite was driving me harder and faster than concern for Ambrose ever had. "And that's why I think you should now read what Strafford once kept from you."

What was it that made Elizabeth agree so readily? Curiosity, I suppose, as much as anything. Once she knew more evidence existed, she had to see it. It was too late then, far too late, to destroy it. However terrible the prospect, she had to look through the door she hadn't known was there.

I fetched the Postscript from the car. Elizabeth had moved into the lounge and was waiting for me there, in her armchair by the fireplace. I sat opposite her and accepted her offer of whisky. Drained by the journey and what had gone before, it was all I was capable of doing: drinking steadily while she read slowly and assiduously through Strafford's final statement, eyes sharp behind her gold-rimmed spectacles, lips pursed with a concentration which defied interpretation. Dora asked if I wanted anything to eat before she went home, but I declined the offer, just sat with Elizabeth, willing her and nerving us through all the pages of Strafford's fate. Her cat came and stretched himself between us, bemused by his mistress's distraction. I thought of Sir Gerald Couchman, seated in the chair I now occupied, warming himself with the same whisky, contemplating the good fortune and outrageous fraud which had brought him Elizabeth as a wife. No doubt as he often had, though with nothing in my case to congratulate myself on, I slowly drifted off to a deep but troubled sleep.

"I've finished, Martin." I started awake. Elizabeth had touched my elbow and was stooping over me with a concerned look in her red-rimmed eyes. "I think you must have been dreaming, my dear."

I pulled myself upright in the chair. "I'm sorry. Have I been asleep long?"

"An hour or so, I think, but I've been concentrating on the Postscript."

"Yes, of course." I rubbed my forehead. "What do you think of it?"

I noticed that darkness had fallen outside and the cat had left us. Elizabeth sat down with a gentle sigh. "I don't know what to say." She was visibly upset. "It says much for Edwin that he wanted to keep this from me, but you were right to tell me, nevertheless."

I strove to find words of reassurance. "Just as you were right to tell me we shouldn't let the past become a burden."

She smiled faintly. "But it's not the past that hurts in this—it's the truth."

"You think it is that then—the truth?"

"Oh yes, without doubt." She inhaled sharply, as if to steady herself. "If you'll excuse me Martin, I think I'll go to bed now. It's late and I must rest, if I can. We'll talk again in the morning."

"Whatever you say." I watched her rise and walk to the door, her spryness displaced by a hunched dejection. "Elizabeth," I called after her. "Will you be all right?"

She turned and summoned a smile. "Don't worry, my dear. An old lady must collect her thoughts. But I will be all right. It's just that I've become a stranger to disappointment. And by the tidings you've brought, my nearest and dearest have disappointed me—to say the very least."

"I'm sorry."

"Don't be. But do be here in the morning. I may need you to hold my hand."

"You can count on me."

"Goodnight then." She left me at that moment, alone in the room, gazing at the Postscript where she'd put it aside. A sleepless night—the only safe kind—stretched ahead of me, a lone, dark watch over Strafford's legacy and last wish: Elizabeth's well-being. I promised Strafford and myself that night that she really could count on me, that I would never allow myself to disappoint her as I'd disappointed others. It was a promise worth making and, as it turned out, one well worth keeping.

Sunday: a sabbath in Sussex, a fresh breeze stirring the rhododendrons in the garden, laundered clouds billowing innocently in the sky, a cottage beneath the Downs where order and calm seemed states of nature. Seemed so and yet were not so, for something was seething in the morning air. The swirling cloud had a quality of whirling acceleration, the church bells struck a strident, frantic note. Normality was out of tune. We were glissading on a plane.

"Will you accompany me to church, Martin?" There was no hint of irony in Elizabeth's voice. She wore an elegant grey frock and a wide-brimmed felt hat. Her expression suggested a disciplined orderliness exerting itself to keep chaos at bay.

We walked to the church in silence, though there were many nods for Elizabeth to acknowledge on the way in. There we sang and prayed in the full-throated, self-regarding company of a wealthy rural congregation.

Filing out afterwards, Elizabeth was obliged to exchange pleasantries with a succession of local churchgoers. Her friendly responses had a strained edge apparent only to me. I was introduced as a grand nephew whose lineage we mercifully didn't have to explain. Only when we were alone in the lane did Elizabeth feel able to express her genuine feelings.

"I'm glad we went," she said. "It was something I needed to do—to prove that not everything had turned upside down."

"Did you think it had?"

"It seemed to—when I read the Postscript."

We'd reached the gates of Quarterleigh. "If it's any consolation, I feel that too—though less personally."

She clasped my hand in hers, cold despite the heat of the day. "It is some consolation, my dear, though alas not enough."

"Would you like to talk about it?"

"I think I must. But first we must address ourselves to Dora's lunch. That, I feel sure, will be as solid as ever."

It was, though neither of us had much stomach for it. As if to prevent me questioning her on other matters, Elizabeth asked about Ambrose's death and I told her everything I knew. Not just Ambrose's contention that he was being watched, but the letter he'd sent me and Timothy's sight of it. Not just the stark facts of his drowning but the insistent belief that it couldn't have been any more an accident than his uncle's death. It was clear that none of the implications escaped Elizabeth—she grew more grave and thoughtful still. My only silence was reserved for Eve. I wasn't yet ready to admit to anyone how easily and completely she'd deceived me. I kidded myself that Elizabeth didn't need to know about it, but that wasn't, of course, the reason for not speaking of it.

After lunch, we went into the garden and sat in deckchairs down by the brook. Dora served coffee there, sunlight played on the water and ducks dabbled beneath the wooded bank opposite us. Our gloom seemed deepened, not lightened, by the summer idyll. Its presence had the force of an eclipse; a black, cosmic shape across the sun.

"You'll want to know how I feel, now Edwin's truth is known," Elizabeth began. "Indeed, it's good of you not to have pressed the point before."

"I had no right to do that."

She smiled weakly. "Perhaps not. But you should be told. The difficulty has been to . . . order a response."

"I can imagine."

"I doubt it." Her tone was sharp, but instantly softened. "Forgive me. I didn't mean to speak harshly. There's been so much for me to . . . understand. And, in all fairness, I doubt if you can imagine what it really means. If I believe Edwin, then my husband becomes a scoundrel, my marriage a farce and my family . . . illegitimate. If I believe Edwin, there can be no excusing what Gerald did . . . what Henry may still be doing."

"And do you believe Edwin?"

"Yes, Martin. I do now. At first, I resisted. Who could not resist the demolition of everything they'd ever taken for granted about their family and their past? What Edwin discovered about Gerald and Henry, about some of his colleagues and some of my friends, seemed too awful to contemplate. I didn't want to believe it. But, the more I read, the less deniable it became. If what the Postscript told me was incredible, then every other explanation was even less credible. In the end, I couldn't pretend even to myself that it wasn't the truth. The pity of it is that I didn't realize that a long time ago. Or, perhaps, as Edwin perceived, that was a mercy."

"In what way?"

"In the way that Edwin was right to withhold the truth 26 years ago. Whatever the lie that was behind our life, Gerald and I were happy together and nothing—absolutely nothing—can change that now. I'm glad Gerald died before I had to face the truth about him. He deceived me, yes, but he was a good husband, if I may use the word. But not to his real wife. That's the worst of it: the hideous unknown of a discarded wife confined in a lunatic asylum, dying without her husband giving the event a second thought, without even knowing that he had a son by her."

"That at least he couldn't be blamed for." I struggled to find some remission of Couch's guilt for Elizabeth's sake. "It was Strafford who decided to keep that from him."

"And so we'll never know what Gerald would have done for him had he realized he existed."

"Never. It'll remain a mystery. Perhaps that's for the best."

"Perhaps. But Gerald's son isn't a mystery any more, is he? I presume he is the same Leo Sellick as hired you?"

"Of course."

"Then he is clearly a wronged man: an innocent party in all this if anyone is. We owe him something. You've met him, you know him. What is it that he wants?"

"I don't know. The simplest way to find out would be to ask him. But I'm not sure I'm ready to do that yet. To say the least, Sellick's been less than frank with me, but, technically, I remain in his employment. It's an invidious position."

Elizabeth leant forward in her deckchair and put her hand on my arm. "My dear, I quite understand that. But you must see that I have to know—and that I have to rely on your good offices for the purpose."

I remembered my secret pledge. "I'll do whatever I can to help. I suppose it sounds absurd to say that I feel bound by Strafford's last words, but I do."

Elizabeth's look was full of meaning. "It doesn't sound absurd. In fact, it's the kind of support I can't do without at the moment."

"So—what can I do?" I didn't pause to consider how little my pledge had once signified.

Elizabeth seemed rejuvenated by the thought of action. "Two things, Martin. Two things that should have been done a long time ago. I want to know the truth—the whole truth, without prevarication—from my son. And I want to offer Gerald's other son whatever form of restitution I can. It's the least that Edwin deserves of me."

"How do you propose to go about it?"

"I suggest I invite Mr Sellick here—to meet his father's family."

It was reasoned, caring, human reaction to the problem, but its appeal bore little examination. "Will he accept?"

"I asked myself that. I wondered why an elderly, wealthy South African should be interested in reconciliation with those who were treated a great deal better by his father than he was himself. But consider the frustration he must have felt after Edwin disappeared from Madeira and the mystification the Memoir must have caused him. We don't know what he made of it, or why he commissioned your research, unless it was an understandable desire to establish whether Edwin really was his father. I think Mr Sellick deserves the benefit of the doubt as far as his motives are concerned."

"It'll be intriguing to see if he accepts your invitation."

"Well, if he does, I want to know Henry's side of it before he arrives. What I propose is that we should despatch a letter to Mr Sellick and, meanwhile, establish with Henry exactly what did happen in 1951."

I was carried along by the buoyant optimism of Elizabeth's intentions. That evening, we composed a letter to Sellick: a brief, unvarnished statement by me of Ambrose's death and the discovery of a Postscript revealing Sellick's own connexion with Strafford, accompanied by an invitation from Elizabeth to visit her at Quarterleigh and heal the breach.

Once the letter was sealed, we agreed to deposit all the evidence in Elizabeth's safe: a substantial, four-square combination version stored in what had been Couch's study, little used since his day. The Memoir and the Postscript joined lesser family papers inside. Before we closed it, Elizabeth pointed to a velvet bag on a low shelf and said that it contained the revolver and harness which—she now knew—Strafford had returned on Sellick's behalf in 1951. Such things were best shut away and, when Elizabeth locked it and spun the combination, I felt a little less insecure than I had.

Then, over laced cocoa, we planned the next move. Because of the Silver Jubilee holiday, we couldn't post the letter to Sellick until Wednesday. What better time to tackle Henry than the present?

"I'd get nothing out of him, my dear," Elizabeth said. "He doesn't think I know where my own interests lie, let alone his. I think it must be you—if you'll agree."

"I'm not sure. You know how little time he has for me, what with Helen and everything."

"Exactly. That's why it must be you. Edwin was right in his judgement of Henry. He needs to learn a little humility. We're none of us too old for that."

"Very well. I'll try. But don't blame me if it doesn't work."

"I shan't. I'm grateful, believe me. At the moment, I don't think I could talk to my son, not after all that I've found out about him."

"When and where should I see him?"

"As soon as possible. Why not tomorrow? I know from Letty that they'll be in London. Henry has to be there for Tuesday's ceremonies and receptions, you see."

"But what do I say to him?"

"Tell him all that we know. Tell him that I have invited Mr Sellick to visit me and that I need to know Henry's part in all this before Mr Sellick arrives. Point out that you are my agent in this matter—I'll give you a letter to that effect. Warn him that if he doesn't tell me what, as his mother, I'm entitled to know, I can do nothing to protect him from Mr Selleck's anger."

"I think he'll deny everything and say nothing."

"That may be so. But he must be given a chance to redeem himself."

I slept unexpectedly well that night and set off early the following morning, driving north through the soft commuter land of Surrey towards London. Strafford's spirit was still with me, urging the vehicle of his uncertain retribution towards its destination, and Eve's memory was waiting to taunt me as soon as I left the refuge of Quarterleigh. Why had she done nothing about my taking her car? What were she and Timothy up to now?

It was a cool day in London, but the city was crowded from

the suburbs in: brightly dressed crowds, bunting in the streets, signs of preparation everywhere for the Jubilee. The carnival mood depressed me. It seemed the worst of times to be there, somehow vaguely indecent to hound Henry on such a day, somehow too much like collecting debts on a Sunday.

Since his children had left home and his political star had risen during the Heath era, Henry had moved into a prestigious Regency residence in Oakment Square, off Cheyne Walk, behind Chelsea Embankment: a place of cooing doves and windowboxes, a fountain playing beneath a statue of the elder Pitt on a small green in the centre of the square, nothing stirring behind the tall windows and broad, brass-knockered doors.

Letty, my former mother-in-law, answered the door. Poor Letty: the precocious young girl with a dimpled grin, who I recalled from glimpses of her wedding photographs, had become a stout, grey-haired lady with a perpetually worried expression.

I tried the impossible, putting her at her ease. "Hello, Letty. How are you?"

"What do you want?" Her tone was neutral but apprehensive.

"I'd like to see Henry, if he's in."

"What on earth do you want with him?" She became more panicky.

"There are things we have to discuss. Has he told you that we've met once or twice recently?"

"Of course." She replied too quickly for me to be sure it was true. "You'd better come in. He's upstairs working."

"On a bank holiday?" I tried to make small talk as I followed her into the hall.

"Yes. He's very busy at present." She hesitated at the foot of the stairs. "Martin, will you come in here for a moment?" She led the way into a front room; the initiative was unlike her.

It was a palely decorated reception room with a rarely used air. The curtains hung stiffly at the windows, the leather-padded furniture shone as in a showroom. Letty closed the door behind us with an excess of furtiveness.

"What is it?" I asked.

"Martin, I'm worried—as you can see. Henry didn't tell me you'd met recently. I learned that from his mother. So I've no idea what's going on between you. But recently Henry's been deeply unhappy. He's overworking and—which I shouldn't tell you—drinking too much. The firm's having some difficulty—which he refuses to explain—and Timothy's no help at all. The party's making great demands on him: too many late night debates, too many councils of war at Flood Street. I'm not sure where it'll end."

"All meat and drink to Henry, surely?"

"Not anymore. He's been moody for a couple of months now. In the past fortnight, it's got much worse. I can hardly talk to him." She was wringing her hands as she spoke.

"What can I . . ."

"It's something to do with whatever's brought you into contact with him, Martin. I know it is. Don't tell me what it is—I don't want to know. All I'm asking you is to leave my husband alone."

"I can't do that, Letty." I felt sorry to have to say it.

"Don't you think you've hurt my family enough already?" She sounded genuinely pained.

I couldn't respond. "Can I see him now?"

"Why not?" Her voice sank with despair. "His study's on the top floor . . . Oh, but you know that."

"Yes." I felt guilty to admit it. "One thing, Letty. You say Henry's been unhappy lately, but it's been worse in the past fortnight?"

"Much worse."

"Did that seem to follow any specific event?"

"No. He came back from a trade conference in Torquay in a black depression—and he hasn't shaken it off. I'm sure you know why."

"I don't know, believe me. How long was he in Torquay?"

"Just a couple of nights. He came back a fortnight ago today."

Torquay, a fortnight before: May 23rd, the day after Ambrose Strafford drowned in Dewford, only ten miles from where Henry was conferring on trade. The coincidence impelled me up the stairs.

Henry had set himself up as a target for me right from the first. Never a step wrong, never short of friends in the right places, never for a moment perturbed by his own hypocrisy. I thought, as I climbed the stairs, of all the reasons why I hated him. A public proponent of probity and economy whose business thrived on bribes and favours. A man of inherited wealth who lectured others on the value of hard work. An outraged father happy to overlook his own notorious peccadilloes. A politician prepared to toe the party line on anything and everything in the belief that office was the reward for all good sycophants—and who'd been proved correct. And now I had evidence that he was also ready to bribe, lie and perhaps even murder his way out of an hereditary embarrassment. For those and all the other ways he embodied the false morality I'd supposedly offended, I hated Henry Couchman.

He was by the window, nursing a whisky glass in his palm, the air thick with stale cigar smoke, the desk scattered with papers, his stare fixed on the outside world.

"I'd like to have a word with you, Henry," I said.

I thought he'd fling the glass at me or try to throw me out, but even his glare lacked fire. He slumped down in an armchair by the window. "I've been expecting you," he said through clenched teeth.

"Why's that?"

He looked at me wearily, with bloodshot eyes. "Call it intuition . . . or just experience. Your kind are all the same."

"Can I sit down?"

"Why not?" From his slur I judged he'd been drinking all morning. "Obviously my wife didn't think to turn away the bloody little lecher who disgraced my daughter."

I sat in a chair on the other side of the desk from him and tried to ignore the insult. "Your mother sent me."

He laughed—a forced guffaw with a surly, intoxicated edge to it. "So she's on your side too: the stupid old bitch."

Suddenly, I felt angry. "I don't think you've the right to talk like that about her."

"Oh you don't?" He smiled unpleasantly. "Radford, why

don't you tell me what your game is? I'm sick of the sight and sound of you?"

"I'll tell you—if you'll listen."

"I'll listen. But God, I need a drink to stomach it." He pulled down a bottle from a trolley beside the chair and poured some whisky into his glass. "Make it bloody good, or, I warn you, you'll regret the day you tried to threaten me."

"Threaten you with what?"

"Stuff your word games, Radford. That's all you ever were, mouth—well, except where schoolgirls were concerned. Get on with it before my patience runs out."

"All right. I've found the Postscript, Henry. The document Strafford left, which his nephew discovered. I'm sure your son told you all about it." I paused for him to respond, but he just twisted in his chair and stared out of the window in silence. "It relates everything that happened when Strafford returned to this country in 1951, up until the day before his death. You know, everything: your father's bigamy, Strafford's total innocence, your botched attempts to blackmail him, your abortive break-in at his nephew's cottage in Devon. All this after you'd claimed never even to have met Strafford, after you'd denounced him as a philanderer, after you'd spent years lecturing me on morality while not even knowing the meaning of the word."

Henry turned and looked at me with hooded indifference. He seemed unusually self-controlled. "I warned you to spell it out quickly, Radford. Is that all you've got to say?"

"Not quite." I held my nerve. "Unlike Strafford, I decided not to leave your mother in ignorance of her husband's and her son's true characters, so I've shown her the Postscript. She knows everything now, you see. That's why she sent me to see you." I rose and handed him Elizabeth's note.

He scanned it briefly, then crumpled it in his hand. "The old man protected her too well," he said. "Cocooned down there in Sussex in her lilywhite world. She understands nothing." The last word was bitterly emphasized. "So, you've fooled an old woman. That's about your mark, isn't it?"

"Listen, Henry. Your secret's out, but that's not the worst of it. There's more you don't know. There's more that Strafford kept even from your father. There was a son by his South African marriage."

"You're trying it on, Radford—and it won't work."

"It will work. I'm not relying on the Postscript for proof. Your father's other son—your half-brother—is alive and well. He hired me to dig into Strafford's past. It was his appearance in Madeira that prompted Strafford to contact your father again in 1951. And your mother's now invited him to visit her and meet the family who spurned him." (I didn't care to let slip that Henry still had time to prevent the invitation being sent.)

Henry jumped from his chair. "This is a bloody lie." He brought his hands down onto the desk with a crash and stooped over it, face working to comprehend and suborn me. "You've cooked up this nonsense to deceive my mother and blacken my family's name. All because we didn't let you get away with screwing that little schoolgirl. All because . . ."

"Shut up, Henry." My sharp but level-toned interruption quietened him. "It's no good trying to bluster your way out of this. The Postscript exists. Leo Sellick lives. The proof is out in the open at last. You're finished, unless . . ."

He sank down in the chair behind the desk. "Unless what?"

"Unless you volunteer what we're going to find out in the end anyway."

"Which is?"

"The part you played in Strafford's supposedly accidental death in 1951."

Henry smirked disconcertingly. "Boy, you just don't understand do you? Do you really think it's as simple as that? Perhaps you and Strafford have more in common than I thought. My father once told me that fools are dangerous, because they don't understand what's in their own interests. You must be a case in point. To think I let you marry my daughter."

"You weren't doing me any favours. I was impressed—yes, God help me, actually impressed—by your family: wealth, political connexions, a knighthood behind you. But what does it all come down to? A coward who got lucky, a bigamous marriage, an inflated, bombastic life built on a lie. And you —Henry Couchman, industrial baron, government minister, pillar of the establishment—what does that make you? Nothing but the bastard son of a . . ."

He swung his chair round, flanked the desk and grabbed my shirt collar. His face, flushed, contorted and angry, was close to mine. His arm shook with the force of his grip. "Shut your mouth, Radford. You haven't the right to speak to me like that. I don't know why I don't . . ."

"Push me under a train? Help me into a river? Why don't you try something like that? It seems to be your speciality."

He wrenched his arm away from me, seemed for a moment shocked by the implications of his action. "So that's it," he muttered. "Christ, you really don't understand."

"Why don't you explain then?"

He walked slowly to the window and spoke with his back turned. "Tell me what my mother wants."

"She wants to know the truth from you about Strafford *before* she meets Sellick."

"Then she's a fool. Like you, she doesn't understand."

"If you wait until Sellick arrives, it'll be too late. Believe me, I know the man."

Suddenly he seemed to cave in, looking at me with a distress that was almost pitiful. "You know already, don't you? You're just dragging it out to punish me for ruining you."

"That's right." I pushed my luck. "Sellick has proof that Strafford's death wasn't an accident. He'll be coming soon to nail you."

"But it was. That's all it was. A horrible bloody accident." He put his hand to his forehead.

"If you can be that sure . . . you must have been there."

He slid his hand down to his mouth. "He was just an old drunk." An old drunk? I'd meant Edwin Strafford, but Henry's admission surely concerned Ambrose. Events slid out of joint. What did his misunderstanding tell me about either death? Everything or nothing? I didn't have time to think while Henry blurted it all out. "Don't you understand? What does it matter that he drowned a few years before he drank himself to death? About as much as the fact that it really was an accident." His look was full of pleading, pleading for me to understand that an obscure death didn't justify his public ruin, pleading for my tacit consent to the logic of his judgement—which I would never give.

"Tell me about the accident, then."

"It was like all accidents—sudden, unexpected, unpredictable: over before I could control it."

"The day we met in Miston, you travelled to Torquay on the pretext of a trade conference."

"It was genuine, but I only decided to go at the last moment, because it meant I could slip up to Dewford without anybody knowing and take a look around. You'd worried me, with your talk about Strafford's accusations of foul play."

"You found Ambrose at the pub in Dewford?"

"I spotted him there, yes—and remembered him from our previous meeting in 1951. I took care he didn't see me, though."

"Not enough care, as it happens. He noticed you."

Henry nodded. "Makes sense, in view of what happened when I went back that night."

"Why did you go back?"

"Because Timothy phoned me in Torquay and told me about Ambrose's letter to you. I'd sent him to buy you off. That sort of thing's his speciality—God knows he must have his uses. We knew you'd been involved with the Randall bitch: Timothy considers he has droit de seigneur over the better-looking incumbents of the Fellowship, but that didn't mean I trusted her, or him. With Strafford mouthing off, it seemed best just to pay up and have done."

"But that didn't work."

"No, and the letter changed everything, because it meant there was evidence to worry about, not just hearsay. I think Timothy actually enjoyed dropping me in the shit where that was concerned."

"So what did you do?"

"I went up to Dewford again. I made for the pub, to see if the old man was there. If he was, I was intending to go back to the cottage and see if I could find that blasted Postscript."

"And was he?"

"Oh yes. The worst of it was he was just coming out and met me in the glare of the porch light. He stank of cider. But he wasn't too addled to recognize me. He remembered me from the pub earlier. And then he remembered me from 1951. Started shouting and swearing—and laughing madly.

"I panicked, the last thing I needed was a row in the street. So I took off, legged it away from the old fool. He followed, but soon appeared to give up. I kept on down the lanes. Inky black they were. Pretty soon I was lost. I came to a bridge over a river and stopped to get my breath back.

"I leant against the parapet, facing downstream, breathing deeply, wondering what the hell I'd got myself into. Then I heard him, panting and cursing.

"'Welcome back, Couchman,' he snarled. 'I've waited a long time to see you again.'

"I protested that I didn't know him, but it did no good.

"'Yes you do,' he said. 'We've met before. I didn't know then that you'd kill my uncle and blight my house.'

"I'd had enough. I tried to break away. But he pushed me back until I was bent over the parapet. He seemed to be forcing me back still further. I summoned the strength to push him off, and somehow, in that scramble in the dark, he fell from the bridge, but whether I pushed him or he simply rolled over the edge I don't know. Whichever it was, I was just relieved to put him safely out of reach. I strained over the parapet for a sight of him but was only too glad that the river and the night had swallowed him. For me, that was enough. I turned and ran. I traced my way by the lights of the village back to where I'd left my car—there was nobody about. So I drove straight back to Torquay. I had one night in a strange hotel to collect my thoughts and put behind me the memory of that mad, frightful moment. It wasn't enough, of course, but, when I got back here on Monday, I felt able to carry on much as normal."

"Letty doesn't think so."

"Well, maybe she's right. But I've tried to put it behind me. When I read about his death in the papers, they called it an accident—and that's all it was. What good would it do to publicize my part in it? Unless, like you, Sellick is just seeking some petty vengeance."

I controlled my anger at his denial of responsibility, for the sake of leading him on. "Sellick's got nothing to do with it."

He looked up sharply. "But you said . . ."

"I said he had proof that Strafford's death wasn't an accident. But I meant Edwin, not Ambrose."

"You bastard," he muttered. He set his jaw and inhaled deeply and stood up, brushing himself down as if to wipe away the stain of his recent humiliation. When he spoke again, his voice had more the strength of the Henry I knew. "You unnerved me for a while, but not anymore. Now I know I was right. You really don't understand—you or this mystery man Sellick: if he exists."

I stepped back. "Oh, he exists. You'd better believe it."

Henry summoned a superior smile. "But he has no proof—not about Edwin Strafford. You know about Ambrose now, but it'll do you no good. I'll deny everything."

I tried to retrench. "Hold on, Henry. Not so fast. Deny it if you like, but what happens if your fingerprints are found in Ambrose's cottage, which you searched for the Postscript after his death?"

He looked genuinely puzzled. "You're stupider than I thought, Radford. Do you suppose I'd be so foolhardy as ever to go near Dewford again after that madness?"

"You were prepared to go back there after a similar madness 26 years ago."

"In 1951 things were different, quite different, though I don't expect your niggling little brain to appreciate the significance of the issues involved. National issues."

"And personal ones?"

"Well, of course, Edwin Strafford frightened me. I had a lot to lose with Attlee's government tottering and a winnable seat there for the taking. I couldn't afford to have Strafford blackening my name—nor could others. When he threatened me, he threatened my party—because of Churchill's involvement in what he was alleging. He threatened the conventions and collusions which politics is built on. It was a threat we couldn't ignore. Even I didn't realize how emphatically that threat had to be negated.

"I panicked when my warning to the leadership about a mad old political maverick seemed to fall on deaf ears. That's why I tried my hand at removing the certificate by force. Strafford thwarted me there. But I needn't have worried, as my father had told me. He always did know how many beans make nine." His voice drifted away into a murmur.

"So what did happen to Strafford?"

He turned and looked at me, as if surprised that I still needed to ask. "Oh, somebody expert in such matters arranged for him to fall under a train. The powers that be ran out of patience and called him in—his time was up. I didn't ask for the hows and whys of it. I didn't want to know them. It was enough that my father and I had brought sufficient pressure to bear in the appropriate quarters. It was enough that Strafford was erased before he could make a nuisance of himself. When the election came in October of that year, I won my seat and the Conservative party won the right to govern. There was no scandal."

"So the conspiracy of silence continued?"

"Yes. But the knowledge is worth nothing to you. It's too big for you to tackle. If my mother's been so stupid as to invite this disinherit South African over, I suggest you persuade her to withdraw the invitation. I suggest you persuade her that politics is more than just banner-waving and hunger-striking."

"She won't stop now."

He walked forward a few paces, turned and faced me. "How about you then, Martin? Will you stop? Let's forget the crap about you dishonouring my daughter. You know that was a sham. I just wanted rid of your pampered, liberal conscience. Perhaps you reminded me of Strafford. But now we're not pretending to like each other—or hate each other—any more." His political nerve was regaining strength all the time, his last-gasp, bareknuckle brawler's instinct for playing on a weakness. "My party's going to win the next election—you can bet on it. This spineless government is its own worst enemy. I'm on a promise of a seat in the Cabinet. That buys a lot of influence, a lot of power."

"What are you saying?"

"I'm saying see reason. For once in your grubbed-together life, stop being a bloody fool, stop being a nothing. It wouldn't involve our seeing anything of each other—you know how repugnant that is. But it would involve your stopping the slide. Why let everybody else snaffle the good things in life?

"We dislike each other—so what? I've learned to live with disliking lots of people. Some of them are my best friends. So Strafford had a raw deal. Why emulate him? I'll donate something to a memorial down at his blasted Barrowteign, if you like. I'm sorry about his nephew. Maybe you were fond of him. Maybe you think I should have gone over that bridge with him. But think carefully—think more carefully than you've ever thought in your life—before you risk going over the bridge along with me."

He looked straight at me in a strangely impersonal way. "If the possibilities interest you, let me know." Then he turned his back on me and resumed his study of a bulky file on his desk. I left without disturbing Letty.

On the drive south, I thought, inevitably, of Eve and Timothy. How much did they know? If Henry hadn't broken into Lodge Cottage, it must have been Timothy—perhaps at Eve's bidding. Did they realize that Henry had been involved in Ambrose's death? Presumably not. So what was their game? Whatever it was, it gave me something to cling to. So long as they and Sellick were exerting their differing influences, Henry's offer lacked the simplicity to impose itself upon me. So long as there were other people and problems to think about, I could avoid confronting my own susceptibility to what he'd said.

Elizabeth was waiting for me at Quarterleigh, eager to know what had happened. I'd rather have delayed telling her, but her manner brooked no postponement. Even so, mine was an edited version. No mention of Henry's contempt for her and the world in general. No mention of his powerful inducements for me to keep silent. No mention of mechanistic rationale of how to live a life. Such things weren't for a mother to hear. Denials that he'd had a direct hand in Edwin Strafford's death, confession and remorse where Ambrose Strafford was concerned—they were different matters and, for Elizabeth's sake, I couldn't help letting them cast Henry in a sympathetic light.

It still wasn't a good enough light to relieve Elizabeth's

distress. Henry had been a party to his father's deceit of her. He'd allowed (if not encouraged) officialdom to eliminate Strafford. He'd tried to cover up his part in Ambrose's death. He had lots of excuses but none of them gave him any esteem in her eyes. It was breakfast-time the following day before she articulated a response. By then, I'd spent a largely sleepless night reproaching myself for what I'd found myself hoping: that Elizabeth would call a halt, would destroy the Postscript, would say that enough was enough. With Henry's offer still eating secretly into my resolution, I no longer felt ready for us to take the irrevocable step which Sellick's arrival was bound to represent. Yet with the Postscript in Elizabeth's keeping, matters were now literally in her hands. If she decided to take the step, I'd have to go with her. And decide she did.

"I trust you agree, Martin, that we should still despatch the letter to Mr Sellick tomorrow," she said, pouring coffee into my cup. "Henry's testimony is in some ways better than I'd feared, in others worse than I'd hoped. It at least gives me the advantage of knowing what wrongs have been done by members of my family. Some of them concern Mr Sellick, some do not. Of those that don't, I think you should advise me what to do about Edwin's nephew." She'd spoken calmly, but I'd watched the stream of coffee waver with her trembling.

"Reluctantly, nothing. The inquest concluded it was an accident. Henry's evidence supports that—though it alters the circumstances. If we believe him, why try to re-open the case?"

"But do we believe him?"

"I think so." A couple of weeks before, I could have rammed the words down my own throat. Now I just gulped coffee to drown the taste of treachery. "It had the ring of truth."

"And what about the letter? Are you happy for it to go?"

"Of course—if you think it can do any good." The implication that it couldn't, dropped delicately between us.

She leant back in her chair. "To do good is perhaps to ask rather a lot—though I have hopes. For the moment, I only propose to see that some form of justice is done to a wronged man." So virtuous, so laudable, so misconceived. How can you wrong the chameleon, for whom mistake and delusion are forms of camouflage? Sellick had already mobilized a chameleon's justice, but we weren't capable of recognizing it.

When we walked, Elizabeth and I together, to the post office in Miston that unremarkable Wednesday morning, to despatch the letter to Sellick, I myself could have asked Strafford's question: which was the dream and which the reality? It had a dreamlike quality, that early stroll in the patchy sunshine, but its consequences were harsher than any reality. When we stopped to put flowers on Couch's grave on the way back, there was in the action as much appeasement as irony. Which was as well, since later there was indeed much to appease.

I didn't expect a reply that week, so reconciled myself to a wait that was bound to be hard on the nerves. Strangely, the days became easier as they passed. Elizabeth and I kept each other supportive company, became comfortable in a routine of spending time harmlessly together, insulated for a while from all the problems certain to beset us.

In fact, we became too comfortable, to the point where I wished I could stay at Quarterleigh forever with Elizabeth in her restful old age, mature and rounded in her judgements and reflections, slowly adjusting to our new-found knowledge, absorbing it as part of her wisdom. I came to understand—in strolls or drives along the Downs—why she felt it important, at the close of her life, to re-open—as some would see it—an old wound. "Because," she said once, "it can't be re-opened if it's never closed. This is a necessary act of healing." Only the very old or the very young could be so hopeful.

As it turned out, we didn't have as long to wait as I'd thought. On Sunday evening, the telephone rang. Elizabeth answered.

"It's for you, Martin—a gentleman named Fowler."

I grabbed the receiver. "Hello—Alec?"

"Yes Martin, it's me." His voice had a gloomy tone, as if he didn't expect me to be pleased to hear him. Perhaps for that reason, he didn't waste his words. "Leo got your letter yesterday. He's flying over tomorrow. But he sent me to make some arrangements in advance."

"Where are you?"

"Here, in Miston. I'm at The Royal Oak. I expected to see you in the bar." The joke fell flat. "Could we meet to talk?"

"Okay. I'll come over straightaway."

I put the phone down, explained to Elizabeth and headed off without delay. The village and the Downs above were huddling in preparation for darkness as a still evening succeeded a breezy day. The lane was quiet, but, in the trees around the church, birds were roosting noisily. The flowers we'd placed on Couch's grave on Wednesday were still fresh, in mind and bloom, but something intangible had changed in the ordered environs of Miston. Alec was waiting for me in the homely bar of The Royal Oak and nothing would ever be the same again.

I found him in the saloon—larger but emptier than the public bar, drinking English beer and smoking French cigarettes in one of the corners by the wide chimneybreast. He smiled and nodded, but waited for me to join him with my drink.

"I didn't expect us to meet again so soon," he said.

"Neither did I."

"It was only a month ago."

"It seems longer. A lot's happened in that time."

"Not to me. Except, of course, these two trips. Your letter came as something of a bombshell."

"I suppose it would." We were fencing, probing conversationally to see if we could put any weight on a friendship we both knew to be bankrupt. "I've only done what Sellick asked."

"And then some." Alec smiled uncertainly. "News of the Postscript took him aback."

"I'm glad something did." I'd tired of the bluff. "Lately, I've had the impression Sellick knew more about what I was doing than I've told him."

"What do you mean?" He smiled, as if he knew all too well.

"I mean he's been checking up on me." It was still only a guess, because Eve had suggested another explanation for my past being divulged to her, but Alec's shiftiness supported my belief that that had only been a ruse.

"In what way?"

"In the way that he's sent you here in advance. Why would that be but to find out what I've been up to?"

Alec looked defensive. "Leo's an old man not used to travelling. He wanted me to book a hotel and, yes, spy out the land here. But there's nothing sinister in it."

"Alec, we've known each other for ten years now. Even if I've acted like a fool at times, don't treat me like one. When we met in London, I told you about my hopes and plans involving Eve Randall. You agreed not to mention them to Leo."

"I remember." His voice had sunk to a murmur.

"Within days, I'd been discredited in Eve's eyes. Somebody had told her all about the end of my teaching career—chapter and verse. I . . ."

"It was me." He looked straight at me, with a frankness in his eyes which had once been charm. "I told her. I encouraged you—with a few insignificant disclosures—to tell me exactly what you were thinking of. When I met her, it was easy to understand why you should throw Leo over for her sake. Ordinarily, I'd have wished you luck."

"But . . ."

"But I'm not a free agent. I'm Leo's errand boy. Let's not dress it up—that's how it is. He sent me to see what progress you were making and, because Eve seemed to be leading you astray—as far as he was concerned—he instructed me to end your association by whatever means I judged necessary. I couldn't see any other way to do it."

I put the only question I could: "Why, Alec? Why sell yourself and me down the river?"

He drew on a cigarette and gazed past me. "Money, old son. It's as simple as that. I ran short of collateral in a cash-conscious age. That magazine I told you was my passport to fame and fortune in Fleet Street—a sick joke. A loss-maker from day one. Sellick let me run up debts with him as if they meant nothing—then, suddenly, called them in. At the same time, I discovered he was the faceless proprietor behind the casino where I'd salved my boredom with some mindless gambling—and lost heavily. I woke up one day in my banana paradise to find a South African capitalist had me by the short and curlies."

"So how did you pay him off?"

"I didn't—hadn't a hope. But Leo offered to commute the debt. A well-qualified, footloose English intellectual in his pocket was just what he was looking for. I'd been set up."

"But why?"

"Because of the Strafford thing—because of you. It was eating away at him for years before I obligingly walked into his web. I couldn't fathom it and I certainly couldn't afford to appear too curious, but what he wanted was some kind of entrée to English intellectual society. He thought I was it and I had to try to live up to that. When I mentioned you as an historian I knew, he was over the moon. I reckon he knew even then about your link with the Couchmans, though I admit it was me who told him why the link had been broken. That pleased him all the more. You were available and known to be antagonistic towards the Couchmans: two qualifications which made you the man for the job."

Now that Alec had said it, it seemed just what I might have expected. "So you didn't invite me to Madeira for a friends' reunion? Sellick's offer wasn't just a lucky windfall? It was part of the scheme."

Alec shrugged apologetically. "That's about the size of it. Leo reckoned it was an offer you couldn't refuse."

"He was right."

"He usually is."

"But why? What's the point? Now you know about his connexion with Strafford, what do you reckon he really wants?"

"I don't know. He wanted you to act as his surrogate. He thought you'd share his motives. That's why Eve was such a threat. What those motives are I can't say. Your guess is as good as mine. It's been like he knew what you'd find all along. None of your reports surprised him—until the last."

"He didn't know about the Postscript then?"

"Definitely not. That was a bolt from the blue. Not to mention the old lady's invitation."

"Why has he accepted?"

"Martin, I'm not paid to solve such riddles. I'm just kept happy with some hack writing and spurious local celebrity. I do his bidding, but I don't have to understand it—or like it."

I looked at him: somehow shrunken in my mind, while I'd

grown—however uncomfortably—in the trials of my task. I should have felt anger or contempt. Instead, I pitied him. "Alec, didn't you ever hesitate to lead me on, knowing what you were getting me into?"

He smiled wryly. "Once or twice. When we met in London, I tried to imply how things really were. But you failed to take the hint and I couldn't risk making it explicit."

"It doesn't say much—for our friendship."

"No. But then Leo enjoys making people face their own inadequacies. So he relished the fact that we were friends, revelled in forcing me to betray you—along the way, as it were, as a sideshow in his larger scheme. As for us, telling you I had no alternative won't wash. I could say I thought the job would be good for you—but I had a bad feeling about it all along. The truth is that Leo's promised to use his money and influence to get me a break in journalism—if I serve him well. After all the false starts and missed opportunities in my life, I just couldn't resist, couldn't let slip what might have been my last chance. For that, I was prepared to play my part in his plans. I didn't realize what it would involve, of course, and, by the time I did, it was too late to back out. Blowing the gaff to Eve was the worst. If that ended something good, I'm truly sorry."

His admission was well-timed. Before discovering Eve with Timothy, I'd have been harder on him and easier on myself. "I'm not sure it did that—though it seemed like it at the time. It turns out Eve wasn't on the level either."

Alec raised his eyebrows fatalistically. "Who is? It must be the age. After the Enlightenment, one day they'll call this the Disillusionment."

"Maybe. But since we are now being . . . honest with each other, tell me why you've come."

"Like I said—to spy out the land."

"That's all?"

"What else would there be?" I challenged him with my eyes, but he wouldn't meet my gaze. I couldn't quite believe him, but his candour had defused my disbelief.

"I don't know, Alec. I didn't know before. Tell me what Leo made of my letter."

"He summoned me to the Quinta yesterday morning,

showed me the letter and told me to travel here by the first available flight and arrange for him to follow on Monday. We didn't debate the matter—we never do. All that reasoned discussion was for your benefit. Leo prefers to give instructions and see them followed. Obviously, he knew the letter would tell me things about him I didn't know, but it didn't seem to bother him. Still, something did. Perhaps the imprecision in your description of the Postscript. How much is there in it you didn't mention?"

As soon as he'd asked the question, I felt reluctant to answer it. Whatever we now admitted to each other, it could never be the same again between us. I've never demanded anything as crude as loyalty from him, but its loss was as keenly felt as its existence had been blandly assumed. "When the time comes, Leo will know."

"When is that time?"

"When he meets Lady Couchman—and her son."

"Well, I'm to collect him from Gatwick Airport tomorrow afternoon. Do you want me to bring him straight here?"

"I suppose so. There's nothing to be gained from delay. I'm sure we all have questions we want answered." We did, but, equally, delay had its appeal. I'd not seen Sellick for two months, not yet spoken to him with the advantage of the knowledge I'd since come by. Before, he'd had the upper hand. Now, I might wrest it from him. But, drinking beer that evening with Alec, 24 hours away from the opportunity, I felt only a sapping inadequacy for the occasion. There were no grounds for any other feeling. "I have a question: why tell me now? You could have kept me guessing about your motives a little longer."

"Could I? You were bound to work out who'd blabbed to Eve. That was a trick we could only play once. Effectively, it blew my cover. But Leo didn't seem to care. You were bound to confront me with it when we next met, which is why I made such a quick getaway at the time. Of course, I could have held out longer, but there are limits even to my obedience. Leo can do without this particular secret—I'm glad it's out in the open." So that was Alec's act of minor heroism—to tell me before he had to. It wasn't enough.

"How do I know the timing of this disclosure isn't Sellick's choice—like everything else?"

"You won't." He drained his glass. "If I were you, I wouldn't trust me. That's the measure of Leo's gift for corruption."

I left him to drink away the evening. It was unlike me not to stay, but I had no wish to, after what he'd said, and there was much to be arranged. I hastened back to Quarterleigh through the velvet darkness and found Elizabeth waiting for me, eager to hear my news.

"Sellick will fly in to Gatwick tomorrow afternoon," I said. "Alec will collect him and bring him here. I hope I was right to assume that's what you'd want."

"You were, Martin. Now that I've taken the step of inviting him, I'd like to see him as soon as possible. And I'd like Henry to be here as well."

"I don't think he'll come. He was hoping you'd withdraw the invitation."

Elizabeth smiled. "I'm sure he didn't seriously expect me to. I shall speak to him now and instruct him to be here."

She went to the telephone and dialled the number.

I listened to her half of the telephone conversation while foreboding gathered in my mind and moved towards a stark conclusion: if I'd been set up in the first place to take the job Sellick had offered, had this invitation and the meeting it was about to lead to been foreseen as well? If so, its purpose was already planned—and it wasn't ours.

Elizabeth had been speaking to Letty, but a change of tone told me Henry had come on the line. "Mr Sellick will be here tomorrow evening. I'd like you to come and meet him over dinner . . . I realize that . . . Possibly—let's just wait and see . . . Yes, he will be . . . Very well then, dear, I'll look forward to seeing you about seven o'clock . . . Bye bye."

She came and sat down. "That was easier than I'd expected. He agreed to come."

"Just like that?" I was puzzled.

"No. He said he was busy and didn't see why you had to be here. But he said he'd come. He didn't sound pleased—in fact, rather low generally—but he consented and that's the main thing. Still, the lack of argument was unlike him. He sounded tired. Perhaps he's sickening for something." She looked thoughtful for a moment. "Once he's here, I can make sure he doesn't take it too badly."

It was wrong and I knew it. Henry should have raged at his mother, refused to have anything to do with Sellick, raced down and tried to prize the Postscript out of our keeping. Why this meek compliance? Why this lack of fire from the arch-fulminator? I was too slow to make the connexions, still too busy forming the questions to guess the answers. Elizabeth was content to wait and see and I, though not content, had to do the same.

I went out at dawn the following morning and walked myself into a physical fatigue with which to face the day. Then I sat with Elizabeth in the conservatory and talked about suffragism to pass the afternoon, though our thoughts were far more on the present, for once, than on the past. Dora began to fuss around in preparation for a grander dinner than she'd served at Quarterleigh in a long time and we knew the evening—with all its uncertain events—would soon arrive.

A taxi crunched up the drive shortly after seven o'clock, true to Alec's phoned estimate. I watched from the lounge as Alec paid off the driver while Sellick climbed—a little stiffly—from the back seat. Immaculately dressed in crested blazer and grey trousers, groomed and slightly self-conscious, but every inch in command. He surveyed the house with his sharp, discriminating eye and betrayed no hint of a reaction. He was the same man who'd charmed and won me in Madeira with his knowing, connoisseur's intellect, but there he'd shone in his proper firmament. Damp-wooded, parochial Sussex didn't quite fit. It viewed him as an outsider while, in his penetrating gaze, he seemed to view it as a conquest—or perhaps an inheritance.

Elizabeth went out to meet him, while I lingered indoors and watched the long-destined moment. I saw her smile and say a word, then extend a hand in greeting. I saw Sellick incline his head and shake her hand. But I also saw that he didn't smile. His lips beneath the pencil-straight moustache didn't even play with the idea. In that moment, my heart sank.

The group filed into the house and joined me in the lounge. Leo's eyes shot across to me as he entered the room and his tongue passed along his lower lip in a sole concession to nervousness. "Why, Martin," he said, "what a pleasure to see you again. I cannot fault your industry over the past two months." He shook my hand before I could avoid it. "I hope you've enjoyed yourself in that time." His look defied me to acknowledge the sarcasm.

"I think I've done what you asked, Leo."

"That and more." He turned to Elizabeth. She looked solemn and dignified in a full-length, dark blue dress with a simple pearl necklace. In her easy grace there was no hint of the inner turmoil she must have felt. "I'm sure, Lady Couchman, you would agree that we owe Màrtin a great debt for making this meeting possible."

"There is much that I owe Martin," she replied in measured tones. "But I feel sure he would be the first to acknowledge that thanks on this occasion are due to you for accepting my invitation and coming such a long way in the interests of . . . reconciliation."

"It was, I assure you, no hardship." There was too much electricity in the atmosphere for my liking. I poured sherry as a distraction and suggested we all sit down. We did, but it made little difference. Elizabeth was trying for something Sellick clearly had no intention of giving. As for Alec, he looked uncomfortable and carefully avoided my eye.

"My son will be arriving later," said Elizabeth. "I hope you'll bear with him in what he's bound to find a difficult encounter."

"It's difficult for all of us, Lady Couchman. After all, few men have to wait until they reach my age to meet their family."

Bravely, Elizabeth persevered. "It has been a long time, it's true, but I hope you accepted my invitation in the spirit in which I issued it, namely that it's never too late to put right old wrongs."

"Oh, I agree wholeheartedly. After all, in English law there is no statute of limitations."

I intervened in an attempt to wrong-foot Sellick. "Tell me, Leo, why did you let me discover your part in Strafford's life rather than volunteer the information? It would, after all, have made my task a good deal easier."

He smiled with patronizing indulgence. "In the first place, Martin, you accepted the terms of my offer and can hardly complain if you had to work for your money. In the second place, I doubt myself if the information would have aided you, quite the reverse. And lastly, of course, I had no idea that you would come upon this . . . Postscript." So measured and so cool, but so careful to avoid mentioning what I'd withheld from him. "When am I to be allowed to see it?" In that last remark, a hint of impatience that was unlike him.

"I think that should await Henry's arrival," Elizabeth said. "You both have an interest in it." I understood her reluctance to reveal the extent of her son's involvement in her husband's fraud to so unyielding a guest, but Sellick seemed to interpret the remark differently.

"I should have thought," he said slowly, "that, as Martin's employer, I had first call on the fruits of his research."

I couldn't let him get away with that. "The Postscript is nobody's property—but Strafford's."

"True. But since Strafford is dead, I own his house and other . . . written work . . . and he has no surviving family, I would contend that it devolves upon me."

Now it was Elizabeth who tried to defuse the situation. "Speaking of Edwin's house, Mr Sellick, why did you buy it all those years ago?"

The reply was sharp. "Because, at the time, it was the only link to any kind of family left open to me. Of course, when I found the Memoir there, even that link was called into question."

Abruptly, Elizabeth rose from her chair. "If you'll excuse me, gentlemen, I'll telephone my daughter-in-law—to be sure my son's on his way. We may have to dine without him." She seemed happier to go than she was anxious about Henry.

"Presumably," I said, "you didn't accept Elizabeth's invitation in the spirit in which it was issued."

"Using all the new-found knowledge that the Postscript has made available to you, Martin, why don't you tell me?"

"The Postscript has told me nothing about you that you don't already know yourself."

"You must let me be the judge of that. Your letter hinted at more than it said."

"It wasn't meant to. I couldn't say much without drawing premature conclusions. For instance, I've read Strafford's account of his meeting with you in 1951, but I'm sure your account would be different."

Sellick eyed me closely. His brow furrowed as if he was trying to glean something from my words that wasn't there. "As you say, I'm sure it would be." But he wasn't going to say how. The certainty hung in the air between us, the certainty that he hadn't come to Sussex to bare his soul but to comb other people's.

Elizabeth returned to the room, looking more strained than when she'd left. "Henry set off in good time to have been here an hour ago," she said. "I can't think where he's got to. We'd better start dinner without him."

Dora had excelled herself in a lost cause: the meal was a country cook's triumph. Unhappily, nobody's thoughts were on food. Sellick became less ambiguous and more overtly bitter as the evening went on, while Elizabeth bore his sarcasm with a martyr's fortitude. Alec ate and drank in glum silence, while my interventions failed to lighten the atmosphere.

My mind went back to the meal in Madeira with which Sellick had feted and beguiled me two months before. How different that had been from this ashen feast in Sussex. I had the sensation that it should never have been, that we four should never have met—Elizabeth struggling to make good her husband's wrongs, Sellick determined to inflict some harsh, hubristic lesson on any of the Couchmans left to face him, Alec embarrassed by his own complicity. As for me, Strafford's trail had shorn me of the delusions which Sellick had exploited so well. They'd fallen away and left him, the arch-manipulator, in clear sight. I watched him, picking at the moistly textured lamb with suspicion, sipping the fine bordeaux without enthusiasm, and recognized him for the first time. Not the cultured recluse or the wealthy free-thinker who'd commissioned my research, but a keen mind narrowly focussed, in whose field of vision we struggled like specimens on a watch-glass.

The tension tripped into dread when Elizabeth, still dignified but increasingly defensive, sought some measure of exoneration for Couch. "You must understand, Mr Sellick, that my husband, though guilty of deserting your mother, never realized that he was also deserting a son. It was not a conscious act of neglect."

Sellick's eyes blazed icily. "I presume you would prefer to call it an unconscious act, Lady Couchman. Or shall we say feckless? Perhaps we could ascribe it to a fault of character common in the English officer class of the turn of the century."

"What fault would that be?" I asked.

"Lady Couchman should be familiar with it: an arrogant assumption that they could go and do exactly as they pleased, without let, hindrance or any obligation to those whose lives they disrupted. We still live today in South Africa—and elsewhere—with the consequences of this peculiarly Anglo-Saxon vanity: that the Empire was your playground."

"You hired me as an historian, Leo, so I ought to tell you what you must know: that's a crude distortion. How can the Afrikaaner community blame apartheid on . . ."

Sellick brought his glass down onto the table with such force I thought it would break. "Forget your liberal pretensions, Martin. Concentrate on cause and effect. Why was my mother's family singled out for massacre by Botha's marauders in 1901? Because they had consorted with—or been duped by—an English officer who guyed their genuine political concerns and deceived their daughter for . . . what? Life, faith, justice? None of these. Merely amusement, merely a certain transient, self-flattering pleasure. They paid for his dalliance with their lives and my mother with her sanity. But when did my father ever even start paying?"

A silence fell. "Never," murmured Elizabeth. "The debt has fallen to me."

"If you accept the debt," said Sellick, "you must honour the payment."

"Wait a minute," I put in. "It sounds as if you've thought about all this for a long time."

"All my adult life, young man."

"Then are you saying that you knew for certain Sir Gerald

Couchman was your father long before I wrote to you about the Postscript, long before you hired me to find out why Strafford resigned?"

"Certainty is a luxury I have only lately been able to afford. Conviction I have long had. As soon as I read the Memoir, I guessed it must be so. I knew Strafford to have been telling me the truth and I concluded that he must have had me confined on Madeira so that he could go home to England and confront Couchman with his suspicions. But what happened? I gave you a genuine problem, though it is true I did not define the question."

"If that's so, why did you let Sir Gerald get away with it?"

"I cannot pursue men beyond the grave. Sir Gerald has eluded me."

"You're being obtuse."

"I beg your pardon?" He bridled. In the background, at the periphery of my mind, I heard the telephone ring and Dora answer it.

"I'm not talking about now. I'm talking about when you first read the Memoir. If you deduced that Sir Gerald Couchman was your father, why didn't you pursue him as you'd mistakenly pursued Strafford?"

Dora came into the room. "It's your daughter-in-law, ma'am. She says it's very urgent." Elizabeth hurried out. Sellick didn't seem to notice her going, but continued to look straight at me.

"It is you who are being obtuse, Martin. It was a year after Strafford's death before I bought Quinta do Porto Novo, and several months after that when I found and read the Memoir. By the time I'd traced Couchman, he was dead."

"It really took you three years to get round to it?"

"What are you suggesting, then?"

"I'm not sure, but there's something . . ." The conversation stopped dead as Elizabeth walked back into the room—deathly pale, suddenly wraithlike: a woman shocked beyond words. "What's wrong?" I said. Alec jumped up and tried to show her to a chair. She waved him away.

"That was Letty," she said in a distracted, dreamlike tone. "The police have contacted her to say that Henry crashed his car on the way down here. He's dead."

Nine

The borderlands between credulity and revelation. Backtracking fast, but still not fast enough. It was as if I had to wind in the sequence of my life before I could reach the point where it began to pay out the line leading to a house of mourning in Sussex. And, even then, I wouldn't have gone back far enough.

Henry's death wasn't the something I'd been stumbling towards in my mental duel with Sellick but, when Elizabeth announced it, it was his face—not hers—I looked at. And for an instant—passing faster than my mind could follow but not than my eye could see—there was, in his look, not surprise, not even indifference, but satisfaction, a faint movement that could have begun a nod of confirmation.

Death triggers a reflex of ritual and formal proceedings which swamps, for a while, too much thought. The shock of Henry going did just that to me. More than anything, I felt for Elizabeth. Whatever Henry had done, she didn't deserve to lose him as her only reward for trying to do what was right.

Dora came to the fore, sitting with her mistress in the lounge all night, making tea and letting her talk of Henry as none of us had known him—a child, a youth and a young man, before anybody had a right to say how he would turn out. When Sellick seemed likely to linger, Alec pushed him to go. We stood in the hall, waiting for the taxi, only Sellick among us at ease.

"Most unfortunate," he said, with meaningful understatement.

"Odd to think," I remarked in a daze, "that you'll never now meet your half-brother."

"It is always odd to think of death."

I looked at him sharply, but he'd prepared a face that told me nothing. "What will you do now?"

"We will be staying at The Dolphin & Anchor Hotel in Chichester—for a week or so. When you're ready to show me the Postscript, contact me there." I heard the taxi pull up outside. "I'll be in touch, Martin. Don't forget—you're still working for me."

They were gone before I could summon a rebuttal. I hadn't, in reality, been working for Sellick since I'd met Eve and he knew that. But, as the taxi rumbled away into the night, his words stayed in my mind. Was I still, without knowing it, doing his bidding?

Morning came—but not a good one. Elizabeth's doctor visited the house and prescribed some sleeping pills. She went upstairs to rest. I drank coffee in the kitchen, while Dora, who'd been delegated to do some telephoning, busied herself needlessly and told me what she knew.

"It's a bad business," she said. "A bad, bad business. Mr. Henry . . . well, you knew Mr Henry. But 'e were a man of substance. Now 'e's just . . . snuffed out. 'Im an' the other feller."

"What other fellow?"

"Seems there was two cars involved—head-on like. Mr Henry was overtaking a lorry on Gibbet Hill, up near Hindhead. Both drivers killed outright. Nobody's said nothing, o' course, but it sounds as if it was Mr Henry's fault. 'E always was 'eadstrong."

"That does sound bad."

She leant against the table beside me. "That Mr Sellick—your friend last night . . ."

"No friend of mine."

"Mmm. Well, I shouldn't say it, but it seemed to me 'e brought bad luck to the house."

"Very likely, Dora, very likely."

The news had come too late for the morning papers, but it had been on the radio. About midday, I answered the door to a reporter from the *Brighton Evening Argus*.

"How's Lady Couchman taken the news?"

"How would you expect?"

"And you are?"

"A friend."

"Fleet Street are beginning to blow this up a bit. How do you see it?"

"As a tragic accident."

"They're saying it could be suicide."

"Why?"

"The lorry driver reckons Mr Couchman pulled out onto the wrong side of the road on a blind bend. Going uphill, he must have known the risks."

"Everyone makes mistakes."

"This one cost another man his life. Mr Couchman's firm has been sliding on the Stock Exchange lately. And he resigned yesterday from the Shadow Cabinet."

"What?"

He looked at me in surprise. "You didn't know, did you?"

What did it mean? I got rid of the reporter and tried to think. The week before, Henry had been prepared to bluff and bluster his way through anything. He'd very neatly got the better of me. Resignation and suicide couldn't have been further from his thoughts. And yet, and yet. Twenty miles from Miston. Could he ever really have arrived? It was as if some weird determinism had forbidden it. How could he and Sellick, the *doppelgängers* of their father's split life, ever really meet without mutual destruction?

Elizabeth saw me in her room that afternoon, a mellow haven of stained beams, blue fabrics and cream papering, with windows looking out across the garden and the wood beyond the brook.

"Where has Mr Sellick gone, Martin?"

"A hotel in Chichester."

She was sitting in an armchair by the window. Only her continual kneading of the wooden arm ends transmitted her state of mind. "I hoped you might say Madeira. I wish now I'd never invited him here. He came for nothing but... satisfaction."

"I'm afraid so."

She looked up at me. "Don't worry, Martin. I don't blame you. I don't blame anyone any more."

"If only everyone could do the same." I sat on the edge of the bed opposite her.

"Henry wasn't a good man. Nor was his father. But they were good to me."

"I know. Truly, I do now know."

"But at what price, Martin?"

I wanted to refute the thought, for her sake and mine. "It was an accident."

"I don't believe that and I don't think you do. I gather he resigned from the Shadow Cabinet yesterday. Why? In what state of mind did he leave London?"

"Who can say?"

"Letty—if anyone."

"And when will you see her?"

"Tomorrow. Helen's collecting her from Oakment Square and bringing her down here. We've decided Henry should be buried here, in Miston, beside his father. The funeral will be on Friday."

"Do you want me to leave before they arrive?"

"It might be best. Dora has said she would be delighted to put you up. I don't want you to be far away."

"I shan't be."

She gazed out of the window. "It'll be best for Letty to come here. I gather the press won't leave her alone. Henry's resignation has made them suspicious. They won't stop until they prove the crash wasn't an accident. If they're right—if we're right—then it's worse than ever, because Henry took an innocent man with him."

"We can't be sure. Nobody can."

"Sadly, Martin, that's no consolation."

Craving any action to occupy the empty hours, I slammed out of the house in the brooding stillness of early evening, intending to take the MG out for a hard drive round the lanes. When I got to it, pulled up on the gravel beside the garage, I stopped dead. There was a note wedged under one of the windscreen wipers. I tugged it free and read it.

"Martin—Want to talk? Find me in the churchyard. E." Was she still there? How long ago had she left the note? I raced to find out.

She was waiting in the lychgate, leaning with her back against one of the pillars. I remember thinking, as I walked along the path towards her, of Strafford's appointment with Elizabeth in the same place, at the same time of day, all those years before.

When I was about ten yards away, Eve pushed herself forwards from the pillar and turned to face me. She was dressed all in black. Her look was severe, unsmiling, combatative.

"Why are you here?" I asked.

"To collect my property."

I tossed her the car keys and she caught them easily. "I'm surprised you didn't report it to the police."

"Are you?"

"You said in your note you wanted to talk."

"No. I asked if you wanted to talk."

"Okay, I will. Let's stick with property. You took me to Braunton Burrows that day so the coast would be clear for Timothy to break into the Bennetts' house looking for the Postscript."

"You think so?"

"I do. Then, when you realized it wasn't there, you persuaded me to hand it over to you. Only I saw you with Timothy before that could happen—and realized what a fool I'd been."

"If I really went to those lengths, wasn't it rather careless of me to be seen with Timothy before the handover?"

"Are you denying it then?"

"I don't have to deny anything, Martin. I don't think you really know what you're accusing me of."

"I'm accusing you of being Timothy Couchman's property from the day you took the Fellowship. All that in Cambridge—all the literary endeavour, all the subtle come-on—was a sham. Everything I said you passed on. Every move I made they knew about. You led me by the nose."

"You led yourself. It was no sham. Do you really think what happened on that beach was play-acting? Do you really think I'd hoax you body and soul for the sake of Timothy Couchman's grubby little cover-up? Or is that just a way of covering up your own past? Do tell me. I'd be fascinated to hear what you really think."

Her eyes and her voice: icy cold on that warm, oppressive evening. Had she chosen the rendezvous to tell me something? Who was misjudging who? She stood stock still, but her look danced with the possibilities she didn't mean me to understand.

I didn't speak, didn't know what to say. With a flash of her eyes that formed a kind of dismissal, Eve moved at last. She walked straight past me without a look or a word and I watched her go as far as the kissing-gate before she looked back, just once. "I hear there's been another accident," she said, and then walked on.

I was still standing in the lychgate a few minutes later when I heard the MG accelerate away up the lane. Eve had gone and, with her going, the first large raindrops began to fall on the path to the church.

Helen and Letty were due at lunchtime the following day, so I packed straight after breakfast and walked across with Dora to her cottage—one of a terrace of workingmen's dwellings near the disused flour mill on the other side of the village. Dora was a war widow—"Mr Bates," as she always referred to him, had gone down on a merchant ship in the Atlantic in 1941—and she lived alone at number 3, Rackenfield, seeing service at Quarterleigh as a means of getting out and being useful. Purposeful bustle was her answer to everything, including Elizabeth's bereavement, so accommodating me in her slightly musty back bedroom was a blessing in disguise.

It also meant she could keep me informed about what was happening at Quarterleigh. After going there to serve lunch, she returned with delighted secrecy to tell me that Letty wanted to see me. Not Elizabeth, as I'd expected, or even Helen, but the one woman I hadn't supposed would think even fleetingly of me at such a time.

I walked directly over to the garden and found Letty wandering among the rhododendrons, fingering the blooms aimlessly. I called to her.

"Hello, Martin." She smiled weakly and moved with a jerky, apprehensive gait.

"I got your message."

We began to walk slowly towards the brook. "Elizabeth has told me everything. Why Henry was so worried after that conference in Torquay. Why you came to see him last week." She stopped and looked challengingly at me. "Did you know this would happen?"

"No—as God's my witness. When I left Henry last week, he was in good spirits."

She turned back and walked on. "That's what I thought. Until . . ."

"Until when?"

"Sunday evening. He had a phone call and went out straight afterwards. Said he had an appointment at his club. He got back a couple of hours later just in time to speak to Elizabeth. He wouldn't talk about that or his appointment, just went up to his study and worked for the rest of the night. Stayed there most of Monday."

"Did you know he'd sent in his resignation?"

"No. He never mentioned it. When he set off that afternoon, I expected to see him . . ." She tailed off into a gentle sob, then recovered herself. "Have you seen the papers this morning?"

"No."

"They're connecting his resignation with the crash—implying suicide, and worse."

"It's just paper talk."

She looked at me with her large, pleading eyes. "No it isn't. We both know that. Henry could never have faced disgrace. Reputation, appearances, respect: they mattered to him. He couldn't have lived without them."

"They weren't threatened."

"He thought they were." She walked on down towards the edge of the brook, but I didn't follow. If she was right, something had happened since he'd bluffed it out the week before.

Something on Sunday, while I'd been meeting Alec at The Royal Oak. And then . . . a blind bend on Gibbet Hill had beckoned him into oblivion.

I went back to Rackenfield and ran over what Letty had said. But it was a riddle without an answer. I couldn't believe Henry had been frightened into suicide by the prospect of meeting his half-brother and I couldn't believe it had been an accident. The truth was waiting for me somewhere, but I couldn't fix it in my sight. It was there, hovering at the edge of my vision. But when I looked in its direction, it vanished.

At breakfast, Dora brought a note saying Elizabeth was staying in her room but wanted to see me that evening. I mooned the day away and then, as soon as I decently could, went round and was shown up to her room. She seemed composed and alert.

She told me that she had arranged for the whole family to meet after the funeral to discuss what she'd originally hoped Henry could agree with Sellick—how to make good the fraud on which Sir Gerald had founded all their fortunes.

"What do you hope will come out of this meeting?" I asked.

"Agreement—and that's where you come in. What I have in mind requires your consent above all others."

"Why me?"

"Because it involves the Postscript and, as the person who found it, you must have the final say in how it is used."

"I passed it over to you, Elizabeth, as the person I thought Strafford would be happiest to have it, so I'll respect your judgement. What do you propose to do with it?"

She looked straight at me. "Destroy it." I must have shown my shock. "I know it seems almost blasphemous in view of all the precautions Edwin took to preserve it. But I've thought about it carefully. In a sense, its contents cost Edwin his life. Had it not existed, Ambrose Strafford would certainly still be alive. And so, very likely, would Henry. I simply can't believe Edwin would want such a high price to be paid for its existence."

"I don't know what to say. After all the efforts I made to find it in the first place . . ."

"I understand how you feel, Martin. It must seem awfully

like a climb-down. It must seem that it suits my family all too well to . . ."

"I don't suspect you of such motives, Elizabeth. Others, perhaps. But not you. I see the logic of what you're saying. It's just that it's awfully hard . . ."

"I realize that, which is why I decided to tell you now, so you could give some thought to it before we meet."

"I can't imagine Sellick agreeing to it."

"I hope he will. He may feel he's had his . . . pound of flesh." She looked past me and I saw her expression harden in a way I hadn't seen before. "If not, I may have to go ahead despite him. You see, the truth is one thing, but I can't let it destroy my whole family. We owe Mr Sellick something, but not everything." She was right. They didn't owe Sellick as much as he was clearly set on taking.

"I'll support whatever you decide."

She grasped my hand. "Thank you, Martin. That's what I was hoping you would say." It was, in truth, all I could say, the least, after all, that I could do for her.

Downstairs, I encountered Helen in the hall. She appeared from the lounge in a way which suggested she'd lain in wait for me.

"I want a word, Martin."

"What about?"

"My father." I followed her back into the room. "The inquest was opened and adjourned this morning. It resumes next Wednesday."

"And now you know all the background?"

"Yes. And the press know they're on to something. It's such a bloody shame." She rarely swore. It was the only sign she gave of her distress. "I don't think he deserved to go this way." She looked at me. "Maybe you think he did—and maybe you're right. What I'm asking wouldn't be for him, but for me—for Laura, if you like."

"And what are you asking?"

"I'm asking you to say nothing about this document Granny has, nothing that would point the coroner towards suicide. If they bring that in, it'll mean my father murdered the other poor man. And the press won't leave it alone until they know everything—about this man Sellick, about Grandfather's other marriage."

I surprised myself by how ready I was to give her some comfort. "Don't worry. I'll say nothing."

She looked taken aback. "Really?"

"Really. I don't want to hurt you."

Surprise changed to bemusement in her face. "I thought you must do. I thought that's why you started this whole business."

"No." I shook my head slowly. "If you can believe it, I was just after the truth all along." It wasn't wholly true, but it wasn't wholly false. "It's not done me such good."

"It's not done any of us much good."

"The truth's like that. I should have learnt as much from history a long time ago." I moved towards the door, but stopped when she spoke again.

"Martin . . . I'm sorry if I misjudged you."

I looked back. "It doesn't matter," I said. Then I left.

What did it matter, after all? A minor misjudgement. I couldn't complain. I'd misjudged life as much as it had misjudged me. I didn't blame Helen for blaming me. I wouldn't have blamed anyone for doing that.

On the way back through the churchyard, I passed a gravedigger at work, shovelling damp clay onto a tarpaulin in a practised rhythm. He nodded to me when he saw me glance in his direction and carried on. To him, just a job of work. To me, the hole he was slowly shaping adjacent to the grave of Sir Gerald Couchman presaged much more than just a burial.

Friday, June 17th was a day of rain in Miston. First light brought a wind-blown drizzle which intensified as the air stilled and settled into a steady, slanting rhythm. Like the gravedigger, it was there before us and would return long after we'd stolen away.

Whatever the rumour, however loud the whispers, officialdom had done Henry proud. A shabby funeral would have been an admission of guilt by association. So the cortège of glistening black limousines that swept silently into the village just before noon were numerous enough, the wreaths large and livid enough, the publicly proclaimed grief unmistakable enough to still—for a while—the clamour of doubt, the raising of questions. Yet the press photographers' shutters clicked, the curious stood and stared. Everyone must have known that the solemnity of the service was only a truce.

The small church was full, mostly of people I didn't recognize: party grandees and their entourage, directors of Couchman Enterprises and some loyal staff, a few villagers there out of respect for Elizabeth. I took my place in a pew beside Dora. She touched my elbow and nodded across at Sellick's measured progress to a seat. He could only have been just behind me, but I hadn't noticed. The thought was a chilling one: that he was at his most dangerous when he was most overlooked.

As the pallbearers carried the brassbound coffin to the altar, my eyes remained on Sellick: a keen-eyed sentinel scanning the black-clad figures and, yes, exchanging one eloquent glance with Timothy that signalled he wasn't the pious mourner he seemed to be.

The family took their places in the pew in front of us. Only Elizabeth turned to acknowledge us. For the rest, Letty's eyes were to the floor, Helen looked straight ahead, Ralph cast his bland antiquarian's gaze to the stained glass and Timothy fingered his lips as if missing a cigarette. Perhaps they'd hoped I wouldn't be there.

As the service proceeded, my mind went back only a matter of weeks to Ambrose's brusque and ill-attended committal in Dewford. Only a matter of weeks? A matter also of revelation and reversal. So much had changed, yet so little had changed. Another tragic accident unsatisfactorily accounted for, another observation of ritual inadequate to the occasion.

And still there was Sellick. What did he think when he let the handful of clammy earth fall heavily onto the coffin where it had been lowered into the grave? What did the emphatic wiping of his gloved hands signify? Nothing to those who wept or wandered away. Something to those who thought they were watching the consignment of a victim.

The lounge at Quarterleigh, with extra chairs and a sideboard loaded by Dora with unwanted salads. The Couchmans, complete with old excisions and late additions, foregathered in distracted poses, some sitting, some standing, shaping and discarding maquettes of conversation, drinking a little, eating less.

Helen and her mother on a settee by the fireplace, talking aimlessly about how the proceedings had gone to take their minds off what the proceedings had meant. Ralph and Timothy by the window, Ralph explaining how to spot fake oil paintings while Timothy looked indolently uninterested and regularly topped up his gin. Elizabeth gently chiding Dora for preparing too much food while remembering, perhaps, a similar occasion 23 years before. Sellick eyeing me with silent threat from the opposite end of the room while toying with a tiny Wedgwood vase.

Elizabeth had evidently slipped out of the room briefly, because, at that moment, I noticed her come back in, carrying the package I knew contained the Postscript. She unwrapped it and laid it on the coffee table in front of Helen and Letty in a way which drew everybody's attention.

"My dears," she said, "you've now all met Mr Sellick"—she pointed over to him—"and you all know what this document is." She patted the Postscript. "The time has come for us to discuss what to do with it. When I first invited Mr Sellick here, it was to make good this family's neglect of him: there is no easier way to word it. But, with Henry's loss, there is no-one left who could be said, even indirectly, to have been a party to that neglect." I looked at Letty: her face grey, expression erased. Then at Helen: hands and eyes moving, uncertain how to take such a candid statement. "With Henry's loss, we have suffered a blow from which we will neither easily nor swiftly recover." Sellick, eyes like diamonds in a face of granite, assaying his disowners. "For that reason, it could be argued that it would be fairest of all to destroy this document, now that only Henry's memory remains to be diminished by its contents." Ralph was fiddling with something in his jacket pocket to cover a mixture of perplexity and embarrassment. Beside him, Timothy reclined languidly against a windowsill and indulged every leisurely nuance of lighting a cigarette. Elizabeth sat down in an armchair behind her. "So now, it's up to you."

Those at the edges of the room moved towards the centre,

eyes focussed on the Postscript. Timothy sat in a chair opposite his sister and stretched out his legs. Sellick walked behind him and took up station by the fireplace, one arm stretched along the oak beam above it, positioned as if in dominion over all of us. I stood behind Elizabeth's chair, while Ralph joined Helen on the settee and took a clumsy hold on her hand.

Letty sat forward and peered at the Postscript. "Nothing can bring Henry back," she said. "But I feel as if this book is in some way responsible for his death. I'd be happier if it was no longer around . . . to trouble us."

I spoke out. "We can hardly blame Strafford for what others make of his words. Any responsibility for Henry's death must surely rest in the present, not the past."

"Very epigrammatical, old man," Timothy drawled. "But what do you actually mean?"

"I mean—old man—that what may have upset Henry to the extent of causing him to crash was whoever or whatever confronted him at his club a few hours earlier. Who or what that was we don't know." I was speaking to Timothy, but looking at Sellick.

"We never will now," put in Helen. "That's just the point. I wish this whole wretched business had never started." She shot me a glare, as if to suggest a decent hostility for Ralph's benefit. "It's gone far enough for heaven's sake. I've lost my father. There are press sniffing round the house. Now I hear the firm's in trouble . . ."

"What's this?" said Ralph. The last remark had him worried, no doubt about his own stake.

"Spot of turbulence," Timothy assured him. "We can ride it out easily—as long as we don't panic."

"The point is," said Helen, "that we can ride it out more easily if we act sensibly where this document is concerned. Why provide our enemies with ammunition to fire at us?"

"What enemies?" I asked.

"There are lots of people who enjoy deriding those who are more successful than they are." She was beginning to sound like her father. "What would happen if this book fell into their hands?"

"My dear," said Elizabeth, "there's no danger of that."

"While it exists, there must always be that danger. Hasn't it done so already?"

"You must mean my hands," I said. "Well, I found it, as anyone could have. I suppose that's your point, isn't it?"

Helen settled back in the settee. "If the cap fits, Martin." She'd soon forgotten the allowances she'd made the day before.

Elizabeth tried to ease the atmosphere by shifting the emphasis. "We've heard nothing from you, Mr Sellick. What have you to say on this matter?"

Sellick brought his arm down from the beam over the fireplace as if swooping across the proscenium of his personal stage. "Well now, Lady Couchman, I don't think you would deny that my origins represent a source of shame for your family, would you?" It sounded like a declaration of war breaking into a trivial domestic squabble and, on the faces of those least prepared for it—Helen, Letty and Ralph—there were looks of shock. But not Timothy's—his was masked by suavity and cigarette smoke—or Elizabeth's, to judge by the firmness of her words.

"No, I would not deny it."

"Nor that the Postscript constitutes proof of that shame?"

"Nor that. I take your point, Mr Sellick. My family has an obvious and vested interest in the destruction of what could be regarded as incriminating evidence."

"So," said Sellick, bending swiftly to the table and seizing the Postscript, "if the contents of this were publicized, you would lose your title, your family its legitimacy and Couchman Enterprises its"—he glanced at Timothy—"resilience."

Elizabeth looked up at him calmly, where he loomed above her, Postscript in hand. "Precisely, Mr Sellick," she said icily. "You hold that power."

He lowered the volume slowly to the table, placed it at the end nearest Elizabeth and stepped back. "Then I agree that it should be destroyed," he announced. "I wish to wield no such power. With Henry's death, let us put it to rest."

I stared at him incredulously. Could he be serious? For Sellick voluntarily to surrender such a powerful instrument of his will contradicted every twist of his plot to bring us to this moment, confounded everything I'd come to believe about him. From the silence which followed, it seemed others felt the same.

Except Timothy. "You're a gentleman, Mr Sellick," he said. "I'm sure we all appreciate the good sense of what you've said."

Elizabeth roused herself. "If that's what you really think, Mr Sellick, I can only say that I'm very grateful to you for such a generous gesture, a gesture we had no right to expect but which I rejoice you have felt able to make."

There was unanimity in the stunned faces round the table, relief edging towards self-congratulation. To them, of course, it made perfect sense and, somehow, to Sellick also. Only I was baffled, yet bound by my earlier promise to leave the matter uncontested.

"There is no need for any form of thanks," Sellick continued. "If the prospect of meeting me here on Monday was in any respect contributory to Henry's accident, I would hope the erasure of this document could serve as a token of my regret." So well-turned, so smoothly toned and yet, I felt certain, so utterly false.

The power of Sellick's words lay not, of course, in honeyed phrases but in the consuming eagerness of his audience to believe them. They were quick to do so, too quick for my mind to assess the significance of his concession or set it against the uncertain inferences of our earlier, unfinished conversation.

It had stopped raining. The sky was grey and still, the garden of Quarterleigh hushed and expectant in a lull of late afternoon. The group moved as if in some secret extension of the funeral's ordered ritual to the incinerator behind the greenhouse. Ralph loaded it with crumpled newspaper and a few sticks of kindling, Timothy sprinkled on some petrol and tossed in a lighted match, the flames licked and spat. Elizabeth handed him the Postscript and asked him to deal with it as agreed. She might not have had the heart to do it herself or to ask me to do it for her. At any rate, it was Timothy, with a dexterity his father would have admired, who tore each page from its binding and cast it into the fire.

For a moment after entering the flame, each page remained untouched, Strafford's fluent handwriting proudly undefiled. Then the yellow rim of the fire's black tide crossed the crinkling paper and consumed the firm-inked script. The smut-specked smoke drifted down the garden towards the brook, stinging my eyes as it passed.

When all the pages had gone Timothy prepared to toss the cover in after them, but I put a restraining hand on his arm. "That's enough," I said. "There's no need to make a meal of it. I'll take that."

"Fair enough, old man," he replied with a twitch of his eyebrows. "Have it as a memento. I wouldn't begrudge you that. After all the efforts you made to stop me getting a sight of it in the first place, it seems only reasonable."

I took the cover from him. "My efforts were nothing compared with yours to find it."

"I'm not sure I know what you mean."

"Breaking into private property—that sort of thing."

"Not my style, Martin. I think you must be thinking of somebody else."

I didn't answer, just shut the cover and walked quickly away into the house. Suddenly, Timothy's squalid ploys didn't seem to matter anymore. The loss of the Postscript left me with a feeling of desolation. It was as if I was mourning Strafford for the first time. And, like Strafford, I didn't pause once the decision had been taken. I marched out of Quarterleigh and left the Couchmans to their own devices.

I drank the evening away at The Royal Oak and woke late at Rackenfield the following morning. The silence of the house told me Dora was out, so I slunk down to the kitchen and made some coffee. I sat sipping it, staring out at the garden in all its mundane summer charm and contemplating the end we'd made the day before with our cauterization of the Couchman family wound.

Or was it the end? It had been too easy to be believed. At the centre of my disbelief stood Sellick. His volte-face had been the least expected anti-climax of all, defusing the set piece family confrontation before it could even begin to tick towards detonation.. For the rest, I knew all the reasons why they would think the Postscript better burned and, indeed, why I'd agreed to support such action. It had been my selfless tribute to Strafford, my attempt to honour his final plea. Yet in its honouring I'd also betrayed him. He whose story deserved to be told had been silenced forever. I winced at the memory of it and at the taste of all I'd drunk to wash away that memory: it had done no good.

When Dora returned, she gave me short shrift.

"Decided to show yourself, I see . . . They've been up an' about for hours at Quarterleigh."

"Oh yes?"

"You'll be able to go back there now. Helen an' Ralph they've taken Mrs Couchman back to London, Mr Timothy's gone off somewheres—and, thank the Lord, that Mr Sellick's nowhere to be seen neither. Jus' like ol' times."

"I don't think it'll ever be that, Dora. It's time for me to leave Miston altogether, not go back to Quarterleigh."

"The mistress 'ouldn't like that. She gave us this note for you."

She handed me an envelope and began clearing up around me. I took out the note and read it.

Quarterleigh, June 17th

My dear Martin,

I am taking the opportunity of some evening repose after a taxing day to write these few lines. They concern what we did today with Edwin's Postscript as well as another matter I shall come to later.

Believe me, I know what a wrench it must have been for you to let us burn the record of Edwin's last thoughts. Yet what else could we do? After Henry's death—with all its attendant circumstances—there seemed to me to be no alternative. I realize how hard it must have been for you to subscribe to the decision. Thank you from the bottom of my heart for doing so. Let us hope that Edwin—as well as Gerald and Henry—can truly now rest in peace.

I wish I could say I was certain that was so, but an unquietness remains in my mind and time alone will tell if it is well-founded. I sincerely hope not.

My reservations are reinforced by my grandson. Before

leaving here today, he asked if he might return on Sunday with an unidentified companion to "discuss one or two points over tea". Naturally, I pressed him for details, but he declined to be specific. I could not, in all honesty, describe Timothy as a doting grandchild. Indeed, of all those gathered here today, he is the one whom I would least have expected to wish to return so soon. So his attentions are puzzling, not to say suspicious.

I wonder, therefore, if I might call upon your assistance once again. If you were here with me when Timothy and his mysterious companion called, I would feel much less vulnerable. Do come if you possibly can. I shall close in the hope of seeing you on Sunday, if not before.

With love from
Elizabeth

This appointment surely had to indicate some new development: but on what lines I couldn't tell. It seemed unlikely to bring comfort to Elizabeth. I gave Dora a brief note to say I would certainly be there.

I killed time and coped with doubt the usual way: too much drink. I'd become a familiar face at The Royal Oak, so was happy enough to prop up the bar there and await the unknown. If I'd only thought or planned to better effect, things might have turned out differently. But I didn't change my style, even when I knew I should.

Sunday afternoon: I woke with a start at Rackenfield after another visit to The Royal Oak. It was gone four o'clock and I should have been at Quarterleigh an hour before. I hurried round there.

Timothy's Porsche was in the drive. As I entered the house, I heard voices from the lounge and went straight in.

Elizabeth looked up from her chair as I walked in. A look of relief passed across her face. Timothy was pacing the carpet in the middle of some statement. "It really does make sense . . ." He stopped when he saw me and scowled. "What do you want?"

"I was invited," I said. "I believe you invited yourself." Our eyes locked.

From the armchair opposite Elizabeth there came the sound of a cup being replaced in a saucer. I swung round. It was Eve, uncrossing her legs elegantly and leaning forward to put the cup and saucer back on the coffee table. "Hello Martin," she said.

I looked at Elizabeth. "Why are they here?"

"They have explained themselves very clearly, Martin. I only wish you'd been here when they arrived."

"I'm sorry I'm late."

Timothy stepped towards me. "Too much at lunchtime, old man?" I ignored him.

"I intended no rebuke," Elizabeth continued. "I only meant that I would have valued your company and advice."

"You're the only one who would," Timothy put in.

"Now that I am here—what's happened?"

"They've put a proposition to me," Elizabeth said. "Perhaps I should say an ultimatum." I sat in the chair beside her and scanned their faces—Timothy's vainly unmoved, Eve's studiously uncommunicative—while she spoke. "They wish me to cooperate in the writing of Miss Randall's book: a study of suffragism with an autobiographical contribution from me, suitably edited. Miss Randall will supply the historical insight and the literary polish. I will supply her with the perfect example she is seeking of an aristocratic corruption of Suffragette values. Is that not so, my dear?" She'd spoken calmly, but I could see her arm trembling where it rested beside me.

Eve carefully avoided my eyes as she spoke. "I happen to believe that interpretation. The Strafford case is a perfect—and a valid—example. He weakened your resolve, just as Lloyd George perverted Christabel Pankhurst's motives to facilitate a sordid political manoeuvre."

"It is also the kind of sensational theme likely to make your name," Elizabeth said. "Pray do not pretend you have some other interest in it."

"But you won't do it," I said to her.

Elizabeth put her hand over mine. "Not of my own volition, Martin. But Miss Randall has me at a disadvantage. She and Timothy have the ear of Mr Sellick."

"So what? Now the Postscript's gone . . ."

"Tell him, Timothy," Elizabeth said.

"All right, though involving him helps nobody. We're all over a barrel, you see, Martin. Leo isn't a vindictive man, but he doesn't propose to go back to Madeira empty-handed. He's sponsoring Eve's research and its publication on the understanding that it'll feature some setting straight of the record where my grandfather is concerned. You should be pleased. Strafford won't come out of it badly."

"And it'll be the truth," Eve put in. "The truth about how Sir Gerald Couchman exploited his marriage under a false name to serve Lloyd George in his deception of the Suffragette and his destruction of Strafford: an exposure of the true nature of Edwardian political life with Lady Couchman as a first-hand witness."

"In the process," said Elizabeth, "Gerald and our marriage will be subjected to public ridicule, my family's name will be dragged through the mud and what little pride and privacy I retain will be lost forever."

"Then why not just tell them to go to hell?"

She looked sharply at Timothy. "For one thing, Martin, I think they're already there. And Timothy will explain the other reason."

"It's what I said, old man. We're over a barrel. Unless we agree to Leo's terms, he will give evidence at the inquest on Wednesday to the effect that he met my father in London a week ago and accused him of murdering Strafford in 1951 and that Papa was so racked by guilt and fear of exposure that he killed himself the following night—along with the other driver. In other words, the whole shooting match."

"Is it true?"

"The meeting? Of course it is. Staff at the Carlton Club could confirm it took place. For the rest, I'm afraid Papa's actions speak for themselves. If you were called, could you deny what he told you about his part in this other Strafford's death?"

"No, but . . ."

"Exactly. But Leo is prepared to say nothing—and you'll do the same. That way, Papa won't be involved. The only member of the family affected will be Grandfather."

"And you're happy to let that happen?"

"No choice, old man. I've had to take charge of the company now. It's continuing prosperity must be my first consideration. Its share price had plummeted and there are ugly rumours circulating. There was a run on even before Papa died, prompted by Leo selling a substantial proxy holding. If we cooperate, he'll buy them back and we'll recover. If not, the scandal following the inquest will finish us."

"Only I don't believe that's all there is to it," said Elizabeth. "I think Mr Sellick has made this worth your while."

Timothy looked impatient. "As I said, Grandmother, I have to salvage what I can for the family. I don't expect you to like Leo's terms. I don't like them myself. But I do expect you to understand."

I looked at Eve. "What has the historian to say?"

Her eyes had a distant, superior sparkle. Only good taste seemed to prevent her smiling. "Nothing. A family quarrel isn't my affair. Setting history straight is. Lady Couchman has my personal guarantee that nothing she tells me will be distorted. The account will be scrupulously accurate."

"But damning?"

"As I said: accurate."

"With all this concern for history, why did Sellick let the Postscript be burned?"

Timothy smiled. "Because he's not an unreasonable man. The Postscript isn't essential to what he wants to achieve."

"And it's superfluous to an understanding of the period in question," said Eve.

I turned to Elizabeth. "What will you do?"

"I don't know. Mr Sellick has generously allocated me time to think. He will call here at noon on Tuesday, the day before the inquest, for my decision."

I looked at the other two. "How can you do this? You call this history? I call it prostitution."

Eve's eyes flashed. "You're in no position to denounce anybody's motives."

"In fact," said Timothy, "you were prepared to let Papa buy your silence, so . . ."

"It wasn't . . ." I made to get up, but Elizabeth restrained me with her hand on my arm.

"Please Martin," she said. "Don't give them the satisfaction of a scene. If you will, just show them out."

Elizabeth stayed in her chair as they moved to the door. Eve looked back at her once, but without pity. Timothy hurried out with the air of a man pleased to be on his way.

I watched from the front door as they walked to the Porsche. Eve waited on the nearside of the car while Timothy went round to the driver's seat.

"Does this please you?" I said to Eve. "Does this give you some satisfaction—to hound an old lady?"

"That's not how I see it."

Timothy opened the door from inside and she lowered herself in. He leant across her to close the door. "You're outclassed, old man," he said. "Why not accept that?" The door slammed and the car pulled away with a crunch of gravel.

I went back into the lounge. Elizabeth was still in the armchair, gazing into the fireplace. I couldn't tell whether she was composed or simply stunned.

"Are you all right?" I said.

"Perfectly. I suppose I should have anticipated this. It was absurd to believe that Mr Sellick meant to leave me in peace."

I sat down opposite her. "I'm afraid it was. And he's found more willing associates than I ever was."

She smiled. "That, my dear, is to your credit. Of my grandson, I shall not speak. As to Miss Randall, I can appreciate how bewitching men must find her. But there is a coldness about her that disturbs me. I do not understand her."

"Neither do I."

"No matter." She sighed. "Mr Sellick will call at noon on Tuesday and I must prepare a reply for him. Odd that he should choose that day."

"It's the day before the inquest."

"I meant the date: June 21st. He will not, I believe, have overlooked its significance."

"Which is?"

"That day in 1910, Gerald met Lloyd George and Christabel Pankhurst and sold them the marriage certificate in Edwin's name. A fateful day indeed. It would seem Mr Sellick expects another bargain to be struck on that date."

A point occurred to me. "It's also Sellick's birthday."

"Yes, of course. Mr Sellick's birthday." She looked thoughtful. "Clearly he hopes to receive a fine present from me."

"And will he?"

"Why yes. I see no alternative."

Nor was there any. I stayed with Elizabeth the rest of the afternoon and evening but our talk took us no further forward, rather backwards, over old ground we'd trodden before: Strafford and Couchman, cause and effect, past and present. Which was better? To co-operate and have her past scoured by the prurient and the curious or to resist and have her present laid waste? One or the other. She had to choose, but her responsibilities to the living—Letty, Helen, Laura, even Timothy—effectively settled the issue. The dead would have to suffer. I spent the night at Quarterleigh, sleeplessly reviewing ways out of the inescapable. There weren't any. Sellick had inherited his father's ability to snare the unwary with deadly efficiency. Still, at the back of my mind, doubt niggled. Why had Sellick allowed the Postscript to be destroyed? Because, surely, there was something in it he feared. But what? It was too late to find out—or was it?

I left Quarterleigh before Elizabeth was up the following morning. If I was to equip us to deal anything like adequately with Sellick when he called, I had to move fast. I caught the first bus into Chichester.

At the Dolphin & Anchor I was told that Alec and Leo had booked out on Saturday, saying they were going to London. The birds had flown.

I wandered disconsolately to the cathedral and sat on a bench on the green, staring up at its slender spire. From within, I could hear the stone-dampened harmony of choir practice. Outside, Monday morning shoppers bustled by me, oblivious of one slumped figure on a bench.

Then, emerging slowly from the angle of a buttress at the eastern end of the cathedral and walking slowly towards me, while gazing up at the decorated stonework, Eve reappeared in my life with an air almost of negligence, as if ours truly was a chance encounter. She tossed back her hair from the collar of a raincoat worn loosely across her shoulders over a thin summer dress and would have walked past without noticing me if I hadn't called out—or so it seemed.

"Sellick's cleared out," I said, walking towards her. She turned and looked at me from behind impenetrable dark glasses. She said nothing. I stopped about five yards from her. "He's cleared out while you two do his dirty work."

"What you're saying means nothing to me, Martin."

"It should. It's an object lesson in how Sellick deals with his . . . employees. People like you and me. Pawns in his game."

"I'm nobody's pawn." Still the level tone, the screen of dark glasses: barriers to keep me out."

"You must know you are. This book . . ."

"Will be a genuine work of historical scholarship."

"It's a complete reversal of what you originally intended. I remember you putting me down for suggesting that Christabel Pankhurst was Lloyd George's dupe."

"I've changed my mind, Martin—about many things."

"Including me?"

"No. That I can truly deny."

I looked at her. An expression of calculated blankness, rebuking me for even seeking an explanation. I flailed for a different approach. "Doesn't it worry you—as an historian—that Sellick agreed to burn the Postscript?"

"It's really none of my business."

"Doesn't it worry you—as a woman—that Sellick is threatening and coercing Elizabeth?"

"By sending Timothy to put his case, he has specifically avoided doing so."

"You must know that's not true. She's dreading his visit tomorrow."

"Needlessly."

"I don't think so and nor do you. Why are you doing this?"

"To advance my career. It's an honourable aspiration, though you called it prostitution."

I moved closer. "What else could I call it when you sell your body to Couchman and your brains to Sellick?"

"That's enough. I don't wish to discuss it anymore." She turned to walk on.

I grabbed her elbow. "You bitch—did what happened on that beach mean nothing to you?"

She froze and the stiffness of her elbow made me let go. Then she turned to face me and slowly removed the dark glasses. Her eyes bore into mine. "It meant something—but not what you thought."

"When we met at Miston Church, you denied you'd simply been keeping me out of the way so Timothy could look for the Postscript."

"I told you the truth. It wasn't as simple as that."

"Then what?"

"Let me ask you a question. You've appointed yourself Elizabeth's protector. But what have you actually done to help her? What will you do to stop Sellick forcing her to comply?"

There was a long pause—a gulf for me to stare across at my own inadequacy—before I heard myself answer in a hollow murmur. "Nothing."

"There's your answer to what Timothy has to offer. He satisfies me, which you never could."

"But when we went to Braunton, and afterwards in Topsham—you can't pretend . . ."

"Oh, but I did. That's just what I did. I pretended . . . everything."

She slid back the dark glasses. I suppose I saw her walk away across the green, but I can't remember. All she'd meant to me ended with that last admission. The point of her pretence escaped me, as it was meant to. But the blatancy of it remained long after she'd gone, staring and grinning at me, her superiority—her deliberate mystery—superimposed on the face of my private demon.

Darkness fell that evening on our thinking time, time ran out in our retreat from Sellick. At Quarterleigh, Elizabeth contemplated the bitter pass a hopeful invitation had brought her to. At Rackenfield, I drunkenly surveyed the road I'd led her down. Those who'd trusted me—Ambrose and Elizabeth—had suffered. Those who'd deceived me—Eve, Timothy and Sellick—stood to triumph. It was too much to take.

But there was no escaping it—even in sleep. Indeed,

dreams were fast and sure enough to find whatever furtive refuge my thoughts might flee to.

"Martin, Martin! Wake up!"

It was Dora, shaking me out of a troubled slumber at Rackenfield. "Wha . . . what's the matter?"

"You've got to get up—I'm worried about the mistress."

I sat up and blearily scanned her face, furrowed by concern. "Okay. What the hell's happened?"

"I think she's planning something . . . drastic."

I pulled on a dressing gown and followed her down to her kitchen. She poured me some tea while I struggled to confront a day I'd hoped would never come. "Tell me slowly, Dora. What's happened?"

"Well, she weren't right all yesterday, as you'd 'ave known if you 'adn't bin drinking yourself silly at The Oak. She went to the safe an' took something out. Then announced she was off to Cap'n Sayers for bridge. But Monday's never bridge night. There were some other reason an' I think I know what it was." She paused.

"Well?"

"She come back about the time I was leaving, not at all 'er usual self. Seemed almost guilty about summut. Went straight upstairs. I found some sheets to take up to the airing cupboard an' from the landing 'eard 'er open an' shut the drawers in that chest just inside the bedroom door."

"So what?"

"Well, it's not as if she'd changed or anything. She came straight back out, closed the door behind 'er—she never does that—an' looked real shocked to see me on the landing. Shooed me down to the kitchen like I were in the way. I knew for certain then there was summut wrong."

"But what?"

"I didn't get a chance to find out until this morning. Straight after breakfast, she took the car out for a drive. I reminded 'er the doctor 'ad told 'er to give up driving, but she wouldn't listen. Anyway, when she'd gone, I went up to 'er room and took a look in the chest o' drawers. That's where I found it—tucked away under some 'ankies in the top drawer."

"Found what?"

Dora looked straight at me. "The gun. That there revolver of Sir Gerald's. The one she's kept locked up all these years. The chambers spun like they'd just bin oiled . . . an' it was loaded."

The words sunk in. "Are you sure?"

"Course I am, boy. Mr Bates used to shoot a bit. 'E taught me enough about guns to know when one of 'em's in a state to be used."

"But why should she take it out of the safe and carry it to the Sayers'?"

" 'Cos Cap'n Sayers is a crack shot. Keeps game birds on 'is land. Even 'as a proper range out the back of 'is 'ouse—a real enthusiast. The sort o' chap who could check over an old gun to see if it still works proper."

I stood up. "We've got to do something. Do you realize what this could mean?"

She nodded. "I'm awful 'fraid she can't face that dratted black sheep Sellick."

"Where's the gun now?"

"Where I found it. It's 'er gun, after all. I got no right to mess with it."

I looked at the clock: nearly nine o'clock. Just three hours to go before Sellick called to receive a ritual surrender. I had to thrust to the back of my mind all the swirling images of fate and failure and concentrate on what one day—one slice of speeding time—might hold for us all.

I flung on some clothes and hurried to Quarterleigh. There was no answer to the doorbell. I peered through the porch window; no sign of life. Anxiously, I scanned around.

Then I heard a car coming along the lane. Sure enough, it turned in at Quarterleigh: the cream Sunbeam, Elizabeth smiling beneath a headscarf as she drove down the drive. I opened the garage doors and she drove inside.

"I didn't expect you so soon," she said as she climbed out.

I smiled. "Couldn't stay away."

"Come inside and tell me why." She led the way with a disturbing, almost feverish energy.

I made some coffee and we drank it in the lounge while I struggled to approach my suspicions. Elizabeth seemed every inch controlled and composed, reclining in an armchair and sipping coffee, confronting Sellick's ultimatum with equanimity. "A golden gaze above a cream dress," as Strafford had recalled on that longest day 67 years before? Not quite. Old age had given Elizabeth a fragile, silvery beauty and a tweed skirt and jacket had succeeded thc Edwardian flounces. Yet something remained, some twinge of her spirit and looks that would have awed Strafford and could still move me. What worried me, though, was the heightened colour in her cheeks, the look in her eye that had lost its usual serenity.

"Where have you been?" I asked. "I thought you didn't drive yourself anymore."

"I drove to Harting Hill, just to prove I still could. I found it . . . exhilarating."

"And did it take your mind off Sellick?"

"No, but it clarified it."

"How?"

She smiled, with just a touch of artifice. "It made me realize how little we should fret over such problems as Mr Sellick may cause us when there is so much beauty in the world." And in you, Elizabeth, and in you.

"So what will you tell him?"

She seemed to pull back her thoughts from a distance. "Oh, that he can have his way. The good name of a very old lady is a small matter, after all." Did she really mean it? I could no longer tell.

"As simple as that?"

"I think so, Martin. It will be a brief and tame encounter. In fact, there's no need for you to remain for it, though I'm grateful to you for coming. I can't help but feel that your presence would only heighten his sense of triumph."

She was trying to get rid of me. I felt sure of it. "Maybe so. I confess I've no alternatives to offer."

"That's because there aren't any."

Somehow, I had to find a way to check on Dora's find. "On Sunday, you mentioned all the anniversaries that fell today. I don't suppose they help."

"No." She sighed. "Edwin's visit to me at Putney: it's one of the descriptions in the Memoir I found especially touching."

"'A golden gaze above a cream dress.'"

"You remember it too." This time her smile was genuine. "Do you know, I still have that dress, hung up in my wardrobe. A genuine antique—rather like its owner. I'm afraid I'd never fit into it now."

I saw my opening. "I'd be fascinated to see it."

"Then I'll show it to you one day."

"How about now—just to pass the time?"

She thought for a moment, then agreed. What reason, after all, could she give to refuse? We'd finished our coffee, the morning stretched ahead and it was a simple request.

We went up to her room. I stood on the threshold while she opened the door of a wardrobe and began sifting through the contents. "I'm sure it's here somewhere," she said.

The chest of drawers was to my right. With Elizabeth's back turned, I'd never have got a better chance. The wardrobe was crammed with the favoured clothes of a long life and the search was evidently going to be lengthy. "I've put all the dresses I'm too old for but can't bear to throw out in here," she mused. "Look at the shoulder-padding on this one . . ."

I eased open the drawer. At one end, as Dora had said, there were some handkerchiefs, not very neatly stacked. "And this cocktail dress turned some heads in 1920, I can tell you . . ."

I parted the handkerchiefs. There it was: somehow larger than I'd envisaged, dull and black, standard officer's issue, Natal Field Forces, 1899. Old maybe, but made to last and made to kill.

Suddenly, silence encroached on my thoughts. I looked up. Elizabeth had stopped talking and was looking into the mirror inside the wardrobe door. It had swung back slowly on its hinges while she'd searched, the reflection moving with it. And now it had moved to me.

"What are you doing, Martin?" she asked levelly.

There was nothing for it but the truth. I lifted the gun out of the drawer. "I was looking for this. It's your husband's service revolver, isn't it?"

She turned and looked at me. "What business of yours if it is?"

"Strictly speaking, none. But I hope our friendship gives me the right to act in your interests."

"And how are you doing that?"

"You used to keep this gun locked away in the safe. You told me so yourself."

"And may I not remove it if I wish to?"

"Of course. But Dora's worried about you and so am I."

"So Dora was spying on me last night."

I moved towards her. "Not spying, Elizabeth. We just wanted to be sure you weren't planning anything . . . foolish."

"You think I'm too old to look after myself?"

"No. But a loaded gun is a dangerous . . ."

"Who says it's loaded?"

"It's easy enough to find out." I fumbled with the gun for a moment in my efforts to open the chambers.

"Let me show you." Holding one of my hands to steady my grip, she slipped back the catch to show a cartridge lodged in the chamber, then closed it. "You're the one who needs protecting from himself, Martin. It is loaded and it is dangerous, but I know how to handle it and you obviously don't. Don't you think it would be safer with me?"

"No." I pulled it away from her and plunged it into my jacket pocket. "I'm sorry, Elizabeth. I can't stand by and let you endanger yourself."

She smiled and walked away to the window, sinking into the armchair with a sigh. "I know you think you're acting for the best, Martin—so I'll overlook the deception you practised to get up here. The problem is: I genuinely believe you ought to let me keep the gun."

"Why?"

"So that I can put an end to all this"—she gazed down into the garden—"bitterness."

I felt sure then that I was right. "There are too many people who are fond of you to let you do that."

She looked up in surprise. "Ah, I see. You thought . . . No, no, that's not it at all."

I walked towards her. "I understand how you must feel. At least, I think I do, though I must admit I hadn't seen you as the sort of person to contemplate . . ."

"Suicide?"

I sat on the broad windowsill and faced her. "Yes."

She smiled. "Then you do understand me, Martin, better

than you think, because it's true: I never would contemplate suicide. And, if I did, it would be something much less messy than shooting myself."

I frowned. "I don't follow. You did get this man Sayers to overhaul the gun?"

"Yes, though without knowing Dora was dogging my footsteps." We exchanged smiles at Dora's kindly expense. "Captain Sayers is an old friend. He's often expressed an interest in Gerald's revolver, so he was only too delighted to take a look at it, check the sighting, oil the moving parts and so forth, then try it out on a target in his range. It showed up remarkably well for such an old weapon."

"Old friend or not, he had no business letting you bring it home loaded."

She grinned mischievously. "As he'd be the first to agree, I just helped myself to half a dozen bullets from the box he'd opened to try out the gun, while his back was turned. I don't suppose he'll miss them."

"But why? What's the point if . . ."

Her eyes met mine. "That's right, Martin. This old lady was going to add something much more dramatic than suicide to her family's catalogue of misfortune. I still would, if you'd only return the gun to me. I think I could use it to good effect."

"You must be joking."

"No. I'm deadly serious. Don't you see? Leo Sellick is an evil man, corrupted by the power he believes he has over us, so much so that he'll never be satisfied with whatever we do to appease him. He'll always come back for more. Well, I don't propose to let that happen. There's only one way to deal with a blackmailer."

"Well, I'm afraid you'll have to find some other way. The gun stays with me. Things just can't be that bad."

"But they are. Don't you think I've racked my brains since Sunday for some way out? There isn't one. So long as Leo Sellick lives, the destruction by degrees of my whole family will be his goal. He has the ability to achieve it and, God knows, he has good reason for wanting to achieve it too. You must let me have the gun back."

"I'm sorry, Elizabeth, I can't do that. I agree Sellick means to embarrass you publicly, but I'm sure that's as far as it goes." I wasn't sure, of course, not at all sure. "You've had a lot of shocks lately. You're under strain. You're bound to get things a little . . . out of proportion."

She sat up sharply. "Don't patronize me, Martin, please. I'm not suffering from senile dementia. It's you who's got this out of proportion. I can't force you to hand back the gun, but please realize that you're depriving me of the only way I can resist Mr Sellick's demands."

I tried to soothe her. "I'll be here when he arrives. Obviously it's unpalatable, but, in the long run, agreeing to his terms might give him less satisfaction than fighting it out."

"You leave me no alternative. I hope you're prepared to take responsibility for what happens."

"I'll have to. In a sense, I'm already responsible. If I'd not taken Sellick's job in the first place . . ."

"He would have found somebody else to do it." The thought seemed to calm her. "I'm glad it was you, Martin. I don't think you could have changed what's happened."

It was good of Elizabeth to say so, but I knew differently. If I'd invested more time in Ambrose and less in Eve, if I'd prevented the invitation being sent to Sellick . . . if, ah, if only. I'd thought myself so clever, making a play for Eve while being paid well to dig out a few historical truths. But it had been the purest self-deception. Every step of the way had been mapped for me by Sellick months before, when my gullible, friend's journey to Madeira—all too ready to act the part written for me—started us down the road to a proud family's humiliation. I'd connived at it myself, but without knowing what it would really mean, without knowing that, in the Couchmans' downfall, Strafford and I would be equal victims. "Render to Elizabeth whatever assistance she may need." It was the only guidance Strafford had left me. With that at least I could still keep faith.

"You could say," mused Elizabeth, filling the silence I'd left, "that I'm the last person to judge Mr Sellick. After all, I misjudged Edwin and Gerald—in very different ways."

"We've all been guilty of misjudgements—Sellick included."

"Then let's hope taking my gun wasn't a misjudgement on your part."

"It's for the best. Sellick doesn't deserve such dramatic treatment."

"Really? We can't forget his connection with my family, you know." She paused and craned her neck slightly to look down into the garden. "What do you suppose was going through Gerald's mind when he took Edwin's place—and name—in Durban? I was married to him for forty years, yet I've no idea."

"You've read what he had to say in the Postscript."

"Yes—and now that's gone too, which proves, I suppose, that Mr Sellick may not be the devil I think him to be." It was said without conviction and its absence was contagious. Why had Sellick let us burn his proof positive?

Later, walking in the garden, I pondered the point. Elizabeth was resting while Dora bustled about—happier now I'd assured her that her mistress was unarmed. I had time, while the last hour ticked away towards noon, to turn over a disturbing thought in my mind.

Nothing had happened that Sellick hadn't planned or foreseen except my discovery of the Postscript. Its destruction had been his only concession to the weakness of others.

Or had it indeed been to the weakness of others? My mind went back to our argument over dinner the week before. He'd been evasive about his movements at the time of Strafford's death, about his reasons for not tracking down Sir Gerald there and then. Was it embarrassment? Did the fact that Strafford outwitted him 26 years before detract from his omniscient image? Or was there something else?

I sat by the brook and watched the water flow by. A few fish shimmered past in the brown depths, heading downstream to where, a quarter of a mile further on, a fisherman sat by the bole of a tree and waited patiently to deceive them. Sun trying to break through the cloud. A rodent stirring leaves in the wood opposite. A fisherman waiting as long as necessary to make his catch. That's when I first guessed how it had really been all those years before, when I realized at last what Sellick was trying to conceal while threatening the Couchmans with exposure. And that's when I heard the church clock strike twelve and call a halt to all my guessing.

I walked round to the front of the house. By the time I got there, the clock was silent. But, contiguous with the fading reverberation of its last chime, there came the sound of a car in the lane. I knew it was Sellick's before I saw the royal blue Daimler nose down the drive, before I saw the grim, spare satisfaction inscribed on his face as he leant forward to speak to the uniformed chauffeur.

I stopped a short distance from the car and watched, without expression or any hint of greeting, as the chauffeur got out and opened Sellick's door. He stepped lightly onto the gravel, said one word—"Wait"—to the chauffeur, then strolled jauntily towards me, imbuing his smile with a delight at its own falsehood. I'd been shown the bohemian recluse in Madeira; we'd all been shown the sober South African when he'd come in response to Elizabeth's invitation. Now, another facet was on view: wealth conspicuous in the flunkey-drive limousine, the elegant clothes, the gold wristwatch and cufflinks, power gouged in an old face, a mask shed by a man of means and menace.

"Good afternoon, Martin," he said. "I wish I could say it came as a pleasant surprise to find you here."

I struggled to keep my temper and my nerve. "I'm here as a friend of the family."

He chuckled icily. "Then have I not achieved a miracle of sorts: to cleave you once more to the family that rejected you?"

"Perhaps. But let's not labour the point. You think you're on top and maybe you are. But I have a few questions that may not leave you there."

"They'll have to wait. I'm here to see Lady Couchman, not debate matters with you. The time for that is over. Is she in?" He turned, without waiting for an answer, and strode towards the door. As he did so, it opened—and Elizabeth stood waiting there for him, slightly hunched, diminished by the reason for their meeting, depressed by the knowledge that she had nothing left to bargain with.

"Mr Sellick," she said. "I see that you are prompt—if nothing else. Would you care to come in?"

"Unless you wish to discuss our business out here."

Elizabeth didn't answer, just turned and led the way into the lounge. She offered Sellick neither a seat nor a drink, merely watched with her deep, reflective eyes his progress to the fireplace. There he stood in all his open arrogance, regarding us with a slight but predatory tilt of his head, amusing himself with our discomfort, assuring himself that he couldn't lose.

"You clearly have no taste for pleasantries," he said. "So I'll dispense with them. Timothy has put my terms to you?"

"Yes." Elizabeth's reply was a hollow murmur.

"Do you accept? Will you give Miss Randall your unconditional cooperation in the writing of her book?"

Elizabeth walked slowly to the window. "I have an answer, Mr Sellick. But first, will you answer three questions of mine?"

"I'll hear them. I don't guarantee to answer them."

"Very well." She turned to look straight at him. "Firstly, Timothy claims to be assisting you because the financial plight of Couchman Enterprises leaves him no choice. Is that true?"

Sellick smiled. I watched his expression hint that he enjoyed giving the answer more than withholding it. "Yes and no. I have undertaken to resume my investment in the company. But you should know that Timothy's so-called mercantile consultancy is in a bad way and so he needs capital for a variety of reasons. I am paying him well for his services."

"Enough to make him forget any loyalty to his family?" asked Elizabeth quietly.

"Yes. Of course, you may feel it is a poor kind of loyalty that can be bought and—and I would agree with you. All I have done is make your grandson's true character apparent to you."

"Thank you." She seemed to intend no irony. "Secondly, did you set out, when you visited Henry in London, to hound him into suicide? After all, we know now that you lied the first time you came here, by pretending you had never met him."

Sellick's smile broadened horribly. "I didn't lie, Lady Couchman. I simply withheld certain facts, which is surely the right of us all." He glanced across at me, as if to say that the only difference between him and me was that he'd known all along what I'd kept from him, whereas I'd never realized till now what he'd kept from me." As for Henry, well, since you ask, you may as well know what passed between us." He paused for effect. "He agreed to meet me at his club—the Carlton, bastion of the Conservative Party—that Sunday night.

"At first, he sought to bluff it out. When I informed him that I meant to deprive him of his good name as surely as his father had deprived me of any name at all, he actually had the temerity to threaten me. He boasted that he wielded influence enough to have me silenced—or worse. He cited as an example Strafford's death in 1951. Did I want to suffer a similar fate?

"I laughed in his face. He had grossly overestimated his own importance: a common flaw in those who inherit wealth and position. He seriously believed, you see, that his political friends had made away with Strafford in order to protect him. Once I had convinced him that such was not the case, his defence was broken. He knew then that he had no way of preventing me from dragging his name through the mire where it belonged, knew that, when he confronted me here, I would show him no mercy. He faced, at best, public disgrace as his father's accessory in bigamy and fraud. At worst—I later learned—he faced exposure as Ambrose Strafford's murderer. So even my threats were more potent than I knew. Where Ambrose's murder could be proved—in the circumstances, nobody would believe it was an accident—Edwin's murder could be surmised. It was bound to turn out that way in the end.

"So you see, I did not set out to drive Henry to suicide. Indeed, I had planned a more lingering and public fate for him. Some part of that could still be arranged if you refuse to co-operate. I think he was simply a weaker and vainer man than even I had supposed. Unable to face what he knew lay ahead, he took the coward's way out."

Elizabeth moved unsteadily to an armchair. I watched her hand clasp the arm as she sank into it, surrendering the stage, as it were, to Sellick, while I remained motionless and silent, a helpless spectator. At last, she spoke. "All you say about my son may be true, Mr. Sellick, but you must understand: he was the only son I had."

"Oh I do understand," Sellick rasped, for the first time admitting vehemence to his voice. "It is you who do not. You still don't comprehend your family's guilt, which you must share: this fine English family with one, favoured son. But not one, Lady Couchman, not in truth. What of . . . the other son? Sir Gerald's forgotten, firstborn foundling? You gave me nothing. What shall I take to pay that debt?"

Elizabeth looked up at him. "You propose to take everything, don't you? My son, my grandson, my good name: everything."

"I shall take a son's due."

"Then my third question . . . why did you let us burn the Postscript?"

"To show you that I didn't need it. I can destroy you without Strafford's help."

It was time I intervened. "That's a lie." Sellick looked towards me as I walked forward. "That's not why you let it happen."

For a long, spaced moment, Sellick's blue eyes fixed me with a cold stare. "You have something to say, Martin?"

"Yes. I want to finish something I was trying to say when news came of Henry's death. It took me a long time to connect it with your part in the destruction of the Postscript, but now I have. You claimed that, by the time you'd deduced from the Memoir who your father really was, Sir Gerald had already died. But there was a three-year gap you couldn't explain away, which is why I didn't believe you. Now you've just confirmed what I think really happened. So let me ask you a fourth question. How did you convince Henry that his political friends hadn't had Strafford killed?"

Sellick's stare began to move towards an unaccountable amusement. "It was a preposterous idea from the first."

"Maybe, but Henry believed it. There's only one way you could have persuaded him otherwise: that's by telling him the truth. By telling him that you killed Strafford."

I'd hoped for a hostile response, but Sellick only smiled. He turned to Elizabeth. "Martin is quite right, Lady Couchman. I killed Edwin Strafford."

Elizabeth looked from one to the other of us and finally up at Sellick. "You murdered Edwin?"

"Yes." He raised his head slightly, as if taking pride in the declaration. "I am free to tell you so now that the Postscript is gone. Without it, there is no evidence to link me with Strafford at thc time of his death. Some years ago, I arranged—with a little judicious bribery—for the record of my birth in Pietermaritzburg to be lost. Thus you will appreciate that, so far as anyone can prove, I am merely a disinterested observer of the Couchman family's death agony. I left Henry in no doubt that I would force his political masters to disown him and deny any part in Strafford's death. Logically, that would have left him as the prime suspect.

"He would have consented as readily as the rest of you in the destruction of the Postscript, in order to clear himself of the charges he knew I would bring against him. Thus he would have played into my hands as you have done. Perhaps, to give him his meagre due, he foresaw that and took the only way out left to him.

"He recognized my account of Strafford's death as the truth as soon as he heard it, and must have realized how easily the public could be led to believe that it was he who played my part."

"And what was your part?"

"You may as well know now. Indeed, I would not wish to spare you it. After all, Lady Couchman"—he bowed faintly in her direction—"my mistake and therefore Strafford's death were all really Sir Gerald's work. Strafford outwitted me in Madeira only because I had no way of guessing what he realized at once from my confrontation of him: that it was Sir Gerald, not he, who was the guilty man.

"Strafford had me shut up for a month in a police cell in Funchal. Like all English gentlemen, he had tame officials to do him favours. Later, I made the Police Chief regret doing him that favour. But, at the time, my thoughts were reserved for Strafford: my father, as I supposed, who'd had me flung into gaol whilst he scurried back to England.

"I followed him. It took me two weeks from my release to track him to Barrowteign, but I found him there, hiding, as I believed, from justice. I proposed to show him no mercy. Yet my arrest in Funchal had made me expect a wily prey. Instead, it was all too easy.

"I reached Dewford on the afternoon of June 4th and learned from the publican in the village that Strafford was staying at Lodge Cottage. He'd made no secret of his return, which puzzled me. But I didn't stop to brood on the point.

"I went straight to Barrowteign. There were workmen everywhere, so nobody paid me much heed as I walked up the drive. When I was about halfway, I saw Strafford come out of the main door of the house and make his way openly towards the cottage. I was surprised. I'd expected him to be lying low, not strolling around the estate as if he owned it. I know now that he had more on his mind than the possibility of being pursued by me.

"I made sure he did not catch sight of me and kept watch on the cottage, waiting for nightfall. Having seen his nephew leave, I felt certain that Strafford would be alone.

"As it happened, Strafford saved me the trouble of a stealthy approach. He came out, lit his pipe and leant against the level crossing gates, looking up and down the railway line. I was becoming anxious that his nephew might return. There was no time to lose.

"I emerged from hiding and challenged him. He treated me with scorn, denying that he owed me anything, openly admitting that he had used his influence to have me confined in Funchal. His calmness—his apparent determination to enrage me—was baffling. But I was a younger and less calculating man then than I am now. His arrogant defiance inspired in me only violence.

"I've thought of it often since and come to admire Strafford for what he did that night: high praise I assure you. He walked out onto the track as if to put the gate between us, but more, I suspect, to lure me to that point. He sensed it was all or nothing, him or me, make or break. He stood little chance, in all conscience, and must have known it. That's what I admire about him. A loser, yes, but a better man than the cheap fraudster who turned out to be my father.

"At that moment, I hated him and wasn't about to let him escape a second time. I pursued him across the track. He seized me, attempted to force me down onto the rails. I heard the train whistle and understood what was in his mind. I remember the shock I felt that the miserable schemer I knew my father to be should be capable—even in dire need—of physical courage. Not that it was ever likely to be enough. I had more than enough strength to overpower him—though not without difficulty, for he fought well. But, once I'd broken free of his grasp, I was able to fell him with one good blow and leap clear of the track with the train nearly upon us, sounding its whistle and braking far too late. Strafford's age was against him. He never had a chance.

"I fled the scene. Strafford was done for—that much was certain. I'd planned a different fate for him, but he'd forced the issue and engineered an honourable death. He'd gone down fighting."

"Fighting to save me," Elizabeth whispered.

"Maybe. At all events, he'd made of me a murderer. There was nothing for it but to return to Madeira at once and hope that nobody would connect me with his death. Nobody did. And parricide didn't seem an unjust way of avenging my mother. I was content."

"Until you found the Memoir?"

"Quite so. The irony of acquiring the Quinta when it came onto the market appealed to me. But I had no idea what was waiting for me there. When I read the Memoir, I understood what Strafford had really been trying to achieve. The Memoir told me enough to identify Sir Gerald as my father, but the circumstances of Strafford's death meant that I could not come here to confront him without the risk of being branded a murderer. Thus, Lady Couchman, your peace of mind was safe.

"But only for a time. Last year, I reflected that Strafford had won you a quarter of a century of unearned complacency. Sir Gerald had—as is the way with such men—died full of cheated years and specious honour. Henry I read of as a rising force in Tory politics. I was wealthy, yes, wealthier than ever, in fact, but not content. I was unknown and forgotten, for all my material success. baulked by Strafford's sacrifice from making the Couchmans pay for their crime.

"I conceived an elegant solution to the problem. I realized that I was wealthy enough to achieve your downfall through mere proxies. For life had taught me—you might say my father had taught me—that all men can be bought and most come pretty cheap at that. Hired hands could protect my anonymity and do my bidding. That was Martin's role—to dig out enough evidence in the cause of historical research to bury you all, without my having to lift a finger. And you did a good job, Martin—no question of it. Until . . . you discovered the Postscript. That was an unexpected difficulty: Strafford's damnable addiction to posterity. Naturally, news of its discovery was disturbing. I had no way of knowing what it might contain to link me with his death, so your references to it were more tantalizing than you knew. There seemed nothing for it but to come at once and brazen it out.

"I tackled Henry first as the weakest link. In his breaking, it became obvious that he had not seen the document, worried though he was about it. There was no harm in telling him the truth when he had even more reason than I to suppress the evidence of it. Once he was dead, the Postscript had only to be destroyed for me to enjoy complete freedom of action. Everybody was very co-operative in bringing that about."

"You've been very clever, Mr Sellick," said Elizabeth falteringly.

"Thank you." He smiled broadly.

"We thought you generous in allowing us to burn it."

"That's what I wanted you to think. Timothy encouraged the idea, as I'd instructed him to."

"And I persuaded Martin not to object."

"Yes. Of course, you should know, Lady Couchman, that, in not objecting, Martin too was only following instructions."

Elizabeth looked at me. "Martin?"

"I . . . I don't know what he means," I stammered.

Sellick beamed. "Yes he does. He's still my employee, you see."

"It's a lie," I shouted. "Just another lie."

Sellick turned towards Elizabeth. "I ask you, Lady Couchman, hasn't Martin done a highly effective job in creating this situation? You've met Miss Randall, another of my . . . employees. She's a bonus payment I arranged for him along the way. You know how much he hates your family. I've only paid him to do what he's always to do: get back at all of you."

My eyes followed this to Elizabeth, hunched in her chair,

wizened and lost. What could she believe when I wasn't certain any more what I believed? She looked up at me and, in her eyes, there was only a terrible doubt. Sellick was right. I couldn't have brought her to this any better if he'd paid me. So what grounds were there for believing he hadn't? I stood speechless, condemned by my own failure to be judged a tainted success.

"If you'll excuse me," said Sellick, "I'll just have something brought in with which to celebrate our agreement. It's something I promised Martin a long time ago." He walked slowly from the room. I heard his voice by the front door, addressing the chauffeur.

In the brief silence of his absence, I stumbled through the rebuttals obvious even to me towards an unconvincing denial. "It's not true, Elizabeth. I'm not working for Sellick any more. I didn't know. . ." I stopped in mid-sentence.

Elizabeth looked up at me. "How can I believe you, Martin? What is there left for me to hold onto? Is this the real reason you took the gun from me?"

I sank into a chair opposite her. There was no answer to give.

Sellick returned to the room. The chauffeur followed him, carrying a wooden box in his arms. He stood it on the table by the window, then withdrew. Sellick lifted from it a napkin-draped bottle in a wicker wine basket and three claret glasses, which he placed in a line on the table. He took the napkin from the bottle and polished each of the glasses in turn, holding them up to the light as he did so. We watched in a trance.

"Today is my birthday," he announced at last. "A date your family should never forget, Lady Couchman. To celebrate that—and your agreement to co-operate—I've brought this bottle: a very special bottle." He lifted it from its basket. I recognized it at once: the 1792 madeira he'd promised as a prize for successful completion of my research into the Strafford mystery. "Originally, I'd intended that we should drink this with Alec at Quint do Porto Novo. But Alec cannot be with us and I don't suppose we shall ever be going back to Madeira together again. So I've brought it here with me in honour of the occasion." He took a penknife from his pocket and cut away the lead from the top of the bottle. "The flight may not have agreed with it and, after all, such vintages are always unpredictable." He returned the bottle to its basket and applied a corkscrew to the neck.

Elizabeth looked at me. "What is this, Martin?"

"My prize for completing the assignment: probably the last bottle in the world of 1792 madeira, left by Strafford in his cellar."

I looked back at Sellick. He'd drilled the corkscrew in. Now he braced the bottle with his hand against the basket and began to pull the cork. I saw his face frown at the skilled and concentrated effort. "This should not be attempted by a novice," he rasped. "You could say I have studied hard for this moment." Slowly but smoothly, the cork emerged. "I think it may be all right, my friends. I think we may be in a unique position to sample a wine once offered to Napoleon." He lifted the bottle from the basket with a reverential air.

"I shan't want any," said Elizabeth.

"Come, come, Lady Couchman. To refuse such an auspicious wine on such an auspicious occasion would be churlish. Surely the widow of a knight would not behave so? I insist you join me in a glass."

"I shall not."

"Lady Couchman," he said, advancing towards her, the bottle in one hand, a glass in the other, "you should know that, when I insist upon something, I have the means to enforce my wish. In this small matter, as, henceforth, in large, you must obey me."

I looked at the salivating triumph in his face. Elizabeth had been right after all. Her forced hand in Eve's book was to be only the start. Now that Sellick had gained the dominance which he deemed his right, he would stop at nothing. Strafford's wine to celebrate Strafford's defeat. Elizabeth to toast an anniversary of her husband's treachery. Me to swallow the bitter vintage of serving him unwillingly but well.

Sellick poured the dark fluid into the glass. It was thick and ruby red. "It is better than I had expected," he said. "Drink, Lady Couchman. Or should I call you Miss Latimer?"

The fire in Elizabeth's eyes outblazed the wine as she looked up. "You may do your worst, Mr Sellick, but I shall not drink."

"You shall." I flinched with the shock and suddenness of his act. He swung the glass and pitched the measure of wine towards her. It drenched her face and neck and splashed down her blouse in a crimson douche. She blinked and coughed once, but didn't move, merely looked, not at Sellick, but at me. Through the wash of madeira that could have been Strafford's blood, her eyes spoke of anguish and accusation. They didn't even flicker when Sellick tossed the glass between us. It smashed into the fireplace, scattering fragments across the hearth.

I stood up. Sellick was walking back to the table, to collect another glass. "I'm sure you'll drink, Martin. As an historian, albeit a hired one, you'll relish a Napoleonic vintage."

Enough. A fractured moment. What had Alec once said? "It's as simple as a worm turning." What was an inadequate historian to do—for once in his sham of a life—but struggle towards an intangible concept concealed between all the words written in and about the past? Honour, loyalty, humanity? No, something much simpler: the right thing to do. "To be, for one fleeting moment, less than a fool." Too hard, Strafford, too hard. Trained to study without conclusion, hired to act for another, never for myself. It was that: a fleeting moment. But for once, for one true, unmet, long-dead friend, for good and all, I turned the tide.

Truth without action was knowledge without honour, was history without Strafford.

It could have been Strafford's hand—but in reality it was mine—that pulled Couch's gun from my jacket pocket as Sellick turned from the table. It could have been a hundred better men—but it had to be me—who raised the gun between two trembling hands and trained it on Sellick in his moment of savoured victory. It could have been any one of a dozen ways he chose to unnerve me, but the one he chose was the only one certain to fail. Perhaps he knew that. Perhaps he couldn't resist one last opportunity to remind me of all the evil I'd happily served—in him and in myself. He took a pace towards me and, as he did so, he smiled. And, as he did so, I pulled the trigger.

I didn't see Sellick fall, just dropped the gun from my jarred hand and stepped towards him. Supine on the carpet, a dark hole in his forehead, his mouth curved open in a frozen smile. Leo Sellick was dead in front of me, his right arm stretched out and hand curled towards the still rocking, felled bottle of 1792 madeira, its blood-red contents gouting onto the pale carpet. It was the last bottle, which nobody would ever drink.

Ten

Why did I do it? That's all they wanted to know. How could I explain that life had stopped for me in that moment, just as it had for Sellick. I hardly remember what happened, in what sequence, at what time, but somebody phoned for the police, while Elizabeth sat talking to me in the lounge, which I wouldn't leave so long as Sellick remained. She was pale, but regally calm.

Later—much later—Elizabeth related snatches of what I'd said in that hushed interval between the act and its flood of consequences.

"You know why I did it?"

"Of course. Before they all come, let me say: it's the finest thing you could ever have done."

"You believed him. When he said I was still working for him."

"God forgive me, yes. It was his gift: to make people think the worst of others. An evil gift."

I remember the police siren gashing the pervasive peace that had followed and forgotten the sudden violence. I remember Elizabeth kissing me on the forehead in stranger and comforting benediction. "You remind me more and more of Edwin. This time, I shan't forsake you." I remember the sun going behind a cloud and the covered shape by the window falling into shadow.

"Why did you do it?"

A rumpled, gravel-voiced inspector sat opposite me, smoking cheap cigarettes. He reminded me—bizarrely—of Marcus Baxter and seemed to say, between his questions: "You bloody fool, Radford. Do you think this proves a damn thing?"

Only what he actually said again and again was "Why did you do it?" I could see the puzzlement in his face. I wasn't the usual sneak thief or drunkard, wasn't even the average rapist or domestic murderer. He didn't know me, or Sellick, or why I'd killed a man on his birthday with his father's gun.

Eventually, unsatisfied, he formally charged me, and invited me to make a statement. There was no pressure or coercion. What I wrote was neither denial nor confession. Even as an explanation it didn't amount to much, because I wasn't speaking to the police or the courts in it or even the public in whose name I was accused. "Leo Sellick was the illegitimate son of Lady Couchman's late husband. I killed him to stop his campaign of harrassment against the Couchman family." Really, it was addressed to Strafford: a dead letter to a dead man. An attempt to tell him his supposed failure had really been a glorious triumph if it could force me to make a stand alongside him. But he couldn't hear.

A sleepless night in a police cell. I was still stunned by the calm that had followed the act, still bathed in an absurd fulfilment.

The mood lingered through the morning. June 22nd: the day after a killing. In Guildford, I knew, the inquest into Henry's death was opening. In Chichester, I lay on my bunk and awaited whatever my action had made inevitable.

In the afternoon, the inspector called for me again. I was taken back to the interrogation room. On the table, there was a thick cellophane bag. It contained the gun.

"It's what you said," he began ruminatively. "An army revolver dating from the turn of the century. We've had it checked. It's in good nick. Lady Couchman confirms it belonged to her husband."

"You've questioned her?"

"Yes—and got more of the same: academic riddles. Only

there's nothing academic about murder." He stared at me for a moment. "If that's what it was."

"What do you mean?"

"You're a weird one—that's a fact. You're no killer. Yet you've killed a man."

"So what happens now?" We were still in the vacuum, the hollow, waiting time.

"You've been charged. Tomorrow, you'll appear in court. Meanwhile, you've got a visitor—your lawyer."

"I don't have a lawyer."

"Sort that out with him. Walter Tremlett: he's known to us. I gather he's Lady Couchman's solicitor." There was a knowing look in his eye that was really just a policeman guessing. "Maybe she's put you on the strength."

"It's not like that." But what was it like? Who was this man, this emissary from Elizabeth? I had no need of a lawyer, no need of a defence—or so I thought.

"Do you want to see him?" He asked, but he knew I would. What else could I do?

They took me back to my cell. A few minutes later, Tremlett was shown in. Rotund, red-faced, half-moon spectacles, receding salt and pepper hair, a country solicitor, in a heavy tweed suit, sweating in the afternoon. He shook my hand clammily.

"Pleased to meet you, Mr Radford."

I sat down on my bunk and he perched on the single chair, cradling a scuffed and bulging briefcase in his lap. "Who sent you, Mr Tremlett?"

"Lady Couchman—as I expect you surmised."

"But why?"

"Young man, somebody in your position needs help."

"Do you really know what that position is?"

"You've been charged with murder, which carries a mandatory life sentence." He smiled disarmingly. "But I imagine you mean rather more than that. Well, as a matter of fact, I do know what your position is, because Lady Couchman has full briefed me. Have they told you what happened at the inquest this morning?"

"No."

"The verdict was accidental death—as we'd hoped. Without Mr Sellick on hand, what else could it be?"

"You tell me." I resented this stranger's assumption of so much knowledge and association.

Once again, the broad, genuine smile. "Mr Radford, I'm here to help you. Do you want to be convicted of murder?"

Since killing Sellick, I'd not stopped to consider more than just the relief it had given me and others. Now I was being forced to confront the actuality of legal retribution. "I've already made a statement admitting that I killed him. It's too late for anything else."

"I've read your statement. It's an admission of homicide, yes, but not murder. That's more than just a fine legal point, as you must realize. Lady Couchman feels beholden to you. She's instructed me to do my best for you. With a good barrister, I think there's every chance of successfully pleading manslaughter and receiving a light sentence."

I looked at him quizzically. "Mr Tremlett, I shot a man in cold blood. How can you dress that up as anything other than murder?"

He pulled off his glasses and sucked one of the arms. "Murder may be commuted to manslaughter on several grounds, one of them being provocation. I think we may be in a position to argue that the killing was provoked."

It had been, but not in any of the ways I expected a court to entertain. "You're not convincing me, let alone judge and jury."

"Bear with me, young man. You've not heard me out. Such a plea would rely upon evidence of the late Mr Sellick's vendetta against the Couchman family and his recent threats towards Lady Couchman. I see his killing as the drastic act of a good friend. I think a jury might see it that way too. Lady Couchman will certainly testify in support of you. I hope your ex-wife may be persuaded to do so also."

"You know a great deal."

"Lady Couchman has told me all that I need to know—which is only prudent."

"I'm grateful to her for trying to help, but I still don't think it'll work. Personal testimony's one thing, but proving Sellick was an unpleasant character isn't enough. You'd have to prove he had a genuine grievance against the Couchmans and was trying to blackmail them. But there *is* no proof, and without proof I'm sunk. The only document confirming Sellick's connexion with the Couchmans was destroyed straight after Henry's funeral. Didn't Elizabeth tell you that?"

"Oh yes. But Lady Couchman visited me at my office here in Chichester the day before the funeral—and deposited with me a copy of that document. I have it with me in my case." I didn't know what to say. Strafford's Postscript—plucked back from the flames. Was it possible? Tremlett pulled a file from his case and handed it to me.

It was—as he'd promised—a complete photocopy of the Postscript. So it was true. The agonized debate, the formal pyre, the dreadful act. And all the time, an anonymous clutch of papers had been waiting in Tremlett's office to give us—whether we wanted it or not—a second chance. Even at desperate need, Elizabeth had remembered Strafford. "Why did she do it?" I said at last. "The whole point was to erase the evidence of Sir Gerald's bigamy."

"And so you did. The copy would have been quite safe with me, unread—until I was instructed to read it, unknown—until it was needed."

"But what for? She couldn't have . . ."

"No." He shook his head. "But from what I know—and from what I imagine you know—is it hard to infer why she would have wanted to keep a secret copy, why she would have saved this last word from Strafford: for her eyes only?"

"No." I'd misjudged her. Elizabeth had succeeded where failure had been inevitable, in standing by both of the men she'd loved. For Strafford's sake, she'd saved the Postscript. For Couch's sake, she'd tried to kill Sellick. And now, for my sake, she'd disinterred the family secret. "But it is only a copy."

"True, but comparison with the original Memoir should verify its authorship. If necessary, I shall go to Madeira to find that."

I looked straight at him. "You're going to great lengths."

He nodded soberly. "Those are my instructions, Mr Radford."

I stood up. "Not if you're to act for me. I appreciate

what you're saying, but there's something you don't quite understand."

He blinked at me owlishly. "Which is?"

"Sellick was threatening Elizabeth with public ruin and humiliation. If we bring all this out in court, we'll be doing the same thing. If I killed him for anything, it was to stop that happening."

He smiled. "I know you think I'm just an ignorant conveyancer, Mr Radford, but, strangely, I had thought of that. It would all be bound to come out. Of course, it wouldn't be slanted as Mr Sellick intended, but it would become public knowledge, which might be just as bad. I think most judges would agree to leave the political connotations strictly alone, which would greatly diminish the story's appeal to the press, but it would inevitably attract the sensation-seekers."

"Exactly."

"I made the point to Lady Couchman in precisely those terms. Like you, I have her interests at heart. I found her response persuasive, so much so that for you to resist would seem ungrateful as well as foolish."

"So persuade me."

"I'll content myself by quoting Lady Couchman's own words. What she said was that Mr Sellick—whatever his background—had no right to demand such a thing of her, but that you—in her judgement—had every right, not least because, of course, you've demanded nothing." A silence fell, warmed by Elizabeth's generosity of spirit. Then Tremlett returned the Postscript to his case and gathered himself together. "Think it over, Mr Radford. I'll attend the court tomorrow. You'll need to have decided by then."

I stood up. "I can't afford to stand on my dignity, Mr Tremlett. I'd be grateful for whatever you can do."

"Very well. We'll give it a try then."

"When you see Elizabeth, tell her . . . tell her I'm honoured to have her support. She'll understand."

"I'm sure she will." He shook my hand. "In fact, I rather think I do myself."

Tremlett had offered me a way out when I'd least expected one. In a way, that only made what followed worse, only made the fragile optimism harder to bear in the stretched, corrosive phase just about to begin.

For the courtroom was only the most formal and visible place of my trial in the months ahead. I knew, I suppose, when I killed Sellick that the penalty for that one act was bound to be long and lingering. And so it proved. A brief appearance in court on June 23rd was immaterial, a plea of manslaughter easy to forget, while I passed the summer in the brick vacuum of Lewes Prison's remand wing, craving the trial to come with all the fervour of a deprived man.

Tremlett worked hard. He got the services of a fine barrister, Clifford Dane, Q.C., an old friend of Henry's, and made that promised trip to Madeira on my behalf. To compound the ironies, Helen came once, to express her stilted version of gratitude. I refrained from telling her that she had nothing to thank me for. There was no point in working off grudges anymore. I was more amazed than she was that it had turned out as it had. I insisted that Nick and Hester be informed and they were good enough to give me a chance to explain at last what I'd involved them in. It can't have made much sense, but they insisted it did.

Aside from Tremlett's progress reports, I saw most of Elizabeth. Our relationship had reverted to those distant, deceptive days when I'd first visited her at Quarterleigh, when we'd explored the past at leisure, ignorant of Ambrose's discovery and what it portended. We talked less of my defence and her part in it than of Strafford and his part in our lives. We'd come to share his memory like a widow and her brother-in-law, we'd come to cherish every trace of him for all the reasons that had prevented her from letting the Postscript be wholly lost.

I asked her about the visitors I didn't receive, but she could tell me nothing. Eve's whereabouts were a mystery and Timothy had vanished to Spain, leaving Couchman Enterprises in the lurch. They'd apparently recovered well without him. Nothing at all was known of Alec, except that he hadn't returned to Madeira.

At last, in early October, the case opened in Lewes Crown Court. One week in a legal itinerary, Regina versus Martin Radford, a weight of jurisprudence to grind down the fact and fantasy. For me, it was the strangest of puppet shows, remote from the events it was supposed to consider, an alien realm of wigs and gowns where what really mattered—Strafford's nobility and Couch's fraud, Sellick's vengeful will and Elizabeth's abiding dignity—held less sway than the whims and strategies of legal technocrats.

"Martin Kenneth Radford, you are charged that, on the twenty-first day of June, in the year of our Lord nineteen hundred and seventy-seven, at Miston, in the county of West Sussex, you did murder Leo Sellick of Madeira, Portugal, a citizen of the Republic of South Africa. How do you plead?"

"Not guilty to murder, but guilty to manslaughter, on grounds of provocation."

Provocation: the crafted key to Dane's mortice-locked defence, or so he thought. To me, it seemed the prosecution's deficiencies rather than Dane's virtuosity that gave me my best chance. It seemed, by a macabre twist, Sellick's self-imposed mystery that might save me in the jury's eyes.

The case against me had been made by the second day, with plodding, constabulary competence. The facts were undisputed and swiftly told. They allowed Dane little chance to impress.

I've often wondered since whether Dane did some deal behind the scenes with Thorndyke, counsel for the prosecution. There was something contrived about their disagreements, something prepared about their approaches, something suspicious about the failure to present Sellick as a tragic, innocent victim of mindless murder. The thought was to recur to me later.

The press and public galleries had filled when Dane opened for the defence. He'd already persuaded me—instructed would be more accurate—that to give evidence myself could prove disastrous. So I had to rely on his professional expertise and the witnesses he called. And they didn't let me down.

Elizabeth was the central figure. She was in the box for a whole day, charming the judge and winning the jury. When she revealed her late husband's secret marriage in South Africa and Sellick's connexion with it, the whole court felt for her. Her decency in seeking to effect a reconciliation was undeniable, her gallantry in resisting Sellick's true intentions irresistible. Did the strain fatally affect her son's driving? She allowed the possibility. We took the hint of probability. Would she have shot Sellick herself if I'd let her? She thought so. We felt we knew so. She spared herself—and us —none of the details of her grandson's treachery or Sellick's final demands. By the end, I saw in some of the jurors' faces the thought that they might—just possibly—have done the same as me. We'd established a kind of fellowship.

"Your witness, Mr Thorndyke."

"No question, m'lud."

No questions? Cross-examining Elizabeth was bound to be a risky business—risky because, if she could have been rattled, it might only have heightened the jury's sympathy for her. But surely the risk had to be taken? Suspicion grew in my mind.

However lax Thorndyke's challenge to our evidence was, the burden of proof remained with us. Handwriting experts were called. Yes, the photocopied Postscript had been written by the author of the Memoir. The jury was given a weekend in which to read the telling extracts. But only extracts. Dane, Thorndyke and the judge had gone into a huddle and emerged with an agreement on that. "Best to keep it brief," I was told. Of course. But somehow I suspected something else.

Strafford's public career wasn't so much as mentioned, far less any hint given that he might have been done down by political enemies. In return—or so it seemed—Thorndyke gave Elizabeth an easy ride and allowed Dane to lead the jury towards the desired verdict. His summing-up was, in its way, a triumph.

"Ladies and gentlemen of the jury, I ask you to consider the salient features of this remarkable case. On the one hand, we have the deceased—Leo Sellick, an elderly, wealthy, South African businessman. Materially, he lacked for nothing. But, on a personal level, he was friendless, secretive and increasingly obsessed with the father who deserted his mother before he was born and condemned him to an orphan's upbringing. When he finally traced his father, the man was dead and beyond his reach. Only his father remained to face his wrath.

"On the other hand, we have the defendant—Martin Radford, a young unemployed history graduate, hired by the deceased to provide the evidence with which to blackmail the Couchmans. Not that my client knew that to be his intention. He embarked innocently on what he thought to be an exercise in historical research.

"We know from Lady Couchman's courageous testimony what that evidence was. We know it may have played a part in her son's death in a car accident on June 13th this year. We know that, only a matter of days after the accident, Sellick presented Lady Couchman with an ultimatum: to co-operate in a dubious literary exposé of her late husband's youthful indiscretion, or let Sellick do his worst.

"My client had every reason to believe he had unwittingly imperilled the welfare of a woman whom he had come to admire—whom I think we have all come to admire. On the afternoon of June 21st he was forced to watch helplessly whilst Sellick abused and harangued Lady Couchman at her home, at one point throwing a glass of wine into her face. It was at that point that my client lost control of himself—momentarily, as any man might. As it happened—solely as a result of his endeavours to protect Lady Couchman from herself—he had a loaded gun on his person. In the heat of the moment and goaded beyond endurance, he drew the gun and fired, killing Sellick instantly.

"So much he readily confesses. To term this murder is, I believe, to distort the truth. The prosecution has failed to challenge the evidence of provocation brought before you. I suggest that a verdict of manslaughter would be sufficient punishment for a man who has already suffered much. I suggest that to be, in the circumstances, your only proper verdict."

So far so good. But the judge was no impressionable juror. He'd scowled and grimaced silently through a week of Dane's florid advocacy with every appearance of a man whose plain tastes were being painfully assaulted. Mr Justic Keppel had the final say and didn't intend to waste it.

"Members of the jury, it is my duty to remind you that your task is a serious and sober one, not to be addressed in an emotional or casual manner. Whatever may have been said against the deceased, remember that he is not here to defend himself.

"This case turns upon a straightforward legal point. It falls to me to offer you straightforward legal advice. The defendant admits homicide but denies murder. He pleads guilty to manslaughter on the ground of provocation, perhaps the least well defined of all the grounds for commution of murder to manslaughter.

"I must therefore draw your attention to the relevant section of the Homicide Act of 1957, which reads as follows. 'Where, on a charge of murder, there is evidence on which the jury can find that the person was provoked to lose his self-control, the question whether the provocation was enough to make a reasonable man do as he did shall be left to be determined by the jury.'

"The matter is therefore in your hands. However, I must first direct you on certain other points. The defence has produced sufficient evidence of provocation to warrant your serious consideration—that is unquestionable. I could have wished"—he shot a glare at Thorndyke—"for a more rigorous examination of that evidence by the prosecution, but no matter. The defendant killed the deceased in the heat of the moment. The absence of cooling time tells in his favour. He might not have done so had he not had a gun on his person at the time. He does not seem to have been carrying that gun with any sinister intent. All that too tells in his favour.

"Yet one factor tells against him. In common law, it is traditionally held that the mode of retaliation must bear a reasonable relationship to the provocation. Thus fists may be answered with fists, but not with a deadly weapon. In this case, mere words—and a technical assault on Lady Couchman—were answered with a bullet. Was such a response truly proportionate to the provocation? I think not. But it is for you to decide."

The jury were out for three hours. Dane and Tremlett came down to my cell to reassure me. Dane was ebulliently confident. "Keppel's last shot won't shake them," he said. "I have them in the palm of my hand. We'll get the right verdict, Mr Radford, never fear."

It was Tremlett who uttered a level-headed word of warning. "The judge seems more hostile than the prosecution. It's worrying. Remember, whatever the verdict, he's the one to pass sentence."

"And what is the maximum sentence for manslaughter?"

"The same as for murder."

The jury were as good as Dane's word. They came back and brought in a verdict of manslaughter. Dane shook my hand vigorously. Elizabeth smiled encouragingly from the public seating above me. Yet Tremlett's words hung in my mind. Keppel's wig-framed, law-lined face was a mask. He adjourned to consider the sentence overnight.

Lewes Crown Court. Tuesday, October 11th. A mild day, sunlight and birdsong venting through the high, open windows. The press gallery packed, awaiting the final pickings. Dane's confident prediction: "He has no choice, Mr Radford, believe me. A light sentence: three years or so. You'll be out in two." But Keppel, brooding and impassive on the bench, had the last word. Faced with his slicing eye and the thoughts I could read behind his censorious brow, I elected to say nothing.

"Martin Kenneth Radford, you have been found guilty of manslaughter. The jury have, in their wisdom, accepted your plea that this is a more appropriate verdict than murder. I agree with them, as I am bound to do.

"Nevertheless, a man has died. However sore his provocation of you, that cannot go unpunished. It is not my intention to allow the idea to gain ground that, simply because a man may seem, by contemporary standards, to be harshly—even brutally—motivated, his killer may excuse himself for that reason. When that day comes, civilized society—which relies upon legal redress for alleged wrongs—will have lost its head. This court, I can assure you, has not lost its head, despite all your learned counsel's polished appeals to the hearts of the jurors.

"I accept that you were provoked into killing Leo Sellick. For that reason—and only for that reason—a verdict of manslaughter and a sentence less than the maximum are appropriate. I do not accept, however, that your retaliation to that provocation can fairly be said to have been proportionate. Amongst the many charges alleged against Leo Sellick, homicide does not feature. That is your offence and the one for which I am bound to impose proportionate punishment. You will go to prison for fifteen years."

"Proportionate punishment."

I wanted to shout at him to stop. I wanted to shout: "You don't understand. Leo Sellick murdered my closest friend on a railway line in Devon 26 years ago. Isn't that proportionate?"

But I said nothing. Silence clamped me with the mute force of a dream. Keppel wouldn't have understood. We'd told him nothing of Strafford. He was just a name, a shadow beyond the shafts of sunlight.

"Proportionate punishment."

The moment had come and gone. The game was won and lost. A prison officer took my arm. Dane muttered a rounded Q.C.'s response. "We'll appeal." I looked up at Elizabeth. She shook her head, as if to say her old, weak best hadn't been good enough. But it had been. You could tell by the pressmen bunching at the exit.

Epilogue

Six months after Keppel had bludgeoned me with a fifteen-year sentence, the Appeal Court reduced it to ten. Dane, who'd have been appalled by even ten first time round, hailed it as a personal accolade. I suppose he had his career to think of. With maximum remission I only had to do another six years and my chances of parole even before that were pretty good. In the autumn of 1979, I was transferred to Ford Open Prison. After the bleakness of Lewes, it was like a holiday camp. I reconciled myself to keeping my nose clean and my head down for the rest of my time. What had once seemed unthinkable became first routine, then just tolerable and finally boring. In the last couple of years at Ford, the Education Officer used my teaching expertise to take the load off his shoulders and getting some of my fellow-inmates through C.S.E.s gave me more satisfaction than any of the work I ever did at Axborough.

My contact with the outside world diminished as my life inside became more self-sufficient. The big break came in the summer of 1978. Elizabeth, who'd written and visited me more than anyone, told me what she'd actually been planning for some time. She'd bought Quinta do Porto Novo from Sellick's estate after lengthy negotiations with a Capetown solicitor.

"I feel sure you, above all people, will understand why," she wrote to me from Quarterleigh. "Life here can never be the same for me following the traumatic events of last year. I am glad to have stayed and done my poor best for you, but now that is settled—not to my satisfaction or, alas, yours—I want to make a complete break. If I wait I shall be too old and frail to do anything about it. I shall be ninety next year and have resolved to confront that milestone with a thorough change.

"So, where better than the equable climate of Madeira? I have been considering it for some time and, at last, all the legal and financial arrangements have been made. Mr Tremlett has been there recently and assures me that the Quinta is in good order. Dora, bless her, has agreed to accompany me, though how she will get on with the Portuguese staff I dread to think. We are combining the journey with a cruise to the Mediterranean, embarking in early September. I shall, of course, be along to see you several times before then. And, when you are free, I shall expect regular visits from you in Madeira.

"I have not felt entirely at ease in this house since Mr Sellick died here. In the house where Edwin found a form of happiness, I hope to regain the peace of mind that he tried so hard to win for me."

Surprised though I was by the news, I found it easy to understand Elizabeth's decision and wished her well, promising to be on hand in Madeira for her hundredth birthday, even though I couldn't be there for her ninetieth. It didn't turn out like that, of course, but it was a happy thought.

After Elizabeth had gone, my contact with her was reduced to regular, bulging airmail letters full of the relish with which she confronted the challenge of a new life so late in the day. "We still keep Edwin's study exactly as it was. I am writing this at his desk. Otherwise, you wouldn't recognize the place. Sprucing it up seems to have given me a new lease of life" . . . "Gabriel (the estate manger) promises a fine harvest this year. Soon, I hope to be able to send you some madeira under my own label" . . . "Dora and Tomás have, I am glad to say, made up their differences" . . . "I look often from this window at the sea and think of England, but without regret—I never expect to come home again now because, you see, I feel truly at home here" . . . "Time cannot erase the sadnesses of life, but it can help us to learn from them the hardest lesson of all: that even one's mistakes are enriching."

So she wrote to me on her 94th birthday. By then, the Parole Board had released me on licence. But I still wasn't free to visit her. Until my normal release date with maximum remission, February 1984, I wasn't allowed to leave the country.

All that changed in November of 1983. Word came from Madeira that Elizabeth had died peacefully in her sleep one night at Quinta do Porto Novo. It was only to be expected, of course, but I felt cheated by it, denied one last, deserved meeting by an unfeeling bureaucracy. The shock broke the trance into which prison life had lulled me. Whatever had then happened, I doubt I could have gone on as before.

In fact, there was no need. At her own request, Elizabeth was buried on Madeira, in the graveyard of a small chapel just down the valley from Quinta do Porto Novo. Helen went out to attend the funeral, though she disapproved of Elizabeth's determination not to be buried with her husband at Miston. It was less symbolic than Helen supposed. By being laid to rest in Madeira, Elizabeth avoided having to choose between the two men she'd loved. I wished I could have been there, but officialdom wouldn't relent.

Then came the bombshell. Tremlett had gone to Madeira to settle Elizabeth's affairs. Early in December, when he returned, he wrote to me with the startling news that Elizabeth had left me in her will the whole estate of Quinta do Porto Novo and a bequest of £210,000, almost all, in fact, of what she had to leave.

While I was dumbstruck, Helen was scandalized. I had to endure several bitter telephone calls and, from as far away as Australia, a lawyer's threat on behalf of Timothy—who'd received nothing—to contest the will. It didn't come to anything. As Tremlett pointed out, Elizabeth's judgement that I needed help far more than either of her grandchildren was undeniably reasonable, even if distasteful to them. I cared little for their protestations. My thoughts and hopes were already bound up in the gist of a letter Elizabeth had left for me.

"I have made Quinta do Porto Novo happy with the memory of Edwin and the promise of a future faithful to its tradition of displaced Englishness. It is my final and finest achievement. What would you have me do with it? Let another passing hotelier snap it up? I think not. Leave it to Helen? She wouldn't want it. Or Timothy? Never. You, Martin, are the only one who understands this place and why I have come here. So take it gladly and treat it well. For you and me, the meaning of your noble action at Quarterleigh six years ago is a bond stronger and more enduring than any certificated lineage. For Edwin to die as he did and for you to be imprisoned as you were, it was unnecessary for me to fail. Permit me, then, this one success. Use your future wisely."

Overnight, I became a wealthy man. Suddenly, I didn't have to be an ex-con clawing his way back anymore. Suddenly, I could do whatever I wanted. It was Elizabeth's gift. The one who'd suffered most from my delving into the past had treated me best. For Strafford, for me, for us all, she'd appeased the past with a bright future.

It took me six months of so to settle here. Six months of fretting about the harvest despite all Gabriel's reassurances, six months of getting used to being accepted—indeed welcomed—by an expatriate English community happily unaware of my past. Not having to explain or excuse myself any more was a strange experience.

But it was one to which I soon adapted. Finally, I realized with mild shock that I was a man of means with nothing to worry about. The Quinta brings in a modest income. That, plus the capital Elizabeth left me, gives me complete security, complete freedom, in fact, to do whatever I want.

Or so I thought.

Then, this morning, just like any other morning, I took a short cut out of the Quinta through the vine groves on its south-facing slope to the Gaula road and walked down towards the chapel where Elizabeth is buried. I rounded the last curve just as a banana lorry passed me, throwing up a cloud of dust in its wake. As it slowly cleared, a car came into view, pulled up on the verge by the railings fronting the tiny, neglected chapel. Clearly, I was not to be alone.

Built in the last century by a Scotsman whose Presbyterian soul couldn't tolerate interment in Roman Catholic soil, St. Andrew's Chapel is undeniable in Madeira but not of it, a slab of local granite forever chilled by a Caledonian memory. Always under-used, latterly forgotten, its small, overgrown burial ground wreathes lily, rhododendron and hibiscus round the gravestones of transplanted Protestants. On hot afternoons, I often walk down there to cool in its perpetual shade, to listen to the eucalyptus pods splitting beneath my feet, to collect water from the spring behind the chapel and replace the flowers on Elizabeth's grave, its stone still white and sharply etched amid all the lichened encroachment.

I pushed open the wicket gate and walked up the short path towards the chapel, brick red paint peeling on its wooden door. Inscribed and barely legible in the stone arch above, a Scotsman's Portuguese joke: BOA MORTE—Death is a happy release. Something made me stop before entering, a faint noise, the click of a camera shutter from the graveyard to my right. I turned and walked towards the sound.

I caught sight of her as I passed the angle of the chapel wall. She was standing by Elizabeth's grave, lowering her camera from where she'd just trained it to photograph the inscription. She could have been any English tourist in her pale blue blouse, full white skirt and open-toed sandals, any English tourist with curiosity and a camera. Only she wasn't. When she swung round at the sound of my steps on the path and a shaft of sunlight through the trees caught her face and hair, I saw that she couldn't be anybody but Eve, her expression composed even if I had surprised her, her eyes fixing and at once assessing the sudden, remembered stranger.

"Hello Martin," she said simply.

I walked slowly towards her. "I never expected to see you again."

"Nor I you."

"Tell me, why do you always choose . . . hallowed ground . . . to meet me? Miston Church, Chichester Cathedral, now here."

She smiled. "I never intended to meet you in Chichester, or here. But it's not inappropriate. Remember the medieval law of sanctuary."

"You think this is my fugitive's refuge?"

"Yours or mine. What differrence does it make?" She turned and walked a few paces to the bench old Tomás crafted from local willow and placed there after Elizabeth died. She sat down and looked up at me in a pose chosen for conciliation—or something subtler.

"You still haven't told me why you came."

"Do you really want to know?"

I stooped to push a tiny lizard down from Elizabeth's gravestone. "I'd really like to know."

"I've just spent a term at the University of Coimbra researching the Spanish occupation of Portugal. Still the academic gypsy, you see. There's a Madeiran on the staff there who sang the island's praises. I decided to come over on the boat from Lisbon for a couple of weeks during the Easter break."

"Just idle curiosity, then?"

"No. Not just that. In fact, not that at all."

"Then why?"

"To see you. I made enquiries in Lisbon and found out you now own the Quinta."

I walked slowly round behind the bench and leant with my back to it, where I could hear Eve clearly but avoid the fixity of her eyes. "I thought that's the last thing you'd want to do."

"So did I, once."

"Then what's changed?"

"You have. We both have. The mystery that bound us has been resolved . . . finished."

"Were we ever bound? You were determined all along to make me tread your path."

"And why not? I knew what I was doing, and why. Of course, that Strafford mystery was interesting in its own right, but I knew more than you thought all along. More about you, too. As soon as Strafford's name came up, I remembered the marriage certificate in the Kendrick Archive. So I strung you along, just to see how far you'd go to please me.

"For all your high-flown male principles you were easily persuaded to sell poor Strafford down the river to suit the theme of my book. I wondered when you'd find out about the Couchman Fellowship, but I reckoned that even when you did, you'd keep quiet about it, and I was right."

"I don't suppose you'll believe it, but that morning—when

I came to Darwin—I was going to call a halt and refuse to co-operate in distorting what I believed about Strafford."

"You seemed to be moving in that direction a couple of days beforehand, but I successfully talked you out of it. Are you sure that wouldn't have happened again?"

"On reflection, no." I wasn't sure, because Eve was right. She could have talked me into anything then.

"I expected it to end there, but Timothy suggested I could wheedle the Postscript out of you—if you had it. And I was vain enough to think: why not? Besides, Timothy promised to pressurize his grandmother into co-operating with the book. I still had my career to think of. At that time, I didn't realize how weak Timothy was—or how strong Elizabeth could be. And I had no idea Timothy's father had killed Ambrose."

"So our trip to Braunton was orchestrated from the first?"

"Not quite. Timothy just wanted you out of the way so he could search the Bennetts' house. I didn't find out till the following morning that the Postscript wasn't there. But the day wasn't wasted."

"I don't understand why you did it. The rest . . . yes. But why that?"

"Because of something you said on the way there. Do you remember we stopped at a pub near Barnstaple and I got you to talk about that girl—Jane Campion? Even then, you couldn't stop portraying yourself as the victim of a ruthless seductress. It sickened me—that you could forget she was just a child, just a vulnerable teenage girl you were supposed to protect. And then I asked you what you thought might have happened to her."

"I remember." I stared at the ground. "I said I imagined she was married with two kids by then, that she'd forgotten all about it."

"That's right! You imagined. You didn't know or care, as you still don't know or care. I looked at you—so soft, so unstretched, so pathetically self-pitying, cruising through life on somebody else's expense account. And I thought: you bastard, it's time you began paying for your past. For what you did to that girl—and for other reasons you could never understand—it's time you began to suffer. And suffer is what I'll make you do.

"What happened on the beach tested me as well as you. I set out in cold blood to seduce you, to take you in so completely that the final rejection, when it came, would break you. I don't think you once guessed, in all we did, that mine was just a courtesan's performance."

I looked up and breathed in deeply. "You're right. I never did guess."

"When you left the next morning, I knew you'd find the Bennetts had been broken into and that you'd rush back to Topsham hoping I could assure you it was all a terrible mistake. So I planned a suitable reception. It was to have been at Book End, but you returned sooner than I expected. I'd been leading Timothy on for weeks. He thought we were going back to the house so that I could yield to his irresistible charms. In fact, he was just a pawn in the game. Still, it achieved its purpose. In some ways, it was even more of a shock for you than I could have hoped."

"Except that it meant Timothy couldn't get his hands on the Postscript."

"That worried him more than me. But I had to follow you, if only to get my car back. Then Sellick showed up and it got better still from my point of view. Timothy revived the idea of putting pressure on his grandmother to contribute to my book, which suited Sellick—and me. Whatever else was tied up with it, the Strafford story was good history. It would have made my name. And that's when it all began to worry me.

"Whatever your failings, Martin, you were never worse than thoughtless. In Leo Sellick, I encountered true evil for the first time in my life. It infected Timothy at once. Then it spread to me. When we visited Lady Couchman, I realized I was condoning a vicious piece of somebody else's revenge."

"But you still went along with it?"

"Oh yes. That was the worst of it. Sellick had a talent for identifying other people's weaknesses—and exploiting them. Mine was academic ambition. His plans were carefully designed to offer me a way of fulfilling that ambition. So I'd have gone along with him all the way, victimizing an old woman without compunction."

"You could just have dropped it."

"But I wouldn't have done. I prided myself on a liberated woman's singlemindedness. Besides, Sellick implied he could get you to do it for him if I didn't—and I believed him."

"That at least wasn't true—not by then."

"No, but, when we met in Chichester, you seemed to confirm it was. I asked you—challenging myself as well as you—what you'd do to protect Lady Couchman. And you said . . ."

"Nothing."

"But the next day, you killed him."

I walked slowly round and faced Elizabeth's grave. "I did it for her."

"I know that now. It was just so . . . unexpected."

"It surprised me at the time. It surprised everyone—even Sellick, I think."

"I went back to Cambridge as soon as I heard about it. Shocked, yes, but also, somewhere in my mind I couldn't own up to, rather pleased that you'd put yourself in a worse position than I could ever have devised for you."

"I'm glad you approved."

"There's no point being bitter about it now, Martin. I'm just trying to explain how it was. Couchman Enterprises wound up the Fellowship straightaway, so, suddenly, I was out of a job and not about to become famous overnight."

"Sorry to have messed it up."

"That's what I'm trying to tell you. Actually, you saved me from a terrible mistake. I left Cambridge that summer, spent a year in Paris, then went back to the States. Female academics have it easier there. It was a good move—for a while. I got on well at Harvard—finally did produce that study of suffragism: a straight academic treatment. I married an attorney with a good practice in Boston."

"Congratulations."

"He died last year."

I stopped short. I didn't have a monopoly on adversity. Even she could suffer. "I'm sorry."

She got up from the bench and walked past me. "It's okay. We had five good years. I've come to terms with his death." She stopped by the chapel wall and looked back at me. "I left

Harvard to make a clean break. Coimbra seemed as far away as I could get from my old life. Then I realized how near it had brought me to you."

"Eve, I'm sorry about the girl. Truly I am. So long ago. I reckon maybe I have paid now."

"I reckon so too."

"And I'm sorry about your husband. But I still don't understand why you came here."

"To seek your forgiveness—this time sincerely."

The lizard had returned to Elizabeth's gravestone, basking on its rough surface where the sun pierced the trees. "Perhaps you underestimated me once. Now you're overestimating me. Prison hasn't turned me into a saint—or any less of a sinner. I'm still just the same weak man, with a thin veil of pride. Forgiveness? So that's what you want. Hallowed ground for absolution. First your plaything, then your eunuch, now your priest. Is that how it's to be?"

"No, Martin. That's not it at all."

"I think it is. Doesn't what Sellick found you capable of tell you something about yourself? Doesn't what you did to me tell you something about the girl—about Jane?"

"What do you mean?"

"Your so-called revenge was just an imitation, a proof, if you like, that I really was her victim, not she mine. Well, you've got what you wanted, what you set out to get from the start, your revenge. So now, just leave me alone." I felt strangely at ease with my own controlled fury.

"If that's how you want it."

"It is."

"Very well." She walked towards me. "I think the worst of it is that we're both right—about each other. But tell me"—she stopped beside me—"what wouldn't Elizabeth have given for a chance to make it up to Strafford?" I looked down at the grave. "That's all I'm suggesting we take—a chance with each other. It would probably never work—but wouldn't it be worth finding out? I only ever looked for the worst in you, Martin. Along the way, the best I discovered was something really rather fine . . . something I might have come to love if I'd allowed myself to."

I stared at her blankly. "It's too late, far too late. What's between us can't be wiped away."

"Of course not. That's just the point. It can divide us—or unite us."

"How could I ever bring myself to believe a word you said? How could I ever forget you might always be giving a courtesan's performance?"

"Neither of us can forget—unless we try together."

"Your memory and your mystery have shimmered at the edge of my mind since that day at Chichester when you told me what you thought of me. Now the truth's out at last, maybe I can finally forget you. That's all I want to do: forget you—not conspire with you in some fiction of a future."

"The pity of it is, Martin, that this is the one time you should believe me—and the one time I can't convince you."

"The one time and the last time. Elizabeth offered to forgive Strafford once, but said she could never forget what he'd supposedly done. Well, I can't forgive you, Eve, I don't have her magnanimity. But I'll try to forget."

"Do you really think you can?"

I didn't reply, just tried to suppress in my face any hint of the truth.

"I'm staying at the Casino Park Hotel in Funchal until next week. Then I'm going to Spain, to research the Habsburg archives at Valladolid. You could contact me at the University there. They know me as Dr Connolly."

"You won't hear from me."

"The invitation's open. I'll be at Valladolid until the end of June." She turned and walked away towards the gate. At the angle of the chapel wall, she paused. I looked towards her quizzically. She raised the camera to her eye and clicked the shutter. "A reminder—in case you don't come."

"I won't."

"We'll see." She looped the camera strap over her shoulder and walked quickly out through the gate. A few moments later came the roar of the car accelerating down the road.

I found myself running out through the gate to the road. I could see the car, a dark shape heading down the hill towards Gaula. Scattered rhododendron blossom was still circling in its wake by the verge. She'd gone. But I could follow—if I wished.

When I returned, I came up here to Strafford's study, to read his Memoir again in the place where it was written, to look at Elizabeth's photograph on the desk where it has always stood, to gaze from the window down the valley towards the sea, as all those who have lived here have done.

Evening is settling over the Quinta. The cicadas are out, scratching away at the blurred edges of the twilight. Doubt is muffled by the onset of night, decision delayed at least until another day.

Yes, she has re-entered my olden haunts. Through the years, the dead scenes, she had tracked me, and now, at last, I know why. What has she found to say of our past? Only the promise, only the vague, bewitching echo of a dream, held out across the dark space wherein I have lacked her. So near at hand, so far from my thoughts until now . . . "I'll be at Valladolid until the end of June." In the months that stretch remorselessly ahead, her invitation will become harder and harder to forget. Acceptance will creep upon me in every unguarded, fatalistic moment. I know it as surely as I know my own weaknesses, as surely as she knows them.

Strafford's face in that gathering of Asquith's Cabinet: I see you, my elusive quarry, but I do not hear you. If you had told me what to expect from a quest after your past, I would never have embarked upon it. But you know that. Your shade, which I tracked and moved in, envelops me now in this place of your displaced being.

What would you do? I know—there is no need to say. But first, I must close the book, Strafford, yours and mine, and, with it, the timeless circle of our acquaintance. Outside, the shadows beckon. To walk into them must always be a choice of random futures. What would you do? I know—there is no need to say. It is now for me to decide.